MAJESTY

JUSTIN HENDRICKSON

Copyright © 2025 Justin Hendrickson
All rights reserved
First Edition

PAGE PUBLISHING
Conneaut Lake, PA

First originally published by Page Publishing 2025

ISBN 979-8-89315-357-6 (pbk)
ISBN 979-8-89315-373-6 (digital)

Printed in the United States of America

I want to dedicate this book to my mother and father.

To my mother: who has instilled me with more light, kindness, compassion, and love than I know what to do with. Her perfect example of pure benevolence and angelic goodness provides me with the unfailing strength and optimism that continue to lead me through every single day, without fail…knowing that things can, often and do, "always get better."

Always and true to the title of "number one fan," she has always been my greatest support and believer. I would be nowhere near where I am, and succeeding in what I am, without you, Mom.

For those who have stated that there are indeed angels among us, I simply need to look to my mother to know how true this is.

To my father: the most magnificent man that I know, who has always known how to perfectly blend incredible strength, fortitude, willpower, and justice, with a level of compassion, understanding, and tenderness that literally melts hearts (mine included). Your wisdom and balance reflect that of a seasoned veteran of another time and realm.

I also devote the purest form of love that I can to him and for his cherished parents…for instilling such profound love of music, the piano, and all creativity to my being.

PROLOGUE

The rain fell softly over the cobblestone streets of Vaerün, casting a silvery shimmer on the kingdom's rustic charm. The quiet town, nestled in the heart of Albyüron, looked like something pulled from the pages of history—its moss-covered thatched rooftops dripping with rainwater, sending thin rivulets down into the cracks between the stones. Lanterns lined the streets, their soft orange glow flickering against the gloom, lighting the path for cloaked figures as they hurried to their destinations.

Wagon wheels rolled lazily along the slick streets, the rhythmic *ca-clack, ca-clack* echoing between stone walls, while horses trod carefully through the narrow alleys. The miller, his cart heavy with flour, exchanged polite nods with the blacksmith, whose soot-streaked face told the tale of a long day at the forge. Down the road, the baker stood in the doorway of his shop, offering a friendly greeting to passersby, the scent of fresh bread wafting through the damp air.

It was another ordinary day in the quiet kingdom of Vaerün—peaceful, perhaps even mundane. But change often comes on the heels of the unexpected, and on this dreary afternoon, something unimaginable was about to unfold.

It happened in an instant.

A blinding flash tore through the overcast sky, ripping apart the veil of clouds. A ring of golden light expanded outward, banishing the dreariness in a heartbeat and revealing a vast, sapphire sky. The rain ceased, and a profound silence fell over the kingdom as every inhabitant, from the baker to the blacksmith, stood frozen, eyes locked skyward. Awe and wonder seized the hearts of the people, for something ancient and powerful was descending from the heavens.

"This feeling…" they would later recall in whispers, "was so familiar, yet beyond comprehension."

The brilliance of the sky deepened as a radiant, all-encompassing light filled the heavens. A soft, rhythmic pulse echoed above, like the beat of a celestial drum, vibrating through the very bones of Vaerün. The sound brought everyone humbly to one knee, their hearts racing, yet stilled by reverence.

Then came the beam—a single golden shaft of light piercing the sky, descending with the speed of a shooting star. It crashed down into the center of the town, sending a cascade of rainbow-hued light spiraling outwards: fiery reds, vibrant greens, and deep purples blending together in a mesmerizing dance of color.

In the heart of this divine spectacle floated a single, golden, angelic feather. Shimmering, glowing with an otherworldly radiance. It hovered in the air, slowly drifting among the crowd, its presence both delicate and terrifying in its Majesty. Beads of light gushed from this majestic icon, sparkling like rain, and as it passed overhead, the people could only gasp… Fully mesmerized by its celestial beauty.

Suddenly, the feather darted through the air, moving with impossible speed and such great purpose, zipping between the people of Vaerün. Some ducked instinctively as it whizzed by, while others watched, their eyes wide with awe and disbelief.

After a dazzling aerial display of light and color, the feather came to a sudden stop before a young farmhand. The man, dressed in tattered clothes and worn from years of hard labor, looked on in disbelief. His eyes widened as he raised a trembling hand, compelled by some unseen force, and lightly touched the feather.

A surge of brilliant light shot forth, enveloping him in an aura of radiant blue. His body shuddered as the light filled him, lifting him slightly off the ground. His once-ordinary blue eyes now glowed with a piercing brilliance, intricate etchings of divine symbols traced across his palms.

Suddenly, a searing heat ignited within his chest, and as he tore back his shirt, an intricate feather design had appeared, etched with radiant precision over his left breast and heart. It shimmered with blue divine energy, a mark of celestial favor—signifying he had been chosen by a power beyond mortal reach.

He was no longer just a farmhand — he had been chosen. A shimmering aura of deep blue Majesty radiated from his being, forming a halo of light that pulsed in harmony with his heartbeat.

Streams of ethereal, water-like beads rippled from his body, moving with a life of their own, flowing gracefully around him as if obeying his unspoken command. Lines of luminous blue traced along the palms of his hands, glowing brighter as he raised them. With a single thought, the nearby puddle stirred, rising into the air in a mesmerizing dance, twisting and spiraling at his command. The world felt as if it breathed through him—he was a Water Majestician, gifted with the sacred power to direct this elemental force to his will.

The onlookers could only watch in awe as the celestial feather resumed its search, weaving through the streets and alleys, leaving trails of vibrant light in its wake. With each touch of the feather, another soul was transformed.

Fire Majesticians erupted in a blaze of scarlet and gold, the air around them shimmering from the heat. Flames curled at their fingertips, ready to burst forth in torrents, while the very ground scorched beneath their feet, bearing the intensity of their new power.

Earth Majesticians glowed with a deep green aura, their presence resonating with the pulse of the land itself. Where they walked, vines and flowers burst from stone and soil alike, bending toward them as if drawn by an ancient bond to the earth's hidden strength.

Wind Majesticians radiated a violet hue, with trails of lightning sparking across their bodies. The air hummed and swirled around them, responding to their every gesture as gusts of wind and strikes of lightning bent to their command, charging the air with electrifying intensity.

Whispers spread quickly through the stunned crowd: For it quickly became apparent that only the purest of hearts, the most selfless and benevolent of souls, were chosen. And by the end of that fateful day, only a select few— even just less than ten percent of Vaerün's population—had been marked by the feather, transformed into Majesticians.

Thus began a new era for Vaerün. The kingdom, once quiet and unassuming, had become the cradle of divine power. The Majesticians, with their godlike abilities, were revered as guardians and protectors, and their presence ushered in a golden age of prosperity, harmony, and peace.

With each passing year, more and more of Vaerün's people aspired to harness the gift of Majesty. Service to the kingdom flourished, trade blossomed, and the arts thrived. Lanterns that once lit the cobbled streets for travelers now cast their warm glow over bustling marketplaces, where Majesticians and common folk alike worked together to build a kingdom of righteousness and goodness.

As a result, the entire kingdom flourished in goodness, righteousness, and benevolence. Service became a way of life, and trade thrived with abundant and generous deals. The focus shifted to the betterment of families, fostering a vibrant vitality across the land for the sake of pure goodness.

Year after year, Majesty continued to return and bless Vaerün (*And the wonderful inhabitants so deserving of its power!*) until the kingdom grew so vast that division became inevitable. Yet, this was considered a fortunate development rather than a setback.

Upon deliberation, each faction of Majesticians chose to establish their own domain, circling Vaerün:

The Wind Majesticians journeyed northward, founding the Kingdom of Wölnas. To the south, the Fire Majesticians established the Kingdom of Fürnas. In the eastern mountains, the Earth Kingdom of Grünas took shape. Lastly, to the west, positioned uniquely on the ocean, lay Wöntylnas, the Kingdom of Water.

Each kingdom bore the name of the first Majestician bestowed with mastery over their respective elements. With their divine powers, the Majesticians sculpted these realms with astonishing architecture, creating kingdoms of unparalleled beauty and perfect construction.

The Kingdom of Wölnas, to the North, is a realm of perpetual tempest. The sky is constantly adorned with dark purple storm clouds and lightning, which ripple through the heavens in a mesmerizing dance. This atmospheric transformation is a direct result of the

Wind Majesticians' continuous use of their Majesty, drawing power from the ether and permanently altering the environment.

The cobblestone streets of Wölnas—a blend of white marble accented with purples and blues—wind through a cityscape dominated by buildings of intricate design and towering spires, piercing the turbulent skies. Amid the howling winds and frequent storms battering the tiled rooftops, the streets glow with the warm orange light of lantern-lit windows, providing a stark contrast to the tumultuous weather. Here, the people of Wölnas have mastered the art of harnessing wind and lightning, making their realm a symbol of dynamic energy and resilient spirit.

To the east, nestled just beyond the Kier Mountains, lies the Earth Kingdom of Grünas, a testament to the harmonious bond between Majesticians and their land.

Carved directly from the mountains, its bastion-like architecture boasts grand halls and towering structures of stone and crystal. Adorned with flowers, vines, and a kaleidoscope of flora, Grünas radiates elegance and strength, with rich earthy hues of greens, browns, and golds seamlessly blending into the natural landscape.

The Majesticians of Grünas wield their powers to cultivate lush gardens and forests, creating a sanctuary where the crisp, pine-scented air mixes with the fragrance of fresh earth.

Waterfalls cascade down mountainsides, feeding clear, sparkling rivers that weave through the kingdom. Grünas stands as a haven of peace and natural beauty, embodying an unbreakable bond between its people and the earth.

To the south lies the Kingdom of Fürnas. The air here is cool and crisp—a result of the Fire Majesticians' constant use of their fiery powers, which unintentionally transformed the very ether and atoms of the air to a cooler climate. Thus, a perpetual fall blankets the land.

The landscape is a tapestry of vibrant reds, oranges, and yellows, with trees forever in the peak of autumn splendor.

The architecture of Fürnas is grand and inviting, with towers of white marble adorned in a spectrum of rich red hues. Lanterns line the cobblestone pathways, emitting a warm, fiery light that casts enchanting shadows in the crisp autumn air of this kingdom clad in eternal fall.

Despite the cool climate, Fürnas exudes an elegant warmth, resonating with the energy of its people, who masterfully wield fire and forge, lending to a vibrant community. Renowned for their culinary prowess, Fürnas is celebrated for its exquisite sweets, pies, and breads, a testament to their deep connection to the permanent season.

To the west, upon the vast ocean, lies the Kingdom of Wöntylnas. This kingdom is a marvel of engineering and beauty, built upon the water and connected to the mainland by a long, elegant marble bridge.

The buildings of Wöntylnas are graceful and fluid, designed to mimic the waves of the ocean. The colors here are predominantly blue and white, with accents of green and silver.

The Water Majesticians have created a true paradise upon the water, with canals and waterways that weave through the kingdom, granting immediate access to Water Majesty for all capable of wielding it.

The air is filled with the sound of gently lapping waves and the salty scent and taste of the sea. The people of Wöntylnas have a deep connection to the ocean, and their ability to command water has allowed them to create a thriving, harmonious society that lives in perfect balance with their beloved marine environment.

Each of these magnificent kingdoms, with their unique characteristics and breathtaking beauty, stands as a testament to the power and benevolence of the Majesticians. Born not just from mastery over the elements, but from pure love, charity, hard work, camaraderie, unwavering faith, and dedication.

Filled with love and admiration, and believing their incredible powers to be gifts from heaven, all four kingdoms gathered together.

In honor of their creator and the heavens above, they built **Laniakéa**, an enormous white tower in the center of Vaerün; symbolizing unity, respect, and camaraderie amongst the four elemental kingdoms, and central Vaerün.

At its base, an archway leads to an incredibly grand spiral staircase, winding up to the top and revealing an open platform with four pedestals, each representing the grandeur and strength of each kingdom. It became a place for Majesticians to gather and humbly express gratitude for their divine gifts.

Truly, never was there a happier time in all of Vaerün.

But in the darkest corners beneath the world, envy and malice festered...

Deep beneath Vaerün, in the forgotten caverns, a sinister force had watched the rise of the Majesticians with growing hatred.

Baehallün, the ancient lord of shadows, seethed with jealousy. How dare the people of Vaerün be granted such divine gifts? How dare they thrive while he remained in the darkness, waiting?

His twisted followers, spirits of malice and temptation, slithered through the cracks of the earth, whispering in complete blackness.

Always aware, always watching, they observed in hatred and anger as the inhabitants of Vaerün were gifted the heavenly power of Majesty and creation.

And so, as Baehallün sat upon his throne of pure blackness, he addressed his followers, hissing through the darkness.

"All of you know our state..." He murkily stated, "You know we've been without bodies since the beginning and that we're told we shall never have one. Well..."

The untold plethora of demonic spirits began to whisper.

"I have an idea, wherein we may *actually* receive the last laugh... And truly come out on top." Baehallün seethed, "It will involve careful temptation, as these, '*Self-righteous Majesticians*' will be so slow to resist. We will need to start small..."

The whispering intensified.

"Go. *Tempt* the Majesticians. Do so in the most subtle ways you can imagine. Don't force anything." With a pause and an evil smile, he finished, "Remember... just as every suit of chain mail has even one small flaw in the tiniest chink, so too does every human soul."

A quiet hush fell upon the caverns.

"Don't bother attacking in their strong areas—you'll never win. Work on that tiny chink," he said, pointing to one of his servants. "For some, it will be patience. Others: swearing, drinking, laziness, fornication. It will take time and the greatest patience. But as you do…"

Wringing his hands together maniacally, he continued, "Their weaknesses will grow larger. Gnaw at it. Drive at it. Attack it!"

One of his spirits hissed, swiping through the air. "It will not take long before their greatest weaknesses are exploited! Do so, and we shall sit back and watch as they destroy one another."

Whispering resumed, louder.

"Our greatest goal is to destroy the family unit. Whether by blood or friendship, family is the strongest bond of light in all of Vaerün. Destroy it, and I assure you…" Baehallün suddenly stood, raising his hands triumphantly. "We shall come out on top!"

With a deafening, unanimous cheer, the translucent spirits rushed up through the ground and into the land of Vaerün.

Flooding the kingdoms and gently descending upon the inhabitants, the spirits began their temptations. And surely, it started small.

Wöntylnas was the first to give in. Approaching the other kingdoms, they began to boast of their intelligence and Majesty. They appointed a king (Indeed, the very first water Majestician!) and began building a castle at the end of Wöntylnas, erecting a tall tower similar to Laniakéa to honor their wisdom and prowess—attributes that they claimed as their own.

Appalled upon learning this, Grünas was the first to step in. But through the careful temptation of Baehallün's spirit followers, Grünas gave in when flattered to assist in the architectural design and creation of Wöntylnas's castle and tower.

Promised a return of the favor, Grünas relented. Soon, Wölnas and Fürnas also wanted their own towers, and before long, all four kingdoms were adorned with grand castles and towers, each falling under the tyranny of kings and queens. (Once more, the *first* Majesticians).

Slowly but surely, Laniakéa grew more and more empty, until it was altogether desolate. The inhabitants of Vaerün became far more interested in worshipping and glorifying themselves and their kings, who stood upon their lofty towers.

To make matters even worse, each kingdom began to practice further moral decline.

Fürnas erected a coliseum, boasting themselves as the most powerful warriors and Majesticians of the land. Wöntylnas, Grünas, and Wölnas, not to be outdone, participated in these battles and began their own practices.

King Vergaus of Wöntylnas established a hall for entrepreneurial ideas, logistics, and scholastic dominance, aiming to conquer Vaerün with intelligence. King Fjalund of Grünas encouraged artistic competition in painting, building, and sculpting. Meanwhile, King Gerund of Wölnas faced darker issues: thievery, mental illness, murder, and brothels abounded in his kingdom, taking advantage of the perpetual stormy weather as the perfect cover for all manner of lasciviousness.

Slowly but surely, "friendly" competition turned into heated debates, escalating into both verbal and physical confrontations.

Just as Baehallün had predicted, the Majesticians and their land began to crumble into severe moral decay.

Having had enough of his kingdom being harassed by robbers, murderers, debaters, and condescension, King Coltin of Fürnas declared a call for war—to be held on the plains in the center of Vaerün.

Not long after sending the message by peregrine falcon, the proposal was unanimously returned from the three opposing kingdoms—civil war was imminent.

What a bleak day it was. As if aware of the impending disaster, the sun hid his face behind dark rain clouds, refusing to give light to these treasonous people.

With the piercing ring of their war horns, each faction approached from the north, south, east, and west. All carried their flag standards and lofty ideals as they charged into battle upon the plains of Vaerün.

Clash, clash, clang! The sounds of razor-sharp swords hacking against one another mixed with the ringing of metal against armor.

The sickening noise of flesh being ripped apart, paired with war cries and shouts, consumed the plains of Vaerün.

Ferocity and axe were the weapons of Fürnas. The razor-sharp daggers of Wöntylnas met the piercing swords of Grünas. All the while, they were buffeted by Wölnas's ranged archers and spear thrusters.

As soon as the factions had fallen by half, a new twist entered the fray. From the four corners of the battlefield came legions of robed Majesticians. Silent, intensely skilled in combat and maneuverability, they blurred across the battlefield like ripples of color.

Shhhgghzzzz, crackled the purple lightning as it tore through the air, decimating metal-suited warriors and opposing Majesticians alike. With focused bolts of lightning and whistling tornadoes, the Wind Majesticians laid siege to the battlefield.

Fsshhrawwwrgggh, roared the flames of the Fire Majesticians, scorching the earth and incinerating warriors. The once beautiful green grass, not yet stained by blood, lay black and charred like the bodies that crumbled to the ground.

Gguuggh…ggguggha! choked warriors and Majesticians as they drowned under the Water Majesticians' control—spheres and tentacles of water suffocating them like a noose. Desperately, they clawed at the water to break free, but to no avail.

Thump, thump, thump, echoed the heart-wrenching sound of bodies hitting the soft earth as they succumbed to death by drowning.

But perhaps the most wretched and abominable sight was the enchanting green and yellow light that filled the air, accompanied by vines, thorns, and flowers of all kinds.

Intended for the greatest good and the most blessed of all, it was an atrocious sight to see the Earth Majesticians use their powers of creation for destruction. The irony was almost unbearable.

Thuuuck, sshiinck! Vines and razor-like foliage pierced through the hearts of warriors and Majesticians. With blood-curdling screams, soldiers fell as their arms, legs, and even heads were severed by the noosing and razor-sharp vines.

From an aerial perspective, the battlefield must have looked spectacular. A dazzling array of rainbow colors glittered below—a chaotic twist of spectrum-encompassing light and magic. It was unbelievable, and for the most sickening of reasons.

And not too far below stood Baehallün and his followers, ready to receive their new prize.

Mechanically extending his fingers and pulling them back toward his palms, Baehallün shouted in excitement as he looked up at the cavernous ceiling.

"This is it! Ha ha ha!" he bellowed. "Stupid heaven! You honestly thought I'd sit back and watch as your Majesticians grew in light and righteousness? Please! Now you've lost! Your power is mine!"

Golden-red, majestic blood began to ooze from the ceiling, falling down and pooling on the cavern floors, running over the rough crags. As it oozed around Baehallün, he carefully knelt to the floor, spread his hands wide, and pressed his fingers into the blood.

At his touch, it immediately turned glossy black and dark. As if the blood were alive and revolted against being touched by such evil, it rippled and writhed.

"You thought you'd banished me, didn't you, heaven?" he mocked, his voice teetering on madness. "You thought you'd cast me out and stripped me of my power? Well, how about this…"

His hands and fingers danced wildly as the black blood began to obey him. On the cavern floors, it swirled. Up the walls, it splashed and climbed. Through the air, it twisted and turned.

"Stupid Majesticians!" he shrieked with laughter. "Didn't you realize that your very blood contained the purest essence of Majesty the moment you accepted it into your heart?"

His spirit followers nodded mechanically as he continued. "Did you ever pause to think of the consequences of giving in to transgression and temptation?"

The swirling black blood began to move faster and faster, as if with agitation and purpose.

"Oh, you certainly should have," he whispered. "For now, your price is worse than death."

With a fierce upward thrust of his hands and fingers vibrating like mad, the sea of black blood rocketed upward, latching onto the ceiling and traveling back through the earth from whence it came.

Clash, clash, clang! The sounds of warfare continued alongside explosions of Majesty.

But ever so subtly, warriors began to disappear from the battlefield, sucked into the earth as if pulled underground by an invisible giant. They were too preoccupied with combat to see the black tentacles of Baehallün's Dark Majesty wrapping around their ankles and dragging them to hell.

Not much time passed before the remaining warriors and Majesticians paused in confusion and fear—only a quarter of the factions were left!

Where did everyone go?

Breathing heavily, they looked around, unaware that the bodies of the dead and even some living had been dragged underground to a fate worse than death.

"That's it! That's it!" Baehallün cackled as bodies fell around him like hail in a summer storm.

"To all my followers…" he whispered eagerly as the thudding of bodies crashed down around them.

In total silence, the spirits leaned in to listen.

"These bodies are yours to have!" Baehallün said sweetly, extending his hands.

"But I must say," he whispered eerily, "you probably would've been much happier in your current state."

As if stabbing the air with his sharp fingers, all his translucent spirits screamed in agony as they were absorbed by the magical black blood that consumed them like a sponge.

Glug, glug, glug, gurgled the Dark Majesty as it stabbed into the bodies of the dead and living, injecting Baehallün's spirits into them.

"Oh, that's right!" Baehallün gleefully continued as he pointed to the new spirits. "From the battlefield above, right? Probably murdered in some gruesome way. Hoping to ascend to heaven?"

It was fortunate they were spirits, for if they had been mortal, their skin surely would have crawled off their bodies at his shrieking laughter. "Come now, that's only for good people! And none of you are, by any means…"

The dark blood continued its work like a factory, absorbing and reanimating every spirit into the bodies.

"Good people," Baehallün finished with a sneer.

Reanimated with the black blood of Dark Majesty, words could barely express the horror of their appearance: occasional hanging mandibles, some with completely black eyes, others white as a ghost.

Black tears streamed down lifeless eyes, fanged teeth with black saliva lined their gums, and black bulging veins marred their arms and faces—revealing the Dark Majesty running through them. Their skin was so pale and sickly that one might prefer to look upon abused leather rather than a creature such as this.

One could only describe these monsters as the very possessed, demonic souls of hell.

Screaming and moaning echoed through the caverns as Baehallün declared over his new faction, "Welcome to the infinite, endless abyss beyond death itself. I call upon the darkness that binds your rotting souls, and with it, I christen you… my legion of nightmare incarnate. Rise as the *Kreaux*—undead, unrelenting, and sworn to serve my will for all of eternity!"

Was it cheering or screeching that filled the caverns as he named them?

"Now go," Baehallün commanded. "Go above and reclaim the rest of my army!"

With razor-sharp fingernails and the dark magical blood of Majesty coursing through their veins, the Kreaux climbed the walls like fleeing spiders about to be squashed.

Boom! Boom! The earth rocked as dirt flew and earthquakes struck the battlefield. The screeching Kreaux clambered their way out of the soft earth and immediately fell upon the warriors and Majesticians, latching onto their bodies with blood-squirting bites and claw-like hands.

It looked as though life-sized insects had been unleashed on the battlefield. Soldiers and Majesticians alike turned their focus upon the Kreaux, confused and terrified as they fought for their lives against the insurmountable foe.

What a sight to behold. They didn't stand a chance. It was as if a blanket of darkness had washed over the battlefield, transforming it in the blink of an eye. Eruptions of tar-like Dark Majesty rocketed from the ground, latching onto bodies—dead and alive—and ruthlessly pulled them underground.

Where could the Majesticians and soldiers even begin? If they weren't being slaughtered by the Kreaux, they were facing something far from human—the twisting, convulsing tentacles of Dark Majesty, which erupted from the ground like vines gone awry, gave them a fight for their very lives.

A few Kreaux fell, blasted by the lightning and fireballs of the Majesticians, but the Dark Majesty was unaffected. In horror, they realized that fleeing was likely their best option.

But it was too late; panting and running for their lives did nothing to save them. As if a monstrous worm lurked beneath the surface, the Dark Majesty moved at an inhuman—no, even Majestic—speed! It burst through the earth, wrapping around fleeing soldiers so tightly it crushed their ribs. The tentacles dragged them down into the ground, some even losing a limb in the process.

From afar, the self-righteous kings watched in horror and confusion from the safe towers of their kingdoms. What in the world—literally—was happening on that battlefield? Dispatching soldiers by horseback to observe the carnage without drawing too close, the kings awaited reports. It didn't take long for the news to return.

Speculation and lack of data left scholars to surmise that a gargantuan, toxic, liquid beast had somehow formed beneath Vaerün's crust and was laying waste on the battlefield.

Being a Majestician himself and able to speak on the wind, King Gerund of Wölnas sent word to the other three kings, demanding that they rendezvous at the grand hall in the Water Kingdom of Wöntylnas, as safely as possible.

Receiving the urgent message, with no time to debate, the four kings met.

At first, debate erupted over who had created the monster. But after thorough thought, consideration, and realizing none of them held the power to produce something so abominable, they deduced it must be a creature of hell itself.

King Fjalund of Grünas sat sorrowfully at the large meeting table, expressing deep remorse and belief that this was punishment for their unforgivable sins.

In quiet reflection, all agreed.

Taking courage, King Coltin of Fürnas—bold as always—stood defiantly, proposing the idea of creating weapons powerful enough to destroy the beast. The idea was met with unanimous agreement, and King Vergaus of Wöntylnas remarked, "It must be a weapon unlike any other."

Reflecting on their times spent worshipping their creator and the heavens at Laniakéa—now nearly forgotten—they deduced that only a sacrifice of great magnitude could forge the weapons necessary to destroy this insurmountable monster.

Wasting no time, the four kings rushed to the underground forge of Wöntylnas. With their Majesty combined, they crafted four small glass spheres: empty, translucent, and eerily compelling. The kings housed the spheres on their belts, strapped securely by a strong band.

Boom! The walls and ground shook violently around them. *What in Vaerün? Boom! Boom!* Earthquakes rocked the forge. As liquid lava spilled over the huge kettles, King Coltin stepped forth to redirect the molten flow.

"Go!" he shouted to his three friends as sweat dripped down his face from repelling the searing, flesh-melting lava.

Once safe, all four kings resurfaced above. To their horror, the Kreaux were already upon Wöntylnas!

"What in the glory of Vaerün..." whispered King Vergaus, shaking his head.

"We're out of time! What do we do?" shouted King Grünas, bursting forth vines and foliage from his palms to create a thorny barricade in front of them.

"Gerund," said King Coltin in a calmed tone, "your Majesty is more adept than all of ours. With the ability to ride the wind and lightning, you have the best chance of placing these spheres atop the four towers!"

"Yes, but…" Gerund worried, "without our Majesty and the emanating energy of our kingdoms to charge them, the weapons are useless!"

Hack, hack, hack! The claws of the Kreaux slashed at the vines.

King Vergaus's eyes rippled with blue light as he elegantly moved his hands, a massive wave of water rising behind them and slamming down on the Kreaux.

"And not just that," Gerund continued, "after they have been charged, they must be unleashed upon Laniakéa!" He pointed east. "How do we accomplish such a feat when that tower is in the center of the battlefield?"

As the Kreaux continued slashing their way through the vines, Coltin unleashed a volley of fireballs, sending the screeching creatures back.

"Well, if I may say," Coltin hollered, "shoot first, ask questions later!"

"Go, Gerund!" shouted Vergaus, unleashing another wave of water. "We'll find a way! This will work!"

Gerund held his breath as he caught the sphere from Vergaus, followed quickly by the others from the remaining kings.

"Dang it!" he muttered as he looked west to see Wöntylnas's tall, white-and-blue tower, no more than a mile away.

Surrounded by crackling lightning, Gerund launched into the air.

Within moments, he descended upon the top of Wöntylnas's tower, striding quickly to the prayer altar set at half his height in the middle of the platform.

His hand flashed and glowed with purple light as he imbued it with lightning. Carefully, he etched a small depression into the pedestal, laying the sphere gently within. Satisfied, he exploded into the air again, this time heading south to Fürnas.

With a wrenching heart, he looked down to see the perpetual-autumn kingdom overrun with Kreaux. Resisting the temptation to help the citizens being slaughtered, he continued to the top of the tower.

With another blast of lightning and careful etching, he set the second sphere in place. Two more remained. He flew east, toward Grünas, deciding to save his own kingdom for last.

Grünas had yet to come under Kreaux attack, but the gates would not hold against the oncoming horde much longer.

"What a pity..." Gerund murmured, observing the women and children huddled together in the thousands, holding one another and weeping, their hopes resting on the backs of the fifty or so soldiers guarding the gate.

There's no way they're going to make it, he thought, seeing the black mass of Kreaux storming up the Kier Mountain Trail toward Grünas.

Tears welled up in his eyes. *What happened?* he thought. *How did we end up this way?* Sorely tempted to intervene, it was as if an angelic voice barred him, reminding him of his duty to place the four weapons.

Steeling himself, he flew to the top of the tower, etched another depression, placed the sphere, and launched north—the final destination; his home of Wölnas.

It felt as though all the powers of hell were combined against him; the storm over Wölnas had intensified tenfold. Even sustaining his Majesty against the storm proved a challenge.

Squinting against the rain and wind, Gerund made out the top of the black-and-purple tower behind his castle, amid the glow of repeated lightning.

With a flicker of hope and an emerging smile, he surfed the lightning to the tower. Nearly slipping on the rain-slick stone, he carefully imbued his hand with lightning and etched the final depression. As he placed the sphere, he knelt and prepared to charge it with energy.

"Ha…ha…ha…ha…" A voice, dry and mocking, echoed on the clouds.

"What the—? Who are you?" Gerund demanded, standing and brandishing his bow. The weapon crackled with purple-and-blue lightning as his Majesty flowed through it.

Zeearrgggh…boom! You'd never think the Majestic wielder of lightning could be struck by it, but there you have it.

Unaware and shocked beyond comprehension, Gerund was blasted off his own tower. Plummeting through the storm and blinking against the rain, he caught sight of the ground approaching fast—less than a second away. Thinking quickly, he extended his hand to guide a bolt of lightning.

Blast! "Agh…agh…agh!" Gerund yelled as he tumbled across the ground, his lightning blast barely enough to break his fall. But it was not enough to prevent a broken leg, broken arm, and fractured ribs.

Coughing blood, wheezing, he sat up and looked around, dizzy and disoriented. Was it the lightning in the sky, or head trauma making the world flash before his eyes?

Trying to prop himself up, he froze in horror as a sloshing sound filled his ears. He scanned his surroundings, his eyes wide with panic—searching for anyone, but finding only the empty darkness of the storm.

Something gripped his legs and squeezed.

In intense agony, he screamed. The pressure around his legs felt like nothing he had ever experienced. Suddenly, he was pulled downward. Thinking fast, he thrust his hands into the earth to anchor himself, fighting to stay above ground.

"Help! Someone, help!" he cried out, gripping the muddy soil. "Coltin! Vergaus! Fjolund!" But there was no response. Only the mocking tickle of laughter carried on the wind.

With one final scream, Gerund was dragged underground by Dark Majesty.

The battlefield was a grotesque sight. All were dead. Dark Majesty oozed and bubbled from the earth, wrapping around bodies and slowly pulling them into the ground—claimed by Baehallün.

Upside-down bodies lay partially consumed, only legs or an arm protruding from the earth. An occasional dead hand, its white fingers entangled in the tar-like substance of the dark blood, reached up in a final, haunting plea.

A small band of scattered Kreaux hissed and wheezed as they dragged even more bodies underground. The eerie sound of the wind battered the flag standards that remained, their once bright colors now tattered and soaked in blood. The red sky overhead loomed heavy with black and gray smoke. The scene reeked of carnage.

As if sent to check on the aftermath of a disaster, the angelic feather of Majesty burst into the sky and descended carefully upon Vaerün, first pausing over the battlefield, only to be screeched at by the Kreaux below. Then, it moved gently through the devastated kingdoms.

The kingdoms were in even worse condition than the battlefield. No one had survived.

Dead women and children lay huddled together, pierced by Kreaux claws and fangs, mauled to death, waiting to be claimed by Dark Majesty. But heaven only knows their spirits had ascended to the almighty heavens above.

As if caressing them, the feather lingered briefly, gently brushing against their pale, dead faces.

With unspeakable lament, the feather drifted through each kingdom, its movements a stark contrast to its last visit. There were no dances, no acrobatic spins, and no exotic flashes of light; it floated as though drifting down a motionless river of air.

Broken buildings, shattered windows, and Dark Majesty filled the lands. It seemed all color had vanished, leaving only monochromatic hues behind.

Wöntylnas's once-thriving Water Kingdom now felt dull and lifeless. Fürnas cast a sepia tone, like an old memory glorifying an age long gone. Grünas's garden paradise stood as a barren wasteland, and the stormy Wölnas seemed haunted beyond measure, its perpetual tempest now a cruel reflection of its fallen state.

With no one left to bestow Majesty upon, the feather slowly lulled back into the heavens above, trails of light flowing from it like tears from an angel.

Now, as fate would have it, vast libraries remained in the kingdoms, preserving a reliquary of knowledge. However, concerning Dark Majesty and the Kreaux, only a few scribbled scrolls lay scattered about on gouged tables in the abandoned halls.

Still having no idea of the true origin of these abominations, the remaining scribes recorded only theories, anatomical drawings, and foreboding messages about the Kreaux and Dark Majesty for the distant travelers who would one day arrive.

As if dealing with a science project gone horribly wrong, future inheritors would find themselves with scant knowledge to work from. And while written histories of Kings Wölnas, Fürnas, Wöntylnas, and Grünas remained, nothing was documented about the magical spheres housed in the pedestals atop each kingdom's tower; there simply hadn't been enough time.

For hundreds of years, Vaerün stood empty—a haunting relic of a once-great kingdom. The streets of cobblestone and moss-covered rooftops, where life once thrived, were now eerily silent, save for the sound of the wind echoing through the abandoned homes.

In the center of it all stood that glorious, heavenly tower… *Laniakéa*, the towering white marble monument of unity, now forsaken. Its once-vibrant rainbow hues, dominantly marble white, with colors of rippling Majesty surging through, once symbolized the power of Majesty itself, still clung faintly to its surface… Now felt twisted, unnatural—an eerie reminder of a forgotten age.

The wind howled through the desolate halls of Laniakéa, no voices echoing in centuries. The spiral staircase that once led the Majesticians to their platform of gratitude now led to nothing but dust, as the towering pedestals stood barren and cold.

Vaerün and its four surrounding kingdoms—Wölnas, Grünas, Fürnas, and Wöntylnas—lay abandoned, the vibrant colors and majestic architecture now faded and cracked, like the hollow remains of a decayed dream.

It was as if the land itself mourned, for the splendor of the past was now just a distant, unsettling memory, and yet… something darker lurked beneath.

Baehallün's plan had always been to wait. The kingdoms lay desolate, but not forgotten. As distant settlers from the far reaches of Albyüron unknowingly began to rediscover Vaerün, they stepped into a quiet trap—one set with patient malice, with an evil stirring beneath the surface.

The marble towers in each kingdom stood entirely still, gleaming like beacons, yet empty and foreboding, as if watching the world. Waiting for the time when their halls would once again be filled with the souls Baehallün desired; his fulfilling mockery to heaven itself.

His hunger had not diminished, and soon, his dark army would rise again… For at long last, ships from distant kingdoms across Albyüron had just touched down upon the Western seashore, near Wöntylnas.

Indeed. After hundreds and hundreds of years, inhabitants had *finally* discovered Vaerün and its four waiting kingdoms.

"Peeeerrrfeeect…" hissed Baehallün as he eagerly awaited in anticipation, watching with his Dark Majesty, beneath the surface…

CHAPTER 1

A New Message

Garon Erbrecht, Wölnas's commander-in-chief, stood atop the crag, staring down into the massive chasm below. It looked like a black ocean, swirling and speckled with moving dots, but upon closer inspection, it was nothing less than a cesspit of Dark Majesty and Kreaux—miles upon miles of it.

Behind him, a short distance away, the gates of Wölnas were raised, clearly preparing for another Kreaux siege. To his left and right, a multitude of soldiers were engaged in brutal combat with the Kreaux.

"Jahrgis! Gyepson!" Garon shouted over the thunder, howling wind, and torrential downpour. "Get those Kreaux away from the gates!"

"Yes, sir!" The armored men saluted, water and mud splashing up as they sprinted across the battlefield.

With a screech from below, Garon quickly turned to face a Kreaux Praetor ascending from the chasm—right in front of him.

Shink! With one swift motion, Garon's gleaming, wing-hilted blade sliced clean through its neck, sending the head flying through the air. With a slight push of his finger, the headless body fell hundreds of feet back down into the chasm.

"Yuhon! Üngir, Loreth!" he shouted down the line to more soldiers. "Turn those trebuchets to the chasm—three o'clock! Blast those Kreaux back to hell where they belong!"

"Yes, Commander!" they replied as they rotated the trebuchets, igniting the weapons.

Slash! Slash! Slash! Garon cut the cords and watched as molten fireballs flung through the air and into the chasm, obliterating the unlucky Kreaux attempting to climb out.

Farther down the cliff edge, warriors dashed around, igniting giant kettles of flammable oil, then tipping them over, sending cascades of "liquid lava" down the cliffs and incinerating more climbing Kreaux.

Shew, shew, shew! Arrows whistled as they were unleashed from the archers, piercing the Kreaux attacking the gates of Wölnas.

All around roared the sounds of Kreaux screeches, clanging weapons, and the yells of men locked in battle.

Constantly engaged in strategy, Garon continued to command his platoon.

"Keep firing!" he shouted, cupping his hands to amplify his voice. "Roll those boulders into the chasm! Cut them to pieces!"

"They find a way around every obstacle we put in their path…" panted a soldier, sliding down against a trebuchet.

"How the hell do we defeat them?" grunted a few soldiers, straining their backs as they pushed boulders.

"That's why you have me," said Garon proudly. "Keep going!"

"Yes, sir!" they cheered in unison, their morale briefly lifted.

Turning to another assistant soldier, Garon gave new orders: "Organize Isolv and Talvald's troops."

"Yes, Commander!" the soldier saluted before departing.

Exhausted from endless hours of combat and issuing commands, Garon approached his drenched and tattered tent. Flinging the flaps open, he stormed to the strategy table, slammed his fists down on the large map, and tried to regain his composure—just in time for an adviser to rush in.

"This is ridiculous," spat the adviser. "According to our records, the Majesty Genocidal War happened over a thousand years ago! Isn't that enough time for an enemy to die off?"

"We're not dealing with any ordinary enemy, Yjalhon," Garon replied sharply. "These are the Kreaux. They are supposedly infused with the very blood of hell."

"I understand that," muttered the adviser, "but surely there's a way to destroy them! Nothing we do seems to work!"

Straightening his back with an audible crack, Garon retorted, "I don't know, and I don't care. My job is to dispatch them, not philosophize about them."

"What? You're not even *slightly* curious?"

Turning fully to face his adviser, Garon said, "Are you deaf? Would you like me to repeat myself?"

"N-no, Commander Garon… my apologies," stammered the adviser, trying to save face as he added, "The new recruits are awaiting your address."

"Hah!" Garon laughed. "In that case, maybe you should give the speech, Yjalhon!" He clapped him on the back, a mix of humor and frustration in his voice.

In their unmarred, silver breastplates and platinum-winged helmets, the new line of recruits stood in the rain, their morale sinking like gazelles thrown to the lions.

"Welcome to Wölnas," Garon declared, withdrawing his sword and pacing the line. "The most dangerous land in all of Vaerün."

A thunderclap and blinding flash of lightning exploded overhead, illuminating the torrential downfall of rain.

No one dared to speak as he bellowed over the storm. "I am Garon Erbrecht, commander-in-chief of Wölnas. Undoubtedly aware, you're here to face an enemy."

Still pacing, he added, "The *Kreaux*. They'll stop at nothing to destroy you. They hate anything that draws breath—they hate life itself. Indeed…They are said to be the very damned souls of hell, risen by the devil himself, to destroy us."

He paused, staring at his blade. "And the way I see it? It's either us or them."

Awkward shuffling and nervous gulps rippled through the recruits, some shifting their boots as the beyond-wet, sticky mud started to absorb them.

"Anything you'd like to add, Yjalhon?" Garon asked his adviser, before shouting, "Oh! And be especially mindful of Mourners and Praetors."

With slight raise of a shaking hand, one brave recruit asked, "Um, Commander... what's a *Praetor?*"

The earth trembled beneath their feet.

What were thought to be mere tremors were now known to be Kreaux heaving their way up from underground, shifting the tectonic plates with their rapid and relentless movement.

With a sound that was equal parts screech and giant's roar, Garon turned just in time to see a Kreaux Praetor—seven-foot-five, muscular beyond comprehension—smash through the ranks of soldiers with a stark white bone club. Mandible hanging, dead, grey flesh.

"**That**, my friend." Garon said, pointing to the hulking behemoth.

Later...

Ticktock. Ticktock. The small clock, its swinging pendulum striking the seconds like a hammer against an anvil, filled Garon's large, spacious, and cozy room in the Wölnas castle.

"Arrrggh..." he grunted, stripping off his battered breastplate and torn undershirt, massaging the purple bruise left from an earlier impact.

Knock, knock! The door burst open as Büteran, the king's posh messenger, complete with an over-the-top, feathered purple hat, strutted in.

"Uh, right? Come on in?" Garon quipped sarcastically, sitting on his bed.

With a dramatic whip of a scroll and in an intentionally irritating voice, Büteran read aloud, "King Jyalhim the Fifth hereby orders Lord Garon to the southern kingdom of Fürnas on strict military business!"

Garon raised an eyebrow as Büteran continued in his squeaky, pompous tone, "There, you are to meet with their Royal Majesties, King and Queen Coltier of Fürnas. You are to depart immediately!"

Groaning heavily, Garon flopped back on his bed and waved dismissively.

"Right, right. Tell His Majesty I'll leave at dawn."

"Yes, Commander," replied the messenger, his voice dripping with condescension.

"Oh, wait, Büteran!" Garon called, just as Büteran was turning away. "Summon my best ten. I want good protection while I'm there."

"As you wish, sir," Büteran snickered as he left.

"Oh, and close the door on your way out!" Garon bellowed.

"As you wish, sir!" Büteran barked back, slamming the door behind him.

"Oh, and make sure you knock next time, jackass!" Garon shouted one last time, clearly at the end of his patience.

"I swear…" he muttered, pulling a pillow over his head. "How about I wear that 'posh fool's outfit,' kiss up to the king all day, while you go out and fight the Kreaux?"

Letting out a deep breath, Garon burst out laughing, picturing Büteran flailing fabulously on the Kreaux battlefield in his ridiculous purple feathered hat.

Awoken by the sound of a thunderclap, Garon groaned as he clambered out of bed, his bare feet touching the cool wooden floor, sending a chill up his spine.

"Top secret business in Fürnas…" he groaned. "The king sure knows how to bait me." With that, he jumped up and pulled on his trousers. Still trying to shake off sleep, he leaned against the cold stone wall and peered out the window.

"For today's weather?" he said sarcastically. "It'll be cloudy, rainy, and stormy—for now and forevermore!"

With a flip of the ornate metal latch at the bottom of the silver window frame, the stained-glass window flew open, slamming against the outside wall as gale-force winds howled through.

"Uh-oh," he muttered as he cupped his hands to gather water from the rain and splashed it on his face—an obvious part of his daily ritual. Reaching out, he pulled the window shut, latching it tightly before chuckling to himself.

"They sure know how to make 'em!" he admired, patting the undamaged window. "Not bad for a thousand-year-old piece of glass."

After splashing his face with fresh rainwater and rubbing it over his upper torso, he quickly dressed, fastening his greaves, breastplate, and the purple Wölnas insignia cloak (worn only by the kingdom's highest order). He secured his sheathed sword and helmet around his waist.

Down in the stable, his ten soldiers were busy preparing the horses. One blessing of living in a kingdom perpetually besieged by storms was that Wölnas's horses were unshakable, unbothered by anything or anyone.

"G'morning, Commander!" shouted his ten soldiers in unison as he entered the stables.

"Today, we ride for Fürnas," Garon announced. "For those of you who've never left Wölnas, we first travel south up and through the Algár Mountain pass. From there, we'll restock supplies at the trail outposts and villages. Any questions?"

"Yes, sir," asked one soldier. "How long will it take to reach Fürnas, sir?"

"By our stallions?" Garon pondered, giving a half-smile. "About five days. By any other horse? Good luck."

The group burst into laughter as they mounted their black stallions. Following Garon's lead, the party departed for Fürnas.

Chapter 2

A Path Less Traveled

From atop the Algár Mountain Pass, they had a perfect view of the Northern Valley housing the Wölnas Kingdom.

Directly above them, the gray clouds and light drizzle of rain showed signs of the storm's retreat as they traveled farther and farther from the storm-ravaged kingdom. However, Wölnas remained as dark as ever, buffeted by the storm overhead.

"Sir, if I may?" muttered a soldier.

"Speak, soldier. What is it?" Garon replied.

"Do you know why Wölnas is incessantly blasted by that tempest?"

Taking a moment to think about it, Garon sighed. "To be absolutely honest, I have no idea. Even the original tomes and scrolls, dating back over a thousand years, can't explain it."

Another soldier rode up, intrigued by the conversation. "You think that's interesting? Did you know that Fürnas is perpetually autumn? The season there never changes!"

With that comment, another soldier chimed in. "That's nothing! Did you know that the Water Kingdom of Wöntylnas is built out on the ocean? Who does stuff like that? How is that even possible?"

One lucky soldier got the last word in. "I'm personally intrigued by Grünas! They say it's like an absolute garden paradise!"

"That's enough!" shouted Garon, silencing everyone.

"If you're all so interested, by all means, go ahead and enjoy your vacation to the other kingdoms! But I have duty in Fürnas. So all of you take care." And with that, Garon cracked the reins and dashed down the path. It didn't take long before all his soldiers immediately followed without hesitation.

Descending down the mountain path and onto the Northern plains of Vaerün, they were greeted by a cool, refreshing breeze carrying the sweet scent of spring flowers. The sun beamed overhead, only to be teased every now and then by passing clouds casting ever-so-light shadows. The rolling green hills appeared to wave at them as the gentle wind tickled the vibrant grass and flowers.

"Gorgeous, isn't it?" said Garon, entranced. "I can't remember the last time I felt sunlight."

Too afraid to say anything for fear of a witty comeback, no one spoke. Instead, they soaked in the stunning vista all around them.

"Anyway! Let's go," Garon said, shaking it off quickly. "The next town is about seven hours from here. If we succeed in reaching it by nightfall, Alansgrú's on me!" (Alansgrú is a dark, molasses-like stout that is extremely popular in the Wölnas Kingdom.)

"Woo, yeah!" shouted the team as they galloped past Garon.

"That's the spirit!" he laughed. "But don't leave your commander behind!"

Thunk, thunk, thunk, thunk, sounded the horses' hooves on the moist earthen pathways as they entered a small village. Tying up their horses in a nearby stable, Garon handed the stable boy eleven pieces of silver—one for each horse.

Since each horse only cost one copper, and with ten copper making one silver, one hundred silver making one gold piece, and one thousand gold pieces making a bar of platinum, one could only imagine how delighted the stable boy was!

Though a humble dwelling, the village was cozy. The thatched rooftops with brown boarded clay walls gave the homes a feeling of comfort. Some even had their doors open!

The rustic windows glowed with the warm orange light of firelit lanterns. And oh, the smell. A boar was roasting on a spit just outside the tavern. With salivating tongues, they could almost taste the heavily seasoned, juicy meat. But no one was more excited than the well-fed middle-aged man turning the crank.

Looking just northwest, one's heart could only melt as a light sprinkle of rain gently fell from the sky. Catching the setting sunlight just right, the raindrops appeared like falling fire. Combining this visual spectacle with the orange light of the windows, the glow of the fire, and the heavenly smell of roasted boar mingled with fresh rain and flowers, it felt like the most alive place on earth.

And what? Oh no… don't tell me someone was baking a fresh loaf of bread! Who needs money when the earth gives you more than you could ever dream of?

"All right, boys, as promised…" said Garon as he took off his gauntlets. "Since we made it by sunset, drinks are on me!"

With a roar of cheers, his men shuffled into the small tavern, eager to get started with their stouts. Garon, on the other hand, approached the man roasting the boar.

The following morning…

"House call!" rapped the maidservant on the inn doors, waking the soldiers. After quickly dressing, their boots clacked against the polished wooden floorboards as they came downstairs to see Garon patiently sitting at one of the small round oak tables, sipping from a steaming mug.

The delicious smell and sound of sizzling pork, bacon, and eggs sent their stomachs growling as they leaned in, anticipating breakfast.

"Sorry, boys. Already ate!" Garon shrugged. "That's what you get for sleeping in."

"Awwwwww!" came the synchronized groans.

"Hah! I kid!" he exclaimed, slapping the table. "Sit down! Sit down! Breakfast is on me!"

Before he could even finish his sentence, the soldiers were already seated at the round oak tables, silverware in hand, salivating as steaming plates of pork slices, scrambled eggs, and fresh-baked bread with sides of fresh-churned butter and kinberry jam were served. They immediately descended upon their plates like a Kreaux upon the unarmed.

Rolling their shoulders and straightening their backs as they stood, the soldiers and Garon gave sincere thanks for the hospitality, paying generously for their meal.

The stable boy nearly collapsed with gratitude as Garon gave him an additional tip.

"Thank you, young man!" Garon said with a smile to the farmhand as he and his men departed on the road once again to the southern Fürnas Kingdom. "Take care!"

The noonday sun cast a quiet warmth on the party, making everyone sleepy and giving them ideas of a nap, especially after that breakfast. The chirping birds flying overhead didn't help, and the rustling leaves of nearby trees beckoned them to rest in their cooling shade.

"Another question for you, sir," said a soldier, attempting to sound bold as he bobbled up and down on his horse.

"If it's going to be another dumb question about kingdoms, Gyepson," retorted Garon without looking over his shoulder, "I'm not interested."

"N-no, sir," Gyepson stammered. "Actually, it was about the town we just visited. It was very peaceful, sir, and I was just curious. Do you think they've ever been victims of a Kreaux attack?"

Before Garon could answer, another soldier piped up. "Doubt it, idiot. Think for a moment! Those people looked like they've never wielded a weapon in their life!"

"Unless you count a shovel, hoe, or hay slinger! Ha ha ha!" added another soldier, prompting laughter from the group.

"Hush!" demanded Garon, immediately silencing the group. "That's enough out of you, Talvald and Jahrgis!" He then turned calmly back to Gyepson. "I can understand your curiosity. But I'm afraid, once again, I don't have the answer to your question."

Some dandelions floated past as he continued, "It is thought that the Kreaux only attack those who summon them with ill intentions, thoughts, and deeds, but…"

Pausing to reflect for a moment, Garon continued, "I grew up in a village just like that. About ten miles east of the one we just passed, near the foothold of the Algár Mountains."

No one said a word as he continued, "I watched as my best friend, Türen, was consumed by a Mourner. The villagers were mauled to death by Kreaux and then dragged underground... all before my very eyes. I, however, was the only one who stood and fought."

There was complete silence. Even the horses seemed to tread softly, their hooves barely making a sound against the earth.

"Oh, and for the record," he snickered, "Talvald and Jahrgis? I was one of those peasant boys who fought for my life with a hay slinger."

Galloping ahead of them, Garon left the boys stumped, feeling like "jackasses" with his parting words.

With a roaring campfire before them and an innumerable host of stars glowing above, Garon, Talvald, and Jahrgis sat around the campfire. The other men were asleep on the ground, resting on makeshift pillows made of balled-up shirts or logs, their silver armor gleaming in the orange firelight.

"So, sir... about earlier..." Talvald swallowed nervously.

"Really sorry, sir. We didn't know," completed Jahrgis.

"Ehhhhh." Garon's hand rolled as he looked away shyly. "Don't worry about it." He offered a slight smile, embarrassed that he'd given away so much about his past.

"If I may be so bold as to ask, Commander," Jahrgis asked quietly, "what happened?"

Letting out a deep sigh and leaning back to rest on one elbow, Garon said, "It's really not worth all the details. We see enough bloodshed every day in Wölnas as it is. You don't need more nightmares put into your heads."

With stark faces, the twins—with black wavy hair, green eyes, and freckles made even more pronounced by the firelight—stared back at him intensely.

"Bah! Fine," he finally gave in. "Short version though! Okay?"

With slight smiles and nods, they agreed. Garon told them, "I had just turned twelve. Hell of a summer, that one! Mom had just finished placing her peach and kinberry pie into the oven."

Looking off and swallowing to regain composure, he continued, "An earthquake hit... or what we thought was an earthquake. Next thing I knew, all I heard was screaming. And a sound I had never heard before. Two sounds, actually."

"What were they, sir?" Talvald asked quietly.

"The first was the screeching of the Kreaux, and the second... was the sound of flesh being ripped apart."

Swallowing nervously, the twins looked away.

"My first thought was to get Pa," Garon said, staring into the fire. "He was always out, tending to the rye fields. My fears were confirmed when my mother yelled for me to get him, demanding that she stay put and hide under the kitchen table. I rushed to find my father."

"Did you find him? Your Pa?" whispered Jahrgis.

Letting out a deep sigh, Garon looked up into the night sky as he answered, "Oh, I found him all right—being mauled to death by four Kreaux!"

"Shüza..." whispered Jahrgis. (*Shüza* is the equivalent of saying "Sh——" in our language.)

Sitting up and massaging his shoulder, Garon finished, "You know what the worst part was? Coming back home to inhale the smell of burned pie. The smoke filled the house."

He leaned forward as tears filled his eyes. Hoarsely, he whispered, "And underneath the table lay a black hole, with black blood oozing around it."

With a disgusted grimace, the twins looked away, their heads hung low.

"So yeah!" exclaimed Garon, breaking the trance. "From there, I grabbed a pitchfork and fled the village, destroying some Kreaux on the way out. I had heard that the Wölnas Kingdom was not far northwest. Always forbidden to go there, on account of it being foreboding, that was the only place I knew I could go to for help."

Talvald shook his head in amazement. "Wow, so you walked all the way there by yourself?"

"Yep. Originally named Gerund after the Wölnas king of old, the current king, Jyalhim the Fifth, fearing future usurpation, renamed me Garon and drafted me into the army. From there, I worked my way up to commander in chief, and here I am!"

Shaking their heads, with no words to say, they looked up at their commander with an entirely new respect.

"Haha, but enough about me, lads!" Garon laughed as he stood up. "Glad to have you on my team."

"Sir, yessir!" muttered the twins in sync.

Garon pointed to Jahrgis as he said, "Jahrgis, take the first watch, followed by Talvald. After your shift, wake me up!"

"Wow!" came the enchanted shouts of the soldiers as they continued down the road, looking eastward to the gargantuan white-marble tower of Laniakéa that seemed to touch the heavens. The midmorning sun wrapped its light around the tower and beamed past, perfectly illuminating the gorgeous structure.

"**Laniakéa**!" called out Garon as they continued riding. "Incredible, isn't it? Tale has it that she was built by the Majesticians of old, over a thousand years ago!"

"Do we have any of their remaining blueprints?" asked the ever-curious Gyepson. "How in Vaerün can an architectural structure of that magnitude still stand, looking as flawless as the day it was built? I'm sure it has absolutely no flaws! It's just like the tower stationed at the back of our castle!"

"No blueprints remain," answered Garon. "And even if they did, it's believed there's no way we could possibly replicate something so structurally perfect and sound." He motioned to Laniakéa. "They possessed ingenuity unlike any other. Our castle and tower share no exception. The other three kingdoms have the same unparalleled design and materials!"

"Woooow..." echoed the additional admiration from the soldiers.

Garon looked forward and, with a hint of sarcasm, added, "It's also believed that their powers helped them build such structures."

"*Powers?* You don't believe in the tales of Majesty, Commander?" inquired Gyepson, never shy to ask another question.

"Hard to believe in something I've never seen," Garon answered flatly. "The tales say that this... *'power'*... called Majesty only chose those who were worthy."

"What? If that's the case, then aren't all of us worthy?" a soldier from the back inquired.

"Hah! You're hardly worthy, Ponüren!" chided Talvald. "I doubt the power of heaven would ever choose a relentless booger-picker like you!"

With horrifying embarrassment, Ponüren immediately pulled his fingers away from his face, clasping them behind his back, looking up into the sky and whistling.

"We're actually doing great on time," Garon changed the subject. "Laniakéa marks the center of Vaerün. Let's push faster! By nightfall, we should reach the town of Fährlund. Hya!" Spurring his stallion faster, the men bolted down the road.

Thump, thump, thump, THUMP! pounded Garon's heart as they entered the small town of Fährlund. Taking in a deep breath, the smell of peach and kinberry pie filled his nostrils. Struck by nostalgia, he momentarily gripped his head, dismounted his stallion, and leaned against it to steady himself.

"Commander!" shouted a few concerned men as they rushed to his side.

"I'm fine!" barked back Garon, causing them to recoil before he calmly added, "I'm fine. Sorry. Jahrgis! Come here."

"Yes, Commander?" Jahrgis asked as he quickly jumped off his horse.

"Take this. You and the men enjoy yourselves," Garon said as he handed Jahrgis a large pouch of silver. "Do whatever you see fit. Just make sure to meet me at the southern end of Fährlund by first dawn."

"But what will you do, Commander?" inquired Talvald politely, trying not to seem too eager to indulge.

"Don't worry about me. Just do as I say," responded Garon, eyes closed as he continued massaging his head.

"Er... as you say, sir!"

With that, the eager soldiers flew down the road, excited to spend their night doing heaven knows what.

Slowly opening his eyes and taking in a deep breath of the fresh evening air, Garon decided to walk his horse to the stable.

What a lovely sight. Looking south, he enjoyed the view of the rolling cobblestone streets. To his left and right lay all sorts of decorative houses, each with wood-post doors, flower boxes overflowing with flora, and colorful tiled rooftops as far as he could see. The clouds above cast their enchanting pink-and-yellow glow, lit aflame by the twilight sun.

"Must be close to Fürnas...," he muttered as his boots clacked on the stone street. "The sky only looks like this around the Fürnas region."

He paused, sniffing the air repeatedly before asking, "Now where is that smell coming from?"

After roughly thirty minutes of wandering and with the help of some townspeople, he reached a small bakery cramped between two homes. The black metal rings on the wooden sign creaked as it swayed overhead, reading *Nan's Bakery*.

Not having had sweets in many years, Garon couldn't believe he had just walked in.

"Well, *well!*" boomed a pleasant voice with a Fürnasian accent (similar to a Southern hospitality twang) as he entered. "Pa always told me my baked goods would land me a handsome angel someday!"

Out shuffled a small, plump woman with beet-red cheeks (covered in flour), wearing a light-blue dress, overly busting bosom, white bonnet and checkered apron.

"Tabatha Tromsdotter at your service!" curtsied the cheerful baker. "But you can just call me Nann!"

"Ah-hem." Garon coughed, shy and unsure of how to respond as he glanced around. "It, uh... smells amazing in here. Is that...?" He trailed off, as he took in a deep whiff. "Peach and kinberry pie?"

"It sure is!" she jubilantly retorted. "Coming out right now! Would you care for a slice?" she asked cheerfully, standing behind the counter stacked with pastries, muffins, breads, and pies.

Opening the black-hatched door behind her, she wielded a wooden board and skillfully shoveled the pie out, setting it on the counter to cool.

"Now!" she huffed, placing her elbows on the counter and staring at him. "What brings the commander over Wölnas's army to these parts?"

Garon turned around to make sure that no one was behind him before asking, "What? How did you know?"

"Hah! Now just because we're out in the country doesn't make us bumsquats!" she boasted. "Whether you believe it or not, I'm actually the founder of Fährlund!"

"That is impressive," he said, walking up as she turned to tend to another oven. "Mayor too?"

"Noooo! No, no!" Nan refused as she pulled out more pastries. "I prefer to bake, as you can see!" She laughed, turning around to pat her large figure. "Though I did pass the title of mayor to my brother, Gürkan."

"Right, I can… just, right." Garon nodded, raising his eyebrows and squeezing his lips together, trying not to laugh.

Always good at changing the subject, he stuck out his hand and exclaimed, "I'm Garon Erbrecht!"

With a smile and a warm, floury hand, she robustly shook his.

"So, let me ask again, Commander," she trailed off, as she brushed down her apron, "what brings you to these parts? Are you afraid Fährlund's gonna be attacked by the Kreaux?"

"To be honest, that's the least of my concerns," he admitted. "My business lies in Fürnas."

Nan leaned in, sensing an opportunity to flirt. "This gets better and better by the moment! Whatever for?"

Feigning secrecy and sarcasm, he continued, "Can't say. Top secret business."

"I see," Nan uttered as she turned to open the oven door, placing another pie inside to bake. "Would it have anything to do with their new weapon?" she asked over her shoulder.

Breaking from his relaxed demeanor, Garon straightened up. "Weapon? Ahem! I mean... what kind of weapon?" he asked, attempting to regain his cool.

"Ha ha! You won't fool me, dear!" she teased with an upraised finger. "Even if you are handsome as I don't know what."

"Not even a little bite?" Garon asked slowly, playfully.

"Oh, I'll give you a bite, all right!" Nan laughed as she cut a fresh slice of pie and handed it to him. "Here! This one's on me, handsome." She winked.

Hot steam wafted from the gooey filling of yellow-and-pinkish-red peaches, oozing out and mixing with the vibrant purple of the kinberries.

Licking his lips and eyes widening, Garon snatched the fork from her hand as she held it up with a knowing look, as if to say, "Uh-huh. Go right ahead, darling. I know the masterpiece I've just created."

"Sor!" choked out Garon with a tiny gap in his mouth to speak. "Wern't yer terl mer abert ders werpern?"

"Ha ha ha! Just for you, hun," Nan said as she tickled his scruffy black goatee. "I'll tell you all I know. Although, to be absolutely honest, I don't know much! Gossip from the people of Fürnas says that King and Queen Coltier discovered an incredibly powerful and treasured weapon."

She then leaned forward, whispering conspiratorially with a hand to the side of her mouth, "One unlike any other that hasn't been seen for over a thousand years!"

"Are you certain?" he asked with a raised eyebrow, while finishing his bite. "How reliable are these sources?"

"Couldn't say, love." She shrugged. "All I know is that people are getting restless since their Majesties refuse to share the weapon with anyone. They say it's too precious and vulnerable in its current state—and needs time to develop."

"What in Vaerün? That doesn't make any sense!" he said, now audible after swallowing another bite of pie.

With a desperate look, he poked at the steaming pie. "And... um... would it be asking too much if..."

"Aren't you just adorable!" She beamed as she scooped up another slice of gooey pie. "You want another slice?"

With the eager nodding of an eight-year-old, Garon accepted another slice of pie.

"Aren't the peaches just the best? They came fresh from the field today!" she claimed proudly.

"No way! For me, it's all about the kinberries!" he retorted.

"Oh, is that so? Well then, I'm sorry, Garon, but there's no way this will ever work. It's only peaches for me," she said coolly, looking away with an upturned nose, folded arms, and a hint of flirtation.

"That's a real shame," he teased back. "I was so sure it would work out."

A slight pause held in the air before he burst out, "Are you kidding me? How in **Vaerün** can you choose peaches over kinberries?"

Pretending to be offended, she retorted, "My, my, *my!* Commander Erbrecht! Do control yourself!" Nan laughed sarcastically as she continued, "Although delicious, they're a little too exotic for me. You know they only grow in the Fürnas region, don't you?"

"They are by far my favorite berries," he admitted. "Perhaps even my favorite food! I had forgotten how amazing they are," he finished, looking up at the ceiling as if staring into heaven.

"Oh, that's right," she said, handing him another slice. "I'd heard that Wölnas is covered in perpetual storm. What on earth do you people feed on?"

"Ohhrrr… thart's errrsy," he mumbled through a mouthful before swallowing. "Mostly tubers and roots. Oh, and lots of meat. But enough about food. Won't you please tell me more about this weapon?" he asked while shoveling another bite of pie into his mouth.

"I'm afraid that's all I know," she admitted. "But for some reason, I assume you're headed there to find out?"

He tilted his head curiously.

"Well, isn't it obvious?" she asked. "You're not here for Fährlund. Wöntylnas is northwest from here, and the closest civilization is to the south, which is Fürnas!"

Boom! The French door slammed open, and the clinking bell nearly flew off its thin bar.

"Sir!" huffed Gyepson as he stormed in, out of breath. "Come quick! Talvald, Jahrgis, Urgen, and Hjalor are all fighting in the tavern!"

"I mean really," Garon stated, standing up and brushing pie crumbs from his hands. "Can't I get one peaceful night away from you deviants? What's going on?"

"Um, well…" Gyepson admitted sheepishly, "Talvald was flirting with a girl in the tavern, but apparently, she was married, but, um… I mean, she was flirting back with him, and so… her husband caught them and… well, yeah."

Looking down and gruffly scratching his neck, Garon turned to Nan.

"It was a pleasure, Tabatha Tromsdotter. May we meet again!" he called as they ran out the door.

"**The pleasure was all mine, handsome!**" she shouted back, laughing out loud.

"Oh, and your pie…" he added, poking his head back in the doorframe. "Amazing. Haven't had pie that delicious since my mom died. So… thank you," he finished, then dashed down the street to rescue his soldiers.

CHAPTER 3

The Kingdom of Fürnas

"Whooooaaa!" The soldiers sighed in awe as they gazed down the open road, seeing a wall of red-, orange-, yellow-, and brown-leaved trees, with red and yellow grass flowing beneath them.

"Haha!" Garon laughed. "I think I've heard you all say that word a few times now on this trip."

"Sir... this is... incredible!" shouted Talvald. "It really is perpetually autumn!"

"No way! Look, look!" Jahrgis bobbled excitedly. "See how the green grass just stops right there? And then—boom! This sudden autumn forest just explodes out of nowhere! That's killer!"

"Come on, come on! I want to see what it looks like inside!" Gyepson shouted, dashing ahead into the forest.

Even Garon joined in the unceasing chorus of "Wow" as they rode through the woods. The late-afternoon sun cast its rays through the leaves, creating a kaleidoscope effect of red and yellow light that illuminated the ground.

Crunch, crunch! The dead leaves crackled beneath their feet. While one might normally consider fallen leaves a nuisance, these leaves seemed to fit perfectly along the forest pathway. It would be a sin to rake or disturb them—they formed an almost sacred, historical carpet that seemed destined to be untouched.

All around, the soldiers found themselves encompassed in a velvet world of warm colors. The air was fresh, clean, and utterly revitalizing. A short while ago, they had been embraced by summer's warmth; now, the cool breeze of this forest transported them into the heart of autumn. The beautiful rustling of leaves in the wind stirred their souls like heavenly music.

Thud! Garon jumped off his stallion and approached a large wooden archway a few feet ahead. Removing his gauntlet, he gently touched the cool wood. It had the texture of the hardest stone, yet appeared utterly brand-new. Carved into the keystone of the archway were the words: *"Kingdom of Fürnas: Home to the Eternal Heavenly Flame."*

"Ahem! Ready, men?" he called out as he remounted his horse.

"Sir!" came the synchronized response.

After less than an hour of travel, the scattered cobblestones beneath them became more tightly packed, transforming the thump, thump, thump of the horses' hooves into a steady clippity-clop. Small cabins began appearing along the streets, and as the inhabitants ran out, "Oohing" and "Aaaahing" at the foreign faction, Garon and his men were delighted by their kind, humble welcome.

Slowly, as the houses became more abundant, the trees grew larger. The ornate white lampposts lining the streets held levitating flames, casting light that added even more color to the rich surroundings. It seemed as if dead leaves, rather than rain, were falling from the massive trees above, filling the air with an enchanting dance of autumn hues.

What a restful place, this kingdom. No one seemed to rush, nor were they lazy. Men, women, and elders stood outside their doorsteps, raking leaves into large piles, only for children to leap in and scatter them. It seemed like they were about to be scolded, but instead, the adults laughed and jumped into the piles right behind them, flinging leaves everywhere!

The happiness, comfort, and love were positively contagious. Although the air held a cool autumn chill, there was an almost tangible warmth that wrapped around one's soul, emanating from the entire kingdom.

"Oh, oh, oh! Hi, Mr. Guy, sir!" shouted an excited young boy as he ran alongside Garon's horse. "Oh, oh! He's so pretty! Can I pet him?"

"Éynath! What do you say?" called out his parents, pausing their leaf-raking.

"Oh, oh!" stammered the boy, "Sorry! May I please pet him, Mr. Guy, sir?"

Laughing and trying to blink away the tears that were strangely forming in his eyes, Garon swallowed, bit his lower lip, and jumped off his horse. Kneeling on one knee, he whispered to the young boy.

"Éynath, was it? I'll do you one better! Up you go!" With a gentle lift, Garon placed him atop his stallion.

"Oh, wow! Oh, wow! Oh, wow!" Éynath shouted. "Mom! Pap! Do you see me? Do you see?"

His parents laughed in gratitude and bowed humbly to Garon, who bowed back. After a few minutes, Garon gently placed Éynath back on the ground, and the boy wrapped his legs around him in a tight hug.

Quickly brushing tears from his eyes, Garon approached the parents.

"Excuse me. I'm Garon Erbrecht, commander-in-chief of Wölnas. I have a summons to report to King and Queen Coltier. Would you please direct me to the castle?"

The family, refusing to simply give directions, insisted that Garon and his men join them for some hearty stew and fresh bread. After some polite denying, Garon eventually gave in.

With full bellies and renewed spirits, they were then directed up the pathway to Fürnas Castle.

Upon arrival, Garon and his soldiers dismounted their horses, an act of respect on royal grounds, regardless of one's status.

The castle was breathtaking. Like Wölnas's castle and Laniakéa, it was constructed of smooth white marble, etched with unique red designs. The pointed rooftops were made of a rare red stone topped with golden spires.

Only two soldiers guarded the massive cherry-wooden doors. Wearing golden breastplates and red-and-white underclothes, they were thrilled to greet Garon and his men. And this wasn't just a formal, obligatory greeting—it was the genuine joy of meeting long-lost friends.

"Garon Erbrecht, right?" said one of the soldiers, shaking his hand vigorously while the other led his horse to the royal stable. "What a pleasure it is to meet you, sir! We are absolutely delighted!"

"Oh, um... likewise!" Garon smiled, his voice vibrating from the enthusiastic handshake.

"We've been anticipating you for some time now. Please, right this way!" the soldier said as he heaved open one of the castle's large white doors.

Impressive emblem, Garon thought, admiring the red-etched design on the castle's doors.

As they entered, Garon and his men stood awestruck, their mouths agape. White marble pillars, lightly marbled with red, lined the grand foyer. A large chandelier of gold and silver hung above them, adorned with crystal that cast a spectrum of rainbow colors as the setting sun gloriously shone through a massive western window.

Large paintings lined the walls, and white furniture held ornate vases. At the top of the grand staircase hung the largest painting—a portrait of King and Queen Coltier with their arms wrapped around a young girl.

Slam! Beneath the portrait, two white doors burst open! What appeared to be an angel came running out.

Her gorgeously long, breath-stealing, shimmering blonde hair twisted and danced through the air. A gossamer white dress trimmed with red flowed around her as she descended the stairs, her heavenly white hand guiding her down the polished wood railing.

She flew into Garon's arms, wrapping him in an embrace. Her dress and hair flowed around him as if her whole being surrounded him, filling him with a sense of joy and belonging he had never dreamed of, let alone thought possible.

And oh... the smell of her hair and dress! How could someone or something smell this divine? Even the peach and kinberry pie he'd had seemed less enchanting in comparison.

"Garon... Erbrecht," Lucy said, pulling back slightly while still holding onto his arms. Her soul-searching, light-blue eyes pierced him, filling him with a feeling one could only describe as indescribable. It was far beyond love at first sight. He felt as if he had met this woman before, as if some deep connection existed between them.

"I am absolutely delighted to meet you!" she exclaimed. "I am Lucy Dolliér, adviser to Their Majesties. I've heard so much about you! Please, come right this way. King and Queen Coltier are expecting you!" she said excitedly, taking his hand and leading him up the staircase.

Wait a second, he thought, following her. I thought it was supposed to be the woman who melts, not the man... right?

My word, he continued to think, completely entranced by this angelic woman. That heart-shaped face... those stunning pink lips. He couldn't even recall what the hallways looked like as they passed by. How could he describe the fierce suits of armor that lined the halls or the intricate crown molding? And the magical flames suspended in the chandeliers? None of it registered.

"Garon, how were your travels? Was everything all right? Have the people of Fürnas treated you well? Are you hungry or thirsty?" Lucy asked as they hurried down the halls, her small hand squeezing his much larger (and gruffer) one.

Sadly, he couldn't utter a single word. He was too entranced by her beauty, her presence, her... everything. Again, there was something familiar about her. Had they met before?

"Garon Erbrecht!" the King and Queen called as they entered the throne room.

Horror! Disdain! Total shock! Garon's fantasy came to a screeching halt. Yet... he still felt the warmth of Lucy's hand in his. Slowly, he turned to look at her with a sad puppy-dog face—the kind dogs make when at the vet. *Please don't leave me...*

"Don't worry. You'll be just fine," she whispered. "We'll have more than enough time to catch up later. You are staying for a while... right?"

Still unable to speak, he sheepishly nodded—then did so profusely.

"Excellent," she whispered. And with that... she was gone.

"Please close the doors behind you on your way out, Ms. Dolliér," called out the king.

"Of course, Your Majesty," she responded.

And with that, they were alone—just Garon, the King, and Queen in the vast hall. Well, and a random assistant guarding some door.

At least they were smiling, and their countenances held nothing but warmth and hospitality. They sat side by side on their throne chairs, hands clasped together, their red coats and gold crowns exuding regality.

Garon turned and looked behind him.

Lucy? he thought as a smile erupted on his face. *What a beautiful name.*

"Garon! Will you please come forward?" called out the king.

As if the entire universe were contained in a single bubble, and as if that bubble had just been popped by the darkest, ugliest, most ruthless needle, Garon stepped forward.

Clearing his throat, Garon took a deep breath and boldly walked up to Their Majesties.

"Greetings, Your Majesties," he said strongly. "I am Garon Erbrecht, commander-in-chief of Wölnas, serving directly under King Jyalhim the Fifth."

King Coltier spoke up first, "It is an honor to make your acquaintance, Garon. I am King Verolt Coltier, and this is my wife, Queen Layna Coltier."

"We understand you're a very busy man," added the queen. "You and your soldiers will find proper housing and accommodations while here in Fürnas. You are permitted to stay here, in the castle, in the guest quarters."

Garon's heart fluttered.

The guest quarters? Does Lucy stay in the castle? Will I get to see her? That'd be perfect!

Suddenly, he mustered all his mental strength to banish thoughts of secret dates and nodded in gratitude.

"That would be… wonderful. Thank you very much, Your Majesty."

"Now, have you heard any rumors about Fürnas of late?" inquired the queen, leaning forward. "Anything regarding... a weapon, perhaps?"

"No, Your Majesty," he lied.

"Hmm... well, in case you had, it's true," she added, leaning back into her chair.

"Hah!" the king laughed. "Although, I doubt our daughter would prefer to be called a weapon."

Right, right... daughters and weapons... weapons and daughters and Lucy and... wait, what?

"Wait, what?" he blurted out, louder and more disrespectfully than he intended. "Your daughter is a weapon?"

Unfazed, the king continued to laugh heartily.

"I suppose it'd be much easier to demonstrate rather than explain."

He turned to a servant guarding the door. "Kirtor, can you please have Jenna come in?"

"Of course, Your Majesty," replied Kirtor, walking away.

After a few moments, he returned with a young girl following behind. Kirtor resumed his post as the girl gracefully approached. She was peculiar! Her reddish-brown hair flowed well past the middle of her back, and her red-and-white dress resembled Lucy's. Her black boots clacked on the floor as she stood before her parents, then turned to face Garon.

"Garon Erbrecht, this is our daughter, Jenna Coltier," boasted the king.

"Jenna, dear... Garon would very much like to see a demonstration of your powers," added the queen.

With a confident nod, she turned to Garon. Observing her closely, he noticed that her irises were slowly moving! Unlike the solid irises of ordinary humans, Jenna's vibrant red eyes swirled as if some magical power resided deep within her. At first, it startled him, but the more he stared, the more comfort and hope they brought him. Truly, this was no ordinary girl.

With a doll-like expression, Jenna raised her left palm—face-up and extended. As if illuminated from within, Jenna's irises began to glow, and soon the red in her eyes danced. As her dress and hair levitated slightly, a faint red glow surrounded her body.

Ffffsshhaawwwrgh! roared the sudden fireball that levitated just above her palm. With a slight twitch of her hand, the flame leaped into the air, dancing obediently to her every command.

The warmth that radiated from her filled Garon with indescribable vitality, hope, and wonder. It was as if someone had opened a door to let in a refreshing breeze, sweeping away stagnant air. He felt consumed by a desire to return somewhere familiar, though he couldn't recall where.

"Incredible," he muttered. While one might expect to be horrified, it felt impossible to fear her powers. They brought only comfort and familiarity.

"This is unbelievable," he said, his eyes following the zipping fireball like a cat chasing a laser pointer. "I had heard stories, but I never believed them. Now that I see it… it's almost like I knew it all along and had just forgotten."

"Thank you, Jenna. That's enough," the king spoke gently.

As if crushing the air in her palm, the flame vanished instantly. Giving a respectful bow, she left the room, accompanied by Kirtor.

"I suppose it would have done us well to ask you this first, but…" the queen shifted nervously. "Do you know what a Majestician is, Garon?"

Clearing his throat, he responded, "Oh, yes! During my training, I spent my free time in our castle library, reading the copied scripts of ancient tomes and manuscripts." Looking toward the door where Jenna exited, he walked closer to Their Majesties. "They spoke of a power called Majesty, wielded by those dubbed Majesticians. But I must confess, my belief was… lacking."

"We understand. We've been there," said the king thoughtfully. "Jenna's only six, but she's incredibly bright. We always knew something was special about her."

"The first moment she opened her eyes, we realized something was different," added the queen. "I'm sure you noticed her eyes as well."

"Yes, Your Majesty. Her irises... they are unbelievable. So then...?"

"Correct, Garon," the queen blurted out. "Jenna is a Majestician! The first to be born in over a thousand years!"

"I'll get right to it," the king declared. "You're here because we'd like you to train her. While none of us have experience with Majesty, we've heard you're the best trainer in all of Vaerün."

The queen placed her hand on the king's shoulder. "Trust us. Some of our best soldiers have trained under you. We've heard first-hand how incredible you are. Your reputation precedes you."

"If you accept, your duration here can be as long or short as you wish, though we request at least a month," said the king.

"We shall pay you ten platinum bars. King Jyalhim has already been compensated on behalf of Wölnas," added the queen.

Ten platinum bars! Holy Kreaux! Considering Garon earned only twenty-five gold a year, the offer was overwhelming. But before he could even think of the money, his thoughts turned to Lucy.

"I'll do it. Absolutely. Thank you very... very... very much!" Garon exclaimed as he repeatedly bowed. "I shall begin tomorrow!"

"No, Garon, thank you! After five days of travel, I'm sure you're exhausted. Would you like Kirtor to show you to your quarters?" the king offered.

"Actually, if you don't mind, may I see your training grounds first?" Garon lied, eager to see Lucy.

The queen nodded with a pleased smile. "Certainly! If you exit through the door behind Kirtor, you'll find the western hall. Follow it, descend two flights of stairs, exit the double doors, and there you'll find the training grounds."

"Fantastic! Never too early to get started, right?" said Garon, already on his way out, Lucy at the forefront of his mind.

Their Majesties exchanged amused glances as the king softly said, "I... suppose? Oh, and Garon, when you're ready to retire, please ask any of our servants. They'll direct you to your quarters."

"Trust me, I know just who to ask," Garon muttered under his breath as he rushed out.

The west hall was as impeccable as the grand foyer and throne room. The polished white granite floor mirrored the light of the setting sun. The suits of armor, holding silver and black axes with the Fürnas flame insignia, seemed to burn with the outline of the sunset.

"Excuse me! Sorry, but could you tell me where I might find Lucy... Lucy..." Garon stammered, stopping a passing servant.

"Dolliér?" answered the servant.

"Yes! Please," Garon replied, smiling nervously.

"I'm not certain, but last I checked, she was in the concert hall, down the northern hall, and—"

"Great! Thank you! Take care!" Garon took off before the servant could finish.

Not jogging but not quite walking either, Garon moved quickly past servants and nobility. Suddenly, he faced a man in oversized armor with a red cloak tied around his neck—another commander.

"Garon Erbrecht!" the commander shouted, jogging to keep up. "What an honor to meet you. I've heard so much! Won't you please come to dinner and—"

"Sorry! Don't have time! Maybe later?" Garon cut him off as he hurried away.

"Oh, well, we'll—" the commander's voice trailed off as Garon reached the end of the hall and descended a staircase, finding another long hall that extended north. This must be it! He ran down the hall, relieved to see no one in sight.

Hold on... what was that? He heard something. Standing still, holding his breath, he strained to listen.

A strange, new sound! It was positively enchanting, yet unfamiliar. And it was beautiful.

Like a spirit pulling him forward with invisible twine, Garon continued. The sound grew louder and clearer. Music! But was it singing? A lyre? A harp? A drum? No, it was different.

The music grew louder as Garon approached two double doors. Thrusting them open, he found Lucy Dolliér sitting at a concert grand piano in the center of a vast concert hall.

The last of the setting sun cast its golden glow through the white curtains, rippling as the wind blew in through the open western windows.

He slowly approached her. The music was unspeakably beautiful, glistening with runs, powerful octaves, crisp arpeggios, and delicate tremolos—all while maintaining a light, captivating melody.

Lucy swayed as she played, enchanted by the music she created, the symbiotic connection between her and the piano clear and obvious.

Garon reached the inward curve of the grand piano, gently setting down his gauntlets to avoid disrupting her. Even sitting, her gossamer dress and flowing blonde hair surrounded her. Was it the music or the breeze? He couldn't tell.

Approaching her side, he leaned against the polished instrument.

"Garon…" Lucy hushed, reducing her playing to a pianissimo. "Do you enjoy the piano?" she asked, eyes closed.

"How did you know it was me, Lucy?" he asked, his heart pounding.

"Easy! I felt your energy," she answered, opening her enchanting blue eyes.

Rubbing his fingers along the piano, he said, "This instrument is called a piano? I've never seen or heard one before. You and your kingdom never cease to amaze me. And Jenna…"

"Oh! So you've met Jenna? Isn't she incredible?" Lucy glowed.

"Undoubtedly!" he exclaimed. "I start training her tomorrow. The pay is unbelievable, but I'd rather…"

Lucy stopped playing and looked directly at him. Standing up, she carefully closed the fallboard and propped lid.

"Do you know what I think, Garon Erbrecht?" she said, stepping closer to him.

He gulped, unable to speak as she entered his personal space.

"I think that even though you try to be tough, your striking green eyes speak nothing but kindness," she whispered, as if searching his soul.

His heart raced as she pressed slightly against him, lifting his jaw and gazing into his eyes. She stood half a foot shorter than him, which was understandable—he was around six foot two.

"Hmm… isn't that interesting?" she said, tilting her head to observe him from another angle.

"Wh-what is?" he croaked.

"At the very center of your eyes lies a tiny ring of yellow. I bet that's the light in you!" she said playfully.

He swallowed hard.

"Your glossy black hair does give a sense of foreboding, though. Maybe you'll turn evil one day?" she whispered in a mock-spooky voice. "Or maybe it's just because it's super messy?" she added, standing on her tiptoes to inspect his hair. "You must feel lucky to have such thick, wavy hair!"

Garon laughed, feeling a bit more comfortable but still shy. "Oh, so now I get a fortune-telling based on my eyes and hair?"

"Perhaps," she responded playfully, ruffling his hair and turning to leave.

"W-wait! Where are you going?" he pleaded sweetly, taking a few steps after her.

"Well, someone needs to show you to your room, right? Come along!" she called back with a smile.

And just like that, Garon and Lucy's bond deepened. Little did they know what their relationship would soon blossom into.

Combat Training

Perhaps it was because Fürnas stood in perpetual fall, but somehow, it felt as if time didn't pass here. Who could believe Garon and his men had already been there for almost six months? Hardly thinking of time or his home kingdom, Garon had quickly fallen in love with Fürnas.

Adored by the king, queen, and the people, he felt a profound sense of belonging. Slowly, his bitterness and disdain for life had melted away, entirely replaced with joy and optimism. It also helped to be adored by a young and peculiar fire Majestician.

The chilled autumn air wrapped around Garon as he stood upon the damp earth of the training grounds. Secretly wishing for the warmth of sunlight, he knew it would be some time before the rising sun beamed above the castle. How frustrating! Why did the training grounds have to be on the western side of the castle? That meant the sun wouldn't reach them until noon. Although he had experienced this every day since arriving, somehow it felt new to him each morning.

"Good morning!" Garon called out to Jenna as she descended the stairs.

"Commander!" she responded, rushing down to greet him.

"Whoa!" he yelled, catching her just in time as she slipped on the frosty stairs.

For some reason, the training grounds felt especially cold this past week.

"That's like... the third time this week!" she shouted in the voice of an adorable and frustrated six-year-old.

Boom! Boom, boom! Fssshhhhhoooooorr! roared the fireballs and continuous flames from her palms as she... defrosted the stairs.

Clap, clap! "Well, that takes care of that," she said proudly, brushing her hands as if finishing a hard day's work. "Shall we begin, Commander?"

Unable to do anything but laugh, Garon knelt to her level, smiling. "Hmmm... what shall we begin with today? Fencing? You've grown quite adept with your rapier!" He nodded toward the small, sheathed rapier at her waist.

"Boooo!" she yelled.

"Haha! Well then... archery?" he asked, curious to see her response.

"Boring. I *hate* bows. They're so awkward to use!" she retorted.

"Right? I'm so with you on that!" he whispered back excitedly.

"Hmmmmm," they both mused in sync.

"Got it!" they exclaimed together.

"How about we spar?" Garon said, standing. "It's been a while since our last match, and it could help warm me up."

Before he even finished, Jenna had already unsheathed her rapier and lunged at him. "My thoughts exactly! Though I feel bad that you suffer so much from the cold," she added playfully.

"Hmmm..." Garon mused as he gracefully avoided her attacks. "Your footing is good, and your stance is perfect. But why are your shoulders so tense?" He finished with a raised eyebrow and a corner smile.

"Oh, bah to you, Commander! You tell me that every single day!" she said, rolling her eyes before charging through the air toward him.

"That's because it's true! Keep it up, and the future queen of Fürnas will look like she's missing her neck!" Garon teased as he swiftly unsheathed his sword, holding against her blow and staring into her intense eyes.

"Yers. Herro. Wert kern er der fer yer, perzent?" Garon mocked, pulling his head down, revealing a mock double chin with scrunched-up skin.

"Perfect! I see you're practicing how to be an old man someday. The double chin suits you nicely!" she quickly spat back.

"Ooooh... you're good!" he laughed, pushing her back with a strong, deflective maneuver.

Seriously though! Were they joking? How in Vaerün was this little girl only six years old? Her linguistic command made her seem at least twenty!

Garon loved training Jenna, almost as much as he loved having breakfast, lunch, dinner, and teatime with Lucy (which was coming up shortly and took place every day after his training with Jenna). It was the perfect time to tell Lucy all about his training sessions with the young fire Majestician—not to mention the improvements in Jenna's skills (both physical and verbal, he noted). Lucy always listened with the greatest interest, especially since the first week of training had been rough... although it did make their first date far less awkward!

"All right, Jenna! Great work! Now, let's practice some of your Majesty," Garon said as he sheathed his sword and took a seat on the stairs to give her ample fire room.

"Yay! Majesty time!" she said with both excitement and sarcasm. "What would you like for today's performance?" she asked, playfully acknowledging that this had been the question of the day for the past six months.

"Hmmm," Garon said, massaging his black goatee as he stared at the ground. "Got it! Okay, so... create a fireball in your left hand, right?"

"Uh-huh... boring!" she replied with a smirk.

"Now, now, let me finish!" he said before continuing slowly, "Shoot it into the air. As it descends, create a ring of fire with your right hand."

"Okay?"

"When the fireball descends at just the right time... squeeze the ring of flame around it with your right hand, and then release. Doing so will—"

"—will shoot the fireball back into the air!" she finished for him.

"Right!" he nodded, smiling at her understanding.

"That will be so much fun, said no one ever," Jenna remarked dryly.

"Oh, that mouth of yours... sometimes it's just too much!" Garon lay back, laughing. "Well, to make it more interesting, let's see you keep it up! I'm keeping score. Ready?"

"I swear, sometimes I just—" she muttered, shaking her head.

"Ready?" he yelled, trying not to laugh. "Go!"

Boom! shot the fireball out of her left hand and into the air. *Boom, boom, boom!* echoed as the fireball was launched back into the air by the ring of fire overhead.

"One, two, three, four, five, six..." Garon counted, his eyes tracking the rising and falling fireball.

"Twenty-seven, twenty-eight, twenty-nine... oops! Almost lost that one! So much for being clever!" he remarked, as she ran around trying to catch and deflect the fireball.

"Oh, shut it! Haha! I bet you lost count, just for 'being clever'!" she fired back.

Ooh... she's good, he thought.

"All right, Jenn, that's good enough for now. Let's call it a day!" he called out after counting past two hundred volleys.

With her feet planted on the ground, hair and training robe flowing around her, Jenna gripped her left wrist for support and blasted the fireball high above her, where it exploded in a burst of flame.

"Woohoo!" Garon cheered as he ran up to hug the huffing Jenna.

"I... swear... huff... huff," Jenna wheezed. "Sometimes I think you're trying to kill me."

"No way. I adore you too much for that," he said sincerely, squeezing her cheeks affectionately.

With a slight pause, she lovingly responded, "I adore you too, Garon."

Their sweet "father-daughter" moment was interrupted as Kirtor came running down the stairs. "Garon, sir... please. Their Majesties request your presence at once," Kirtor huffed, clearly out of breath and obviously out of shape.

"What's wrong, Kirtor?" Garon asked, lifting Jenna and placing her on his right shoulder.

"I don't know, sir, but I know it's urgent," Kirtor said, turning to leave.

"There goes your teatime with Lucy," Jenna whispered in Garon's ear.

"What? How do you know about that?" he demanded playfully.

"I'm not telling!" she teased, looking up. "But... I think you two make the most beautiful couple I've ever seen," she whispered again. "But I don't think your daughter will be as cool as me!" she declared, throwing her hands into the air.

Unable to speak, his throat seized with embarrassment, and his cheeks flushed as he let out a choked laugh.

"Say... has it gotten colder here?" Garon asked, attempting to divert the conversation, as they ascended the stairs; Jenna bobbing up and down on his shoulder.

"Look at you, changing the subject!" she teased with a big smile, while leaning around, so as to look him right in the face.

But he had a point. It had gotten colder—much colder! Was that frost on the ground? And why were the stairs slippery again?

"Oh... you know what? I guess that means the rumors are true after all," Jenna said, staring into the pink sky overhead.

"Rumors?" Garon inquired, carefully stepping on the slippery grass.

"Well, you know how we've been talking about the cold on the training grounds for the past couple of weeks, right?" she asked.

"Right."

"Well... I've been doing some research in the library."

"You? Researching?" he asked with a laugh.

"Well, it's not like your thick skull would do it for us!" she shot back immediately.

"Well played… well played," he admitted, tossing his head back in defeat.

"No one really knows how old Majesty is, how it came to be, or why it exists. But it's clear it's been around for a really… really long time."

"Uh-huh?"

"It's believed that the Majesticians of antiquity lived in this area long before any buildings were constructed… let alone the kingdom!" she continued.

"Right?"

"It's also believed they were fire Majesticians who claimed this part of Vaerün for themselves."

"Fascinating!" he exclaimed.

"But what's even more fascinating is why the land is always in autumn!"

"Well, I could've told you that, smarty!" Garon mocked lovingly.

"I'm not done yet!" Jenna retorted, lightly bopping him on the head. "Here, stop for a moment."

Garon immediately obeyed.

"See? Now that we're farther from the training grounds, doesn't it feel a little warmer? And look! The grass isn't frosty anymore!" she said, pointing to the red grass.

"Wait just a moment. You can't be hinting that your Majesty causes the cold, can you?" Garon asked, looking up at her in astonishment.

"That's exactly what the texts said! They believe that the price for using Fire Majesty repeatedly is that the energy has to come from somewhere—so it gets absorbed from living things!"

"Which would… explain the perpetual autumn in Fürnas!" Garon said jubilantly. "But… wow. That would take an enormous amount of Fire Majesty. I wonder what could've happened to affect such a large part of Vaerün?"

"Sadly, they believe it was a civil war among the fire Majesticians," Jenna answered, her voice tinged with sadness.

"What a shame," Garon replied, nodding his thanks to a servant who held the castle door open for them, while they entered.

"But hold on now! If that's the case, wouldn't I be... well, dead?" Garon asked. "I watch you perform Majesty every day, and I only feel invigorated when you do so!"

"It may sound strange, but... when I cast Majesty, I feel as if a whole world of invisible energy surrounds me. It doesn't seem to come from any single direction—it flows from everywhere," Jenna explained.

"Wow. Continue?" Garon pleaded, leaning in as they walked.

"Here... close your eyes," Jenna said, gently placing her hands over his eyes to guide him. "Black, right? Now, imagine millions—no, billions—of tiny red-and-orange dots, swirling all around you in every direction."

"Crazy... I'd be completely overwhelmed!" Garon responded, his voice low with awe.

"No, not at all! It's actually... beautiful. Imagine your arms, hands, and legs composed of those glowing dots, too," she continued softly.

"Okay... I'm imagining," Garon whispered, smiling.

"Now... as you extend your hand, picture all those dots obeying your every will. Free to do anything you command!" Jenna's voice brimmed with excitement.

"That's madness! How could you resist the urge to control them all?" he asked.

"Simple... I don't want to," she said matter-of-factly, removing her hands from his eyes. "This... energy... it's so stunningly beautiful, I wouldn't dare disrupt its harmony."

"Wait, don't tell me that—" Garon began.

"Don't worry—they don't die. Matter can be moved and changed, but never destroyed," Jenna interrupted with a warm smile. "Just like our spirits, it's eternal." She rested her left hand over his heart.

"Okay, but that still doesn't explain the cold!" Garon stated, his brows furrowed.

"Oh! That's right, sorry! Momentary... paradigm shift," Jenna said, shaking her head like a distracted professor.

(Again... she was only *six!*)

"When I repeatedly cast Majesty, the energy is transformed into fire. After the fire dissipates, the energy disperses back into the ether to be, well…"

"Reused?" Garon offered.

"Precisely!" Jenna chirped.

"Wouldn't Fürnas have recovered by now, then? I mean, things still grow here… but why do they grow in autumn colors?" Garon puzzled.

"Like I said, energy can be moved or changed, but not destroyed. The energy's still here—it's just been altered by whatever those ruthless fire Majesticians did," Jenna explained as they reached the throne room doors.

"It all makes sense now. The colors, the cold air, the constant seasonal shift. Jenna, you're amazing. Thanks for figuring this out. From now on, you're my go-to researcher!" Garon said sincerely.

Jenna blushed, looking down shyly. "You know… I find it odd you're not a Majestician yourself, Garon."

"What do you mean?" Garon asked, setting her down.

"The energy that glows from people… it's usually pretty dull. But yours… it moves just like mine," she said with excitement.

"Hmm… let's see… ha! Ha ha!" Garon said playfully as he thrust his palm outward.

Nothing happened…

"Sorry, Jenn. Looks like your 'inner eye' might need some examining!" he teased.

"Doubt it. There's only one other person who has that energy, too."

"Oh, yeah? And who's that?" Garon asked, bending down to hug her.

"Why, Lucy, of course! Speaking of which, I should tell her you're going to be late for tea," Jenna said as she gave Garon a quick kiss on the cheek.

"Wait, no, Jenn! Agh!" Garon called out.

Dang, she was fast! Down the hall she zipped! Going, going, and… gone. Man, he loved that little girl. There was something about her… like the feeling of a long-lost friend from a past life, brought back to harass him in the body of a child with the intelligence of a scholar.

"Your Majesties... how may I be of service?" Garon asked, bowing before the king and queen in the throne room.

"Garon... we have troubling news." Solemnly stated the king. "King Jyalhim the Fifth has requested your immediate return to Wölnas. Your lieutenant has fallen in battle, and none are skilled enough to take his place,"

Perhaps it was Fürnas's charm melting his heart, but this news struck Garon hard. He and the lieutenant were hardly friends, but suddenly, the weight of responsibility crushed him. Was it because he'd neglected his kingdom? Had the six months in Fürnas softened his resolve? The Kreaux! How could he have almost forgotten?

"The Kreaux?" Garon asked, almost sheepishly, like a child confessing a forgotten chore.

"Yes, Garon. We're so thankful for your service here, and we confess we've grown very fond of you. You're family," the queen said warmly.

"And Jenna utterly adores you. She's going to be affected most of all," added the king.

Jenna? Affected? Impossible. No one would be more affected than him. But that's war. Even in love and happiness, somewhere out there someone was being ripped apart by fangs, shredded by claws, or crushed by a Praetor.

"R-right," Garon muttered. "So then..."

"Your men left this morning. They care deeply for you. They said they'd handle things themselves so you could stay here," the queen said.

"Oh! Well, if that's the case, then..." Garon said, not wanting to leave.

"But I'm afraid it's not possible. The letter is signed, stamped, and sealed by His Majesty, King Jyalhim the Fifth. It must be fulfilled as per your contract with Wölnas's army," added the king.

It felt like a rusted, ugly needle had pierced the bubble of Garon's perfect world. He growled under his breath.

"I understand, Your Majesties. It has been my absolute privilege to serve you and your precious daughter," Garon said proudly.

"No, Garon. The pleasure has been all ours," the queen smiled gently.

"As promised… please take this, Garon," said the king, motioning to a servant holding two bags filled with twenty platinum bars.

"Thank you, Your Majesties, but… I do not want your money," Garon replied.

"What? Nonsense! It would be treason not to accept this!" the king insisted, with a mild but serious tone.

"I feel… my heart desires something else," Garon said, looking at them both.

"Oh? And what might that be, Garon?" asked the queen, her smile twisting with suspicion, already knowing the answer.

"There are actually two things I want, and they are worth more than all the platinum in Vaerün… nay, Albyüron!" Garon exclaimed.

"And what may they be?" the queen asked.

"Well… once my contract with Wölnas's army is fulfilled, which will be in less than two years, I'd like to return to Fürnas and live out my days here," Garon said, shyly.

"Done! We'll have your name added to our kingdom roster immediately. Scribe?" the king called out.

"Yes, Your Majesty?" the scribe, Kirtor, responded, quill in hand over rustic parchment.

"Add Garon Erbrecht's name under First Commander in our upper echelon of the kingdom roster. See to it immediately!" the king ordered.

Wow. An honor indeed. Above even their own commander, born and raised in Fürnas.

"Th-thank you very, very much," Garon barely managed to say.

The queen leaned in, smiling knowingly. "And… your *second* request?"

"I desire Lucy Dolliér's hand in marriage," Garon said boldly.
Total silence.

Shoot! Why did he say it so fast? What if they refused? Would Kirtor be called back in, to help blot his name from the roster?

"I was going to request this a few days hence, but..." Garon said quickly, while trying to soften his delivery, before trailing off. "Given the circumstances, it seems I must ask now -"

"We grant you permission, with our highest blessing," King Coltier said without hesitation, cutting him off.

"Wh-what...? Thank you! Most sincerely!" Garon beamed.

"And knowing this... you must take your pay," the queen added, smiling.

"Please forgive me, but I must refuse." Garon replied firmly. "Your blessing means more than all the wealth in Vaerün,"

The queen clapped her hands together. "You'll be done with your obligations in a year and a half, then?"

"Yes. I'm twenty-eight now, and my contract will be fulfilled on my thirtieth birthday," Garon explained.

"Hmm... so that means your birthday is around Vulhaahnin?" the king asked, rubbing his chin thoughtfully.

"Close! It's actually on the twentieth of Vulhaaner," Garon responded.

(A Quick Guide to Birthdays & Months in Vaerün)
In Vaerün, the year is divided into four quarters:

- **January-March = Aahn**
- **April-June = Vuhlaahn**
- **July-September = Feraahn**
- **October-December = Wölntaahn**

And then each quarter is further divided:

- **Aahn = January, Aahnin = February, Aahner = March**
- **Vuhlaahn = April, Vuhlaahnin = May, Vuhlaahner = June**
- **Feraahn = July, Feraahnin = August, Feraahner = September**
- **Wölntaahn = October, Wölntaahnin = November, Wölntaahner = December**

Easy, right?

"Excellent! Then we'll know the exact day to celebrate your birthday!" the queen exclaimed, beaming.

"But hold on… as we're nearing Aahn, you must have celebrated your twenty-eighth birthday just before you arrived here in Fürnas about six months ago?" the king added, eyes twinkling with the realization.

"Bah, don't worry about that!" Garon grinned, waving his hands nonchalantly.

The king and queen exchanged a knowing look and then nodded at Garon with warm smiles.

As Garon bowed deeply and prepared to leave the throne room, he heard footsteps fast approaching from behind. He turned just in time to see the king and queen rushing to embrace him. His heart nearly melted—never had he been hugged by royalty, let alone with such affection.

"We love you, Garon. And we eagerly await your return home!" the queen said warmly.

"You have no idea how much that means to me," he whispered back, his voice thick with emotion.

Stepping back to take in their appearance, he admired the regal couple before him: the king with his strong blue eyes and square jaw, the queen with her soft brown eyes and high cheekbones, both adorned with golden crowns embellished with rubies and topaz. They truly were a majestic sight.

"Oh! Well, now. I've just realized we have a slight dilemma," the queen remarked, turning to her husband with mock worry.

"Oh! We're going to need a new adviser!" the king exclaimed, feigning surprise.

Pausing for just a moment, Garon clapped his hands together, accidentally causing his gauntlets to ring out. "I know the perfect person you should interview. She'd make an exceptional adviser!" Garon said confidently.

"Do tell?" the queen asked with intrigue.

"She lives in a town called Fährlund, just a few hours north of your kingdom border. She's not only an outrageous baker but has major experience in 'higher end' affairs. I truly believe she'd serve you well," Garon explained, smiling at the thought of peach and kinberry pie already filling his mind. "I'll be passing through on my way back to Wölnas. I'll be sure to send her your way for an interview!"

"Perfect!" the king exclaimed. "If you're recommending her, we can only imagine her prestige."

After receiving the most heartfelt blessings from Their Majesties, Garon was officially dismissed. As he climbed the steps to the tearoom, eager to return to Wölnas and complete the necessary battles ahead, his thoughts raced. This castle truly had it all! Pausing at the top of the staircase, he gazed through the golden-framed windows, admiring the autumn leaves that continued to fall like a beautiful dream over the castle grounds. Light and color flooded the room from the open southwestern windows, and he paused to marvel at the distant glistening ocean.

How wonderful it would be to have an ocean view rather than the Kreaux chasm back in Wölnas, Garon thought to himself as he took the final step to the tearoom.

Lucy sat at their usual table, cup in hand, waiting for him. No matter how many times he saw her, it always felt like the first time. Her exquisite dresses, her stunning long blonde hair, and those penetrating blue eyes that captivated his soul. A servant pulled out his chair, and as he sat, Garon leaned in to kiss her before he began explaining… everything.

"You're leaving Fürnas, then…?" Lucy's voice was small, her heart heavy with sorrow.

"I am," Garon nodded, trying to keep his voice steady.

Lucy's glare was sharp and intense. How could he leave her like this? His face didn't show any longing, remorse, or sadness. In fact… he seemed almost happy. How dare he! Anger and frustration burned within her, and she nearly slapped him as she stood up abruptly.

"Wait! Lucy! Please. Hear me out. I have one last request… Will you do this for me?" Garon pleaded.

"What is it, Garon Erbrecht?" she asked coldly, voice trembling.

"Please… play that piece for me again. I so desperately want to hear it before leaving Fürnas. Please?" Garon's voice softened as he humbly asked.

She sighed. How could she say no to those striking green eyes? Not to mention, that handsomely etched face always looked too strange when it appeared sad.

"As you wish... come on, then," she answered, marching down the stairs.

Garon followed closely behind, hiding the growing smile and excitement that stirred within him—knowing what was about to unfold, one of the biggest moments of his life.

Eaaarrggh! The old concert hall doors creaked open, accompanied by the warm, aged scent of wood. **Clip, clop, clip, clop!** Their boots echoed on the polished floor as they entered.

Garon bit his lip hard, so hard that another layer might've broken skin. His heart raced as Lucy approached the piano, and he half-expected it to echo in the hall like a beating drum.

Here we go...

"All right, Garon. Just for you, okay?" Lucy said sweetly, as she opened the fallboard...

The hall filled with the sound of her gasping shriek. There, resting on the ebony-and-ivory keys, lay an ornately decorated pile of autumn leaves. And on top of them sat a wedding ring.

With one hand over her mouth and the other over her heart, Lucy let out a cry of joy, tears streaming down her face. Garon gently guided her to sit on the bench, and then he knelt down before her, taking her hands in his.

"Lucy Dolliér... never has my heart felt so alive, so full of hope and life until I met you. It was as if an angel swept down from the heavens the day you descended those stairs and... saved me," Garon whispered, his voice thick with emotion.

She sat, breathless, eyes locked on his.

"You've done the impossible. By some magnificent miracle, you've pieced back together my shattered soul and given me life once more."

Tears streamed from her eyes, her lips trembling as she tried to speak, but no words came.

"Lucy Dolliér... will you give me the most superb... the grandest honor...?" Garon's heart pounded so hard he thought it might burst.

"Will you marry me?"

"Yes!" she screamed, leaping into his arms. "Yes! Yes, yes, yes! Infinity yes!"

And then they kissed. Garon lifted her up, spinning her around in an elegant dance, like the very embodiment of a fairy-tale come to life. Her dress flowed around them, her blonde hair catching the light, cascading like silk. His strong arms crossed over her back, holding her close. Sunlight burst through the western windows, casting a radiant glow upon the floor, intensifying their beauty, their passion, their love.

As they left the concert hall, Lucy explained there were some things she needed to handle first, suggesting Garon go ahead and meet her at the base of the castle path, right below the tailor. And so, they set off, temporarily parting ways.

"Garon?" came the small, broken voice behind him.

Garon turned to see Jenna standing at the top of the grand staircase, her eyes filled with sadness. "Where are you going?" she asked, tears beginning to well up.

Facing away, Garon swallowed hard, trying to fight back his own tears. Kneeling down, he waited as Jenna descended the stairs toward him. "Jenna... precious Jenna... I'm needed back in Wölnas. The Kreaux are getting worse, and my king... he needs me."

"But... what about our training? Who will I pick on?" she asked, her small voice quivering.

"Come now, I'll be back soon enough. I just have to give those Kreaux a good beating, that's all," Garon said, forcing a smile.

"No, Garon, don't go! I... I have a really bad feeling about this," she pleaded. "Take me with you! I can help! I'll burn those monsters to a crisp!"

"Ha! I'm sure you would, you little firebolt. But this... I have to do alone. I promise I'll come back. Okay?" Garon assured her.

Jenna sniffled, wiping away a tear. "Okay... but will you do me one favor?"

"Anything, Jenn. What is it?" Garon whispered, leaning in close.

"Will you… will you bring your daughter back with you?" she asked softly.

"Daughter? I don't have a—" Garon began to say.

"Don't worry. You will. Bring her back, okay? Promise me! She's supposed to be my best friend," Jenna exclaimed earnestly.

Garon's cheeks flushed as he considered her words. With a deep breath, he answered, "It's a deal." And he pulled her into a tight hug, one that neither wanted to end.

Jenna kissed his cheek and pulled away, tears spilling freely.

"You be good now, okay? And try not to make everyone feel too stupid with that brain of yours," he teased, holding back his own tears.

"O-okay." She hiccuped, taking a step back, then another.

Garon turned and walked away, the massive castle doors swinging open one last time.

"Wait, Garon!" Jenna called out.

"Yes, princess?" he asked, turning around.

Boom! Garon was nearly knocked off his feet as she rushed into his arms, the blazing force of her Majesty enveloping him.

"I love you," she whispered, kissing his cheek one final time.

With one last embrace, tears running down his face, Garon squeezed her tight and whispered back, "I love you too, Jenna."

And with that, Garon turned his back and left Castle Fürnas.

With his black stallion trotting slowly beside him, Garon walked down the castle pathway and into the town market. He gently held his left hand out, palm upturned, catching some of the vibrant, falling Autunn leaves. With a gentle caress of the thumb, he looked up just in time, snapping out of his stupor, to see Lucy sitting on top of her mare. (Whoops! Almost walking past your fiancée probably isn't a good idea.)

"Are you ready?" she asked, while sitting upon her striking white mare, satchels and bags attached to the saddle.

"As sad as I am to leave this kingdom… knowing that I have you by my side, I could live anywhere in Vaerün and still be happy," Garon said quietly.

Lucy rested against the neck of her horse and stared at him adoringly. "Without a doubt, I truly feel the same way."

"But… I would be lying if I were to tell you that I wouldn't dearly miss it here." He said, shaking his head and taking in the vast colored canopy above. So many things have happened since my arrival! I feel robbed of time. Six months just wasn't enough,"

"Don't worry. We'll be back!" She optimistically replied. "As you just said, time passes so quickly. A year and a half will be nothing! Before you know it, we'll be standing on this very spot once again, this time to stay for *good!*"

He smiled at her. How could he not? That contagious optimism and light of hers was just what he needed. After all, he really, *really* didn't want to go back to Wölnas.

"Wait. Hold up," he said, approaching her mare, trying to investigate the filled saddlebags.

Lucy pulled the reins on her horse, forcing her to back up. "*Ah, ah, ah!* Didn't anyone ever tell you not to go through a lady's belongings?" she teased.

Although he knew she was partly kidding, Garon couldn't help but feel a bit embarrassed. "Oh! Right! Right. I am so sorry… ahem! But I have some bad news," he said, petting the white steed.

"What is it?" Lucy inquired.

"I don't think we can bring your mare. My horse was bred in Wölnas, and he's used to the constant siege of the storm. Thus, I'm afraid—"

"I hadn't even thought of that!" Lucy interrupted with total shock and relization. "Keina doesn't spook too easily. But then, she's never been exposed to an unending storm, so…"

"Exactly. *So…*" Garon leaned in cautiously to grab the satchels. "I promise I won't look in them. May I?" he asked, placing a hand on one bag and raising the other in a gentlemanly manner.

"You may," she said slowly, as if speaking like royalty. "But no peeking!"

"All right, all right!" He laughed.

Pull. Tug.

"Um, Lucy, dear... What is in these things?" he chided. "Did you pack the whole dresser in here?"

"Only a few dresses!" she squeaked back in a girly voice as she dismounted her mare and jumped onto Garon's stallion.

"Okay, umm... give me a moment," he muttered, struggling with the weight of the heavy bags.

Clink, clink! rang the bags as he heaved them off the mare. "What in Vaerün... how do dresses clink? And how many are in here?" he cried out, hefting the bags over his shoulders and catching the attention of some amused onlookers. Some inhabitants ran up to assist but were turned away by the "proud manliness" of his raised hand.

"You ask too many questions!" Lucy quickly said, trying to hold back the laughter bubbling up inside her.

"Merciful goodness of the—" he muttered as he held his breath, quickly attaching the bags to his stallion's saddle.

"Yay!" Lucy clapped, with a hint of sarcasm, and patted him on the head as if to say, "Job well done!" "Well, come on now! Aren't you ready to go?" she asked excitedly, still hinting with just a bit of added sarcasm.

"One..." He huffed. "Second..." There was more huffing... and then a deep breath. "Okay! Let's go," he finished, jumping on his stallion and wrapping his arms around his fiancée while handing the reins of the mare to a helpful citizen.

"Shall we?" he whispered quietly into her ear.

"We shall." She nodded, cracking the reins and heading down the pathway, her dress and flowing hair cascading around them. There was just something extraordinary about seeing her on horseback that stirred something within him—even if it *was* his...

CHAPTER 5

The Kingdom of Wölnas

Garon and Lucy paused atop the Algár Mountain pass, looking down into the northern valley that held the Wölnas Kingdom. The constant storm, as ever, still refused to cease.

With a disgruntled look, fearing rebuke, Garon had to ask, "Soo... this is Wölnas. I know it's a far cry from the comforting beauty of Fürnas, but... what do you think? Can you possibly endure this hell for a year and a half?"

"Are you kidding? This is incredible! I've never seen anything like it!" Lucy responded, delighted. "And you said this storm never lets up? Ever?"

"Never," he answered truthfully.

"How in Vaerün is that even possible?" she asked, her voice full of curiosity.

"Actually, thanks to a genius little girl, I think I might have an idea," Garon said, as they began to descend the mountain pass and entered the storm-swept kingdom.

"Wow! So you're telling me that something terrible must have happened here, thousands of years ago? Like an ancient battle among wind Majesticians?" Lucy shouted over the noise of the storm.

Now in the shop district of Wölnas, the howling wind and clapping thunder made it difficult to talk.

"Yeah! Or something like that! That's just my guess, though!" Garon returned, also shouting over the storm.

"Aren't people ever afraid of being struck by lightning?" Lucy asked, ducking every few seconds as lightning flashed and illuminated the sky. She was clearly anxious, but everyone else looked calm.

"Nah!" Garon responded. "See the needles on those spires? Way up on those towers?" He pointed upwards, where long silver needles burst with purple-and-white light as they were struck by lightning.

"Incredible!" Lucy shouted as she continued to observe the white-and-purple stone buildings. After a moment of awe, her eyes moved to the inhabitants.

How peculiar they looked! Everyone seemed to wear identical outfits, aside from the color of their robes. Strange helms covered their heads and faces, and cloaks attached at the rear rim whipped through the stormy air. Though their features were obscured outside, one could clearly identify them through the warm, lantern-lit windows of the shops, where busy hands unclasped buckles and straps, revealing faces. Women with flowing hair or men with scruffy beards and shaggy wet hair were visible as they removed their helms, shedding the storm's condensation.

"Follow me!" Garon shouted. "Let's get out of this storm!"

"After you!" Lucy replied, captivated by the bouncing purple lightning trapped inside the clear spheres on the streetlamps.

Slam! The door burst open as Garon kicked it. They were soaked through, rainwater dripping off them as they entered the house. The storm seemed to have waited until they were three blocks from Garon's (now Lucy's) home before letting loose. And why did Mrs. Bürgohen have to stop and talk to them? She stood dry and warm in her doorway, a roaring fire behind her, while Garon and Lucy sat drenched on their horse.

Garon breathed heavily as he carried Lucy inside, her wet blonde hair and dress stuck to her body like plastic wrap.

"I can say one thing for certain," he panted.

"Yes, love?" she asked, looking up into his green eyes.

"There's never a dull moment in Wölnas!" he exclaimed, kissing her soaked brow.

"I can see that! But I thought you lived in the castle? You spoke highly of your room there!" Lucy said, looking around. "I was hardly expecting to come home to a gorgeous two-story house with five bedrooms! What in Vaerün do you do with all this space?"

"It was... well, I'm shy to say, but..." Garon paused. "It was lonely here, by myself," he admitted softly.

"Awwww, really, dear? But look at the neighbors you have!" Lucy exclaimed.

"My point exactly! And speaking of which... did you really have to stop and chat with Mrs. Bürgohen?" Garon questioned.

"What? Oh no, you will not put that back on me!" Lucy retorted playfully, with a slight edge to her voice. "You're the one who wanted me to meet her!"

"Okay, yeah, but—" Garon continued as he headed into the other room to grab a towel. "Did you have to go on and on about the piano and needlework?" he questioned from the other side of the wall.

"Oh, sure. Sure! So the next time someone asks what I like to do, I'm just supposed to say, 'I'm sorry, but could you please, for all that is good, shut up?'" Lucy joked, before adding, "And no, Mrs. Bürgohen, I don't care about your apple bake. But clearly, from your voluptuous girth, you do!"

"Look, I'm just saying," Garon replied as he reentered the room, voice muffled while he stripped off his soaked gear and shirt. "You need to watch out. I'm going to be at the chasm every day from day-break till sundown," he added, tossing a towel to Lucy.

"And?" she asked, rolling her hand in the air for him to continue.

"And... that means you need to watch out for the bored house witches and their sniveling crocheting friends! You're fresh meat, and you're beautiful. You really think they won't want to spend every moment with you while their husbands, or whatever they are, are off fighting at the chasm?"

Lucy paused, glaring at him fiercely with her piercing blue eyes. Garon pretended not to notice.

"And yes. That includes Mrs. Bürgohen. With her apple bake and bratty kids, who will undoubtedly demand piano lessons," Garon finished.

"Piano lessons? Up until some months ago, you didn't even know what a piano was! How could that get past you when the people of your kingdom play too?" Lucy demanded.

"Hm, well… it might have something to do with the fact that I spent night and day at that forsaken chasm trying to defend those cheeky, lazy people so that they could safely play an instrument that I didn't even know existed!" he yelled.

"You know what? Ever since we've left Fürnas, I've heard you complain about nothing but that stupid Kreaux chasm. Well, where is it?" she sharply questioned, turning around with hands waving in the air as if searching for it.

"How could you miss it from atop the Algár Mountain pass? It looks like a massive black scar running along the northern end of Vaerün!" he exclaimed. "Which also happens to be the north and northeastern border of Wölnas!"

"Oh? Well, maybe you should just show me!" Lucy challenged, stepping forward to meet his advance.

"Maybe I will!" Garon returned, staring into her eyes, her wet dress still dripping, the water beading on her beautiful face.

"Let's go then! Right now!" she demanded, slapping her hand to his warm, bare chest.

"Right now?" he questioned, wrapping his arms around her.

"Right… now," she whispered.

And then they kissed—passionately. The only sounds around them were the thunder crashing above and the ticking of the pendulum and gears from the wooden wall clock.

"Dear, wake up! There's something I want to show you," Lucy whispered as Garon looked up at the hanging clock in his room, which read six-oh-nine in the morning.

"Ugh… what is it?" he asked, rolling over in his four-poster bed and pulling a pillow over his head, clearly irritated by the endless sounds of wind and thunder.

"Come with me. It's a surprise! I've been dying to show you this since we left Fürnas, and now I cannot wait any longer!" she demanded, her footsteps echoing down the cold wood floor of the staircase.

"Grrr… only because I love you, Lucy," Garon grumbled, jumping out of bed, slipping into trousers, a tattered shirt, and weathered leather boots.

Clunk, clunk, clunk, the floorboards creaked beneath his feet, reminding him of his room back in Fürnas. The smooth oak railing under his hand evoked warm, recent memories, though somehow, they already felt distant.

"What is it, love? Oh, and how did you sleep?" he asked through a yawn, bringing a hand to his mouth.

Lucy brimmed with excitement as she kneeled on the floor, both hands upon the satchels she had so adamantly refused to let him look in.

"Oh, decently, I suppose. How on earth do you sleep amid the crashing thunder, howling wind, and lightning flashes? They cast such horrifying shadows in the room! I nearly burned through three candles last night!" she exclaimed.

"You get used to it after about a week. Trust me. And holy Kreaux, three candles? That's the equivalent of six hours! Why didn't you come wake me?" he demanded.

(For those curious, no, they didn't sleep together—they were not yet married. And no, they hadn't "done anything" yet, for those who might have thought it implied!)

"Absolutely not. You resume work in just six days, right after our wedding! You're going to need all the sleep you can get!" she answered.

"Minus the wedding, I couldn't give three shüzas about work," Garon replied coldly.

With a raised eyebrow, a blank look, and a cold stare, she replied, "I know. That's why I'm worried. I don't need you fighting Kreaux and giving orders to soldiers while running on inadequate sleep!"

Ooh, she had a point. Thankfully, Garon could use the excuse of just waking up to cloud his judgment.

"Now, come here!" she said, reaching up and pulling him down. "Please, go ahead and open the bags. You have my permission."

Garon squinted his eyes, giving her the look that said, *"Are you sure? What on earth are you planning, woman?"* Nevertheless, he knelt down in front of her and opened the left bag first.

"No. Freakin'. Way." There, nestled in the burlap satchel, lay ten platinum bars.

"What?" Garon exclaimed, rushing to loosen the other satchel and finding ten more platinum bars. His heart pounded, and his throat tightened as he fell back on his bent knees, completely overwhelmed.

Lucy's face was aglow.

"No. No! We have to send them back! I told them I wouldn't accept this!" Garon shouted.

"'Them,' dear? There is no 'them.' Only *her*," Lucy said, waiting for him to catch on.

"What?" he asked in a low voice. "Oh no. What a goober!" Garon exclaimed, jumping to his feet. "Jenna! Was it—"

With a slow head nod, and biting her lower lip to hide her smile, Lucy confirmed, "Yes. She figured since you wouldn't accept the payment from her parents, you'd have to accept it from her."

"Unbelievable!" he cried.

In deep thought and emotion, he crumpled back onto the cool floor. "But... I can't, we just don't—"

"Shhhh!" Lucy pressed a finger to his lips. "Also... there is one more thing," she added, handing him a sealed wax letter with the Fürnas crest imprinted on it.

With a slight tilt of his head and a look of curiosity, he grabbed the envelope, carefully opened it, and pulled out a letter. The familiar smell of cinnamon and kinberries filled his nose—the scent of Castle Fürnas—mixed with the fresh aroma of autumn leaves.

Hardly able to speak, he slowly read the letter aloud:

"Dearest Garon,"

"We cannot thank you enough for taking the time out of your undoubtedly busy life, schedule, and routine to travel all the way down here to the Fürnas

Kingdom, to assist, teach, and guide in what may have seemed a petty and fruitless task. Like us, without having a clue about Majesty, what it is, or how it even works, you've done a profound job in instructing our little Jenna… somehow guiding her to establish a deeper connection with a power that you don't even wield."

"Having no difficulty or attempting to repress emotion, it is with the greatest and utmost sincerity that we express our deepest appreciation for you. Tasked with a burden that may have seemed daunting at first, you delivered and exceeded our expectations in every way."

"You are a profound man, Garon Erbrecht. Having not even left yet, the whole castle and kingdom prematurely suffer from the missing hole that is your bright person. Undoubtedly, you shall excel in Wölnas. You are not hailed and claimed as the best instructor for no reason. Return to your home kingdom, Garon Erbrecht, and seize the day! Destroy and banish those Kreaux back to the oblivion whence they came! May the light of our eternal creator, distilled in each of us, radiate forth from your glowing countenance, further banishing the Kreaux! May your sword always fight for truth, blessed in righteous desires for preservation, defense, goodness, and benevolence in all its glorious splendor."

"Our lives have been forever touched by you, Garon Erbrecht. But beyond us… lies a heart most precious, sincere, and powerful beyond comprehension. Opened and abounding in the outpouring of a light, hope, and belief so strong that could only have been fostered upon your strength, compassion, sincerity, and adoration. And that heart… that most tiny heart… is our precious daughter, Jenna Coltier. Who, above all, most eagerly awaits your return."

"So as not to rest entirely upon the bittersweet words of departure, let us leave you with a positive note. We love you, Garon. Though you return to Wölnas, know that a portion of your heart beats as true and lively as the colored leaves of our kingdom. Here we stay, waiting for you and your beautiful wife, Lucy, whom we additionally adore beyond measure, to return to us, your family."

"May your next days be filled with hope, optimism, and joy that shall lead you back home to us for good."

"Most Sincerely, Your Family,"

"Verolt Coltier"
"Layna Coltier"
"Jenna Coltier"

P.S. *"I can only imagine that you're going to refuse the platinum from my parents, Garon. As I have already anticipated this, you don't have a choice accepting it from me. And so help me if they are returned via caravan. I'll carefully melt your eyebrows and beard off so as to scar the skin in such a way that they'll never grow back! You'll look so weird! And may that foreboding thought run through your mind as you and your wife-to-be enjoy it."* — *Jenna, your goddaughter*

Lucy watched in unspeakable joy as her husband-to-be slowly dropped the letter, tears rolling down his face and disappearing into his short, stubbly, black scruff.

As he attempted to speak, his voice only whistled and cracked, seized by emotion.

"You have no idea how much you're loved, Garon Erbrecht," Lucy said, throwing her arms around him.

The stairway to the basement was cold and unwelcoming (as are most basements). Lucy followed Garon with a lit candle as he unlocked the metal doors and entered the dark room.

"Where should we put them?" Lucy asked, motioning to the platinum bars.

"Where I put the rest of my gold!" Garon exclaimed, opening another door cleverly disguised as part of the stone wall.

Clink, clink! sounded the bags as he set them upon a massive pile of glittering gold that reflected the candlelight.

"It's good to know we're set for life," Lucy said honestly.

"Hah! And then some. I won't lie; we have more money than I care to know what to do with. If you ever need any, for anything at all," Garon said, turning to her, "please, come and take as you wish." He finished by opening her free hand and placing the key to the vault inside.

"Garon? What? No… you don't have to—" Lucy started before being cut off.

"Nonsense! You're going to be my wife! Perhaps someday, I'll be able to afford all of Vaerün. But until then, this vault is absolutely yours to do with as you see fit," he finished boldly, walking back up the stairs.

She carefully observed the large vault and the piles of gold. It made sense—he had been working for the Wölnas military force for several years. (And unlike our world, you better believe that Vaerün paid its soldiers most handsomely.)

Lucy closed the large stone door, carefully pulling a table in front of it. As she left the basement (locking it too), she squinted at the vault key, its platinum glinting in the candlelight. It was beautiful! The grip was formed into a circle, with a diamond shape inside, housing the Wölnas crest, all crafted from amethyst. She gripped the key tightly and ascended the stairs.

"I need you to leave the house, please," Garon said to Lucy as she reached the top of the stairs, her arms folded in curiosity.

"What? Is everything okay?" she asked, her heart momentarily sinking.

"Yes. But I have a surprise for you. And for you to receive it, I need you to leave for a while," Garon said, placing an arm around her shoulders and guiding her to the front door.

"Oh, really? Well then, it looks like I have no choice, 'Commander!'" she teased, playfully saluting him.

"Trust me. You'll love it. At least, I hope you will," he finished shyly, poking his index fingers together.

How cute! It was so fun to see a rugged, masculine commander look so shy and boyish.

"All right. When would you like me back?" Lucy asked, opening the door to the relatively calm day outside.

Garon glanced at the clock for a brief moment. "It's about seven-oh-five, so… be back here by noon. That'll be more than enough time. We can go out for lunch!"

"It's a date then. Where are you taking me?" she asked, leaning in to kiss him.

Wrapping his arms around her and kissing her about four times, he responded, "The Sneaky Snake! Haha!"

"The what?" Lucy asked, pulling back with a skeptical look.

"Ha ha!" Garon laughed out loud. "That's what it's called! It was the bartender Gürbak's idea to name it that."

"How romantic. You're taking me to a tavern?" Lucy snapped back.

"Don't knock it until you've tried it!" Garon countered, holding up a finger. "Don't worry. I won't drink. But shüza, the food there is to die for! Will you please just try it for me?" he begged, giving her a puppy-dog expression, his green eyes glistening.

"Oh, all right! Besides… I'm going to have a word with this Gürbak about the name of his tavern," Lucy said, fastening her purple cloak around her neck.

"Um… where's your helm?" Garon asked, noticing she was without the standard face-covering headgear.

"No. Just no. Those things look creepy. I'll take soaking wet hair any day over that ugly, horse-like mask!" Lucy proclaimed.

And with that, she marched out the door into the windy weather. (Thankfully, it wasn't raining—yet—putting Garon's heart at ease.)

Running through the cobblestone streets, Garon's mind was consumed by the mission at hand. The wind whipped at his military cloak as he exchanged quick greetings with passersby. Suddenly, the ground trembled beneath him, and instinct took over—his hand darted to the absent sword at his side.

An earthquake. A strong one.

The gasps of nearby citizens, gripping handcarts and storefronts for stability, confirmed the magnitude. Not altogether surprised—these tremors occurred now and then—the large ones usually indicated something worse.

"*Praetors*," Garon muttered under his breath.

Although very rare, sometimes Praetors surfaced near Wölnas, only to be struck down by tower archers and soldiers alike. Not only that, but (Thankfully) the Kreaux found it nearly impossible to dig through the stone foundations of homes and cobblestone streets. They were typically smart enough to stay in groups, attacking the kingdom from the outside.

Still, that quake was big. *I hope the men have it contained,* Garon thought to himself. "Hang in there, guys… I'll be there to help you tomorrow," he whispered aloud.

But worse than the Kreaux came the fear of the chasm splitting apart Wölnas. Not an improbable scenario, as the northern chasm had sent fissures growing some fifty yards away from Wölnas over the past five years. You can imagine their fear—a massive quake could split the fissure directly through Wölnas, breaching the kingdom walls and leaving it vulnerable to siege.

"Are you okay?" Garon asked, running up to some elderly citizens gripping their canes in terror.

"Yes, Commander, thank you," they quickly answered, as he helped them up.

Trying to shake off his concern, Garon continued down the street, heading toward the western district.

Known for its woodcarvers, clockmakers, and forges, the western district was home to craftsmen and engineers of all kinds. If something needed to be created, this was the place to go.

"Fjaltünd's Forge… Térom's Clocks…" Garon murmured as he read the swinging wooden signs above.

"Aha! Kéith's Pianos!" he exclaimed, rushing inside the shop, a bell clinking overhead.

The smell of freshly cut wood filled his nostrils. Five grand pianos stood atop the smooth stone floor of the shop. Garon looked around, noticing various unfamiliar instruments hanging on the walls.

"Hello!" came the gruff voice of an elderly man, pushing past a curtain from the back of the shop, probably his crafting area.

"I'm Kéith! Like 'em?" the man asked, leaning against one of the pianos and shaking Garon's hand vigorously. "How might I assist our commander-in-chief on this slightly pleasant day?" Kéith smiled, revealing a strong character despite his gruff demeanor. His wavy gray hair, streaked with silver, framed a wrinkled face of experience. He wore a brown leather apron, splattered with stains from his craft, over a long-sleeved shirt.

"It's a pleasure to meet you, Kéith. As you already know who I am, I'll get straight to business," Garon said, not mincing words. "My wife-to-be in one week—"

"Congratulations!" exclaimed the shop owner, interrupting him with bold enthusiasm.

Slightly surprised, Garon smiled before continuing, "Thank you very much, Kéith. I—"

"Don't call me sir. It's Kéith!" he barked playfully.

Embarrassed, Garon nodded. "My apologies, Kéith. As I was saying, my wife-to-be is an exceptional piano player—"

"Pianist," Kéith corrected sharply.

"Right. Pianist," Garon repeated flatly before pressing on for the fourth time, "and I need—"

"Exceptional, huh?" Kéith interrupted again. "If she's exceptional, and she's your wife-to-be, you need to get her something top of the line," he added as he walked over to the largest piano in the shop. "This here is my parlor grand. It's a Héndrjksen & Sons, handcrafted by yours truly," he said, slapping the top of the piano.

"Wonderful! I'll take it! How much?" Garon asked, reaching for the small satchel of coins at his belt.

"How much?" Kéith snapped. "Don't you want to play the dang thing first? It could be a piece of junk for all you know—not to mention an insult to me and my craft!" he practically hollered.

"Oh! I apologize!" Garon exclaimed, further embarrassed and raising his hands in defense. "To be honest, I don't play; I just—"

"They never do. They never do," Kéith spat, interrupting again. "Everyone just wants them for a dang decoration. Do you have any idea what goes into making this instrument?"

"Errr, I..." Garon stammered, starting to regret the idea but holding fast for Lucy.

"Thousands of parts go into the creation of just one instrument. You hear me?" Kéith raised a finger. "Sigh... It's okay," he added, calming down. "At least you help keep me in business. *Mary!*" he yelled toward the back.

"Yes, Kéith?" asked an elegantly dressed woman, emerging from behind the curtain.

Her snow-white hair curled gracefully around her kind face. Though slightly stern, her gentle manner and ornate attire, with pearls and chains adorning her neck, exuded dignity and respect.

With no preparation needed, just like Lucy, Mary immediately sat on the bench that Kéith had pulled out for her and began to play on the brown and black keys. It was beautiful! Just like Lucy's playing—melodic and graceful.

"As you can see, not at all in an attempt to sell my husband's instruments, of course! But from the sheer melodic singing, I must confess this is a piano of quality, and I recommend it with my utmost endorsement. I am sure your wife, undoubtedly a better pianist than I, will love it," she finished humbly, rolling her fingers across the keys in a dazzling glissando finish.

"I'll take it!" Garon exclaimed, already picturing Lucy's delighted reaction. "How much?" he asked, again reaching for his small satchel of money.

"About fifty gold," Kéith answered shortly. "But since you're newlyweds-to-be, I'll take forty."

"Thank you very much! I'll also need it delivered to—"

"Today, right? That'll cost one more gold," Kéith interrupted, yet again.

"Please, it's going to number seven of—" Garon tried to say before being interrupted for what felt like the umpteenth time.

"No."

"Pardon?" Garon asked, looking up.

"No! Clearly, you have the day off, so help my boys move it! The training will do you good. That way, if you ever need to move it again, you'll know how," Kéith said with a spunky grin.

"Got me there," Garon murmured.

"Jön! Matt! C'mere!" shouted Kéith.

What a bold shop owner! Although one might mistake his brashness for rudeness, there was something humorous about it—it was as if he knew he was being clever and enjoyed seeing how others reacted to his wit.

Within seconds, two young men rushed in. One was a bit taller than the other and clearly older. Both had dark brown hair and eyes, and were a bit on the skinny side, but their faces radiated excitement and a sense of adventure.

"Garon, these are our boys, Jön and Matt," Mary said with polite quietness, introducing her teenage sons.

"It's an honor, sir! We know all about you! Thank you for defending our kingdom," Jön said, shaking Garon's hand with a hidden strength.

"I've got the dolly, Pops!" exclaimed Matt excitedly.

"Let's get to it then! Mary, love, thank you," Kéith said to his wife as she got up from the piano bench.

With a gentle handshake to Garon, Mary disappeared behind the curtain.

"Jön, prop the board on top of the dolly. Garon, come here. Matt, stand back for a sec," ordered Kéith.

As the piano rolled down the streets, pushed by Garon, Kéith, and his sons, they passed by some wounded soldiers just re-entering the gates. Their armor had been slashed clean across the torsos, and dark-red stains revealed the severity of the wounds beneath. With arms barely able to hold up the cloth stretcher they carried, the soldiers cast a somber glance at Garon.

Garon's blood ran cold. But why? He had seen this before, many times over. Had his time in Fürnas dulled his senses? Or was it the image of himself pushing an expensive, beautiful instrument home for his soon-to-be wife amid the chaos of war? Or perhaps it was the gloomy stare from the soldiers, as if to say with their eyes, *Must be nice, Commander.*

Pushing the thoughts aside, Garon continued to help transport the piano. Shortly after, they arrived at Garon's house, ready to set up the grand piano in the parlor room for Lucy.

"All right, Matt, when I tell you to, pull the dolly out from underneath and get out of the way!" Kéith barked.

"Right, Pops!" responded Matt cheerfully.

In just a few minutes, the piano was set in its new place, and Kéith dismissed his sons back to the shop as he pulled out a toolkit and began to tune the instrument. Curious but not wanting to interrupt any further, Garon quietly walked upstairs to organize some space in the rooms for Lucy, eagerly awaiting the completion of Kéith's work downstairs.

"How is it already eleven-thirty?" Garon muttered under his breath, running downstairs to check the clock.

Having just finished tuning, Kéith stood beside Garon, toolkit in hand. "Y'know, Jön is pretty handy with clocks. If the thing ever breaks on you, let me know," Kéith said, pointing to the grandfather clock and shaking Garon's hand.

"Wait a second. Please, hang on for just a moment..." Garon said, rushing down to the basement. After a few moments, he returned with another satchel. "This is for you and your family. I refuse for you to refuse it!" he demanded.

"No, I—"

"Will take it!" Garon finished, interrupting *him* this time, while handing over a satchel.

"I said—" Kéith attempted to interrupt, while shakily taking the satchel, voice cracking.

"That you will take it! Goodbye, Mr. Héndrjksen, and thank you. Come to our wedding, will you? I'll send a personal invitation!" Garon declared as he gently but firmly pushed the old man out the door. "Take care!" he finished, closing and locking the door behind him.

Unbeknownst to him, on the other side of the door rested a weeping, humble man, giving thanks to heaven above for the additional two hundred gold coins.

Garon stood eagerly in the foyer, arms folded, waiting for Lucy to open the door at any second.

The grinding gears of the lock sent chills down his spine as Lucy stepped in, kicking the mud from her boots at the doorframe before entering.

"Come with me," Garon said quickly, immediately grabbing her and placing his hands over her eyes.

"But dear, I haven't even taken my boots off yet—" she laughed.

"Don't care. Come with me. Okay! Are you ready?" he asked excitedly as they stood in the parlor.

"I'm ready," she said, trying to contain her excitement.

"All right... one... two... three... four!" Garon pulled his hands away, revealing the polished, solid oak grand piano in front of Lucy. Elegantly etched in gold upon the fallboard was the name "Lucy."

Unable to speak, hands clasped over her mouth, tears fell from her eyes and rolled down her raised arms.

"Do you like it?" he whispered in her ear, wrapping his arms around her. "I had him etch your name into it as proof that it is *your* piano!" Garon exclaimed spiritedly.

"L-like it?" she stammered as she walked over to the large, polished instrument, the purple lightning flashes streaming through the surrounding bay windows reflecting off its glossy surface.

Unable to say anything, Lucy demonstrated her answer with action.

Ding! echoed the crisp, clear sound of a single piano note, solidly pressed by one of her fingers. As if the acoustics of their home were meant for this instrument, the note rang through the room and surrounding halls, loud and clear.

The following notes slowly unveiled a growing melody, full of passion and romance. Her left hand rose gracefully to join the right, adding depth and harmony to the enchanting tune.

Eyes absolutely fixated on her delicate, dancing fingers, Garon squatted down, observing her every move and soaking in the spellbinding music for what would last another hour.

This newly composed piece, performed with love, came to a heart-wrenching close as her left hand faded in a low bass, *ritardando* tremolo, mixed with the serene cascade of rolling arpeggios, ending in the romantically nostalgic key of E minor.

Neither dared to move as she slowly lifted her hands from the keys, resting them in her lap. Garon could have sworn that his heart-pounding breath was disrupting the stillness of the moment.

Lips clenched together, tearstained face, and an expression that seemed to say, *You've just given me the earth*, Lucy turned to Garon, still unable to speak.

"Oof!" he exhaled as she leaped from the bench and tackled him to the ground. Her arms squeezed him so tightly, he hadn't realized that someone so small could possess such strength! Unable to speak himself on account of her emotional reaction and the beautiful piece she'd just performed, all he could do was hold her back and kiss her blond head.

As promised, Lucy followed Garon to their lunch date at the Sneaky Snake. She feared the tavern would be filled with rough men donned in eye patches, scraggly beards, and tattoos—gold teeth with rotten breath—but to her surprise, it was quite the opposite. Instead, the atmosphere was warm and lively, filled with plain soldiers enjoying their Alansgrú stout, alongside ordinary townsfolk and their wives, sharing a nice (albeit windy) quiet lunch.

Mr. Gürbak, Lucy noted, was delightful. Sporting a twanged accent (its origin unknown), he was a positively jubilant man with rosy red cheeks, a receding hairline, and a massive beer belly bulging behind a brown apron. He kept a steady rhythm, constantly polishing glass steins behind his well-kept wooden bar. Overcome by excitement for the soon-to-be-married couple, Gürbak provided freshly roasted boar, seasoned potatoes, and a generous slice of sweet potato pie for dessert—all for free—in honor of their upcoming wedding.

With full bellies and spirits lifted, they returned home, where Lucy immediately dashed to her piano. She thrust open the lid, propped it up on the stand, and flipped open the fallboard, squealing in delight as her fingers ran over her name, etched in gold. The day melted away as she played piece after piece, every melody drifting through the home like a fresh breeze through open windows.

The following five days were enormously busy. Garon found himself juggling between cleaning and organizing their slightly dusty house, and making frequent trips to Wölnas Castle to oversee the preparations for the wedding. The grand hall was to host the ceremony, and lucky for him, Gyepson, a close friend, had taken on the burden of organizing invitations.

Lucy, on the other hand, spent her time meeting with Mrs. Éinovin, the town seamstress. While Mrs. Éinovin was a master of her craft, her appearance left Lucy unsettled. Bone-thin with a gaunt face, she looked more like the town mortician than a seamstress. Her cold, dimly lit home, which smelled of mildew and aged parchment, added to the eerie atmosphere. Lucy couldn't have been happier to leave, her discomfort palpable as she hurried down the streets to Mrs. Bürgohen's, to finalize the wedding menu. *I'll take her undisciplined, unruly children over that coffin-laden house any day*, Lucy thought, shuddering at the image of open caskets lining the basement.

As is often the case when time is full, it seemed to fly. And so, the day of their wedding finally arrived.

The grand hall of Wölnas Castle looked resplendent. Lanterns and chandeliers hung high on the walls and ceiling, casting a warm glow over white tablecloths, polished silverware, and gleaming wine glasses. White linen streamers, with a faint purplish-blue hue, fluttered around the room, illuminated by the unceasing lightning captured within orbs that adorned the walls—still trapped by the wind Majesticians of old.

Dressed in his black-and-purple-lined captain's coat—customary military royalty attire for such a day—Garon struggled to retain his composure as he greeted guests, each adorned in tight tuxes and elegant gowns. Talvald and Jahrgis, ever his mischievous comrades, followed him around, making inappropriate and baited comments about "this evening's events," a clear indication that they had already had a bit too much to drink.

"I will not say this again, you two. Leave me be, or I'll have you both—" But Garon stopped short, his stern tone lost as he noticed the sudden drop in his friends' expressions, their faces going slack and eyes wide. They weren't looking at him; they were looking past him.

Slowly, he turned around.

It was Fürnas all over again. His mouth fell open, breath catching in his throat. There, above the grand staircase, was Lucy. She stood like a vision in her jaw-dropping wedding dress, one hand gently resting on the metallic railing, her eyes fixated only on Garon.

Descending the marble stairs, her white-gloved hand skimmed the gunmetal gray banister. Her dress flowed around her like an ethereal mist, and the purple sash perfectly accentuated her delicate figure. Her golden hair cascaded down her back in soft waves, catching the light of the room.

Gulp. Garon swallowed hard, trying to steady his breath. This angel was coming straight to him, her presence casting away every shadow in the hall. She was about to be his wife—and the thought was almost too much to bear.

They moved toward each other, footsteps echoing in the grand hall. The tension in the room was palpable; the electricity between them almost tangible. Closer and closer, until…

Lucy leaped into his arms, and he spun her around, her hair and dress swirling like a storm in itself. He gently set her down, and together, hand-in-hand, they ascended to the altar, ready to accept the bonds of holy matrimony. With the ceremony complete, the grand hall erupted in cheers, whistles, and applause as Garon and Lucy Erbrecht shared their first kiss as husband and wife.

Following the ceremony, a feast ensued. Mouths were stuffed with succulent roasted boar, imported kinberries, garlic-sautéed potatoes in cream sauce, and freshly baked bread. Everything was paired with rich wine gravy, prepared specially for the celebratory banquet.

Of course, who could forget dessert? Mrs. Bürgohen, with her "voluptuous girth," had labored for days to prepare a spread that no one could resist. In Garon's honor, she baked over twenty peach and kinberry pies. And for Lucy, a white cake stuffed with creamed strawberries, topped with a silky chocolate ganache, stole the hearts of many. Not to mention the miniature sticky buns, lined with gooey cinnamon and drizzled with melted honey icing—every bite was heavenly.

"Go on, get outta here, you two!" Jahrgis shouted, rallying the entire crowd behind him as Garon helped Lucy onto a beautiful white mare, laced with purple and white ribbons.

"Thank you!" Lucy called out, waving both hands excitedly.

Garon jumped on behind her, and together they rode off into the stormy, lightning-rippled sky, heading toward their official home as newlyweds.

"Ha ha ha!" They laughed as they nearly stumbled through the doorway, drenched from the downpour.

"Really, it's like it's a—" Garon started to say before Lucy cut him off.

"Curse, right? Every time we pass Mrs. Éinovin's house, just three blocks from home, it starts to rain!" Lucy finished his thought, giggling.

"I've always been suspicious about that place," Garon muttered as he wrung his black hair dry, droplets splashing on the wooden floor.

"No, you did not just say that! I know you didn't!" Lucy exclaimed, poking his nose playfully. "I swear to you, I thought the exact same thing after leaving her house last week!"

Their hushing laughter filled the room as they looked into each other's eyes. The intensity between them grew, blossoming into a love that could no longer be contained. Without another word, Garon swept Lucy off her feet and slowly ascended the staircase to their master bedroom, the candlelight flickering and casting warm shadows around them.

Isaac Erbrecht

Dink, donk, burnk, pank, gink! The random notes from Lucy's piano burst out as ten-year-old Gerbin—Mrs. Bürgohen's oldest son and Lucy's newest student—banged on the keys.

"A-all right, Gerbin. I have to ask…," Lucy spoke calmly, though her eye twitched, hands clasped nervously in her lap. "Did you practice at all this past week?" she blurted out.

"I promise I did, Mrs. Erberck"—he could never say her name right—"but the keys kept sticking! It made it hard to practice!" exclaimed Gerbin, his chubby face rippling with each word.

"Sticking?" Lucy asked in fear, her face scrunching up as she anticipated the reply she knew was coming.

"Yeah! The keys haven't worked well since I played after eating all the leftover sticky buns and pies from your wedding!" Gerbin said, matter-of-factly.

"Um. Gerbin… you do know that was over ten months ago… right?"

"Of course, Mrs. Erberck!" he replied with a facial expression that practically shouted, *duh!*

"Gerbin, did you at least wash your hands after you ate said sticky buns and pies?" she asked, already horrified by what she knew the answer would be.

"I don't ever wash my hands after anything, ma'am," Gerbin responded earnestly.

With a cough that barely held back the rising nausea in her throat, Lucy stood up and motioned for Gerbin to follow.

"Thank you, Gerbin. Tell your mom today's lesson is on me. Take care!" she exclaimed as she gently (but firmly) pushed him out the door.

"But I've only been here for five min—" he called out.

"Thank you, Gerbin! Take care!" she shouted, slamming the door shut and leaning against it, eyes closed in relief.

A sudden realization hit, and her eyes snapped open. She rushed to the kitchen, grabbed a linen towel, soaked it in the washtub of rainwater, lathered on some handmade soap, and hurried back to the piano, gingerly dabbing at the sticky keys.

Why? Why? she asked herself over and over. Why did she agree to teach the Bürgohen boys and their unruly friends piano? (Mrs. Bürgohen was quite persuasive.) And why did they all smell like rotten fruit and cheese? Did they never bathe? Between the booger flicking and armpit fart noises, Gerbin was the worst. (And no ten-year-old should be that fat with a voice that deep.) Yet, the incalculable freckles on his chubby face, nestled beneath that scrunched, matted red hair, made him slightly more tolerable.

"Lucy?" Garon called out as he entered, pulling off his sweating helm, his black hair flinging droplets of sweat around.

"Thank heaven above for a mental paradigm shift!" Lucy cried, still gently dabbing at the piano keys.

"What's going on?" Garon asked, stepping into the parlor. "Um, everything okay?" he asked, half sarcastically, as he pointed to the washrag.

"I don't even know where to begin," Lucy replied, scrubbing the keys.

"Ha ha... let me guess. Gerbin?" he questioned, wrapping his arms around her and massaging the large bulge of her lower abdomen.

"How did you know?" she replied in mock surprise, her voice pitched high.

"Dear," Garon said as he turned her around, taking the washrag and tossing it into the bucket, "you're due to have the baby any day now. Please... I think it's time for the piano lessons to stop."

Lucy looked at him with sorrowful eyes.

"At least for now!" he added quickly with a smile. "I think you should give yourself at *least* six months."

"But not too many months after that, your contract will be fulfilled! And we can return to Fürnas!" she said hopefully.

"Exactly! So…" He trailed off.

"I should probably just tell everyone I'm done teaching, then," she said with a hint of sadness, finishing his sentence.

He nodded sympathetically. "I really think it's for the best."

"I agree," she said sincerely. "Oh my gosh… Fürnas is going to flip when they learn I've started teaching!"

"Hmm… between our return, a newborn, and your becoming a piano teacher, we may have our hands a little too full. Think we should just stay here for a while?" Garon asked, hardly waiting for her reply.

"Heck no!" she blurted out, then caught herself, shame crossing her face. "I mean… I'm sorry, dear, it's just that Wölnas isn't exactly…" She trailed off, letting out a holler as the baby kicked.

Garon's eyes widened with excitement and concern. "Is it time?" he asked eagerly.

"N-no… not yet. Soon though…" she huffed. "Dear, can you do me a favor?" she asked as Garon pulled out the piano bench and helped her sit.

"Anything for you," he said immediately, dropping to one knee and taking her hands in his.

"It may sound silly, but… I'm craving Mrs. Bürgohen's strawberry tarts."

"Oh! I'll go by her place right now and ask her to bake you some," he said, standing up.

"I already put in the order this morning. Do you have any money on you? The payment is fifty silvers," Lucy said, almost shyly.

"Fifty silvers!" he exclaimed. "How many did you order?"

"Well… about five of them, and I may have also asked for them to be stuffed with roast boar, sauerkraut, and topped with pickled beets," she answered in a hushed, shy tone.

Garon paused, scratching his head as he processed the... interesting combination. "I, um... well, okay. I do have the silver on me, so I guess I'll be right back!" he said, kissing her forehead.

"Why does it always start raining every time I pass Mrs. Éinovin's house?" Garon mumbled, carrying the large metal platter of tarts back home. Although an odd combination, the aroma of the baked goods wafted through the linen cover, flaring his nostrils with each step.

"Lucy?" Garon called out as he kicked his boots against the doorframe to knock off mud, swinging the door open.

There was no response.

"Dear? I have your, um... well, I have your tarts!" He paused, trying to figure out what exactly to call them.

Again, no response. He walked into the parlor to find the piano completely closed up. With scrunched lips and a raised eyebrow, he moved to the kitchen. She wasn't there either. Gently setting the tray down on the kitchen table, he decided to check upstairs.

Sure enough, there she was, sound asleep on their four-poster bed, exhausted and snoring lightly. He softened his breath, carefully unstrapping his leather and metal-covered war boots, placing them aside as he tiptoed over to his sleeping wife.

How funny, he thought, gazing at her beautiful, smooth skin and rippling blond hair. Just a year and a half ago, he couldn't have cared less about dying on the battlefield. But now, as he sat down, slowly caressing her face and lower abdomen, more than ever, he desperately wanted to live. How quickly things change! In less than eight months, he would be rid of this terrible kingdom.

Suddenly, the glass stein of water on the nightstand began to ripple and shake. No, the whole house began to tremble!

"**Damn it!** Another one?" Garon swore under his breath, gripping the nightstand for balance.

After just a few moments, the shaking stopped. Squinting, he bit his lower lip, staring at Lucy intensely. Not a stir! His heart momentarily dropped as he placed a finger under her nose. Yep, still breathing. Gracious, she must be exhausted.

Click, click! The sound of armor latches echoed as Garon unclasped his breastplate, setting it on the armor holder.

"Garon? You're back!" Lucy yelled as she suddenly sat up, nearly giving him a heart attack.

"How in Vaerün can you sleep through an earthquake, but the latches on my armor wake you up?" he demanded, half-joking, half-serious.

"There was an earthquake?" she asked cutely, (But most sincerely) while looking around.

"Yes! Less than a minute ago!" he exclaimed.

"Gracious! I'm glad we're okay," Lucy sighed. "What took so long? I've been waiting for over an hour and a half!" she suddenly demanded.

"Right. Sorry about that. Olga [Bürgohen] had to finish baking three more tarts," he said as he sat down on the bed next to her. "Want me to bring one up to you?" he asked excitedly.

"It'll only further add to my love and adoration for you," she said simply.

Like an excited puppy fetching a leash, Garon rushed downstairs, heart beating at the thought of pleasing his wife.

Clink! The fork hit the marble plate as he accidentally dropped it, nearly breaking a tart as he scooped it onto the dish. Thank goodness it didn't—he probably would have lost his head.

"Jahrgta?" asked Lucy, looking up as Garon gently set the plate on her lap. Immediately, she took her hands from caressing the smooth metal bands and small amethyst of her wedding necklace, grabbed the plate and fork, and dug into the tart.

"Excuse me?" Garon demanded, raising an eyebrow and leaning in.

"Or Zölko?" she asked again, smiling slightly.

"Thank the heavens above." Garon sighed in relief as he sat next to her on the fluffy bed. "For a moment, I... no, never mind," he said, dismissing the fleeting thought that she might be suggesting names for someone else's child.

"What do you think of those names? Or maybe... Gerund Junior?" she asked whimsically, chomping on the tart and rubbing her abdomen.

"One problem, dear," Garon countered, "I think it's going to be a girl. Those are boy names."

"Oh, don't worry about that. I'm almost positive it's going to be a boy," she replied simply.

"What? No way! Jenna wanted us to bring back a little girl for her!" Garon objected.

"Despite what the lovely princess may want, even royalty doesn't always get what they want," Lucy said coolly.

A boy? Garon's head reeled at the thought. It wasn't that he didn't want a boy, but… how on earth would he be a father to him? His own dad was never there! Not that it mattered, since he lost him at a young age anyway. Girls were just so much easier to handle! Besides, he already had some practice with Jenna. Maybe that was it—maybe he enjoyed his short godfather moments with her so much that he wanted a little girl of his own. Or maybe it was the idea of seeing Jenna's face light up when they returned to Fürnas with a little girl, fulfilling his promise to her.

"Well, we don't know for sure if it'll be a boy or not… right?" Garon asked quietly, squinting in contemplation.

"It's true. But somehow, my heart tells me it's going to be a boy," Lucy said. "Would you humor me, please? Just tell me… what would you want to name him if it is a boy?" she asked, smiling warmly at her husband.

"Hmm…" He paused, tossing his head thoughtfully as typical boy names ran through his mind.

"Isaac," he suddenly declared, as if placing the last piece of a puzzle. How it rang out! His heart raced, and his blood ran cold with excitement. "Yes. Isaac. *Definitely,* Isaac."

"Isaac?" Lucy whispered, sitting her empty plate down and massaging her belly with both hands. "*Isaac Erbrecht,*" she whispered again.

A chill ran down Garon's spine as he looked at the goosebumps on his arms.

"Isaac Erbrecht," he muttered. Perhaps it would be a boy after all? Maybe Lucy was onto something. Again and again, he repeated the name in his mind as he lay down next to her, rested his head against her, and quickly fell asleep, imagining what it would be like to have a son.

"Commander, look out!" Talvald shouted as he ran in front of Garon. *Clang, clang!* echoed his shield as it absorbed the blows from a sudden Kreaux attack.

"Talvald?" Garon questioned dreamily. "Talvald!" he exclaimed, snapping out of his daze and rushing around him, his long silver blade slicing through the Kreaux, now drenched in fresh black blood.

The battlefield spun around him as if he'd drunk too much Alansgrú the night before. All around, his units fought desperately against the Kreaux, screams and clashes filling the air. Yet all Garon could think of was his wife. Frustration and anger boiled inside him.

Why did it have to be this morning that she went into labor? Curse this position, forcing him to service on the battlefield! And curse Wölnas for being so damn dark and stormy all the time! But worst of all, curse these Kreaux—these relentless creatures that ruined every day of his life!

"My apologies, Talvald! Is your arm okay?" Garon asked, wrapping an arm around one of his best friends and examining his shield arm.

"Y-yes, Commander. It's a little sprained but still usable," Talvald replied, shaking his arm out. "Been through worse than this. Ha ha, remember when that Praetor crushed my leg?" he said, laughing for some comic relief.

"That was unfair. I swear that was one of the biggest clubs I've ever seen a Praetor wield!" Garon immediately replied, joining in on the humor.

"Sir, I know you're worried about your wife," Talvald said as he pierced his sword through an oncoming, screeching Kreaux. "You said she's in labor?" he shouted to Garon while engaging more of the attackers.

"Aye, she is! I can't lie to you… I'm worried sick," Garon admitted, sinking his sword into a nearby Kreaux, followed by a swift kick to its abdomen.

"When's your relief coming?" Talvald asked, raising his shield just in time to block the razor-sharp, black claws swooping down upon him.

"It's about three, right? The lieutenant should be here around seven," Garon answered as he cut down yet another Kreaux.

"Man, that's Boar shüza!" shouted Jahrgis as he ran up to help fend off the growing number of Kreaux attacking Garon and his twin brother. "Why the hell are they making you work when your freakin' wife is in labor?" he demanded, unleashing three arrows from his bow in rapid succession.

"That's what I was just asking!" Talvald exclaimed as he pushed over the Kreaux in front of him, its head freshly pierced by one of Jahrgis's arrows, black blood oozing down.

"Shüza, man!" Jahrgis yelled, nocking more arrows and felling more Kreaux.

"It's all right," Garon said loudly to be heard over the thunder and rain. "At least I have you guys here to help me out," he finished as he tackled a Kreaux to the ground, beating it relentlessly.

"Hey, Jahrgis!" Talvald shouted as he dragged a Kreaux out from underneath Garon and held it up. "Another target practice!"

The squealing Kreaux flailed every which way, its limbs struggling against Talvald's grip.

"Give me some numbers!" Jahrgis called out as he nocked his bow, shutting one eye and readying to fire.

"Five for the chest, ten for the kneecaps, and—" Talvald started before being cut off by Garon.

"Fifty for the hands and feet," Garon finished, standing up and brushing some mud off his silver armor.

Shink, shink, shink, shink, shink, shink! The arrows pierced the Kreaux, who hung lifeless above the ground.

"Point tally, please?" Jahrgis called out.

"Gotta watch my six while I add it up!" Garon replied as he approached the Kreaux.

Arrows flew around them from Jahrgis's bow, mixed with the cacophony of yelling and screeching from the ongoing battle. But what could anyone say? They were used to it.

"Let's see here," Garon said, counting the arrows in the Kreaux's body held by Talvald. "Five, ten... fifteen... fifteen for the chest!" he cried out to Jahrgis. "Three arrows... two in one knee, one in the other, so... thirty for the knees!" he shouted again. "Fifty... fifty, fifty, fifty. Two hundred for the hands and feet!" he yelled out, finishing.

"Not bad! Two hundred and forty-five, huh?" called out Jahrgis, still firing his bow at advancing Kreaux.

"Next time, add another arrow in the kneecap, and you'll beat last week's record of two hundred and fifty!" Garon laughed.

With great strength, Talvald hurled the body through the air.

Shink, shink! Two more arrows pierced the flying body before it hit the ground with a thud.

"You'll find those two arrows just hit a foot and a hand," Jahrgis said as he approached, finished with fending off the additional Kreaux. "So that puts me at three hundred and forty-five!" he added cockily, wiping dirt from his nose.

Garon and Talvald inspected the body. Dang, he was a good shot! Sure enough, another arrow was embedded in the left foot and one in the left hand. With nods of approval, they both clapped for Jahrgis's mastery of the bow.

"Thank you, thank you. I'll be here all evening," Jahrgis said, bowing dramatically.

"And tomorrow. And the next day. And the day after that," Talvald added sarcastically.

"And the day after that, and the day after that... and so on and so forth, for how many years, Jahrgis?" Garon asked curiously as he withdrew his sword to fend off an approaching Kreaux, arms flailing wildly.

"Hmm..." Jahrgis mused, stroking his goatee and acting as if they were having a casual tavern conversation amidst the battle. "Why, I believe I have about four left!" he said with a grin.

"Man! You suck, Jahrgis!" Talvald shouted. "You get out one year ahead of me. What am I supposed to do by myself? Garon will be gone, and who will I have to tally up points with?" he demanded.

"Ha ha, well, I'm sure Erycks or Polner would be happy to play. They're both good shots. Although Erycks uses a crossbow and

Polner a recurve, like me," Jahrgis said. "Oh, but there's one problem, Talvald. I know you forget frequently, but we're twins. We finish at the same time," he said, clapping Talvald on the shoulder in a brotherly way.

"What will you guys do after... hold up..." Garon trailed off, taking a few steps forward.

"What in Vaerün?" Talvald said slowly, squinting as he joined Garon.

"No way..." Jahrgis said as he stepped up beside them.

In the distance, at the crag edge of the chasm, an overwhelming wave of Kreaux surged. A black, moving sea of creatures, bent on utterly destroying the Wölnas faction. Beneath their feet, the earth began to quake as a massive earthquake struck, forcing them to their hands and knees. All around, Kreaux clawed their way out of the drenched, muddy ground, screeching and seizing soldiers left and right.

As the tremors ceased, the three men quickly rose to their feet.

"Commander! What do we do?" screamed Jahrgis as he unleashed a storm of arrows, nocking five every second.

"The Kreaux have never attacked like this!" Talvald yelled, battling three at once.

Garon swallowed hard, looking around in horror. For every one of his men, at least four Kreaux surrounded them—too many. One Kreaux was more than enough to handle; two were nearly overwhelming. Three? Without help, they were doomed.

His heart raced, desperate for a plan—anything! If he didn't act fast, his entire army would be annihilated.

Boom. Boom. Boom. The ground quaked beneath them. *Boom!* Dirt exploded everywhere as Praetor after Praetor burst through the ground, clubs and arms swinging to attack. What the heck? As if one wasn't bad enough!

With the fiery red insignia of Fürnas reflecting off the lightning, Garon unleashed his Fürnas blade—a gift from King and Queen Coltier—and charged into battle.

Agggh! Arrggh! Gulk, gulk! echoed the cries of his men, ripped and shredded by Kreaux claws and fangs. *Ughaw, golk!* sounded the crushing blows as the monstrous clubs of the hulking Praetors smashed down.

"Commander! Help!" some soldiers screamed, running toward Garon, only to have their heads and arms slashed off right in front of him.

With all his fervor and an indescribable mix of anger and fear, Garon's blade met the Kreaux.

Shink! Shink, Shink, Slash! rang the blade as it sliced off Kreaux heads, legs, and arms. *Shuk, shuk, shuk!* sounded the sword piercing Kreaux chests and torsos.

"Garon! Look out!" Jahrgis screamed from a short distance away.

Garon turned just in time to raise his sword, blocking the massive club of a Praetor coming down on him.

Iiiiiinnnnnggg! vibrated the blade as it met the club. Nearly dropping the weapon from the impact, Garon tightened his grip, the trembling hilt sending waves of pain through his hands.

Shew, shew, shew! Arrows whistled past, and Garon watched as the Praetor swayed left and right.

"Uh-oh!" he shouted, barely jumping out of the way in time to avoid being crushed by the massive giant. "Wow..." he muttered, staring at the seven silver arrows embedded in the Praetor's back.

"Got your back, Commander!" Jahrgis yelled, rapidly firing upon the other Kreaux.

For a split second, everything seemed to pause as Garon's eyes filled with tears. Though he was their commander, never had he felt so cared for. After all, Jahrgis could have died saving his life.

"Jahrgis!" Garon yelled, voice cracking with emotion. "Don't do that again. You could have died with your back turned like that!" he finished.

"Naaah, don't you worry 'bout me, Commander. I got your back! Now shut up and get back to work. You've got a kid to go home to soon!" Jahrgis called out. "Besides, you're distracting me!"

What more could he do than laugh? And with that, Garon turned back to engage the Kreaux.

Eeeeeeeee reeeeeee! pierced the storming air, the blood-quivering, ear-shattering sound of Kreaux Mourners.

"What in Vaerün is going on here?" Garon and Talvald said almost in unison, their backs nearly pressed together as they fought side by side.

It was true. The Kreaux had never attacked like this! Sure, it was a battlefield, and that chasm was crawling with them, but this… no, this was as if someone had unleashed hell itself upon them.

Unable to cover his ears, Garon's eyes watered as he ran, sword in both hands, extending toward the Kreaux Mourner. Around her lay the bodies of nine soldiers, their deaths obvious from the abominable banshee-like screeching that shattered their helmeted heads.

"Damn you!" Garon shouted. "They didn't even have a shüza's chance!"

Not wearing his helm, Garon's life was spared as he bolted toward the banshee. But there were consequences—he felt a warm trickle of blood ooze out of his ears as he drew closer. His heart filled with dread as he realized this might be the last time he ever heard again. Gradually, the soul-racking torment of the banshee's screech dissipated.

Thhhuunk! Garon felt the vibration of his blade as it ran the banshee through. Filled with raging anger, he barely heard his own voice as he yelled, slamming the creature to the ground. The horrifying thoughts flashed through his mind—he might never hear his newborn's first words, or Lucy's music, ever again.

Why? Why was he even in this stupid war? Why hadn't he traveled south to Fürnas when his town fell apart, instead of heading north to this hellhole of a kingdom? Such thoughts raged as he beat the banshee's body with his fists, venting every feeling of frustration and despair he held inside.

"Germander. Grrrmander!" came Talvald's muffled voice as he struggled to pull Garon away from the banshee.

Barely holding back tears, Garon let Talvald help him to his feet. *Please, please… don't let my hearing be gone,* he thought repeatedly, the tinnitus unbearable.

"Just a moment, Talvald. I just need a moment…" Garon muttered, unable to hear his own voice as he pulled his sword from the banshee, still hearing only the ringing in his ears.

"Wrrgis hrs brn njrd," said Talvald, though it sounded muffled to Garon as he led him past the attacking Kreaux.

"Talvald, I said I need a moment," Garon repeated.

"Wr drnt thnk hrs grrna mrk it, srr," Talvald's voice muffled for the third time.

"What, are you deaf? Like I am now?" Garon shouted, frustrated, ripping his hand away from Talvald and stabbing a Kreaux about to seize upon them. "I said I need a moment!"

"I'm sorry, Commander. It's just that… Jahrgis has been injured, and I thought you'd like to know," Talvald said, exasperatedly.

"Wait. What did you just say?" Garon's blood pumped faster as he realized he could hear again.

"Jahrgis, sir. He's been injured. He needs help!" Talvald repeated.

Oh, happy day! He could hear again! Thank the heavens and the almighty Creator! Garon laughed with relief, confusing Talvald as he burst out in joy.

"Right, let's go. Show me the way to him, Talvald!" Garon exclaimed as he followed.

The Kreaux siege didn't relent. In fact, it was getting much, much worse. And to make matters even more dire, the storm intensified tenfold. Thunder clapped every few seconds. Lightning sizzled and flashed above them almost continuously. The wind howled and whistled with gale force, making the Kreaux go ballistic.

"Not too far away, sir!" Talvald yelled, helping Garon cut through the swarming Kreaux.

There's no way we're going to survive this, Garon thought as he fought on. *There's just no way. There's too many, and nowhere near enough of us. My wife… my darling wife…* Suddenly, he paused, thinking of Lucy playing her elegant music at the piano. Then he thought of Fürnas and Jenna… and his soon-to-be son.

"Wait, son?" Garon said aloud, pulling his long, silver Fürnas blade from a Kreaux's stomach.

"I'm sorry, sir?" Talvald asked, running his blade through another Kreaux. Both were practically caked in black Kreaux blood.

"Talvald, I don't think we're gonna make it," Garon said, exhausted.

"No, no, sir! See? He's right there!" Talvald said excitedly, albeit out of breath, as they spotted Jahrgis kneeling just ten feet away, still firing his bow at the oncoming Kreaux.

"Jahrgis!" Garon shouted. "Hang in there, buddy. We're coming for you."

Suddenly, Garon froze. His heart began to pound. As if he hadn't been breathing hard at all this whole time, suddenly, that was all he heard. It was as if the world around him had gone still, and he was the only thing left alive. Overwhelmed with an all-consuming fiery feeling, he found himself dropping to both knees, his sword sinking into the ground before him, hands barely gripping the hilt.

"What is happening?" he whispered. "Am I... dying?"

No, not dying... but *living!* Living and breathing in a way he had never felt before. As if someone had injected his spirit with an eternal flame, Garon looked around. Whatever was happening, this effect was gripping everyone and everything around him. All his soldiers had fallen to their knees, some mirroring him with their hands on their sword hilts pierced into the ground. Others had their heads raised to the heavens, tears streaming down their blood-and-mud-caked faces, all facing the same direction—toward the sky over Wölnas.

Even the Kreaux had fallen to the ground... stunned, as if struck by the most powerful tranquilizer imaginable! Some lay lifeless, while others screamed and thrashed their heads violently, as though injected with a horrific poison. For the first time, Garon felt a pang of pity for the creatures. As terrifying as they were, they suddenly seemed insignificant, reduced to pitiful beings upon the face of Vaerün.

Garon's eyes rose to the sky. The lightning had stopped—and so had the rain and wind! All was quiet and still. Even the dark purple storm clouds above had paused, as if waiting for something incredible to happen.

Boom... echoed a sound from above, high in the heavens.

Squinting, Garon looked up to see a glorious, golden-yellow-and-white feather descending through the storm clouds, surrounded by what seemed to be a barrier of light.

The feather hovered elegantly in the sky, dancing among the clouds above the Wölnas Kingdom.

"What is it?" murmured the citizens of the kingdom below as they pointed up. Was it a messenger? An angelic being? "No, it's too small for that," some would have said. Or was it a feather from the wings of the Almighty Creator himself?

Whatever it was, they knew one thing: it was alive with its own grace, and by far the most glorious sight to behold. (It had to be! It was not every day—or ever—that the eternally raging storm of Wölnas came to a complete halt.) Later, when asked to describe what it felt like to see the feather of Majesty descend upon Wölnas for the first time in a thousand years, the response was unanimous: "It felt as if a portion of the Creator himself had graced us with his glory. And desperately, we never wanted him to leave."

Swish... swish... flip! danced the feather of Majesty in the air, still high in the clouds. Knowing its exact target, it seemed to survey the scene below. Within the kingdom's walls, people stood perfectly still, some kneeling and others pointing in awe. Outside, on the battlefield, countless soldiers knelt, overwhelmed by the sight.

"I must see this for myself!" the feather seemed to say, if it could speak.

"What... in... Vaerün..." Garon whispered as the feather dashed down from the sky, casting rippling rays of resplendent light. Was he losing his mind? Or was it really headed toward them?

No, it couldn't be...

It was! It was headed straight for him!

As if God himself had wrapped his arms around him, Garon took in a deep breath as the feather whipped around him. His lungs felt as though they might burst from the sheer vitality and splendor that encircled him in a sublime cyclone of light.

And there it was again—that feeling. The powerful feeling of familiarity that consumed his soul, just like when he saw Jenna perform Majesty for the first time. It was a divine sensation that filled his soul with unspeakable joy.

"No, wait! Please, come back," Garon uttered, hand outstretched toward the feather as it left him and encircled other soldiers.

"Shut up!" He found himself thinking, stomping his boot on an annoying, wailing creature on the ground. Wait a second—that creature was a Kreaux! And not just that one—all of them! Every Kreaux was fidgeting and holding their heads in a fetal position on the ground, crying and mourning in a way he had never seen before.

But why? Garon dismissed the thought as his eyes refocused on the feather.

As if God had whispered, "Okay, that's enough. Now remember why you're here!" the feather whipped back into the sky, holding its position over Wölnas one last time before rocketing down at an angle and disappearing entirely beneath the kingdom walls.

As the ripple of golden light faded, Garon struggled to tear his eyes away from what he had just witnessed.

"Commander, look out!" Talvald screamed at the top of his lungs.

Still in a daze, Garon turned around slowly, but not quickly enough.

Slash, slash, slish! His flesh tore open as black, razor claws gouged deep wounds in his back.

The sheer momentum of the blow forced Garon to turn. The Kreaux stood before him—shaggy black hair, pure-white eyes, black veins pulsating within, and white fanged teeth lined with black saliva and gums.

Shink! Shink, shink, shink, shink! Arrows whistled past, obliterating the attacking Kreaux.

Barely able to speak, Garon turned to see Jahrgis unleashing arrow after arrow upon his attacker.

"Jah… Jahrgis, no… stop," Garon mumbled, his vision blurring from the mortal wounds.

Garon's eyes widened as his heart pounded faster. There, behind Jahrgis, stood a Praetor.

Unable to shout, Garon grabbed Talvald and turned him to face Jahrgis.

"Jaaahrgiisss!" screamed Talvald, horror-stricken. With all his might, he charged, sword at the ready, his hands like stone.

But there just wasn't enough time.

Slaaaammm! The immense, white club came down upon Jahrgis, crushing him into the earth.

"How?" Garon muttered as images of Jahrgis flooded his mind. From their early days in the force, training and laughing together, to pranking others in the mess hall, to riding to Fürnas... and now this—so many moments, all flooding in at once.

How did we go from something so glorious... so heavenly... to something so unspeakably tragic? Garon thought, his face stoic.

As if he'd lost all hope, feeling he'd never again see that comforting, angelic light, Garon dropped his sword and fell to his knees.

Devastated and filled with a hatred like no other, Talvald unleashed a rage so fine upon the Praetor that the hell below might have difficulty distinguishing its remains.

"Get up, Dad!" a young male voice suddenly echoed in Garon's mind.

"What?" Garon muttered aloud as the voice struck his mind with the same feeling, wonder and joy that had just filled him some moments ago.

"Don't let them win! You can't! Never... ever! Give up! We need you!" rang out the voice, pure and clear.

"Whose voice is that?" Garon questioned. "Why does it feel so... *familiar?*"

With a newfound vigor, Garon gripped the hilt of his sword with a strength that could have crushed it were it not made from the adamantine forges of Fürnas. Filled with anger at the death of one of his best friends and spurred by a sudden hope, Garon unleashed his wrath upon the Kreaux.

Shink, shink! Slop. Shlick, guk! echoed the sounds of Kreaux body parts being sliced and limbs being severed. Garon couldn't stop; he wouldn't. Was it pure adrenaline? Or was it the image of Jahrgis—his freckles, green eyes, and black hair—that fueled his relentless fight? Or maybe it was the voice of the young man he'd just—

"Isaac? Isaac Erbrecht?" the voice echoed again in his mind. "I love it, Dad! Thank you so much!" it rang out, loud and clear.

Garon laughed, his face reflecting a look of disbelief. "You're welcome, Isaac," he muttered quietly.

Had he lost too much blood? Was he losing his mind? Yeah, maybe. But as long as it lasted, why not give in to it?

"I'm sorry, son. I'm so sorry I won't get to meet you," Garon said aloud, not caring who heard him.

No way, Dad! You will meet me. You just have to! Help is on the way, coming for you right now! Don't give up! the voice shouted in his head, so loud it nearly brought him to his knees again.

"What? No... how is that possible?" Garon muttered in shock as he saw entire platoons of Wölnas soldiers racing to aid them. At the front charged their lieutenants, dressed in white-and-purple armor, spears held out for battle.

"Frackin' crap... I don't want to die here... Please help me, Isaac..." Garon mumbled, falling to the ground, mud splattering as his vision went blurry.

With his eyelids blinking heavily, he exerted all his energy to watch as the fresh platoons raced past him. Overcome with fatigue, his eyes closed.

Wait a moment, Garon thought to himself. *That feather... and that voice... Isaac! You're here!*

Suddenly, he felt the strong grip of hands upon him. Was it Kreaux or soldiers?

Oh well. I guess it doesn't really matter anymore... He thought, as he slowly passed out upon the muddy battlefield.

Isaac... Isaac. The name ran through Garon's mind as he slowly awoke to the sound of whispering around him, though he pretended to still be asleep.

"Who is that...?" Garon thought to himself, while he twitched in his bed.

"I'm so sorry again about your brother, Talvald. Please let us know if there's anything we can do," Lucy said.

"Thank you, Mrs. E. Hard to believe it's already been a week and a half!" Talvald kindly replied, though slightly choked up.

A week and a half? Had he really been out that long?

"But," Talvald continued, "I'm concerned about Garon. That was no normal Kreaux that attacked him! Please, you have to believe me!"

"I do, kind one. I really do," she said softly.

"You should've seen the eyes, Mrs. E... They were unlike any I've ever seen."

"I don't get it. Why did it only go after Garon, though? You said he just melted away after he attacked?!" Lucy demanded, confused. "Is that even possible?!"

"Please, Mrs. E! I know it sounds crazy, but I'm telling the truth! The moment he slashed the commander, he just... melted into the earth! As if into black goo or gunk or something!" Talvald said, exasperated.

Lucy sighed.

Man, did he love it when she sighed like that. Garon struggled to hold back a smile.

"All I know," Lucy continued, "is that something's wrong. Look at his face! And arms! And don't even get me started on the wound on his back..." She trailed off.

"When was the last time you checked on it?" Talvald whispered.

"About three days ago."

Talvald whispered so low Garon could barely hear him, "Do you think he's been... infected?"

"I pray to heaven above that isn't the case. Besides, have you ever heard of Kreaux infecting people?" she whispered back.

"N-no, ma'am. As far as I've seen, they chomp, chew, slash, and destroy... oh! And frequently take the dead underground. But no, never infect," he said with a sigh.

How much more of this could he take? What were they talking about?

"The king says we should—"

"I know what the king said, Talvald!" Lucy interrupted sharply. "I... I know." She calmed herself. "I just... I can't. We don't know what the situation really is until he wakes up!"

All right, that's enough.

"What are you two talking about?" Garon asked, sitting up and opening his eyes.

Why is it still dark? he wondered. "Oh! Whoops," he said, pulling bandages off his eyes. "What the... why is everything in black and white?" he asked, looking around their master bedroom. Sure, it usually lacked color, but not like this! He looked to his left at Lucy and Talvald, who both screamed.

"G-Garon!"

"Commander!"

Lucy and Talvald said at the same time.

Garon threw off the blankets and swung his legs to the side of the bed, attempting to stand. But Lucy and Talvald rushed to him.

"H-hang on a moment, Commander! You've been out for—"

"A week and a half, yeah, I just heard," Garon finished.

"Dear, please wait... something—" Lucy tried to say.

"I've been infected, right?" he finished for her. "Is that why everything's black and white?" he asked, standing up.

What the—? Why are they stepping back? Garon wondered as Lucy and Talvald backed away, fear in their eyes and hands raised defensively, as if he were about to attack.

"Wait a sec, hold on, why are you two..." He trailed off as he looked at his raised hands.

Why were his fingernails so long, sharp, and... black? And putting the color aside, why did his skin look so pale?

Hardly listening to Lucy, he rushed past them to look into their standing mirror, barely making out her words, "Garon, dear, please, don't..."

What. In. Vaerün... he thought.

"*Infected*" might be putting it lightly.

His cheeks looked sunken in, revealing the skull structure beneath. His hair was a mess and felt dead. The reflection of his sharp, black fingernails looked unnervingly eerie, and when he smiled, he nearly recoiled at the sight of his own fanged canines and black saliva staring back at him.

But worst of all were his eyes. As if someone had dripped black beads of ink into them, they appeared clouded with a film of blackness.

"No... what happened to me?" Garon yelled as he (easily) shredded the shirt off his torso. Turning around, head over shoulder, he nearly recoiled again to see no visible sign of injury upon his back.

"What?"

"That's not possible!" Talvald and Lucy said in sync, both leaning forward in disbelief.

"No, no, no. No," Lucy said desperately as she walked over to Garon, running her hands over his back. "Brrr!" she shivered, yanking her hands away.

"Huh?" Garon asked, placing his own hand on top of his skin. It was then that he realized something even worse. Rather than feeling cold, warm, or *anything*, he felt... nothing.

"What's happened? I don't understand! The last thing I remember was being encircled by that feather, and now here I am, and... why?" he asked, beginning to cry.

Even his voice sounded different—thicker, as though he had fangs lodged in his mouth. Why were Talvald and Lucy staring at him like that? He was crying, for heaven's sake!

Oh... that's why, he thought as he turned back to look in the mirror. Black tears were streaming down his face.

"Commander. What was the last thing you thought of before you got attacked on the battlefield?" Talvald asked, trying to restrain his fear.

"I was... thinking of the feather," Garon answered honestly. "And my son, Isaac."

"Isaac? How did you know about Isaac?" Lucy asked.

"Know? What do you mean, 'know'? I don't *know* anything!" he exclaimed back. "It's just, when I saw the feather, for some reason, I thought of him. And I even thought I heard his voice in my mind!"

Lucy and Talvald exchanged looks.

"Okay, well... don't get mad, but..." Lucy muttered.

Then it hit him. Lucy had been in labor that day on the battlefield. And if it had already been a week and a half... and seeing her now-flat abdomen beneath her violet dress...

"Where is he?" Garon asked coldly. "My son."

"He's..." Lucy trailed off.

"Where's my son? Why didn't you tell me?" he spat, black saliva flying everywhere.

"Commander, please!" Talvald shouted as he and Lucy followed Garon, who fled the room.

"Honey, please, hang on. He's downstairs in his crib! But he's asleep. Please don't—" Lucy said, breathless and nearly tripping as she hurried down the stairs after him.

Garon's heart pounded. *Get out of my eyes!* he yelled internally as he rubbed them furiously. It took a moment for him to realize that the black strings he saw were the new, pulsing black veins in his eyeballs.

"Shhh, dear, please... don't wake him!" Lucy whispered.

Not in the family room... not in the living room... not in the kitchen... *Where was he?* Then it hit him—the parlor.

"Ah!" Garon exclaimed in excitement as he entered the parlor. There, next to the grand piano, sat a wooden crib with the Wölnas insignia carved into it and the name *Isaac Erbrecht* engraved on the side.

"It was... a gift," Lucy muttered, motioning to the crib. "From the Héndrjksens."

"The who?" Garon hissed, nearly fainting at the sound of his own voice.

Why am I feeling so angry? He had just woken up, and no one was to blame. Lucy surely planned to tell him about Isaac! And why was his heart beating so fast and hard? It felt like someone had replaced his heart with a mechanical pump.

"Um, dear... the piano makers. Don't you remember?" Lucy whispered, concerned.

The piano makers? Who? Garon thought, shaking his head as he struggled to recall. *Argh*, the frustration of trying to remember made him want to break something!

"Commander, please. Let's just sit down for a moment and have some tea, okay?" Talvald asked gently.

"I'll get the kettle ready!" Lucy added quickly, eager to help.

"No. I want to hold my son!" Garon said, his voice leveling out.

"Dear, please... don't wake him!" implored Lucy.

"Why does it matter? No one woke me a week and a half ago to hold him!" Garon said as he walked to the crib.

"Honey, we tried. You were unconscious!" Lucy explained.

He didn't care. All he wanted was to hold his son. As he looked into the crib, he couldn't help but smile at the beautiful infant wrapped in a large white cloth, a tiny head poking out with a small tuft of blond hair.

"I-Isaac," he muttered as he reached in to pick him up, fingers extended.

Then it hit him. He quickly pulled his hands back, horrified at his own claw-like hands poised to pick up his son.

"Oh, Isaac..." he barely whispered as black tears streamed down his face. Once again, he reached out, desperate to hold him, only to pull back once more. It was as if he felt unworthy to touch something so precious, so sacred. Somehow, upon staring at his son, he was filled with that same feeling he had when gazing upon the feather of Majesty.

"Lucy," Garon said, still staring forward.

"Y-yes, dear?" Lucy asked softly.

"The day Isaac was born... did anything strange happen?"

"Well..."

"Answer me, damn it!" he screamed, turning around, black spit flying everywhere.

Lucy and Talvald covered their mouths as Isaac let out a soft moan in his crib.

"Commander, I'm sorry for this, but please, come this way," Talvald said bravely, stepping forward to grab Garon's hand and lead him out of the room, Lucy trailing behind.

"Get your hand off me! I am **your** commander!" Garon roared as he ripped his hand away from Talvald.

"Agggh!" Talvald cried out as he fell to his knees, blood seeping from his palm and wrist.

"T-Talvald, I'm..." Garon stammered, kneeling beside him. Sorrow and realization suddenly overcoming to what he'd just done.

"Garon? Why? Can you please just sit down?" Lucy demanded, though still remaining calm, as she pulled out a chair and sat him down.

"Talvald..." Lucy whispered maternally as she stared at Talvald's hand and wrist. "That's going to need stitches... immediately. Come with me," she said, wrapping his hand in a clean kitchen cloth.

"I-I'll take him to..." Garon began.

"No!" they both said in sync.

"N-no. Garon, dear, please stay here and watch Isaac," Lucy said as she placed an arm around Talvald. "And I know this is going to sound terrible, but... please don't pick him up until I get back and we trim your nails," she said as they left down the hallway.

Garon swallowed repeatedly, about fifty times in a minute. Not hold his son? What parent would ever want to hear those words? And to make it worse, how could he have done that to Talvald? He didn't mean to... or did he? *Actually, it felt good. As a matter of fact, it was a shame he didn't cut off his whole arm!*

"**Agggghhhh!**" Garon shrieked, holding his head and shaking it violently. Suddenly, he stopped. Down the hall, from the parlor room, he heard his son crying.

What a great opportunity! I know she told me not to hold him, but... he thought as he hurried into the parlor room. *She didn't say anything about not comforting him if he started crying!*

Garon tried to smile as warmly as possible as he looked down at his son. Was it possible? Garon's eyes widened as he leaned closer to the crib, swearing that the irises looking back up at him were dancing and moving, just like Jenna's did.

But damn it all. What's the color? he wondered, his vision only showing the irises in black and white. *My son... my precious son,* Garon thought, tears filling his eyes as he reached out. *More than anything, I just want to—*

Kill you, boomed a sudden and random voice within his head. So deep, so profound, so evil that it made his whole frame quake.

"N-no. More than anything, I just want to hold you," Garon said aloud, trying to reassure himself of his sanity.

Duhn ***duhn****. Duhn* ***duhn****. Duhn* ***duhn****,* thundered his heart. Why would he think something that abominable, and so unspeakably heinous? *Were those even his own thoughts?* Or was it the infection? And if so, what on Vaerün had infected him?

"I-Isaac," Garon said aloud, his voice unsteady, as his shaking claw-like hand wrapped around the wooden bar of the crib.

As Garon spoke to his son, he found himself calming down. And it wasn't just him—Isaac stopped crying too, as if eager to hear his father's voice.

CHAPTER 7

Farewell, Kingdom of Wölnas

"Garon?" Lucy called as the front door swung open, his boots knocking fresh mud off the frame. The familiar sound filled her with a relief she hadn't felt in days.

"I'm right here," came his slightly muffled voice from around the corner.

Her heart leapt as she entered the parlor and found him lying on the floor beside Isaac's crib. He looked more himself—the darkness in his eyes had lightened, and a hint of color had returned to his skin.

"How are you feeling?" Lucy knelt beside him, pressing a gentle kiss to his forehead, her scarf tumbling over his face.

"Forget me—how's Talvald?" Garon pushed himself up, his hands trembling with an unspoken urgency. He reached out cautiously, his sharp nails hovering near Lucy's skin, a reminder of the changes overtaking him.

"Well… it'll take some time, but he'll be all right."

"Did he need stitches?" Garon's eyes narrowed, bracing for an answer.

"About thirty."

Silence pierced the room, sharp as a newly forged blade.

Lucy continued quickly, trying to ease the tension. "Don't worry, he's fine, really! In fact, he was… excited. Said it was a good reason to get drunk on Alansgrú."

"Hah!" Garon chuckled, some comfort returning to his voice.

"You should have seen him after he got drunk! He actually paid you a compliment. Said, 'It's not every day you get stitched up by your commander in chief!'"

Garon pressed a hand over his mouth, stifling a laugh so as not to wake Isaac. He motioned with a nod, and they left the parlor, walking down the hall to the living room, where they settled on the velvet couch in front of the fireplace.

"There's something I need to tell you, and it's… kind of important…" Lucy's voice trailed off as they sat down. Her fingers nervously traced the patterns on the velvet.

"What is it?" Garon's voice held a curious edge, a flicker of concern in his eyes.

"That day, when Isaac was born… about an hour after his birth, something happened." She hesitated, unable to meet his gaze.

Garon nodded, urging her to continue.

"Something very peculiar. But… I don't really know how to describe it."

"Can you try? Is it… bad?"

"I don't know. I don't think so, but it makes me fear for Isaac's future."

"Well, what is it, then?" Garon demanded, anxiety tightening his voice, his posture straightening as his heart began to race.

"His birth took place in our bedroom, upstairs. Mrs. Bürgohen and Mrs. Éinovin were there to help." Lucy paused, gathering her thoughts. "Right after they delivered him, something entered the room."

"Entered the room?" Garon's eyes narrowed. "What do you mean?"

"Earlier, when Talvald asked you what you were thinking about before you were attacked by the Kreaux… you mentioned a feather and Isaac. Right?"

"Right."

"Well, I don't know if it's the same feather, but this one… it was heavenly, brilliant beyond description. It descended into the room as if a gift from an angel."

Garon's heart pounded faster, and Lucy could see the flicker of recognition.

"It spun through the air, encircling me, before it flew into Isaac, disappearing." Her voice trembled. "What do you think it means?"

"Well, I…" Garon hesitated, words failing him.

"There's more," Lucy continued. "After it disappeared, Isaac's body emanated this most beautiful light."

"Perhaps… he's been chosen by heaven for something?" Garon mused, uncertainty thick in his voice.

"That's what scares me!" Lucy's voice cracked. "If he's chosen, then doesn't that mean he'll have to face terrible things? Do you think someone will try to hurt him? Or… kill him?" Horror filled her eyes.

"Lucy, please, calm down." Garon placed his hands on hers, trying to steady both her and himself. The black claws that were now his nails glinted in the firelight, a stark reminder of their struggles.

Lucy exhaled, trying to steady herself. "Only a few months left until we can return to Fürnas. I want to go back as soon as possible."

"You have no idea," Garon muttered under his breath.

"I believe it's the safest place to raise Isaac."

"Come now!" Garon grinned. "He seems to be doing quite well in the midst of Wölnas's storm."

"Really, Garon?" Lucy arched an eyebrow.

"Like our stallions—born and raised in storm—look how well they handle catastrophe! If Isaac has a great work to do, at least he'll have the strength to face it."

Lucy fell silent, staring at him. "Those born in the storm are the likeliest to survive it," Garon said, his voice sincere.

She smiled at him, a "*Thank you*" reflecting within her eyes.

"I can say one thing for sure…" Garon leaned back, looking into the fire. "It makes sense that light dwells within him. Being near him… fills me with a peace and protection like nothing else."

"And he loves the piano!" Lucy suddenly exclaimed, her eyes lighting up.

"Haha! So that's why you have his crib right next to it!" Garon laughed. "That reminds me, did you ask anyone else what they thought of the feather?"

"No," Lucy replied, shaking her head. "I asked Olga [Bürgohen] and Beatrice [Éinovin] to keep it a secret until I knew more."

"Please... you asked the two biggest gossips to keep a secret?" Garon teased. "Bless your heart."

"I know... but I have to trust them. I had no choice—they were right there to witness it!" Lucy's voice trembled with an edge of desperation.

"Well, tomorrow, while I'm at work, maybe you could go to the library to see if there's any information." Garon draped his arms over the back of the couch, letting out a sigh.

"About that..." Lucy looked down at the floor. "I received a letter from King Jyalhim about your return to work."

"Oh, perfect!" Garon's voice dripped with sarcasm as he stood. "Where is it? It's getting cold in here. I'll use it to start a fire."

"I felt you'd say that," Lucy admitted shyly. "So I read it before you could do that."

"And then you burned it?" he asked eagerly.

"And then I burned it."

"Well, what did our kingly 'Shüza' have to say?"

Lucy bit her lower lip, afraid to respond. "He said you're not allowed to return to work or leave the house. If so, you'll be executed."

"Aaand he wonders why everyone hates him," Garon muttered, throwing up his hands.

"He fears that, with the way you look, you'll cause panic if the citizens see you."

"Oh, come on, it's not that bad! Is it?" He leaned in, seeking reassurance.

"It's... pretty bad, dear," Lucy answered honestly.

"Well, frack him then! Let's leave here and return to Fürnas!" Garon exclaimed.

Lucy's blood ran cold, and additional silence temporary filled the room.

"I would love nothing more," Her voice wavered with desperation, "but we need to find a way to cure you first."

"But—"

"Do you really think Jenna would like to see you like this?" Lucy challenged.

Suddenly, a vision of playing with Jenna crept into his mind. Garon imagined himself accidentally piercing one of her doll's eyes with his claws, or even skewering kinberries at the dinner table and waving them around on his claws to make her laugh. He couldn't help but let out a chuckle. The humor of the scenario *momentarily* lifting the weight of everything else currently going on.

For that most fleeting moment, it felt almost normal—*like the old days*. And yet, in the back of his mind, he knew things would never quite be that simple again.

"If it's Jenna we're talking about, then—"

"Don't even finish that sentence," she interrupted sharply.

Silence settled over them. He simply had to break it. "Does the king know about Isaac?"

"Like I said," Lucy answered, irritation tinging her voice, "the only ones who know are you, me, Olga, and Beatrice."

Garon nodded slowly. "Why does this sound so familiar?" he mused, just before a horrifying voice hissed in his mind: *She's lying to you.*

"Wait." Garon straightened, eyes narrowing. "You don't know anything about what's going on with Isaac, do you?"

"N-no, I don't," Lucy stammered, looking away.

"Are you sure?" Garon pressed, leaning closer. "Promise me you're telling the truth?"

"I really don't know. It's just..." Lucy continued, but the voice in Garon's mind shouted again: *She's still lying to you! She knows WHO and WHAT Isaac truly is!*

"You okay, dear?" Lucy reached out to touch him. "Why are you holding your head?"

Garon slapped her hand away, his voice suddenly cold. "Lucy. I demand you tell me the truth about Isaac. You know something, and if you don't tell me, so help me... I SWEAR I'll find out."

Horrified, Lucy sat still. *Who was this man sitting across from her?* "It's conjecture, but... I believe our son is a Majestician," she said finally, though slowly and quite carefully.

"What?" Garon's eyes widened.

"Just like Jenna. I believe Isaac has been chosen by… Majesty."

"**Majesty**?" Garon echoed, guffawing.

"When I was King and Queen Coltier's adviser, I had to know the history of Fürnas." She quickly responded.

"Okay?" Garon's voice dripped with sarcasm.

"Ancient texts describe an angelic feather descending from heaven, bestowing the power of Majesty on the chosen."

Images of Jenna casting fire and wielding flames flooded Garon's mind.

"So Isaac's like Jenna?" Garon asked, his curiosity piqued. His gaze couldn't be contained, he simply had to look around the room.

"I think so, but… that's what's strange." Lucy's gaze drifted away.

"**What's** strange?" Garon's irritation grew, suddenly looking back at her with tremendous fixation.

"When Jenna was born, a feather dashed through her and then ascended back into the heavens, and a fiery red aura surrounded her," Lucy explained.

"So?" Garon waved his hand dismissively.

"When Isaac was born, the feather stayed *in* him… It never left."

"All right, big deal. Is that all?" Garon's agitation flared further without warning.

"There's more to it than that!" Lucy pressed on, frustration in her eyes. "When Majesticians are chosen, their auras glow in colors representing their elements—blue for water, green for earth, purple for wind, red for fire."

"And?" He spat.

"Isaac's aura was pure light. And his eyes—have you seen them? Golden yellow, unlike any Majestician before him. And… Come on!" She emphatically spoke, "Have you ever met anyone with yellow eyes?"

Garon shifted uneasily, the voice in his mind whispering: *She's hiding something.*

"I'm color-blind, remember?" he snapped back sarcastically.

Lucy's face tightened. "I'm telling you… Isaac, our *son*, is unlike any other Majestician. And it worries me."

"Why does any of this matter?" Garon's voice twisted, his irritation morphing into something darker. "It's all so… dumb. Are you sure you didn't just imagine this? He's just a baby!"

Lucy's hand flew to her mouth in shock. "How can you say that?"

"And even if he was chosen by some 'Majesty,' so what?" Garon's voice rose, a snarl forming on his lips. "Like Jenna, he'll grow up thinking he's special."

"Garon?" Lucy's voice was soft, unsure who she was speaking to.

"News flash!" Garon's eyes glinted with a cruel amusement and pure sarcasm. "NO ONE is special. Everyone tries so hard to be somebody, only to end up being a *nobody*."

Lucy's fear tightened, arms wrapping around her body as if to protect herself.

"And you want to tell me that *THAT* baby boy," Garon pointed down the hall, "is supposed to be the most special of them all?" He laughed darkly. "HA! I **bet**… he'll grow up feeling the most insignificant of all."

Slap! Lucy's hand stung against his cheek. It happened so quickly, nothing else could be said for a few moments.

"How dare you," she whispered, her voice trembling with rage. "I don't know what complete *filth* has poisoned your mind, but I'll be DAMNED to the very hell with all the Kreaux to sit here while you insult our precious son!!"

And with that, she stood and walked away, her dress and hair flowing behind, leaving Garon to be stunned in total silence.

The following weeks were a challenge. Confined to the house, Garon found it hard to keep busy—sharpening swords, polishing armor, cleaning hallways. He had even found a dead rat in one of the suits and used it to play a trick on Lucy, leaving it in the kitchen sink.

Cutting down his claws was the most grueling task. Why did it feel like clipping bones instead of nails? And they grew back in just three days. The pain was worth it, though, for those few fleeting moments he could hold Isaac.

"Everything okay?" Garon asked as Lucy came up from the basement.

"Oh, yeah!" She answered quickly. "Just leaving something for Isaac," she added as she walked by, absently touching the key dangling from her wedding necklace.

"Leaving something? Like what?" Garon followed her, curiosity piqued.

"Don't you worry about it!" she replied playfully, wagging a finger. "It's nothing that concerns you."

"Well, curse me for asking!" he retorted, feigning offense.

Lucy laughed. "It's nothing bad, Garon. Just something for when he's older."

"Okay... but how's he going to get it when we're moving to Fürnas?" he asked.

"It's just a letter, Garon! When we move the contents of our vault, it will come with us," she said, rolling her eyes.

"You wrote a letter to our baby?" Garon's expression softened, making his otherwise frightening appearance almost endearing.

"If he could read, then yes," Lucy said sarcastically.

"Can I read it?" Garon took a step toward the basement.

"Absolutely not! The letter is for *Isaac*, not you, silly!"

"Ooooh... **cold**," he laughed.

"Just like you, dear," she gently stated, while guiding him away from the basement.

Knock, knock, knock! Three loud bangs on the front door.

"Is that Mrs. Bürgohen?" Garon's eyes glinted with mischief. "Or even better... Mrs. Éinovin? Oh, how I'd love to scare the shüza out of that woman!"

"No, dear, let's not." Lucy sighed, pulling on his ear and dragging him away.

"Aww, come on! Just one last scare!" Garon pleaded, rubbing his hands together like a mischievous child.

"Stay behind the door," Lucy demanded of him, as she opened it.

"O-oh!" Garon heard of Lucy, "How may I help you?" Her voice shook.

"We're here for Garon Erbrecht," said the lieutenant, ten soldiers standing behind him and a metal cage on a handcart.

"What is this about?" Lucy tried to close the door, but the lieutenant's armored boot kept it open.

"We've learned that Talvald received a near-mortal wound from Garon Erbrecht, who turned on him without cause."

"No, it was an accident!" She spat in *too* much honesty, clearly filled with panic. "Surely Talvald told you that?"

"Thanks to his heavy dose of Alansgrú, we got all the details," the lieutenant said coyly.

"Really?" Garon stepped from behind the door, swinging it wide open, unable to contain himself a moment further. "Of course, *any* drunk man will tell you his deepest secrets. No shüza!" He spat.

The soldiers recoiled in fear at the sight of their transformed commander.

"C-*Commander?*" whispered Gyepson, pushing to the front.

"**Stand back, Gyepson!**" barked the lieutenant.

"So, the rumors are true, then... Don't worry, we'll get you back to normal," Gyepson said optimistically.

"I have two questions," Garon said, leaning casually in the doorway, totally ignoring Gyepson. "One, did you interrogate Talvald after he sobered up?"

"That information is classified," the lieutenant replied nervously.

"Well, it concerns me, considering you're all on my doorstep to throw me into that cage," Garon snapped, finger quickly pointing at the handcart just behind the group.

"And your second question?"

"Oh, right... Why the hell are you on my doorstep?" Garon's eyes blazed.

Clang! With a single kick, Garon sent the lieutenant flying back into the soldiers, effortlessly knocking all of them over.

The next moments were chaos. Blood sprayed as Garon slashed at the soldiers, claws flashing in the early morning light. Screams pierced the air as Garon fought with a ferocity and strength that none could match.

Lucy's voice was drowned out in the pandemonium, her pleas for peace ignored as the battle raged.

And oh, how her heart shattered as she beheld Garon—no, *not* Garon—an animal, a **Kreaux**. His eyes, fully black. The veins in his body pulsated with black venom.

It ended quickly, though not as Lucy wished.

Caged, Garon howled and thrashed, his black claws scraping the unyielding platinum bars. Contained, but far from subdued.

Lucy's emotions were in turmoil. There was her husband, being dragged away in a cage, and soldiers lay bleeding on the ground. She looked to the disappearing handcart, only three of the eleven soldiers still pulling it toward the castle, all of them limping and bloodied.

Then, she saw them—the dead soldiers. Cold realization gripped her. And Isaac... how long had he been crying?

Who in Vaerün should she help first?

Looking between the fallen soldiers and the house, her mother's instinct demand her to run inside and grab Isaac. By the time she returned with water and clean cloths, the scene was swarming with citizens, platoons of soldiers, and lieutenants.

Shüza... This was only the beginning of her troubles.

"Lucy Erbrecht!" shouted the inquisitor.

"Yes?" Lucy bobbled Isaac, trying to soothe him in her arms, her voice brave.

The throne room of Wölnas was a world apart from Fürnas. The black and purple marble floors were cold, and the large tapestries were like blown-up battle standards. Purple lightning crackled in glass orbs that hung high above, casting harsh shadows across the walls. Everything was metal—dark, gray, and unwelcoming.

"**Answer** my **question!**" demanded the inquisitor, spit flying.

MAJESTY

Lucy suppressed a laugh as she took in his ridiculous outfit—an over-the-top fluffy purple hat, topped with an enormous feather, and a face so wrinkled it made a bulldog look elegant.

"I'm sorry, Inquisitor. Please repeat your question," she said, her smile barely contained.

"Vhat was you doing on shaid day of shaid incident?" he repeated, jowls wobbling as he spoke.

"Ha ha ha!" Lucy burst out laughing, clearly unable to hold it in any longer.

"**Enough**," came the deep, commanding voice of King Jyalhim. "I'll take care of this. Inquisitor, you are dismissed without another word." The king finished, with a dismissive hand.

The Wölnas inquisitor, not daring to argue, bowed deeply and scurried away. Lucy sighed with relief.

"Lucy Erbrecht, formerly Lucy Dolliér of the Fürnas Kingdom. Correct?" The king's voice was cold.

"Correct, Your Majesty," Lucy replied steadily, unafraid to respond.

"Is this a conspiracy against Wölnas?"

"Excuse me?" Lucy's voice held a raised eyebrow.

The king shuffled some papers, laying them to the side. "You were King and Queen Coltier's most *trusted* adviser... Were you not?"

"Correct."

"Then why did you come to Wölnas?" He leaned forward, eyes narrowing.

"I came to Wölnas with and FOR my husband, Garon Erbrecht."

"But that's where you lie. You didn't come here with your **husband**." The king's voice dripped with sarcasm. "You came here with your... man toy."

Lucy's blood boiled. "I'm sorry?"

"How long were you two together before you got married?" the king pressed.

"That's hard to answer, Your Majesty. We—"

"Exactly my point. You seduced my commander with your provocative ways. We know how desperate you women of Fürnas are," he added coolly.

"Excuse me?" Lucy's voice trembled with rage.

Goodness GRACIOUS. No wonder Garon hated this man.

"You waited to marry until you arrived here. And since then, nothing but trouble has followed."

"How so, Your Majesty?" she asked, fighting to keep her voice steady.

"For **one**, only men play the piano in my kingdom, wench."

Lucy's eyes narrowed. *Oh no, he didn't.*

"For **two**, only... well, you know, stay in the homes of unmarried men."

"It was only for a week—"

"For **three**, what is that strange, glowing, fiery thing that came from the sky? Practically scared my kingdom to death!"

"Try reading your history books, you—"

"**And four!**" he barked. "How does my commander receive a nearly fatal wound, only to have it disappear after resting in your house?"

"What does that have to do with—"

"Sounds like dark magic to me!" the king spat, happily interrupting her. "No one has ever been infected by Kreaux venom before!"

Lucy's heart pounded. Never had she felt the urge to punch someone as she did now. "What are you implying?"

"You've *tricked* my soldiers, *infected* my commander, and summoned a strange weapon that attacked from the skies—all from Fürnas!"

"Your Majesty," Talvald stood, raising his hand, "if I may?"

"What is it, Talvald?" the king snapped.

"With all respect, Your Majesty, I can't help but think all these events are coincidental."

"Coincidence?" scoffed the king.

"Yes, Your Majesty. Lucy has been nothing but a blessing, as has Garon, who has served loyally as commander in chief of Wölnas's armies for many years now."

The king massaged his forehead, clearly frustrated.

"And while YOUR accusations clearly *ATTEMPT* to ring true," He continued, "I have some good news, indeed... The jury finds

Lucy Erbrecht not guilty of treason or conspiracy," Talvald continued. "Quite frankly? She's been nothing but a victim of strange circumstances."

Whispering filled the hall, as the king examined the royalties and lower classes alike in their stations, staring at their king with intent and pure disdained hatred.

The king exhaled, realizing he was outnumbered. "Very well. Lucy Erbrecht is not guilty."

Before anyone could cheer, he added, "However, Garon's contract will be fulfilled in one month. When that time comes, I demand that you, Garon, and your son leave Wölnas immediately."

No one said anything.

The king continued, "I! Or... -ahem- WE don't want that... THING here in our kingdom." he finished, accusingly pointing to the ground, implying the dungeons beneath.

Lucy nodded. *Fine with me,* she thought, dismissing the king's demand.

What was she feeling? Relief? Anger? Frustration? Perhaps all of the above.

Lucy's breathing grew heavy as she wound down the narrow passage, lit by the eerie purple glow of lightning lanterns.

"I suppose Garon was onto something," she whispered to Isaac, tickling his nose. "Not even this wretched place can dim your brilliance."

Isaac giggled, his tiny hand touching her cheek, and a feeling of comfort washed over her. Light rippled in his eyes, golden and pure.

A man's agonized scream echoed through the dungeon, the stone amplifying the sound. Lucy clutched Isaac tightly, unsure if she was protecting him or seeking protection herself. With every step, the air grew colder, the chains hanging from the walls clinking ominously.

"What is this place?" she whispered as she walked past bloodstained torture devices.

"Hello, Lucy!" The rough voice startled her, an unfamiliar terror filling her bones.

"Garon?" Lucy turned, gripping the rusted bars of a cell.

"Hello, Lucy!" Garon grinned, twitching like a broken puppet. His black eyes glistened, and dark, putrid saliva dripped from his mouth. His hair was wild, and he looked utterly deranged. Chains bound his hands behind his back, forcing him to the floor.

"Oh…" Lucy's hand covered her nose as the stench hit her—dozens of uneaten food plates, rotting, maggots squirming.

"G-Garon, have you…"

The words stuck in her throat; mouth suddenly dry. She couldn't swallow, and it felt like her head was being squeezed in a vise.

"Not feeling well?" Garon's head tilted at an unnatural angle.

"Y-y-you're not G-G…"

The saliva in her mouth dried up completely. She choked, hacking for air as if she were being strangled. And then came the laugh—dark and twisted, like a bass drum pounding underwater. Why was his hand outstretched, clawed fingers twisting as if gripping the air? No one had power like this… did they?

Lucy's vision blurred, her breath choked out, and the world began to darken.

But then—then came a bright light, emanating from Isaac, his tiny hand outstretched toward his father. Light rippled from his tiny being, filling the dungeon with warmth and life.

"Lucy… Isaac… please, get out of here." Garon's voice echoed faintly. "I'm so sorry. I'm not going to make it."

"Garon!" Lucy shouted. "What are you talking about?"

"Please, leave Wölnas. Forget about me. He's going to kill everyone, and he wants Isaac most of all!"

"Isaac?" Lucy's eyes darted to her son, his glowing hand held toward his father.

"No, Garon! We have to save you!" Lucy cried.

"Go to Fürnas, meet the king and queen, and…"

"Garon! How do I help you?" Her voice quivering with pure desperation, for the love of her life.

"Find Jenna… Isaac must—"

The voice choked off. A dark scream of countless voices filling the air. Lucy fled down the dungeon halls, Isaac's light guiding her.

Once outside, the storm clouds above seemed almost welcoming compared to the horrors of the dungeon below. Drenched in rain, Lucy returned to their house, barely acknowledging the passersby as she hurried down the cobblestone streets.

She threw open the front door, kicking the mud from her boots, but the empty silence of the house filled her with total unease. The ticking of the grandfather clock was the only sound. Once pleasant and inviting, it now sounded fully foreboding.

"Oh, Isaac... what do I... Isaac?" Lucy paused, studying his face. Were those tears beneath his eyelids? She clutched him tightly, sliding down the door in sobs.

After a moment, thoughts of Fürnas flooded her mind—the **Coltiers, Jenna...** and the piano. **The piano!** She had forgotten it was right there in the parlor.

With hurried footsteps, she laid Isaac in his crib and walked upstairs to change, inhaling the sweet scent of cinnamon and kinberries from her clothes.

"If we're to return to Fürnas, I think it's time to get into the spirit of it," Lucy smiled, pulling out a bright dress—the very one she wore when she met Garon.

Changing into the red-and-white dress, she lay on their bed, head resting on the fluffy pillows... It wasn't long before her eyes began to close.

"*Please...*" She quietly thought to herself, "*Let this nightmare end...*" and thus she began to hope once more, filling her mind with fantastical creations of her beloved home kingdom.

"*You're here!*" Lucy shouted atop the grand staircase, staring down at Garon.

"*Lucy Dolliér, is it? Please come down!*" Garon extended his hand toward her, the grand staircase of Fürnas echoing with her delicate steps. *Clip-clop, clip-clop, clip-clop.*

Oh, her *BELOVED* kingdom! How she missed Fürnas—the chandeliers, the kind servants, the benevolent king and queen, perpetual Autumn splendor... Baked goods all around and Jenna... Oh, dearest, sweet, Jenna! Always with her bright smile.

"*Garon, dear, please turn around!*" Lucy called, as she reached him at the bottom of the staircase, his back turned to her.

"*Lucy... why did it end like this?*" Garon's voice trembled. "There was only one month left. I wanted to return with you and Isaac to live out our days."

"What are you talking about, dear? We are here! And we're here to stay!"

"*I tried so hard, Lucy... to fight it.*" Garon wept. "*Why did this happen to me? I tried to do everything right. Was I not good enough?*"

"Garon..." Lucy's hand trembled as she reached for him. "*Turn around.*"

"*It's all gone wrong.*" Garon's voice broke. "*I'll never be good enough—not for you, Fürnas, Jenna, or Isaac.*"

With all her strength, Lucy turned him around—and was met with the transformed face of a monster.

"You think THIS is okay?" Garon roared, his fangs bared. "*Do you? DO YOU!? It's all gone wrong!*"

CRZZZRACK!!! Burst the lightning above their home, awaking Lucy with a start and immediate gasp for air.

The curtains of the bed swayed, the phantom breeze of the room chilling her to the bone.

Panic gripped her in a way that it had never done so before. Being the king and queen's adviser, she was taught to remain calm in even the most *unsettling* of circumstances.

But no... Something was wrong. Something was *off*, this time around.

"*Take the sword*". Echoed the words loud and clear in her mind, as she fixated upon the intricate red and gold patterns of Garon's sheathed blade; recently gifted from Fürnas's beloved rulers, and ever so regally resting against his dresser.

Without hesitation, the sword was immediately thrown overhead, belt fastened around her waist.

"Isaac!" she screamed in panic, as the thud of the cold wooden steps of their grand staircase met her bare feet.

"!!!" Lucy's eyes shattered open as it hit her… The front door was wide open, freezing storm rain littering the foyer.

Slip! She crashed to the ground, sliding on a cold, sticky liquid.

Lucy's heart sank as she looked out the front door, hands trembling as she shakily examined her hand.

Blood. Blood *everywhere*. It wasn't hers.

The brilliant, incessant strikes of lightning overhead flashed eerily upon the bodies which lay strewn in the streets… Rain pouring over them, blood running over and through the cobblestones.

She couldn't help but scream as she beheld the inexplicable carnage that now adorned the streets. Suddenly, it hit her…

"Isaac! My baby!" She turned around and immediately followed the trail of blood to the parlor.

The crib was empty… The piano completely gouged with claw marks, blood dripping into the polished white keys.

Her heart pounded, breaths coming fast and shallow.

"Think, Lucy. *Think*," she whispered and demanded of herself, forcing to stay calm.

With attempted composure, down the eastern streets she ran, following the trail of blood—different from the others. A beloved pet dog, stammering and bleeding, leaving erratic marks.

"L-Lucy…" Came a weak voice from the side—Mrs. Éinovin, against a wall, her abdomen slashed open.

"**Beatrice!**" Lucy cried, rushing to her friend's side.

"H-he took him… Garon… to the chasm…" Mrs. Éinovin's voice faded, her head lulling lifelessly.

Horror filled Lucy as she witnessed her new friend leave this world.

Without any time to grieve, she could only run as fast as humanly possible to the eastern gates, pushing through the cracked opening to the battlefield beyond.

"**Where IS everyone?!**" She demanded of herself, scanning the muddy battlefield that was usually relent with soldiers and Kreaux.

No… No one. It was mortifyingly empty.

Empty, save for *one figure*—a man clutching something over the chasm, some two hundred feet away.

"***Garon!***" she shouted, while running with all her might to him.

"Oh, Lucy," Garon said sarcastically and uninterested, holding Isaac over the abyss.

Below, Kreaux hands clawed, desperate to reach the child... Their screeching filling the chasm below.

"What are you doing?" Lucy's voice cracked as she approached.

"Doing? Oh! You mean *him?*" Garon caressed Isaac's head, his claws coming dangerously close to his soft skin.

"Give me our son!" Lucy demanded.

"*GARON?* Who's Garon? I'm not he. Or rather... *this* isn't Garon anymore!" His voice rang with a cruel amusement. "Stupid girl. Have you any idea who you are attempting to address?"

Lucy stood bold and defiant. Heart pounding, she didn't dare take her eyes off his.

"Baehallün; author of all darkness, to your pleasure." hissed the words from Garon's lips.

"***Liar!***" Lucy unsheathed the Fürnas blade, gripping it tightly.

Garon laughed. "If you really are the author of all darkness, then you're a liar!" Lucy shouted over the thunder.

"Oh, I can assure you, my dear... this is the truth." Garon's black eyes locked onto hers. "I can see into people's souls—their deepest, darkest emotions. And Garon's? He was filled with jealousy. Envious of Majesty, of its power."

"Wait... Garon knew about Majesty?" Lucy's voice shook.

"Of course. You weren't the only one well-versed in history." Garon paced back and forth, Isaac still in his grasp. "He wanted that power for *himself.*"

"NEVER!" Lucy shouted. "Let him GO!"

"Let him *go?*" Garon sneered. "I only remain with those who *want* me, dear one."

Lucy's heart cracked. "You lie!"

"Garon wanted power. And oh, if you could've only *FELT* his jealousy as he watched that *STUPID* feather of Majesty descending from the heavens! It was then... I knew I had found my *perfect* host." Garon's voice dripped with pleasure. "But enough of this. It's time to end it."

Lightning crashed, splitting the sky, as the world itself seemed to be torn apart by their struggle.

SHHHZZZING! The Fürnas blade sang as Lucy drew it, a brilliant, razor-sharp gleam piercing the storm, tip pointing straight towards Baehallün. Her blue eyes burned with an uncontainable intensity, a mother's resolve blazing like the heavens themselves. Every flash of lightning accentuated the wild fury within her face.

"Spawn of hell..." Lucy's voice thundered, the words reverberating with divine fury... Thunder crashing above. "I don't care *who* you are or *what* power you think you hold. You'll learn today the full wrath of a mother who will give anything—***everything***—to protect her ***son!***"

For just a fleeting moment, Baehallün's dark eyes flickered with hesitation, but the darkness roared back, and he grinned. "Foolish woman!" he taunted.

Lucy charged, a storm unto herself, blade raised high. Their swords met with a CRACK of steel, her Fürnas blade flaring bright, shedding sparks like stars in the night sky.

CLANG! CLANG! Each strike resounded with fury—Lucy's desperate, frenzied defiance and Baehallün's merciless drive. Dancing like shadows and light across a dark tapestry, crashing against each other in a tempest of sparks and steel.

"Isaac's power is too great, too pure!" Baehallün spat upon her, as they met in direct clash, driving his blade hard against hers. "He'll grow to be a weapon of heaven, and I will NOT let that happen! This is *MY* army and *MY* world!!"

"You will ***never*** take him!" Lucy roared, voice booming, cracking like the very thunder overhead. Eyes continuously blazing with unyielding resolve.

Baehallün's dark smile only deepened as he hacked at Lucy's defenses, pushing her back with brutal strikes. "Oh, Lucy..." he hissed, "Sweet, *sweet Lucy*... you still don't understand, do you? Your husband is already lost... and your son will be next."

With a savage thrust, he broke through Lucy's guard, blade cutting deep into her shoulder, and blood pouring like a river onto the rain-soaked ground beneath. Lucy staggered, pain flooding her senses, but her eyes never wavered, sword kept steady.

"**Garon!**" Lucy suddenly and desperately cried, voice trembling with the intensity of her love and anguish. "I know you're in there! Fight him—fight for me, for Isaac—fight for yourself!"

For an agonizing heartbeat, the world seemed to stop. The storm's rage dulled to a low roar, and the darkness recoiled. Garon's face, hidden behind the mask of Baehallün, softened—that cruel smile faltered, and the pure, raw agony of Garon broke through, like a light struggling against a choking shadow.

"Lucy..." Garon gasped, fighting to breathe. "I... I never wanted this... I... love you... I'm so sorry."

Lucy's heart leapt, hope flaring in her chest. With trembling hands, she lowered the Fürnas blade, searching his face for truth, *praying* for him to win this battle.

"That dress..." Garon whispered and examined, tears streaming down his cheeks, mixing with the rain. "The very dress you wore... when we first met."

"*Garon?*" Lucy desperately inquired, her eyes wet with tears, but still she clung to the hope that this was real.

He gave a weak, broken laugh. "Yeah... Hah! Leave it to my wife... to fight me with my own sword, huh?"

"And where... did you get it?" Lucy whispered through her sobs, testing the man she loved one last time.

"From King and Queen Coltier... of Fürnas." Garon's voice was choked, but the love, the sincerity and pure honesty was there. He fought against the chains of darkness, gripping his head as if to tear it away. "Lucy... you have to go—NOW! Take Isaac... mount my steed, and ride... to Fürnas... Go NOW, before it's too late!"

Lucy's breath caught, a sob tearing through her throat. "No... Garon, *no!* You have to beat this! Snap out of it, *please!*" Her hands shook violently as she dropped the Fürnas blade, and instead, cupped his face, brushing the wet hair from his forehead. "**Fight this, Garon!** Fight him, and then come join us... I need you—I can't..." She sobbed, "I can't live without the love of my life!" She clung to him desperately, trying to pull him from the abyss.

For a brief, blessed second, Garon's eyes were once again his own. He lifted his shaking hands, clasping hers, and for a moment, the darkness seemed to fade. "Lucy... I'll try... I'll... I'll try..."

"**Run!**" he suddenly gasped and choked out, the words rasping from his throat. "Run, Lucy! Go NOW! Take Isaac, flee to Fürnas! Take nothing—take no one—save for Isaac! I will... I'll find you... just *GO!*"

With tears streaming down her face, Lucy swallowed the pain, the heartbreak, and turned away, holding Isaac tightly to her chest.

Heart pounding, she immediately obeyed. And thus, dashed with all her might.

With every step away from Garon, her heart seemed to shatter even further. *She ran, oh my, did she run...!* The world around her a blur of rain and mud, her only focus to get to safety—to save her son.

Fifty feet... Sixty... Her breath ragged and feet pounding the wet earth—

SHRRRRAACK!

Lucy stumbled mid-step. The wind leaving her lungs in a gasp. A cold, searing pain radiated through her chest as she slowly looked down to see the bloodstained blade—the *very same sword* that had been gifted to Garon by her beloved rulers of Fürnas—piercing straight through her, running her through.

She fell, collapsing to her knees, her body trembling violently as the blade was torn from her, and she crumpled to the ground, mud and blood mingling with the rain that pounded the earth. Her white and red Fürnas dress, once so beautiful, was now caked with the mire of battle, sticking to her skin like a wet shroud. Her golden, angelic hair clung to her face in dirty strands, plastered with mud and streaked with crimson.

Gasping, struggling for air, she lay on her side, her shaking hands still gripping Isaac, holding him to her chest. Her eyes, though dimming, stayed fixed on her precious son—his innocent, wide eyes staring up at her, full of unknowing wonder. She could feel the life ebbing from her with every labored breath, the world fading to darkness.

"Isaac..." she whispered, each word a tremor, each breath a struggle. Her fingers carressing his lion-like, golden blonde hair. "Worry... not, precious... angel. Heaven will... *never* be far... from you. How can it be? For it dwells within you... Mom will... always, **always**... protect you..." Her trembling lips pressed a final, fleeting kiss to his tiny forehead as her voice faded, and her breath stilled. A final tear ran down her cheek as her faded blue eyes started at her beloved son.

Baehallün's cruel laughter cut through the storm as he looked down at her, the dark glee of triumph shining in his eyes. "Such a noble death, for such a foolish woman," he sneered, mockingly bowing over her fallen form. "But alas, death is the fate of all who oppose me!"

He turned to Isaac, raising his sword, ready to claim the final victory. "Now, let's end this—"

BOOOOOM!

A burst of blinding light erupted from Isaac, surrounding him in a divine, golden barrier that pushed Baehallün back. The dark figure shielded his eyes, teeth bared in frustration as he staggered, the brilliance of the light cutting through the storm like a sunburst. The barrier shimmered with a strength beyond earthly might, glowing brighter and brighter with every heartbeat.

"What... what is this?" Baehallün snarled, his voice trembling with fury. Dark Majesty coiled around him like living smoke, and he raised his sword, the blade dripping with the black venom of his power. He slashed at the barrier, each strike ringing out like a thunderclap.

BOOM! BOOM! The barrier flared, absorbing the darkness, standing firm against every vicious swing. Baehallün's rage erupted, and he hacked at it with all the might of Dark Majesty, his blade crashing against the light in a flurry of sparks and shadow.

BOOOOM! Each strike sent shockwaves through the storm, the pure wall of light rippling like a roaring sea, but it held, unyielding and true.

"FALL! FALL!" Baehallün screamed in a twisted frenzy, pouring every ounce of his dark energy into the final blow. Black veins of shadow coursed up his sword as he lunged, his roar echoing through the storm, aiming to shatter the divine shield once and for all—

BOOOOOOOOM!!!

The barrier erupted in a shockwave of pure, heavenly light, blasting Baehallün back with a force like the wrath of a thousand suns. He screamed as his form was hurled through the air, black blood spraying like rain, and he tumbled headlong into the chasm below, his scream fading into the endless dark.

The storm, silenced, gave way to a serene calm as the divine light continued to surround Isaac, who lay quietly, his tiny hand reaching for the sky as the golden glow enveloped him like a cocoon—pure, bright, and filled with a power that no darkness could touch.

And above, in that moment, the clouds parted, and a beam of light from the heavens shone down upon the child, as if all the angels of Vaerün looked down with their blessing, wrapping him in a promise that darkness would never have the final say.

CHAPTER 8

The Siege of Fürnas

"Jenna, dear, please wake up!" called the ethereal voice of Lucy.

Jenna rolled over in her large princess bed and reached out a hand, searching for a pillow to cover her head as she usually did whenever Lucy woke her.

"Nooo, Lucy! A princess needs her sleep…" whined Jenna, her voice muffled beneath the pillow, annoyed by the rays of light that she assumed were from the sunrise.

"I cannot tell you what it means to me to see you again." Lucy's voice was soft and angelic, a warm smile spreading across her face as light flowed from her white robes.

"I'll say…" mumbled Jenna from under the pillow. "Tabatha is cool, but no one matches up to you, Lucy."

"Oh, how I *wish* we had more time. But alas, it has altogether run out. Please take Isaac with you, and go to your parents," said Lucy as she gently laid a baby boy at the foot of Jenna's bed.

"Take Isaac, and go to my parents. Got it," mumbled Jenna, still half-asleep, waving a hand lazily through the air.

"I have to go, Jenna! Please, hurry! The Kreaux will be upon your kingdom soon!" said Lucy in her final words before vanishing.

"Right, right. I'm sure they will, Lucy. I'm sure they will," Jenna mumbled, her hand flopping down beside her. Unbeknownst to her that there truly was a baby at the end of her bed, both she and Isaac fell back asleep.

"Stop crying, Isaac. I'm trying to sleep!" Jenna muttered from beneath the pillow. But Isaac did *not* stop crying.

"I said, Isaac—" Jenna started to shout, but then her eyes shot open. She sat up quickly, squinting her eyes. Was there really a baby at the end of her bed? Furiously rubbing her eyes, she leaned forward so far that she toppled onto her stomach.

"Wait - what in the absolute - Why is there a *baby* on my *bed?*" she shouted, hands outstretched. Silence answered.

She tapped her nose repeatedly as her eyes darted left and right in deep thought. *Did someone drop him off? Where did he come from?* The questions raced through her mind before she flung the covers off and leapt from her bed.

"***Lucy!***" she screamed. With her heart racing and emotions spiraling, she paced back and forth on the floor, the cold marble beneath her bare feet waking her up fully. "Or was it a dream?" she asked herself, tapping her forehead as she tried to recall.

"Oh, that's right... Isaac, was it?" Jenna said as she walked over to the crying baby and gently picked him up, rocking him back and forth.

"*Isaac...*" echoed a voice in her head. The baby immediately stopped crying and stared into her eyes.

"Wait a second," Jenna said as she looked into his eyes, realization dawning on her. "Your eyes are like mine!" she exclaimed, observing the dancing light within his yellow irises.

Please, Jenna, hurry! The Kreaux will be upon your kingdom soon... Lucy's voice echoed in Jenna's head as a slight tremor shook the floor beneath her feet.

Bam! Her bedroom door slammed open as she kicked it wide open, nearly knocking it off its hinges. She ran down the hallway, leaving her west wing chambers behind.

"Sorry, don't have time to talk!" she yelled to servants who tried to ask her something—probably where she was going, though she paid them no attention.

Long brown and reddish hair flowing behind, evening dress trailing her as she ran, and a heavenly child in her arms, one might say she looked like a younger and more exotic version of Lucy.

"Brrr!" She shivered as she dashed across the large outdoor catwalk connecting the west wing to the east wing. "I probably should've put on some boots," she muttered, her feet gripping the cold marble floor.

Slam! Her parents' bedroom door burst open as Jenna barged in, nearly giving the sleeping king and queen a heart attack.

"Jenna?" the king and queen said in sync, blinking at her.

"What's wrong, darling?" asked Layna, sitting up.

"Mom, Dad, something's wrong! I think something's happened to Lucy!" Jenna quickly recounted the heavenly visit.

"Are you sure that wasn't just a dream, Jenna?" Verolt asked, leaning back in bed.

"Oh, of course, Dad!" Jenna replied with a sarcastic smile. "But hopefully your dream fairy will bring you something useful. Mine just brought me a baby." She glanced sadly at Isaac.

Layna snickered as she got out of bed. With a tilted head and a warm smile, she approached Jenna, kneeled down, and brushed Isaac's blond head. "He's beautiful," Layna said as she looked into his eyes. "Wait a moment…"

"Yeah. I think he's a Majestician, like me," Jenna said knowingly, expecting what her mother was about to say.

"**What?**" Verolt demanded, quickly stepping out of bed to look at Isaac.

"No way!" Jenna shouted, pulling Isaac away from her father. "Ask the dream fairy for your own baby!" she said, nose in the air.

Already used to her sarcasm and fiery spirit, Verolt kneeled beside Layna, examining Isaac's eyes. "It's true," he said in awe. "They're just like Jenna's."

"What is it, Mom?" asked Jenna curiously, as Layna covered her mouth in shock.

"You said the angel called him *Isaac*, right?" Layna asked.

Jenna nodded.

"And you said the angel was Lucy?" Verolt asked.

"It's hard to say, Daddy," Jenna answered simply. "I never got to see her, but her voice sounded just like Lucy's."

"Why are you giving Isaac that look?" Verolt asked, noticing the odd expression on Layna's face.

"How can you not?" Layna retorted. "Have none of you truly looked at him? Tell me, who does he look like?"

Verolt and Jenna's response was cut short by a tremendous earthquake, followed by the sound of thunder.

"Earthquakes and thunder in Fürnas?" Layna gasped as she wrapped her arms around Jenna and Isaac. "We've never had—"

"Daddy! Where are you going?" Jenna shouted as Verolt ascended the spiral staircase in their room.

"Wait there, you two—or three! I'm just going to take a quick look!" he shouted back, climbing swiftly.

"What in Vaerün..." Verolt muttered as he reached the top and peered out the northern window. His hands fumbled for a telescope on the small table, and with the advantageous height of the tower, he gazed past the autumn treetops of the kingdom to see a tidal wave of rippling storm clouds consuming the sky, with legions of Kreaux below.

"Verolt! What did you see?" Layna asked frantically as she saw the horror-stricken look on his face.

"Kreaux. Masses of them. And a storm beyond description, approaching from the north," he said, his face pale.

"What do we do?" Layna whispered, placing one hand on Jenna's shoulder, the other covering her mouth.

"Tabatha!" Verolt shouted as he stormed into the hallway.

"Yes, Your Majesty?" came a voice from down the hall.

"A massive host of Kreaux and a storm beyond description approach from the north," Verolt commanded. "Gather my commanders and have them meet me in the royal meeting hall immediately!"

"It shall be done, Your Majesty!" echoed her voice in response.

With determination, Verolt reentered the room. "Jenna, Layna, get dressed," he ordered shortly before losing his temper. "Damn it, Layna! Where are you going?"

"I'll be right back! I have to tell Tabatha something!" Layna shouted as she fled their chambers.

"Shüza, we don't have time for this!" Verolt swore before shaking his head to calm himself. "Jenna. Go get dressed."

"But what about—" Jenna began, glancing down at Isaac.

"Take him with you!" yelled Verolt as he entered the massive closet and began changing into his war gear.

Before Jenna could even reach her chambers, the castle fell into chaos. Servants darted in every direction, some even screaming for reasons Jenna could not comprehend.

How is it that a child and a baby can be calmer than adults in a situation like this? she thought as she dodged screaming servants amid another earthquake.

"What should I wear, Isaac?" Jenna asked the baby as she rummaged through her closet. "This one or this one?" She motioned to two ornately red and white dresses on hangers.

Propped up on a makeshift seat of blankets on her bed, Isaac gurgled adorably, smiling playfully.

"Good choice. I like this one too," Jenna said, choosing the dress in her left hand and tossing the other onto her cherrywood dresser. Isaac tilted his head curiously as Jenna attached the oversized sheath containing a rapier to her waist.

"Oh, this? This is my rapier!" she said proudly, patting the sheathed blade. "If the Kreaux are coming, it's high time I use some of the moves Garon taught me!"

"Jenna, dear!" Layna shouted as Jenna stood on the landing above the grand staircase of the royal meeting hall. Jenna gripped the railing, peering down at her parents, soldiers, commanders, and lieutenants, all hustling in urgent conversation.

"Cooool…" Jenna muttered as she stood on tiptoes, watching people disappear into doors below the landing.

"Jenna, come down here!" Verolt's voice boomed a little too loudly.

Sensitive despite her fiery nature, Jenna hated being yelled at, especially when she'd done nothing wrong—like lighting the tailcoats of servants on fire, boiling water instantly for tea, or burning grass (which she never understood).

"Perhaps I should've..." Jenna mumbled as she held Isaac close, overwhelmed by the tall soldiers towering over her.

"All I need here is Commander Hürom and his five soldiers. The rest of you, leave us!" Verolt commanded, waving his hands.

Thank heaven above, thought Jenna as the hall emptied, leaving only Commander Hürom, his five soldiers, Jenna, Isaac, and her parents.

"Jenna. Are you prepared to fight?" her father's voice echoed in the great acoustical hall.

"Oh!" Jenna shouted, both surprised and excited. "Y-yes, Daddy. I—"

"No way," Layna interrupted, stepping forward to take Isaac from Jenna's arms. "She's still too young, and—"

"And we need her, I know!" Verolt shouted back. "But her powers are the most effective weapon against the Kreaux!"

"Yes, but she's still too young! And it's not just us who need her—it's all of Vaerün!" Layna argued.

Verolt glanced around, desperate, searching for something or someone. "Tabatha!" he screamed suddenly, forcing Jenna to cover her ears. "Tromsdotter! Ugh! Where is she?" he yelled, hands shaking.

"Would you calm down for just a few moments, please?" Layna demanded as she approached her husband, recognizing his unraveling nerves. "I asked her to do something for me. She should be back any moment!"

The queen looked around before feeling a small tug on her dress. She glanced down to see Jenna, eagerly pulling on it. "Don't worry about me, Mom. I can fight! I'll show those nasty Kreaux who's boss!" Jenna said, attempting to unsheathe her large rapier.

"That's very kind of you, Jenna, but—"

Time ran out again as another earthquake struck, sending everyone to their knees. *Earrrrgggghhh!* hissed the Kreaux's bloodcurdling screech from outside.

"Hürom and men, prepare yourselves!" Verolt roared.

Jenna breathed in the scent of cinnamon and kinberries from her mother's dress as Layna clutched her daughter close, hands shaking.

"Agggghhh!" screamed the Kreaux as they burst into the hall, claws and fangs bared.

"Haaaaah!" shouted the soldiers and the king as they charged at the Kreaux flooding in.

Jenna's heart pounded so quickly she imagined pulling it out, attaching little wheels, and entering it in a chariot derby. She'd never seen the Kreaux before—creatures she'd trained to fight since childhood—but the reality of seeing them was indescribable.

She squeezed her hands as the majestic flame within her roared to life. Fury gripped her as she watched soldiers she knew fall to the Kreaux's razor-sharp claws.

"No, Jenna, please don't!" her mother begged, pulling her closer as Layna, too, witnessed the slaughter of their beloved soldiers.

In that moment, Jenna managed to look at her mother's arm, holding Isaac. "How is he staying so calm?" Jenna asked herself as she watched Isaac remain peaceful amid the horror.

"Close the doors, Hürom!" the king thundered as he brought his claymore down upon a Kreaux, splitting it in two.

Poor Hürom—asking him to close those doors was like asking a man to fight against roaring floodwaters.

When the king realized that Hürom couldn't do it alone, he attempted to hack his way forward to help. But...

Reeeeeeeeee! Eeeeeee! The air-shattering screeches of the Kreaux Mourners pierced through the grand hall like jagged glass.

Tsshh...tshh...tshhh! The windows imploded in violent bursts, unable to withstand the assaulting sound waves, sending shards flying throughout the air.

Jenna's hands flew to her ears instinctively as pain shot through her head. Tears streamed down her face, blurring vision as she pressed her back against the pillar for cover.

All around, soldiers fell to their knees, clutching their now blood-pouring ears, anguished cries lost amidst such horrific screeching.

Without hesitation, Kreaux swarmed in, seizing their moment of chaos.

MAJESTY

"Wh-what's happening?" Jenna whimpered, voice thin and trembling. She felt something wet hit her head and looked up in terror.

Her mother, Queen Layna, was standing over her, mouth open in a silent scream, eyes wide with desperation.

Blood flowed freely from Layna's ears, staining down her cheeks and hair. Yet, amidst her own agony, Layna clasped Jenna and Isaac's heads together, forcing their foreheads to touch, as she shielded both their ears with trembling hands.

"Stay close... stay close..." Layna's voice came in shallow gasps, trying to be heard over the relentless screeching. Her hands pressed tighter against their ears, desperate to protect her children, even as she shook with the pain overtaking her own body. Jenna could feel her mother's warmth, hear the erratic thumping of her heart beneath the blood and chaos. Layna's nails dug into their scalps as if anchoring them to her through the madness.

Jenna's eyes welled with more tears as she looked up at her mother's contorted face, feeling the surge of love and fear all at once. Even through the blinding pain, her mother's fierce determination to protect them was clear. And though Layna's scream was silent, its agony wrapped around Jenna's heart like an unbreakable chain.

In that moment, nothing else existed. Just the shattering screams, the crushing pressure in her ears, and her mother's trembling, blood-soaked hands shielding her and Isaac from the storm of chaos that was consuming everything around them.

But before Jenna could process the scene, the hall shook again.

A monstrous Praetor thundered in with its massive, white bone club. Hürom and his soldiers were tossed like rag dolls as the giant swung its weapon, sending them flying. Verolt, being the largest man in the hall, repeatedly stabbed the Praetor, black blood seeping down its purple-and-black-skinned body.

Huugghwaaggghh! roared the Praetor as it swung its club, sending Verolt crashing into the wall.

And then suddenly... Time itself seemed to slow. Something within Jenna snapped. Amid the chaos, she darted out from behind the pillar, hands thrust in front of her. The fury within her roared like a blazing inferno.

"*Haaaa!*" Jenna screamed with hands forced into the air. Flames erupted from her palms, twisting like a dragon and engulfing the Praetor, reducing its giant body to a blazing torch.

Screeches, along with a black fluid pulsed from the burning behemoth—was it blood? No, it was skin melting off of flesh and marrow.

With hands still raised, she brought them together and unleashed a storm of fireballs, obliterating Kreaux one after another.

"*HAAAAA!!!!*" she continued, feeling a storm of rage and joy. *Finally! Finally, I am able to fulfill what I was sent here to do!* she thought triumphantly.

But suddenly, a hand gripped her wrist and yanked her away. "Wait, no, *no!* The fight's *that* way, damn it!" Jenna protested as the Kreaux grew farther away from vision.

Realization landed upon her, as Jenna realized her mom had picked her up and was swiftly fleeing away.

Boom! The doors beneath the grand staircase slammed shut with a deafening thud, cutting off the horrifying sounds of battle from the hall beyond. Jenna's breath came in ragged gasps as she pressed her back against the wall, heart still pounding in her chest. The sudden silence felt like a shock—unnatural, as if the storm of chaos was only held at bay by the thin, fragile barrier of the door.

Layna quickly locked the doors and, with trembling hands, grabbed a sword from a nearby suit of armor, jamming it between the handles to further barricade the entrance. The clang of metal echoed ominously in the quiet, and for a moment, it seemed they had a brief reprieve.

But Jenna's mind was still in the battle. Her hands tingled with the memory of the fire she had summoned, the burning heat that coursed through her veins as she had unleashed her power. She had felt invincible, ready to fight alongside the soldiers.

I could have helped them, she thought, her pulse racing again. *I could have saved them.*

"Jenna, come with me," Layna's voice broke through her thoughts, firm but weary. Without looking back, the queen gripped her daughter's wrist and began leading her down the hall with intensity and speed.

"But, Mom, I—" Jenna protested, glancing back at the sealed door, heart wrenching with guilt. She could still feel the heat of her Majesty power in her palms, the rush of adrenaline demanding she return to the fray. "Mom, please! I need to go back and help! Didn't you see me? I was—"

Layna's steps faltered, but she didn't turn around. Her ears were still bleeding, Jenna realized with a pang of dread. The sound of battle must have shattered her mother's hearing, and yet she had stayed so strong, shielding them both. Jenna's protests faltered as she realized that Layna's mind was focused not on the battle they had just escaped, but on what still lay ahead—what dangers they still faced.

"But wait..." Jenna hesitated. "This leads to the back part of the castle! Why the *back*?"

Dust rained down from the ceiling as the castle continued to quake. Jenna's anxiety spiked as the sound of screeching Kreaux grew louder behind the shaking doors.

"**Nanny!**" Jenna exclaimed, delighted as Nanny Tromsdotter opened a set of doors further down the hall, opening the way for them ahead.

"This way, *this way!*" ushered the voice of their delightfully plump adviser.

Despite the catastrophe, Jenna smiled at the sight of Nanny, with her rosy cheeks and ever-familiar white bonnet and checkered apron that seemed to struggle to contain her voluptuous frame.

"Your Majesty, I have secured a wagon for passage to Aerlund," Nanny said, holding open the large doors.

The courtyard outside was beautiful and freshly groomed, with trimmed hedges and statues of King and Queen Coltier. And there, behind them, were white horses harnessed to a Fürnas carriage.

"Fährlund?" the queen shouted. "No, no, that's to the north!"

"No, my queen," said Nanny, cupping her hand to the queen's ear. "***Aerlund***, to the southeast!"

"Oh, Aerlund. Perfect! That's far enough!" Layna shouted, barely hearing.

Jenna's flames surged as she looked behind her to see the doors shaking violently, Kreaux squealing just on the other side.

"Jenna, dear, come quick!" urged Nanny as she helped her into the carriage, assisting her into the plush seat.

Queen Layna quickly handed Isaac to Nanny, who struggled to step into the coach's seat. "Listen, Jenna," Layna said, tears streaming down her fair face as she held Jenna's hand. "Under no circumstances, *WHATSOEVER* are you to leave Aerlund until you receive word from me or your father that it is safe to return to Fürnas. <u>*Do you understand?!*</u>"

Hating being yelled at and overwhelmed by emotions, Jenna broke into tears. *How did all this happen in just an hour?* Just hours ago, she had brushed her hair and gotten her nightly kiss from her parents, as always.

"PROMISE ME!" Layna demanded as the Kreaux's screeches echoed down the hall.

"I promise, Mom!" Jenna sobbed, choking on her tears.

"That's my baby. I love you more than you can even begin to comprehend!" the queen exclaimed, hugging Jenna tightly and kissing her forehead.

No, please don't let go, thought Jenna as her mother pulled away.

"Now, Nann!" Layna ordered as she unsheathed her rapier and turned to face the Kreaux flooding in.

Whu-pish! cracked the whip as Nanny sent the carriage bolting down the path.

Jenna's eyes blurred with tears as she watched her mother fight the Kreaux.

"Nanny, please, we need to warn these inhabitants that Fürnas is—" Jenna began, seeing townspeople out on late evening strolls as the carriage sped past.

"I'd love to, but we must get you away, dear one!" shouted Nanny over the roaring wind as the carriage raced down the trail.

Isaac looked into Jenna's eyes and smiled, and Jenna buried her face into his tiny chest. "Please be okay, Mom and Dad!" she cried softly, feeling Isaac's small hands wrap around her neck in an innocent embrace.

They rode through the night, Nanny and Jenna taking turns sharing stories to stay awake.

"Ooh, ooh! And I can't wait for him to meet Isaac!" Jenna said as she looked down into Isaac's golden eyes, his adorable smile staring back at her.

"Perhaps he'll want to godfather him too?" asked Nanny with a raised eyebrow.

"No way! I'm his only godchild. And besides…" Jenna's voice trailed off as she hugged Isaac. "He promised to bring back a daughter for me to play with!"

Nanny laughed and shook her head. "Looks like we have a lot to look forward to!"

"Now it's my turn for questions," Jenna said, with an almost evil smile. "How do you know about Garon?"

"Well, now…" huffed Nanny as she turned around and cracked the reins, sending the carriage forth again. "There's some matters that don't concern you, princess!"

"If you don't tell me," Jenna threatened, "I'll jump out of this carriage and run back to Fürnas! And I know you can't catch me."

"Ooooh, you're evil!" Nanny laughed, playing along. "Well, all right… it was a beautiful evening in Fährlund…"

"Uh-huh?" Jenna uttered as she rested her head on one palm, smiling. "Oh! So this was when you were still Fährlund's baker?"

"Right. About seven months before I became adviser to your parents."

"Okay. Continue?" asked Jenna curiously.

"So, like I was saying…" Nanny continued, "It was a cool evening in Fährlund, and I had just finished pulling some fresh peach and kinberry pies out of the oven. My goodness!" She suddenly broke her thought. "Never have I met a man who loved peach and kinberry pie so much!"

Jenna let out a girly laugh, followed by Isaac joining in sympathetically.

And Nanny continued to tell the story of how she met Garon Erbrecht... perhaps with a few embellishments, to add just a little bit of spice. (But maybe the romantic kiss she received from the ruggedly handsome, green-eyed, black-haired commander of Wölnas was a bit overkill.)

Somehow, Jenna managed to stay awake the entire night as Nanny told her story. (Exactly how many embellishments did she add?)

"Oh! That's Aerlund in the distance," said Nanny, cutting into her story as they came to a pause atop the eastern hill on the seemingly never-ending trail of Ryúnion.

The sun was barely rising, and about another mile down the hill, upon the Ryúnion trail, Jenna looked down into the eastern valley to see the most charming little town.

"It looks so much like Fährlund!" exclaimed Jenna, head popped out of the carriage window, hair blowing in the refreshing morning breeze.

"That's because the mayor of Aerlund is my cousin. His name is Inglethöp."

"Wow." Jenna snickered, trying not to laugh. "What a name."

"As you know, I helped design the construction of Fährlund."

"Right?" Jenna nodded. "Wait. So is this a family thing going on? Isn't the mayor of Fährlund your—"

"We're not going to talk about him," spat Nanny, interrupting Jenna. "Let's just say that my cousin grew tired of Fährlund's mayor and his condescending ways."

"Oh! And so that led him to build Aerlund?"

"Yes. It's almost entirely constructed after Fährlund as I gave him the blueprints."

"Bravo!" Jenna clapped sincerely. "Talk about dedication! That must have taken a lot of guts for Inglethöp to come all the way out here and build a town!"

"Undoubtedly," said Nanny, cracking the reins once more.

"That reminds me..." Jenna said shyly. "Um. Why did we flee to Aerlund instead of Fährlund? Did you and your—"

"I said we shan't say his name!" spat Nanny angrily, interrupting Jenna again.

"O-oh. Right." Jenna giggled quietly. "Did we not go to Fährlund because of the unpleasant terms that you and the mayor left off on?"

"I mean really!" Nanny spouted off. "Why'd he have to do me like that? His own sister!"

Jenna bit her lower lip as she smiled, trying not to laugh for what she knew would be the umpteenth time of hearing this story. She stuck her hand out the window and felt the cool breeze as they descended the hill, the new rays of morning sunlight imbuing the green plains around them with life and vitality.

"It's not my fault," spat Nanny, "that the king and queen of Fürnas requested me!" She shook her head and momentarily jumped as she cracked the reins.

Jenna's heart momentarily plunged as the carriage shook, fearing that the Kreaux might be nearby from the earthquake she'd just—

Oh. Wait. It was just from Nanny's monstrous size.

"And not only that," continued Nanny. "Don't be bitter that Wölnas's gorgeous commander in chief referred me instead of you!" Nanny continued to shout to the air. "I already gave you the title of mayor. What more does your piggly, trouser-bustin' butt want?"

Tears began to squeeze from Jenna's eyelids. The stitches in her sides were becoming unbearable.

"It's because you're a fat, greedy son of a Kreaux's dirty uncle!" Nanny exclaimed as she shuffled her shoulders. "And you wonder why Inglethöp left your fat ass in the first place!"

Jenna roared out laughing. She had to wrap her arms around Isaac so as not to drop him from loss of strength.

"O-oh!" said Nanny as she turned to look at Jenna, embarrassed. "Goodness me. Forgive me, princess, please! I beg your forgiveness."

"Not at all, Nanny! It's great! I don't blame you," she said, wiping away her tears.

"And anyway…" Nanny trailed off. "We didn't go to Fährlund because the storm and Kreaux that fell upon Fürnas came from the north."

"I understand." Jenna nodded. "Do you think that Fährlund and your brother are okay?"

"Oh, I'm sure they're fine," said Nanny nonchalantly. "Fährlund is some few hours north of Fürnas."

"Right…" Jenna said uncomfortably as a strange feeling gripped her. "But what if the storm began farther up north and passed through Fährlund? Is what I meant."

"It'd give that great loaf a run for his position!" thundered Nanny defiantly. "I'd love to see how he'd handle a disaster like that!"

Jenna smiled and sighed. What more could she say? Thank goodness that they pulled into Aerlund just in time to banish any growing thoughts of disaster.

"It's just like Fährlund!" Jenna said as the carriage strolled through the cobblestone streets.

"Isn't it lovely?" asked Nanny as they rolled by the comforting homes with wooden boards attached to the walls and flower boxes hanging underneath the just-opened windows, orange light coming through from candlelit lamps.

"You said it was about a year ago that you went, right? To Fährlund?" asked Nanny, purposefully creating conversation so as to ignore the curious rubberneckers as they passed by.

"Yep." Jenna nodded. "I had to beg my parents for them to give me permission to ride with Mr. Tendúr. And even then, we were accompanied by ten soldiers."

"Oh, the caravan trader!" exclaimed Nanny, surprised. "Such a sweet old man. He has so many odd trinkets and collectibles!"

"He also helps us sell the kinberries that grow only in Fürnas! I figured it'd be a perfect excuse for me to see Fährlund."

"Look at you, clever little thing," finished Nanny as they pulled up to the mayor's large, two-story stone building at the southern end of Aerlund.

"Now what kind of reunion is this?" bumbled Nanny as she climbed out of the coach's seat. "I sent word by peregrine falcon two days ago! He knew we'd be arriving around this time!"

"The mayor?" asked Jenna as she stepped out, gently handing Isaac to Nanny.

"My cousin Inglethöp!" finished Nanny. "I swear… you think we would've gotten a little more southern hospitality! And not only that, it's not every day you're greeted by the princess of Fürnas!"

"Don't even worry about that. I'm just Jenna!" Jenna smiled as she climbed the stone steps to the double doors of the building. "Perhaps he's just busy?"

Nanny was already wheezing, and she was only on the third step (out of eight). "B-busy or n-not…" She huffed, "You d-don't… do family l-like this!"

"Hello?" Jenna called out as she pushed open one of the large front doors and entered. "Are you here, Mr. Mayor Inglethöp?" She had to cough to mask her laugh.

What an interesting place! The dark-green-carpeted floor beneath Jenna's feet felt soft and squishy as she bounced upon it. To her left and right ascended two staircases leading up to a unified, long corridor. The wall in front of her had two more double doors, and my goodness did this man like clocks. They were everywhere! About four grandfather clocks stood, placed in the four corners of the large foyer, and wall clocks littered the surface in such a way that she could barely make out the wallpaper underneath.

"Is that Jenna Coltier?" echoed the voice of what sounded to be a normal man, above. "And, Tabatha, are you—"

"I'm coming!" wheezed poor Nanny as she finally entered the building, her poor face beyond beet-red.

"Coming, coming! Be right down," sounded the voice above them again.

Jenna and Nanny looked at each other and shrugged in sync.

Oh, my merciful, thought Jenna as the mayor came down the steps.

How on Vaerün was it possible to have chicken legs, sticks for arms, a skeleton's chest, and yet have a belly that big?

"No way…" Jenna muttered as she shook her head. *Seriously… how many pigs is he hiding under that jacket of his? He has to! That's just not possible!*

Giving the young Jenna some credit, Mayor Inglethöp was quite a peculiar sight. His green-and-purple pinstriped top hat was far too small for his large head. The gray hair that shot out beneath it made Einstein's hair look tame, and I'm sorry, but the monocle just made his oddly shaped head much, much worse.

The skintight gray cloth that sucked to his legs that some may have questioned to be his pants made an elephant's trunk look ginormous. And why? Why did he have to wear that purple blazer? It was as if he was begging to accent his malnourished upper torso! Wrap that in with the protruding buttons from his white shirt underneath, bulging out from an oversized belly, mixed with (how many?) pocket watches in every pocket, and you have, undoubtedly, what many would call a great piece of work. (I kid you not. If I could paint a picture of him, I would gladly sell it at an art exhibition that'd potentially put Picasso to shame.)

"There's my Inglethöp!" bumbled Nanny as she pulled her cousin into a strong hug.

"Wow." Jenna winced as she heard countless bones in Inglethöp's body reposition from the robust embrace.

As if used to it, Mayor Inglethöp simply cleared his throat and brushed his jacket off as he smiled. "I can always look forward to a realignment when I see you, Tabatha!"

"When are you going to learn to share?" barked Nanny as she kneeled a little and spoke to his bulging abdomen. "Can't you see the rest of him is starving?"

Poor Jenna. She felt so embarrassed as she let out a shrieking laugh.

"Princess Jenna!" exclaimed Inglethöp, as if seeing his granddaughter again after a long time. "Welcome to Aerlund, dear one, welcome!" he said as he kneeled down and took her hands into his.

"Th-thank you, Mayor!" said Jenna, a little shy.

"Please call me Uncle Ingle!" he said as he stared at her with his large, piercing blue eyes.

"Uh, o-okay!" said Jenna, now even more shy.

"And where is the love?" roared Nanny behind them. "Here I was telling young Jenna all about the southern hospitality of Aerlund, and for what?" Nanny paused for "dramatic effect" as she placed her large hands and arms on her monstrous hips. "Nothing! Not a greeting of any kind!"

"I sincerely apologize." Inglethöp bowed as he got up. "But if I may, Tabatha…" he said, turning around, "I know that you and your brother didn't leave on good terms, but how can you possibly be so happy?"

"Excuse me?" she asked, leaning forward with a little bit of threat.

"Oh no…" said Inglethöp as he rested into an awkward position on his bony little legs. "Do you not know?"

"Know what?" Nanny huffed, eyes widening.

Whatever Inglethöp must have whispered into Nanny's ear, it must have been something terrible for Jenna to see her react like that.

"Jenna, dear," said Inglethöp in his tired, kind voice as he kneeled again, his gray bushy eyebrows slightly raised. "Why don't you go on ahead up to my office?"

"But… what about Isaac?" Jenna politely asked.

"Oh!" said Inglethöp as he rotated around. "How terribly rude of me! We hadn't been introduced," he said with a sorrowful look. "How about I stay here and get acquainted with him for just a moment while you go ahead and snack on some fresh apple tarts, just baked by Mrs. Sumergön?" he asked with a wink.

"Apple tart?" Jenna asked excitedly.

"Yes." He nodded with a crooked teeth smile. "Go up these stairs and down the hallway. My office is all the way at the end! You'll find it on my desk, freshly baked. Grab a fork from the cup holder and dig in!" he finished as he lovingly pushed her toward the stairs.

"Oh yay, oh yay, oh yay!" exclaimed Jenna, momentarily acting her age.

"It should still be steaming!" he shouted up to her as she disappeared down the hallway.

Jenna pushed the polished brown door open and ran in, huffing.

"Apple tart!" she shouted in her head as she approached his desk.

Sure enough, there, on a silver plate, sat a freshly baked (and still steaming!) apple tart.

It didn't take long for Jenna to find the fork handles sticking out of a beaten, metallic cup, sitting on his dark, cherrywood desk.

His office is pretty cool! she thought as she immediately caved the fork past the crispy exterior and into the gooey filling of the apple tart.

Similar to the downstairs foyer, his office did have some more embellishments—clocks... and lots of them, just like downstairs. *Oh, wow!* Jenna couldn't help but notice the sleeping bird tucked away in its cage, resting peacefully amidst the corner of the room. (He looked like a cockatiel!) But the stacks of frayed and stained papers upon his desk gave her that same boring feeling that she used to get when she'd watch Lucy do her work.

"Ooh!" said Jenna as she walked around the large room, examining the busts. "King Jyalhim the Fifth of Wölnas... ooh, he does look like a tool," mumbled Jenna as she walked past the statue.

"King and Queen Närveln of Wöntylnas," she said as she observed the two additional busts. "King and Queen Grünas of... Grünas?" Jenna questioned with a snicker. "Wow. How original," she said as she took a bite of the apple tart for the first time. "And..." She continued mumbling again as she walked to the last two statues.

The timing really didn't seem fair. Having just been hit by the reminiscent taste of cinnamon upon her tongue (of which her kingdom was known for, in addition to kinberries as we know) combined with seeing the two busts that read the names *King and Queen Coltier,* her response would only seem natural.

Clatter, clatter, thunk, sounded the plate and fork as it clanked and thudded to the carpet floor.

"Jenna!" screamed Nanny as she rushed in, holding Isaac, cheeks beet-red again. "What's wrong, dear one?" Nanny huffed, before she realized, "Oh... oh no, dear one."

"Who'za what'za put'za it'za?" asked the mayor as he fumbled in. His heart sank as he saw the young girl with her arms wrapped around the two statues of her parents, and Nanny wrapped around her, both of them crying. *Oh... that's why she's crying.*

"I'm so sorry," he said as he slowly walked over to them. "I'll get rid of these immediately."

"No! No, please don't!" yelled Jenna as she gripped the statues tighter.

"What a day for bad news and memories, isn't it, dear one?" choked Nanny through sobbed tears.

"Wh-what do you mean?" asked Jenna as she calmed down. Her mercy and compassion kicked in again as she turned and watched Nanny flop to the ground, holding and kissing Isaac, tears streaming down her rosy cheeks.

Inglethöp knelt down beside Jenna and put an arm around her. "Fährlund... was destroyed a few days ago, by a terrible storm and Kreaux siege that came from the north."

With the familiar feeling of emotional daggers piercing her, Jenna tilted her head and stared at the mayor with eyes wide as saucers, "Wh-what?"

The caged bird began to chirp and squawk in the background, adding to the strange arrhythmic sounds of the incessant *ticktock, ticktock* coming from the multitude of clocks all around them.

"Wyllmourn, the closest neighboring town that lies about two hours northwest from Fährlund, learned about the siege from one of its inhabitants."

"How?" asked Jenna as she calmed down.

"Wyllmourn and Fährlund are pretty new towns, only about ten years old, built around the same time."

Jenna nodded.

"Their inhabitants trade goods back and forth every week. This time, it was Wyllmourn's turn." Inglethöp paused as he swallowed. "When the trader from Wyllmourn was about twenty minutes away from Fährlund, he described what looked to him like a massive storm approaching from the northeast, some miles away."

"Okay?" asked Jenna, motioning for him to continue.

"He decided to rest in his caravan, waiting for the storm to pass by." Inglethöp swallowed again, then continued, "When he arrived some hours later, he found Fährlund to be under complete attack by the storm and Kreaux."

"Well, what in Vaerün?" demanded Jenna. "Did he stop and help? Or at least find help?"

"I'm sorry, Jenna, but just like ourselves and Wyllmourn, Fährlund is not a part of any of the kingdoms. What soldiers we do have are numbered."

"Right, yeah, I understand that," argued Jenna. "But shouldn't he have sought the help of Wöntylnas? Surely they—"

Inglethöp interrupted Jenna while shaking his head. "No, Jenna. The kingdoms do not help towns and villages like us. They figure that, since we're not bringing them additional prosperity and safety, why should they for us?"

"That's ridiculous!" yelled Jenna as she slammed her boot against the floor, startling everyone in the room (even the bird).

"Not really," said Nanny as she wiped away her tears. "It actually makes a lot of sense. We chose to separate ourselves from the kingdoms and thereby from their powers and resources, choosing instead to rely upon ourselves and our resources." Nanny coughed, then continued, "Why should we be allowed to seek them for anything, when they seek us for nothing?"

"It's not like that, though!" argued Jenna. "Not at all! Where is the compassion? The mercy by our Creator above? If people need help, then help them!" she yelled. "Why does it have to be about, 'Well, you did this for me, so let me do this for you'? That doesn't make any sense!"

Jenna's dress began to levitate as the red fiery aura emanated from her body.

"J-Jenna, dear…" stammered Nanny. "Please calm down."

"No!" fought Jenna. "I hate the people of Vaerün! Why is everyone so greedy? It's because of their selfish ways that the Kreaux exist in the first place!"

Inglethöp began to crawl backward on all fours as he covered his face with his arm, shielding himself from what he feared might soon be a force to be reckoned with.

Papers and book pages began to flip and slap through the air, mixed with some bird feathers as the warm, red energy of Jenna's Majesty began to radiate through the room.

Suddenly, Isaac began to cry. And with that, Jenna immediately calmed down (but for a moment…) until a flood of emotions hit her, forcing her to leave the room in tears.

After Nanny successfully calmed Isaac down, Inglethöp let out a big sigh and placed a hand on Nanny's shoulder. "So," he muttered, "those were the powers you were talking about?"

"Hah." She flatly laughed. "You haven't seen anything. Trust me."

Inglethöp extended a hand out and attempted to help his cousin up. "The poor thing… it's just too much. Waaay too much on such a young girl."

"Too much on them both!" extended Nanny as she brushed Isaac's blond hair.

"Albeit horrifying," Inglethöp continued, "I am honored to be in the presence of two Majesticians," he said as he stared into Isaac's dancing eyes.

"You always were obsessed with reading about them as a kid," piped up Nanny.

"It's just hard to believe that the thing of legends, and two of them, at that, are here in my town," he said as he shook his head. "I'm positively honored. Although, I fear I won't have them long."

"If I may be honest," whispered Tabatha, "I think you may get your wish. For I believe we will be here a lot longer than we'd both anticipated."

"Naturally, I'm delighted!" he responded with a surprised look. "If I may be bold, how *long* do you think…?"

CHAPTER 9

The Town of Aerlund

Isaac looked up into the blue sky, took a deep breath of the refreshing morning air, and exhaled through his mouth, slowly closing his eyes. The morning sunlight was positively radiant! The golden beams penetrated the pure white clouds above as they ever so slowly drifted across the sky. Almost as if meant to absorb the sun, his golden eyes easily stared into the piercing light without any pain or wincing. The breeze tugged at the white cloak around his neck.

"*Light...* Most precious and eternal." Isaac muttered aloud.

As if some gentle force had overtaken him, he slowly pushed his head back into a lull and simultaneously raised his hands, gently resting them against the growing warmth of the stone wall of their house.

"*'That man is clearly an angel from heaven,'*" were words often whispered among the simple people of Aerlund. And who could argue? With his long white jacket adorned with golden buttons and blue trim (not to forget the upturned collar!), white pants, white-and-blue boots (complete with metallic steel toes!), and flowing white cloak clasped by a striking silver brooch, Isaac cut a figure like no other.

His benevolence was accented by a strong, masculine jaw and facial structure, etched golden eyes, and nearly glowing blond hair. His entire presence radiated the courage of a lion, the warmth and compassion of a loving child, the humility of the poorest peasant, and the strength and determination that would put Colosseum warriors to shame.

"Ever wonder what it goes to?" Jenna asked as she stepped out the front door and leaned against the wall beside him.

Isaac tilted his head in confusion (as he often did), before realizing she was talking about the necklace and key he was rolling between his fingers.

"Sometimes," Isaac replied simply, resting his head against folded arms behind his head.

"But... I have a feeling I'll find out someday," he finished with a smile.

"Yeah." Jenna laughed. "Too bad we'll never leave this place."

Isaac broke his trance and looked boldly at Jenna. "What? Nonsense." His expression softened into a gentle smile. "I have a feeling it'll be much sooner than you think." He trailed off as he lulled back into his restful position against the wall.

Jenna sighed and laughed. "Always the optimist, aren't we, Isaac?" She looked past him, taking in the beauty of Aerlund.

Rows of trees in elegantly decorated planters perfectly lined the descending, snaking cobblestone streets. Each house looked like polished gems, with the morning sunlight reflecting off their neatly placed, artfully crafted stone rooftops. Windows were opening everywhere, and brilliant white curtains fluttered into the morning breeze with helpless fashion.

"Aren't you glad our home is on the northern end of Aerlund?" asked Isaac, breaking Jenna's gaze.

"Huh?" She shook her head, pulled from her thoughts.

"And how convenient for us to be on a hill," Isaac said, motioning down the southern road. "We get the perfect view!"

"It's true," she agreed, looking down the southern pathway leading into the busier streets of Aerlund.

She could never forget that day, nearly twenty years ago. Nann and Inglethöp had been in such a heated debate about where to build their house! Uncle Ingle had wanted them to live close to him; his argument was that he had never had children and wanted to help look after his newly adopted nephew, Isaac, and niece, Jenna.

"No," Nann had barked back then, "we will not be moving right next to you just so you can study and observe their powers, you coot!"

After a lengthy discussion, they decided that their home would be built on the northern end of Aerlund, in case another storm or Kreaux siege ever attacked from the north. That way, they would be prepared.

"After the forest has been burned to the ground," Isaac said suddenly, snapping Jenna out of her thoughts, "nothing could be more beautiful than to see the vibrant little saplings emerging from the ashes."

Jenna raised an eyebrow and smiled. "What, Isaac?"

"It's kind of the same as us, right?" he asked, staring into her moving red eyes. "Except in this case, we're the emerging saplings."

"And from the ash is right," Jenna mumbled.

The moment stretched longer as she came and rested against the warm stone wall, mirroring his pose.

As if royalty had been misplaced in a humble (albeit cozy) town, that was precisely how Isaac and Jenna looked amid the people of Aerlund—and even the buildings themselves.

Perhaps it was their attire? Next to Isaac's pure, enchanting wardrobe and countenance stood Jenna, just a few inches shorter than him. With her white, red, and black jacket-dress combo (complete with golden trim), adorned with the red rose insignia of Fürnas on the neatly folded lapels, white princess gloves, black belts with golden rose buckles, and dark-brown and burgundy boots, her presence was nothing short of commanding. Add to that her waist-length, glossy, flowing walnut brown-and-burgundy hair, neatly pulled behind her shoulders to reveal a fair, elegant heart-shaped face, and it was easy to see why the two of them stood out like (beautiful) sore thumbs.

"I'd say it's about that time, right?" Jenna asked as she pushed away from the wall, her long hair flowing behind her.

"Aww, come on…," Isaac responded awkwardly, "can't we take a break, please? Just one day?"

"Absolutely not!" Jenna barked back. "Commander Garon wouldn't let me take a break, and I know he wouldn't let you either!"

"But—" Isaac began.

"No buts!" Jenna snapped, pointing a finger at him. "And no barriers this time!"

Isaac took a few steps away, turning his back to her. "But I hate sparring! I hate combat in general! It all seems so unnecessary. Why does there need to be violence in Vaerün in the first place?" he demanded, turning back around.

Jenna giggled, furthering his slight agitation.

"I'm sorry, I'm sorry," she continued, stifling her laughter as he stared at her. "It's just that… you sound just like him—Garon. He said the same thing."

Isaac tilted his head. "Huh? But you said he was the commander-in-chief over Wölnas!" He shook his head in confusion. "How does someone who hates combat become the leader of an army who dictates it?"

Jenna's face suddenly turned serious. "I asked him the very same question. And I bet you know the answer."

Isaac paused, looking at the ground before raising his eyes to meet hers. "To protect, right?"

"Clichéd, I know, but," Jenna said, "look at the good that's come from our protection." She motioned downhill to Aerlund. "How many times have we rescued these people from random Kreaux attacks?"

"I know, but—" Isaac's words trailed off as a most incredible scent filled the air. It was a smell so sweet… so deliciously cunning and full of delight that even words failed to describe it. It was as if this heavenly aroma and the mischievous breeze conspired together in a secret combination to create pure ecstasy.

"Waffles. Fresh waffles," Isaac muttered in a trance-like state.

Damn you, Mrs. Sumergön! Jenna silently cursed as she took in a deep breath of her own.

"Kinberry jam," Isaac said, looking from Jenna down the southern path.

With speed and strength that no normal man possessed, Isaac rocketed off—down, down, down… and gone.

"Oh! There he is again," Jenna muttered, spotting him atop the hill passing by the Wilburns' house—and gone.

"Oh! There he is again, now passing Mrs. Aulburn, and—"

"Please say hi to her. Please say hi to her. **Please say hi to her!**" Jenna chanted as she watched Isaac pass by the waving Mrs. Aulburn from afar. "**Damn it!**" she shouted, stomping the ground in frustration.

"I'll be hearing about this later," Jenna mumbled, as she rubbed her forehead. "Mrs. Aulburn hates to be ignored, especially by Isaac and me. Ugh, the lecture will never cease!" she said as she massaged her brows, hoping to dispel the headache forming over the last minute.

The double front doors of their ornate two-story home creaked open as Jenna walked into the foyer.

"Jenna!" shouted Nann as she rushed down the stairs, gripping her apron and dress in one hand, her shawl fluttering behind. "Won't you please..." She paused to catch her breath before reaching the bottom of the chestnut wooden stairs.

"Nann!" Jenna exclaimed, her face lighting up with a smile.

With arms outstretched, Jenna ran right up to her, just as she reached the last step, and pulled the short, plump woman into a tight, loving embrace.

"Jenna!" huffed Nann. "Good morning!"

"Good morning!"

"Where is Isaac? I was going to make the both of you some breakfast!" Nann chimed.

Here we go, thought Jenna as Nann took in a deep breath and continued, "How does potato hash with garlic, onion, and bell pepper, served alongside some scrambled eggs topped with freshly grated cheddar cheese..."

Jenna could only smile, as she did every day, at what she knew as "Nann's breakfast menu."

"Buttermilk biscuits with freshly churned butter," continued Nann. "Sausage links, sizzling bacon, and some freshly whipped-up butter waffles with warmed kinberry syrup?"

"Hmm... how does that sound?" Jenna playfully rolled her eyes up toward the ceiling, pretending to contemplate. "I think that sounds amazing," she concluded with a decisive nod.

"Then I shall get started!" Nann declared as she headed toward the grand kitchen. "Oh, but," she paused and turned around, "where's Isaac?"

"Hah!" blurted Jenna. "Um..." she continued, trying to regain composure, "I'm afraid we may have already lost him to waffles and kinberry jam from downtown."

"Well, give me a hell sandwich with some devil in between!" Nann burst out in her rich southern accent. "You go get that boy right now, and tell him if he doesn't come back posthaste, it'll be floor scrubbin' for a month!"

Damn, thought Jenna, *A month?*

Suddenly, the image of Isaac on all fours, his heavenly white wardrobe stained with mop water and blond hair tied back while scrubbing all seven of their rooms plus the concert hall that was their basement, filled her mind.

"Yes, Nann," Jenna said, snapping out of the vision. "I'll go get him right away."

"Girly, have you any idea the danger he's truly in?" asked Nann as she walked up to Jenna.

Nann's round face was simply adorable! No one could resist the infectious joy that radiated from her presence. Even Mr. Turgeon—a bitter, decrepit, and miserable old man—couldn't help but crack a smile when Nann was around.

"Ma'am?" Jenna asked respectfully.

"M'dear..." Nann said, placing her warm, tiny, soft hands upon Jenna's cheeks, "it's not the waffles I'm afraid of. It's the she-devil serving them that I'm afraid of!"

Jenna burst into laughter and embraced Nann. "Do you really think that Mrs. Sumergön is trying to set her daughter up with Isaac?"

"Oh, I know she is!" Nann continued. "But what's it to me? I just don't want to see you lose the man of your dreams to some girl who's gonna end up lookin' like me!" thundered Nann. "Or already does..." she added, raising an eyebrow.

Now Jenna was roaring with laughter. "You stop that now! You're lovely and beautiful, and we adore you just the way you are!" she said, wiping away a tear.

"What makes you so sure Isaac won't fall for her?" asked Nann, suddenly serious, with both hands on her hips.

"That's because HrFA," Jenna said, "Just like the lovely Ms. Sumergön is nothing but a dopp! A full-blown, evil, conniving, dirty, fat, grease-eating HrFA." [HrFA = "Her Royal Fat A———," an acronym that Jenna and Nann came up with to describe Mrs. Sumergön's daughter.]

Nann doubled over with laughter, unable to breathe, both hands propped upon her knees as she attempted to pull in oxygen to restore color to her crimson cheeks.

Jenna bit her lower lip to stifle her laughter, then helped Nann before her upper body weight cut off the circulation to her hands.

With effort, Nann stood properly and sniffled in an attempt to control her laughter and tears. Relief came as they stepped outside and stood on the cobblestone street.

"I swear, what does that woman put in those waffles?" asked Jenna, sniffing the air.

"Probably swaps the buttermilk out for Alansgrù," replied Nann with a simple shrug.

"Hey!" Jenna exclaimed, as if a revelation hit her, "That makes so much sense! Spike the waffles, get Isaac drunk, and set him up with her daughter!"

Something between a snort and a snicker came from Nann as she nodded. "Undoubtedly. Well, go rescue our darling man before it's too late."

"Yes, ma'am! Be right back!" Jenna shouted, already some ten feet away, dashing down the path.

Clink, clink, ca-clink, sllllasssh! chimed the sounds of Isaac and Jenna dueling in the training grounds behind their house.

With intense glares, they pushed against each other, Jenna's (now suitably sized) rapier clashing with Isaac's silver arm braces.

"Do you know what I don't understand?" Jenna grunted, trying to push Isaac back. "How is it that someone who catches onto things faster than anyone I've ever met…"

Isaac smiled and raised an eyebrow at her, as if to say, "Go on?"

"…resorts to using something that was intended for defense as offense?" Jenna finished, the two of them pushing each other back and landing on their feet.

"Hmm…" Isaac hummed with a nonchalant expression as he held up an arm, deflecting her blows. "I guess it's because this is how I feel most comfortable."

"I don't understand. Not one bit," chided Jenna, launching attack after attack, forcing him to raise both arms in defense.

"Yes, you do!" he argued, shoving her back and taking advantage of the opportunity to unleash a flurry of martial-arts-like moves upon her.

"No, I really don't!" she shot back through gritted teeth.

"Yes, you really do!" Isaac insisted.

With simultaneous backflips, both adjusted their footing. Isaac gripped one of his arm braces and tightened it.

"It's just like how you hate using bows, right?" he asked, shaking his head and flinging sweat from his shimmering blond hair. "Well, apply that to me! Except instead of bows," he added with a hint of sarcasm, "apply it to all weapons!"

Voooom! A blast of light shot from Isaac's palms, only to be deflected by a burst of flame from Jenna.

"See? Got you!" said Isaac triumphantly.

"No, that's not it," Jenna said, trying to hide her smile as she momentarily glanced down.

"Then what is it?" Isaac asked, sending waves of Light Majesty her way.

"Garon and I had a similar conversation, that's all!" she said, slicing through the Majesty with her blade.

"Well then, there you go!" Isaac said, holding up a hand and easily reflecting some of the fireballs that Jenna cast at him. "Thanks, Garon!" he shouted to the sky.

"You about ready to take a break?" Jenna said, a little tired. "We've been going at it for about three hours now."

"Aw, come on?" Isaac teased; fists raised. "I thought you wanted to spar!"

"Yes, well…" Jenna burped. "It also helps to let your food settle after one of Nann's monster breakfasts."

"Oooh… yeah. Got me there. All right! Let's take a break, Jenn!" Isaac agreed, lowering his fists.

Knock, knock, knock, sounded the door of the mayor's office.

"Come on in!" shouted Inglethöp.

In came Nann, wheezing and huffing. "Sometimes…" she said between bated breaths, "I think you built those stairs… 'cause you knew they'd get to me."

"Haha! Nonsense!" Inglethöp retorted. "I love you, Tabatha! That's exactly why I had them installed—to give you some exercise."

"Oh, you devil," Nann huffed.

After a pause, both started laughing.

"So what can I do for you?" asked Nann as she took a seat at his desk.

"Well…" Inglethöp sighed, rotating the quill pen between his fingers. "Mr. Tendúr's caravan is just outside the borders of Fürnas."

"What?" exclaimed Nann, nearly jumping out of her seat. "And how is it?" she demanded.

"Well… it's hard to say," Inglethöp said thoughtfully, continuing, "He's seen quite a few of those Fürnas folk scattered throughout the diverse villages, towns, and kingdoms of Vaerün during his travels these past years."

"But what of Fürnas—"

"I know, I know," interrupted Inglethöp. "I'm getting to it!" he exclaimed in his southern accent. "Said it's not like it used to be. Said about only one-tenth of the people remain."

Nann's eyes drooped as she slumped back into her chair. "But what of the king and queen?"

"And that's where it gets even more interesting," Inglethöp said, leaning forward. "Tendúr said the castle's like a ghost town... no one there. But... Tendúr found something on a table in the foyer."

Nann swallowed.

"A letter. Addressed to 'Jenna Coltier, Princess of Fürnas,'" Inglethöp whispered, as if fearful of being overheard.

"Well, where is it then?" Nann demanded.

"Well, daggum it," Inglethöp replied with a "Guh-doy!" kind of look. "What do you mean, 'Where is it?' Why, it's with Mr. Tendúr, of course!"

"Mr. Tendúr!" Nann barked, "Why didn't he just bring it here directly?" She finished, in a whisper.

"Tabatha," Inglethöp said gently, "one, he wants to deliver it to her personally. Two, he considered it a matter of grave importance and didn't want it intercepted!"

Nann sat down and let out a big sigh. *Oops...* She hadn't thought of that.

"As you know," Inglethöp continued, "Fürnas is about three days from here by horseback."

"Right?" Nann said, raising an eyebrow.

"Mr. Tendúr is quite old and rather... slow."

"Oh, just like you!" Nann teased with a hand wave.

"With his caravan," said Inglethöp, ignoring her, "it'll easily take him about six to seven days to get here."

"What?" Nann spat. "There's no way! We can't wait that long!" she said, standing up.

"I know, I know!" shouted the mayor, motioning his hands up and down to calm her down. "That's why... I have a proposition."

"What is it?" Nann asked suspiciously.

"Now, don't you go jumping down my throat, but..." Inglethöp paused, then blurted out, "I think Jenna should go on ahead, meet him, and get it herself."

Nann shook her head. And then she continued. And then she shook it some more. "Absolutely not!" she barked. "I promised to not let her leave here until we got word from her mother that it's safe to leave!"

"I know you're worried about her safety too, dear, but..." Inglethöp trailed off. "They've been here for almost twenty years. It's high time they leave Aerlund and help others besides ourselves!"

"My ears can barely believe they're hearing you of all coots say this!" Nann stormed. "You're the one who wanted to keep them here in the first place!"

"I know, I know!" he retorted. "But how on earth are two such souls, imbued with the power of heaven itself, supposed to stay here and rot, when we know full well that their work is beyond this tiny town?"

Nann took a deep breath and massaged her forehead.

"Besides," Inglethöp continued, "it's a great opportunity. They can both leave Aerlund and experience some of the outside world. And Mr. Tendúr won't have to travel so far."

"They can meet up!" Nann suddenly thought aloud. "But just Jenna." She added, "Isaac can stay here in case, in case..."

"Don't finish that sentence," Inglethöp responded. "And yes, I agree. Besides, this occasion is just for Jenna, considering the letter is addressed to her."

"Well then! I'll go tell her right now," said Nann, turning to leave.

"Tabatha, wait," Inglethöp said, stopping her. "There's one more thing."

Nann turned around, raising her hands. "What is it, Inglethöp?"

"Perhaps the timing couldn't be better, but... Professor Vandergaus has discovered something very important."

Nann's face turned serious as she immediately came back to sit down in front of her cousin.

"What is it?" she asked nervously.

"He found something... and you're not going to like it," Inglethöp said. "It's been weighing on me ever since I received the news," he finished, pulling a sealed letter from a locked drawer and handing it to her.

"No... I thought it was just a myth!" she spat, throwing the letter onto the desk.

"Apparently not," he said, shaking his head.

"It looks like the time has finally come for Isaac and Jenna to meet up with him," Nann said slowly and sadly, as if not wanting to say the words at all.

"Like I just said," he finished, "perhaps the timing couldn't be better."

"Stairs," Nann muttered to herself as she huffed just outside Jenna's door. *"Why the stairs?"*

The etched oak door creaked under her weight as she leaned against it, listening to the beautiful soprano voice emanating from the other side.

"Such music!" Nann whispered, raising her hand to trace one of the grooves in the door.

After what felt like an hour of listening, Nann snapped herself out of the spell and knocked loudly at the door.

There was no response.

"Jenna, dear?" Nann rapped on the door a few more times.

Again, there was no response.

Nann smiled to herself, acknowledging that she'd come back later to try again. But as she began to walk away, the door swung open, releasing a surge of warm, pleasant heat and vibrant light-red colors.

"Nann!" said Jenna, a little surprised. "Good morning! Is everything all right?" she inquired with slight concern. "You look a little out of it."

"Oh, yes, yes," Nann said, clearly spellbound. "Yes!" she exclaimed, shaking her head to break free from the daze. "Sorry to bother you, m'dear."

"How insulting!" Jenna retorted, feigning offense. "You never bother me, Nann!"

With her mind still on the music, Nann reached out to place her hand on Jenna's shoulder. "Beautiful, my love… just beautiful!" she exclaimed. "You absolutely inspire me." She shook her head as she gazed up at the ceiling. "Between you and Isaac, I constantly ask myself what I could've done to deserve the honor of living with two Majesticians like yourselves!"

Nann took a deep breath and sighed as if in a dazed romance.

"Oh, Nann, you're too sweet!" Jenna smiled, straightening up. "I assure you, not a day goes by when we don't speak of our gratitude to have you as our wonderful, loving mother figure."

Jenna paused, then continued, "You mean everything to us. And we're so thankful for all that you do. Truly, from the depths of my heart, thank you."

Nann's eyes glistened, and her lips quivered.

Not wanting to see Nann cry—knowing it would make her cry—Jenna quickly asked, "Where's Isaac? What's he doing?" She raised an eyebrow and added, "I know he's quite fond of sleeping in on weekends."

"Just like you, m'dear!" Nann piped up, pointing to the floor. "Down in the concert hall, playing heavenly music on that piano of his."

Jenna laughed and nodded. "Right, right. That was my second guess!"

An awkward pause filled the air, making Jenna uneasy—a feeling that something was wrong.

Nann beamed, "It's a beautiful morning! Shall we step outside for a breath of fresh air?"

"That sounds lovely!" Jenna said, closing her bedroom door behind her. "I could use a break, anyway."

Down the hallway they walked, passing the busts of Jenna's parents (personally requested from Uncle Ingle), massive framed artwork depicting ancient Majesticians, and numerous statues. The awkward sound of their footsteps on the hardwood floor made both of them uncomfortable until Nann finally broke the silence.

"Jenna, my dear," Nann said slowly as they walked down the corridor.

"What is it, Nann?" Jenna asked.

"Do you remember Mr. Tendúr?"

"Of course! The caravan trader!" Jenna beamed. "He helped sell Fürnas's kinberries!"

"That's right!" Nann exclaimed, momentarily smiling before the smile faded. "Well… how shall I put this?"

They were now at the top of the grand staircase, in the foyer. Multicolored beams of light cast rippling colors upon the foyer as they shone through the large stained-glass eastern windows.

Jenna took Nann by the hand, and they both slowly descended the stairs.

"Oh no," Jenna mumbled. "Did the poor thing finally pass away?" she inquired. "Last I saw him, he was already up there in numbers! And now"—Jenna's face slightly reflected some horror—"if he just passed, that'd put him at, what, a hundred plus?"

Nann did something between a wheeze and a laugh. "You're so funny, Jenn! I assure you, Mr. Tendúr is still alive and well. And he's only eighty-two."

"Only eighty-two, she says," muttered Jenna. "Ow!" she yelped as Nann pinched her ear.

"None of that now!" Nann exclaimed. "Is this how you talk behind my back too?" she asked with a smile.

"No, no, ma'am," Jenna said, trying to free her ear. "Not everyone is blessed to stay thirty forever!"

Ooooh, clever girl, that Jenna! Nann immediately let go of her ear and gave something between a giggle and a snort. "Why, who, little old me?" she asked shyly. "Why, thank you, dear! Y'know I turn sixty-two on the third of Feraahn!"

"How could I forget, Nann?" Jenna asked, raising her hands in playful surrender, before her face once again expressed horror. "How is that only two months away? I can't believe we're already in Vuhlaahnin!"

"I keep tryin' to tell people that the Creator has sped up time!" Nann barked, waving her hands as if to say, "Duh!"

Jenna placed both hands on the two golden knobs of the large front doors and pulled them open. The immediate rush of the cool morning breeze compelled them both to take in a deep breath of the nourishing air.

After a short moment, they looked at each other and said in sync, "That never gets old."

"We're getting off track!" Nann snapped playfully, scrunching her face like a bulldog.

"Ow!" Jenna laughed as Nann jokingly slapped her arm. "All right, all right!" Jenna exclaimed, brushing her arm. "So, Mr. Tendúr, right?" she asked. "What about him?"

Nann took Jenna's hand and led her outside, where they sat on the front steps. She looked up into the sky and then at Jenna. "Well, I suppose I'd better just spit it out."

Jenna smiled, tilting her head curiously (something she picked up from Isaac).

"Mr. Tendúr's just been to Fürnas," Nann said quickly.

"What!" Jenna shouted, literally jumping up. "And how was it?! Is it safe? Are there still inhabitants?! What of my parents?!" she demanded.

Nann laughed and motioned for her to sit again, gently helping her down. "You sound just like me. That's exactly how I said it when I found out!"

Jenna's eyes widened as she stared at Nann in anticipation.

"Ahem!" Nann cleared her throat. "Well, I suppose there's no beating around it," she said, resting back on her hands. "Only one-tenth of the people remain. A lot of the buildings are vacant."

"Okay, but what of—" Jenna tried to ask.

"The castle's like a ghost town," Nann said, interrupting her.

Jenna's face melted as she flopped down onto the cool stone.

"But—" continued Nann, sparking interest, "there may be some good news yet!"

"Lirk wert?" Jenna mumbled through her hands pressed against her face.

"There was a letter," Nann whispered excitedly, "addressed to, 'Jenna Coltier, Princess of Fürnas.'" Nann stared at Jenna, waiting for the response she knew was coming. "He found it in the foyer, on one of the tables."

"What?" Jenna asked, sitting up, her long hair wrapping around her and Nann as the breeze blew. "A letter for me? From who? Is it from my parents?" she demanded with wide eyes.

Nann shook her head. "I don't know, dear, but—"

"What do you mean you don't know?" Jenna interrupted, exasperated.

"Jenna, dear, please hear me out!" Nann urged, calming her down. "There's more good news if you'll just listen for a sec!"

Jenna swallowed and nodded apologetically.

"Mr. Tendúr wants to give the letter to you personally," Nann said, squinting her eyes. "He's on his way to Aerlund even as we speak."

"Oh my gosh, really?" Jenna asked excitedly. "Will he be here soon then?" Her smile and enthusiasm quickly faded. "Oh… wait. Never mind. With his speed, he probably won't be here until next Vuhlaahnin."

And with that, Jenna flopped down again, hidden beneath her mass of hair.

"You're probably right about that one," Nann admitted mournfully as she lay down next to her. "That's why," she said simply, "I figured you should go ahead and meet him."

"What!" Jenna screamed, bolting upright. "Me? *Really?* You aren't serious, are you?" Her enthusiasm was contagious, helping Nann sit up as well.

"I am dead serious, dear," Nann said with certainty. "Uncle Ingle and I were talking, and well…"

Nann couldn't help but laugh as Jenna's eyes stared at her with the intensity of a just-landed alien.

"Now come on, Jenna!" Nann laughed. "I can't think when you're starin' at me like that with those big ol' movin' eyes of yours!"

Jenna blinked repeatedly, then smiled. "Sorry, sorry!" she apologized. "But please, go ahead."

"Like I was sayin'," Nann continued. "We've held you two here long enough, Uncle Ingle and I," she said, looking down. "So you go on ahead. Meet up with Mr. Tendúr! He's on the Western Ryúnion Trail." Nann placed a hand on Jenna's shoulder. "Grab a horse and go get your letter."

Jenna was overwhelmed. What could she say? She hadn't left Aerlund since she arrived, twenty years ago! "But what about Isaac?" she quickly asked.

"Isaac can stay here," Nann responded. "It'd be useful to have him here in case, in case—"

"Don't even go there," Jenna interrupted flatly. "The Kreaux haven't attacked in some time, and everything will be okay. Besides…" she added flippantly, "if I were the Kreaux, I wouldn't dare go up against him."

"Or you, for that matter!" Nann added with a sharp point of her finger.

"Thanks, Nann. But really," Jenna said, widening her eyes and shaking her head, "he's no joke. And you wanna know the most ironic part?" she asked with a slight laugh.

Nann scrunched her face and made a silly expression that said, *Try me.*

"He makes destroying them look so damn easy!" Jenna shouted, laughing. "I guess that's what happens when you're a Majestician sent from heaven," she finished, shaking her head in disbelief.

"If you ask me," Nann whispered, "you're both from heaven."

And with that, Nann threw her arms around Jenna and pulled her into a strong embrace.

"Awww, Nann," Jenna murmured as she melted into her arms.

Isaac breathed deeply, letting out a relaxing sigh as he looked up at the enormous, oak-beamed ceiling of their concert hall. The twisting and turning designs of the golden paint that danced across the ceiling rippled like the very Majesty he cast. As his gaze came down, it rested upon the large, white concert grand piano that stood before him.

The hall was huge! Many thought it a waste of space, arguing that it would make an excellent ballroom (too bad there weren't enough people in Aerlund for that!). Although the hall was frequented by Isaac and Jenna for practice and performing duets, it was Isaac's sanctuary. Here, he spent most of his time playing and creating beautiful music on his piano.

Isaac's dancing, light-filled translucent yellow eyes soaked in the morning sunlight as it streamed through the eastern arch windows to his left.

MAJESTY

Always so humble, gratitude welled within him as he gently ran his fingers across the ebony-and-ivory keys. With the lid propped open at its highest, the clean, beautiful light filled the hall, reflecting perfectly off the golden plate and illustrious silver strings of the piano, as if begging for the motion and vibration that were about to occur.

As he turned his head toward the glorious sunlight cascading through the towering, etched glass windows in the whitely painted walls, Isaac held his breath in anticipation of what was about to begin. With a radiant and gentle smile, he slowly raised both hands toward the descending light and opened his fingers, as if to catch the incoming beams.

I wish for the eternal glory and splendor of heaven's light, he spoke in his mind, clenching his fists tightly before releasing a ripple of light from his palms.

Isaac sat down at the bench, brushing his masculine, flowing coat and cloak behind him. He depressed a single key and hummed in unison, then up a perfect fifth, and then up an octave. The very air seemed to vibrate, glowing around him.

Then, without hesitation, he burst into action! His fingers danced and flew across the keyboard, each key utterly yielding to his command, technique, skill, and prowess.

Streams of light rushed forth from the piano, twisting throughout the room, crashing together and exploding into bursts of radiant, pure white energy. As his music grew in grandeur and splendor, the light streams combined until they formed a full, all-consuming brilliance emanating from the instrument and his entire being.

With his back turned to the entryway of the concert hall (and utterly engulfed in his music), he didn't see Jenna standing in the doorway.

This, Jenna thought to herself as she quietly and elegantly walked in, *is exactly what makes him so special. It's why people love and adore him so!*

Her long, streaming hair twisted through the air with her flowing jacket-and-dress combo as she slowly advanced toward Isaac. *His Majesty and being have such influence for good!* she continued to think.

I cannot help but wonder if he knows… just how special he really is. And how much he's loved.

The whizzing, twisting streams of light, as if alive, began to encircle her, wrapping around her whole body in extravagant patterns and formations. Her breathing intensified as each step became more deliberate—her entire focus on Isaac.

As if beckoned by an unseen power, Jenna touched a few fingers to her throat, opened her mouth, and held a single note before continuing with a melody that synced perfectly with Isaac's music.

What happened next was nearly indescribable. The streams of light that emanated from Isaac's Majesty, sensing the familiarity of Jenna's, began to vibrate through the air with a strange rhythm, dancing furiously around her, as if to inspect her.

Just as no one can express the passion of a first kiss or convey a favorite scent, taste, or song, no words could fully express how wondrous, beautiful, and Majestic the unfolding sight was.

The accompanying music of her mesmerizing voice was passionate—powerful, fiery, and intense—yet still elegant, mesmerizing, and utterly sincere.

The golden streams of Isaac's light mixed with the newly radiating flames of Jenna's Majesty, transforming into dashing, dazzling, whirring rivers of yellow and red streams of untold beauty.

Taking her time purposefully, Jenna eventually stood directly behind Isaac. She held the last note of her soul-enchanting voice, gently placing a hand on top of Isaac's head.

Isaac stopped playing immediately, sitting perfectly still. The dazzling display continued to flow, then slowly ceased. All was as it had been.

Always afraid of showing too much emotion, Jenna suddenly ruffled Isaac's hair, breaking the moment.

"Grrr… ha ha!" Isaac laughed as he turned to her. "Surely by now, you'd have found another way to get my attention?" He continued to laugh, shaking his head in an attempt to fix his messy hair.

"Trust me, Isaac," Jenna retorted. "That's the only way I can get your attention when you're playing the piano." She tossed her head back and forth, looking away playfully. "Or maybe I'll summon a pillar of flame upon you next time?"

Isaac stared at her nonchalantly. "Nah, that's okay. I'll take you messing up my hair."

"Now!" Jenna interjected. "I am here on very important news, I assure you," she said with a whimsical smile as she paced back and forth.

Isaac smiled, tilting his head in curiosity. "Oh?"

"Do you remember Mr. Tendúr, the caravan trader?" Jenna asked seriously, stopping to stare at Isaac.

"I do," Isaac nodded. "He's delivered kinberries here a couple of times," he added, his mouth beginning to water.

"Well…" Jenna sighed, squatting on the floor and recounting all that Nann had told her.

"I can hardly believe it!" Isaac exclaimed. "You get to leave Aerlund… for the first time in twenty years! That's great!" he shouted enthusiastically.

"It is hard to believe, isn't it…" Jenna trailed off before catching herself. "Do you want to come see me off?"

"Of course I do!" Isaac boomed, swiftly jumping off the bench and helping her off the ground. "You go ahead. I'll be right there!"

"Meet me in the foyer, okay?" Jenna asked cutely.

As she jogged toward the entryway, hair flowing behind and boots clacking on the wood floor, Isaac gently pushed in his bench, shut the fallboard, and closed the lid to his piano—his ritual when he finished playing.

Isaac walked up the stairs to find Nann embracing Jenna with tears in her eyes.

He could only smile as he felt their emotions. Jenna had a small satchel attached to one of her loose-fitting belts (probably filled with provisions for the road) and was obviously trying to hold back tears of her own.

"My word, how long is she going to be gone?" Isaac teased, hinting at some comic relief.

Nann and Jenna laughed as they pulled away from their embrace.

"It depends on how far up the Ryúnion Trail Mr. Tendúr is," Jenna responded. "So I could be gone anywhere from half a day to…"

Nann interrupted her, "I'd give two and a half days max."

Isaac tossed his head back and forth. "That works," he said, pulling Jenna and Nann into a hug. "By the way…" he muttered into Jenna's ear, "can I ask you a favor?"

"Yes, Isaac," Jenna replied, already knowing what he was going to ask. "If Mr. Tendúr has any kinberries, I promise to bring some back to you."

Nann's body rippled like a fat caterpillar in a miniature slinky as Isaac jumped up and down for joy. With their final embrace, Isaac and Nann bid Jenna farewell at the front door.

"Um, aren't you going to take a horse?" Isaac asked, raising an eyebrow as he looked around.

"Who needs a horse when you have Majesty?" Jenna responded sarcastically.

"But—" Isaac started.

"Sometimes it's best not to ask questions, Isaac," Nann interrupted.

Isaac simply shrugged. "Well then! Please be safe, princess," he said, bowing to Jenna sincerely.

"Oh, that's right," Nann suddenly said, catching the attention of both Isaac and Jenna.

"Yes, Nann?" Isaac asked politely.

"There's something I need to tell you two…" Nann trailed off. "But… perhaps it can wait until Jenna returns," she added, deciding not to share the heart-wrenching news right before the trip.

"Here we go," Jenna quipped sarcastically. "The classic, 'Let me leave you on a cliffhanger right before you leave on a trip' thing!"

Isaac started laughing. "Pretty good timing, Nann! Come on, what is it?"

Nann bit her lip, mulling over whether to share the news she received from the mayor. "Hmm… nah," she said suddenly, met by playful booing from Isaac and Jenna.

"Please, Nann? You can't just—" Jenna started.

"I can do as I please!" Nann bristled, snapping rhythmically. "And I please to tell you that it can wait until you get back!"

"Mercy of mercies!" Isaac remarked.

"Well then," Isaac said, motioning to Jenna, "hurry up and go! Then come back so she can tell us!"

"Exactly!" Jenna nodded in agreement. "All right, bye, you two! See you when I get back!" she yelled, heading down the street.

"I love you!" Isaac exclaimed, cupping his hands around his mouth.

Jenna stopped dead in her tracks, her face growing hot as the blood rushed to it. With her back to Isaac, she called out, "I... take care!" Why couldn't she say it back? Maybe it was all the tragedy that had affected her life, making her emotionally constipated. Or maybe it was because she felt something for that wonderful, masculine, and angelic man. Nah! That'd be weird... or would it?

"Trust me," Nann said, placing a hand on Isaac's shoulder, "I know she loves you too."

Isaac simply smiled, watching Jenna disappear in the distance. "Even if she doesn't, that's okay," he said with a shrug. "I just want the people I love to know, in case anything ever happens to me."

"Oh, Isaac," Nann said. "Such young love! How adorable! How it takes me back."

"Young love?" Isaac questioned with a smile and raised eyebrow. "Do you know something about Jenna that I don't, Nann?"

Nann immediately broke the daydream trance she had fallen into. "What? Of course not!" she stated, upturning her nose and looking away. "That girl doesn't open up to anyone!"

Isaac stared at her with a look that said, *Really? Seriously?*

Nann laughed, placing a hand on her face and dismissing Isaac with the other. "Oh, don't you give me that stare of yours! You know I love you, Garon!" she exclaimed.

"And I love you too, Nann!" Isaac beamed, squeezing her tightly and giving her a kiss on the cheek. "But... who's Garon?"

"Well, plums and puddin'!" Nann exclaimed in her rich southern accent. "Did I say Garon?" Her face turned beet-red as she added,

"My goodness, am I sorry, Isaac! The subject of love always puts him in my mind!"

Isaac tilted his head, raising an eyebrow.

"Also doesn't help that you look so much like him!" Nann continued. "I swear, that look you just gave me matched his perfectly on that day in my bakery, so many years back."

Having the desire to return to his piano rather than hearing about some random love love story, Isaac bowed humbly to Nann and started to walk up the stairs. "I love you, Nann!" he shouted as he turned around. "Thank you for being so wonderful!"

With his white cloak flowing behind, Isaac disappeared back into the house and down the stairs, likely to play the piano once more.

Nann held her cheek and shook her head, muttering, "They just don't make 'em like you anymore, boy."

CHAPTER 10

Farewell, Aerlund

The wind whipped and churned Jenna's hair and jacket-dress combo as she turned around one last time atop the western hill of the Ryúnion Trail to gaze at Aerlund below.

It truly was a beautiful town. The colorful rooftops gave it a vibrant, picturesque look. (*To us, it would seem like a Thomas Kinkade painting brought to life.*) And it was so peaceful.

She took a deep breath of the fresh morning air, smiled with vigor, and threw her hands into the air, shouting, "I'm free!"

Her laughter, the kind that makes your heart flutter, rang through the air, forcing a smile on anyone who could have heard it. Jenna spun around before bolting down the western Ryúnion Trail.

She couldn't stop smiling; she hadn't felt this free in over twenty years! Sure, she had known the beauty of a gentle breeze, the occasional storm, and the enchantment of Aerlund, but being out in the open—on this trail, surrounded by rolling green plains dotted with flowers and scattered trees, the cool wind alive with energy—was something else entirely. It felt like God Himself was breathing His life-giving breath down upon her and the world.

Down the path she flew, driven forward by her roaring flame Majesty.

"All right, Mr. Tendúr," Jenna said under her breath as she stared at the setting sun on the horizon, taking in the gorgeous array of oranges, yellows, and pinks that filled the sky. "It's been going on a day and a half now, so hopefully I find you soon."

Suddenly, her heart grew heavy yet hopeful as she fully took in the sunset. It reminded her so much of Fürnas's sunsets, ones she had dearly loved as a little girl.

"Hah," she laughed quietly. "It's been a while since I've seen a sunset like this."

She thought of her precious kingdom, though it was still some distance away. How was it faring? What had happened after she, Nann, and Isaac had fled all those years ago? Nann had said some people stayed—how were they doing? And her parents... had they survived the siege?

Jenna stopped abruptly, dirt and earth spraying everywhere as she slammed her feet into the ground. She sniffed the air, and the fresh, clean scent of campfire smoke filled her nostrils.

She dove to the ground and began to army-crawl on the damp earth, hustling up a small hill in front of her.

"Hehe," Jenna whispered with a sly smile. "I've finally found you, Mr. Tendúr!"

With her fiercely dancing, fiery red eyes, she stared at the old man some twenty feet away like a predator stalking its prey. *Let's see if you remember me after all these years*, she thought, smirking as she crawled to the top of the ridge, hiding behind a log for a better view of his caravan below.

Hmm... how shall I get his attention? A vision came to her of throwing a fireball into the sky and exploding it as she jumped out from behind the log. But then she imagined him having a heart attack, and her having to explain to Nann and Isaac that poor Mr. Tendúr had died of "natural causes." That thought won out over the temptation.

"All right, shoulder angel, you win this one!" she muttered.

Sighing quietly, Jenna closed her eyes. When she reopened them, she extended her hand slightly and focused on Mr. Tendúr's campfire. A piercingly beautiful, yet quiet, melody began to flow from her lips as she rhythmically waved her hand in short, deliberate motions.

Mr. Tendúr noticed instantly. He erupted into a smile, focusing intently on the now-living flame that was his campfire.

Jenna smiled, watching the old man's delight. Deciding to take it a step further, she clenched her fist. The fire reacted to her invisible grip, and as she unclenched her fist and moved her hand melodically through the air, the flame leaped from its confines, whirring around in controlled, docile beauty.

Her melody grew in intensity, and the flame responded, sizzling and crackling as it belched golden sparks of magical fire, flying around with dazzling speed.

Mr. Tendúr leaped to his feet, eyes glued to the beautiful, dancing flame of her Majesty. He refused to look away for even a second.

Jenna extended her index finger, rotating her wrist, and the flame obeyed, zipping around Mr. Tendúr. In a childlike response, he raised his hands and exclaimed, "Wooow!"

Ripples of orange, yellow, and gold flames swirled around his fingers as he reached out to touch the living fire. He smiled as he felt an incredible energy rush through him upon contact. Somehow, he knew it wouldn't harm him.

Jenna gleamed a white-teethed smile as she watched Mr. Tendúr enjoy her gift.

After a few moments, she commanded the flame back into its original housing, ceasing her song and bringing her hand to rest. Still smiling, she pushed herself up, dusted off, and walked down the path.

Wow, Jenna thought as she approached Mr. Tendúr. *He doesn't look bad for his age!* His shoulder-length gray hair swayed gently in the breeze. His face wasn't heavily wrinkled, and his familiar, kind blue eyes gleamed with warmth. His bright gray tailcoat, more colorful than even the gaudiest court jester's attire, seemed alive with his fantastic personality. And how, on Vaerün, did he keep his white pants and shirt so pristine?

To Jenna's surprise, Mr. Tendúr had tears streaming down his face when she reached him. He pulled her into a loving embrace. She hugged him back, laughing softly. He reminded her so much of her beloved Fürnas Kingdom. That, and he was like the awesome grandfather she never had.

"Your Majesty... Majesty Jenna Coltier!" he beamed as he pulled back, still holding her arms. "My, how you've grown! It is such an honor to see you again!" He paused, still smiling. "And what a surprise! I wasn't expecting to be met!"

Jenna laughed and hugged him tightly again. After a short moment, they both sat down on a makeshift seat—a log near his campfire.

"Nanny Tromsdotter has—" Jenna began, but Mr. Tendúr interrupted.

"Oh! Tabatha! Of course she would," Mr. Tendúr said, looking into the fire and shaking his head. "How is she doing? I miss that woman so much! It's been years!"

Jenna nodded, smiling. "It has been quite some time."

"And by heaven," Mr. Tendúr continued, "how long has it been since I've seen you, my beautiful Majesty?" He raised her hand and kissed it gallantly.

Jenna blushed slightly, bowing her head. "It's been many years, sir," she replied honestly.

"Goodness, how time flies!" Mr. Tendúr said, looking into her eyes. "You have no idea how happy I am to see you." He paused, then added, "But what brings you to me so soon?"

Feeling a bit ashamed that she couldn't have waited longer, Jenna swallowed and said confidently, "To be honest, sir, Nann told me you've been to Fürnas, and..."

He interrupted her again, this time with a loud, "Oh! Yes! Fürnas!"

Jenna shifted uncomfortably on the rough log and asked, "How is it?"

Mr. Tendúr leaned forward, looking intently into the fire. "It's kind of sad, really. Not many people left. Everyone's scattered to other kingdoms, towns, and villages."

"I see," Jenna muttered.

"Lots of buildings are destroyed," he continued. "But somehow, they don't look too scary. They're covered in vines, grass, and leaves."

Jenna bit her lip and nodded.

"The castle shows signs of a struggle long past," Mr. Tendúr added solemnly. Then suddenly, as if recalling something crucial, he exclaimed, "But I found a letter! Addressed to you!"

Jenna's heart leaped. She had nearly forgotten that the letter was the whole reason she had come to see him. Excitement surged through her.

"A letter?" she asked eagerly, her body tense with anticipation. "Oh, please, Mr. Tendúr, will you give it to me?"

"Give it to you?" he teased. "I cannot *give* what isn't mine, dear!" he added playfully. "Here, come with me."

In his usual gentlemanly manner, Mr. Tendúr bowed, offering her his hand to help her up.

Jenna's heart raced with excitement as she followed Mr. Tendúr to his caravan. She couldn't decide if she was more eager to get the letter or to finally see the inside of his legendary traveling home. Her heart practically leaped out of her chest as they approached.

The caravan was fascinating. The smell was pungent but strangely pleasant—salty, fruity, and flowery, with a touch of old wood. Glass bottles and dented canisters lined the stained wooden shelves, filled with all sorts of odds and ends. One thing caught her eye: an ancient candle, its wick barely holding a flame atop a massive pile of wax that had melted down to the floor—who knew how long ago?

"There really is life on other stars," Jenna mumbled to herself as she poked at a glass jar holding what appeared to be a miniature gremlin covered in boils and black spikes protruding from its back like a porcupine.

"A Gerdpolüs!" Mr. Tendúr shouted over his shoulder, somehow knowing what she was looking at. "Nasty creatures!" he exclaimed, shaking his head.

"Worse than the Kreaux?" Jenna asked, still poking at the jar.

Mr. Tendúr turned sharply, as if she had just insulted him. "Nothing is worse than the Kreaux," he said firmly, pointing a finger at her.

Jenna gulped, regretting the comparison. Desperate to change the subject, she quickly asked, "Um… where are they from? I've never seen one before."

Her tactic worked. Mr. Tendúr laughed as he walked over and gave the jar a poke himself.

"Smart girl!" he exclaimed. "They're not from Vaerün."

"Oh?" Jenna replied, genuinely curious.

"Nope!" He smiled. "They're from the northern continent of Kohlkhüran."

Jenna's eyes widened in amazement. "Are you serious?" she exclaimed. "You've been to Kohlkhüran? How?"

Mr. Tendúr placed a hand on her shoulder and led her further into the caravan. "Don't worry, Your Majesty. You'll travel much more of Albyüron than I ever have."

"But—" Jenna started to ask, but he cut her off.

"It was some time ago, at least twenty-five years," Mr. Tendúr said. "And let me tell you, sea travel is *not* my strong suit," he added, holding his stomach as if recalling an unpleasant memory.

"That's a shame," Jenna said, disappointed.

"Speaking of travel," Mr. Tendúr said with a smile as he handed her the sealed letter, "I believe this is for you. And what do you know? It will take you on a journey far greater than mine!"

Jenna's heart skipped a beat as she stared at the envelope in his hand. The red wax seal bore the Fürnas crest, gleaming in the dim candlelight. Apprehensive but excited, she took the letter and carefully broke the wax seal, pulling out the parchment inside.

She began to read:

To Her Dearest Majesty, My Jenna Coltier,

It is with the greatest humility that I send you this letter.

I hope you are in good spirits and strength, despite the circumstances that have befallen you and your beloved kingdom.

Hoping this letter may reach you, and knowing you will understand its urgency, I implore you to seek out the kingdom of Wöntylnas as soon as you find this letter.

There isn't a day that goes by that I do not miss your most precious smile and quirky, snarky sarcasm! You are destined for great things, Jenna. I have absolute faith in you, and I know your parents would have, too. I am deeply sorry for your loss.

I have suffered tragedies of my own, princess—losses no mortal should bear. Though I cannot tell you where I am, know that I am well.

Just as you, my beloved kingdom of Wölnas has fallen. You might be wondering about Lucy, dear Jenna. Sometimes, betrayal comes from those we least expect. And there will always come a time when we must pick a side. It is my sincerest hope that you will choose the correct side: mine.

You once told me, so many years ago, that you felt as though no one understood you. Well, now, more than ever, I completely relate. And that is why I need you.

My beloved Jenna… how I miss you. Were my heart not locked away, the pain would be more than I could bear.

Make haste to Wöntylnas when you find this letter, princess. Know that someday, we will meet face-to-face. And at that time, you must choose a side. It is my hope that you will choose me.

Until then, my precious goddaughter, know that I cannot wait to hold you in my arms once again.

Always,
Your Godfather,
Garon Erbrecht

P.S. *Rule those flames that shall soon burn upon your home. With the blood upon this letter, know that it was spilled for your cause.*

Jenna's heart pounded as she finished reading. *Garon?* Her godfather, Garon Erbrecht, had written this letter to her? She smiled, tears streaming down her face as she hugged the letter close to her chest. She kissed the letter gently.

But then, confusion struck her. The letter was obviously written after the destruction of Fürnas, but why did it smell like cinnamon? The scent immediately filled her with memories of her mother and her kingdom—both of which constantly smelled of cinnamon. And… the wax seal—it belonged to Fürnas! Had Garon been there that day, twenty years ago during the siege?

"Mr. Tendúr!" Jenna called, her voice trembling.

"Yes, Your Majesty?" Mr. Tendúr replied, stepping forward.

"How old do you think this letter is?" Jenna asked quickly, handing it to him.

Mr. Tendúr examined the letter closely, holding it up to the light. After a moment, he said, "It's hard to say exactly, Your Majesty. But…" He trailed off as he gently ran his fingers along the parchment. "Vulfothis."

"I'm sorry?" Jenna asked, confused.

"Vulfothis!" Mr. Tendúr exclaimed. "It's a type of parchment made from the Vulföthen beasts, unique to the Fürnas domain."

"Oh," Jenna said, nodding as she remembered the fluffy Vulföth beasts, a cross between a bear and a lion. "I thought they were nearly extinct. I only saw a few during my time in Fürnas."

"You're correct, Your Majesty," Mr. Tendúr said. "They're long gone now. This letter was likely composed around the time of the siege, some twenty years ago."

Jenna stared at the letter, her mind racing. *It sounds like he wrote it just for me!*

"Poor thing," Jenna whispered as she ran her fingers along the dried, bloodstained paper. "He must have gone through so much to send this to me."

Little did Jenna know, it was not Garon's blood on the letter, but the blood of her very parents. Garon had personally slain them, his claw-like hands dripping their blood onto the parchment as he wrote to his goddaughter.

"What's wrong, Jenna?" Mr. Tendúr asked gently, placing a hand on her shoulder.

Jenna held her head, overwhelmed by the weight of the letter. "I just… I have so many questions. This letter sounds like it was written for me just recently. And yet, it couldn't possibly be, based on what I know."

"So, what are you thinking?" Mr. Tendúr asked, motioning with his hand.

Jenna hesitated. "I know it's going to sound crazy, but… the way this letter is worded, it feels as if the person who wrote it already knew what was going to happen. Almost like… they could see the future."

Mr. Tendúr raised his eyebrows. "Well, it's a good thing no one has that kind of power, right?"

"Right," Jenna muttered, gripping the letter. But doubt crept into her thoughts. What if Garon *did* know something? Something she didn't?

She sighed deeply, pushing the troubling thoughts aside. "Well, I guess I'd better be on my way. Now that you don't need to come to Aerlund, where will you go?"

"Don't need to come to Aerlund?" Mr. Tendúr exclaimed. "Of course, I need to come to Aerlund!"

Jenna tilted her head, smiling. "Oh?"

"I've been traveling for quite some time now," he said, leaning wearily against one of the wooden shelves. "I could use a rest, and what better place than Aerlund?"

"That's an excellent idea!" Jenna said enthusiastically. "Do you know where you'll be staying?"

"Not just yet," Mr. Tendúr replied honestly. "But I'm sure Mayor Inglethöp will help me find a place. I've known him for quite some time, you know," he added with a wink.

Jenna thought for a moment, then a bright idea lit up her face. "Why don't you stay with us? Isaac, Nann, and I would love to have you!"

Mr. Tendúr's eyes widened in surprise. "Really? No, no, I couldn't possibly—"

"Refuse!" Jenna interrupted with a playful grin. "We have more room than we know what to do with."

"But—" Mr. Tendúr tried to protest, but Jenna cut him off again.

"Trust me," she said, crossing her arms. "Even if you refuse, I'll still tell Isaac and Nann. And I guarantee their reaction will be very different than mine!"

Mr. Tendúr chuckled, shaking his head in defeat as they both stepped outside the caravan. "Well, it seems I haven't much of a choice, do I?"

The night sky above them was breathtaking. Deep blues and purples blended with the last hints of orange from the setting sun. Stars twinkled like diamonds scattered across velvet, casting a soft glow over the land.

Mr. Tendúr leaned against the side of his caravan and sighed contentedly. After a moment, he noticed Jenna's serious expression as she gazed at the sky.

"Your Majesty, is something the matter?" he asked, concerned.

Jenna squinted, biting her lower lip as she clutched the letter in her hand. "I'm not sure… I have so many questions, and there's just so much that doesn't add up."

Mr. Tendúr placed a reassuring hand on her shoulder. "Well, sometimes it's best to hold on to what we *do* know before we assume too much about what we don't."

Jenna nodded, grateful for his advice. "You're right. Thank you, Mr. Tendúr."

"Absolutely!" he replied with a grin. "And that reminds me—would you like to ride with me to Aerlund?"

You can't, a familiar-sounding female voice whispered in her mind.

"I'm sorry?" Jenna said, startled, looking around.

Mr. Tendúr raised an eyebrow. "Oh! I really should speak up. I said, would you like to ride with me back to Aerlund?"

The voice spoke again, louder this time: *Please, don't! It'll be too late!*

Jenna looked around, trying to locate the source of the voice, but saw no one other than herself and Mr. Tendúr.

"It'll take me about five or six days to get there with old Belana," Mr. Tendúr continued, pointing to his old horse grazing nearby.

Jenna's heart raced as she held her chest, ignoring him. *What do you mean, it'll be too late?* she asked internally, but the voice didn't respond.

"I'm so sorry, Mr. Tendúr," Jenna said abruptly, her tone more serious. "But I have a strange feeling I need to get back to Aerlund immediately."

Mr. Tendúr smiled warmly. "No apologies necessary, dear one! Is there anything I can get you for the road?"

"Oh!" Jenna shouted so loudly that both Mr. Tendúr and his horse jumped. "Do you have any kinberries? Isaac is a huge fan."

"Isaac?" Mr. Tendúr said with wide eyes. "The Light Majestician?"

"The very same."

"Well, in that case, it would be my *honor*!" Mr. Tendúr said, rushing into his caravan. "Wait right here!"

Jenna looked up at the mesmerizing sky, her thoughts swirling. Who was the voice she'd heard? Why had it warned her?

A few minutes later, Mr. Tendúr returned with a small burlap sack tied with a red ribbon. "It's not much," he said, handing it to Jenna. "But I'm delighted to give it to such a remarkable man."

"Thank you so much!" Jenna beamed. She reached for her coin pouch but was swiftly interrupted.

"Absolutely not!" Mr. Tendúr cried, waving his hands and stepping back.

"Come on, Mr. Tendúr," Jenna urged, trying to hand him the coins.

After a brief but warmhearted debate, Mr. Tendúr had an idea. "Tell you what," he said, "I'll take the coins, but then I'll find a different place to stay in Aerlund. Deal?"

"That's just unfair!" Jenna laughed. "Fine!" she agreed reluctantly, taking the small bag of kinberries.

"You're such a… such a…" Jenna teased, searching for the right words. "Such a Gerdpolüs!"

Mr. Tendúr burst into laughter. "Now, now," he replied, patting his back, "I may not have spikes, but trust me, I've got boils right—"

"All right, thank you, Mr. Tendúr!" Jenna interrupted, laughing as she hugged him tightly, then turned and blasted down the eastern trail.

"Was it something I said?" Mr. Tendúr called after her, cupping his hands around his mouth.

"Can't wait to see you in Aerlund!" Jenna shouted back. "Your room will be all set up!"

"Where's your house?" he called.

"The first house through the northern gate! You can't miss it!" Jenna replied, her voice fading as she disappeared into the distance.

Being alone isn't always easy, especially since it gives us the time to think about things we'd rather not. This was exactly how Jenna felt as she returned home to Aerlund.

Thankfully, the thoughts racing through her mind propelled her speed—she was only about an hour away from the town.

"Not bad timing," she muttered as she glanced up into the night sky. *But how, why, and what is the story behind this letter?* she thought, pressing forward. *And Lucy betrayed him? How is that even possible?* The thoughts swirled relentlessly. *Lucy was one of the most heavenly people I've ever known. Could she really have betrayed him?*

Suddenly, a memory began to flood Jenna's mind…

About Five Years Ago

It was a cool, brisk evening in Aerlund. Jenna had just finished arguing with Uncle Ingle, a group of townspeople, and another self-righteous citizen of Aerlund. The argument was about whether the townspeople should engage in combat with the Kreaux or leave the fighting to Jenna and Isaac, since their powers were far more effective.

The debate ended badly. Neither Isaac nor Jenna were treated well. Isaac had finished his statement first and left the building, while Jenna, more passionate, stayed to deliver a longer address—only to receive more rejection and ridicule. Both had been in favor of the townspeople defending themselves.

Jenna stormed out of City Hall, stomping down the stairs, cursing under her breath. If it weren't for Isaac's shining countenance, she would have missed him entirely. He was leaning gently against the guardrail of the staircase, looking heavenward.

Isaac smiled his gentle smile and then asked, "It... didn't go too well, did it?"

"'Go well'? Ha!" Jenna roared. "What a joke! These people are idiots!"

She swiftly turned and looked up the stairs, shaking her fist. "That's right—idiots! I said it! And I damn well hope you can all hear me!"

Isaac laughed heartily, embracing his friend in an attempt to console her.

"It's all right, Jenn," he said. "We'll manage. At least if people aren't involved, no one can get injured."

"Besides us!" she retorted, pacing up and down the steps. "Oh sure," she began, mimicking a cutesy voice, "'Leave the kids with magical powers to save our fat, ugly hides from the Kreaux!'"

She quickly turned around, adopting a deeper voice, "What a capital idea! With them out there fighting, it'll give us more time on the john!"

Isaac shook his head, laughing despite himself. He grabbed Jenna, trying not to chuckle too much. "Nice rhyming, Jenn!" he exclaimed. "But I really almost prefer it this way. I really do."

"That's not the point!" she shouted. "Why did it have to turn into a debate? Why couldn't they just tell us nicely that they'd prefer to leave the combat to us?"

Isaac narrowed his eyes slightly, still smiling gently. "But nooo, no!" Jenna continued, pacing again. "I had to piss them off by arguing! Ugh!" She stomped her foot, and a wave of flames fanned out from beneath her boot.

"Jenna, I know these people love you," Isaac said softly. "I really do. They're grateful for your strength in defending their lives and homes."

"Doubt it," she quickly replied. "Not everyone can be heaven-sent like you, Isaac." She sat down on the steps and shook her head. "I'm just the fire witch from a Kreaux-ransacked kingdom."

Isaac sat beside her.

"Personality differences aside," he said, "I must tell you something important."

Jenna rested her chin on her knees, turning to Isaac. "What is it?"

Isaac gazed at her earnestly. "Always, always assume that people's intentions are good. Assume that their hearts are in the right place and that they're doing the best they can with what little understanding they have."

Jenna blinked, absorbing his words.

"In doing so, you'll be able to trust people more," Isaac continued. "You'll have compassion on your side. And you'll give light back to the world. To do the opposite robs humanity of the light and integrity it deserves."

The world around her slowly returned, as Jenna hugged the small satchel of kinberries, whispering to herself, "Thank you, Isaac. I've lost count of how many times you've saved me from myself."

Her gratitude was interrupted by an unpleasant sound. She froze, her eyes narrowing.

"Who's there?" she demanded, her voice firm as she slammed her feet into the ground. Dirt and earth sprayed in all directions.

Focusing her hearing, she recognized the sinister, whispering sound that sent chills down her spine. The same sound she heard whenever the Kreaux were near.

Shiiiiiink! The unmistakable sound of her rapier unsheathing filled the air.

"Kreaux," Jenna growled. She scanned her surroundings, ready for the inevitable fight. "Let's get this over with."

She raised her palm and launched a large fireball into the air, its blinding light illuminating the plains like an early sunrise.

With her hand still held high, she thrust it down, raising her rapier in her other hand just in time to absorb the fireball. Her sword now glowed with the infused flame, a fire-imbued blade of lethal energy.

"Now I'm ready," Jenna muttered, her eyes fixed on the shadows ahead.

She listened again. Silence. The dark whispers had stopped.

"Really?" Jenna called out mockingly. "Looks like some Kreaux actually have brains!"

Though outwardly tough, Jenna felt a twinge of nervousness. She was used to fighting alongside Isaac, and without him, a sense of unease crept in.

"Isaac," she whispered aloud, his name a beacon of strength. "It's so late. I wonder what you're doing now?"

She tossed the flaming blade back and forth, her nerves settling as she focused on the path ahead. "Guess I'll find out soon enough," she said before breaking into a run.

Too bad she didn't ask the same question the night before.

Their Home, the Previous Night, at the Same Time...

"Isaac!" shouted Nann as she burst through Isaac's door.

"I'm coming! I'm coming!" Isaac called back, leaping out of bed.

With both hands beneath his bottom, he momentarily levitated with the aid of his wind-Light Majesty before landing squarely in his boots, which had been neatly placed on the floor.

"Where are they?" he shouted, still groggy. "The Kreaux! I'll take care of them for you!"

Nann couldn't help but giggle as she watched the shirtless, pantless Isaac trudge past her into the hallway, wearing only his underpants and boots.

"Isaac, dear, I'm sorry to do this," Nann began as she pinched him, immediately waking him up.

"Ow, Nann!" Isaac cried, rubbing his arm.

"Besides," Nann continued, "I don't think our beloved Light Majestician would want to fight the Kreaux in just his underpants and boots, now would he?" she teased, hands on her hips, smiling.

Isaac, still embarrassed, rushed back into his room, quickly dressing. "What's going on, Nann? Everything okay?" he called out.

Nann smiled as she admired the artwork on the hallway walls and replied, "Why, yes! Er, well, no?" she questioned. "It's Mrs. Bürgohen again, dear."

"Oh no," said Isaac, his voice rising in concern. "Is she suffering from another spell?"

"I'm afraid she is!" Nann yelled back. "Her sister, Ertha Fügenhod, is down in the foyer right now, waiting for you!"

"I'm coming right now," Isaac said as he walked out of his room, fastening the clasp of his cloak around his neck.

Only the sound of Nann's huffed breathing could be heard as they quickly walked down the halls and descended the grand staircase into the foyer.

"I'm so sorry about this," said Mrs. Fügenhod apologetically to Isaac as he reached the bottom of the stairs.

Ms. Ertha Fügenhod looked nothing like her sister. She was quite slim, always dressed nicely (her wristwatch, gemmed necklace, and dresses were always quaint!), and her grayish-white hair was pulled back with a lovely crested ponytail holder. Although slightly awkward and easily startled, she was sweet and generous—a lady who looked great for being in her sixties!

"Not at all, Mrs. Fügenhod!" Isaac smiled, trying to open his eyes wider to hide his sleepiness. "I'll be right back, Nann!" he exclaimed, opening the door for Mrs. Fügenhod.

"I'll wait up for you!" Nann called out.

"No, no, please don't!" Isaac said, closing the door behind him. "Go to bed! If you don't, I'll eat Mrs. Sumergön's waffles for breakfast!"

And wouldn't you know, just like that, Nann began to take off her apron and hat to retire for the night.

"This is so embarrassing," said poor Mrs. Fügenhod as she and Isaac quickly walked down the cold stone streets of Aerlund.

It was almost three in the morning, so the town was mostly deserted. But the fresh scent of damp flowers wafted from the flower boxes, and the orange glow of light coming from some windows always brought a cozy, comforting feeling.

"Not at all!" Isaac replied, his white wardrobe and shimmering blond hair reflecting the moonlight above. "It's not your fault, and I'm happy to help, so please," he continued, "don't even give it another thought."

"Oh, Isaac," uttered Mrs. Fügenhod in gratitude, "whatever would we do without you?"

Isaac smiled humbly and looked forward.

"You truly are a gift from heaven," she finished.

"Thank you very much, Mrs. Fügenhod," he said, taking a deep breath before exhaling slowly. "If I may be so bold, how long has your sister been like this?"

Mrs. Fügenhod looked ahead as she pondered his question. "Well," she said, "ever since the day she arrived here, really. Probably about twenty years ago." She glanced up at the sky before continuing, "She's from Wölnas."

"You said she's from Wölnas, right?" asked Isaac. "I can't believe the same storm and Kreaux siege that terrorized Fürnas hit Wölnas too!"

"Some people believe," said Mrs. Fügenhod, "that the storm actually started in Wölnas!"

"Really?" inquired Isaac curiously. "So it started in Wölnas and just kept heading south, all the way to Fürnas?"

"Now don't quote me on that!" Mrs. Fügenhod quickly added. "That's just conjecture from the grapevine."

Isaac nodded, still listening intently.

"But I do know," Mrs. Fügenhod added, "whatever happened in Wölnas was bad enough to scramble her brains."

"I can only imagine," Isaac said as they came to a stop in front of Mrs. Fügenhod's house, where the anguished wails of Mrs. Bürgohen could be heard through the front door.

"Well, what do you expect?" said Mrs. Fügenhod, her eyes wide as she looked at Isaac. "You can't just watch as your children and husband are slaughtered before your very eyes and expect to walk away with all your marbles!"

Isaac shook his head, unable to find words.

"I'm just glad she made it," Mrs. Fügenhod continued, hand on the doorknob. "Poor thing had to witness all that and then ride a horse for about seven days to get here, after being mortally wounded! She should've died!"

"Why here?" Isaac asked gently, tilting his head to change the subject.

"I'm the only family she has. We lost the rest in a Kreaux siege as kids," Mrs. Fügenhod said as she opened the door.

Isaac slowly followed her into the living room. It was filled with the kind of odds and ends one might expect in an older person's home. The furniture was delightfully quaint, although the grandfather clock looked a bit too large for the small space. The knitted doilies under every vase, fruit bowl, and candy dish added a pleasant touch.

"No!" came the desperate shouts of Mrs. Bürgohen from the other room. "No! No! You stay back, you monster!"

Isaac swallowed and then smiled slightly as he walked into the larger parlor. (Why wasn't the grandfather clock in here?)

There, in an old rocking chair covered from the waist down with a knitted blanket, sat Mrs. Bürgohen. Her eyes were sunken and darted around frantically. She had lost so much weight that she was thinner than her sister, and her hair looked like twigs and branches sticking out from her head.

Isaac slowly approached and knelt in front of her, taking her hands in his.

"Please!" she cried, looking at Isaac in terror and desperation, her freezing hands trembling in his. "Please don't let him kill them! He's going to kill Gerbin! And Berg, and Hünd!"

Isaac swallowed hard, tears forming in his eyes. The way she looked and screamed, it felt like she was reliving it all over again.

Suddenly, her eyes looked straight past him.

"Nooo! Get away! Get away from them! My babies! My precious babies!" screamed Mrs. Bürgohen at the top of her lungs. "No! No ho ho no!" Her cries were so heart-wrenching, they almost sounded like she was laughing.

Tears rolled down Isaac's face. He simply couldn't bear one more moment.

Voom...voom...vooom! The momentary ripples of rainbow light pulsed through the air as they emanated from his hands.

Mrs. Bürgohen immediately stopped crying and stared into the glowing light coming from Isaac's palms.

"Olga Bürgohen," said Isaac in a profound voice as he placed his right hand over her heart and his left hand on her face, "we are strangers in a distant land... sent to do the will of our Father." He paused as his voice cracked with emotion. "And although we suffer in ways that are incomprehensible, we must not give up. We must not let go. We must fight! Hold steadfast and strong!"

The rippling light from his hands began to pulse faster and faster!

"We are his light upon Vaerün: Creators, Children of a god."

Mrs. Bürgohen's breathing became a hushed whisper as Isaac's Light Majesty slowly faded from his palms. Gently, he lifted one of her hands to his lips, kissed it softly, and then neatly placed it atop the other.

Believing she was asleep, Isaac slowly stood. Behind him, Mrs. Fügenhod stood in silent tears, witnessing the profound scene.

"Isaac?" whispered Mrs. Bürgohen just as Isaac turned to leave.

Shocked that she knew his name, he looked back at Mrs. Fügenhod, his expression questioning, "She knows my name?"

Mrs. Fügenhod shook her head repeatedly, quietly whispering, "She must have heard it. I never told her."

"Yes, Mrs. Bürgohen?" Isaac asked, sweetly kneeling in front of her once more.

"Isaac... Isaac. Isaac..." she repeated, gently caressing his face.

"Yes. That's me." Isaac nodded slowly.

"Isaac... Lucy... Isaac..." she kept repeating. To anyone else, she seemed like a poor, mentally ill woman who knew only two names: Isaac and Lucy.

"Ah!" she suddenly exclaimed, making both Isaac and Mrs. Fügenhod jump. "Lucy!" she blurted out, pointing toward the upright piano in the room.

Isaac turned to Mrs. Fügenhod, confused.

"I… think she wants you to play the piano?" Mrs. Fügenhod said as she opened the fallboard.

"Oh. Oh!" Isaac caught on quickly. "You want me to play the piano for you?" he asked again, pointing to the instrument.

Mrs. Bürgohen nodded eagerly, like an excited child, her gaze darting between Isaac and the piano. "Isaac! Isaac!" she cried, followed by, "Lucy, Lucy, Lucy!"

"Lucy? Is that what you named the piano?" Isaac asked as he pulled out the bench and sat down, giving an inquisitive look to Mrs. Fügenhod.

"Beats me," mouthed Mrs. Fügenhod.

Deciding to play along, Isaac began a soothing melody on the piano, his fingers dancing across the keys.

"Isaac… Lucy… Isaac, Lucy…" Mrs. Bürgohen murmured as she gradually drifted to sleep.

Isaac continued playing for the devastated and mentally ill Olga Bürgohen of Wölnas, the only comfort he could offer.

"For you!" mouthed Mrs. Fügenhod as she placed a pie on the top of the piano for Isaac. "When you're done!" she added silently.

"Is that the sun?" Isaac asked as he saw the dark sky change to shades of purple, blue, and orange.

Unbeknownst to him, always thinking of others before himself, he had unintentionally stayed awake the entire night, playing for the comfort of Mrs. Bürgohen.

I think… I need some sleep, he thought as he gently ended the long, long, looong composition. He closed the fallboard with still hands and rose from the bench.

His heart momentarily raced as he heard Mrs. Bürgohen utter in her sleep, "Isaac… Lucy…"

After realizing she was still asleep, he silently (and swiftly) grabbed his pie and left for home.

A piece of parchment paper, scribbled with the words, "Thank you, Isaac. We owe you now and forevermore," was tacked onto the front door. He gently pulled it off the nail and read it.

Service, he thought to himself. *Never convenient.* He then smiled. *But always worth it.*

And with that, the poor young man went home to get some much-needed rest, unaware of what would unfold the following night.

As Jenna approached the final hill on the ryúnion trail overlooking Aerlund, the pungent scent of smoke filled her nostrils. Her eyes shot open as she faintly heard the sound of the battle bell.

Gong, gong, gong! Its sound pierced the chill evening air, as if the very atmosphere itself were screaming in anguish.

With all her strength, she sprinted to the top of the hill and looked down upon Aerlund.

Jenna's breathing stopped. Her heart pounded so fiercely that her eyes began to quiver from the strain, the shock, and the horror.

Aerlund was on fire! Though still some distance away, the distinct sound of terrified screams reached her ears.

What? How? Who? she thought in a whirlwind of confusion and panic, struggling to make sense of the madness below.

Fueled by adrenaline and the roaring fire of her Majesty, Jenna descended the hill like a blazing missile.

Why did she have to enter through the western archway? The scene was unspeakable. There were already so many dead, and the Kreaux frantically dragged bodies to whom knew where, while others screeched and tore through the streets, hunting for more victims.

As familiar as she was with the sight of flames and the colors of fire, nothing was more gut-wrenching than to see the stark red blood of her beloved people filling the cracks of the cobblestone streets.

Why! she screamed internally, trying to process the chaos.

Those who weren't dead screamed in terror as they tried to flee from the Kreaux's flesh-rending claws and sharp fangs. A few brave souls attempted to fight back with pitchforks and makeshift weapons, but to little avail. The flames Jenna wielded in combat, usually a source of triumph, were now consuming homes, shops, and even people running in flaming agony.

I can't watch this another minute, she thought, gritting her teeth.

Jenna planted her feet firmly and thrust her sword skyward. With her arm fully extended, she closed her eyes and began to hum softly.

Her hair and dress rippled and danced, as the air vibrated with her Majesty's power, radiating a fiery spectrum of colors. Her eyes slowly opened, glowing with the same flames that swirled within her soul.

Then, her raised arm clapped down into her other hand, gripping her sword. As they collided, a powerful flaming aura exploded from Jenna, rushing forth like a tidal wave across all of Aerlund.

The savage flames that consumed the town died out completely, extinguished by the overwhelming force of her power.

"Takes care of that," Jenna began, but—

Fffssshhrrawrrrr! The flames roared back to life as if conjured by a force far darker than her own.

Startled and shocked, Jenna gripped her sword even tighter and unleashed another wave of Majesty. But again, to no avail—the flames briefly subsided only to explode back with even greater ferocity.

Rather than question the mysterious force, she shook her head and made up her mind. "It's no use. I have to find Isaac," she said boldly, running down the street. "Something is terribly wrong. These are flames of darkness."

She fought her way down the treacherous path to her home. With Kreaux attacking from every side, she did her best to save the remaining citizens from their black, venomous claws, fangs, and maws.

Ear-piercing, blood-curdling screeches filled the air. Though her face showed only fierce determination, Jenna's insides twisted with fear. Silently and swiftly, she unleashed her etched, rose-ornamented rapier upon the Kreaux, felling them as she ran past like a hot knife through butter—only this was a razor-sharp blade through Kreaux flesh.

Really? Jenna thought, pausing for a moment, eyeing the Kreaux blocking the street ahead.

Like mechanical beasts, their wretched heads spun, cracked, and sickeningly turned to face her, staring with their soul-angering gazes.

A moment of silence.

Then, in an instant, they tripped and trampled upon each other in their desperate attempt to destroy their most hated prey: a Majestician.

Almost unfazed, Jenna cut through the Kreaux like wind through leaves. None could touch her, let alone harm her.

And then it happened—an arrow whistled through the air.

Jenna barely managed to dodge, but not without consequence. That warm, wet feeling was unmistakable. As if time itself had slowed, she looked down at her arm, watching blood ooze down her sleeve, dripping to the ground.

Completely stoic, Jenna turned to face the Kreaux archer who fired the shot, their eyes meeting.

Damn, I hate the Kreaux. Those streams of black tears continuously running down its face, that dead, pale skin reflecting the fire's glow, that greasy black hair twisting in the wind... and those long, sharp black fingernails.

And then, oh, the final insult—the smile. That sick, twisted smile of fangs, with hideous black saliva lining the gums and teeth.

Jenna's fiery hair and eyes burned brighter as she took in the scene. The welling heat from the burning buildings was unbearable around them, yet no one turned away. Suddenly, an explosion of glass erupted beside her, threatening to shred her to pieces.

In what might seem a fatal moment for any other, time seemed to stop as Jenna raised her hand, the indents on her palm glowing with a furious, fiery light. The shards came to a complete standstill, as though commanded by an unseen force.

Jenna's smile turned almost maniacal as she focused on the Kreaux archer, her fingers trembling with energy. Even the nearby Kreaux dared not move.

"I don't suppose," Jenna spoke quietly, her voice clear and cutting, "you know what happens when you heat up glass, do you, little archer?"

The Kreaux archer's smile vanished.

"That's right," she said as the shards began to dance and transform in the air. "Basically… you have liquid lava."

The archer had no time to react. Thousands of drops of liquid lava, orange and glowing like molten gold, rushed through the air, cutting through the Kreaux like liquid flame.

"How is it…" Jenna shouted as her glowing hands weaved through the air, "that you think you can come to my town—" the Kreaux's screams rose to an almost unbearable pitch— "and get away with it?"

None of them stood a chance.

The ground was covered in Kreaux bodies, but Jenna wasn't done—oh no. For although the archer was bleeding the black ooze of Dark Majesty, he still stood.

She raised both hands, and everything seemed to pause once more. In an ornate pattern, her hands danced through the air. Liquid lava shards transformed into an orange cage around the Kreaux archer, moving so fast it was almost impossible to see. He looked around in horror and began to scream with rage.

"Aww, what's wrong? Angry?" Jenna teased. "Well, I can assure you that it's nothing compared to mine!" With a sharp motion, she slammed her glowing palm into her other hand, gripping her rapier.

Without hesitation, the liquid lava encased the archer, tearing him apart in an instant, fully dismembering him.

"And that's that," Jenna said as she waved her hand. The lava, now controlled, shot forward in streams, incinerating any remaining Kreaux in its path.

Though briefly triumphant, a feeling of dread and sorrow washed over her as she noticed the citizens' screams had faded. All that remained was the crackling of the fires consuming the town and, occasionally, the shattering of more glass.

Attempting to focus, Jenna ran faster toward her home on the northern end of Aerlund.

Was it the time it took to reach her house that irritated her—the struggle of fighting Kreaux, dodging burning debris—or the sight of the dead, murdered people she loved so dearly? Perhaps it was the suffocating smell of burning homes or the horror of seeing Kreaux clawing at the stone walls of her mansion, trying to break in. Or perhaps it was all of the above.

Regardless, no one could blame the Kreaux for screeching and attempting to flee as Jenna levitated, her Majesty ablaze, streams of fire consuming the unfortunate creatures who didn't escape in time.

"What the heck, you two!?" she hissed under her breath, directing her frustration toward Isaac and Nann as she tried to open the locked front doors of her home.

"Nann? Isaac?" Jenna cried out, shaking the rattling doors.

No response.

"To hell with this," she muttered, blasting the door open with a surge of her Fire Majesty.

How heart-wrenching it was—like the siege of Fürnas all over again. Jenna's heart pounded as she entered the foyer and looked up. The upstairs was already a roaring inferno, flames consuming everything in their path. The air was thick, choking her lungs with smoke and heat. Not even Jenna could make it through those flames unscathed. All she could do was pray that neither Nann nor Isaac were up there—because if they were, there was no way they'd survive.

"Nann! Isaac!" Jenna shouted, coughing as she held her sleeve to her mouth.

With smoke flooding into the foyer and no path forward, Jenna descended the long, winding staircase to the concert hall. Halfway down, the smoke had not yet reached, and she could finally breathe clean air.

What? No... Jenna thought as the faint sound of piano music reached her ears.

Clip, clop. Clip, clop. Her boots echoed on the hardwood stairs as she ran down them.

Bursting through the concert hall doors, Jenna stopped dead in her tracks. Shocked, angry, and relieved all at once, she saw Isaac sitting at the piano, playing with his eyes closed, completely absorbed in the music. More surprising still, a shimmering, glowing, light-emitting barrier encased him.

"A barrier?" Jenna demanded as she ran toward him.

"What the heck—" But as she drew near, the barrier's power knocked her back, slamming her to the ground.

"**Isaac!**" Jenna screamed, tears welling in her eyes.

Isaac continued to sway within the safety and comfort of his barrier, oblivious to the chaos around them.

Reeeeee! shrieked the sounds of Kreaux all around.

Jenna's panic escalated as she desperately tried to figure out what to do. With little choice left, she stepped back, raised her hand, and a roaring fireball shot forth from her palm, streaking toward Isaac's barrier.

Aaaaahhh! she screamed, ducking as the fireball ricocheted off the barrier and exploded against the high-vaulted ceiling, setting the wooden beams aflame.

"What in Vaerün?" Isaac exclaimed, lowering the barrier, suddenly aware of the danger around him.

"Isaac!" Jenna shouted, rushing up to him and hugging him, then promptly slapped him.

"Ow! What the—" he started, rubbing his face. "What was that for—"

"What are you doing!" Jenna yelled. "Do you hate Aerlund that much that you'd rather sit here playing your freakin' piano under the protection of your barrier while the town and people burn?!"

"What are you talking about, Jenna?" Isaac demanded, finally standing, his calm demeanor wavering for the first time.

Just then, his eyes flew open as he turned to see Kreaux flooding into the concert hall.

Now, when Isaac faced Kreaux, his expression was always one of two things: pity, as if sorrowful for their existence, or an angelic smile filled with the gentleness and mercy of a loving being. And either expression was accented by the slight tilt of his sad, heavenly eyes.

As the Kreaux charged, Isaac raised his right hand, the indentations on his palm glowing with twisting yellow and white light.

Waves of Majesty pulsed through the air, bringing the Kreaux to their knees.

"Care to join me?" he asked politely, motioning to Jenna.

"With pleasure," Jenna replied, dashing toward the Kreaux, her rapier flashing as she cut them down with unyielding speed.

Once the Kreaux were dispatched, she turned to Isaac, watching him move with elegant precision. Every motion of his fingers sent streams of living light rippling through the air like an ethereal piano composition, their path impossible to predict as they zipped and whirred through the space.

Amazing, Jenna thought, watching him. *It's as if the whole world is his keyboard, and he's playing a song of light.*

Eaaarrgghh! screamed the Kreaux as the streams of light pierced through the glass windows, decimating those outside.

"Isaac," called out Jenna, her voice rising over the roar of the flames now consuming the ceiling above, "we have to get out of here!"

Isaac immediately lowered his hands, the light dissipating as he ceased his Majesty.

How on Vaerün does he manage to stay so calm? Jenna wondered as she stared at Isaac, standing serene in the midst of chaos.

"Right!" Isaac agreed. "Here. Come take my hand, and I'll lead us out!"

But suddenly, the splintering sound of wood filled the room. They both looked up to see one of the burning beams above begin to fall.

"Jenna!" Isaac screamed—perhaps for the first time in his life. "*Look out!*"

Down came the swinging, massive wooden beam.

"Aaahhh!" Jenna cried, raising her arms and closing her eyes.

Was she dead? Was anything broken? The force that knocked her down was intense, that much was clear. But nothing felt broken. In fear, she moved her arms, hands, legs, and feet. They all worked—but how?

Jenna opened her eyes and gasped, bringing a hand to her mouth. There, right in front of her, was Isaac—trapped under the massive wooden beam.

Unbeknownst to her, Isaac had used his Wind-Light Majesty to propel himself forward, shoving her back and taking the crushing blow himself.

"Isaac!" she screamed, her voice breaking as she tried to lift the massive beam.

The thing was heavy—much heavier than expected—but not impossible for a Majestician.

Jenna yelled, screamed, and roared as her Majesty filled her with strength, lifting the beam off Isaac and hurling it some distance away.

She immediately knelt down to inspect him. Thank heaven above, he was still breathing. His head was covered in blood, but nothing appeared to be broken. Still, seeing Isaac's face covered in blood was almost too much to bear.

With shaking hands, Jenna gently lifted a piece of her dress and wiped the blood from his face. A strange thought crept in—was she unworthy to even do that? Was it because he saved her, or because of something else entirely?

Boom. Boom. Boom. The ground beneath them trembled and shook.

"Hell…" Jenna cursed under her breath, "really? *Praetors?*"

Flaming debris crashed down around them. Aware that she was running out of time, Jenna's eyes glowed with the red hues of her internal Majesty as she lifted Isaac and slung him over her shoulder.

Though he was larger and by no means light, she felt an unexpected strength surge within her as she carried her beloved friend, running as fast as she could toward the back wall of the concert hall.

What to do, what to do! Panic rose in Jenna's chest as her eyes darted around for an escape route. Exiting through the main entrance was now impossible, with the flames from above spreading downward, and burning debris cascading around them.

"Line of the night, I guess," Jenna muttered, taking a few steps back before blasting a hole through the wall, shouting, "To hell with this!"

Thankfully, the training grounds were located behind their home and the concert hall.

Suddenly, Jenna strained her ears; a distant voice, frantic and familiar, seemed to be calling out from the south. It sounded like Nann.

And she was right. As Jenna sprinted down the cobblestone streets, she ran into her surrogate mother, leading a group of panicked townspeople.

Oh, Nann... how could one even begin to describe just how hardcore this woman was? A voluptuous figure, wearing the same country-blue dress beneath a bloodstained apron, bonnet perched firmly atop her head, and wielding a black, bloodstained sword gripped tightly in her stout hands.

"N-Nann!" Jenna exclaimed, trying to repress a wave of emotion.

"Jenna!" Nann shouted, lowering her sword. "I've been searching for you for the past hour!"

Jenna was at a loss for words. There was so much she wanted to say.

"Isaac's unconscious," she blurted, the first thought to escape her mouth.

"I can see that," Nann replied, breathing heavily. "But there's something important I must tell you. Listen closely."

Jenna stepped closer, nodding, trying to steady her own breath from the strain of carrying Isaac.

"Take this path and go north," Nann huffed. "All the way to the northern gate of Aerlund. You'll find a horse tied to a stake. Take him and ride into the Aerbön Woods."

Jenna nodded, focusing intently on every word.

"Find Professor Vandergaus and tell him you've received his letter."

"What?" Jenna demanded sharply. "What letter? And who is—"

She was cut off by the screeching of Kreaux and the rumbling earth beneath the Praetors' approach.

"There isn't time to explain, Jenna!" Nann yelled. "Now, do as I say!"

Tears welled in Jenna's eyes as she stared into Nann's determined blue gaze. "Please, Nann... I can't lose you too. I just can't."

Nann's lip quivered as she pulled Jenna into a fierce embrace, whispering, "Yours and Isaac's survival is paramount, Jenna." And with that, she pushed her back. "I have to rescue Uncle Ingle's sorry ass. And let me tell you, I've no intention of dying in this sorry hellhole!"

Jenna couldn't help but let out a tiny chuckle amidst the chaos.

"Now go, girlie!" Nann shouted as she turned to rally the other townsfolk.

Jenna's heart swelled as she ran, and after a few moments, she couldn't help but turn and shout, "Nann!"

"Damn it, Jenna, what now?" Nann roared in response.

"I… I love you!" The words finally burst from Jenna's lips.

For a moment, there was silence. Jenna's breath hitched in her throat, fearing she might not hear a response.

Suddenly, the clang of a metal sword hitting the ground echoed through the chaos, and before she knew it, the stout woman Jenna so dearly loved charged toward her.

"Oof!" Jenna grunted, almost dropping Isaac as Nann collided with her, wrapping her in a fierce hug.

"My precious girlie, Jenna," Nann whispered through bated breath and tears. "I love you too. So, so much."

With that, Jenna watched Nann bolt down the path, disappearing into the smoke and flames of Kreaux-sieged Aerlund.

A fierce determination flashed across Jenna's face as she ran through the burning streets of Aerlund, Isaac limp and unconscious on her shoulder, blood still trickling down his forehead.

Go north. Go north. Go north! Jenna repeated the mantra in her mind, as if it were the only thought and goal in existence.

What felt like an eternity passed as Jenna dodged exploding glass from superheated buildings and avoided flaming debris. It wasn't without struggle—Jenna endured cuts and lacerations, too afraid to stop and check on Isaac—but she finally caught sight of the northern gate.

Perhaps she was too focused, or perhaps too emotional; either way, Jenna never looked back as she dashed down the stone path, leaving behind the blazing inferno that was once her home.

MAJESTY

Almost there, almost there, almost there! The words rang in her mind as she kept her eyes fixed on the northern gate, growing closer with each stride.

Thankfully, no Kreaux were in sight, and she thanked the heavens that her family's mansion—now a flaming ruin some thirty feet behind her—was the farthest northern house in Aerlund, sparing her from more burning debris.

Boom. Boom. Boom. Boom. The sound that echoed through the air was heart-wrenching, blood-chilling, and terrifyingly unfamiliar.

"What is that?" Jenna whispered, looking around in panic. Was it a Praetor?

Oh, shoot! she thought, realizing she had completely forgotten about the Praetors.

But a deeper sense told her that whatever she was hearing was far worse than any Praetor... far worse, demanding her immediate attention.

Jenna's heart felt like it might stop. As if the booming sound wasn't dreadful enough, it faded into the background as two more sounds filled the air—sounds she hated more than anything in Vaerün: the soul-gripping whispers of Dark Majesty and the sickening, contorting slop of black, tar-like blood spilling from some dark, ancient source.

Jenna took a step back, then steadied herself, squinting to see through the ash and sparks flying through the air. There, amid the chaos, something began to take shape—a bubbling, slopping silhouette of a being. Was this creature formed by Dark Majesty? Or was it Dark Majesty itself?

Steeling herself, Jenna gripped the rose-hilted rapier, ready for whatever came. Was this the creature responsible for conjuring the dark flames and hiding their nature? What evil force could wield such dark power?

The sickening goo-like sounds ceased, but the *Boom. Boom. Boom. Boom.* continued.

At first, it was difficult to discern its form, but as it slowly advanced, taking deliberate, rhythmic steps, Jenna realized it was a man—a tall man draped in a black robe, darker than the void.

Jenna recoiled as she saw the figure cloaked in black, his head bowed forward, hidden beneath a deep cowl. From the hood's empty void, Dark Majesty seeped out like a malevolent mist, pouring down to the ground in thick, twisting tendrils. The darkness dripped and oozed, almost alive in its grotesque movement, obscuring any hint of a face and filling the air with a foreboding presence.

She swallowed hard, trying to control the fear rising in her throat. Should she attack? Speak? Or just run? Was this even a person, or some dark manifestation?

"And who do I have the pleasure of standing before me?" the creature hissed, his voice like nails on a chalkboard.

Jenna winced. *Did Mourners and Kreaux have a demon baby?* she thought. *Because that's what this sounds like!*

Waving a finger in mock scolding, Jenna raised her rapier, saying, "Ah, ah, ah! Didn't hell teach you it's rude to demand the names of royalty?" she taunted, as the fiery aura of her Majesty ignited around her.

"But of course, princess!" the creature sneered, bowing sarcastically.

"What are you, anyway?" Jenna demanded confidently, standing her ground.

Ignoring the question, the robed figure pointed toward the flaming wreckage of Aerlund. "Do you care for my Majesty?" he hissed. "You seem frustrated that mine is more powerful than yours!"

Jenna's blood boiled.

"*Your* Majesty?" she spat. "Darkness doesn't *wield* Majesty. Only heroes chosen by heaven wield Majesty."

In an instant, the robed figure became a blur, shifting faster than Jenna's eyes could follow. Shadows twisted and merged, and Dark Majesty crackled and surged around him like living flames.

With a sudden, violent motion, this dark Majestician unleashed a torrent of black fire, seething and wild, that roared toward Jenna with the force of a storm, threatening to consume everything in its path.

"Ha ha ha!" Jenna yelled, deflecting fireballs with her sword.

"Majesty, is it?" she mocked, thrusting her rapier forward, launching her own barrage of fireballs like a flaming gun.

Wow, he was fast! Did he even move, or was it some kind of teleportation? The first few fireballs he dodged effortlessly, but by the ninth and tenth, Jenna was gaining speed.

Boom! Fireballs exploded as they collided. Jenna was forced back, the sheer force and heat of his return blast sending her flying. She cursed under her breath, frustrated by the hindrance of having to carry Isaac.

"Poor *thing*," mocked the robed man, "handicapped by that rag doll."

"Agggghhhrrr!" roared Jenna as she gripped the hilt of her sword, holding it up and unleashing a continuous breath of flames as if from a dragon's maw.

"Ooooh!" the man mocked, raising his dead white hands to repel the fire with his own. "That is some Majesty!"

Jenna braced herself and unleashed another wave of fire, pushing back against the opposing force that came her way.

"But," whispered the man, his voice dripping with malice as he began to conduct in a four-four-beat pattern, "I still think mine is better."

Jenna watched in both agitation and curiosity, unable to understand what he was doing. With each rhythmic pulsation of his hand—up, down, left, right—the same dreadful sound echoed through the air: Boom. Boom. Boom. Boom.

Reeeeee! screeched the Kreaux as they swarmed from all directions, some clawing their way out of the damp earth around them.

Jenna's breathing intensified as she scanned the massive host of Kreaux surrounding her. The corner of her lip curled up into a slight smile.

"Oh, how I do love a challenge," Jenna muttered, eyeing her enemies with determination.

Suddenly, the tempo of the man's conducting picked up. With every movement of his hand, the Kreaux followed as if they were marionettes under his command. And then, in a split second, he stopped, and silence fell over the chaos.

It would've been hard for anyone to guess that she was weighed down by Isaac.

Her silver, rose-etched rapier danced through the air, slicing through Kreaux after Kreaux. Dead hands, arms, torsos, and heads flew in every direction. With every opening she found, her supporting hand—still holding Isaac—shot waves of fireballs.

"Ah!" Jenna screamed as sharp claws tore into her back and legs.

Come on, Jenna, you can do more than this! Isaac's familiar words echoed in her mind as she looked around, defending both herself and him from the relentless Kreaux.

And then a brilliant idea sparked in her mind.

Frrroooarr! Jenna unleashed a circulating wave of fire, momentarily repelling the Kreaux. With her feet dug into the ground and knees bent, she launched herself backward with all her might, flying through the air.

Her hand reached over her shoulder as she stared intensely at the flaming wreckage of their home. "Let this be a lesson," she growled, stretching her hand toward her home, the flames dancing in response, "to any Kreaux that dare attack my home again!"

And with a flick of her wrist, the flames leaped from their inferno, exploding through the air like a tsunami of fire toward the Kreaux and the robed man. A surge of power and Majesty poured from Jenna's open palm.

"Haaaaahhhh!" Jenna screamed as she landed, raising her other hand to join the first, amplifying the wave of fire fivefold. Her dress and hair whipped wildly in the scorching wind.

Catching her breath, Jenna felt a sudden chill. All the Kreaux lay decimated, but to her bafflement and anger, the robed man remained unharmed, protected by a wall of flames.

Unsure of what to do next, Jenna stared at the man, demanding, "Just who are you?"

"Ah, ah, ah!" he mocked, echoing her earlier taunt with cruel irony. "Didn't heaven teach you that it's rude to demand the names of royalty?"

"*Royalty?*" Jenna scoffed, incredulous. "WHAT royalty? There's no royalty that—"

Her attention was abruptly diverted as the robed man extended his palm. The black, tar-like matter of Dark Majesty twisted up his robe, morphing into a long, sinister sword.

She barely had time to react as he lunged, slashing with an intensity and speed she had never endured, not even in her most rigorous training.

Oddly, he never once targeted Isaac, though the opportunity was clear. No, all his hatred and fury seemed focused entirely on Jenna.

Dark Majesty or not, Jenna knew one thing for sure—his blade was just as sharp as hers, if not sharper.

She howled in pain as his sword nicked and cut her across her arms and midsection—wounds she hadn't felt since her training with Garon years ago.

Why can't I get him? she screamed internally as he continued to dodge every move, every slice.

But then a righteous anger grew inside her—the kind that rises when all you love and cherish is under threat, when the kingdom and town you hold dear are dying at the hands of those who hate all that is living and good.

And as the fiery glow inside her eyes danced, she unleashed a volley of fireballs and imbued her rapier with such heat, it appeared freshly forged.

"Ha ha," the robed man laughed, his voice dark and menacing. "I remember giving that very same look once! Those eyes… the passion… **the fire!**"

Clang, clang, clang! Shiiiiiiiirrrr! The swords collided again and again, scraping and sparking with each strike.

Boom! Fsshhhhroooarrr! The sounds of their flame-wielding Majesty echoed as they battled furiously.

"HAAAHH!!" Jenna screamed, raising both hands and finally overpowering the robed man's Dark Majesty.

Realizing he was about to lose, the man knelt, raising his hands to shield himself from her consuming flames.

Jenna's rapier pointed down at him, her fury palpable. "Do you—" she started, but her words were cut off.

The man's boney, white-knuckled hands moved with impossible speed. A black, fiery surge of Dark Majesty rocketed forth from his palm, sending Jenna careening backward, briefly knocking her unconscious.

"No!" she screamed when she came to, frantically thinking of Isaac.

"No! No!" Her frantic gaze darted left and right until she realized she was lying on her back, struggling to breathe—likely with broken ribs. Propping herself up on her knees, she was met with the sight of a rippling black sword, inches from her face. Refusing to look up, Jenna's eyes lifted only enough to see Isaac lying motionless, about twelve feet away.

Jenna's head dropped as tears ran down her ash-covered face, revealing the fair skin beneath. She was battered, beaten, and broken. Her cuts meshed into the fabric of her dress, and her white princess gloves were stained with blood and soot.

She couldn't hear the robed man's words. The world around her seemed to dissolve into chaos, but her gaze was locked on one thing—the Kreaux, slowly closing in around Isaac, their claws twitching in anticipation. Terror clawed at her chest, choking her.

"ISAAC!" she screamed, desperation and pure panic cracking her voice. "**NO!!** Don't let them take you!" She reached out with trembling, bloodied hands, body too broken to move, every ounce of will fighting against her fading strength.

And then... Something miraculous and terrifying happened. Isaac's eyes flung open, but they weren't the eyes of the friend she knew. Glorious, celestial rays of light burst forth, as if too powerful to be contained by mortal eyelids. Unconscious yet perfectly regal, he began to rise. With an ethereal grace, he stood, arms outstretched to the heavens as if summoning a power far beyond his understanding. White cloak and golden hair billowing around him, caught in the radiant spiral of his own inner Majesty, now flooding out in wind-like waves of blinding brilliance.

Jenna's breath caught in her throat. It was impossible to swallow. Blinking through the burning light, struggling to keep her vision clear, to make sense of what she was seeing.

Isaac lifted off the ground as though weightless, hands reaching upward, heavenward, Majesty erupting like a beacon from realms beyond their earthly world.

"...Isaac?" she whispered, voice trembling, as darkness began to creep into the corners of her sight. And in that one breath, as if every ounce of strength had given out at once, Jenna collapsed. The last image burned into her mind: Isaac, a figure of pure, undeniable light and majestic glory.

Unconsciousness claimed her just as the surrounding scene erupted with divine power.

What Jenna could not see—and would never fully understand—was what followed. The heavens themselves seemed to open... And from that swirling portal of light, a heavenly ray descended, encircling Isaac. A celestial figure, an angel of such perfect fierceness and beauty, came rushing down from the heavens at breakneck speed.

Long, golden hair flowed like molten silk. A robe of purest white rippling around her like living sunlight. Never had a face been so full of love as this, and though neither Jenna nor Isaac could know... This was none other than Lucy, his precious and beloved mother, coming to her son in a moment of infinite grace.

Isaac, caught in his spiritual trance, reached up as if welcoming the divine presence, instinctively seeking comfort from above. And then, in a blinding burst, angelic arms, accompanied by tears streaming down faces, were wrapped around one another—a mother's embrace to her son. Light poured out from their touch, cascading over the town in a wave of radiant Majesty.

The Kreaux were instantaneously consumed by the brightness, twisted forms dissolving to nothing, only remembered by the shrillest of shrieks one can imagine.

The dark-robed Majestician vanished, swallowed by the celestial tide in the blink of an eye. Destroyed by such sublime destruction, or fleeing at the last moment?

The sound of crackling, burning buildings was all that pulled Jenna back to reality.

What just happened? she thought, dazed. *Where did he go? That robed man...*

Like the rest of the Kreaux, he was indeed gone.

And what of—Jenna thought as she looked forward.

"**Isaac!**" she screamed, finally breaking the silence.

Ignoring her pain, Jenna immediately pushed herself up and rushed to Isaac's side. Sorrow visibly expressed upon her face, quickly brought to awareness that he was still unconscious.

Was everything that happened just a dream? No, it couldn't have been... Jenna wondered, glancing at the bleeding gash on Isaac's head.

The pain of her broken ribs sunk in as she struggled to lift Isaac again from off the ground. Cuts and lacerations stinging, but pressing on, she scooped him up. Almost forgetting her task at hand, she suddenly remembered the northern gate to the Aerbön Woods.

Upon reaching the northern gates, Jenna fought an overwhelming urge to look back. Every step feeling like her heart was being dragged through shards of glass. But she couldn't help it—she had to see, **and** had to take one last look... At everything she was leaving behind.

Ever so slowly, she turned around. The scream that left her was quiet and strangled, a sound of devastation from the truest depths of her soul.

Her beautiful Aerlund... reduced to ruin. The town she'd known so intimately—cobblestone streets, ivy-wrapped beams of quaint homes, the warm glow of tavern lights—all gone. Now it was just smoldering wreckage, a place where dark fire had run wild and unchecked.

Embers filled the air like lost souls, swirling in the black and red of a sky incessantly choking on smoke. The darkness above was like a suffocating shroud, heavy with grief, ash, and a despair that felt almost alive.

"My... my *home*—" she choked, unable to steady the quiver in her voice.

And then it hit her. The scent of burning timber filled her nose, striking with a cruel, familiar intensity.

It was the same smell as that day, twenty years ago—that same, wretched day in Fürnas. That same bitter, acrid sting of smoke, taste of ash, taste of a world going up in flames.

The memories ceaselessly came crashing in, relentless and suffocating: A collapse of her kingdom, the screaming, fires devouring everything in their path. It was as though the past had cruelly come back to haunt her, fully superimposed on this burning town.

With a shake of her head, Jenna pulled herself into reality as she once again took in Aerlund.

It was all painstakingly visible. Shattered glass windows of homes she once loved, broken teeth of wood jutting out from disfigured walls, the cozy taverns that used to glow with laughter and warmth now just charred frames—hollow, empty skeletons where joy used to thrive. The streets, those beloved cobblestones she'd run across as a child, now strewn with debris and destruction—burning fabric, broken carts, fallen signs—all of it reduced to rubble and flame.

Tears fell. Hot and fast, cutting tracks through the soot on her cheeks. The realization of her nails digging into her palms via clenched fists, pain grounding her, anchoring her to this awful reality. Every breath felt like swallowing knives, each glimpse of fire twisting the blade ever deeper. It was like losing her life twice—two worlds, two homes, destroyed by the same relentless force. And now she stood in the wreckage of both, helpless to stop it.

"I failed you... *I failed you all*," she whispered to no one, voice lost in the roar of flames.

With a slow turn around, Jenna heaved Isaac into the saddle.

Her fingers shook as she gripped the reins of the horse tighter, knuckles pale, her body fighting the urge to collapse under the weight of that familiar, gut-wrenching despair.

"There's going to be so much..." Jenna wheezed as she limped down the path, holding the horse's reins, "so much to talk about when you wake up, Isaac." She finished most quietly, as her eyes slowly looked up, observing the broken and charred sign overhead that read, *'Aerlund'*.

Chapter 11

The Water Majestician

The sound of horse hooves trotting on damp earth filled Jenna's ears as she loosely held the reins of the horse carrying Isaac. Had there been any passersby on the cool, damp forest trail, they would have either screamed in terror or rushed to aid upon seeing the bloody, tattered bodies of both Isaac and Jenna.

Exactly how long had she been traveling now? Hours? Days? Jenna had entirely lost track of time. Too many thoughts and images were running through her mind from the trauma she had just experienced.

Oh, Nann... she thought worriedly. *Where are you? Did you survive? I hope you're okay.*

Jenna shook her head, pushing thoughts of her beloved Nann aside, then to Uncle Ingle, and finally to Mr. Tendúr, who would be arriving in just a few days.

"Shüza!" Jenna swore aloud. "Mr. Tendúr! I had entirely forgotten!"

The horse whinnied as Jenna subconsciously gripped the reins tighter to calm it. She began talking to herself, muttering anxiously.

"Why, hello, Mr. Tendúr!" Jenna suddenly exclaimed to the air, as if speaking with the old man himself. "Welcome to Aerlund! Welcome!" She sarcastically smiled and gave a mocking bow. "I *do* hope you enjoy your stay."

Jenna's expression twisted into an exaggerated form of hospitality as she playfully continued her mock tour of the burning ruins that had been Aerlund.

"Right this *way*, Mr. Tendúr! Let me show you to your living quarters!" She motioned to the empty air. "I *do* hope you find your incinerated room to be quite comfortable!"

"What's that?" she added, cocking her head, "Why, no! We figured the Kreaux do a *much* better job than just your average bellboy!" Jenna snickered, whimsically, imagining Mr. Tendúr's horrified expression, when he sees the Kreaux holding the door open for him.

Suddenly, an image of a Kreaux, awkwardly smiling, filled Jenna's mind. She pictured the creature assisting Mr. Tendúr with his luggage—its polished claw-like fingernails, dead white skin, black eyes, and fanged teeth lined with black saliva. To add to the insanity, she dressed it in a neat bellboy's outfit, complete with a hat, suspenders, slacks, and an engraved nametag reading '*Greesee*'.

"Now, Mr. Tendúr!" Jenna exclaimed, while raising her voice theatrically, pointing to a large mushroom on the side of the path. "I'll have *none* of that! Complaints concerning the incinerating heat and ash covered floords have already been filed by other guests."

She looked up into the dark canopy overhead and continued, rolling her eyes, "As I've told the other visitors... perhaps instead of complaining, you could use this *extraordinary* opportunity to reflect on the mysteries of heaven and hell. Why, take young Greesee here for example," she added sympathetically, motioning to an enormous flower, similar to a rafflesia.

"*He* enjoys these circumstances, don't you, Greesee?" she demanded, as she took one of the flower petals and nodded it up and down.

"Now, Mr. Tendúr," she continued, addressing the mushroom again, "we'll be expecting you at Mayor Inglethöp's this evening! I am assured you love the theatre? Tonight's *fiery* performance will be by none other than our favorite Conductor!" (*The name she had given the black-robed man.*)

Jenna smiled for a moment as she imagined the Kreaux bellboy clapping his clawed hands together excitedly. "Oh!" she exclaimed.

"But do be careful on your way over! The flaming debris crashing down and exploding glass might cause some... *minor* complications."

With a flourish, Jenna bowed to the mushroom. "Please make yourself comfortable. We do *hope* you enjoy your stay in Hell-lund—I mean, Aerlund! And of course, if you need anything, Greesee is right here to assist you. Toodle-pah!"

"Ugghhh..." moaned Isaac, his eyes slowly opening. "Jenna?"

"Aggghh, my aching head..." He grunted as he pushed himself up, holding his head in his hands.

Isaac blinked repeatedly as he slowly regained focus, only to see Jenna kneeling down, caressing a mushroom.

"Perhaps," he said with wide eyes, "I've hit my head even worse than I thought."

"Oh! Isaac!" Jenna exclaimed happily as she walked over to him. "I'm so happy to see you're awake! In case you haven't noticed, we're in the Aerbön woods. Pretty, huh?" she asked excitedly.

"Um, Jenna?" Isaac politely inquired. "Two questions. One, what were you just doing? And two, what happened?"

Jenna raised her eyebrows and smiled widely as she pointed to the mushroom. "I was talking with Mr. Tendúr! He was complaining about the incinerating heat of Hell-lund."

"Uh-huh..." Isaac replied suspiciously, raising an eyebrow.

"But I assured him it'd be fine," Jenna said whimsically. "Besides, Greesee here doesn't mind it at all, do you, Greesee?" she added, "tickling" the petals of the massive flower.

"Jenna..." Isaac mumbled as he slowly dismounted the horse, holding his head. "Forget the second question. I have a new one."

"Of course, Isaac! What is it?" she asked, leaning closer to hear him.

Isaac's emotions welled with sorrow and compassion as he looked at his beloved friend. She was cut all over, lacerations slowly oozing blood, and her long hair was mostly matted and crispy, glued to her scalp by dried blood. Ash covered her like someone had pushed her into a soot pile.

"How long..." He swallowed nervously, afraid of the answer. "How long have we been on this trail? How long... have you been without sleep?"

Jenna tapped her chin and raised an eyebrow, pacing in thought. "Hmmm…" she hummed. "Well, let's see… Shut it, Mr. Tendúr!" she suddenly yelled, pointing at the mushroom. "I'm talking to Isaac right now, so wait your turn!"

Isaac blinked repeatedly, still unsure if he was hallucinating or suffering from a concussion.

"As I was saying, before I was so rudely interrupted!" Jenna rolled her eyes, folding her arms and turning her back to the mushroom. "I'd say it's been about two and a half now, if I'm certain!"

"Two and a half days?" Isaac bellowed. "And with those injuries? No wonder you're hallucinating!" He exclaimed as he rushed over to her, helping her to kneel.

"Nooooonsense!" Jenna laughed whimsically. "I am so okay right now! Right, guys?" she asked, looking around and nodding at the surrounding foliage of the forest.

"No, Jenn," Isaac said, shaking his head. "You are sooo not okay right now." With that, he gently lifted his left, bloodstained hand and placed it on her cheek, staring directly into her eyes.

"Ooooh, how pretty!" Jenna said, rocking back and forth and staring back at him. "Since when did you add blue to your yellow eyes, Isaac?" she questioned. "They look like the skkkyyyy!" She giggled.

Isaac sighed as he momentarily closed his eyes. With his right hand extended upward, his palm reaching out, he looked up as if speaking to someone beyond the canopy.

"May the light of divinity grace us in this, one of our darkest hours," he spoke, the dancing lights of yellow and blue racing around his irises, light emanating from his body.

"Battered and broken we appear to be," he recited, Majesty filling him, "tossed and turned by our enemies."

Tears, imbued with sunlight, rolled down his face and fell to the ground, shining as they descended. A beam of light pierced through the dark canopy overhead, radiating down upon his open palm, filling it with light.

"But upon thy glorious light we stand," Isaac finished, "knowing our deliverance… is always at hand."

If the forest had eyes that *we* could see, surely, they would be as wide as a child's being served a nice, fresh slab of kinberry pie.

There was something majestic about Isaac as he knelt there on the ground. How could someone wearing such a grotesquely bloodstained white wardrobe, looking so battered and defeated, emit so much hope, strength, and unwavering faith?

The streams and beads of light that radiated from him were so clean and pure, carrying a sense of life and vitality. Truly enough, life and vitality they did indeed carry. As soon as he had absorbed enough light from above, he gently closed his fist and held what appeared to be an orb of pure, glowing light.

"No, Isaac," said Jenna wearily, attempting to hold up her hand. "That's for you—"

But it was too late. Isaac had already crushed the tiny orb of glowing light in his hand. Streams of light danced, twisted, and swirled around Jenna, wrapping around her wounds and instantly healing them.

After a few moments, Isaac raised his hand skyward once more, and the streams of light rushed up and through the canopy, disappearing.

"Isaac… why?" Jenna asked with tears in her eyes as he rested against her. "You needed that far more than I!"

"Don't worry, Jenna," he sighed wearily. "That's the beautiful part about Majesty."

Isaac rolled his shoulders as he stood up and extended a hand, helping Jenna to her feet.

"It is eternal—to be used now and forevermore," he said with a smile.

"Yes, but—" Jenna started, but Isaac interrupted.

"It's not Majesty's fault!" exclaimed Isaac. "The ether from which Majesty is drawn is in infinite abundance. I cannot blame it for my lack of mental, emotional, and spiritual deficits that restrict me from accessing it more fully."

Jenna raised an eyebrow. "You speak of Majesty as though it is a living thing!"

MAJESTY

Isaac tilted his head in confusion. "Is it not? Look around you." He motioned to the forest. "Every single thing you see had to first be created by the ether of Majesty before it could be created tangibly."

Jenna looked around and nodded quietly, recalling a conversation with Garon many years ago on the training grounds of Fürnas, where they spoke of Majesty similarly.

"And I suppose we should consider ourselves special," said Jenna, in an awed tone, "that we have control over such power."

"'Control' is such a terrible word," said Isaac boldly. "One of many words I detest; it comes straight from hell."

Jenna couldn't help but laugh at the sternness and sincerity in his voice.

"No," Isaac continued. "I believe the word 'access' fits just fine."

"Ah, I see," said Jenna as she gripped the reins of the horse. Isaac gently took them from her hand and helped her into the saddle before taking the reins himself.

"So we don't control the power of Majesty," she added. "We access it."

Isaac smiled and nodded.

"Do you truly believe," Isaac said in absolute humility, "that even for a moment, I could do something as miraculous as this?" He pointed to her freshly healed wounds, peeking through her slightly torn dress.

"Well, you did—" she tried to say.

"Absolutely not," Isaac interrupted, pointing up to the canopy. "That, and only that, was possible through the power of divinity. That's why I had to return it as soon as I was finished."

Jenna raised an eyebrow and asked sincerely, "Do you really have to return it, though?"

"What do you mean?" Isaac asked with a smile.

"Perhaps I access Majesty differently, but..." Jenna momentarily trailed off before continuing. "When I cast Majesty, I get the whole ether thing, mind you!"

Isaac nodded and motioned for her to go on.

"But..." she shyly admitted, "it just feels like it's there to be used. And the more I take and utilize, the more powerful I feel. Isn't it difficult to just… return it? I mean, look! If you would've just kept it, you could've healed yourself too!"

Isaac shook his head. "There is power in righteous suffering, Jenna."

She swallowed nervously as he continued, "As there is power in righteous sacrifice. Yes, I could have easily kept the light for myself and used it to heal my injuries. But why?" he questioned. "I'm all right now. By grace above, I'm alive, well, and soundly intact."

"That's debatable," Jenna said with another raised eyebrow as she scanned him up and down.

He simply smiled. "The ether is there for everyone, Jenna. And I can explain to you why I enjoy returning it instead of keeping it."

"Yes?" she asked in suspense.

"No greater joy is experienced from giving rather than taking," he said in a heroic voice.

Jenna looked at him flatly and said, "Well… gee. Uh, thanks, Isaac. You sound like one of those secluded monks up in the frozen heights of the Kier Mountains."

He tilted his head again, giving that slightly confused look that said, *Oh, I'm sorry, did I do it again?*

"And why are you putting me on the horse?" she demanded. "You're the one that's still injured, not me!"

"Now that's easy," he simply said. "Because I'm not the one surviving on two and a half days of no sleep."

Ooooh, that mouth of his… Sometimes he did have a little sass to him.

"Well, yeah, but—" she tried to protest.

"Yeah, no. Sorry, Jenn, no arguments this time. Sleep well."

With that, Isaac tugged on the reins and began walking alongside the horse as Jenna leaned forward and rested on the mane. Without hesitation, sleep overtook her…

(Do you know those weird, random dreams you have when you've been running on too little sleep?) Yeah, *those* were the dreams Jenna was having as she fell asleep on the horse. *(But really, you've gotta think- who wouldn't have strange dreams hobbling up and down on a horse?)*

No greater joy is experienced from giving rather than taking, Isaac's words repeated in her mind as she dreamed of him casting his Majesty in a black and empty void.

It makes so much sense! she exclaimed to the dream Isaac. *That's why you utilize Majesty the way you do!*

Dream Isaac nodded, touching the black void—a ripple of light emanated, followed by a stream of racing light that stood in stark contrast to the infinite blackness behind it.

Duh! she exclaimed as she watched. *You're literally accessing the ether itself—as if momentarily setting it free to do its work! But why?*

That's easy, responded dream Isaac. *Because the ether of light automatically seeks the destruction of darkness. I simply set it free to do what it was designed to do, and when it's done, it returns whence it came.*

That is incredible. I wish I could wield Majesty in such a way, Jenna said sadly.

I'm sorry, Jenna, responded Isaac sorrowfully. *But I don't think heaven would ever allow a Kreaux as evil as yourself to access the power of Majesty.*

What? cried Jenna. *Isaac, how could you say such a thing?*

Dream Isaac raised his hands, rippling explosions of light emanating from his palms.

No, Isaac, what are you doing? I thought you loved me! she cried out, shielding her eyes from the blinding light, only to see dead-white hands in black-robed sleeves.

I'm sorry, Jenna, but heaven cannot love hell. It's just not possible.

As if someone had flipped the angle around, Jenna screamed in her mind as she looked at herself, wearing a robe blacker than hell, and Dark Majesty dripping out of the hood.

"Noooo!" she screamed as Isaac's powerful Light Majesty whipped through the air toward her.

Jenna bolted upright, gasping deeply, sweat and tears dripping down her face.

"Jenna?" asked Isaac in his kind and benevolent tone. "Are you okay?"

"Yes..." she huffed. "It was a nightmare..."

Isaac's sad eyes melted like a puppy dog's as he said, "Oh no… I am so sorry! Is there anything I can do for you? Here, please have some water!" he exclaimed, unfastening a ceramic jar of water from the saddle.

Jenna quickly uncorked it and gulped down the fresh, cold water.

"Would you like to talk about it?" he asked politely.

"No, not really. I think…" She faded off.

"That it's because you didn't get enough sleep?" he finished, posing a question.

There again was that mouth, at the most random times!

All she could do was laugh. "I'm afraid you've got me there. Not to mention everything that happened in Aerlund… it was so awful."

"Speaking of Aerlund," Isaac added, "would you care to explain what exactly happened?"

"Well…" Jenna sat up, straightening her back. "I'll start with my trip to Mr. Tendúr."

Isaac nodded, looking forward as he listened to Jenna recap, in full detail, her entire trip from meeting with Mr. Tendúr until their current moment in the Aerbön woods.

"A letter? From Garon Erbrecht himself?" Isaac asked excitedly. "How fascinating! But who would have thought that his wife, Lucy, would betray him?"

"That's what I said!" Jenna exclaimed.

"But I could've sworn you told me she was the nicest woman you'd ever met?"

"No," Jenna replied. "She wasn't just nice. That woman was *angelic*!"

Isaac smiled widely as he looked up at her, then forward again.

"Wow… I wish I could have met her," he said sadly.

"Don't worry, I'm sure you will someday!" Jenna said optimistically.

"You think so?" he asked. "But I thought you said they lived in the Wölnas Kingdom? And we know that it was destroyed during the Kreaux siege some twenty years ago, just like Fürnas."

"That may be true," Jenna replied, "but who's to say they didn't survive? Besides… if there's anything I know about either of them, it's that they're fighters like you've never experienced."

Isaac laughed and nodded. "Fantastic! I can't wait to learn a lesson or two from them."

"But you hate combat!" spat Jenna.

"That may be true," said Isaac with a head toss, "but I wouldn't mind some lessons from the commander-in-chief of Wölnas, and as for Lucy…" he said thoughtfully. "I mean piano lessons."

Isaac looked up at Jenna curiously and asked, "You… did say she was a pianist, didn't you?"

Jenna nodded profusely. "Oh, yes! Yes, yes. A pianist like no other…" She trailed off before continuing. "To be honest, the only other pianist who compares to her is you."

"Pleaaaase!" Isaac responded, both humbly and sarcastically. "That's a dishonor to compare someone of her prestige with someone like me, who is entirely self-taught."

"Be that as it may…" Jenna mumbled. "For some strange reason, your music reminds me so much of hers."

The situation grew a little awkward.

Isaac broke the ice by asking another question, "And what's this about another letter from Uncle Ingle?"

"Hah!" Jenna laughed. "Beats me. Isn't it the best, always being left out of the loop? I cannot tell you how many questions I have at this very moment."

"At the very least," Isaac said quickly, trying not to get overwhelmed, "it'd be nice to know why we must meet this Professor Vandergaus."

"Or why Garon's letter speaks of the Wöntylnas Kingdom," added Jenna.

"Or who that angel was that came to our aid," added Isaac.

"Or why your eyes now have blue in them after she touched you," added Jenna.

"Or why Nann didn't just come with us," added Isaac.

"Or why we've been traveling in this stupid forest for over two days now and haven't found anything," Jenna added, always with a sassy finish.

Both of them started laughing but quickly stopped.

"Okay. Either the head trauma is starting to get to me," Isaac muttered as he looked around, "or I'm losing it."

"You hear that too?" Jenna asked excitedly.

"I do!" he answered with a nod. "That music, it's beautiful."

Isaac halted the horse momentarily, holding up his hand as if to still the air. There, all around them, hovered the enchanting sound of a harp, both far off and yet very, very near.

"But where is it coming from?" Jenna asked as she too looked around, squinting her eyes.

"Hmmm…" Isaac said quietly, looking around for a place to tie up the horse.

"Why not tie him up over there, next to that broken-down cottage?" Jenna suggested, pointing to a moss-covered pole beside a small, sagging wooden cottage.

"That's a great idea!" Isaac exclaimed as Jenna jumped off the horse to walk beside him.

"Wait a second," they both said in sync, looking at each other. "A cottage!"

They quickly darted through the trees and hastily tied the reins to the wooden pole as Isaac knocked at the bowed, sorry excuse of a door.

One must ask, who builds a cottage in the heart of the woods? And goodness, was it interesting! It was the type of cottage that you'd expect an old swamp witch to be living in. Perhaps it looked decent when it was erected, but now it looked as if the designer stood back and said, "Yep. I want a U-shaped cottage!" And so it looked from the obvious years of continuous rainfall.

The ivy and green moss entangled the walls and roof in such a way that it was no wonder Isaac and Jenna had barely noticed it. Although the dark brown, curling wood shingles of the walls and roof, barely visible underneath all that ivy and moss, did give it a unique look.

"Why, oh why…" Jenna bellowed, raising her arms over her head.

Isaac smiled, placing his hand upon her back. "It's all right, Jenna. It's only sprinkling!"

And although Jenna hated the rain or any manner of precipitation, Isaac loved it. And who could blame him? Compared to the music of the heavens, not much can stand against the soul-invigorating sound of gentle rain falling upon the innumerable leaves and foliage of the forest.

Tink, tink, tink, tink, rang the charming sound of water droplets splattering on the clear glass jars and metal teacups randomly scattered upon the peeling wooden table next to the side of the house.

"Well, what now—" Jenna began, but Isaac raised a hand to stop her.

"Do you feel that?" he questioned, narrowing his eyes.

"Why, yes, Isaac, I most certainly do!" she responded with a goofy grin and an exaggeratedly high voice.

"Really?" he asked excitedly.

"Yes! It's called the rain!" she said, nodding up and down with wide eyes and a smile.

Isaac stared at her and simply sighed as he walked toward the source of the music.

"That's not what I was talking about," he said coldly. "It's the ether. Someone is using Majesty," he added, continuing his walk.

The ether? Jenna thought, scowling cutely as she stomped through the damp earth beneath her feet. *How on Vaerün does that boy feel things that even I can't?*

"Sometimes I wonder if he just makes all this up," she mumbled under her breath accidentally.

"I'm sorry?" Isaac questioned without turning around, gripping a tree branch and swinging over a large tree root.

"Shüza, did I say that out loud?" she demanded, embarrassed.

He sighed and smiled. "It's okay, Jenna. I'm used to no one believing me."

Ooooh, the awful burn…

"You aren't the first, and you're certainly not the last," he finished, so sadly.

Jenna gulped as her face grew hot. If there was one thing she hated more than the Kreaux, it was hurting or offending Isaac. To do so was about the equivalent of hurting a sleeping puppy or kitten that had done nothing wrong but only desired to be loved.

One can only imagine how much more stupid she felt when they suddenly found themselves standing in a large and beautiful clearing. Instead of the dark green grass of the forest, this grass was bright green and vibrant. The gentle sound of a gargling brook flowed into either a very large pond or a small lake, situated at the center of the clearing.

Brilliant, vivaciously yellow daffodils were everywhere, lulling left and right either from the pleasant breeze or the gorgeous harp music. (Or heck, why not both?) There, complementing the scene, sat a man in blue garb on a wooden log, right next to the brook.

Isaac couldn't help but smile as he watched the water ripple and cascade through the air, directed by the man's hand, while he played the harp with his other hand resting on his leg.

"Excuse me!" Isaac called out as he approached the young man.

"Isaac!" hissed Jenna as she momentarily stood her ground, then followed him with an, "Ugh!"

The man immediately ceased playing the harp, as well as controlling the water, though he did not turn around.

"My name is Isaac," said Isaac politely as he approached the man. "And this here is Jenna. We're from Aerlund, and—"

"Is there anything else you'd like to tell him, Isaac?" Jenna spat angrily, crossing her arms.

"Ha ha!" the man laughed as he stood up, still facing away from them. "Sounds like something I'd say!" he exclaimed as he turned around. "I'm James, and whooaaa…" He dropped to one knee, the water behind him bursting as his hand flung backward.

See what I mean? Okay, so he's not a passerby, but his reaction is normal considering how Isaac and Jenna looked in their battered state.

James's black hair was slicked back and pulled into a small ponytail. His dark blue vest with silver buttons and white trim bore intricate designs and patterns of the Wöntylnas Kingdom, though unbeknownst to Isaac and Jenna. His brown leather pants and dark brown boots further brought out the blue of his upper vestments and dark blue cloak. At first, one might think he looked a little snobby, with those high cheekbones and striking blue eyes and all, but beneath his appearance, he was really calm and laid-back—what many would consider *cool*. To add to his unique character, his vocal accent was reminiscent of what our modern world would consider an Australian accent.

"What's wrong?" Isaac questioned, stepping forward to help James up.

"Um, Isaac?" said Jenna between pursed lips, raising a finger. "It might have something to do with your bloodstained face, blood-caked hair, and blood-covered wardrobe."

"Wh-what's your excuse then?" James asked in shock, pointing at Jenna. "I know ten years is a long time to be in the Aerbön woods, but has fashion changed this much that—"

"Ten years?" Jenna boomed, stepping forward, knocking the poor guy back to the ground. "You've been in this wretched forest for over ten years?"

"Jenna, please—" Isaac tried to interject, hands raised, but James interrupted.

"Is that a problem?" James piped up, quickly setting his harp down and unsheathing two gleaming silver daggers.

"Oh ho!" Jenna shouted as she unsheathed her rose-etched rapier. "Is this how it's going down?"

"Would you both just please—" Isaac tried again. But it was too late.

Hack, hack, hack. Slaaasssh! rang the daggers and sword as they repeatedly clashed, again and again, wielded by James and Jenna.

"What a way to introduce yourself!" James shouted, amidst the ringing blades. "Jenna, was it?"

"No, no, James!" Jenna spat back, holding her sword in a defensive stance, glaring into his mesmerizing, dancing blue irises. "I'm far more interested in you!"

"Whoa, now wait a second—" Isaac tried again.

"I agree with Isaac!" James shouted as he shoved Jenna back. "Hold on. Those eyes..." He momentarily lowered his arms, squinting as he looked deeply into Jenna's eyes.

"Your irises..." he mumbled, tilting his head this way and that. "They're like—"

"Yes, genius, we're like you," Jenna belted sarcastically, rolling her sword in her hand, clearly itching for more combat.

Ignoring her, James carefully approached Isaac as if inspecting a sleeping lion.

"And... how about you?" he quietly asked, gripping Isaac's shoulders while looking deeply into his eyes.

"I must confess," Isaac beamed, "that we certainly weren't expecting to meet another Majestician out in the Aerbön woods."

"Indeed?" James questioned slowly.

"Now hold up juuust a moment," Jenna yelled, "I want to talk about why you've been out here in the forest for ten years. And about my dress. So what if it's the latest fashion?" she boomed.

But James's focus was entirely on Isaac. "I don't understand..." he mumbled, gripping Isaac's chin and tilting his head, inspecting his eyes. "The texts of antiquity did indeed describe the Majesticians of old, housing irises of moving light and color, in direct correspondence to his or her element of earth, fire, wind, or water. But...," he trailed off, "yours are different, Isaac."

"Well, wouldya look'it that!" Jenna proclaimed in a "hillbilly" accent. "'parently we gotsa genius on our hands, Isaac!" she belted with a bucktoothed grin.

In shock and surprise, Jenna and Isaac watched as James darted back (for reasons unknown to them), threw his arms behind his back, and suddenly brought them forward—waves of twisting water gurgling and rushing through the air with tremendous force, right toward Jenna!

Shhhhh! Ssssshhhhhh! Boooom! hissed and echoed the sounds of steam and force as Jenna's Fire Majesty collided with James's Water Majesty.

"Whoa, whoa, whoa!" Isaac said, raising his hands, attempting to calm the two battling Majesticians.

"What's your problem?" Jenna yelled, holding both hands in front of her to create a firewall, stopping the crashing waves descending furiously upon her.

"My problem?" James roared in response. "You're the ones who came out of nowhere and ruined my peaceful morning!"

"And for that, we apologize—" Isaac tried to interject before both of them shouted:

"Shut up!"

Isaac sadly shook his head, taking a few steps back and waiting for them to duke it out.

"Who wants to be out in this dismal forest in the first place?" Jenna shouted, cartwheeling to dodge water whips and launching fireballs.

"Me, that's who!" James retorted as he imbued his daggers with water, slashing through Jenna's fireballs and disintegrating them.

Perhaps Jenna was too enraged to notice, or maybe she couldn't tell from the distance, but Isaac immediately saw James's voice begin to crack, and tears filled his eyes during their duel.

"To get away from—" James shouted as he unleashed wave after forceful wave, "no-good." Boom. "Wretched." Boom. "Evil people." Boom. "Like you!"

"Evil?" Jenna spat. "Ho hooooo, boy, you don't even know what evil is!"

"Haaaaaa!" both of them shouted in sync as their glowing palms radiated the explosive power of water and Fire Majesty.

"Enough!" roared Isaac, his powerful, silencing, and humbling voice forming a barrier around his raised hands, slamming both Jenna and James backward.

With a look upon his face that would send the fiercest wolf whimpering back to its den, Isaac stood in righteous fury, his cloak, wardrobe, and partially bloody red hair dancing furiously in the wind of his Majesty, boosting the unintentional intimidation factor.

James and Jenna lay on their backs, arms and hands raised as shields in fear of being struck down.

"Why are you two fighting?" Isaac roared. "Is there not enough of that happening all around us, upon our beloved land of Vaerün?"

Neither of them dared move as he continued, "If you have the time and energy to use your divine powers of Majesty to destroy one another," Isaac thundered, "then at least give our Creator the respect he deserves and return his power back to him before you run each other through with those wretched blades of yours!"

Both Jenna and James felt as if they'd just been reprimanded by one of heaven's mightiest archangels. Neither of them could say a word as they stared at Isaac. The colorful irises of his eyes danced furiously, along with his wardrobe. Was he even breathing? He looked like a statue; so still was his hold upon the barrier surrounding him, keeping the two at bay.

After a few moments, Isaac lowered his hands, dropping the barrier. He let out a deep sigh and sat on the ground as if his legs had just given out on him.

"I-I'm sorry," they both tried to say around the same time.

"Don't apologize to me," retorted Isaac. "Apologize to each other, and apologize to Him for the awful ways in which you used His powers," Isaac finished boldly, pointing up to the sky.

Once the apologies were said, James approached Isaac and plopped down in front of him, reaching out to touch the platinum silver necklace and key with the Wölnas amethyst that was exposed upon Isaac's breast. (It must have come out during the casting of his Majesty.)

"Is that..." James gawked, gently touching Isaac's necklace and key. "Platinum?"

"It is," Jenna answered for Isaac. "And before you ask, he doesn't know what it goes to or how he got it."

"Is that true?" James asked curiously, slightly lifting the key and inspecting the purple gem housed in the handle.

"It is," Isaac nodded seriously.

Well... James thought. *Surely he knows that's the Wölnas insignia and gem, right?* he questioned internally, staring at the small purple gem in the key.

Fearful of additional reproach, James slowly dropped the key and figured that now wasn't the best time to pry for additional information or personal questions.

"You're injured, Isaac," James said compassionately. "Please... will you come back with me to my cabin so that I may tend to your wounds?"

As if he had forgotten everything that had just happened, Isaac looked at James with his radiant, kind eyes, smiled, and said, "That would be wonderful, and I would be in your debt. Thank you, James!"

Surprised but happy, James stood and helped Isaac up. "Not at all! The pleasure is all mine."

"Oh, and that reminds me," Jenna butted in. "Do you have a needle, by chance, James?" she questioned, motioning to her dress. "Seeing as how you don't care for my 'fashion.'"

James burst out laughing. "I do. But do you blame me for asking? I mean, really, that's such a strange dress you have on!"

"If you think I'd purchase a dress like this," Jenna argued, "much less wear it, then you really do have water for brains, James."

James tilted his head in confusion and looked at Isaac.

"Trust me," Isaac said, "her wounds were far worse than mine before I healed them. That's why her dress looks the way it does."

"What?" James roared, startling some birds in the nearby trees. "Healed her? You can heal?"

"Yes," Jenna responded before Isaac could. "But he doesn't like to heal himself. And it has to be under unique circumstances."

"Like what?" demanded James, utterly intrigued.

"Well," Jenna shrugged, "that is a conversation for the way back to your cottage. Along with many more, I'm sure."

"First the eyes," James counted on his fingers. "Then the barrier, and now healing... is there anything else you can do, Isaac?" he questioned in awe.

Shy and embarrassed, Isaac waved his hands in rejection. "You give me too much credit. I am simply the one who opens the vault, not the one who owns the stores."

"What?" James asked in confusion. "I don't understand. I've never even heard or read about any Majestician like you! Never!" he exclaimed.

"That's because there has never been anyone like Isaac," Jenna said simply but truthfully. "Now, are you going to gawk at my beloved friend, or are you going to take us back to your cottage?"

James continued to shake his head, unsure what to say.

"Besides…" Isaac smiled as he placed his hand upon James's shoulder, "I've never met a water Majestician. I am far more interested in hearing all about your unique abilities!"

Hook, bait… and done.

"Well, now…" James said, rubbing the back of his head, shy. "I'm not that special, buuut…"

And thus, James went on to tell Isaac and Jenna all about his powers as a water Majestician as they returned to his cabin.

James had to jiggle the creaking door a number of times before it finally opened.

"Fascinating…" Isaac uttered as he stepped in, followed by Jenna, who said nothing.

Somehow, the cottage seemed much bigger on the inside. The kitchen table was lined with countless beakers, flasks, and all sorts of rotating glass tubes with vials, all housing some sort of odd-colored liquids, and each liquid doing something different. Some were entirely still, some were bubbling, and others were twisting and moving as if alive.

Although not fancy, the bed in the corner was neatly made, and the pillows were lightly fluffed. The few pieces of furniture each had their special place, and all was very organized (except for the desk next to the kitchen table that had accidentally overflowed with scribbled notes, texts, and tomes).

Although bizarre, the smell was more than pleasant. Jenna took particular notice of the large black cauldron with a lid on it, placed in the fireplace with a roaring fire beneath it.

"You wouldn't by chance..." Jenna mumbled, spellbound as she took in a deep breath. "...be cooking anything in that pot... would you?"

James walked over to the fireplace, lifted the large iron lid, and picked up a wooden spoon to stir the concoction inside.

"Sure am!" he responded excitedly. "Have either of you ever had roasted acorn squash soup?"

Isaac stared at Jenna intently. "We've had roasted pumpkin soup but not acorn squash."

"Well then," James said as he continued stirring and adding seasoning, "you'll be in for a treat! I personally find the flavor profile to be more dense than pumpkin."

Bold and a little nosy, Jenna walked over to his desk and began inspecting the notes while Isaac politely stood in the entryway, hands gently clasped together.

"Surely there couldn't be two more opposite people," James smirked as he turned around, noticing the two on either side of the room, "in all of Vaerün."

Isaac smiled, and Jenna simply ignored him.

"Isaac, please take a seat!" James exclaimed as he pulled out an old cushioned chair. "You're making me nervous!"

"My apologies," Isaac responded as he graciously sat. "Thank you very much!"

"Remind me again what all this is about?" Jenna questioned as she continued flipping through James's notes.

"Weren't you paying attention to anything I was saying on the way here?" James asked, agitated.

"Not really," Jenna answered honestly. "It all sounded pretty boring. You lost me at Wöntylnas."

James leaned in closely to Isaac and whispered in his ear, "Is she always like this?"

Isaac gently cupped his hand to James's ear and whispered back, "Don't worry. She'll warm up to you. It just takes time."

"I'll explain over dinner," said James. "Jenna!" he suddenly blurted out, causing her to jump.

"For all that is good," Jenna shouted, startled. "What, James?"

Isaac couldn't help but smile as James pointed to a polished wooden cabinet in the corner of the room.

"Would you please grab three bowls and some spoons out of that cabinet?" he asked. "While I tend to Isaac's wounds?"

Jenna's agitation melted as she suddenly felt warmth and compassion—entirely caught off guard by the request.

"Y-yes, of course," she quickly said. "Would you like me to fill each bowl?"

"That'd be great!" James said with a smile. "It'll only take me a few minutes to clean up Isaac, and that'll give enough time for the soup to cool."

"Stay seated, Isaac, and please don't move," said James with ushered hands as he took an empty bowl off the cramped table and walked outside.

Isaac found his head nodding off as he fought to stay awake. The sound of the gently falling rain pitter-pattering outside was hard enough, but with the heavenly smell of James's fresh soup and the additional sound of it sloshing into bowls by Jenna, it brought too much comfort and the feeling of home.

"O-kay!" James said loudly as he walked back in, startling poor Isaac.

"Really?" Jenna questioned sarcastically, motioning to James's filled bowl of water with her dripping spoon. "Just rainwater? Yeah. Wow. Gonna do a whole lot with that!" she exclaimed as she turned back around to resume her task.

"Not to insult your intelligence," James returned, "but do you have any idea the nutritional and mineral concentrations contained in rainwater?"

"Well—" Jenna tried to interject.

"And perhaps you aren't aware," James continued, "but the Aerbön woods is the richest forest in all of Vaerün."

"That makes sense." Isaac nodded. "The Aerbön woods run parallel with the Kier Mountains and so—"

James interrupted in excitement. "Exactly! The Kier Mountains are dense with minerals. Between the precipitation and the descending flow of water from the ice caps, they directly feed this area, which is now the Aerbön woods."

Jenna slowly turned around with two bowls in hand and one further up her arm. The look on her face extended the sentiment of, *Really? Just really?*

"What?" said James shyly, realizing she was glaring at the kitchen table, full of lab equipment.

"Oh! How embarrassing—" He cut off as he set the splashing bowl of water on the floor. "So sorry, Jenna, this'll only take a sec."

Both Isaac and Jenna watched in fascination as James moved his hands through the air. The glass lab equipment on the table vibrated and, as if picked up by invisible hands, levitated through the air and settled into an empty space on the floor next to it.

"How'd you do that?" Jenna asked, slowly setting the bowls down on the now-available kitchen table.

"That was easy," he confidently replied. "I simply commanded the liquid in the equipment to move it. And now, back to Isaac…" he muttered, kneeling down to pick up the bowl.

There was a debate that went back and forth for some time as to whether Jenna should leave the room while Isaac took off his upper wardrobe to give James easier access to address his wounds. But the men finally lost when Jenna "logically" refused to stand out in the rain (although James's internal guess was that she just wanted to see Isaac shirtless).

Despite Isaac's flushed cheeks, James continued to address his wounds.

"Well, don't just stand there!" James shouted to Jenna, who was staring intently at Isaac. "Take his cloak and garment and wash them in the tub right there!"

"Um. There's no water in it?" Jenna questioned sarcastically, lifting the empty wooden tub at the foot of the bed.

James sighed, stood up again, walked over to her, and took the washtub. He dropped it near the entryway and flung the door open. With a repeated motion of his hands, a twisting wave of fresh rainwater formed and slammed into the tub, knocking it backward and splashing water all over the wooden floor of the cottage.

"Hey!" Jenna shouted, lifting her dress and doing a slight dance to avoid getting wet.

With a roll of his hands, the water sprang to life and leaped back outside as he closed the door.

"There!" he said shortly, motioning to the full tub as he sat back down to tend to Isaac's wounds.

What more could she say? Isaac bit his lower lip to keep from laughing. Jenna merely grunted, slung his bloodstained white cloak and upper garments into the tub, and began scrubbing them, the water immediately turning red.

"I still can't believe you got cracked in the head by a rafter beam," said James, shaking his head as he controlled a small amount of rolling water that continued to flow across Isaac's gashed head.

"It was worth it," Isaac said honestly.

Jenna said nothing.

"And you did it to save her?" James questioned with a slight hint of sarcasm, motioning over his shoulder to Jenna.

"Oh, don't worry," she quickly responded. "I can guarantee you that he'll save your sorry hide many times from this time forward."

"And what makes you so certain that I'm going with you in the first place?" James retorted, looking over his shoulder at her. "All because of a letter you got from a certain Garon Erbrecht?"

"It does make sense," Isaac answered before Jenna could. "You are from the kingdom of Wöntylnas."

"Not only that," Jenna interjected, "but you said that your uncle is Professor Vandergaus himself! And Nann told us to find him!"

Isaac looked at Jenna curiously. "Are you sure Nann didn't know James was out here in the forest? And that she just wanted us to meet up with him?"

James raised an eyebrow. "I sure hope not. I've had enough stalkers in my day."

"Are you about done yet?" Jenna asked a little rudely, wringing out Isaac's freshly washed cloak and upper garments, quickly drying them with a heated wave of her Majesty.

"The soup is going to get cold," she finished.

"Did you ask Isaac the same thing when he was healing you?" James demanded.

"Of course not!" Jenna answered, appalled. "We didn't have any soup in the middle of the forest at that time!"

James stared blankly at Isaac, who gave a scrunched-up smile that said, *Yeah, that's Jenna.*

Not desiring to wait any longer, Jenna sat down at the table and began enjoying her hot soup as she watched James tend to Isaac's wounds.

After about twenty minutes of repeated washing and cleaning, Isaac looked revived from the clean and nourishing rainwater treatment of James's Water Majesty.

"That should do it!" James piped up as he opened the door and tossed the red water outside.

"Thank you so much, James!" Isaac exclaimed as he ran across the floor, quickly dressed, and latched his cloak around his neck.

With his back turned, Isaac didn't see Jenna as she gave a silent, *damn it!* look (although James, who had just reentered, was now smiling widely).

You know those conversations with friends or family that are so good you end up sitting at the table for hours, going back for seconds, thirds, and fourths on food? That was exactly what happened between Isaac, Jenna, and James as they talked well into the night.

"I don't know why," James said, holding his head, "but learning that you're a princess just makes it so much worse."

"Don't give it another thought," Jenna said, folding her arms and leaning back. "From what I hear, it sounds like I don't have much of a kingdom to return to anyway."

"I don't believe that," Isaac said, leaning forward. "Mr. Tendúr told you that some people remain in Fürnas and that there are others scattered across Vaerün. You should summon them back to their home!"

"Not right now," Jenna said, playing with her soup spoon. "Besides, we need to go to Wöntylnas, per my letter from Garon and Nann's request to find Professor Vandergaus."

"What's wrong, James?" Isaac asked, always aware of anyone's suffering.

"Oh… Sorry," James mumbled quietly.

Perhaps for the first time since meeting him, Jenna asked compassionately, "Is it because of Wöntylnas? I'm sorry, I don't mean to keep talking about it—"

"No, no," James quickly replied. "I mean, yes, it is, but it's not your fault. I understand that you need to go there."

"I still can't believe it," Isaac said, massaging the back of his head. "Why on Vaerün is the kingdom of Wöntylnas intent on poisoning itself?"

"Easy," James responded. "You poison the food, you poison the people. You poison the man-made medicine they purchase, and you repeat the vicious cycle."

"But for what?" Jenna asked. "Why poison the people just to give them medicine that'll further kill them?"

"Wöntylnas is rich," James explained. "Most of the inhabitants are extremely wealthy. However, the aristocracy desires even more wealth."

Isaac tilted his head as James continued. "It's a little something I like to call *Secret Combinations*. As you know, Wöntylnas is founded on its vast knowledge and intelligence, only rivaled by Grünas. And even they have secluded themselves some thirty years ago."

"Right?" Jenna said.

"Well, there are many scientists in Wöntylnas… and many lawyers. And many doctors, musicians, theologians—the list goes on and on and on."

"So?" Isaac added.

"So… the scientists are paid to make their faulty 'medicine.' The doctors and theologians make money when they push it on the people. You keep feeding the people the poisoned food, and they continue taking a medicine they think will help them."

Isaac and Jenna stared intently at James, intrigued by what he was saying.

"I get it," Jenna said. "It's a cycle of money that just continues circulating."

"That's correct," James nodded.

"But hold on," Isaac interjected. "If you keep doing that, won't the people run out of money? Or worse, die?"

"Of course!" James exclaimed.

"But that's awful! And evil!" Isaac spat, infuriated.

"Yes! It is!" James said in a *duh* manner. "And that's why I tried helping them."

"I understand…" Jenna muttered. "That's why everyone ridiculed you, forcing you to move all the way out here into the middle of the Aerbön woods."

"There's more to it than that," James said. "Like I said earlier, both the water and especially the rainwater possess unique healing attributes, qualities, and properties." He pointed down to his vast number of flasks, vials, and test tubes. "The aristocracy of Wöntylnas has concocted a powerful poison—both in the food, but most prominently in the medicine."

"Hah!" Isaac blurted unintentionally, hearing the word "medicine" used in such a terrible way.

James continued, pointing to his equipment. "I moved out here for two reasons. One, Wöntylnas hates me. They think I'm some sort of freak with my Majesty, and they don't believe in my work or research in my attempt to heal them."

"Can't say I blame them." Jenna shrugged. "I mean, really, you're twenty now, and you left Wöntylnas at ten? Who wants to listen to a conceited brat with powers try to tell them how to live and heal their crappy lives?"

"Jenna!" Isaac blurted out.

"It's true." James nodded. "But I'm still trying."

Isaac nodded and gestured with his hand. "Anyway. You were saying?"

"And two," James continued, "to access the healing power in the waters of this forest. With my Majesty, I figured it wouldn't be too hard to concoct a remedy."

Both Isaac and Jenna leaned forward eagerly. "And… did you do so?" Jenna asked.

"Originally, it was actually rather easy!" James beamed. "The body is made from the earth. And therefore, the earth should be able to heal it, right?"

"Of course," Isaac and Jenna agreed logically.

"But what happens..." James said darkly, "when you add something so dark, and so evil, no matter how small the concentration... to said poison?"

"Okay. You lost me," Jenna said with a blank expression, sitting back again.

"No, no, hold on," James continued. "I'm telling you that the contents of the original poison are very easy to neutralize and heal! It's easy!"

"That's fantastic! So you have the remedy?" Isaac asked excitedly. "Then let's go give it to them!"

James wagged his finger. "No. You misunderstand. I'm trying to say that something else has been added to this poison. Something that even I cannot undo with all my knowledge, intelligence, and even Majesty."

Jenna nervously asked, "What on Vaerün could possibly be added to a poison to make it so deadly and dangerous?"

James stood up from the table, walked over and picked up a glass vial, and returned, holding it up. A strange, black, moving, tar-like goo twisted inside the vial, as if alive.

"This," James said fiercely.

Isaac and Jenna squinted and leaned forward in unison to inspect the vial, refusing to touch it.

"What is that?" Jenna demanded.

"I don't know," James said, shaking his head. "But it is something that cannot be destroyed, undone, or cured."

"It looks so much like Kreaux blood!" Isaac exclaimed with a tilted expression.

"That was my first guess!" James returned. "But when have you ever seen Kreaux blood move all on its own like this?"

Suddenly, Jenna bolted up from the table as the memory of the black-robed man filled her mind—the vision of him conjuring a black sword from the black, moving matter of (what none of them knew as) Dark Majesty.

"Wait a sec," she blurted out. "That looks just like the stuff that robed guy commanded when he conjured a sword that day in Aerlund!"

Isaac looked at James. "Is there really no information regarding this substance? Even in all of Wöntylnas?"

James shook his head. "Nothing. Even while I was there, no data could be found on it. But I have surmised that whatever it is, it links directly to the Kreaux. Perhaps even worse."

"Worse?" Jenna demanded. "What could possibly be worse than the Kreaux?"

Boom. Boom. Boom. Boom, echoed the heart-wrenching pulsation all around them.

The cottage rocked with each quake as the lab equipment clacked and clattered along the wooden floor from the vibrations, each pulse sending a dreadful feeling up the spines of the three Majesticians.

"What is that?" James muttered, placing a hand over his rapidly beating heart. "Is it a Praetor?"

"Do you even know what a Praetor is?" Jenna yelled.

"Jenna," Isaac said calmly, "you spoke of a pulsation similar to a Praetor's when that robed man attacked you. Is this it?"

"But that's impossible," Jenna quickly replied. "How could he find us all the way out here?"

Reeeeeeee! screeched the ear-penetrating voices of the Kreaux all around the cabin as the three Majesticians stood.

Jenna quickly opened the door, only to slam it shut again as she saw a flood of Kreaux storming around the cottage outside.

"Afraid to fight?" James asked cynically, unsheathing his two silver daggers.

"Um," Jenna said, "can't really be afraid to fight when there's nowhere to fight."

The three of them had to shield their eyes as splinters flew through the air, the Kreaux stabbing and hacking their way in.

The intensely repeating sound of *boom, boom, boom, boom!* grew faster until it sounded as if it were right outside.

"What is that sound?" James yelled as they all listened to the whistling noise growing louder.

Jenna's eyes burst open as she recognized the all-too-familiar sound of an oncoming fireball. "Everyone, get dow—" she shouted.

Boooooom! roared the exploded walls and debris all around as splinters, glass, and rubble stormed around them.

Voom, voom, voom, voom, voom! rippled the heavenly light of Isaac's barrier as the dust settled, revealing the three unharmed Majesticians inside.

"Hoooolllyyy shüza," James said, looking around inside the barrier in awe.

"Told ya," Jenna said nonchalantly, clapping James on the shoulder. "And we haven't even left your cottage yet!"

Isaac winced and recoiled as the Kreaux hacked and jabbed at the barrier with their fierce claws. Arrows exploded in splinters and flying metal shards as they fired upon the barrier.

"That's enough, Jahrgis!" hissed the voice of the conductor upon the air. "I'll take care of this."

As if an invisible force had blown the Kreaux back, they flew through the air as the conductor advanced toward the barrier, left hand conducting and right hand holding another fireball.

"Isaac!" Jenna screamed, holding onto him. "That's him! That's the man I was talking about!"

"Is that the same substance as…?" James mumbled, focusing intently on the black, dripping matter constantly oozing from the conductor's hood.

Boom. Boom! Boom, boom! sounded the incinerating fireballs as they crashed into the barrier, Isaac holding steadfast with his extended, light-glowing hands.

His face looked nothing short of heroic as his furious glare focused entirely upon the conductor through the rippling waves of light.

The yellow, white, and blue light of his irises danced furiously as he sustained the protective dome.

"Isaac… yes, Isaac!" hissed the voice of the robed man as he held up both hands, unleashing an unceasing inferno of flames upon the barrier. "How nice to see you awake this time!"

"What do we do?" Jenna quietly demanded of James. "How do we help him?"

James looked around the battered remains of his cottage, when suddenly his vision focused upon a rug.

"You're not going to like it, but…" he whispered, "there's a trap-door beneath that rug that leads to an underground tunnel."

"Where does it lead?" Jenna asked quickly.

"West. That's all I know."

"West? That's it?" she asked sharply. "We don't even get a, 'What it was built for,' or 'How long said underground tunnel is'?"

"It's either that," James barked back, "or we stay here and fight this demonic Kreaux and his awful army!"

Isaac's eyes began to wince shut as sweat dripped down his face.

"What's the matter, Isaac?" hissed the conductor. "Jenna and James? Don't want to fight?"

James and Jenna swallowed at hearing the conductor say their names. How did he know?

Suddenly, the conductor jumped back, holding out his hand as the dark sword formed in his grip once again.

Hack, hack, slaaash! Hack, hack, hack, hack! rang the sound of "metal" and Majesty as they collided, sparks of Isaac's barrier flying through the air.

Fffsshhhawwwrrrrggghh! exploded the flames from the conductor's opposing hand as he blasted and hacked at the barrier without abandon.

Fresh blood ran down Isaac's face as the gash on his head reopened from the sustained siege. His raised hands and body began to shake and tremble as he received each and every blow, refusing to drop the barrier.

Hold on, James thought as he observed the conductor. Kreaux can't use Majesty… And the last fire Majestician was…

"Okay, James!" Jenna exclaimed suddenly. "I can't take it! I can't watch Isaac suffer like this! We'll take your tunnel!"

"I've got it!" James shouted at the top of his lungs. "King Coltin Fürnas!"

Suddenly, the conductor immediately stopped firing and hacking at Isaac's barrier, taking a momentary step back.

"Now, James!" Jenna screamed.

The wrecked table and debris flew back as James forcibly kicked it, revealing a metallic trapdoor. He knelt and whispered an incantation.

"Hurry up, James!" Jenna screeched as the conductor held up his hands, charging a large fireball.

With the last words said, the metal door flung open.

"Come on, Isaac," Jenna yelled, gripping his arm and pulling him toward the trapdoor. "Let's go!"

She ignited a fireball for light in her hand as she quickly descended the metal bars leading into the black abyssal hole.

"After you, Isaac!" James yelled.

"No!" retorted Isaac. "I need to protect you! If I go before you, you'll—"

"Be just fine!" he quickly responded. "Now go!"

And with that, James shoved Isaac down.

James's heart pounded like crazy as he slammed his hands forward, a huge wave of water just meeting the intense fireball coming his way.

"Jahrgis! Fire!" screeched the conductor.

Arrows hissed and whistled past James as he quickly took one last look at the wreckage of his cottage and descended the trapdoor.

Slam! rang the metal door as James pulled it down and waved his hand back and forth, sealing it with another incantation.

CHAPTER 12

A Prison Like No Other

The light of Jenna's fireball cast the only glow from below as she continued to descend the long metal bars of the ladder, which seemed to extend endlessly downward.

"Ugh!" she shouted up. "James, are you drooling up there? It's getting on my hair!"

Isaac blinked as he looked at the dimly lit scene of his hands upon the bars. Some black substance was dripping on them. It was warm and sticky.

Whoosh! rippled the sound of his Majesty as he raised his glowing palm to reveal the blood dripping down his hands and arms.

"James?" said Isaac in a cracking voice. "Are you okay?" He looked up to see an arrow piercing straight through James's right shoulder, blood steadily dripping down.

"Nooooo!" hissed and screeched the horrifying voice of the conductor from above. "I will get you, Isaac Erbrecht!"

"Wait," said Jenna, suddenly stopping dead on the metal bars. "Wait, wait, wait… Did he just say—"

Neither Isaac nor James said anything.

With laughter that bordered on the insane, Jenna continued in shock, "That's just not possible, right? He did just say *Erbrecht*, right?"

Again, neither of them spoke a word.

"Right!" demanded Jenna. "Why aren't you two saying anything? And damn it, what is dripping on me?"

"James is bleeding, Jenna," said Isaac matter-of-factly. "He was struck by an arrow—in his right shoulder."

Jenna brought her flame closer to her forearms and inspected the red blood that had spilled upon her elbow-length gloves.

"Oh…" she muttered, embarrassed. "Isaac, can you—"

"I know," He responded calmly, while assessing James' wounds. "But I need sunlight in order to heal him."

"Well then, let's hurry it up!" exclaimed Jenna, hastening down the ladder.

Bar after bar, they climbed down for what seemed like over ten minutes until finally, Jenna called out, "Sorry, James, not trying to be that kind of hoo-ha, but how far does this ladder go? I thought tunnels were supposed to extend horizontally, not vertically!"

With labored breaths, James shakily replied, "I don't know. Never been down here."

"Maybe we should—" Isaac started.

"To hell with this," said Jenna, exasperated, as she thrust a fireball down the passage.

For about fifty feet, it flew downward until it finally exploded at the bottom.

"Really?" James shouted through bated breath. "What if there's something flammable down there?"

"Doubt it," she responded, kicking her feet out and gripping the bars to slide the rest of the way down.

"Oi, is she something else!" he said in a mix of agitation and amazement.

"Trust me." Isaac laughed. "She wears on you."

Naturally, Jenna was already at the bottom and walking around by the time Isaac had helped James descend the last few bars. Isaac raised his hand, his Majesty casting more light to reveal the room they were in.

A rusted metal desk lay overturned on its side, some of its legs scattered around the room from Jenna's fireball. Nearby, charred book covers mixed with moldy, rotten ones.

Two out of the four massive stone walls held rows upon rows of rusted keys, easily numbering in the thousands.

"Is any of it legible?" Isaac asked as Jenna flipped through a massive mold-covered book, pausing on some of the more preserved center pages.

Jenna squinted in confusion and disgust as she examined the pages.

"Yes, but…" she quietly responded.

"But what?" asked James, huffing and gripping his shoulder.

"It's just… names," she said, flipping another page. "Just rows and rows of names."

"You said you don't know what this place is, right, James?" asked Isaac as he gently inspected the arrow lodged through James's shoulder.

"I honestly don't," he responded sincerely. "All I know is that my uncle told me to never come down here, except in an absolute emergency."

Isaac and Jenna stared at him.

"Well," Jenna said, "I'd consider having your cottage blown apart, being shot through the shoulder, and saving your friends from hell as an *emergency*!"

"Oh no!" Isaac suddenly exclaimed, his voice echoing around them. "Your cottage! And equipment, and research!"

"Don't worry about that," James quickly responded, slightly shaking his head. "I've got it all up here," he said, pointing to his head with a trembling hand.

"We need to get out of here," Isaac said as he walked to the northern part of the room and opened the only door.

Both Jenna and James winced at the squealing sound of the metal door as Isaac forced it open, a freezing blast of wind rushing into the room.

"I've heard Kreaux that sound more pleasant than that," James said honestly.

"And said!" agreed Jenna.

The three Majesticians squinted as they stepped through the door, peering into the darkness beyond.

"I wouldn't say so much a tunnel," Jenna said sarcastically, "as it is a corridor."

"A very, very, very *loooong* corridor," James agreed as they observed the burning light of Jenna's fireball, which she cast down the corridor, where it disappeared into the darkness.

"Well, at least there's only one way to go!" Isaac tried to say optimistically.

Once through the door, it didn't take long to notice a solid wall to their right and in front of them. The only opening was the corridor to their left, running west.

After about ten feet, they began to take notice of the numerous metal doors with cutout boxes at the top, lined with metal bars, accompanying the northern and southern walls to their left and right.

"I'll give ten gold to whoever looks in one of those doors," said James, trying to offer comic relief as they all looked dead ahead and kept walking.

"Not on your life," said Jenna boldly.

With one arm around James, Isaac held up his other hand to give more light. The stone walls had an almost rainbow sheen from years of moisture running down them. Strangely, all the doors they passed were not rusted, though their design suggested they were quite old.

Empty black lanterns lined the high ceiling, adding to the foreboding atmosphere.

"Jenna," said Isaac as he suddenly stopped, "I need your help."

"What is it?" she asked, turning around.

For a moment, she almost wished she hadn't. James's eyes were rolling back in his head, his skin was extremely pale, and his face was dripping sweat.

"Was that arrow poisoned?" she asked as she quickly knelt before the two.

Isaac placed a hand on James's forehead and shook his head. "No. But he's losing too much blood. Until we can get outside, I need you to brand the wound."

Jenna started to panic, repeatedly shaking her head. "I can't, Isaac! No!"

Despite her sarcasm and constant snarkiness, Jenna hated hurting people, even for their own good. Perhaps it was because of the incident years ago when she first discovered her Majesty and accidentally set one of the servants on fire.

"Yes, you can," responded Isaac faithfully. "Don't worry. I'll heal him as soon as we get out! But if you don't, he could die, Jenna!"

"Fine," she said through gritted teeth, looking away with closed eyes. "But you have to take care of the arrow first!"

Isaac touched the air with his finger. A single stream of light extended out as he quickly came down and sliced cleanly through the arrowhead. With a slight grimace and Jenna looking away, he quickly grabbed the tail end of the arrow and pulled it out of James.

Naturally, James screamed in pain, his voice booming and echoing down the abyssal corridor.

"All right, Jenna…" said Isaac as he stepped back, "it's your turn."

With her lips sucked in and eyes scrunched tight, Jenna gently knelt in front of James, observing the dark red circular wound in his shoulder. She began to cry as she placed a hand on James's knee.

"What if the shock kills him?" she suddenly said. "I could never live with myself! Why can't you just heal him?" she pleaded to Isaac.

He frowned and responded, "I'd love nothing more. But to instantly heal the flesh of man requires a power far beyond my own. I need heaven's light in order for that."

"Dang it, Jenna," said James through gritted teeth. "Just do it! I'll live! Come on. Gotta help you two to Wöntylnas!"

She smiled gratefully as she wiped away the tears. "Besides," James continued, "who'll pick on you other than me? Definitely not Isaac."

"Very well…" she said.

With that, she slowly removed the glove from her right hand. The indentations in her palm began to glow a furious red as she held her hand before his wound. Through gritted teeth, she pressed her palm against his shoulder.

The hissing sound of burning flesh echoed in addition to James's atrocious screams as she sealed both sides of the wound.

Deciding a few moments of rest would do him good, they struck up a conversation.

"Soo…" Jenna said awkwardly, "neither of you answered my question."

James and Isaac looked at each other.

"What question?" they asked in unison.

"The conductor." She responded, "Don't play me for a fool. He said Isaac's last name was Erbrecht. Didn't he?"

Isaac looked at the ground, but James answered, "I don't know much about this, Lucy, but doesn't it make sense?"

Jenna stared at him with a side-glance and squinted eyes.

"You said that this Garon Erbrecht you know is the commander in chief over Wölnas, right?"

She nodded.

"Look at his key!" James exclaimed as he reached out and held up the dangling key around Isaac's neck. "Surely you noticed that this gem and insignia belong to Wölnas?"

"I get that!" retorted Jenna, a little rudely. "But that doesn't explain much! He was delivered to me *from heaven*!" she said rhythmically.

"Right. As a baby. Makes *so* much sense…" James sighed. "Trust me, it is a fascinating story. But I have a question that should solve this right now."

Isaac and Jenna looked at him in anticipation as James asked her, "Does he look like them?"

"What?" asked Jenna, almost pretending she didn't hear.

"Does. He. LOOK. Like. Them?" asked James again, agitated this time. "This… Garon and Lucy? You said he was your trainer, and she was your adviser. They both moved to Wölnas to be wed, waiting for him to finish his contract. Is it not possible during that time that just maybe they had a son?"

Jenna glared at him. *How rude for him to lecture her on her two favorite people!*

"Hmph." She grunted.

"Forget for a moment the circumstances on which he was given to you," said James, waving his hand dismissively. "Let's pretend you're meeting Isaac for the first time, and he's just been introduced by his parents, Garon and Lucy. Does. He. Look. Like. Them?"

Jenna sighed as she bravely looked up and stared into Isaac's kind, gentle, yet bold and heroic face. She shuffled on her knees and took his chin into her hand. With narrowed eyes, she examined him, moving his face this way and that.

He did have Lucy's chin. And those strong features of his jaw and cheekbones definitely belonged to Garon. The messy hair screamed Garon, but the rippling, shimmering blond color roared Lucy. That nose was Lucy's for sure. But those long eyebrows were Garon's.

His strong eye structure hinted at Garon's as well. But the sadness reflected in them spoke of his mother. And although his eye color was dominantly yellow, the newly added small streams of blue struck her soul with the same feeling she received when she looked into Lucy's eyes.

Jenna brought both her hands over her mouth as she began to cry. Without a doubt, the very son of Garon and Lucy, Isaac Erbrecht, knelt before her!

She began to laugh through her tears as she threw her arms around him and sobbed. "Isaac! You really are Isaac Erbrecht! How did I never notice before? You look just like them!"

James sighed as he leaned back against the wall, saying, "Sometimes I'm just too smart for my own good."

A little shy and unsure of what to say, Isaac embraced Jenna back and muttered, "Isaac? Isaac Erbrecht."

"But wait," Jenna said suddenly, pulling back, "that doesn't make sense. Where are Garon and Lucy then? And that angel that delivered you to me—"

"Annnnd that's where we're going to stop for now," said James, struggling a little to push himself up.

Jenna looked at him with a mix of confusion, irritation, and curiosity.

"Sometimes it's best not to ask questions when we don't have all the data we need to achieve the correct answers," he said sincerely.

"I agree with James, Jenna," Isaac said, smiling at her. "If I really am their son—"

"Oh, trust me, you are." Jenna nearly gawked. "You look just like them. I'm only ashamed I didn't notice sooner."

"We'll get the answers someday, I'm sure!" he finished. "But for now, we need to get out of here."

"Yes," she said as she stood up. "This place is really starting to wear on me… It's, well, it's…" She trailed off.

"Evil," said Isaac and James in unison.

"I don't know what this place is," Isaac furthered, "but whatever it is, something terrible happened here. The negative energy is nearly unbearable."

Jenna swallowed as she continued walking forward, followed by Isaac and James.

After over an hour of traveling, James began to shake.

"Are you okay?" Isaac kindly asked as he put his arm around James again.

"I sealed his wounds," interjected Jenna. "Are you sure that arrow wasn't poisoned?"

"It's n-n-not th-that," said James shakily. "S-so cold."

Isaac smiled and motioned to swap with Jenna. "This is your area of expertise, Jenn. Can you warm him up?"

"Can I warm him up… please!" she mocked as she threw an arm around James. The warm red glow that surrounded her began to flow around James as he slowly stopped shaking.

"Th-thank… thank you," he gratefully said.

Suddenly, a freezing cold blast of air whooshed past them, accompanied by the sounds of screams and moans, instantly sending chills up their spines.

"Umm," said Isaac as he raised his hands, preparing for combat.

James began to profusely shake again, somehow affected far worse than Isaac and Jenna.

"We need to get out of here," Jenna said, trying not to panic. "Something's really wrong."

"Not going to get out… not going to get out," repeated James, shaking his head repeatedly.

"I'm sorry?" asked Isaac as he turned to James.

"Not gonna get out. Not gonna get out. Not gonna get out… can't get out…" he continued repeating.

Jenna slapped James hard, snapping him out of it.

"Really?" she asked. "As if this place isn't bad enough, and here you are making it ten times worse!"

"S-sorry," James stammered, still shaking a little.

Jenna sighed as she gripped him tighter and unleashed another wave of warmth.

"Saaay, I have a question for you, now that I think about it!" she exclaimed.

"Wh-what is it?" he asked as he warmed up, all of them continuing down the corridor.

"That conductor guy… thingy… thing… thing," said Jenna, unsure of what to call him. "I could've sworn I heard you call him Coltin Fürnas. That was the name of the king of Fürnas some thousand years ago."

"R-right." James shook. "It just m-made sense to me."

"How do you figure?" she asked.

"Well," he continued, "K-king Fürnas was the l-last fire Majestician b-before you, known to r-record."

Isaac turned around and listened as he walked backward.

"You really think the conductor is King Coltin Fürnas?" he asked quizzically. "Turned into a Kreaux for all these years?"

"A-at first it was j-just c-c-conjecture," stammered James. "But I th-think it makes sense. Wh-when we get to Wö-Wö-Wöntylnas, I'll show you my n-notes."

"Sorry, James," said Jenna plainly. "Still doesn't make a lick of sense to me."

"No, he may be onto something," said Isaac as he tapped his chin. "When he called out his name, the conductor stopped attacking my barrier for a moment. It may really be him!"

"Well, if it is," mumbled Jenna, "it'd make sense why he hates me so much."

"James?" cried Isaac as he watched James nearly crumble to the floor from a shaking fit.

The sound of *Ha... ha... ha... ha!* chased down the corridor as the black lanterns overhead burst to life with blue fire.

Jenna's heart fell as she peered down the corridor. There, standing amid the darkness, was the robed conductor, his black robe so dark and so evil that it made the surrounding darkness pale in comparison.

"It's him!" she screamed, pointing down the hall, immediately catching Isaac's attention.

Isaac whipped around as his hands exploded with rays of light that shot down the corridor like twisting rockets.

The conductor smashed the streams of light out of the way as he held up his own hands.

Dark blue jets of water, looking as though they were mixed with black tar, streamed through the air and into the openings of the doors all around them.

"What is he doing?" yelled Jenna as she focused on the dark Water Majesty.

"I don't get it," muttered Isaac as he held his hands up. "It's not possible for anyone to wield more than one element—Kreaux or not."

"I hope my prisoners keep you in good company!" hissed the conductor's different, unfamiliar voice as he manipulated the black streams of water.

The sounds of screams, gargling, and drowning began to surround them, echoing through the barred windows of the prison doors.

"Ha!" shouted Isaac and Jenna simultaneously as they fired light and fire down the hall.

Ha ha ha ha... echoed the conductor's voice as he disappeared just in time before the Majesty hit him.

The chaotic screams and sounds were unbearable. *To us, it probably sounded like a modern-day Titanic scene, when the ship had just sunk and everyone was drowning and screaming.*

Jenna's eyes shattered open as white, dripping wet, dead hands gripped the metal bars of the doors. She could only scream as faces—young and old, male and female—pressed against the bars next to their hands. Their eyes were completely white. Their skin was whiter than snow yet paler than… well, who knows what. Their hair looked grim and plastered down from water, and their entire appearance was waterlogged.

"They were…" mumbled Isaac as he stood in the center of the hallway, trying to avoid the hands reaching out to grab him.

"Drowned," said James creepily as he was slammed against one of the doors by multiple hands.

"Let him go!" hollered Jenna as she tried to pull him off. She nearly vomited when, instinctively, she gripped the hands that were pulling him. They felt slimy and colder than any cold she'd ever experienced. One might have felt more comfortable touching a bare, dead body than this.

"To hell with this," she said as she unsheathed her rapier and sliced away at the dead hands and arms, the dark blue and tar-like water flowing out of them.

"What in Vaerün?" Isaac mumbled as he stared.

"James," shouted Jenna, slapping him, "snap out of it!"

"Not gonna get out. Not gonna get out. Not gonna get out. Can't get out…" he mumbled repeatedly.

"So heaven help me," she said, repeatedly slapping him. "Snap. **Out. Of. It.**"

"Jenna?" questioned Isaac politely. "We have <u>another</u> problem."

What a grim sight. With the dim blue light from the hanging lanterns, the pale-white, damp skin of the innumerable hands and arms of the dead twisted, twitched, and turned through the small spaces of the bars, as far as the eye could see in both directions.

The screaming, hollering, wailing, and drowning sounds were unbearable, though Isaac hardly ever showed signs of distress. But James was suffering the worst.

Suddenly, water began to splash onto the stone floor beneath their feet as the faces of the dead pressed against the bars, opened their mouths, and released an unceasing flow of water. And oh, how they twitched and squirmed as they did so! Some of their eyes opened so wide that the black veins within might burst at any moment. But perhaps even more disturbing were the ones with closed eyelids, appearing even more haunting.

Blast, boom, boom, fssshhhrawwwrggh, roared fireballs and flaming waves of fire as Jenna shot at the dead, to some avail. With each impact, they exploded into the same dark, tar-like water.

"Isaac! Help me!" hollered Jenna as she fired again and again, still holding up James with her other arm.

Isaac's eyes danced furiously as he took in the scene around him. The water was now past their knees and filling even faster. Whatever panic was setting in, it sure didn't show.

"It's not going to work," Isaac called out.

"What?" screamed Jenna, alternating her attacks and looking at him. "So we're just supposed to drown down here?"

"Not gonna get out… not gonna get out… can't escape the water prison…" mumbled James, his eyes rolled back in his head.

"No," said Isaac as he waded toward his friends and put an arm around them, stopping Jenna's casting. "But there's too many. We can't stop all of them. This corridor extends for miles."

"So what do I do?" Jenna asked, panicking.

"Nothing." Isaac smiled as he pulled the floating James closer to him.

"Nothing?" she spat, demanding.

"Correct." He nodded. "You don't have to do anything."

Isaac put both of his hands together as if in prayer and recited, "Master of Goodness, Truth, and Light, save us from this, an untimely blight."

Flat rays of light began to burst from between his palms as he finished in his bold and heroic voice, as if his voice alone could shake the hell around them:

"Though darkness untamed shall strive to prevail, shield us right now, with thy unbreakable veil!"

Whooosh… Voosh. Voosh. Voosh, rippled and danced the waves of light as Isaac released his hands and held them up, a heavenly barrier of pure light forming around them.

Jenna's mouth dropped as she quickly felt her feet touch the ground again.

It was both horrifying and mesmerizing to stand on dry ground, while all around them, outside the barrier, water continued to rise

As if someone were pressing a wet hand against a windshield, so too sounded and looked the hands of the dead as they continuously pulled down against Isaac's barrier.

"Shall we?" Isaac smiled as his cloak and rippling blond hair levitated gently from his casting Majesty.

Jenna stared into his dancing eyes, mesmerized by the yellow-and-blue light swimming in his irises.

"Y-yes," she stammered, unable to look away. Although she had experienced the heavenly grace of his protective and powerful barriers on a number of occasions, it never ceased to amaze her. Just who was this man, anyway, to conjure and wield a power so divine and unbreakable?

"James should regain himself in a moment," Isaac continued, looking forward and breaking the trance upon Jenna. "Take my arm, Jenna, and take his, and let's get out of here," he finished with strength and courage.

"R-right," Jenna stammered again as she wrapped an arm around Isaac's and another around James's.

For some reason, fearful of breaking his concentration, Jenna said nothing for the next passing hours. The echoes of the gargling moans of the dead on the outside of the barrier were extremely unpleasant to hear. And yet somehow, she was filled with peace and serenity. Indeed, she felt more pity for the lost souls on the other side of the barrier rather than fear.

"Whooooaaa…" mumbled James as he slowly came around, observing the barrier around them.

Taking advantage of the opportunity, Jenna looked at him and said, "Did I not tell you? This is the second time he's saved you!"

"Saved *us*," James quickly spat back. "Don't put all this back on me!"

When they finally reached the end of the tunnel, none could be happier than James.

"Thank our Creator above. There's the ladder!" he exclaimed.

"Yeah, but one problem," said Jenna.

The circumstances they were in proved difficult for traversing the ladder.

"James," said Isaac, "you opened and sealed the last door with an incantation. Is this one the same?"

"Yes, sir," James nodded, slightly intimidated by Isaac's constantly radiating Majesty.

"Well, then," Isaac continued, "you'll need to ascend first. I'll follow second, and Jenna third. That way, you both will stay within my barrier."

"Don't have to tell me twice," said James as he quickly climbed the ladder, followed by Isaac and then Jenna.

"Hey, that's my line!" cried Jenna.

"So I've heard!"

After about ten minutes of climbing, the water level had ceased, allowing Isaac to lower his barrier.

Upon finally reaching the top, James placed a hand upon the metal trapdoor and mumbled an incantation. With a burst of blue energy, the door flew open, and out he quickly climbed.

"Never... in all my life," beamed Jenna as she spun around. "Have I been happier to see the—whoa!" she suddenly blurted out, interrupting herself as she stared with Isaac and James.

For all their gazes were transfixed upon the massive, marbled white tower of Laniakéa, some miles northeast of them.

"Never seen Laniakéa?" asked James a little condescendingly.

Unabashed, Isaac quickly answered, "No. But there's something about it that just feels so familiar."

"Thanks, Isaac, but I was actually asking Jenna."

"No, you were just trying to embarrass me," said Jenna as she slightly stuck her tongue out at him. "But that's what you get. Isaac always has my back... even when he doesn't mean to."

Isaac took a few steps forward, his hand outstretched toward the tower.

"Please... can we go? I feel so drawn to that tower," he said, mesmerized and almost as if asking someone who wasn't present.

"I haven't any objections," answered James. "But although it looks close, it's still about an hour or so from us by foot."

"Well, you two can go on ahead, but I'm continuing to Wöntylnas," said Jenna, spoiling the moment.

"You go right on ahead, princess," said James, waving goodbye to her. "We'll catch up with you later. Oh, and by the way, do you even know where we are?"

Jenna looked all around her, observing the open, rolling green fields, with only a few rocks scattered here and there.

"Umm… it looks kind of similar to the Ryúnion Trail?" she half said, half-asked.

"Hah!" James laughed. "The Ryúnion Trail? Sure! Just keep going south for another day or so, and you might hit it!"

Jenna made a funny face as she tried to hide her embarrassment.

"No, this is the Néor Plains." James smiled as he took a deep breath of fresh air. "We're less than two days away from the Wöntylnas Kingdom."

"Isaac?" Jenna asked as she walked up and placed a hand on his shoulder, ignoring James.

"Yes, Jenn?"

"I want to visit Laniakéa too. I really do. But…" She trailed off.

"Say no more, Jenn." Isaac smiled as he turned his back to the monstrous tower. "I have a feeling we'll go there someday. For now, it's important for us to continue to Wöntylnas. I haven't forgotten."

"Thank you, Isaac!" she beamed. "Besides, now that we know that Garon's your father, aren't you curious if he might be there?"

James gave a blank stare as he tapped his foot. "You really have a way with words, you know that?"

Jenna ignored him again and tugged on Isaac's jacket, pulling him along.

"Let's go, Isaac!" she shouted.

"One problem, princess!" cried out James, laughing. "Wöntylnas is west—not north!"

With her nose upturned, she goofily stepped to her left and continued marching west, pulling Isaac along.

James couldn't help but laugh as he caught up with them, his blue cloak flying through the air.

Although the sun was at its highest point, it didn't feel hot at all. No, it was the perfect temperature. And the wind that whipped and churned around them, carrying the fresh scent of flowers and all sorts of earthy aromas, could only further invigorate them.

Isaac mimicked Jenna, slamming his boots into the ground, kicking up dirt and earth every which way.

"Whoa, whoa," yelled James. "Where's the fire?"

"That's the problem!" Isaac exclaimed, quickly turning around. "Your shoulder! Jenna just recently branded it with fire. I need to heal you!"

"What's wrong, James?" Jenna questioned as she folded her arms, her long hair and jacket-dress combo whipping in the air around her.

James bobbled up and down as he bit his lower lip and smiled, looking like a kid ready to lose his cool in a toy store.

"To be honest," he said, "she did a great job mending it. Buuut... I really want to see what it looks like when Isaac heals it!"

"You don't believe he can?" questioned Jenna sharply as she unfolded her arms.

"It's not that," said James, scratching the back of his head. "I've just never experienced anything like it. I mean really, let's be fair," he said, giving a head nod to Jenna. "What did you do the first time you saw it?"

"Hmm... well," Jenna mumbled as she held her chin.

Suddenly, the memory hit her. She was helping to mend the roof on their mansion-like home in Aerlund when she was seventeen and had accidentally slipped on one of the broken tiles, falling two stories to the ground. Oh, how that pain was unlike any she'd ever experienced! And she was certain that her leg wasn't supposed to be bent that way. And boy, could she remember screaming and crying like no other... only to watch as the ten-year-old, angelic boy came running out of the house.

Perhaps more devastated than she was, tears streamed down young Isaac's face as he cried and cried. And then she remembered the shocking look on his face when he thrust his hands to the heavens and pleaded for help. The rays of light that descended down from above and filled the palms of his hands with the most extraordinary glow were indescribable.

From there, she remembered him staring at the light himself, in great curiosity. And of further interest was when the light suddenly turned into zipping streams and surrounded her leg, placing it in the right direction and mending the broken bones. Oh, the shock on her face and his and Nann's and Uncle Ingle's and—

"Why are you crying?" James asked, snapping her out of it.

She quickly nodded and wiped away the tears. "I don't blame you at all, James. And yes, the first time I saw it was an experience like no other."

Isaac smiled.

"Go ahead, Isaac," motioned Jenna. "Show him what you're made of!"

"You're kind, really. Both of you." Isaac smiled graciously. "But I keep trying to tell you that it's *his* power, not mine, that does the healing," he admitted as he pointed to the azure sky above them.

James quickly pulled down the right part of his vest as he almost gleefully revealed the scorched scars of Jenna's patchwork healing.

Isaac looked up into the sky as he held up his hands to the sun. His cloak and hair floated gently, carried by his Majesty's power

"Battered and broken we appear to be," he began reciting, "tossed and turned by our enemies."

Angled beams of light radiated through the air as they filled his palms with light. Jenna smiled, and James's mouth dropped open.

"But upon thy glorious light we stand," finished Isaac, "knowing our deliverance… is always at hand."

Isaac looked down at James, momentarily causing him to recoil as he felt the burst of his Majesty and power—unlike anything he'd ever experienced as he stared back into his glowing yellow-and-blue eyes.

With his hands holding two orbs of pure light, Isaac kneeled in front of James. Suddenly, he crushed the Majestic orbs in his hands, releasing the flowing, zipping rays of light. The rays circled around James's shoulder until they disappeared into him in an eye-shielding blast.

Unable to say anything, James slowly opened his eyes and inspected his shoulder, completely healed and back to normal (albeit still a little pale).

"**Yep,**" said Jenna with a laugh. "I remember my reaction being quite similar to yours when he first did it to me."

"I… what do I even say?" stammered James as he rubbed the healed wound again and again.

"Uh, how about, 'Thank you'?" commanded Jenna.

"Jenna, it's not like that," said Isaac before he was squeezed in a tight embrace by James.

"No. She's right," cried James. "Thank you so much, Isaac! Thank you, thank you!"

Slightly shocked, not used to such gratitude, Isaac wrapped his arms around James and squeezed him back, saying, "O-of course, James! My pleasure! But I just borrowed the power. I didn't really do much!"

"Do much?" mocked James. "You healed my arm! Your power or not, you accessed it to heal me, and for that"—he choked up—"I am most thankful."

Isaac gave him one final squeeze before letting go and nodding.

"Wow." James shook his head. "Just wow."

Their journey toward Wöntylnas proved to be a little less than ideal. Though they were engaged by the Kreaux a few times, it was nothing they couldn't handle. Thankfully, they didn't encounter the conductor again.

For them, the sorrowful part came from stumbling upon randomly destroyed homes in the middle of nowhere, obvious victims of the Kreaux. And even worse was the small town of Dürdéngon, in the western Néor region, that had just been attacked.

Though familiar with the destruction and carnage left by the Kreaux, it never ceased to shake the Majesticians. Perhaps it was even more devastating for them, on account of their unique gifts, powers, and sensitivities.

Isaac was delighted to have the opportunity to heal a couple of families and displaced survivors, but alas, they left nearly empty-handed in the way of food and drink (although Jenna did gain access to a needle and thread, which she quickly used to mend their clothes from the unceasing rips, shreds, and tears of combat and travel).

By nightfall, they had reached the entrance to the Wéljelnin Pass, an upheaved valley with winding twists and paths through rough and smooth rock alike, upon misty sand.

"Not a bad use of your cloak there!" admired Isaac as he watched James lie down and use his cloak as both a blanket and pillow.

"It's actually pretty comfortable. You should give it a try!" he responded, fluffing his makeshift pillow. "Oh, and thanks for the fire, Jenna!" he added.

Jenna stood some feet away with her arms folded, staring up into the starry sky overhead.

"Anytime," she simply responded, hardly audible.

"Jenna?" said Isaac in his compassionate and concerned voice. "Will you not be resting?"

"No, no, Isaac. Don't worry about me!" She turned around with a smile. "I'm just enjoying the night stars."

Isaac stared from her and then to James, who muttered, "I'd just leave it at that for now. Don't want to upset her."

With a concerned look and bitten lower lip, Isaac observed the slow-moving energy around her that was sadness.

"Come now, Isaac," said James, breaking his concentration as he unlatched Isaac's cloak. "Let me help you. Give it a shot!"

In a kindly, forceful way, James pushed Isaac's head down to rest upon the newly made "pillow" of Isaac's cloak.

Still concerned, Isaac began to lose the battle, finding it harder and harder to focus on his beloved friend and easier and easier to focus on the inside of his eyelids.

Isaac gasped in terror as he found himself suspended in a vast expanse of dark clouds.

He quickly held his hands up and attempted to cast Majesty for light, but nothing happened.

As if delayed, he had to shield his eyes when a sudden flash of blinding light illuminated the air. He waited for the light to dissipate, but it did not! Trying to focus as hard as he could, he could barely make out the silhouette of what appeared to be a woman with a flowing white robe.

"Isaac? Is it you? It is! It's really you!" cried the angel.

"Who are you?" asked Isaac with squinted eyes. "And where are we?"

"Oh, how I wish we had more time!" rang the ethereal voice of the angel through the air.

"Time for what?" demanded Isaac, feeling (for the first time in a very long time) a little agitated.

"Don't forget about him, Isaac! He needs you! All of you, Jenna and James! Like you, he has suffered so much loss."

"Please, who are you talking about?" asked Isaac, trying to reach out to the angel, only to feel an invisible energy stop him.

"He's waiting for you, Isaac! Don't leave him alone in his kingdom!" responded the voice.

"Arrggh," grunted Isaac, finally losing his patience (only because of his great desire to help). "Why won't you tell me who he is? What is his name?"

"Gage, Isaac!" responded the angel.

He sighed in gratitude at the thought of hearing a name.

"Don't forget it, my love! And please, don't forget about him! He's been lost for so many years!"

"Why are we talking about him when we should be talking about—" yelled Isaac in a surge of sudden and unexpected emotion.

"Please, Isaac, gather the spheres, the weapons! I'll be there to aid you!" echoed and interrupted the angel's voice.

"No, wait!" screamed Isaac as he reached out to the fading angel. "Please, don't leave me! Don't leave me again!"

"My baby! I'm always with you!" screamed the angel as she, too, reached out for Isaac's hand, barely missing his fingers.

"You are a hero like no other, my beloved, charged by heaven itself," echoed the fading words of the angel. "Legions of angels stand at your back, ever ready to combat the powers of hell with you."

"Please... please don't..." cried Isaac with both hands outstretched now, tears streaming down his face.

His emotions were so powerful he couldn't utter any more.

"Fight, Isaac, fight!" shook the air around them from the angel's voice. "Gather the spheres. Climb Laniakéa. Obliterate the evil that torments Vaerün!"

"Please..." whispered Isaac, unable to speak at all.

"Prevail against hell! Shake its very foundations with your light and Majesty!"

"No!" Isaac screamed, finally able to. "Mom! My beloved and precious mother, come back!" he screamed in hysterics.

"Isaac, **wake up!**" Jenna exclaimed, as she shook him awake.

His cloak was drenched with sweat as he sat up and brushed the tears and perspiration from his face.

"Are you okay?" she asked, holding the back of her hand to his forehead. "You have a terrible fever. Was it a nightmare?"

"It... it was... no!" he suddenly blurted out, "What was his name? **I forgot his name!**"

Jenna sat back and raised her eyebrows in shock. "What name? Isaac... you need to rest more!"

"**No!**" he shouted, jumping up.

James stirred slightly, then continued snoring.

"Dang it, what was his **name?**" Isaac yelled in outrage, pacing back and forth.

"Isaac... Isaac, dear," Jenna said as she stopped him, placing both hands on his cheeks. Her touch felt warm, and the bare skin of her hands was comforting. (It was a rare treat to feel her hands, as she almost always wore her white princess gloves.)

Isaac immediately calmed as he stared into her beautiful eyes and glistening, porcelain-like skin. Her heart-shaped face was stunning, framed perfectly by her flowing hair.

He gulped as his face flushed.

"Oh my..." she spoke even more softly, "You really are getting a fever... and it's spreading to your cheeks. Please... rest with me for a moment."

Why was she suddenly acting this way? And her voice... had she ever spoken so sweetly to Isaac before? Whatever heat he felt before was now reaching overwhelming levels as she pulled his head close to her bosom, running her small, delicate fingers through his thick, messy blond hair.

"J-Jenna," he muttered.

"Shhhhh, Isaac... rest," she gently said, slowly rocking him back and forth.

"But... the name," he shyly protested.

"I know, honey, I know," she sweetly said. "I'm sure you'll remember tomorrow."

Honey? When had she ever called him that? For a moment, Isaac had convinced himself he'd surely entered another dream. So, he decided to go along with it.

"But, dear..." he responded softly, "it's very important. And I promised not to forget it."

Agh! Why did she have to smell so sweet?

"You smell beautiful," he muttered, swaying back and forth with her.

"Oh, you like it?" she asked, pausing for a moment. "It's my own personal perfume... a combination of rosehips and cinnamon."

"It's... divine. Just like you," he whispered, wrapping an arm around her.

For a dream, her heart sure was beating fast.

"No, Isaac," she whispered as she kissed his head, "the only divine thing upon Vaerün is you."

"But what is divinity," he whispered, pulling back to look up into her eyes, "without its angels?"

His heart was about to burst as he felt the invisible, powerful pull of his lips to hers.

I do not want this dream to end, he thought as his arm moved up and around her neck, the creamy smooth texture of her hair flowing against his strong, masculine hand.

Suddenly, they both bolted apart as James's loud snoring (that would put a grizzly bear to shame) boomed through their "camp."

Shüza! Isaac swore in his mind (perhaps for the first time ever) as he realized that it wasn't a dream.

"S-sorry!" exclaimed Jenna, quickly running her fingers through her hair and walking away, completely embarrassed.

"Wait!" whispered Isaac as loudly as he could.

But it was too late—she was already too far away.

So many thoughts flooded his mind as he fell back down on his "pillow." Whatever concerns he had about the dream he had just experienced were now almost entirely gone. And honestly? He really didn't care. All his attention and focus were on the scene that had just happened! It wasn't a dream! And thus for the next hour or so, he replayed again and again in his mind the wonderful feelings and joy he'd just experienced.

"Good morning!" shouted the words of James, waking up Isaac.

Isaac dared not open his eyes as he heard Jenna happily respond, "Good morning, James!"

What? "Good morning, James!" Since when was Jenna ever that nice to James? Maybe it was because of what happened between her and Isaac last night…

"Uh, how'd you sleep?" James asked, clearly surprised at her kindness.

"Oh, very well," beamed Jenna's voice. "Thank you! How about yourself?"

"Uhm," he muttered, "good! Really good. This thing makes the best pillow, you know that?"

"I can only imagine!" Her voice laughed. "Isaac seems to be enjoying it too. Look how he's still knocked out!"

Isaac's heart dropped as she said his name. And somehow, for some strange new reason, he longed to hear her say it again. But why? She'd said his name countless times before. Why was this time any different?

"Should we wake him up?" James whispered.

"Nah… let him sleep a little longer." Jenna quietly giggled.

Isaac tried to discreetly swallow as the attention focused on him.

"Haha! Whatever he's dreaming about," laughed James, "it must be nice. Look how red his face is turning!"

"I hope he's not having a nightmare," Jenna muttered.

Oh gosh, why? Isaac's face grew hot as he felt the cool shade of Jenna's shadow cast over his closed eyelids. And there was the smell of rose and cinnamon. His heart began beating faster and faster as he felt her presence draw closer to his. And he nearly choked on his saliva when her hand touched his forehead.

"He all right?" asked James.

"I don't know. He's had a fever since last night," she responded, sounding concerned.

"Well, the poor guy hasn't eaten much in the way of food."

"I know, he's so sweet! He's been giving a lot of his portions to me," Jenna said kindly.

How much more of this can I take? Thank goodness her hand didn't travel to his heart, or she'd panic! However, holding back that smile couldn't last forever.

"Ugh!" James yelled in disgust. "I can't wait to reach Wöntylnas."

"Um. I thought you hated your kingdom?" Jenna asked with a raised eyebrow.

"I hate the people," James answered with a pointed finger. "But the food is to die for!"

"Literally," retorted Jenna. "I thought you said it was poisoned?"

"About ninety percent of it is," he answered honestly. "But if you know where to go, like I do, then you're fine."

"Riiiiiight," Jenna sighed.

"Oh, trust me. You say that now, but wait till we get there and you have some fresh pancakes with drizzled honey and kinberry syrup."

Isaac nearly fainted upon hearing the word *kinberry*.

"That's right! I keep forgetting that a lot of places import kinberries for all sorts of jams, spreads, and syrups," said Jenna proudly.

"Gotta thank your kingdom for that." James smiled. "Although I hope there are still some inhabitants exporting it from Fürnas to Wöntylnas."

"Trust me when I say, I'm certain there are," she answered confidently.

"Oh. My. Gosh!" she suddenly screamed, startling James and even Isaac, who still pretended to be asleep.

"What? What's wrong?" James demanded.

"I completely forgot to give those kinberries to Isaac!"

Isaac's heart literally fell at these words, and it took every ounce of mental strength for him not to bounce up.

"Um?" James looked at her like she was crazy.

"You don't get it," she said, with a devastated expression. "Isaac *looooves* anything kinberry-related."

"Can't blame him." James shrugged. "The berry is fabled to have been sent from heaven. And seeing how angelic he is, it only makes sense that he'd be drawn to it."

"Lore aside," continued Jenna, "I can't believe I didn't give them to him."

"Where'd you leave them?"

"On your kitchen table."

I knew I smelled kinberries in that bag! Isaac yelled in his mind.

James scratched the small patch of his newly growing black goatee. "Well," he smirked, "that's a damn shame."

Unable to take any more, Isaac pretended to "wake up," stretching and yawning loudly.

"Isaac!" Jenna and James shouted in sync.

"Good morning, you two!" beamed Isaac. "How'd you sleep?"

"Very well, thank you." Jenna fought to mow down James verbally as she stared at him.

"We were just talking about—" James started.

"How it's fascinating that it's going to take us a day to get through this, uh… what's it called again, James?" Jenna asked as she gave a stern glare to James.

He momentarily stared at her in confusion, then quickly caught on as he responded, "Oh! Uh, it's called the Wéljelnin Pass."

"What a fascinating name!" Isaac exclaimed. "Do you know where it comes from?"

"Sure do!" James answered proudly. "King Vergaus Wöntylnas, the last water Majestician over a thousand years ago, named the pass after his wife, Wéljelnin."

"What a mouthful, that," said Jenna blankly.

"No, no, it's easy! Here, try after me," James encouraged. "Veil."

"Veil," Isaac and Jenna said in sync.

"Zhel."

"Zhel," they copied.

"Neen!"

"Neen," they finished.

"Right! Exactly!" James smiled. "Veil-zhel-neen!"

Jenna tossed her head back and forth as she repeated the name and said, "Ohhh, okay. Once you break it down like that, it is pretty easy."

"And it's a pretty name too!" complimented Isaac.

"Oh?" Jenna turned. "You think it's *pretty?*"

Isaac's cheeks grew hot as his heart raced.

"N-no! I mean, it's not as pretty as *Jenna,* of course," he quickly said.

James raised an eyebrow, and Jenna's smile could've melted even the coldest heart.

"I mean," Isaac quickly said, flustered, "that's not what—I just—Agh!"

Jenna started laughing as she came up and hugged him, causing him to blush even more.

"It's okay," she whispered. "I know what you mean."

"You do—"

"All right. So," interrupted James, "are you both ready to go?"

"Yes!" boomed Isaac. "I can't wait to try those pancakes with kinberry syrup!"

Oh. Shüza.

Jenna slugged him in the arm repeatedly (playfully, of course) as she yelled, "I knew it! I just knew you weren't asleep! Dang you, Isaac Erbrecht!"

James laughed as Isaac began running around in circles (undoubtedly enjoying the new affection).

The wind whistled and howled around them as they trudged through the squishy sand under their boots. Every now and then, Jenna and James would let out a swear word or two when the sand kicked up into their eyes from the random gusts of wind.

Peculiar and new in sight to Isaac and Jenna, James could only smile as he continued to talk about the vast canyon crag they were walking through.

"Unique, isn't it?" he questioned them as he ran his hand along the smooth, polished stone walls—carved by the many years of sand blasting.

"I'd love to say yes," Jenna responded, "but my eyes have so much sand in them, I'm afraid I'm going to have to get back to you on that."

"It is definitely unique," Isaac answered with his typical smile. "Do you know how it came to be?"

"Bah…" James replied, flipping his hand. "There's a whole lot of conjecture. But one story of lore stands out to me."

"Do tell?" Jenna asked.

"Well, it's believed that Majesticians have been around as long as Vaerün itself," he started.

"Okay?" Isaac asked.

"And between us and the Majesticians that existed over a thousand years ago, we received our powers from a heavenly, angelic feather that descends out of heaven."

"That's how it goes!" added Jenna.

"Well, it's believed that many, many, maaany years before them, Majesticians used to get their power from falling stars."

"No, thank you," Jenna said boldly.

"I'm sorry?" James asked, confused.

"I said no, thank you!" she repeated. "I'll take receiving my power from a feather any day over being slammed down by a frackin' falling star!"

Isaac couldn't help but laugh. Why? A lot of the times, he didn't used to laugh at her. Why did she suddenly seem so much funnier?

"Were that the case, I'd agree," continued James as he kicked up a slew of sand, "but in their case, it is said that the essence of Majesty was contained in the stardust upon their exploding impact."

"That's pretty cool!" exclaimed Isaac.

"I agree!" piped up Jenna, causing him to blush a little. "But… what does that have to do with this canyon?" she asked.

"It is believed that this was the most concentrated area of starfall," motioned James as he knelt down and scooped the sand. "And this is the very essence of stardust from so many millennia ago!"

"No way?" Isaac and Jenna said in sync.

"Is it really true?" Isaac asked as he kneeled down to scoop the sand.

"It is!" beamed James. "I used to come out here all the time. And what I did really helped my powers grow."

"Really? What did you do?" asked Jenna excitedly.

"It probably sounds strange," James continued, "but you have to rub the sand on your body."

"Um. What?" she asked with a raised eyebrow.

"I know it sounds weird," he said as he tossed his head, "and it doesn't have to be a lot. You can even just rub it on your arms. See? Isaac's doing it!"

Jenna watched in horror and embarrassment as she looked at Isaac, who had already pulled up his sleeves and was rubbing the fine grit sand upon his arms.

"James," Jenna said flatly, "you are perhaps the biggest *Gerdpölus* I've ever met. And you're lucky I don't set you on fire at this very moment."

James did something between a "Ha ha" and "Hee hee" as he tried to run ahead, only to trip and fall face-first into the squishy sand.

Ever the compassionate one, Isaac reached out his hand in concern as he immediately tried to help him up. But to his surprise, he was stopped by Jenna's strong hand.

"No. Just, no," she said as she shook her head.

"What? Why not, Jenna?" he asked sadly.

"Isaac. Dear," she said, turning to him, causing his face to flush a little. "You don't help up the people who tried to trip you."

"But—"

"No buts on this one," Jenna said as they both stepped over James.

"Whoooa!" James cried out as twisting rays of light wrapped around him and helped him up, secretly cast from Isaac behind his back.

"Is it seriously going to take us until nightfall to get through here?" Jenna asked a few hours later.

"The funny part about it," answered James, "is that it's not the distance that takes so long but rather the trudging through the sand!"

"Especially when you're wearing boots," mumbled Isaac as he lifted his tired legs, one after the other, pulling each foot out from the squishy sand.

"You better say it!" exclaimed Jenna. "I'm a little confused, though, James," she muttered.

"About what?"

"You said Wöntylnas is pretty much on the other side of this canyon, right?" she asked.

"That's correct."

"Well then… why do we have to camp out another night rather than just stay in the kingdom?"

"Two reasons," he responded. "One: It's not a direct entrance into Wöntylnas. There's a couple of hours' worth of trekking we have to do across the Wöntylnas prairies."

"Okay?"

"And two: we'd be entering Wöntylnas past nightfall. And no one gets in or out of the bridge gate without written consent of King Närvein."

"Sounds fancy," said Isaac.

"Sounds stupid," added Jenna. "What kind of pompous, overfluffed, bougie people are we talking about here? Ridiculous… this is a free land, thank you very much, and I'll be damned if I let anyone tell me where I can or cannot go!"

James threw both of his hands in the air as he said, "Trust me when I say that you may hear me repeat the words a million times: *and you wonder why I left.*"

Isaac couldn't help but laugh as he said, "Come on, James. Is it really that bad?"

With a hand clapping on his shoulder, James picked up the pace and walked past Isaac as he said, "Trust me on this one, mate. You'll see for yourself."

Almost hoping for a repeat of last night, Isaac eagerly stared at Jenna's back as he rested on his cloak "pillow" again. Just like last night, Jenna stood a few feet away, arms folded, staring up into the stars. Thank goodness they were out of that canyon.

Dang it, not again, thought Isaac, as his eyelids grew heavy, quickly falling asleep.

Although in a similar dark space, this time, there was no heavenly appearance. Everything was just black.

Did you forget, Isaac? echoed the words of the angel through the blankness.

Of course not! his voice echoed back. *Gage. Right? That's his name.*

No, Isaac. Did you forget about me?

I could never forget about you, Mom!

It's all right, Isaac. It looks like the payment for our sacrifices is to be forgotten.

What do you mean? he asked.

You've forgotten about me, and she is going to forget about you.

That's not possible. She could never forget about me, he responded.

What if she didn't have a choice?

Isaac bolted up as the same familiar, uncomfortable feeling of sweat rolled down his face.

Thank heaven, he thought as he wiped the sweat away. *I must've just fallen asleep.*

Jenna was still standing a few feet away, arms folded, eyes on the sky. *How long has James been snoring?* Had he really only just fallen asleep? How long had Jenna been standing there?

As quietly as possible, Isaac pushed himself up and slowly walked over to her.

"O-oh…" she stammered shyly. "Good evening, Isaac."

He cleared his throat and responded, "G-good evening, Jenna."

After an awkward pause, he spoke up, "It's… a beautiful evening, isn't it?"

"Yes. The stars are gorgeous. I can't stop staring at them."

Isaac swallowed repeatedly, holding back the words he desperately wanted to say: *Gorgeous, like you, and I can't stop staring at you either.*

"Were you having another bad dream?" she asked without looking at him.

He tilted his head slightly and asked, "How did you know I was having a bad dream?"

She quietly giggled and said, "You're so cute. Do you think you're the only one who can read emotions and energy?"

Isaac swallowed again, his face growing hot.

"What were they about?" she asked. "Your dreams."

Isaac nervously ruffled his hair. "To be honest, I don't know."

"What? What do you mean you don't know?"

"It probably sounds odd, but..." He paused for a moment, then continued, "When I'm having them, they feel so... familiar. But then, when I wake up, they're just... gone."

"I completely relate," Jenna said, still looking up. "Because I suffer from the same thing. It really is terrible."

"Perhaps it's our minds trying to protect us from something?" Isaac asked optimistically.

"Or perhaps it's our hearts trying to prevent us from getting hurt," she sadly responded.

The overwhelming desire to place his arm around her was growing unbearable. Just when he was about to, she suddenly turned and stared him directly in the eyes, blurting out, "Have you ever just wanted to run away?"

Isaac's eyes grew wide as he tried to respond.

"It just feels so... impossible—life." She continued, "No matter how hard we try, no matter what we do... the Kreaux continue to attack. We fight and fight, but to no avail."

"Are you still thinking about Dürdéngon?" asked Isaac quietly.

"No matter how hard we try, no matter how hard we fight... it never pays off," she answered.

Jenna walked away for a moment, holding the side of her head, then returned.

"My question is, when will it pay off? When will the fighting stop?" she asked. "And why were we stuck with this unbearable burden? Why on Vaerün did Majesty only choose us?"

Isaac swallowed, feeling suddenly powerless to say anything.

"We've watched so many good people die, Isaac," she continued. "And as if that isn't bad enough, we've had to watch them perish in ways that no one should!"

Isaac slowly looked to the ground, unable to make eye contact, bracing himself for what he knew was coming.

"I mean, really," she continued, "ripped apart? Mauled to death? Cut into pieces? Infected? Bodies pulled underground?"

Unable to say anything, he looked up into her eyes and placed a hand on her shoulder.

"And what about us?" she asked, tears beginning to form in her eyes. "We're the ones who suffer even more. Why? Because we get to witness all of it and continue to live!"

Isaac had to fight back his own tears as he continued to listen.

"Knowing... that we aren't strong enough to save everyone," she went on. "Knowing that we're all alone. Knowing that we must give up our own desires for the sake of the greater good."

Jenna's hands were shaking, when suddenly she became infuriated. "Knowing that good is *constantly* thwarted by darkness and evil! Why must we be justice and light? And when will it end, Isaac? When?"

With a quiet breath, Isaac began to speak. "I feel... that we are strangers in a distant land, sent to do the will of our Father. And we must not give up. We must not let go. We must fight! Hold steadfast and strong! I am His light, and you are His fire upon the world."

He paused for a moment, then finished, "We are Creators of a sublime origin; Majesticians. And no matter what, Jenna, we must never give up. **Never!**"

Tears rolled down Jenna's cheeks as Isaac gently shook her, staring deeply into her eyes.

"And no matter what darkness attacks you, no matter what storm beats upon you, no matter what hell strives to prevail against you... never stop fighting. You hear me?"

With that statement, Isaac stepped back, and his Light Majesty began to emanate around him as he declared, "There will come a day, Jenna, when all will be well. When light and justice seize the day!

Darkness will be cast down. Every wrong shall be made right. Hell will. Be. Broken! And that day, Jenna…"

Perhaps unbeknownst to him, Isaac was practically glowing like the sun—so much so that Jenna almost had to shield her eyes—as he finished heroically and majestically, "…is what we fight for!"

In slight shock, Isaac further extended his arms when Jenna melted into them, sobbing, both kneeling to the ground in a sincere embrace.

CHAPTER 13

The Kingdom of Wöntylnas

"Now that..." Jenna muttered, "is a bridge."

James motioned his hand out as he slightly bowed. "Welcome to the kingdom of Wöntylnas! Or rather, the bridge leading to Wöntylnas, anyway."

"This is incredible," said Isaac, shaking his head, flabbergasted by the enormous white bridge.

They had just finished crossing the Wöntylnas prairie, and to their delight, it didn't take much time—only a little over an hour. Thus, they had the entire day left to explore the beautiful, intriguing, and enchanting water kingdom, as it was still bright and early.

Clip, clop. Clip, clop. Clip, clop, tapped the sounds of their boots on the glossy white stones. The white-and-blue lampposts lining the bridge still burned with blue fire, and although the kingdom was still some distance away, out on the ocean, they felt as if they were already there the moment they set foot on that beautifully ornate bridge.

Jenna's thick hair whipped in the salty breeze.

"Exactly how long do you think it'll take for us to reach the kingdom?"

"That all depends on how fast you want to move," James smiled.

"How about we use our Majesty to help us get—" Isaac began to suggest.

James threw himself in front of Isaac, pulling his hands down and hissing, "No! No! No! No Majesty!"

Tap tap tap tap tap, sounded Jenna's foot as she irritably tapped it, arms folded. "First, he says we need permission to enter or exit the forsaken place, and now he says we can't even use Majesty?"

James turned to Jenna and gave her a 'really?' sort of look. "That's only if we're trying to enter or exit at nighttime!"

"I don't understand, though," said Isaac. "Why can't we use Majesty?"

James let out a deep sigh and motioned for his friends to move to the side of the bridge, trying to avoid a scene as some people began to cross their path.

"Please…" he whispered. "I know you probably think I'm crazy, but you two have to trust me—you've never been here before!"

Jenna's irritation faded as she noticed how sincere James was being. And of course, Isaac smiled and nodded.

"These people…," James continued, "are like no other. I don't know what it's like to grow up in Fürnas or Aerlund, but here… let's just say they do things differently."

Jenna threw her arms behind her head as she continued walking. "All right, James. We trust you. No Majesty then."

"No matter what?"

"Well now," she said, holding her chin in deep thought, "I can't promise anything, but I really will try."

James gave Isaac a desperate look that said, *please help me out?*

"It'll be all right, James," Isaac reassured him. "A massive majority of people's worries never come to pass."

Poor James took a deep breath as his friends continued moving ahead. How could he possibly explain it to them? Oh, well. They'd see soon enough.

For the next twenty minutes, the trio encountered passersby after passersby, and to Isaac's dismay, the people did not grow any kinder.

The first group merely frowned and quickened their pace, pulling their children along as though they were escaping some unseen threat.

"Good morning!" Isaac called again to a well-dressed woman with a towering hat, who responded by glaring at him over her shoulder before muttering something under her breath.

The next man, carrying an armful of scrolls, glanced at them warily, clutching his belongings closer to his chest as though expecting them to pounce. Without a word, he veered to the far edge of the bridge.

"That's odd," Isaac whispered, shaking his head. "Maybe I'm just not loud enough?"

"No, Isaac," Jenna cut in dryly, "It's not you."

Another group approached—a pair of older women in elaborate gowns, speaking animatedly. Isaac gave them his most charming smile and waved. "Good morning, ladies!"

Without missing a beat, one of them huffed loudly, raising her hand dismissively. The other narrowed her eyes and whispered something to her companion before both quickened their steps.

"That was rude," Jenna growled, folding her arms across her chest. "Seriously rude."

But Isaac, ever the optimist, tried again when two young men passed, laughing between themselves. "Morning!"

One glanced at Isaac, a look of surprise flashing across his face, but instead of responding, he threw up his hand in a hurried gesture and mouthed, "Don't talk to me."

Jenna's patience had reached its limit. "Isaac, do me a favor," she said in a low voice.

"Naturally, Jenn! What can I do for you?"

She stepped in front of him, causing him to stop. "Please, stop greeting people. Because the next rude response we get will have me fighting. Okay?"

James threw an arm around her and raised a finger. "Thus it starts."

"Thus *what* starts?" questioned Isaac.

"My saying: *And you wonder why I left!*" Chided James.

Isaac and Jenna watched as James skipped forward a few feet and then turned around to face them. "And the best part? We haven't even officially entered yet!"

Jenna momentarily stopped as she ran her fingers along the enormous, ornate, open, blue metal gates of Wöntylnas. In awe and admiration, she looked up so far that it caused her neck to crack as it bent back.

"I'm beginning to see why you said no one gets in or out at night."

"That's the truth, miss!" James said, clapping her on the back.

Isaac walked up to James and placed a hand on his shoulder, whispering to him. "James, I just thought of something."

"What is it, mate?"

"I understand that you don't want us to use Majesty, but… won't people know we're Majesticians when they see our eyes?"

"Not only that," chimed in Jenna, "won't our wardrobe stand out just a little bit?"

James laughed out loud, causing both of them to stare. "Yes, but not in the way you think. As nicely as you think we may be dressed, these people will indeed outdress you and me both."

"Really?" Jenna asked, spinning around as the dress portion of her wardrobe elegantly turned through the air.

"At least, they'll think so," James finished with a grunt. "And as for our eyes," he continued to Isaac, "don't worry about that. People do alterations to their bodies here all the time."

Isaac's mouth dropped in horror as Jenna spoke for him. "What? What do you mean, alterations?"

"I already told you, Wöntylnas isn't the place you think it is," James answered. "It may appear beautiful, have no doubt about that."

And boy, was he right. The twisting and turning white-stoned streets, lined with blue mortar, were very elegant. Statues of robed men and women, battle commanders, and strong-featured individuals holding books were everywhere! The buildings—they were tall, composed of beautiful white stone. Their dark-blue, shimmering rooftops mirrored the sky above and the ocean beneath. Despite being built on top of the ocean, exposed to the ravages of the elements, one might be left baffled at how everything looked so perfectly clean, shimmering, and brand-new.

"But beneath all the superfluous glitz and glimmer," James continued, "lies a kingdom full of darkness and secrets."

Jenna shook her head, still unable to believe that people could make alterations to their bodies.

"Yes, but, you didn't explain how—"

"Didn't I tell you, or didn't you know, that this kingdom is founded upon principles of intellectual prowess?"

Neither of them responded.

"There are many doctors and scientists who've delved deep into anatomy and chemistry. You don't think, even for a moment, that they'd use any of their skills to gain money?"

Isaac covered his mouth, stunned. "Yes, but to alter the human body? Even if such practices exist—"

"Oh, I assure you, they do," interrupted James.

"Isn't that just—"

"Evil," said Jenna boldly. "You're messing with creation."

James rubbed his shoulder, still unable to believe that Isaac actually healed it. "And do you seriously think these people care about that?"

"By heaven, I sure hope so!" answered Isaac indignantly.

"You give these people too much credit," James responded flippantly. "Don't worry. Give it about a week, and you'll understand just why I feel the way I do about this place."

Isaac and Jenna gawked as a woman passed by with a partially shaved head and overly large bosom and buttocks.

James smiled largely as he motioned to the passing woman. "And you're worried about someone judging our eyes? *Pleeaaaase…*"

The trip to the castle, situated at the westernmost end of the kingdom, proved to be a bit of an eye-opener for both Isaac and Jenna.

"Don't worry," Isaac reassured Jenna with a smile. "You're beautiful… and you look just fine," he whispered.

Jenna gave him a grateful look as she stopped fidgeting with her bosom, midsection, and buttocks. It was taking quite a toll on her to see such seemingly perfect women stroll this way and that down the streets, flaunting their exquisite figures and curves.

"Oh? Do you like what you see?" Jenna asked bitterly, noticing Isaac's gaze.

"N-no, it's not that!" he quickly answered. "I just don't know how anyone can walk around like that and feel comfortable! I'd feel so ashamed!"

True enough! One can only imagine the poor young man's shock, who grew up entirely in the country (with clothed people, at that!) as his vision was freshly exposed to the almost entirely nude women walking around with strange pieces of cloth and fabric barely covering their private areas.

And you wonder why I left! echoed the voice of James, some five feet in front of them.

"And do you like what you see?" questioned Isaac as he felt insecure for the first time.

The two men they passed had just left the bathhouse. Visually pleasing (according to the standards of Wöntylnas), they were extremely fit with rippling muscles, slicked-back hair, chiseled jaws and faces, and perfectly manicured eyebrows and facial hair. And, similar to the women, these men wore little more than strange cloths covering only their most private areas, with naught but a string girded around their hips.

"N-no!" barked back Jenna. "I just can't believe this! How on Vaerün has our Creator not zapped this wretched kingdom into the ocean yet?"

Again, some feet in front of them, James couldn't help but laugh. "Annnnd you wonder why I left!" he repeated.

"Oh… my… heaven!" shrieked Isaac as the fresh smell of pastries, baked goods, and kinberries filled his nostrils!

They'd just entered the restaurant district. Jenna and even James were both taking their time as they, too, enjoyed the heavenly smells.

James cast his fierce, moving blue eyes upon Jenna and Isaac. "I swear… it may smell like heaven"—he sighed—"but it will take naught but one bite to send you straight to hell."

Isaac gave something between a whimper and a cry as James wrapped an arm around him. "Don't you worry, mate! You'll get real food soon enough. And it'll be much better than this poisoned trash!"

And with that thought, they continued moving forward. Panic momentarily set in when they turned around and realized that Jenna was no longer behind them.

Grunts, swearing, verbal attacks, glares, and obscenities fell upon Isaac and James as their white-and-blue cloaks danced through the air, accidentally brushing the many citizens of the busy streets as they retraced their steps. Both had their hands cupped to their mouths as they repeatedly called for their friend.

"Jenna? Jenna! Jenna?"

Isaac nearly had the wind knocked out of him as James brought him to an abrupt halt with his arm across his chest.

It didn't take long for them to realize the commotion that was taking place under the open patio, canopied dining area of a fancy restaurant café called *Zhü Heltenöv*. Between the whispering and pointing inhabitants, it was pretty easy to make out Jenna's long, flowing brown hair and red dress, which stood out like a sore thumb amid all the blue and white.

She was arguing profusely with a lady seated at a table. And the worst part? The woman simply had her eyes closed and nose upturned! She wasn't responding to Jenna at all! No wonder she was so infuriated!

It probably didn't help that the woman was dressed so fancily. And how old was she? Perhaps one of those women James had mentioned, with all the physical alterations. That white dress of hers was so tight upon her body, one could only wonder how she could breathe in it. (Was she even breathing?) And that hat—putting an umbrella to shame!

Unsure of what to do, Isaac stood still in the street as he watched James run up and grab Jenna. "Jenna, what are you doing? That's—"

"Get off me, James!" she spat back as he pulled her away. "I'm not done with her yet!"

Unfortunately, the scene caused some unwanted attention, but, surprisingly, not from Jenna's debate.

"Jjjjjaaames?" rolled the name off the tongue of the woman as they just set foot onto the street. "Is that Jjjjaames Vandergaus?"

Ugh! Her snobby voice was enough to make anyone want to regurgitate.

James took a deep breath as he closed his eyes and sighed, back still turned to her. "Yes, Mrs. Minlöuian. It is I."

Mrs. Minlöuian carefully rose from her chair. With an additionally careful and gentle push, she slid it back in. "That is Professor Minlöuian to you, *thhhaaank you very much*!"

Ugh! Why did she always have to roll a word in every sentence?

She was quite tall—or was it the high heels she was wearing? Either way, it made Jenna's and James's blood boil as she carefully walked over to them, looking down her nose.

"What on Vaerün are you doing back here?" she demanded. "I thought you were banished!"

James gave something between a snicker and a laugh. "No one banishes me from anywhere, let alone my own kingdom."

Ooooh, you go, James! Jenna cheered in her mind as she tightened her grip on his arm in excitement.

Mrs. Minlöuian gave something between a snicker and a snort as she looked at Jenna. "I suppose it'd only make sense that this barbaric girl is your friend, then?"

Unable to hear what was going on but fearful of gathering attention, Isaac walked up just in time to stop the growing heated debate.

"Oh? And just who is this?" questioned Mrs. Minlöuian with a slight raise of her hand toward Isaac.

"I'm Isaac, ma'am. Pleased to meet you!" he exclaimed, extending a hand.

Mrs. Minlöuian slowly extended her hand, and everyone was quite (although expectedly) disappointed when she reached for a fan instead of returning his handshake.

"Young man, do not **ever** address me as '*ma'am!*'" she scolded him, pointed finger and upturned nose. "Should we ever have the displeasure of crossing paths again, I am *Professor Minlöuian*! Master concert artist of the *pianato*."

Isaac's heart dropped as he strived to hold back his excitement, even amid her excessive rudeness. Another pianist? No way! "You play the—"

"No one...," Jenna boomed, "and I mean no one—is a master of anything!"

Mrs. Minlöuian simply smiled and looked up as she retorted, "But, miss... surely you must be incorrect?" She began to fan herself as she continued, as if talking to the air, "Why, you've mastered the art of ignorance, unrestraint, contempt, foolishness, and idiocy!"

Jenna's blood boiled as she strove in every possible way to restrain her Majesty.

"And to make matters worse," Mrs. Minlöuian went on, "she doesn't even know how to bathe!" She pinched her nose. "But then again, I cannot place all the blame upon you."

Fearing the worst was yet to come, Isaac and James each wrapped an arm around Jenna and began to lead her away.

But Mrs. Minlöuian wasn't through. Oh no... she still had more to say.

"No, a majority of the blame must go to the filthy, uneducated, ill-tempered, barbaric, and foolish excuses that must be your parents."

"Oof!" Isaac and James exclaimed as they were pulled back by Jenna, who stopped dead in her tracks.

"Oh? Have I struck a nerve?" questioned Mrs. Minlöuian with a twisted smile, making a strange sort of squawking noise that must have been her laugh. "Forgive me, I retract that statement about your parents, for I'm sure you have none. Yes, indeed, how very blind of me!" she finished. "For you fit the perfect description of a *bastard child!*"

Isaac and James looked at each other in absolute horror.

This is it! This is it for my kingdom, thought James as he looked dead forward. *I hope Wöntylnas is prepared to become the next Aerlund.*

Merciful Creator of heaven and Vaerün, begged Isaac in his mind as he closed his eyes, *may thy eternal power calm the raging inferno that is undoubtedly storming within my precious friend at this very moment. Save her from this demon, I pray.*

With a moment's pause, Mrs. Minlöuian internally rejoicing in her self-proclaimed victory, Jenna slowly turned around.

"Mrs. Minlöuian... was it?" she calmly asked, her eyes glaring with a roaring fire. "I have only one thing to say to you."

Mrs. Minlöuian discreetly swallowed, undoubtedly witnessing the storm of barely contained fire in Jenna's eyes.

"There is only one Master..." Jenna quietly said, pointing upward, "and that is our eternal Creator."

With that, Jenna threw her arms around Isaac and James and quickly walked down the street, continuing toward the western end of Wöntylnas.

Neither Isaac nor James dared to say anything for the next few moments. Finally, unable to take it any longer, Isaac spoke up. "Jenna, are you—"

"Honestly! Who does she think she is?" Jenna suddenly boomed. "What a wretched woman! I **hate** the people here."

James snickered and snorted, trying to repress a laugh. "Yes, well... it doesn't help that you had to pick a fight with the snootiest woman in all of Wöntylnas, its famed concert pianist and instructor."

"I don't give a shüza who she is!" roared Jenna. "And I mean really—all of that over a grape?"

"Whoa, whoa, whoa!" exclaimed James as he brought the two to a screeching halt. "I need to make sure I heard that right. Did you just say that *all* of that... was started over a grape? Ha ha! This I've gotta hear!"

Jenna tossed her head as she flipped her hair and closed her eyes. "Not much to say. You and Isaac were a few feet in front of me when suddenly I heard this snobby wench to my left arguing with the servant."

"That's 'waiter,'" interjected James.

"Whatever. So anyway, she was complaining to this waiter that the grapes she had ordered had been delivered with the *'skins still on them!'*"

Isaac blinked repeatedly as James laughed. "Wait, what? Are you serious right now?"

"I swear!" exclaimed Jenna. "Now I tried to ignore it. I really did!"

"What was the topper then?" Isaac smiled.

"The topper was when she demanded that they throw away those perfectly good grapes, bring her new ones—[skin off them, mind you!]—and give them to her for free!"

James ran his fingers through his slicked-back hair and grimaced. "Ooooh yeah... that's rough."

Isaac stroked his shimmering, newly growing blond beard as he pondered. "To be honest, I don't think I'd have been able to keep my mouth closed either. That's positively asinine."

James tossed his hands in the air as they continued toward the castle. "I'm not kidding when I say that both of you are going to get tired of me repeating—"

"Oh, trust me," interrupted Jenna, "we haven't even been here an hour, and I get why you left!"

"And said," agreed Isaac.

"Not as impressive as my castle, but I suppose it'll do," said Jenna as she tossed her head back and forth in observance.

The gleaming white marbled stairs reflected the morning sunlight as they led up to the ornate, grand castle of Wöntylnas.

After climbing about fifty steps, Jenna was shocked when they were stopped by two soldiers barring the platinum silver gates that led through to the castle beyond.

"State your business," they said in sync, unsheathing their silver daggers, prepared for combat.

"What a way to be greeted." Isaac frowned.

Jenna folded her arms as she laughed sarcastically. "Nonsense! According to the way this kingdom runs, why, I'd expect nothing less! Much less than my kingdom that allowed any visitors."

"Günholdt? Kolkür?" James questioned; hands outstretched. "I know it's been ten years, but come on, guys. I'm offended."

The soldiers looked at each other, then removed their blue-and-silver helms as they shouted in unison, "James Vandergaus!"

"Always a pleasure to see you two jerks!" James shouted back, nooging both of their heads.

"I know, I know. You have questions, I'm sure! But right now, I need to get my two friends to the castle."

The soldiers immediately opened the gate as Günholdt quickly said, "Of course, of course, James! We're sure you're here on very important business."

James shook his head in exhaustion as he responded, "Oh, you haven't a clue! A business like no other!"

Kolkür spoke to James as the three of them passed by. "Please, tell your uncle that we said hello!"

James turned around and raised an eyebrow as he questioned, "My uncle?"

Kolkür looked at his partner in equal confusion as they both stared at James. "Are you not going to see your uncle?"

"Oh!" James suddenly shouted in surprise. "Oh, of course we are! After we get some breakfast."

Isaac and Jenna couldn't help but laugh as the soldiers looked at each other with that same "really?" sort of look.

"Right. Well, give our regards to your uncle when you're finished with your… breakfast." Günholdt nodded as he placed his helm back upon his head.

"Will do!" beamed James. "Take care!"

Jenna gave a slight push to James once they were out of earshot of the soldiers. "Thanks for introducing us, James."

James gripped the large golden handle of the castle door as he heaved it open. "Don't worry. I have a feeling we'll be here long enough for you to get acquainted."

Isaac and Jenna quickly responded in unison, albeit both for different reasons, "We don't need to get acquainted."

"Indeed?" responded James, a little taken aback.

The interior of the castle was stunning. Rippling pillars of pure water lay suspended between the floor and ceiling. The white marbled floor, accented by smears of all different blue hues, complemented the white marble statues of angels in flowing robes.

The sound of running water came from all directions as it flowed through silver channels within the floor, leading from room to room. And there, in the center of the foyer, was the focal point of the grand staircase: a white marbled statue of King Vergaus Wöntylnas with his hands outstretched, depicting him casting Water Majesty.

"Umm…" whispered Jenna to James, "isn't your current king a little upset about a statue that's not him?"

"Not at all! King Närvein isn't like that. He's actually pretty cool and laid-back."

Isaac observed the statue and smiled as he ran his fingers along the cool, smooth stone. "That doesn't make sense. If Wöntylnas is corrupted, wouldn't its king be too?" he asked further.

"Well, what do you expect?" James shrugged. "He's only thirty-five. And it'd be hard for you, too, I'm sure, if your servants were older than you and working secret combinations behind your back!"

Isaac turned around and shook his head. "That's got to be tough. My heart goes out to him."

James waved his finger as he began to ascend the grand staircase. "But that's why he has my uncle, the Magister Professor Vandergaus, as one of his leading servants and assistants. Now come on! Come meet him! Isn't that why you're here?"

Jenna gave Isaac a nervous look. He returned with his typical calm smile as they both followed James up the grand staircase and down the long corridor.

She had to run a little faster to catch up with James. "If I may be bold, James... what happened to your parents? How'd your uncle find you?"

His response was entirely calm as he continued looking forward. "Don't even worry! And I don't know who my parents are. They abandoned me at birth. Professor Vandergaus rescued me from the streets of Wöntylnas and adopted me as his 'nephew' rather than son."

Jenna covered her mouth in shock. Isaac was speechless.

"I'm... so sorry. I... I had no idea," she quietly said.

"Not at all!" beamed James. "I'm grateful. Professor Vandergaus didn't have to take me in or adopt me."

"But your parents? That's so cruel of them to—"

"I like to think," he interrupted her, "that there's more to the story. I can't blame them when I don't have all the details. And I have great hope that I'll meet them someday! And then I'll be able to get all my answers."

Isaac smiled as he grasped James's shoulder. "That's very admirable of you! Never lose hope!"

"No way. Never!" thundered James as he placed his hands upon the golden handles of the throne room doors. "Well, this is it. Are you prepared to meet King Närvein and Professor Vandergaus?"

Isaac and Jenna nodded with excitement as he opened the doors and entered, both following behind.

So, *this* is where all the water was coming from! Atop the stairs that led to the throne, high on the left and right sides, gushed two small waterfalls that emptied into two silver basins, held by elegant female marbled statues. The water then emptied into the silver channels that flowed throughout the castle.

Stemming from the same construction and design, albeit in different colors, Jenna smiled as she rubbed her hand along the smooth white, blue, and golden pillars, flooding her mind with memories and thoughts of her parents' throne room.

It didn't take but a few seconds to realize that no one was seated upon the throne.

James gave a nervous chuckle as he turned to his friends. "They must have just… stepped out for a second. Hold on really quick, okay?"

Both politely nodded. Jenna walked around as Isaac stood in the same place with his hands calmly clasped together.

"King Närvein! Uncle!" cried out James as he stepped forward.

His voice boomed and echoed through the hall, but there was no response.

"Heeelloooo?" He tried again. But to no avail.

James bit his lower lip as he turned around and rushed up to his friends.

"Why do you look so happy?" asked Jenna cautiously.

"Because now," he answered, "we get to go and have breakfast!"

Isaac and Jenna looked at each other as their hearts momentarily skipped a beat, the unmistakable feeling of saliva welling in their mouths.

With hands rubbing together, James bolted past them and called for them to follow.

"Please… right this way! You're going to love Chef Volkan's food! And don't worry," he said as he suddenly turned around, "it's all safe to eat, seeming as it's all meant for the aristocracy."

"Don't mind me if you see me stealing some and giving it to the poor," said Jenna truthfully.

"Can't mind when I've done the same," replied James as he turned around.

"You two are awesome." Isaac smiled as he followed.

Similar to a posh café, the three friends couldn't quit smiling as they sat in one of four mid-sized rooms that made up the divided dining hall. But they were smart; they chose the room and table with the western ocean view.

"It's still hard to believe that ten years passed that fast!" beamed Chef Volkan as he arrived, pushing a silver cart full of food.

It was so hard for Isaac to not pay attention as Jenna was served first, then James, and finally himself.

He had to quickly swallow and shut his mouth to prevent the drool from falling as the fat hand of Chef Volkan placed multiple plates in front of him. The steaming French toast with powdered sugar, drizzled with kinberry syrup, scrambled eggs with fire-roasted tomatoes and onions, roasted boar with sautéed greens, and hash browns mixed with peppers and onions nearly caused him to faint.

"Th-thank you, Chef Volkan," Isaac muttered as he dug his fork into the French toast.

"Eat up, Isaac and Jenna! Any friend of James is more than welcome!" he exclaimed as he pushed the cart away, back into the kitchen.

Jenna's eyes widened as she gave Isaac an accusing smile. "Isaac! I'm shocked! It's not like you to eat without saying—"

"Ohr drn't wery," he said with his mouth full of French toast. "I olrdy blersd irt."

"Well, damn," said James blankly. "The guy must really love food."

"It's not so much that," added Jenna, "as it is the kinberry syrup adjoining the French toast," she said as Isaac dabbed his already dripping French toast onto Jenna's to soak up more syrup.

"For me, it's all about the hash browns." James winked.

"That reminds me. Would you like me to pay for this?" Jenna asked as she reached for a small pouch attached to one of her many belts.

James nearly choked on his potatoes as he spat, "What? You have money?"

She couldn't help but laugh as she sincerely answered, "Far more than I possibly know what to do with."

He quickly swallowed and leaned forward. "That's right! I keep forgetting you're the princess of Fürnas!"

"It comes with its quirks." She shrugged. "And one of those quirks happens to be a secret vault, hidden in the castle dungeon with loads of gold and platinum bars."

James leaned back as he scooped up more hash browns. "That's just crazy. What does one even do with all that money?"

"I always tell people that money is just an outlet. Big deal." She answered, "It is not at all necessary to survive."

James swallowed his hash browns and pointed to Isaac. "What about you, Isaac? Got any dirt?"

"No. And even if I did, Jenna refuses for me to use it."

James looked at Jenna and raised his eyebrow. "Why would we need to use any money that he'd have when I have a whole vault full myself?"

He tossed his head back and forth as he went to cut his roasted boar. "Can't argue with that. Oh! And no, Chef Volkan would kill me if we gave him any money. No, as long as we're here, the food is always free."

Isaac's eyes partially lulled back into his head as James's words echoed in his head, as if someone had just drugged him, *always free... always free... always free...*

"Well then. Shall we try this again?" James asked as he held his hands upon the golden handles of the throne room doors.

With full bellies and spirits, the three were much more prepared to meet with the king and James's uncle.

And imagine their delight when they entered to find both of them there!

"James!" cried Professor Vandergaus as he dashed down the steps and pulled his nephew into a strong, loving embrace.

How rude! Jenna thought as she watched the scene. *Why didn't he say anything?*

As if able to read her mind, she suddenly picked up on what was happening as Isaac tapped her shoulder and motioned for her to listen.

Perhaps she'd forgotten that Majesticians have emotions too, but she was still pretty shocked upon hearing James's sob and cry as he rocked back and forth in the arms of his beloved uncle.

Although she was one to talk, as the scene momentarily brought her back to think of the times when she, too, had rocked back and forth in the loving embrace of her precious parents and even Nann and Uncle Ingle.

The sting of emotions got her every time as she felt a little embarrassed. Although, she quickly felt better as her gaze fell upon Isaac to notice that he was crying too. But was he crying for the same reason as her? Or was he just happy to see James happy?

King Närvein smiled in patience as James eagerly introduced his friends.

"Uncle, I am so delighted to introduce you to my friends!"

Now able to get a better view of him up close, Isaac and Jenna smiled widely as they shook hands.

And this was James's adopted uncle? They looked so much alike! The salt-and-pepper hair, slicked back into a ponytail, mirrored James's own style. Even their facial structures shared a striking resemblance, and those blue eyes—though not as animated as James's—closely matched his nephew's. Their wardrobes were also quite similar, but Professor Vandergaus's attire had an added elegance: silver and gold threading adorned the dark-blue vest, and a fluffy-rimmed, blue-and-black cloak draped over one shoulder. Though the gray-and-black goatee gave him a more intimidating presence, there was nothing but kindness and hospitality in his demeanor.

"This is Isaac, our dear friend, and beloved Light Majestician to Vaerün!" James exclaimed as he motioned to his new, precious friend.

Isaac's voice vibrated a little as Professor Vandergaus grasped his hand with both of his. "P-pleasure to m-meet you, Professor!" stammered Isaac.

"Isaac?" He glowed, while observing the pendant around his neck. "Why, your necklace reminds me strictly of the great commander-in-chief over the northern wind kingdom of Wölnas! Right, James?"

"It looks the very same, sir!" exclaimed Jenna as she stepped up next to him.

With a corner smile, hardly containing his excitement, James motioned to Jenna as he said, "And this is Jenna Coltier, princess of Fürnas!"

Professor Vandergaus could hardly contain his excitement as he profusely shook her hand and then finally brought both Isaac and Jenna into a bear-squeezed hug. "I cannot tell you what it possibly means to me to finally meet you two," he muttered before blurting out, "Oh! Gracious, where are my manners?"

With the smell of sweet smoke and spearmint flowing behind him, he politely and quickly motioned for them to ascend the stairs with him, to meet King Närvein.

A little shy, but in strong spirits, Isaac and Jenna followed Professor Vandergaus and James up the marbled stairs to meet the water king sitting upon his throne.

Undoubtedly, his appearance screamed nothing but *king*. His thick, black, wavy hair just came to his shoulders. The dominantly silver crown, accented with gold trim and blue gems that sat upon his head, further added to the shine of his glossy hair. His features were very strong, completely visible from his neatly shaved face. And like Professor Vandergaus and James, he had striking blue eyes.

His wardrobe was beautiful and impressionable. Silken white pants, cast against blue-and-white boots, lined with gold and silver, made James a little jealous. His heavily ornamented captain's coat laid open to reveal a fluffy white shirt underneath (perhaps a little flirtatious or striving to be independent). A little bit of black chest hair lay barely visible, revealed from the unbuttoned top. And to wrap it all together, a fluffy rimmed cloak around his shoulders, similar to Professor Vandergaus's, although better!

One can imagine their surprise when King Närvein himself stood up, walked over, and embraced each of the Majesticians! "I cannot tell you just how happy I am to meet all of you," he sincerely said after the embraces. "James, thank you very much for taking the time to find and bring these two Majesticians here! I'm sure the trek hasn't been easy."

Jenna snickered a little, and Isaac just smiled, as both looked at James, eager to hear his reply.

At first, the thought came to him of just lying. But then, always striving to have integrity, he told the truth. "Your Majesty, to be honest, our meeting was not intended. Isaac and Jenna barely escaped their burning home of Aerlund, and their story is probably the one of which you desire to hear."

Certainly, everyone was a little shocked.

Professor Vandergaus appeared sad, disappointed, and surprised as he asked Jenna and Isaac, "Did Mayor Inglethöp not deliver my letter to you? I sent it some time ago and never received word. Is that not why you're here?"

Jenna's face melted a little as she, too, told the truth. "No, sir… we know nothing of a letter. When Aerlund fell under siege of the Kreaux, our surrogate mother, Nanny Tromsdotter, told us to find a certain Professor Vandergaus in the Aerbön woods. She said it was imperative that we find you!"

Professor Vandergaus massaged his goatee as he nodded. "Fascinating… very clever of her." "Clever, sir?" asked Isaac. "The code in which she said it," he responded. "I explained, in my letter, that I had finally found the answers to the sealed towers, located at the back of each castle, in each kingdom."

The three Majesticians focused upon him as he continued, "I further explained that Isaac and Jenna needed to meet with my nephew, James Vandergaus, and the only water Majestician upon Vaerün as soon as possible, and to come here to Wöntylnas."

Seeing that they were intrigued, he continued, "When I said that she said it in code, I believe it was clever of her because she knew if she said, 'Water Majestician' around the Kreaux, they probably would have beaten you to poor James. And although my nephew is quite powerful, I fear to think how those circumstances would've turned out."

"Please hold just a moment, Professor," said Jenna as she held her head. "There are so many questions I have, and I'm sure Isaac and James do too, and—"

King Närvein placed a hand on Professor Vandergaus's shoulder as he interrupted, "Pardon me, Princess Coltier. But Jéid, why not utilize the library for this conversation? That way, you can all sit comfortably as I'm sure you have a lot to talk about."

Professor Vandergaus thought for a moment and then nodded. "Capital idea, Your Majesty. Shall you be joining?"

"I have other matters to attend to. But I shall anticipate a full report when you are finished."

"Very well then. Isaac, James, and Jenna, please follow me!" exclaimed Professor Vandergaus as he led the way to the library.

It didn't take long to clear out the vast library of bookworms, scholars, and students as Professor Vandergaus ordered immediate vacancy by command of the king.

Isaac and Jenna took advantage of the short opportunity as they looked out the enormous glass windows and stared out into the deep blue ocean. The wonderful, old, and sweet smell of aged tomes, texts, scrolls, and books filled their nostrils as they looked all around at the towering walls that held an incalculable number of books. All around them, tables laid scattered with parchment paper and additional tomes and books.

The ceiling held multiple crystal chandeliers, with their blue-and-gold emitting lights. And above them laid a rich and ornately painted ceiling depicting the heavens and clouds above, with angels blowing their trumpets.

Professor Vandergaus walked up and clapped his hand upon the large table that was in front of them. "Excellent choice! I do so love an ocean view."

James quickly pulled out a chair and sat down. "Aren't they the best? We had a similar view just some stories below us in the dining hall!"

Professor Vandergaus was the last to sit as he did so with interest. "Oh! So, you had some of Chef Volkan's cooking, now did you?" he asked as he looked excitedly at Isaac and Jenna. "What did you think? Wasn't it fantastic?"

"It truly was superb," answered Jenna. "Some of the best roasted boar I've ever had."

"The French toast was to die for," added Isaac. "Also, that kinberry syrup was divine."

Professor Vandergaus smiled and laughed as he clapped. "Fantastic! I'm sure, as James told you, that you're welcome to eat at any time. No charge at all!"

Poor Isaac felt quite embarrassed as he missed the next few minutes of conversation, too busy fantasizing about stacks and stacks of unlimited French toast, smothered and dripping with kinberry syrup.

His attention was brought back when Professor Vandergaus laughed his distinct laugh. "No, no, of course not! I don't want to hear the personal details of your life story. Those are for you and are meant to be kept private. No, I simply desire to hear what happened from the time of Aerlund's demise until now. Oh, and please, call me Jéid. It's so much easier than Professor Vandergaus!"

And so, thankfully, Isaac caught on as James, Jenna, and he recapped to Jéid all that had happened from Aerlund's demise to their current arrival.

"Ha ha ha!" boomed Jéid's laughter. "Mercy of mercies! I cannot believe you took them through that ancient water prison!"

Jenna's eye twitched for a moment as she quietly asked, "Water prison?"

"Yes, didn't you tell them, James? Surely, with how studious you are, you'd have known what you were getting yourself into? Why do you think I told you to use it only in cases of emergencies?"

Isaac and Jenna slowly turned their heads to James, expecting an answer.

"Wait, hold on. You misunderstand!" he exclaimed, both trying to get out of trouble and telling the truth. "I swear I didn't know what it was! Please, Uncle. Care to explain?"

"Sure, sure," said Jéid as he nonchalantly waved his hand. "Over a thousand years ago, during the Majesty Genocidal War... You all know of that, right?" he quickly interjected.

They nodded their heads, and so he continued.

"Wöntylnas, with its water Majesticians, was said to have been the most ruthless. They created that tunnel for the very purpose of trapping their prisoners of war. And once they were done torturing them for information, they filled up the entire tunnel [all fifteen miles, mind you] and drowned the prisoners with their Majesty."

Jenna covered her mouth and shook her head as every hair on her body stood up.

"No wonder I was so affected by it then," mumbled James. "The ghosts probably saw me as the biggest threat since I'm a water Majestician."

Jéid, still chuckling, placed a hand on James's shoulder. "Don't fret, James. The tunnel has long since been dormant. But now that it's surfaced... well, let's just say I hope you didn't disturb any resting spirits!"

Jenna rolled her eyes and gave a shiver. "Oh, well that's just wonderful! So now we might have angry ghosts following us? Wonderful... just wonderful!"

Isaac, trying to lighten the mood, forced a smile. "Well, at least we made it through! And all in one piece!"

Jéid laughed heartily once more. "Yes, yes. And that, my dear friends, is all that matters."

A silence hung over the table for a few moments as they each took in the revelations of the day. The pale blue glow from the chandeliers cast gentle shadows on their faces, each of them lost in thought for a brief moment.

Jéid finally leaned in, the energy in his voice turning a touch more serious. "Now then, let's talk about why I called for you in the first place."

Isaac, Jenna, and James sat up a little straighter, sensing the shift in the conversation.

"As I mentioned, I sent a letter to Mayor Inglethöp of Aerlund, but since you were unaware of it... Well, perhaps it's even more important that you're here now."

"What did you find, Professor?" Isaac asked, the curiosity clear in his tone.

Jéid's eyes twinkled. "The final words of King Vergaus Wöntylnas himself. And not only do they reveal what the Kreaux really are... they describe how to destroy them. For good."

Jenna, James, and Isaac nearly fainted as they immediately leaned in so close that their heads almost touched.

"What? Are you certain?" Jenna and James demanded in sync.

"Destroy them? For **good?**" Isaac added.

"Yes! It's true!" Jéid's excitement was palpable. "And that's why I'm so concerned about this letter Jenna has received from someone claiming to be Garon."

Isaac's eyes narrowed in thought as he sat up suddenly. "I get it."

James looked at him in confusion. "Would you care to explain then? Because even I'm not following."

Isaac leaned back slightly, looking between Jéid and Jenna. "Jéid, when exactly did you make this discovery? The final words of King Wöntylnas?"

Jéid held his chin as he thought for a moment. "Why, about a month ago!"

"Exactly," said Isaac as he put the pieces together. "Jenna, do you remember how strange Nann was acting before you left to meet Mr. Tendúr?"

Jenna thought for a moment, recalling how nervous Nann had indeed been acting before she left. Nann had mentioned something "very important" to share but chose to wait, so as not to ruin Jenna's trip.

"Yes," she admitted. "Yes, I do."

Isaac turned back to Jéid, his voice low. "Exactly what did you say in your letter to Mayor Inglethöp?"

Jéid placed his palm face down upon the cool wooden table as he admitted, "I wrote that I had made a decisive discovery for the destruction of the Kreaux, one that requires the last remaining Majesticians of our time."

"And did you explain what that discovery was?" Isaac pressed on.

"Yes," Jéid confirmed. "I explained that it involves the towers at the back of each castle, in every kingdom, and that Isaac and Jenna were to meet up with my nephew, James, in the Aerbön Woods, and come to Wöntylnas immediately!"

Jenna's heart began beating faster and faster as the realization hit her. "I get it… So it would be impossible for that letter to be from Garon, then! Seeing as how he's supposed to be dead, and how you just made that discovery about King Wöntylnas!"

"Exactly," Jéid said sharply, raising a hand. "And that is why I am panicking, trying to figure out who could have intercepted my letter, had enough knowledge to pose as Garon, and what their motives might be!"

Feeling suddenly like the letter was cursed, Jenna quickly dropped it on the table, and they all stared at it.

"Are you sure this Mr. Tendúr fellow can be trusted?" asked Jéid.

"If you don't believe me on anything else, believe me on this: Mr. Tendúr is, next to Isaac, perhaps the most benevolent man on Vaerün, and he would never lie or do such a dark deed," Jenna asserted.

Isaac, finally breaking the tension with a deep breath, added, "The way I see it, there are only two possibilities. Either the letter really is from Garon, somehow… or someone intercepted Jéid's letter and is spying on us."

"But how?" Jéid asked, leaning back in his chair. "Let's pretend, for argument's sake, that Garon is alive. The only other person I've shared my research and findings with is King Närvein himself, who is sworn to secrecy, lest accusations arise that could lead to the usurpation of his kingdom!"

"Was the letter tampered with when Mayor Inglethöp received it?" asked James.

Isaac and Jenna looked at each other, then shook their heads. "Like we both said, we never saw the letter," Isaac answered. "But if there's one thing I know about Uncle Ingle and Nann, they would have told us right away if anything strange had happened with it."

James stood up and took a deep breath. "That's true... They probably would have taken it as some sign of an impending attack."

Jéid's eyes widened as he slowly retracted from the letter on the table, as if it were something horrid and evil. "If that really is from Garon... then," he whispered, afraid to voice his thoughts, "he would have to possess powers of perception and sight beyond any mortal, even beyond Majesticians."

Jenna reached for the letter, scanned it quickly, then folded it up and tossed it back down. "And as we've said, that's just not possible."

Everyone seemed quite shocked when Isaac spoke gravely, "This is disturbing. Something is *very* wrong." For anyone else to say it, it was okay, almost... expected. But when Isaac spoke like this? It was as if someone had just unleashed a bad omen that was surely going to come to pass.

Jéid, snapping them out of the looming daze, spoke up, "Isaac... Jenna... and my nephew, I must show you the words of King Wöntylnas. You need to understand what's at stake."

Jenna and James's eyes widened as they exclaimed almost in unison, "Yes! Show us what he said! What must we do to defeat the Kreaux?"

Jéid picked up his cloak from the back of his chair and draped it upon his shoulders, his expression changing to one of hesitation. "Forgive me, my dear friends... but I'm going to hold off."

"What? Really?" exclaimed Jenna and James, both leaning in, eyes wide with disbelief.

"Whatever, or whoever sent that letter, they know too much. And until I can gather more information and make sense of it, I will not reveal anything further."

"So you brought us all the way here just to have us sit and wait?" demanded Jenna, her eyes glowing with anger.

"I'm sorry, Jenna," Jéid said, his concern evident, "but it's for your safety. All of you. Give me just one week—max—and I promise

I will reveal all. No, better than that, I'll let you personally read his notes yourselves."

The three Majesticians sighed as they slumped down into their chairs.

"Well then... what do we do for the next week?" Jenna asked, pressing her face into her hands.

"Come now, it's not so bad!" Jéid tried optimistically. "Do you like music? We have some of the finest performers in—"

"Trust me," interrupted Jenna, "we've met some of your 'finest' performers."

Jéid stared at James curiously and then quickly caught on. "Ah, so you've already had an introduction to Wöntylnas'... unique musical scene, then?"

"Soooo!" Jenna deflected, leaning back in her chair with a raised brow. "What are you going to be investigating for the next week while we wait, Uncle?"

"Just some intel gathering, if you will. I'm going to head personally up to the Kingdom of Wölnas to see if there are any survivors from the recent attacks and to gather any intelligence on this matter."

"And if there are?" asked Isaac curiously, leaning forward, unable to hide his interest.

Jéid's eyes flickered with intensity as he answered, "If there are, then I'll interrogate them about the current standings and whereabouts of Garon. We must know the truth."

Isaac sat back, processing the gravity of the situation. "I see... I understand."

"Now please, don't look so glum!" Jéid said, attempting to lighten the mood with a bright smile. "Spend this time getting acquainted with the finer aspects of Wöntylnas! And, James, I've personally seen to it that you and your friends are staying in the most esteemed quarters, right here in the castle."

"Thank you very much, Uncle," James replied, his tone a mixture of gratitude and lingering concern.

With that, James, Isaac, and Jenna each gave a hug of farewell to Jéid Vandergaus as he left the library. His cloak fluttered behind him as he strode toward the throne room to begin his journey.

"Well... what do we do now?" Jenna sighed, massaging her temples as if to stave off a headache.

"Can we go eat?" Isaac quickly asked, his face brightening at the mere thought of food.

Jenna and James couldn't help but laugh at his earnestness. They both stood up, nodding in agreement.

"Sounds good to me," Jenna said, trying to lift her own spirits. "Lunch does sound pretty good."

"And after that," added James, "let's check out our quarters! I'm curious to see what sort of fancy place my uncle has set us up in."

Isaac held back a moment, his fingers drumming a soft rhythm on the wooden table. James noticed and called out, "Oi! Everything all right, Isaac?"

Jenna placed a gentle hand on James's arm and shook her head with a knowing smile. "Don't worry about him. His fingers just do that when he hasn't played the piano in some time."

James tilted his head, looking from Isaac's tapping fingers to Jenna's calm, understanding expression. "You know, you're probably going to hate me for saying this... but maybe he could take some lessons with Mrs. Minlöuian while we stay here for the week?" he suggested, half-joking.

Jenna gave him a smirk and a playful clap on the shoulder as she walked toward the exit, "You're funny, James. Real funny."

"I actually think it'd be a great idea!" Isaac chimed in, surprising them both. He stepped up to James with a bright, hopeful look. "Besides, she needs to learn a very important lesson."

James turned to Isaac, an eyebrow raised in curiosity and mild concern. "Teach her a lesson? What in Vaerün are you talking about?"

Isaac's smile widened as he walked forward, turning back briefly to look over his shoulder. "No one is ever done learning, and we can all learn something—from anything and anyone."

James's eyes opened wide as he massaged his scalp, trying to ease the tension from the day's events. "Oh, Isaac... you don't know who you're dealing with. But it'll be interesting to see what happens, that's for sure," he muttered.

Lessons to Be Learned

Isaac stared up at the ceiling as he lay upon the fluffy, blue-and-white comforter of his king-sized bed. For being just one of fifteen bedrooms in the guests' quarters, it sure was huge! It was probably about half the size of his (now destroyed) concert hall back in Aerlund. Well, okay, maybe not that big, but... close!

How grateful he was to have a room with an eastern window! For he loved to watch the rays of the morning sun as they streamed into his room.

Surely, he was quite used to the grandness of the home he grew up in, but this took it to a whole new level. I mean really, who needs five sofas, two coffee tables, and three armoires in their bedroom? The two glass coffee tables with silver legs accented the marble floor beautifully. But he certainly wasn't used to staying in a room equipped with four water pillars, nor was he accustomed to the constant sound of running water as a tiny river wound through one of the walls, fed a fountain that could only be left to the imagination, and flowed back through another wall.

Knock, knock, knock! The massive white wooden doors banged loudly as he shouted, "Come in!"

His heart momentarily plummeted as Jenna walked in. She always managed to make his heart do that—skip a beat or drop out entirely—but today was different. There was something about the way she closed the door gently behind her, leaning against it for a second as if steadying herself. A shadow seemed to hang over her expression, and Isaac instantly sat up, running his fingers through his hair to tame it, fluffing his collar out of sheer habit.

"J-Jenn! Good morning! What a wonderful surprise." He tried to sound casual, but the knot forming in his stomach betrayed him.

Jenna didn't say anything at first, and that only made the tension worse. Her eyes lingered on the floor for a moment, and she took a slow breath before finally looking up and meeting his gaze. He noticed the tiny, almost imperceptible frown that marred her usually bright expression. This was serious.

With her clip-clopping boots, long flowing hair, dress, and smile, Jenna was every bit the picture of beauty and grace, yet today, there was something fragile—uncertain—behind her eyes. Isaac feared he might faint when she sat down right next to him on the bed, her shoulder brushing his as she settled in close. He tried to steady his breathing, his heart pounding in his chest.

"I'm surprised to see you in here! Normally, you would have wolfed down your breakfast at Chef Volkan's by now." Jenna's voice was soft, almost teasing, but there was a sadness beneath it that Isaac couldn't quite place.

"O-oh. Yes, I suppose you're right." Isaac's voice wavered, and he felt his face flush as she turned toward him, her white-gloved hands reaching up to cradle his face. She was close now—so close he could feel the warmth of her breath.

"What's on your mind?" Jenna's tone was gentle but probing. "It must be something, for you to be holding off on steaming French toast and piping-hot kinberry syrup."

Isaac tried to shrug it off, but her eyes bore into his, and he felt utterly unable to lie. How could he ever lie to her, when she looked at him like that—with all the love and concern in the world?

"I'm just a little sad, that's all," he admitted, though the words felt small compared to what he actually felt. Jenna gave him a small, reassuring smile, but it didn't quite reach her eyes.

"What are you sad about, darling one?" she asked as she stood up and pulled open the large, white, crosshatched windows, immediately letting in the cool ocean breeze. The scent of the sea filled the room, and Isaac closed his eyes for a moment, letting it wash over him. Anything to distract from the nervousness building inside.

"Is it the weather? Today does look rather gloomy."

He took a deep breath, trying to steady himself. "It sure does now! You just missed the sun, I'm afraid." Isaac tried to keep his voice light, but it cracked on the last word.

Her boots clacked on the floor as she pulled him up and spun him around in a circle. "Soooo? Are you going to tell me, or am I going to have to force it out of you?"

The poor guy nearly fainted as his voice cracked again. "A-and how would you do that?"

She stopped spinning him and collapsed back onto his bed, laughing softly—a sound that would normally set his heart fluttering, but today, it only made the heaviness of the moment grow.

When the laughter faded, Jenna's expression became serious again. She reached out and took his hand in both of hers, the warmth of her fingers steadying him. For a long moment, she just held it, her eyes flickering as if she were gathering the strength to say what needed to be said.

"Isaac," she began, her voice low and trembling slightly. "I… I need to tell you something. Something important."

Isaac's smile faded, his eyes searching her face. "Jenn? What is it?"

Jenna bit her lip and looked away, her fingers tightening around his hand. "Some intel came back, Isaac. From the palace… Regarding *Wölnas*."

He could feel his pulse quickening, the tension in the room growing unbearable. "Intel?" he whispered. "What do you mean? What… what did you find?"

Her eyes were suddenly swimming with emotion as she met his gaze, and Isaac could see just how difficult this was for her to say. "It's about your… your family," she said softly. "About who you are."

Isaac's breath hitched, and he shook his head, a sick feeling rising in his stomach. "My family? Jenn, I… I don't understand."

"It's about Garon and Lucy Erbrecht," Jenna pressed on, her voice cracking with the effort. "Isaac… it's almost certain now. All the evidence points to it—you're their son."

Gently, she brought her porcelain like-hand to his face, brushing his hair back. "And honestly? Now that I take an even greater look into your handsome face…"

"*Handsome…? Did she just-*"

"You really do look just like them. You have your dad's strong facial structure and your mom's heavenly gentleness."

The words hung in the air, heavy and inescapable, and for a moment, Isaac felt like the world had stopped spinning. His breath caught in his throat, and his entire body seemed to go numb. He stared at Jenna, his eyes wide and uncomprehending. "I… I'm their… son?" he whispered, as if saying it aloud might somehow make it less real. "But… how? Why?"

"I know," Jenna said, her own voice choked with emotion. "It's a lot to take in. And I wish I could give you all the answers, but… we don't know everything. Not yet."

"But… but what about them?" Isaac's voice was trembling now, desperation creeping into his words. "Where are they? Are they… are they alive?"

Jenna's face crumpled, and she squeezed his hand even tighter, as if to give him all the comfort she could. "No one knows," she said, her voice barely above a whisper. "No one knows where they are, Isaac. Or if they survived the siege of Wölnas."

The reality of it crashed over him like a wave, and Isaac felt tears spring to his eyes. He wanted to say something, anything, but all he could do was shake his head, trying to make sense of it all. "But… why would they leave me?" he said, his voice breaking. "Why… why wouldn't they come back?"

"I wish I knew," Jenna said, her tears spilling over as she pulled him into a fierce, desperate embrace. "I wish I had all the answers. But all I can tell you is… you're not alone. You have us. And no matter what, we'll find out the truth together."

Isaac clung to her as if she were his only anchor in a storm-tossed sea, the reality of his parentage crashing into him with every heartbeat. Garon and Lucy Erbrecht. His parents. Who were they? And why had they vanished, leaving him to a life without knowing?

Where are you?

The question echoed through his mind like a haunting melody, unanswered and unresolved, a mystery waiting to be unraveled.

"Were they... Bad people?" Isaac desperately asked.

Jenna immediately placed a hand on his leg and spoke to him compassionately.

"Oh no, no, dear."

There it was again. *Dear. Honey. Merciful heavens above!*

"I can promise you that Garon and Lucy Erbrecht were by far the most *amazing* people I ever had the pleasure of knowing. They'd never do anything malicious, let alone think of it!"

Although... Jenna raised an eyebrow. "Garon *did* love to play an awful lot of tricks on me. One time, I woke up all sticky... Couldn't figure out why, 'til I realized that he'd swapped my doll in the middle of the night, with a kinberry loaf."

Isaac erupted in laughter.

"Yep. Jelly was *EVERYWHERE*, let me tell you that. Kinda sucks when you think you are squeezing your favorite dollie, only for it to be a sticky jam loaf!" She finished, sarcastically

Isaac sniffled from the pollen that had just blown in, now sneezing and laughing at the same time.

"That's why I'm having so much difficulty swallowing this story!" she further exclaimed.

"I just wish I knew more," Isaac said as he stood up and paced back and forth.

"And for that, I don't blame you, dear. But please, hold on to what you do know, and just keep moving forward! Like James said, don't jump to conclusions when you don't have all the data."

Isaac stood still for a moment, clearly in deep thought. Jenna's heart fluttered as she watched his shimmering blond hair and heavenly wardrobe twist and turn in the breeze.

"Do you miss them?" he suddenly asked as he looked up, startling her.

Suddenly, she felt herself choking up as she swallowed and shook her head.

"I used to... but honestly? Not anymore."

Isaac's eyes widened; he hardly knew how to respond.

"What? Why not? Did they do something to hurt or offend you, last you saw them?"

She shook her head no as she continued to stare at him, unable to take her gaze away.

"How can I miss them when I see and feel both of them in you?"

Isaac swallowed as he clasped his hands together.

"You have every ounce of your father's strength, fortitude, and unwavering determination. Yet you have the kindness, compassion, and unfailing love of your mother."

She stood up and walked over to him, gently holding his hands in hers, staring directly into his eyes, her own glistening in the reflection of his.

"It is as if someone took every bit of their good sides and combined them together, creating you."

Isaac's head turned a little, his eyebrows drooping in an *Awwww* expression.

"No one is perfect on our land of Vaerün, or in Albyüron for that matter. But never has anyone come as close to divinity and perfection as you, Isaac Erbrecht."

Dang it, Isaac. Give her a compliment back! he shouted in his mind as his throat, once again, refused to obey.

"And I'm sorry, but I refuse to let someone so amazing, beautiful, and talented sit here in a room and sulk all day!"

Isaac stammered a little as she began pulling him toward the door.

"Wh-where are we going?"

"Why, to breakfast, silly!"

And with that, his heart fluttered off to La La Land for the next ten minutes as they traversed the massive castle, down to the café-like dining hall.

Naturally (as with all of us), his spirits immediately began to lift as he filled his empty stomach with waffles (they were on today's menu), boar sausage, Chef Volkan's rendition of huevos rancheros, steaming buttermilk biscuits, and fresh berries—all crowned with piping-hot, cinnamon pumpkin cocoa. (Like the kinberries, the cinnamon was imported from Fürnas!)

"Are you really considering taking lessons with Mrs. Minlöuian?" Jenna asked with concern as she held the warm mug of cocoa in her bare hands.

"I'm honestly just curious how she instructs! Not to mention, I've never had a teacher before."

Isaac set his fork down for a moment as he noticed the concern and seriousness on Jenna's face.

"What's wrong? Do you really think it's that bad of an idea?"

Jenna began rotating the spoon in her mug as she responded, "It's just... you remind me so much of your mom. And I'm ashamed that I never picked up on it! Like you, she was really a phenomenal pianist."

"Thank you, Jenna, but I have so much to improve upon. That's why I need an instructor—so I can be phenomenal like her! How am I supposed to impress her someday if I can't play as well as she did?"

Jenna took a nice, long, *sloooow* sip and then set her mug back down.

"There are two things wrong with that. One, I'll bet you'd be shocked to hear that, like you, she was entirely self-taught! And two, not only do you play as well as she did, I'd go so far as to say you're better. I'm sure you'd impress her far more by not taking lessons with that evil wench!"

Isaac quickly finished another bite of his waffle, eager to respond.

"She was self-taught too? Amazing. I had no idea! And your compliments mean so much to me. Thank you, from the bottom of my heart."

"Isaac. We've already been here for three days now! In just four more, Jéid is supposed to be back, and then we can leave! Wouldn't it be a waste to begin lessons only to leave? What if you end up enjoying them?"

Jenna's heart plunged for a moment as she watched Isaac's eyes glisten.

"Isaac! Dear, what's wrong?" she exclaimed as she nearly knocked over her cocoa reaching for his hands.

Startled, he quickly calmed her down and said, "Nothing, nothing! I'm sorry. I didn't mean to make you worry. I just can't imagine what it'd be like to actually have something to look forward to."

Her heart fell again as her hands fumbled to grasp hold of his. More than anything, her greatest desire was to just see him happy.

"If that is how you feel about it, then nothing would make me happier than to see you try."

Isaac's sleeve nearly dragged through his syrupy waffle (thank goodness Jenna rescued it in time) as he exclaimed, "Really? Oh, thank you! When do you think I should try talking to her?"

Jenna motioned down to his plate for him to finish his breakfast.

"Why not right now? Finish up your meal, and we'll ask James where we can find her!"

He looked left and right, observing the posh people that sat at the other tables.

"Speaking of James, where is our dear friend?"

Jenna's head rolled back as she finished the last of her cocoa and then set her mug down with a dull thud.

"He's in the library. Said he was searching for something important?"

"Ohn?" questioned Isaac through his sleeve-covered mouth. "Wert erbert?"

She couldn't help but giggle at just how cute he sounded.

"Well," she paused as she tossed her fork back and forth playfully, "I'm not sure about all the details, but he said it had something to do with the conductor? Or conductors?"

"Grim subject," Isaac said, now able to speak after swallowing. "Not to mention frightening. You said you don't know any more details?"

Jenna looked out the western window to her right, taking in the beautiful ocean view some distance below them.

"Oh! That's right. I do remember one other thing. He mentioned something about the Majestician Kings of Antiquity. And that's honestly the last thing I recall."

Isaac stood up and pushed in his chair, quickly walking over to help her up.

"Got me even more curious now. Shall we see what he's dug up?" he asked as he held out his elbow.

With a shy smile, she wrapped her arm around his and replied, "Let's!"

Isaac's mouth dropped as he and Jenna entered the library. It. Was. A. Mess! Books lay opened and scattered everywhere, and all sorts of frayed parchment papers were dispersed and sprinkled about on the floor and tables that had been huddled together.

"My word. I'm sure King Närvein would hardly approve of the way his people left his library!"

With two hands plastered down upon the table, James looked up with his mouth slightly open.

"Oi! Isaac and Jenna, good to see you! And no, trust me, he's used to things looking much worse than this by the time I'm done with my research."

"Hold on just a moment," Jenna said as she picked up a piece of parchment that she had just stepped on. "You mean to tell us that all of this is your doing?"

James looked around and scrunched up his lips.

"Yep. Pretty much! Oh, come now, don't you two give me those looks! You think this is bad? You should see how it looks when my uncle is done!"

Isaac rubbed his eyes as he slowly walked up to the table, Jenna right by his side.

"By the way…" James muttered, approaching Isaac and placing a hand on his shoulder, "We'll figure this out, mate. 'Bout your parents, alrighto? Alrighto!"

Isaac provided a sincere smile.

"Hmm… what first?" Jenna asked, looking back and forth between Isaac and James.

"Sorry?" they both asked at the same time.

"Well, Isaac has two questions for you, James. And I'm just trying to figure out which one he should ask first!"

Thud! sounded the huge tome as James closed it with one hand, now fully providing his dear friend with undivided attention. "Ask away, Isaac!"

"I've decided that I'd like to try taking lessons with Mrs. Minlöuian."

James's hand slipped out from underneath him on an ill-placed piece of parchment paper as papers scattered through the air.

"What? Are you serious? And you don't mind this?" he demanded of Jenna.

She simply shrugged and smiled.

"Couldn't hurt to try," Jenna whispered.

"Besides," Isaac hurriedly added, "we only have four days left here. If it doesn't work out, it makes it that much easier to quit."

James mumbled under his breath as he scooped up the papers and began stacking them, keeping track of his notes.

"Aaand… what happens if you do like them?"

"Then he has something to look forward to!" Jenna answered for him.

"Righto, righto. Well then! I'd direct you to her house myself, but I see no point, as all you have to do is go down the northern street—seven houses till you've reached hers."

Jenna nearly tripped forward as the arm that was holding her up slipped off Isaac's shoulder.

"You seriously mean to tell us that *that* wench lives in the castle district?"

Tap. Tap. James shuffled his notes on the table.

"Oh, come now, would you expect anything less? She *is* a part of the aristocracy! Wait, hold up a sec, Isaac!"

Isaac quickly turned around, trying to quell his excitement.

"What is it, James?"

James motioned to Jenna and asked, "Jenna here said you had two questions, did you not, mate?"

Isaac pulled the huge wooden doors open and shouted back, "It's not that important. I'll ask when I come back!"

With a look of sadness and a hint of sarcasm, Jenna shouted back to him, "Don't worry! I… I mean *we'll* be right here when you get back!"

More papers scattered through the air as James additionally shouted, "Seventh house, Isaac!"

Isaac ignored the fancily dressed people who were pointing and whispering about him as he walked down the street.

Five… six… seven, he counted in his mind as he approached the seventh house down the castle street.

"That's so strange," he muttered to himself as he observed the house. "It's pretty, but… shouldn't it be much bigger for the castle district? Why, our home back in Aerlund was larger than this!"

And so it was! It certainly had a charm to it, though. The sun had just come out again and bathed the eastern-faced, two-story home in light. The top windows were open, and the white-and-blue floating curtains twirled and leaped, as if waving to him. The pastel flowers, neatly placed in their flower boxes beneath the windows, brought him a feeling of homesickness as he walked up to the large front double doors.

"What are you doing?" called out a voice.

Curious and slightly embarrassed, Isaac turned around to see an older, swanky-dressed man with a cane facing directly toward him. He pulled his hand away from the door (on which he was just about to knock) and approached the man on the street.

"I'm sorry, sir?" Isaac asked politely.

"Did you not hear me the first time? I asked, 'What are you doing?'" the man demanded, stamping the end of his cane on the white-stoned street.

Isaac smiled as he gestured toward the house.

"Why, I'm going to—"

"Do you *mind*?" yelled the man, interrupting him as he made raspberry sounds and flaunted his hands, clearly irritated and offended by Isaac's white cloak, which had barely touched and clung to his leg from the ocean breeze.

Isaac immediately pulled his cloak back, twisting it up and wrapping it around his neck like a scarf.

"My sincerest apologies, sir! I didn't mean to offend."

"Well, you did! When was the last time that thing was washed? It smells of… roasted boar and kinberry syrup!"

A big smile spread across his face as Isaac confessed, "You have a good nose! I just ate breakfast with my—"

Crack! echoed the sharp sound of the man's cane as he slammed it into the ground again.

"You've just eaten breakfast in that garb, and you dare to enter the public with the very same? Young man, I know not who you are, but you are obviously in the wrong district."

The man raised his cane and pointed northeast as he said, "You'll find the lower-class district that way."

Oh, how I wish I had Jenna with me, Isaac sighed in his mind as he tried to be bold. Poor guy! He'd never had to deal with people like this before!

"And I know not what business you have knocking at our most esteemed concert pianist's house. She already has servants."

The snobby man turned his back to Isaac. "Now leave this area before I summon the authorities."

Isaac quickly dashed in front of the man, hoping to explain and clear his name. Imagine his surprise when the man began yelling and screaming.

"Help, help!" he cried, "I'm being attacked by a lawless delinquent!"

Before things could get too out of hand, Isaac raised his hands in a calming gesture and had to yell to soothe the man, "Please, good sir, my name is Isaac Erbrecht! I am here on official business with..."

Suddenly realizing that saying James's name might not be the best idea, he quickly finished, "Jéid Vandergaus and King Närvein himself!"

The man suddenly sized him up and down, poking him in the gut with his cane.

Although Isaac was the most patient person you'd ever meet, even he had his limits. And he hated to be hurt physically—especially by the sharp jabs of a stupid cane!

"How dare you make such accusations!" the man spat as Isaac stepped back, avoiding another poke.

"They're not accusations. It's the truth!" Isaac quickly said, his fingers beginning to move.

Oh, he was having so much difficulty restraining himself from casting a barrier! How much longer could he take being poked by this jerk? And wasn't he too old for this? Shouldn't he be taking a nap or playing cards or… or… something, other than this?

The man gave a disgusted look and motioned to Isaac's twitching, moving fingers.

"And just what are you doing now?"

Isaac took a deep breath, clasped his hands together, and forced himself not to use Majesty.

"Sir, I promise you that I truly am here on official business with King Närveid and Professor Jéid Vandergaus," he said calmly but boldly. "I am a pianist and was told that Mrs. Minlöuian is a fantastic teacher. I simply wanted to see if she'd be willing to give me lessons. That's all!"

"Hah! Ha ha!" mocked the man. "Give you lessons?"

Feeling indignant, Isaac waved his hand through the air as he finished, "But if it's going to be this big of a deal, then I don't even want to—"

Imagine his surprise when, as he attempted to take a step back, he bumped right into (yep, you guessed it!) Mrs. Minlöuian. Before he could get a word out, she was already speaking.

"You want to take lessons from me?" she gawked. "My dear boy, do you even know what it is that I teach?"

"Doubt it!" exclaimed the man. "Why don't you just admit it, young man? You are from the ghetto, and you wanted to see if Mrs. Minlöuian was in need of servants. Or perhaps you wanted her autograph, in an attempt to sell it for some petty coin?"

Isaac's eye slightly twitched as he thought, *yes. It's a very good thing that Jenna isn't here. There's no way the conversation would have gotten even this far.*

He cleared his throat as he decided to ignore the man.

"Yes, Mrs. Minlöuian. You are a concert pianist, and you give instruction for the piano."

The man laughed again as he jabbed Isaac in the side of the ribs.

"Do you see what I mean? Look at him, calling it a *piano*. Hah!"

Refusing to open his mouth or move, for fear of doing something he might regret, Isaac simply stood still.

"I remember you, Isaac Erbrecht," said Mrs. Minlöuian with her upturned nose. "I recall meeting you just a few days ago with your devilish and most barbaric friend, in addition to the company of James Vandergaus."

Isaac's knuckles cracked, and he feared his lower lip might have begun bleeding as he fought to maintain self-control from the sharp jabs of the cane.

"James?" mocked the man. "James Vandergaus? That's who you're here with? Well, doesn't it all make sense then! Riffraff sticks with riffraff. Now, young man, I'm beginning to lose my patience."

You haven't a clue, thought Isaac as his knuckles turned white from clenching.

"But I shall give you the benefit of the doubt, seeing as your ears may be full of the dirt on which you no doubt sleep upon!" the man spat, pointing northeast again. "It is that way to the ghetto. Now I shall give you five seconds to leave us before I summon the authorities!"

"You may summon the authorities as you see fit," Isaac nodded. "But I can assure you that you're the one who shall feel the fool when you learn that I am indeed telling the truth."

Before the man could unleash another nasty word, Mrs. Minlöuian spoke up.

"He is telling the truth, I'm afraid. I've heard it from Mévon myself. He, that loathsome wretch, Jenna—"

(Magister Mévon was the immediate commanding authority beneath King Närvein and a 'dear friend' to Mrs. Minlöuian herself.)

"Don't call her that," snapped Isaac in righteous anger, interrupting her. "You may be a part of the aristocracy of this kingdom, but I will not stand by and listen as you bad-mouth not only my beloved friend but also the princess of the Fürnas Kingdom!"

This time, before Mrs. Minlöuian could say anything, the man spoke up.

"Well, now things are making more and more sense by the moment! A broken-down, trashy princess for a broken-down, trashy kingdom!"

"Oh, there shall be broken-down trash by the time I'm done, I assure you," roared Isaac as he, for the first time ever, lost his cool.

Thank the Almighty Creator above that Mrs. Minlöuian's husband came rushing up to break up the imminent destruction.

"Löunda! Mr. Débchet! Mercy of mercies, can you give the poor young man a break? Do you not know that this poor man has just recently lost his beloved home?"

How on Vaerün does this kind man fit in with these people? Isaac thought as he observed Mr. Minlöuian.

For indeed, Mr. Minlöuian appeared like any regular person you might meet in any ordinary town or village. With his neatly combed gray hair, gray-and-blue checkered button-up shirt, suspenders, gray slacks, and leather shoes, he'd have fit in perfectly in Aerlund!

No one said a word. What could anyone say?

Mr. Minlöuian gently placed one hand on Mr. Débchet's cane, which was still touching Isaac's ribs, lowered it down, and placed another on his shoulder, turning him around.

"I do believe that it is about time for your brunch, is it not, Mr. Débchet?" Mr. Minlöuian kindly said as he pushed him down the road. "Do take care now!"

And truly enough, that rotten old man dared not turn around and say a single word as he continued walking. Although Isaac did detect the burning energy of his pure bitterness and negativity as he slowly faded down the street.

"And, dear," continued Mr. Minlöuian, "if you do not want to teach this young man, then so be it. But so that we do not waste each other's time, can we not resolve this immediately?"

Mrs. Minlöuian tightened the scarf around her neck, cleared her throat, and coldly asked, "What experience do you have? Where have you studied? What credentials do you hold?"

Credentials? Isaac thought, *Why do I need a piece of paper to prove what I'm capable of doing?* He verbally responded, "I am self-taught, ma— I mean, Professor Minlöuian. Although I did host regular concerts in my home, back in Aerlund," Isaac added honestly.

Mrs. Minlöuian's eyes widened in horror and anger.

"Self-taught? Young man, do you have any clue how many students beg for me to be their teacher? Many have traveled abroad from all over Albyüron, just to become one of my pupils, and yet you dare to—"

"Ah-ha-hem!" cleared the throat of Mr. Minlöuian as he glared at his wife.

With huffed breathing and agitation, she gripped her handbag and quickly turned around, walking up to the front door of their home.

"You have two minutes, Isaac Erbrecht, to show me what you can do. And if it's not good enough, we are through! And I must have your word that you shall never bother me again!"

Delighted at the opportunity to show her just what he was capable of, Isaac gleefully replied, "I am very grateful for this opportunity, Professor. I hope not to let you down."

Mr. Minlöuian gave Isaac a kind wink as she said, with her back turned to them, "We shall see about that."

The interior of their home was stunning. Angelic, marbled statues with harps in hand were neatly placed in corners and against the crown-molded white walls. A giant golden treble clef was engraved and centered on the tiled floor of the foyer.

And there, right before him, sat a beautiful, white, concert grand piano, centered in the clearing of the grand staircase.

"Ah, ah, ah!" she scolded as Isaac quickly dashed up in an attempt to play it.

"My goodness… please do not tell me that you are as barbaric as your friend?" questioned the snooty voice behind him.

Isaac stopped dead in his tracks as he watched her disappear into the parlor room to her right.

"What makes you think that you have the right to play on my esteemed Héndrjks and Sons piano, when I have yet to esteem your worth?"

"You haven't the right to esteem anyone's worth," argued Isaac in his mind as he quietly nodded and followed her.

She gently lifted the fallboard of one of two pianos that sat in the parlor. Naturally, out of the two, she chose for him to play on the worst one. The keys were badly cracked and damaged. The finish was peeling. And it was terribly out of tune. Indeed, one might've thought that this was a piano from hell, tuned by its angels.

Isaac quietly pulled out the creaky wooden bench and sat to play.

With a sigh that sounded like the world was about to end, she asked, "I may be asking too much, but are you acquainted with the works of Gözern? Bécken? Or Müsalae, to name a few?"

Without saying anything, Isaac nodded. And despite how terrible this demon piano sounded, he dared not let it show as he did his best, performing some of the esteemed works from memory.

"Sloppy. Terribly sloppy," she said as she shook her head and paced back and forth. "Where did you learn your technique? The Gerdpölus institution?"

Isaac said nothing but continued to play.

"And my heavens," she belted, "why must your rhythm be played in constant rubato? Have you issues with your heart?"

"Not only that," she continued as she whipped out her fan and began fanning her perspiring face, "but clearly you are uneducated. Bécken is meant to be played with the most careful and intricate of articulations."

Isaac said nothing but continued to play.

To add insult to injury, she continued, "Yes… now, if you were playing Vhochén or Alkyür, perhaps I'd let it slide! But this, no, this is just terrible."

Isaac said nothing but continued to play.

"Stop, stop, stop!" she finally shouted as she stomped her foot.

Naturally, he immediately pulled his hands away from the keys but refused to look up.

"Ugh! I need some water," Mrs. Minlöuian said in great exasperation as she stormed out of the parlor.

The broken, cracked keys of black and white began to ripple and move as Isaac looked at them in silence, through the forming tears in his eyes.

Isaac rang a female voice inside his mind, kind, pleasant, sweet, and most familiar.

My darling one, why do you perform the music of dead men, when Vaerün and Albyüron are in such desperate need of yours?

Isaac's eyes opened wide in realization as the voice finished, *without it, surely mankind shall mourn the loss of a music so heavenly and divine as to fill their souls with hope, comfort, and peace like no other. If you do not play your music, then who will?*

As the voice faded, Isaac slowly closed the fallboard, pushed in the bench, and silently pulled out the bench next to him, sitting at the nicer (and more in-tune) piano. As he lifted the fallboard to this piano, imagine his delight to see that none of the keys were broken or cracked!

Feeling as though heaven favored him in this choice, the sunlight streamed into the room from the large eastern window as he slowly lifted his gentle, elegant, and masculine hands to the keys.

Beginning in the softest *pianissimo,* the index and middle fingers of his right hand vibrated and blurred as he began one of his compositions with a light and fluttering trill.

Without Mrs. Minlöuian (albeit very temporarily) around to bark insults and critique, he focused and listened as the piano sang the heavenly music he played—a music like no other.

Oh, how he missed the piano! And he simply couldn't stop. How long had he been playing now? Oh well. It didn't matter, especially as he was coming to the grand finale!

His hands crisscrossed this way and that as he performed run after run, accompanied by roaring bass octaves, rippling fourfold trills, and tremolos.

Duhnh! echoed the triumphant sound of the chorded octave as he brought his incredible piece to a close. All was silent again, except for the sound of his excited breathing. Although he could have sworn that just for a moment, he'd heard the roaring cheers of heaven from above.

Suddenly, his heart fell as he heard the voice of Mr. Minlöuian behind him.

"Bravo, Isaac, bravo," he muttered as he rested in the archway, tears running down his face. "If I may be so bold, I'd dare to say… that, that was your music. Wasn't it?"

Isaac swallowed nervously as he gave a head nod and slowly turned around.

"Never have I heard such music like *that*." Mr. Minlöuian continued, "And never would I have guessed that anyone could make such a percussive instrument sing in such a way as you've just done!"

"Th-thank you," Isaac stammered.

"Your music must go out—" Mr. Minlöuian tried before being interrupted by his wife, who came bolting into the parlor.

"What was that music you were playing just now?" she demanded, pretending not to have overheard the conversation between her husband and Isaac.

He didn't even get a chance to respond before she continued, "That's enough for today. I have a lot to consider and think about."

Feeling as though she could see his spirit, and through some diabolical means remove it from his body and shatter it into a million pieces upon the ground, so too did Isaac feel as she tore into him.

"You've obviously no idea what the word '*technique*' means. We need to get your heart checked to make sure you understand the word 'rhythm.' Perhaps next time, if there is a next time, I shall stand next to you and tick into your ear!"

Refusing to hear another word, her husband shook his head and left the room.

"Your interpretation is nonexistent, as is your respect for the composers and their styles," she said.

Isaac slowly stood up, pushed in the bench, and closed the fallboard as he turned around.

"Leave me," she said, staring straight past him. "You shall receive a letter first thing in the morning if I desire to continue."

With courageous and admirable restraint, he began to leave.

"Oh, and Isaac?" she asked as he walked by, placing a hand on his shoulder to stop him.

He said nothing but listened as she said, "It is an insult to me, the piano, the composers of old, yourself, and our Creator for you to even attempt to compose when you haven't even a clue how to perform the basics."

And with those last words, Isaac left the concert artist's house.

Feeling as though his whole world had come crashing down, he hardly paid attention to the ever-judgmental inhabitants of Wöntylnas who pointed, mocked, and whispered about him as he returned to the castle.

Have you ever been so broken down, distraught, and just plain hurt that you didn't even want to talk to the people closest to you? That was exactly how Isaac felt as he decided to go straight to his room and sleep, instead of checking in on Jenna and James.

Shiiiiink! sounded the metal rings of the curtains as Isaac pulled the outer, dark-blue curtains closed over the windows, making the room all but entirely dark.

Suddenly, a burst of heavenly light filled the room; a gleaming sphere of pure light suspended from his palm as he lay upon his bed.

Streams of light began to zoom and twist through the room as he shattered the sphere with his index finger.

Am I really so bad of a person, he thought as he stared at the light he was commanding and directing, *that I must constantly suffer so much and be treated so poorly?*

A single tear descended from his glowing eyes as it rolled down his strong face.

If everyone only knew... just how good my intentions are for their sakes, Vaerün, and all of Albyüron, would they still treat me this way?

And with that thought, Isaac fell asleep, comforted only by the unceasing streams of Light Majesty that continued to stir and fly around his room.

"One... two... three!" James and Jenna said in sync as they combined their fire and Water Majesty, creating a hissing steam that filled Isaac's room.

"R-really, you two?" He coughed as he sat up in his bed, waving the steam away from his face.

Both of them burst into laughter. Jenna sat down on Isaac's bed as James went to open the window.

"I'm going to assume," said Jenna with a concerned smile, "that your lesson didn't go too well, did it?"

Isaac rolled over so that he didn't have to look at her as he asked, "What makes you think that?"

James playfully rocked him back and forth as he said, "Well, you missed lunch. And dinner. Chef Volkan was worried about you, y'know! Said, *'Somethin' must be up for Isaac to miss my cookin'.'*

"And of course, I missed—I mean, we missed you too," Jenna stammered.

"So?" James quickly asked. "What's the verdict? Go or no go?"

"Well, seeing as how—" Isaac began to say as he sat up and then stopped as he noticed James holding a sealed letter addressed directly to him.

James raised a corner smile as he said, "Must've done something to get her attention! This is the fourth one she's sent. And her servant has come to the castle twice already!"

"Twice? Exactly what time is it?" Isaac demanded as he stood up.

"It's only nine," Jenna answered as she continued to sit upon his bed.

Isaac went over to his dresser and panicked when he noticed his cloak wasn't there, only to realize that it was still clasped around his neck (obviously from falling asleep, still wearing it).

"Mercy. What time does she wake up, then? Six?" he asked, half-joking, half-serious.

"Nah. Three!" James returned.

Isaac and Jenna exclaimed at the same time, "Are you serious?"

"Of course!" he immediately responded. "It'd have to be!"

Jenna stood up and placed a hand on her hip as she asked, "And just why is that?"

James turned around and waved his hand as he answered, "Easy! That's what time the witching hour begins!"

Isaac couldn't help but laugh as he imagined Mrs. Minlöuian standing over a large black pot in her kitchen, adding all sorts of random ingredients and laughing maniacally.

His attention was broken as Jenna asked, "Well, are you going to open it or what?"

He had completely forgotten all about the letter! It probably didn't help that James had just left it on the bed.

Isaac closed his eyes as he took a deep breath and then grabbed the letter, opening it and silently reading it.

Jenna placed a hand on his shoulder as she asked, "Is it what you hoped for?"

He slightly scrunched his face, clearly mulling something over in his head.

"I'm not sure. She said that she'll accept me as her student, but only if I follow her instructions exactly."

His face began to grow hot as Jenna wrapped an arm around him and led him to his door.

"You see, and this is exactly why you should forget this whole mess and just come have breakfast with James and I!"

They stopped in the large corridor as Isaac said, "I'd love nothing more, Jenna, but I'd like to get started as soon as possible. And to be honest, I'm not very hungry at the moment."

It was an obvious lie!

Jenna placed both hands on his shoulders and looked him dead in the eye.

"Isaac... my darling one, why are you so bent on taking piano lessons from this wench? You are the most incredible man I know. Why must you be 'instructed' on something that's already been given to you?"

He slightly tilted his head as he asked, "What do you mean?"

"Isaac," she said quietly to avoid attention from the passing servants, "whether you remember or not, you already learned how to play the piano in heaven."

Isaac smiled graciously as she continued, "We all have gifts, and when we're able to pick up something and suddenly do it with extraordinary proficiency, does it not ring a bell that we've done this before?"

"Yes, but—"

"For each of us," she interrupted as she held up a finger, "talent lies within us like a covered, dusty chest in the dungeon. We simply need to dust it off and open it up to receive the forgotten treasure within!"

Isaac's eyes looked away from Jenna as he pondered what she'd just said.

"My question to you is," she continued as she looked directly into his eyes, "why do you feel the need to be instructed on something that was already taught to you personally from, but who do you know, our Almighty Creator, in the celestial realms above?"

"That is very kind of you, Jenn, but—"

"All I have to say to you, Isaac Erbrecht," she interrupted again, "is that you don't need to take lessons for something you already know. And she may have received validation from man, but you've received validation from above. And that is something no man can even begin to compare to."

And with that, Jenna boldly (but elegantly) walked down the hall, her gorgeously long hair flowing behind her.

Isaac's heart felt incredibly heavy as he approached the front door to the Minlöuian's home. The fifteen minutes it took to get there gave him time to ponder Jenna's words. Why did he suddenly feel as though he were a servant, responding to a master's call?

"Ugh..." He shivered as his shoulders shook from the thought.

Just as his mind began to change, and he turned around to walk away, the front door flew open. And there stood Mr. Minlöuian.

"Isaac!" he shouted, with an enormous smile on his face. "Welcome, welcome! Do come on in. Mrs. Minlöuian is in the parlor, just like yesterday. Good luck!"

Isaac's heart fell, and he had to swallow a few times as he entered the parlor.

Mrs. Minlöuian was standing directly in front of the better piano and had her right hand gestured to the open fallboard and lifted lid of the demonic one.

"I trust you read my letter, then?" she asked, with her eyes closed, somehow knowing it was Isaac.

"Yes, Professor," he simply answered.

"And why, may I ask, did it take four letters and two house calls to get your attention?"

He said nothing as she continued, "I know not where you're from, but here, we do things differently. And that means waking up at five a.m. sharp every day to begin your technical practices upon the *pianato*."

Again, he said nothing but nodded.

"And we do not do that here," she said with a disgusted face. "None of that head nodding. You are to strictly address me as Professor and reply always in the positive of 'Yes' or negative of 'No.' Is that understood?"

"Yes, Professor," he quickly responded.

"Good. Now that we've handled that, let us begin. Oh no, no!" she suddenly snapped as she stopped him from pulling out the piano bench.

For a moment, he was delighted!

Yay! he thought. *She is going to let me play the good piano!*

Imagine the poor young man's surprise when it couldn't have been further from the truth.

"No, no. Heavens no. After seeing you bang upon my poor piano yesterday, I have deemed it necessary to start with the basics."

Bang upon your piano? My hands are probably the kindest things that have ever touched that instrument! he rationalized in his mind as he stared at the terrible, broken-down piano. *And basics?*

However, he simply and humbly agreed.

"Very well, Professor. I shall do as you say."

A sick and evil smile stole across her face.

Suddenly, he truly felt as though he were serving a demonic master, whose only desire was to torture and demean him in every way possible. Yes, indeed… she was a demonic master that wore an umbrella for a hat (exaggeration, of course), a dress that would have difficulty breathing on a lamppost, and a dolled-up face that made powdered sugar look dark.

"Yes, yes, you shall." She nodded as she motioned to the center of the room. "Stand there."

"All right. Now what?" he blankly asked as he followed her instructions.

Her hand suddenly flung beside her as she picked up a glass jar from off the piano. Inside were tons of old, wooden buttons.

"I'm going to have you start with an exercise. And don't you dare rush this," she snapped as she unfurled a long, old piece of text and set it upon the music rack.

Upon closer inspection, Isaac realized it was an old layout of the keyboard. The sketch was rather faded, and the ends were frayed. His eyebrows creased as he looked at the blotched, creepy happy faces on the keys that were smiling back at him.

It was as if her life had suddenly derived the greatest pleasure in seeing him suffer.

"One by one, I want you to take a button out of the jar and place it upon the correct key. Make sure you use the map."

A slight panic set in as Isaac suddenly felt as though everything he knew was being questioned.

"I don't understand, Professor," he tried to say. "I already know all the keys and—"

Snap! rang her hand as it came whipping down upon the wooden frame of the piano.

"Do you want to be my pupil or not?" she demanded.

"Y-yes, Professor, but I—" he tried.

"Then do as I say! Anything else is obviously an open rejection to my superior instruction and shall have you banished from my home and tutelage!"

He had to blink a few times to prevent his eye from twitching as he reached into the jar and held up one of the buttons.

E, it said, also equipped with a blotched and smeared black smiley face!

For the glory of the heavens above, it was as if Mrs. Minlöuian were the demon instructor from hell, sent to bind and torture him. That broken and twisted piano was her assistant, and to top it all off, she had used her demonic powers to trap the innocent souls of her previous students within these poor wooden buttons and sealed within that parchment paper. And merciful heavens, he was going to be next!

The whole room could hear Isaac as he swallowed and walked up to the piano.

"All right… let me see," he mumbled as he stared at the parchment paper and found the key that also had an *E* written upon it.

"That goes… right here, then!" he exclaimed happily as he set the button upon the key.

"Very good, Isaac!" Mrs. Minlöuian exclaimed proudly—so proudly that it made him feel uncomfortable.

"Th-thank you!" he stammered as he reached into the jar she was holding up and pulled out another button.

"This one's a… *B*!" he beamed as he looked up at the map again, found the key, and set it upon it.

"Well, now look at you!" she said with a smile. "I can't believe how good you are at this!"

"Thank you, Professor, I really—" He stopped dead in his tracks.

Who was that laughing at him? It sounded so awful and scary! And it sounded very far away.

"I'm sorry?" he asked as he looked around.

"Oh!" she exclaimed jubilantly as she repeated, "I just can't believe how good you are at this! Now continue on! Next button!" she exclaimed as she held up the jar once more.

Isaac's insides began to churn as he heard the laughter again.

Why was he doing this? He felt like the biggest fool. And why did he suddenly feel like crying?

And how demeaning! For I can tell you that this situation would have been just as insulting as trying to teach a master of linguistics the ABCs, although the difference lies in that they wouldn't have dared to suffer such insults, compared to the painfully humble and angelic Isaac Erbrecht.

After all eighty-eight of the twisted, smiling, demonic buttons looked up at him from their appropriate housing upon those broken and cracked demonic piano keys, Mrs. Minlöuian clapped repetitively, as if cheering for a child who just said their first word.

"Bravo, Isaac, bravo! And now let us move on to the next exercise."

Clink, clink. Clink, clink, clink, clink, clink! sounded the wooden buttons as Isaac hastily scooped them into the glass jar, eager to remove Baehallün's smiling wooden buttons that just wouldn't stop staring at him.

"Here, let me help you with these, Professor!" he exclaimed.

"Thank you, Isaac," she said as she began to leave the parlor. "Please follow me."

Feeling both uneasy and curious, he followed her as she led the way out into their backyard.

The neatly trimmed hedges lined their unexpectedly small backyard. And just like the water channels that ran through the castle, a similar one ran right through their backyard, feeding and circulating the water of a strange and peculiar fountain.

Mrs. Minlöuian gave him a rather strange smile as she approached the fountain.

"I purposefully had this fountain made to assist my students that have…" With a momentary pause, her eyes widened as she finished, "unique challenges with rhythm."

Isaac approached the fountain as she maneuvered a series of levers. Instead of the water fanning out, it suddenly drastically reduced as the top bowl retained its water and ceased to flow over.

Tun. Tun. Tun. Tun, sounded the awful, eye-twitching sound of a single droplet of water repeatedly landing in the bowl of water below it.

It's not too late to run! echoed a voice in his head as he quickly dismissed it with a slight smile.

Clap. Clap. Clap. Clap, snapped the sounds of Mrs. Minlöuian's hands as she clapped in unison with the water droplets.

"Get it?" she coldly said. "**This. Is. Rhythm,**" she also said in unison.

"You don't need to take lessons for something you already know," echoed the still-fresh words of Jenna through his mind as he began clapping in sync with Mrs. Minlöuian.

"Oh no, you poor thing, you!" she exclaimed as she pulled another lever.

The dripping water slowed down significantly, causing it to grate on his nerves even more!

"That was probably much too fast for you! Let's start slower…" she muttered in a baby-like voice, with her lower lip puckered out.

Have you ever been in those circumstances that you know you shouldn't be in, and yet for some strange and stupid reason, you do it anyway? Yeah. I'm sure you can imagine, but that was exactly how Isaac felt as he continued to be demeaned more and more with each passing moment.

Thank heaven that's over with, Isaac thought as he quickly ran down the hall leading to the library of the castle. *Although maybe she's just testing me? I'm sure the lessons will get better!*

Isaac's spirits immediately began to lift as he opened up the huge wooden doors and entered the library.

Tiny streams of water and fire, emanating blue-and-red light, and dispersing beads of energy were dancing and flowing through the humongous hall.

His ears perked up as he heard Jenna's crisp and beautiful voice, singing with enchanting harp music. As he swiftly ran past the tables and bookshelves, his being nearly collapsed with relief as he saw Jenna standing and singing next to James, who was seated and playing his harp.

Trying to retain his joy and to suppress the incredible effect that their music and Majesty were having upon him, Isaac had to ask as he approached, "I thought you said no Majesty was allowed in Wöntylnas, James?"

Both of them immediately ceased performing.

"It's a good thing we have the library all to ourselves!" exclaimed Jenna.

James just scratched the back of his head.

"My bad. But you know what's funny about it? I'm not even casting Majesty when I play my harp. It just sorta comes out."

Jenna tossed her head back and forth as she lifted it up and ran her fingers through her hair.

"I know exactly what you mean. Nevertheless, sorry to you, James and Isaac."

James rested back in his chair as he motioned to Isaac.

"How was your lesson, mate? You don't look very happy."

Isaac shook his head, breaking out of the trance that he fell into as he recalled the terrible morning he'd just had.

"No, no, don't worry about me! It went just fine," he lied.

And although James nodded happily for him, Jenna gave him a raised eyebrow and a smile that said, *Really, Isaac? You may be able to fool him, but you can't fool me.*

Isaac cleared his throat as he approached the table next to them, literally overflowing with books and notes.

"Did you… find whatever it is you're looking for?" he asked as he rummaged through some of the papers.

"Pch!" mocked James. "We wish!"

"No, *you* wish!" Jenna quickly defended as she slammed a book shut. "I couldn't care less about whether or not it's true."

Intrigued, Isaac asked, "Whether or not what's true?"

Jenna gave a silly face as she made fun of James.

"He's under the crazy notion that the conductor we ran into—"

"Conductors!" James quickly corrected.

"Right, right," she corrected with raised hands, "the conductors that we ran into are the very Majestician kings of antiquity."

Isaac's heart dropped as he recalled Professor Vandergaus mentioning that the lookouts who witnessed the storming Kreaux siege some twenty years ago did indeed describe five hooded figures leading the legion.

"See, Isaac gets it!" James exclaimed as he motioned to him, already sensing that he'd figured it out. "You're thinking about how my uncle mentioned the five robed figures who led the charge some twenty years ago, aren't you, Isaac?"

"Not only that," Isaac answered, "but you should've seen it, Jenn, when James called out the name of Coltin Fürnas to the conductor who attacked us at Aerlund and James's cottage."

Jenna rolled her eyes as she flippantly waved her hand.

"I know, I know. James won't quit shoving it down my throat!"

Ever intrigued, Isaac placed a hand to his chin as he thought out loud, "Hold on just a moment… If that is indeed true, then the Conductor who attacked us in the water prison was none other than—"

"The last water Majestician before me," James said, finishing his sentence, "King Vergaus Wöntylnas."

The chair clawed against the wooden floor as Jenna pulled it out and sat upon it, kicking her feet up on another one and resting back.

"Yeah, too bad you didn't call out his name to see if it was him!" She laughed.

"And just for that," James said as he shoved her feet off the chair, "you get to call out his name the next time we see him."

Neither Isaac nor Jenna said a word as a cold silence fell upon the room. To make up for the misplaced sentence, James quickly said, "I mean… if we see them again. And we probably won't, for all we know!"

Isaac approached the table and began to flip through some of the open books.

"So what's all the research for then?"

James stood up and cracked his back as he answered, "Looking for anything that might confirm it!"

"I keep telling him that it's a waste of time," Jenna said in an uninterested sort of voice. "And not only that, but it doesn't matter. Even if we come in contact again, we'll just destroy them—like all the rest of the Kreaux!"

Obviously determined, James walked over to the nearest shelf and pulled down some more books.

That poor table creaked and groaned as he dropped the additional books onto the overflowing mess.

"Research is not a waste of time!" he exclaimed as he opened one of the books. "Look how much my uncle has learned from it!"

Jenna forcefully flipped page after page of one of the books as she added, "Not to mention that it took him nearly his entire life before he found the piece of parchment containing King Wöntylnas's final words!"

Not desiring to see his friends fight, especially after already being drained from dealing with Mrs. Minlöuian, Isaac attempted to change the subject.

"I'm starving! Either of you hungry? Let's go get some lunch! I bet Chef Volkan's whipped up something tasty!"

His world could only further come crashing down as they answered.

"We just ate some twenty minutes before you came in," James flatly said as he began flipping through some of the new books.

Jenna sat up and frowned, clearly hurt by seeing the pain in Isaac's expression.

"I'm sorry, dear…" she faded off before trying to rescue the situation. "But to be honest, I could use a break from all this research. And some of that cinnamon hot cocoa sounds fantastic right about now!"

"Really? You don't mind?" he asked with a relieved smile.

She practically jumped into his arms as she responded, "Mind? Why, nothing would make me happier!"

"Yes, yes. Both of you go on. Get outta here," James happily said as he continued to pour over one of the books, not looking up.

"Don't have to tell me twice!" they said in sync.

"But!" James called out as they were already leaving. "I could really use both of your help, when you have the free time!"

"Isaac doesn't have the time to be helping us. I'm sure he'll have his hands full with practicing!" Jenna shouted back, "But I'll be sure to come and help when we're done!"

How could he break it to her? There's just no way! She'd throw a fit if he told her the truth about his lessons!

And thus he consoled himself in his mind that the lessons would get better. They just had to. Right?

But unfortunately, they did not. As a matter of fact, they got worse—much worse. It was as if Mrs. Minlöuian was sitting at home while he wasn't there, trying to devise terrible and demonic ways to torture him for his next lesson.

I mean really! Why did he have to sit there and play "Roll-A-Tart" (our version of "Pat-A-Cake") with some of her students? Don't get it wrong; kids are great and all, but he wasn't a kid! Was he?

And why did she have to constantly gloat about her other students who were far more talented than he was? (Or so she said.) Why did it matter how fast little six-year-old Chénchin could play Alkyür's "Waking Dream"? Besides, I'm sure he could play that fast too if his parents had locked him in the dungeon with a piano for twelve hours out of the day! And to add to the hellhole of a situation, Jenna continued to interrogate him as to the quality of his lessons. And in order to avoid confrontation, he had to continuously lie to her.

To make matters even worse, Professor Vandergaus did not return when he said he was going to. Were it not for the consoling words of King Närveid, who received a letter by peregrine falcon from the professor himself, Isaac and the party were prepared to go and find him!

The throne room doors closed behind them as James pulled them shut. The three friends had just finished receiving an audience with King Närveid.

"A few extra days is one thing, but an additional two weeks?" barked James.

Jenna placed a hand to her head as she stormed down the hall with them.

"I know. Something's wrong. Wölnas is only about three days there and three days back from here."

Isaac placed his hands upon their shoulders as he strove to console them.

"I'm concerned just like you two, but aren't you glad to hear that he'll be back by tomorrow evening?"

James ran his fingers through his slicked-back hair as he answered, "Yes, but it would've been nice to know!"

"I agree with James," Jenna said. "Three weeks to spend in this dreadful kingdom has been more than enough for me!"

Oh, how those words hurt Isaac more than anything! For they hadn't a clue as to just how much he'd suffered through his atrocious lessons with Mrs. Minlöuian and her dreadfully conceited students! Nor were they the ones that had to endure the constant critique and judgments from the upper class every time he went to and from her house!

"I know," Isaac said as he suddenly stopped and pulled both of them into a hug.

"But I have a feeling that everything is going to be just fine. You'll see! I bet you that we'll be leaving here in just a couple more days!"

Grateful for his unceasing optimism, they both embraced him back.

"It's true," Jenna whispered, "Thank you, Isaac."

"Yes, thank you, mate!" James exclaimed, then asked, "By the way, you're going to be late, aren't you? I thought your lesson started at nine?"

Isaac's heart plunged as he dashed down the hall and ran into the foyer to observe the incredibly ornate gold-and-silver clock that read the time, 8:57, above the doors.

Jenna had to shout after him as he nearly flew down the grand staircase.

"Don't let her bully you!"

Both Jenna and James gave each other a concerned look as Isaac flew out the front doors of the castle.

Isaac's heart pounded as he ran down the street.

"Sorry, sorry, so sorry!" he shouted as his cloak whipped and churned through the air, accidentally brushing up against the swearing passersby on the street.

Ugh! he thought. *I wish I could just use Majesty. I would've been there by now!*

Knock. Knock. Knock! sounded the Minlöuians' door as Isaac quickly rapped on it.

He brushed his wardrobe down and readjusted his cloak as he strove to lower his huffing breathing.

There was no answer.

"Hello? Professor, are you home?" he called out as he knocked again.

A slight panic set in as he thought, *What do I do? Do I dare knock again?*

After about five minutes of waiting, he knocked one last time and waited an additional two more minutes.

Again, there was no answer.

Feeling almost relieved to be free, he turned around and walked away. He was only partway down the path when the door opened from behind.

"Well now, look who decided to show up!" exclaimed Mrs. Minlöuian nastily.

"Professor!" Isaac shouted as he turned around and ran up to the door. "I am so, so sorry! Please forgive me for being late!"

"We shall discuss this momentarily. Come in," she said with a hollow expression.

Ever the optimist that everything was just fine, Isaac entered and followed her into the parlor.

"Take a seat," she said as she pulled out the piano bench to the better piano for him. "We're going to do things a little differently today."

"O-oh!" he stammered for a moment, "We are? Well, excellent! I shall follow your instruction!"

For a moment, it actually looked like she gave him a sincere smile!

Here we go, Isaac! he thought happily as he took his seat at the piano. *After weeks of dealing with torture and humiliating kiddie lessons, she is finally going to let me play how I really can!*

"What would you like me to do, Professor?" he asked with a smile.

"I would like for you to please play one of your compositions for me."

He nearly fainted.

"I-I'm sorry?"

"That's right!" she said with a strange smile and a clap to his back. "Go right on ahead!"

"Well, all right!" he beamed. "Which piece would you like to hear?"

Her strange smile turned to a disgruntled frown as she asked, "What do you mean, 'Which piece'? Exactly how many have you composed?"

Isaac bit his lower lip as he looked up and thought about it.

"Hmm...I would have to say at least fifty!"

She nearly fell off her chair as she demanded, "Fifty?"

"That's right!" He smiled, feeling benevolently proud of his accomplishments.

Something just wasn't right. Why was she smiling like that? And to make it even stranger, she took off her hat and bowed as she motioned back to the foyer.

"Well then...for someone who has composed fifty pieces, I dare say that you rightfully deserve to play on none other than a Héndrjk & Sons concert grand piano!"

Isaac blinked a few times. He wasn't sure how to take it. Although he got the obvious sarcasm, was there a hint of sincerity in there too?

Nevertheless, he didn't want to argue, and so he went along with it.

"That's...very kind of you, Professor, but—"

"No, no, Isaac. I absolutely insist!" she exclaimed as she walked back into the foyer, lifted up the fallboard, opened the massive lid, propping it up and pulling out the bench for him, motioning for him to sit.

Feeling rather uncomfortable, he wasn't too sure what to do.

"Well, don't be shy!" she exclaimed as she forcefully made him sit and pushed him in. "This is where you belong!"

Again, he didn't know how to take that.

"If I may, what would you like me to—"

"You may play anything you like, Master Erbrecht!" she interrupted.

With a sincere smile, he said, "Very well, then. I shall play one of my favorite pieces for you. It's called *'Majesty.'*"

Isaac closed his eyes and bowed his head in humble prayer (as he always did right before a performance). When he was finished, without opening his eyes, he slowly raised his hands to the keys, preparing to play the first notes, when—

"Don't you dare touch those keys!" Mrs. Minlöuian bellowed so loudly and suddenly that Isaac nearly had a heart attack from his still-closed eyes.

His eyes burst open as he immediately pulled his hands back and stared at the fuming Mrs. Minlöuian.

What happened to her? Who would've thought she had so many veins! They were quite readily bulging out of her temples, forehead, and neck! And was it healthy for anyone's face to turn that red? And my word, the bags that formed under her eyes, were they always there? Truly, it was as if she'd transformed, right before his very eyes.

"I'm sorry, I—" Isaac attempted.

"Shut up!" she screamed. "Just. Shut up! How dare you waste my time, forcing me to wait fourteen minutes for you!"

Isaac's face melted as he tried to respond, "I really didn't mean—"

"Do you know what, Isaac Erbrecht?" she said as her face vibrated back and forth in sync with her raised, shaking finger.

"You are the most terrible man I've ever met! You pretend to be some sort of heavenly soul, always trying to play the humble, kind, and compassionate act. Well, I say that you are a **demon!**"

He clasped his hands together as he tried to explain.

"Professor, I—"

"I never should have wasted my time with you! I mean *really*." She nearly shoved him off the bench as she sat down and pretended to play, mocking him, "Oh, look at me, I'm Isaac Erbrecht! I've never had a teacher but watch as I recite and perform my own compositions, when I know not a Shüza about what I'm even doing!"

Isaac's eyes were growing wider by the moment. Naturally, he was shocked. But she continued on.

"I know what game you're playing," she said viciously as she raised a finger at him. "You want to play me for the fool! You think you're some sort of prodigy, trying to get attention and accolades from me, the greatest concert artist and teacher of all time!"

A spark began to flicker within him as these ridiculous accusations continued to be thrown at him.

"Now hold on just a moment—" he tried before being interrupted again!

"You think that some sort of…reverse psychology will work on me, do you?"

He truly attempted to resolve things but only got mowed down again.

"Well, let me tell you something, Isaac. I heard that composition you played for my husband. And let me tell you…" she said in the most threatening and hostile voice as she stood up and attempted to size him down, "that I have never heard a more barbaric, unimaginative, redundant, amateur, dreadful, and sloppily played piece in my life!"

Both Mrs. Minlöuian and the room began to dance and sway as Isaac viewed both from the swimming tears that were forming in his eyes.

"You are a disgrace to this divine instrument! And surely, you'd be doing both it and me a favor by never touching another one again!"

He was utterly shocked. He hadn't a clue of what to say. After all, what do you say to something like that?

She waved her hands as if shooing a fly away as she finished, "Now get out of my house. Get away from me. And most of all, get away from this glorious instrument before you dare insult me or it any further!"

As if she had some sort of horrifying power, he felt as though his body were moving on its own, dictated by her very willpower in banishing him from her home.

With his back turned to her, his eye twitched a little as he heard her whisper to her piano as she stroked it, "There, there, my darling one… He didn't touch you. That filthy, ignorant peasant didn't lay his putrid, grimy fingers upon your glorious keys."

Perhaps if it would've been left at that, he would've left as commanded. But things have a very interesting way of changing, as Mrs. Minlöuian just had to add, "Isaac. Hold on just a moment."

His back was still to her, and he said nothing as she said, "If anyone asks, you were never my student. I simply hired you to be my servant."

She slowly stood as she continued, "And should you say otherwise? Friend of King Närveid or not, you do not want to mess with the people I know…for I can assure you that my friends are so high in power that they are the ones who govern King Närveid."

His fingers began to move and twitch as she finished, "Should you fight, I shall personally see to it that you and your unworthy, filthy, and barbaric friends are properly eliminated!"

Did he mean to? Was it a reaction from every terrible thing she'd said? Or was it because she'd threatened his friends? Maybe it was because she threatened Jenna.

But intended to or not, he suddenly spun around in his Majestic fury. A barrier of light exploded through the air as he thrust his hands up, surrounding both him and Mrs. Minlöuian.

Her mouth instantly dropped as she screamed in terror and ran into the barrier; trapped from the inside, her (now obvious) wig-and-hat combo launched off her balding head.

"Mrs. Minlöuian," he said in righteous fury, his eyes glowing and dancing as his whole being emanated the splendor and glory of his Light Majesty, "did you know that as a Majestician, I have the ability to read people's emotions?"

She lay upon the ground, with one hand raised in front of her as she looked up at him in terror.

"And do you know what your emotions have said, ever since you heard me play for your husband?" he quietly asked.

She said nothing.

"Jealousy," he simply said, before saying, "I do not need your validation to prove my talents. I don't need your permission or approval to say that I am a composer, pianist, and Majestician."

There she lay, still speechless, as he continued, "Like the flowing waters, roaring fires, rays of the sun…the strength of the trees and the freedom of the creatures of this magnificent world, do you think they need validation or a paper certificate to tell them what they are or what they can do?"

Either from horror or sorrow, it was hard to say, but the tears that rolled down her face were nothing short of noticeable.

"No!" he shouted as he flung his hand forward, causing her to recoil back against the domed light in further terror.

"Because they already know what and who they are, and all of them…" he said as he waved his finger, "and myself shall be damned if we need approval, permission, and validation to do what we were designed and created to do!"

With a wave of his hand, the barrier instantly disappeared, causing Mrs. Minlöuian to flop down onto the floor.

"Oh...I'm sorry. Just a couple more things," he said as he turned around again, after walking away. "You say that you are the teacher, no? Well, are we not *all* teachers and students? For I have a couple of lessons for *you*."

She shuddered in fear as he walked past her and rubbed his hands along the concert grand piano.

"Amazing...isn't it?" he questioned. "A black-and-white instrument, similar to the black ink and white pages used to create stories of a book, is it not?"

Mrs. Minlöuian looked up and swallowed as he continued, "It is as if the piano is all but one infinite round of ink and pages, and our fingers, hands, and bodies are the pen. Free to create and edit as many stories as we like!"

Isaac then took a few steps back and began tapping on the air, unleashing his streaming rays of Light Majesty.

"May I ask you a question, Mrs. Minlöuian?" he respectfully asked. "How is it that you can feel so accomplished and conceited in saying that you've mastered the piano?"

Her eye twitched as she looked up at him and hoarsely whispered in anger, "What do you mean?"

"Well, let's say that you really are the master of the piano." He smiled as he continued directing his Majesty. "That's not really saying much...is it?"

Her breathing began to huff as she undoubtedly withheld her anger in fear.

"You know, of course, that the keys of the piano, being eighty-eight, are turned in half-steps. Right?"

Was that a twitch or a head nod she gave? Either way, he continued, "Well, how can you feel so accomplished, mastering something so small?" he questioned with a head tilt. "After all, why do we not create a keyboard with one hundred and seventy-six keys, tuned to eighth steps?"

Mrs. Minlöuian's expression looked horrified as she quickly caught on.

"Or…" he continued, "even something as crazy as three hundred and fifty-two keys, tuned to sixteenth steps?

"I'm sure you can imagine," he said with a smile as he continued touching the air, "why I truly *don't* understand how you can be conceited, in the efforts of 'Mastering' something so limited. Also, it looks as though you're wondering what I'm doing, right?"

Her attention and focus looked this way and that as she watched the zipping rays of light zoom and flow past her.

"Right now, I am unleashing the musical notes of the ether. Basically, I am playing an ethereal piano. And I'd love nothing more than to tell you the range of music I hear, but I must sadly and honestly confess that it is without your hearing range. So, you *clearly* wouldn't understand."

With her mouth dropped again, she hadn't a clue as to what to say.

Isaac suddenly clenched his fists together, causing his Majesty to cease.

"Oh, and you're more than welcome to report me to your, *'friends of power,'*" he said as he turned around to walk out. "But I must warn you, those that dig pits for heaven's children shall find themselves falling **in it,** instead."

And with that, he left Mrs. Minlöuian utterly flabbergasted as he walked out her front door and gently closed it behind him, never again to return.

CHAPTER 15

James's Sacrifice

"This is going to be hard, you know," said Jenna as she, once again, had her feet kicked up on a chair in the library. "Waiting up all night for your uncle to return."

James picked up a stack of dusty books and set them down on the side of the table, giving it some relief.

"Nonsense! There's still so much work to be done!" he exclaimed as he pushed the wooden ladder down and then climbed up multiple shelves to get more books.

Jenna threw her arms behind her neck as she leaned back even further and closed her eyes. "I am tired of all this research," she complained. "I admire you and your uncle and your love for it, but by my word, the Creator didn't give it to everyone!"

"And said," James quietly mumbled as he descended the ladder and dropped more books, startling Jenna.

"Look, I know it's not very fun," he said as he looked at her, "but can you at least help me until Isaac gets back?"

Jenna sat up and looked at the clock, then back at James as she answered, "Sure! I don't suppose thirty-seven minutes would kill me!"

She startled him as she suddenly jumped into the air excitedly, and then immediately restrained herself.

"Umm...," James said, raising an eyebrow and recoiling slightly, "what was all that about?"

She massaged her forehead as she stared at the floor and said, "Well, you know how Isaac acts strange every time he goes to his lessons? And comes back sad?"

James tossed his head back and forth as he thought about it. "I've noticed a bit, yeah," he agreed.

"I was thinking," she continued, "that I could go and grab him some lunch! That way, when he gets here in the next thirty-five minutes or so, he'll have something to eat!"

He gave her a suspicious smile. "You don't happen to, I don't know… like Isaac a little, do you?"

Jenna nearly blasted the poor table holding all the books across the room as she accidentally flipped it up in a shocked response.

"What? That's madness!" she spat, kneeling to help pick up the books.

But there was no fooling James, who was laughing hysterically as he sat on his behind, supported by his hands.

With a sour expression and beet-red face, Jenna immediately stood, whipped around, and said bitterly, "I'm going to get Isaac some lunch."

"Whoa, whoa, wait! Stop!" James exclaimed, ceasing his laughter. "I really think Isaac'd be much happier if we all went."

Jenna was still so embarrassed that she couldn't turn around. With added sympathy, James saved her from the situation as he suggested, "But hey, I know he loves sweets, right? How about you go on ahead and see what Chef Volkan's whipped up in the name of desserts and bring it back for him?"

As if she suddenly forgot everything that just happened, she spun around and faced James. "That's a great idea! He'll be so happy! Thanks, James!"

And with that, she turned around and bolted out.

Isaac pushed open the doors of the library and entered to see his friends knocked out asleep on the already bowed table.

The gold-and-blue light of the chandeliers cast a decent amount of light, but the flame that was suspended over their research table (clearly cast by Jenna's Majesty) brought a feeling of comfort and warmth.

He immediately noticed the slice of peach and kinberry pie just to the left of Jenna's elbow, fork neatly resting on the white-and-blue plate.

A shimmering, weeping sphere of light danced to life as he held up his right palm. With a gentle push, it began to slowly circle around Jenna's suspended flame, adding more light to the huge room.

Jenna's eyes slowly blinked open as she heard the gentle clatter of the empty plate and fork being set down, in addition to the sound of *pitter-pattering.*

What in Vaerün...? she thought sleepily as she fully opened her eyes to see Isaac standing there, drenched and dripping water all over the floor.

"Isaac!" she shouted, nearly knocking over the table again and practically giving James a heart attack.

"Hey, you two," Isaac mumbled, "I'm so sorry to have taken so long. I hope you didn't wait up all this time just for me!"

James tried to respond but was suddenly interrupted by his and Jenna's growling stomachs.

With a concerned look, Isaac glanced back and forth between the two. "Oh no! Please don't tell me you haven't eaten all day?"

James squinted for a moment, then widened his eyes when he looked at the massive hanging clock on the wall, which read the time—10:23.

"No, no, mate!" he quickly answered, lying. "We just slept through dinner, is all!"

"That's right!" added Jenna. "But enough about us. I have two questions. One, why on Vaerün did your piano lesson take up the whole day? And two, why are you soaking wet?"

Isaac watched the trailing flame zoom around him as Jenna commanded a gentle stream of her Fire Majesty around him, instantly drying him.

"Thank you, Jenn!" he exclaimed. "To start with, I'm soaking wet because it's pouring rain outside at the moment."

Jenna and James immediately looked toward the massive western windows and saw the downpour.

"And well..." Isaac trailed off for a moment before continuing, "I guess it's time I told you two the truth about my piano lessons."

For the next hour and a half, Isaac recapped to both his friends every single terrible, atrocious, and utterly demeaning piano lesson he had with Mrs. Minlöuian.

By this time, James had gone through three books (he was a great multitasker) and was starting his fourth. Jenna was pacing back and forth.

"Can I ask you a favor, Isaac?" Jenna suddenly asked, stopping and staring at him.

"I know, Jenn." He sighed. "I promise to not lie ever again. I'm really sor—"

"That's not it," she interrupted as she walked up and hugged him. "No, I was going to ask you, to please... never, ever let anyone treat you like that again. Do you promise?"

He squeezed her back as he answered, "I promise. I'm so sorry."

James laughed as he looked up from the large tome and pointed to Isaac. "But, oi! Way to stick it to the old wench with your final remarks, mate!"

Jenna looked off and said on a tangent, "That woman, though! I swear, you would've found kinder competition in the Fürnas coliseum when I was a girl!"

Isaac could only shake his head as he admitted, "Competition... I hate that word."

Jenna and James stared at him as he continued, "Does anyone realize just how terrible competition really is? I mean, let's think about this for a moment, okay?"

"Okay?" they nervously asked.

Isaac half-snickered as he said, "We only exist because of our Creator above. Is that not true?"

"It is," they agreed.

"Think about it," he continued. "If competition existed in the heavens above, then we wouldn't exist. For our Creator would be *competing* with other creators!"

"That's true," James nodded. "He'd be far more interested in competing with other cosmos creators like himself, rather than tending to us weak and frail beings."

Jenna gripped her head as she confessed, "Leave it to you, Isaac, to think of such things."

"It's true," he admitted. "I just think competition is another unnecessary evil—"

The library doors smashed open, and in a panic, Isaac and Jenna immediately ceased their light-giving Majesty.

To their great surprise, in marched King Närveid.

"King Närveid!" James shouted, immediately slamming a book shut.

"James, your uncle, he—" huffed King Närveid, attempting to catch his breath.

"This can't be good," Isaac whispered to Jenna. "For the very king of Wöntylnas to personally visit us, something must be—"

"Just returned," interrupted the king as he finally caught his breath. "I've come to you just as fast as I can."

James's heart began to race as he approached the king, a little frantic. "Is everything okay? Why hasn't he come in himself? What's going on?" he bombarded with questions.

"Please, come with me, and I'll explain along the way," answered the king as he turned around and swiftly walked out of the library.

No wonder he was huffing! You'd be huffing too if you had to wear all that heavy kingly clothing! Or queenly, for you ladies.

The three friends looked at one another for a moment and immediately followed.

Clip, clop. Clip, clop. Clip, clop, echoed the sounds of their boots upon the smooth marble floor of the corridor.

"Jenn," whispered Isaac as he reached out and grabbed her hand, "are you okay?"

To his surprise, she immediately clenched it back, sending chills up his spine from her freezing grip.

"S-sorry..." she quietly stammered. "Just... really bad memories, that's all."

And bad memories indeed! For minus the Wöntylnas Kingdom, it was on a very stormy night just like this that she, too, followed royalty (albeit her mother) down corridor after corridor. The lightning and thunder strikes outside, in addition to the downpouring rain, didn't help.

"Jenna?" he asked as he squeezed her hand and sent a wave of his Light Majesty into her. "It'll be okay. Don't worry. I'm always here to protect you."

How could her heart not melt as she received the heavenly comfort that was not only his Light Majesty but also those strong, loving, and compassionate glowing yellow eyes of his, in addition to that beautiful smile?

Both of them momentarily forgot that they were running directly behind James and King Närveid.

"I'm sorry," Jenna honestly said. "I'm afraid we haven't heard you two. Can you please explain what's going on?"

King Närveid slightly turned his head but continued to look forward as he answered, "Yes. Jéid Vandergaus has just returned some twenty minutes ago, but it is as if he's lost his mind."

"What?" yelled Isaac. "What do you mean?"

"That's what I said!" piped up James. "How does one of the most intelligent men in Vaerün go on a trip and come back, only to be fit for the funny farm?"

Where did the time go? It was as if someone had sped it up! They'd all but forgotten the beautiful halls and corridors they'd just run down as they finally reached their destination—a certain dread falling upon them.

All their hearts (including King Närveid himself) began to race as they found themselves outside of a white door, with a blue archway surrounding it. A strange and fearful moaning was coming from the other side.

"I am not good at explaining these things," said King Närveid as he placed a hand upon the golden handle. "So it might just be easier for you to see for yourselves."

Without hesitation, James immediately turned the handle and walked in, followed by Isaac and Jenna.

The king stopped Isaac as he quietly explained, "I'm sorry, but I can't join you. Please, when you're finished, come see me."

"Yes, Your Majesty, you have our word," responded Isaac.

The aura of the room was forlorn, hopeless, and positively dreadful. And there, on one of the freshly made beds, lay Professor Vandergaus.

His hair was a mess, and his cheekbones were terribly sunken in. Had he eaten at all? He looked the very image of death! It didn't help that his clothes were positively filthy and shredded!

James rushed up to his uncle and immediately fell to his knees as he observed his eyes rolling back and forth into his skull.

"Uncle! Uncle!" he yelled. "What happened? Please, talk to me!"

As James tried to get a response from his uncle, Jenna stood so close to Isaac that she was touching him.

"This... energy. It's the very same as the conductor's, isn't it?" she whispered so low Isaac barely heard her.

"I agree," he replied. "But... how?"

"Isaac! Isaac," James frantically cried out as he rushed on all fours over to his friend and tugged on his white coat. "Please! Can you heal him?"

Isaac swallowed as he looked at Jenna and then at James.

"James..." he said as he knelt beside Jéid's bed. "I would love to, but it's not daylight, and so I can't—"

"What? Are you kidding me?" James shouted back. "Look at him! If you don't do something, he'll die!"

Jenna squeezed Isaac as James rushed back over to his uncle, kissing the back of his hands in frantic love and desperation.

"Isaac," she said as she turned to him, looking him directly in the eyes, "I know you said... that you can't heal without the power of the sun, but... I agree with James. If you don't try something, I genuinely believe he will die."

Isaac's eyes looked left and right in deep thought.

"Please, mate!" cried James. "I'll do anything! I'll have King Närveid give you whatever you desire. Just please—"

He was silenced as Isaac raised his right hand and began tapping shortly on the air, unleashing the beautiful streams of rippling light.

"James…" he said with compassion and sincerity as he knelt down next to him at Jéid's bedside. "My only desire, just like you, is to see this wonderful and innocent man healed."

James's face melted with gratitude as tears streamed down his face.

"And you have my word," continued Isaac as he clasped the shoulder of his dear friend, tears also streaming down his face, "that I will do whatever I can!"

"Thank you, Isaac Erbrecht!" James exclaimed as he shook Isaac with fervent love and gratitude. "Thank you!"

Jenna bowed her knees a little as she bent over to help James up and away from the bedside, giving more room for Isaac to do his work.

"Battered and broken, we appear to be…" came the majestic, healing words from Isaac's mouth as he moved his fingers, controlling the streaming rays of light. "Tossed and turned by our enemies!"

With a thrust of his palm, the streams of light blasted into Jéid, causing him to convulse furiously as Isaac continued, "But upon thy glorious light, we stand, knowing our deliverance is always at hand!"

Jenna and James had to shield their eyes as Isaac clasped his right hand with Jéid's, unleashing a blinding flash of light.

"Aaah!" Isaac screamed as his vision was suddenly and entirely centered on the black holes of eye sockets and a gaping maw—a ghastly white, dead face staring at him.

The vision worsened as he noticed the increase in the number of horrific, dead faces against a black background. The audible sound of lightning and thunder mixed with rain.

Suddenly, he found himself standing on a cobblestone street. As if his vision had been expanded, he began to take notice of the buildings around him and the raging storm of black-and-purple clouds high above him.

What he did not know was that the vision he was having was of his very home kingdom. Indeed, it was the kingdom of Wölnas!

His blood ran cold, heart feeling as though it would burst through his chest as the laughter (*Like no other*) continued… as if hell itself were making him a joke and he the last living soul, surrounded by the countless visages of horrifying spirits encircling by the thousands. Suddenly, he blacked out.

"Isaac!" cried out a voice.

There's that voice again… Isaac thought in this black space. *Who are you? You sound so familiar to me.*

Please, dear, wake up! Don't give in to the darkness! Don't let him take you! echoed the voice of Lucy all around him.

Wait, please… please don't wake me yet. I must see you! he exclaimed as he watched his hand reach out before him.

And there, in return, appeared the glowing image of an angelic woman—cloaked in white light and utterly indiscernible. She, too, had her hand outstretched to him.

It's going to be all right, darling, whispered her voice. *I'm always here for you, and I will never leave your side.*

"No!" he shouted as he thrust his hand out. "I can't—"

The vision came to an abrupt end as his hand shot out and gripped hers, causing an explosion of light.

"Isaac… from the depths of my soul, thank you," sounded the hushed words of Jéid as he clasped Isaac's hand back.

He had almost entirely forgotten that he was in King Närveid's castle, in Wöntylnas! How long was he in that vision? It seemed like forever. But as he came to and finally opened his eyes, he realized that it must've only been a moment!

"Professor…" he mumbled as he stared into the glossy, grateful eyes of Professor Vandergaus, still clutching his hand. "I'm so glad to see that you're all right!"

"Only because of you, Isaac. You saved me," whispered Jéid as a tear streamed down his face.

James dashed over and threw one arm around Isaac (forcing him onto the bed, face down) and another around his beloved uncle.

"Uncle!" he shouted. "You're okay! Oh, Isaac, thank you. Thank you, mate!"

And as quickly as he'd flopped down, he was suddenly pulled up and into a massive embrace and repeatedly kissed on his cheeks by James.

"Now now," roared Jenna as she rushed over and threw her arms around Isaac, shielding him. "That's enough of that!"

Jéid began to laugh, but after a short moment, he released a coughing fit.

"Hold on there, Uncle," James said as he waved his hand and created a fresh, pure stream of water, filling a cup by the bedside and handing it to him.

Jéid immediately took it and guzzled down the water, streams of it rolling down his chin.

"Ahh!" he said, refreshed. "Nothing like the pure streams of heavenly, Majestic water to revive the body!"

"Uncle," James said, a little stern, "what happened?"

Jéid propped himself up against the headboard as he immediately apologized, "I know, I know, I'm so sorry to all of you! I didn't mean to keep you waiting so long."

Isaac waved his hands compassionately as he said, "It's okay, Jéid. We just want to know what happened!"

"Well..." he started.

"Don't you think you two are being a little rude?" Jenna questioned as she tapped on Isaac's and James's shoulders.

"No, no, it's all right!" Jéid quickly defended. "I have to tell you right now. We're running out of time."

"What do you mean?" all of them asked, albeit at different times.

"Well, please don't be mad at me, but..." He trailed off as he reached into his battered coat and pulled out a very old, folded piece of parchment paper.

"Who would like to read?" he asked as he held it out.

"Isaac," Jenna and James said in sync.

Isaac quickly took the paper and unfolded it.

"Be a dear and read it out loud for us, will you, Isaac?" asked Jéid politely.

He slowly nodded as he unfolded the paper. The writing was extremely neat and elegant yet obviously rushed. The ink was smeared in many places, and black blotches glared back at him, instantly reminding him of the horrifying vision he'd just had.

With a deep breath, he read:

To any Majestician who should find this,

We've run out of time. The Kreaux are, even now, falling upon us in incalculable legions—all of them the very men and women who were once our fairest and most beloved brothers and sisters.

But we deserve this. To have none other than the very powers of hell awakened and unleashed upon us. Indeed, a punishment for the very gravest of sins in which we so callously and freely committed.

Fearful and confident in knowing that the very powers that were gifted to us by heaven have now been turned against us, to be the very execution from our existence, may prove as a devastating reminder to any who may survive or find this letter.

But should any Majesticians survive this, our most deserved genocide, or should heaven ever again decide to grace any benevolent soul with the sacred power of its unfathomable Majesty, I must beg—finish what we started.

In this, our last attempt, we, the kings of Vaerün, and perhaps its last Majesticians, have used our powers to create a weapon like no other: a weapon solely created to obliterate the Kreaux for good.

Climb the towers. (Blotched part) back of our castles, in each kingdom, according to (blotched part) element.

I must profusely apologize that it must fall to you, for in order to activate the weapons, you must (badly blotched part).

They're here. Time is gone. Gerund has just perished. Coltin's dead. Fjalund's consumed. All hope is lost.

I seal this letter with my tears.
(Blotched part)

> *Begging the mercies and forgiveness*
> *of divinity, reader, and Creator,*
> *King Vergaus Nöleid Wöntylnas*

No one said a word as Isaac finished the letter, gently folded it up, and went to hand it back to Jéid.

"No," he said, waving his hands in rejection. "Please keep it. It's addressed to you, after all."

"When I arrived at the northern Algár Mountain pass," he spoke after no one further said anything, "I was engaged by a number of Kreaux. Thankfully, I had swift Kölvun to help me out."

James snickered as he mumbled, "I swear… best horse we have, if you ask me."

"But," Jéid continued, "the moment I reached the top of the pass and looked down into the northern valley that is Wölnas, I should've just listened to my instincts… and turned back."

"What was it like?" Jenna asked. "Why didn't you?"

"Well, have you ever walked past an abandoned house that just gave you the jitters, something fierce?" he asked.

All three of them nodded.

"Then take that, and make it a kingdom," he stoically said. "And add a massive ravine running right through it, like a black scar. And add the unceasing storm raging over it, of which it's known for, and you have yourself Wölnas."

James shuffled nervously as he admitted, "That does sound pretty bad."

"Oh, no!" Jéid laughed. "That's nothing, I assure you, compared to when I actually entered that forsaken kingdom!"

Isaac's eyes burst open as he recalled the exact vision of which he'd just seen.

"Spirits," Jéid muttered, "everywhere. Ghosts of the dead—undoubtedly the inhabitants, haunting the whole kingdom. Black sockets and gaping maws. Translucent and still wearing their frayed clothing."

Jenna covered her mouth as he continued, "To be honest, I'd rather have engaged the Kreaux than to have witnessed and experienced that."

"That is terrible," admitted Isaac as he placed a hand on his leg. "But then why did you stay so long?"

"I admit I shouldn't have." Jéid nodded. "But I'm sure as James can attest here, that we researchers will do whatever it takes to prove or disprove a hypothesis."

"Maybe I'm a little lost," said Jenna, "but shouldn't you have known that Garon Erbrecht wasn't there the moment you arrived? I mean, obviously your hypothesis about Wölnas's destruction was true!"

"Oh, Jenna..." muttered Jéid, "I'm so embarrassed to admit, but you're right. I should've left when it was confirmed. But that's not the hypothesis I'm talking about."

James looked up at the ceiling as he said, "No. You're referencing King Wöntylnas's letter."

"That's correct," he agreed. "I wanted to confirm if it was true or not! So... I headed to the back of the castle, in search of the pathway leading to the enormous tower behind it."

"And was it true? Did you find the weapons it talks about?" Jenna curiously asked.

"I don't know. First of all, it was hard enough to get to the back of the castle. I was attacked by Kreaux and possessed suits of armor, and navigating past the abyssal holes and fissures from years of decay and earthquakes proved very difficult."

"Is that what took so much time?" Isaac asked.

"Let me finish," he said with a waved hand. "So yes, I reached the back of the castle, and I found the door leading to the bridge of the tower."

Everyone slightly jumped as he shouted, "It was incredible! The most impressive workmanship I've ever seen. It had the engraved emblem of Wölnas carefully etched into its massive platinum front and looked as though brand-new."

"Wait a second…," said James in deep thought. "That sounds just like the door at the back of our castle, except ours has the Wöntylnas emblem!"

"Right!" Jéid excitedly explained. "But what fascinated me even more was the fact that I was blown back by a powerful electric field when I tried to open it!"

Everyone looked at Jéid in awe but said nothing.

"And thus, my research was confirmed," he said with folded arms. "This letter was truly written by none other than King Wöntylnas himself, during the great and devastating Majesty Genocidal War, some thousand years ago."

"But James just mentioned the very same door at the back of this castle, here in Wöntylnas," Jenna said. "Wasn't that enough to prove his letter?"

"My dear," he quickly defended, "any good researcher and scientist will tell you that you must check your hypothesis at least twice in order to confirm it."

No one said anything as he added, "Besides, my main goal really was to confirm as to whether or not Garon Erbrecht was there."

Isaac straightened up as he asked, "And… he obviously was not, as we previously discussed… right?"

Jéid placed a hand on Isaac's shoulder as he answered, "I'm afraid so, Isaac. I'm sorry. And thus continues our ongoing issue of the mysterious letter writer to Jenna Coltier, left for her in her very kingdom."

"Hold on," interrupted James. "I still want to know why it took you so long to come back! What happened?"

Jéid's face fell a little as he was forced to say, "It was terrible. On my way out of the castle, I came face-to-face with a man wearing a robe blacker than night, with some strange black venomous goo dripping out of his overdrawn hood!"

"The conductor!" yelled the three of them in sync as they all looked at one another.

"What?" Jéid curiously asked, before answering, "Is that what you call him? How fascinating, for I could've sworn I heard the Kreaux call him Gerund."

"Gerund?" shouted James as he nearly flew into the air. "Like, Gerund Wölnas? The Ancient King Of Antiquity?"

Isaac and Jenna looked at each other as Jéid answered, "Now don't quote me on that. For that's what I was just going to explain—that on my way out, before I left the castle, I fell down some ten feet into one of the fissures, in the castle."

Everyone's eyes widened as he continued, "I honestly thought I was going to die down there, especially after being stuck a whole week! Thank heaven I had my rations of bread and water on me."

"So how'd you get out?" demanded James, irritated.

"That's what's so disturbing." He admitted, "The whole time I was there, in addition to the spirits, I saw, repeatedly, at some distance, this robed man."

Jenna spoke up and said, "Ah, but I bet you just thought he was a part of the specters?"

"That's right," he agreed. "But imagine to my surprise when one of the final times I attempted to climb out of that fissure, a hand so cold that one might have thought that death himself were there to escort me to my eternal resting place should help me out."

"What?" shouted Jenna and James, nearly in sync.

"He helped you?" demanded James.

"I'm not so sure about that," mumbled Jéid. "It probably would've been better for me to die in that ravine."

A strange fear gripped Isaac as he reached out and asked, "What happened, Professor?"

"It's strange to describe…" He slowly continued, "But the moment he touched my hand, it was as if legions and legions of spirits were whispering and shouting in my head."

Everyone's hair stood on end as he continued, "And you may think me psychotic, Isaac, but all I could think of was you."

"Me?" he curiously asked.

"Yes." He nodded. "I mean not to scare you, but it was as if he was using me as a tracking device to find you."

Shiiiink! rang the shimmering, gleaming sound of Jenna's rapier as she unsheathed it.

"Let that creep even try to hurt Isaac!" she yelled. "He thinks hell is hot? Oh ho, clearly he hasn't felt my flames!"

James motioned for her to sheathe her rapier as he asked, "But hold on, Uncle, I need to know something. You said his name was Gerund, right?"

"Yes," said Jéid. "Among the whispers I heard when he gripped my hand also echoed the words, 'Gerund. Gerund… Gerund. Gerund! Gerund… Gerund,' again and again and again."

"That proves it then," James said as he turned around and faced Isaac and Jenna. "The conductors are the Majestician Kings of Antiquity."

Isaac nodded in agreement. Then he said, "It makes sense to me. Perhaps that's why they're able to use Majesty?"

"Clever for you to pick up on that, nephew," added Jéid. "But I think there's more to it than that."

"Like what?" asked Jenna.

Jéid massaged his forehead as he said, "Well, according to my research, the Kreaux were once human beings and Majesticians—just like you three!"

"Are you serious?" Jenna asked in awe, alongside Isaac and James.

"Yes," answered Jéid, "but it's rumored that the kings, before they were kings, were actually the first Majesticians!"

"I see," said Isaac, figuring it out. "And according to King Wöntylnas, whatever brought about the Kreaux was believed to have been their fault."

"And so," added Jenna softly, "it would only make sense that their punishment be the worst…"

No one said a word as everyone sat in quiet, eerie contemplation.

Finally, and always being the one to move an awkward situation forward, Isaac spoke up.

"So, what should we do?" he asked.

This was followed by Jenna, who added, "And although you didn't see Garon in Wölnas, it's still possible that he may have escaped and written that letter to me!"

At first, he opened his mouth to argue, but then thinking better of it, Jéid said, "It is possible, Jenna. But I fear that we have another problem on our hands."

A sense of foreboding filled the room as James asked, "What is it, Uncle?"

"That robed man, what you have deemed as a conductor," answered Jéid, "followed me at a distance, mind you, all the way from Wölnas to the southern Algár Mountain pass."

The room began to feel darker and colder as he continued, "It is my fear… that for whatever reason, he is after Isaac."

"Pcchh!" spat Jenna playfully. "Please! Perhaps none of you believe me when I say, let him even try!"

"It's not that, Jenna," said Jéid seriously as he shook his head. "Not to scare you three, but I don't think you have a clue as to the powers of darkness that are striving to combine together to destroy you."

In silence, the three friends looked at one another.

"And there's one last thing…," he said as he looked down, "something I didn't tell you."

Perhaps in fear, Jenna accidentally shouted, "Well, what is it?"

"After he pulled me up, the conductor grabbed King Wöntylnas's letter, observed it for a moment, let out a howling shriek, then dropped it to the floor."

Jenna and James raised their eyebrows as they looked at each other.

"Okay, and…?" James asked, with a roll of his hand.

"You don't get it, do you?" Jéid asked, this time in agitation.

"I do." Isaac nodded. "He knows that we know about the weapons and that we're going to strive to destroy them, the Kreaux."

Without saying a word, Jéid motioned to Isaac as his expression said, "Thank you, Isaac."

It was obvious that Jenna and James immediately got it, as a look of terror reflected upon their faces.

"Hoooold up…" James echoed. "You just said he followed you some way back, right? So that means he knows you're coming back to Wöntylnas!"

"But I thought you said Wöntylnas is impervious to Kreaux attacks?" demanded Jenna.

"Nothing is impervious to anything, dear," said Jéid boldly. "All I know is that our greatest enemy knows that we're trying to destroy them."

"And for us… that cannot be good," added Isaac.

Jenna repeatedly shook her head as she said, "As if being the last three Majesticians on Vaerün wasn't—"

"Four," interrupted Jéid.

"What?" she demanded. "There's another one? Who?"

"Gage Grünas," answered Jéid proudly, "the earth Majestician, of the eastern Grünas Kingdom."

Gage… Gage. Gage? Isaac mulled the name over and over again in his mind. *Why do I feel I've heard that name before?*

"Wow," said James with a shocked but blank expression. "My mind is totally blown right now."

Suddenly, a slight earthquake hit, causing everyone to grip onto the nearest item. (In this case, Jenna gripped Isaac.)

When it ceased, Jéid slowly looked up to the three friends.

James looked from his friends and stared at his uncle as he slowly asked, "I thought Wöntylnas was built upon the water. How can we have earthquakes?"

"And this is why you should've finished Wöntylnas's history!" he exclaimed as he answered. "It rests upon the ocean, but its foundation goes deep down into the ocean floor. So yes, we can still have earthquakes."

After a few moments of waiting and straining their ears, Jenna spoke up.

"Well, I don't hear anyone screaming, so it doesn't sound like the Kreaux are attacking."

"To be honest," confessed Jéid, "I fear for something far worse than a Kreaux siege."

"What might that be, Jéid?" asked Isaac concernedly.

"The sought destruction of Vaerün's last Majesticians," he coldly admitted.

Jenna and James gulped, but Isaac stared at him calmly, hands folded.

"It would appear that we, too, are running out of time then," Isaac said. "If the enemy knows our intentions, we must move forward."

"Yes!" hissed Jéid excitedly. "Go! Activate the weapons, for only you can! Destroy the Kreaux from Vaerün once and for all!"

"Well, what are we waiting for?" Jenna asked as she turned around, preparing to open the door.

"Where are you going?" James asked, when suddenly he found himself being pulled by her hand. "Whoa, whoa, Jenna, what—"

She rolled her eyes as she said, "Well, duh, James! It only makes sense to start with you first since we are in your kingdom!"

Jéid looked from Isaac to James as he agreed, "Jenna's right, James. You should start with your weapon. And please hurry. I fear that earthquake may signal something terrible."

"Will you not be joining us, Professor?" asked Isaac innocently.

"If there's one thing I've learned"—he slightly laughed—"it's that this task was meant for you Majesticians and you alone. I go with you in spirit and eagerly await your return."

James and Jenna gave him a hug as they said their goodbyes, followed by Isaac.

Jéid gripped Isaac's arm as he whispered into his ear, "Isaac. Heaven forbid something should happen after James activates that weapon. Do not stop. Find the earth Majestician Gage Grünas as soon as possible!"

Isaac stared intently into Jéid's eyes as he said, "You have my word, Professor. But I can only hope that everything will be just fine."

"Me too, Isaac, me too," he muttered.

"Okay, wait. Hold on a second," James said as the three of them came to a screeching halt in the long castle corridor.

"What is it, James?" Isaac kindly asked.

"Not trying to be funny, but… let's say all hell breaks loose when I activate this 'weapon.'"

"Right?" Jenna said sarcastically.

"Well, I'm just saying," he continued, "that it prooobably wouldn't be too good of an idea to have to deal with some sort of disaster when running on no sleep. Am I right?"

Isaac couldn't help but laugh as he saw the look on Jenna's face that basically said, *Guh-doy.*

"I must confess, James," admitted Jenna, "that I hadn't thought of that."

"Not only that," he added, "but the moment I'm done, we should head—"

"Straight to Fürnas!" she interrupted and demanded, "And neither of you shall dissuade me. Go find the earth Majestician all you want, but I am going to my kingdom."

Isaac and James looked at each other and smiled.

"We'd never separate from you, Jenn!" Isaac happily exclaimed.

"Too right you, that!" James agreed with Isaac. "We've waited this long to meet him. Besides, it makes sense to go in a loop!"

"That's true," agreed Isaac. "Starting here, going south to Fürnas, east to Grünas, then north to…" He faded off when Jenna quietly finished for him.

"Wölnas."

"Oi! None of that!" said James as he snapped his fingers. "Happy talk, okay? Lots o' hope and optimism! Okay? Now let's get some rest so that we can wake up and have a proper Chef Volkan breakfast!"

Isaac and Jenna looked at him and said in sync, "You got it!"

The following day, after breakfast, they met with King Närveid in the royal meeting hall to discuss everything that had transpired with Professor Vandergaus the previous night.

"I understand," the king nodded as he sat upon his throne. "We can only hope that these 'weapons' will do what they're said to do."

"And with your permission," said James, "we will head to the back of the castle right now so that I may activate it."

Everyone jumped as a clap of thunder struck overhead.

"Call me crazy," muttered Jenna to Isaac, "but for some reason, I just don't have a good feeling about this."

"I agree," he whispered back to her.

"You two talking about something you'd like to share?" questioned James as he turned around to face them.

Unabashedly, Isaac admitted, "We're just concerned that this may not be what it's chalked up to be. What if it's a trap?"

Jenna looked very concerned as she looked out the window, then back to James.

"Not only that, but don't you find it strange that the whole time we've been here, there hasn't been a single storm, and now all of a sudden there is?"

James ignored another thunderclap as he glared at his friends.

"You wouldn't happen to be accusing my uncle of bringing back some bad omen, would you?"

Isaac motioned his hand up and down to calm his dear friend.

"Not at all, James. We're just worried!"

"Do you seriously think this whole thing is just a setup?" James demanded.

"No, James," returned Jenna, "we don't! We love and trust Professor Vandergaus, just like we love and trust you!"

"But seeing as how this is your kingdom, and only you can charge this 'weapon,' don't you feel the least bit apprehensive?" Isaac asked in great concern.

King Närveid stood as he agreed with Isaac and Jenna.

"Your friends have a point, James. You do not have to go through with this!"

James shook his head in anger for a moment and then calmed down.

"Thank you... all of you. But for some reason, I just have this strange feeling that everything is going to be okay. And that we need to do this!"

Everyone quietly listened as he continued, "My uncle believes in King Wöntylnas's words, and so do I. Not only that, but I know you do too, Isaac and Jenna!"

Isaac stepped forward as he placed a hand on James's shoulder.

"Yes, James, we do. But we just don't want anything bad to happen to you, that's all!"

He laughed as he, in turn, placed a hand on Isaac's shoulder and said, "Thank you, mate. Really. But one gift that continuously gets me through anything is my hope." He shrugged as he continued, "I just… I always have this hope that everything will be okay! It's what's gotten me through life!"

Isaac stared at him for a moment and then pulled him into a big embrace as he said, "I believe you."

James squeezed him back and then jumped back excitedly.

"Well, then! Shall we get to it?"

"You're not, I dunno… excited, are you?" Jenna asked with a slight smile.

He smiled and gave her a very gentle punch in the arm as he answered, "Are you kidding? These 'weapons' are supposed to be strong enough to obliterate the Kreaux! How could I not be excited?"

King Närveid beckoned for the Majesticians to follow him as he approached a small wooden door at the back of the throne room.

"I'm sure you remember, James, but take this door through and—"

"Yes, Your Majesty," interrupted James. "I remember, thank you!"

And with that, he quickly bowed to the king, thrust open the door, and ran in.

"What a way to talk to a king," Isaac said as he respectfully bowed to the king.

King Närveid laughed and bowed back to Isaac.

"Don't worry, I'm not offended. I find his character to be quite…"

"Jubilant?" asked Jenna a little sarcastically as she too bowed to the king.

"That's a good way of putting it!" he admitted. "Good luck to all of you. Please be careful."

The door creaked shut as the king closed it behind them.

"I… kind of feel like we've stepped back in time a little," said Jenna as she observed the long corridor with Isaac and James.

The smell was very old but not unpleasant (kind of sweet, actually). Although the flooring was the same marble structure, it looked newer, as if this part of the castle were built after the main one (which indeed it was, unbeknownst to them). There were cobwebs everywhere—lining suits of armor, paintings, and decor that just didn't coincide with the times. Strangely enough, all of it seemed much more… advanced than today's aptitudes.

"I take it that no one ever comes back here?" asked Isaac as he and Jenna followed James and continued to observe.

"No need," he answered. "And you'll see why."

No one said anything as they continued down the immensely long corridor for over five minutes.

"Kind of brings back some bad memories, doesn't it?" Jenna laughed a little to ease the quiet tension.

"Hardly," said James, still walking forward. "I'll take this any day over that terrible haunted—"

"So!" interrupted Isaac, "We about there, James?"

"See for yourself!" he responded as he began running.

Surely enough, they reached the end of the corridor to find another wooden door.

James quickly opened it and led the other two into the room.

"Yeah. I can see why no one comes back here," said Jenna as she looked around the room. "Hardly worth traveling down a quarter-mile corridor just to reach another room."

Isaac observed the large, strange metal door that had the Wöntylnas emblem deeply engraved upon it. Minus the large, ornate door, the room was a little boring. The floor and walls were nothing but stone.

"Fascinating!" he exclaimed as he took a step back and looked it up and down.

After a couple of moments, he took a few steps back and motioned for James.

"Well then, go on ahead! Open it!"

James paused for a moment as he bit his lower lip in suspense.

"What are you waiting for?" Jenna asked as she stared at him suspiciously. "Haven't you done this before?"

"No," he answered. "This is as far as I've ever gone. To be honest, that door scares me."

"Why?" Isaac asked as he further observed it and quietly said, "It just seems like a normal door. Minus the fact there's no handle."

"Right? That's just it!" James yelled. "What kind of door doesn't have a handle?"

"Well… maybe you should try touching it!" Jenna spoke up as she pushed him from behind.

Isaac approached him as he said, "Again, if you don't want to do this, James, you don't have to!"

"It's true," agreed Jenna. "If you're getting a bad feeling about this, it may be good to listen. Let's just turn back!"

"No way!" he exclaimed. "New things are always scary. Let's push forward!"

James walked up to the door and placed his right palm onto the emblem. A blue wave of rippling energy coursed from his hand and pulsed over the door, instantly causing it to swing open.

The three of them raised their arms to shield their faces from the blast of cold, wet ocean air that flew into the room.

In curiosity and excitement, they stepped through the open doorway and found themselves upon a large, white stone bridge. It was very similar to Wöntylnas's main bridge, albeit not as wide and much smaller.

James squinted as he pointed to the huge, tall, white-and-blue stone tower that lay over the long stone bridge.

It was beautiful and very similar to Laniakéa, albeit much smaller, and adding in the blue stones and ornate blue patterns.

"Exactly how far up does it go?" Isaac asked in shock as he looked up. "It kind of reminds me of a lighthouse…"

The tower rose high into the sky and then disappeared amid the layer of dark-gray clouds.

James held up a hand over his brows to shield his eyes from the rain as he looked up.

"Well, according to my research, all of the towers were built nearly to the same height as Laniakéa! Although they are much smaller in size."

Jenna looked at him in amazement as she asked, "Why so tall?"

"Well, like Laniakéa," he answered, "they were built to honor the heavens and their Creator."

"Incredible..." muttered Isaac as he looked forward. "It truly is a splendor to behold."

Jenna began to have flashbacks of her home kingdom as she thought, *It looks just like mine, back at home... just with different colors.*

Isaac couldn't help but laugh after ten minutes had passed from them walking on the bridge.

"They sure knew how to build them, didn't they?"

"One thing's for sure...," Jenna added, "back then, you sure had to be in shape to pray to divinity!"

"This is nothing," responded James as he pointed up to the tower that was slowly growing closer. "What do you want to bet that we have to climb that next?"

Thankfully, the rain was finally letting up, although the dark clouds remained overhead. And every now and then, a ray of the late morning sun would come through, only to be covered up again.

"Nearly there!" beamed James as he suddenly picked up the pace and pointed to the massive, open archway of the tower just ahead.

The three of them suddenly stopped dead in their tracks. A terrible dread began to fall upon them as they heard that horrid sound. Indeed, it was that same gut-wrenching, hair-raising, throat-swallowing sound that always signified the coming of the Kreaux—the sound of dark whispers.

James had turned around, only to notice that Isaac and Jenna were already facing the same way. For there, some fifty feet away, stood the conductor.

I'm sure they had so many questions, but it was cut rather short as he reached into his black robe and pulled out two black daggers, dripping with Dark Majesty.

"Go, James!" shouted Isaac as he thrust his palm forward, casting one of the whistling daggers back with a blast of light.

"No, mate! I—"

"Damn it, James," cried Jenna as she unsheathed her rapier and launched fireballs with her opposing hand. "Do as he says, or you'll have to fight him and me!"

With something between a growl and a grunt, James continued down the bridge.

"Hurry up, you two!"

Tethered with Dark Majesty, the black-and-blue water stuck to the daggers like glue as they whistled and stabbed through the air, striving to bring down Isaac and Jenna.

Boom, boom, zzzeeearrgh! flashed and exploded the fanning waves of Jenna's flames, blasting through the air from her slicing sword, as Isaac did backflips and side strafes, deflecting the infected daggers with well-placed casts of Light Majesty.

With the additional boost of water jets from James's Majesty, he launched himself through the archway and looked back at his friends.

"Come on, mates!" he cried with cupped hands. "Nearly there!"

Rrrrah! shouted Jenna as she launched a wall of fire and light that consumed the entire bridge.

In anticipation and disappointment, they watched as the conductor cut through and dispersed it with his dark Water Majesty and razor-sharp daggers.

"Haaaa!" shouted Jenna as she strived to charge but was interrupted when Isaac yanked her back.

"What? What?" She looked at Isaac in dismay and shock. "How could you—"

And then she caught on as she noticed that Isaac was pointing to the conductor.

He was laughing! But not only was he laughing, he'd actually stopped attacking!

Isaac squinted as he tried to figure out what was going on.

"Why is he—?"

"Doesn't matter," interrupted Jenna as she forcefully grabbed his arm and tugged him down the bridge. "Can't reason with crazy!"

The archway grew closer and closer as they saw James beckoning them through.

Booom! rippled the blue light barrier as it slammed Isaac and Jenna back.

After a moment of gaining their wits, terror began to sink into them as they realized why the conductor was laughing.

"I get it...," muttered Isaac. "He knows that only James can go through."

Jenna's eyes grew wide as she realized, "If that's the case, then he must be—"

"James!" shouted Isaac, interrupting Jenna. "Go! We'll hold him off!"

"No way, mate. I—"

Both Isaac and Jenna turned their backs to the slowly advancing conductor as they raised their palms and ignited them.

"Like I just said," muttered Jenna menacingly, "it's not just the conductor you'll have to worry about, if you come back through."

"Oi, you guys are terrible!" yelled James as he slammed his fists against the ground, then jumped up and began to run up the spiral staircase.

"Just wait till I get back. You'll both be sorry!" echoed his voice as he disappeared up the stairs.

Isaac turned to Jenna and smiled.

"Not bad tactics, miss."

"Truly." She nodded pleasantly. "Now... shall we whup this Majestician wannabe?"

"After you, darling!" He bowed.

Her feet were moving so fast that she probably could've run on the water below them as her hands roared behind her like rockets with bursting fire.

Come on... come on... come on, mumbled Isaac as his fingers gripped the air, shaking, vibrating, and charging.

Now, Isaac! he shouted in his mind as he watched Jenna leap high into the air and explode her sword down, as if the Creator himself had sent his divine weapon to destroy.

"Haaaa!" he yelled as he stabbed the air with his fingers, unleashing ten enormous and rocketing streams of light that dashed through the air with unforeseen speed and straight for the conductor.

James practically hugged the wall as the entire tower momentarily shook.

"Give 'em hell for me, mates!" he barely muttered as he began to run up the seemingly never-ending stairs.

After what felt like "too long," he placed a hand against the cold stone wall and sought to catch his breath.

The quakes and sounds of exploding Majesty could no longer be heard.

Exactly how long have I been climbing? he thought as he slowly inched over to the railing and looked over. *And how far up am I? Does this never end?*

Indeed, he was so far up that as he looked down, all he could see was the meshed white of the stairs appearing as if they'd combined together.

"Damn it!" he shouted as he brought his fist down on the railing and then began running up again. "Hold out for me, mates! I'm hurrying!"

The conductor's hands danced like mad as the black ropes turned this way and that, continuously commanding his daggers. Through the air they flipped and slashed, like blurs of black—one engaging Jenna, the other, Isaac.

"Isaac!" shouted Jenna as she continued to deflect the black, magical dagger. Her dress was torn and cut in some areas, accented and stained by the sharp inflictions.

"Jenn?" he shouted back as he unleashed a series of light rays in martial arts-like fashion.

Shink, shink, clink, shiiiink, sha-shink, shink! cut the sounds of the spark-casting blades as Jenna responded, "I have an idea! Can you give us some cover for a sec?"

"I'll try!" he shouted as he blasted himself into the air and momentarily levitated.

Like an angelic seraphim, he floated, arms and hands outstretched, his white cloak and wardrobe twisting and turning through the air, casted about by his emanating Light Majesty.

"Haaa!" he shouted in fury as he unleashed two devastating beams of roaring Light Majesty down upon the conductor.

Not even with his Dark Majesty could the conductor have been prepared for this attack as he was blown back by the immense wave and beams of light.

With a swift descent, Isaac quickly ran up to Jenna and shouted in his commanding voice, as he clapped his hands together, "*Never to turn, never to fail, shield us with thy unceasing veil!*"

Vooom! Voom. Voom. Voom. Voom, echoed and pulsed the sounds of his incredible Light Majesty as he separated his hands and held up his palms, casting a rippling light barrier around him and Jenna.

Although her heart was racing, she couldn't help but let a tear fall helplessly from her eye and down to the ground as she looked all around at this glorious power that could only be heaven-sent. And although she'd experienced this a number of times, it always felt brand-new.

Despite the terrible battle they were currently engaged in, it was as if time momentarily stood still within this bastion of light.

Jenna slowly turned to him.

"Who... are you... Isaac, Erbrecht?" she quietly and humbly asked as she stared at the fierce, powerfully unwavering, yet kind and gentle man that was her beloved Isaac.

James's heart began to race as he squinted his eyes to shield the incredibly bright light that suddenly fell upon him from high above. He slowly looked up to see that, in just another hundred steps or so, he'd be at the top!

With great nervousness and anxiety, and in seeking comfort, he thought, *what's that prayer that Isaac is always saying? Oh!*

And thus, at the same time, unbeknownst to them, as James continued to ascend the stairs, looking heavenward, Isaac looked forward, both of them facing their fears as they both said in unison, "*I... am a stranger, in a distant land... sent to do the will of my Father.*"

James's speed began to pick up as he continued running up, and Isaac's barrier rippled and shone as sweat began to drip down his face as he sustained blow after unceasing blow of the furious conductor.

"I will not give up! I will not let go."

Almost there! Just another fifty steps, James!

Boom, boom. Boom, boom. Boom, boom, boom! sounded the ringing barrier as it deflected the intense attacks from the battered conductor.

"I will fight. Hold steadfast, and strong, for I am his."

"**Water!**" cried James as he was just ten steps away.

"**Light!**" cried Isaac as he was dripping sweat, sustaining the siege of blows.

"Upon the earth. A creator, a Majestician."

And with those final words, James took in a deep breath as the heavenly noonday rays of the glorious sun shone down upon him, and Isaac finished hearing the last of Jenna's words as he exploded his barrier, sending out a force field of light.

Momentarily spellbound, James had all but forgotten his mission as he looked around at the massive landing that was the top of the tower. He ran to the eastern railing and was quickly taken by surprise.

What kind of metal is this? he thought as he touched and looked at the gleaming, polished railing that was unmarred by the elements.

His thoughts were entirely changed, once again, as his mouth dropped. For there, far to the northeast and southeast, he could make out the towers of Wölnas and Fürnas. But it wasn't nearly as breathtaking as the massive, ornate, and white tower of Laniakéa that stood a little taller than the other towers, directly east of his direction.

Don't forget what you're here for, James, echoed a voice in his mind as he suddenly snapped out of it and turned around.

But my, who could blame him? For as he turned around and walked west, toward the small marble and granite pedestal that held a small, glass sphere, his eyes were filled with the visage of the heavenly blue sky and white fluffy clouds and the rippling ocean that consumed the western view.

"Snap out of it, James!" he shouted out loud as he violently shook his head and slapped himself. "Your friends are down there, and they need your help!"

He quickly approached the small pedestal.

It was beautiful and very ornately designed. And like the railing (and heck, for the rest of the tower too), it showed absolutely no signs of weathering or decay but looked as though brand-new.

Suddenly, he found himself getting a little angry as he observed the small, empty glass sphere that sat in a depression upon the pedestal.

"Is this a joke?" he asked as he tilted his head this way and that, observing the sphere. "This little sphere is supposed to be a weapon?"

And just like that, he swiftly turned around, his blue cloak spinning through the air behind him.

"What a joke!" he shouted in anger. "My friends could be dead right now, and all for what?"

He nearly fell forward as a blast of light bloomed from behind him. With great anxiety, fear, and (undoubtedly) curiosity, he turned around.

There, next to the pedestal, stood Lucy Erbrecht.

"Hello, James Vandergaus," her gentle and ethereal voice sounded.

"H-h-hello?" He choked and stammered as he gazed upon the beautiful, heavenly woman.

Her flowing long blond hair, mixed with the pure-white dress robe she was wearing, twisted and churned in the air from the clean, gentle breeze.

"I am delighted to meet you," she said as she slightly bowed. "And yes, I must agree with you that in its current state, this sphere doesn't look like much of a weapon."

"I-if I may, umm…," he stammered, before finally asking, "Who are you?"

She smiled as she humbly answered, "My name is Lucy."

James's eyes burst open as he nearly tripped. "Lucy? Hold up, surely not, Lucy, Lucy? Like, Lucy Erbrecht?"

With a sincere smile, she nodded and confirmed, "I am indeed the very same. And yes… I am Isaac's mother."

Something between a whistle and a cough repeatedly came from James's mouth as it stood gaping open.

"But if I may," she continued with a sad look, "please don't tell him or Jenna yet. For it's not yet their time to know."

"I-it… I—" he stammered, still flabbergasted.

"Please, James," she interrupted with a slightly fearful look, "they need your help. For even now, they are engaged with King Vergaus Wöntylnas."

"I knew it!" he shouted as he jumped up and down. "I knew the conductors were the Majestician kings of old!"

"James, please," she said, trying to get his attention.

"But hold up just a moment," he said quickly as he paced back and forth. "Eyewitness accounts talk of five robed men who led the Kreaux siege that day, some twenty years ago!"

"Unless if I'm losing my mind, or if the account was wrong, Vaerün only has four kingdoms," he continued, until he stopped pacing and stared at her. "Who is the fifth robed figure?"

Lucy shook her head as she answered, "I'm sorry, James, but I can't tell you that."

"What?" he shouted. "Now that's just a load of—"

"James, please," she slightly shouted, casting a rippling energy, "Jenna and my son need you right now! They need your Majesty!"

As if someone had just shaken him up and down, James received his wits.

"I apologize, Lucy." He humbly bowed. "What will you have me do? How do I activate this weapon?" he asked as he approached the pedestal.

"It requires sacrifice," she forlornly said, "as do all of them."

"A sacrifice?" he curiously asked as he kneeled down on the indented kneeling stone, placed before the pedestal.

"Yes."

"Well, what kind of sacrifice?" He slightly laughed. "I haven't much to give, and I didn't bring anything up with me—"

"Not a sacrifice of anything material, James," she politely interrupted, "but rather one of most precious worth."

He swallowed as he stared at her and then at the small, empty sphere.

"Can't I just, I don't know… charge it with my power or something?" he nervously asked.

"But that's just it," she answered. "You will be doing just that. For sacrifice is the greatest power of all."

"I don't really understand, but… is it really necessary?"

"Yes. It is the only way to permanently rid Vaerün of the Kreaux."

His face reflected a couple of disgruntled looks as he said, "And did it really have to be me, to do this?"

"You may not remember," she said as she kneeled next to him and placed a hand on his shoulder, "but you promised to fulfill this very act, before you were born. You knew what you were getting into, and that is why you were chosen as one of the last Majesticians to fight and destroy Baehallün and his legions of Kreaux!"

With a sorrowful but very sincere look, he stared into her charming and enchanting blue eyes.

In return, she smiled back and explained, "It is why you have been given a portion of our Creator's power—to access and command his very water."

"I'll do it," he quietly said as his whole being vibrated and glowed with the blue energy of his Majesty. "How do I fulfill what I've promised?"

Lucy closed her eyes. Although fearful herself, she tried to show strength as she said, "Place your hands upon the sphere, James. It'll do the rest."

For the final time, James stared at the small, empty glass sphere. Although it looked harmless, as it reflected the surrounding blue sky and white clouds, he just knew something bad was going to happen. It was that same foreboding feeling he'd experienced the day he'd first discovered that door leading out to this very tower.

With a deep breath, he raised his trembling hands and placed them upon the glass sphere.

At first, nothing happened. It felt smooth and cool to the touch. But suddenly, he began to hear voices in his head as a pain, indeed an unbearable pain unlike any he'd ever experienced, began to pull upon his whole being. And then followed a series of visions and memories.

"What's the matter, freak?" shouted one of the bullies as he kicked and punched the young eight-year-old James in the grungy alleys of Wöntylnas.

The poor young James, with his messy black hair and blue eyes, had his hands raised up, striving to defend himself from the five bullies that were assaulting him.

"Yeah, what's wrong, freak?" roared another bully, much larger than the first, as he slammed a metal cup over his head, causing blood to drip down his pale face.

"Awwww, look at 'im...," added another bully as he socked him in the chest and knocked the wind out of him. "Cryin' again? No wonder Mommy and Daddy threw him away! Ha ha!"

Tears were indeed streaming down James's face, but not for long as he nearly fell unconscious. Blood gushed out from the side of his skull as the fourth bully slammed him in the head with a broken brick, causing his beautiful blue eyes to momentarily lull into the back of his head.

"Naaah, Gérx," chided the fifth bully as he wrapped an arm around the small young James and lifted him off the ground, choking him by the neck. "They din't want him, on accounta' him bein' a monster!"

"Now, now, boys...," mocked the first bully (obviously the leader) as he pounded his fist against his palm. "We promised to do this quick and easy."

He approached James and whispered into his ear, "They sent us, you know... your parents. They sent us to kill you, demon!"

And with that, James became their personal punching bag as each of the bullies took turns beating the living daylights out of him.

Was it from the blows or the lack of oxygen from him being strangled? Either way, he began to see his small life slip away as the whole scene grew ever blurrier.

Shiiiink! pierced the air of the unsheathed sword of Jéid Vandergaus as he glared down the bullies with an anger and fury like no other.

He didn't even have to say a word as the five bullies screamed and dashed away, throwing poor James to the side.

"James... James!" cried the words of Professor Vandergaus as he carefully rushed over and picked up the broken and malnourished boy.

"James," he whispered into his ear, "don't give up, James. Don't give up hope!"

"Aaaaaggghhhh!" James screamed in torturous pain as blue lightning exploded from the glass sphere.

His black hair and blue cloak were flying like mad as his whole being was unable to let go of the sphere. Blue energy continued to flow from James's hands and into the sphere.

"Please!" he screamed at the top of his lungs. "Please don't! I can't! Lucy, help me!"

Tears streamed down Lucy's face in helpless abandon as she fell to her knees and wrapped her arms around James, her head resting on his shoulder as she broke down crying.

Another vision began to consume his mind.

He was sitting in one of the side rooms at Castle Wöntylnas as Professor Vandergaus, King Närveid, and some other men were debating back and forth.

"He cannot stay here. There's a reason his parents abandoned him," hissed the voice of a bitter old man.

"That's enough, Taldrön!" boomed the younger voice of King Närveid.

"It's true!" hissed another voice. "And should he stay here, the entire kingdom of Wöntylnas shall be thrown into pandemonium and chaos!"

"I don't understand you. Any of you, minus King Närveid!" shouted Professor Vandergaus. "Shouldn't we be delighted and honored to be blessed with the first water Majestician in over a thousand years? Is this really how we're going to thank heaven above for such a divine and precious gift?"

"He is no Majestician," hissed Taldrön's voice. "He is a demon! And the sooner he leaves our beloved kingdom, the sooner these terrible rumors can cease, and peace be restored!"

"Oh, you mean like, poisoning our food supply and killing our people so that you can make a profit?" roared Professor Vandergaus's voice.

The audible sound of men fighting and hitting one another echoed in the other room.

Bursts of blue Majesty and rings of light exploded repetitively from the sphere as it continued charging.

James's skin began to turn paler. Every vein in his hands, face, and neck were positively magnified as they bulged against his tightened skin. His mouth couldn't possibly stretch any further as he continued to scream and beg for help.

"P-p-please!" he begged as he began to furiously convulse. "L-L-L-Luuucy… S-s-s-save me fr-fr-from th-th-this h-hell!"

Lucy's arms squeezed him tightly as her glowing angel tears fell upon his shoulder. As if a light Majestician like Isaac, her whole being emanated the same heavenly light and splendor as she held on to James, imparting some of her angelic comfort to him.

His eyes squeezed shut as his mouth came to a forceful close. For the pain was so horrendous that he couldn't even scream anymore.

If any of you have ever been unlucky enough to have something jabbed or inserted into a fresh or even a healing wound, that was how James's mind felt—as though someone were invading it in the most barbaric of ways possible, searching for every single thought, feeling, and emotion of despair, mixed with hope.

"Aaaaggghh!" he screamed again as another memory came to his mind.

It was some months after his encounters with the bullies, and he was tired of being judged by the Wöntylnas inhabitants. And so he'd decided to leave for good.

He was out upon the Wöntylnas plains, when suddenly a strange, black mist surrounded him. The green grass beneath his feet began to wither and die. And truly, for a time, he felt as though he were standing at hell's gates.

"Jaaames…" hissed a voice so evil and unspeakable that words cannot even describe it.

"Wh-who are you?" cried out James as he looked all around in search for the source of the voice.

"Come with me, James," hissed the voice. "Serve me… and I shall treat you like a king!"

Was the voice coming from below? Or all around? It was impossible to tell.

"S-serve you?" he muttered in terror.

"Serve with me, and I shall give you power like no other!" continued the voice. "All you have to do is call my name. It's—"

"No, James! Don't do it!" screamed two voices in his head. "Our beloved, don't give in to despair! Don't give up hope!"

Although he knew not whom the voices belonged to, they didn't sound unfamiliar.

"Will you s-s-serve me?" demanded the unnamed voice.

"Never!" cried the young James as he slammed his hands through the air, casting his Water Majesty.

"You shall perish!" hissed the voice as it slowly dispersed. "You, and the rest of them!"

The vision came to a close, but James's eyes were still closed. A multitude of voices whispered over and over again in his head: *Don't give up hope, James. Hope… hope… don't give up hope! Don't let go of hope. Hope. Hope. Hope! Hope.*

"Rrrrrr-**aggghhh**!" he yelled as he finally heaved himself off the sphere, casting himself backward.

Lucy immediately grabbed him with her heavenly strength and gently sat him upon his feet.

He was still shaking as he stared at his hands. As he huffed and breathed, the air turned misty, as if he were standing in a frozen tundra.

"Wh-what… happened?" he stammered as he stared at the sphere.

To his shock, it was now glowing as it revealed the blue light within its clear casing.

"And wh-why…"—he shivered—"is it s-so… c-c-cold?"

Lucy was still crying, and she hardly knew what to say. But with strength and determination, she finally said, "James… as you know, in order to charge these weapons, a terrible sacrifice must be given."

Still shaking, he wrapped his cloak around himself as he woozily slumped down onto the ground.

His eyes were now a sharp, frosty blue. His skin was even paler, and he now had a gleaming, silver streak running through his jet-black hair and goatee.

Lucy suddenly broke down crying as she fell before James and grasped his freezing cold hands.

"My dear James... it's going to be okay! I promise!"

Still shaking, he slowly looked into her eyes.

"N-no, L-L-Lucy... t-th-there's n-no h-h-hope l-left," he stammered.

Lucy suddenly broke down crying as she fell before James and grasped his freezing cold hands.

"My dear James... it's going to be okay! I promise!"

Still shaking, he slowly looked into her eyes.

"N-no, L-L-Lucy... t-th-there's n-no h-h-hope l-left," he stammered.

"No, James!" she shouted, as if refusing to believe it herself. "Please, dear." She threw her arms around him once more and squeezed him tightly.

But he just sat there and did nothing.

"Trouble..." she muttered through her tears, "does not last always. For this, too, shall pass."

Suddenly, his mind caught hold of Isaac and Jenna. As if somehow his concern and love for them had just quadrupled, he suddenly jumped up, causing Lucy to fly back through the air and gracefully land down.

"Isaac! Jenna!" he shouted. "They need my help!"

In awe and amazement, Lucy stared at James.

"J-James!" she stammered. "You've just lost all your hope! Are you sure you—"

"They need me!" he exclaimed as he ran over to the pedestal. "I may have lost hope for myself, but not for those two!"

Neither Lucy nor he could have anticipated what would happen next. For the second he grabbed the blue sphere, it began to shake and vibrate within his hand—so much that he had to grip it with the other one to stabilize it.

"Aggghhh!" he shouted as a massive blizzard erupted from the sphere and surrounded them.

Both of their eyes widened as they heard the sound of a wolf howling among them.

The blizzard disappeared, and there, before them, stood a beautiful, blue-eyed, white-, gray-, and black-coated wolf (with intricate and ornate designs etched into his coat). Even on all fours, he stood but a foot shorter than James. He was huge!

Lucy laughed as she, once again, shook her head in shock and amazement.

"Wh-what is he?" stammered James as the large wolf approached and lovingly rubbed against him.

"That..." choked up Lucy, as she pointed, "is your hope, James."

"My... hope?" he whispered as he ran his hand along the wolf's coat.

"What will you name him?" she asked as she approached and joined in, petting him.

"Hmm...," he hummed as he thought about it and then said, "**Ruvíag**."

"Ruvíag?" Lucy asked with a slight head tilt. "Why Ruvíag?"

"Begging all pardons," James politely said, "it's... personal."

Lucy humbly bowed as she said, "I absolutely understand."

In return of humility and respect, James bowed (followed by Ruvíag) before Lucy as he began to descend the stairs.

"Wait! Please hold a moment, James," beckoned Lucy after him.

He turned around and asked, "What is it, Lucy?"

She extended her index finger and zipped it through the air in an ornate pattern. As if the air had just become her heavenly forge, the gleaming string of light ceased to reveal a strange, metallic-like silver netting.

"Hm? What's that for?" he curiously asked.

She approached him and pressed her finger to his lip as she attached the small, intricate, silver web to the right side of his belt.

"For your sphere," she whispered. "This lacing is special. It will prevent anyone and anything from getting it, so long as you don't relinquish it! Do you promise?"

He gripped the sphere tightly as he and Ruvíag nodded in sync.

"I promise, Lucy."

"Very good then," she whispered as she pushed him forth.

"Oh, and James?" she called after him once more.

His eyes began to lull a little as he wobbled back and forth. In a sudden burst of snow, Ruvíag disappeared.

"Ha ha!" Lucy compassionately laughed. "That's what I was going to ask, but it was obviously just confirmed."

"What's that?" he weakly asked.

"It would appear that it takes an incredible amount of Majesty to sustain Ruvíag," she said as she held him up. "I'd advise you to only use such power when in dire needs."

And with that, she held up her palms and imbued him with some of her power, returning some strength to him.

"You know," he said with a half-smile as he was partway down the stairs, "this is going to be really hard, you know, not telling Isaac that I just met his mother."

With a quivering lip and immediate tears that rushed down her gentle smile, she quietly whispered, "You have no… idea."

And with that, James gave one last bow and dashed down the stairs.

"He sure doesn't mind taking his time, does he?" howled Jenna as she made repetitive jabs and slices at the swiftly dodging conductor.

"In all fairness," huffed Isaac as he was combating both of the daggers with blades of light, "he hasn't been gone too long!"

Both of them were cut up and mildly bleeding. They were drenched in sweat, and it looked as though they'd been tossed down in the water below them, only to resurface.

"Jenna!" yelled Isaac. "Look out!" He shoved her out of the way just in time, from a black water tentacle that came slamming down from over the side of the bridge.

"What in Vaerün?" she huffed before shouting, "Now that's just cheating! We're out of our element here!"

Refusing to say a word, the conductor just laughed.

His hands extended high into the air, revealing his white, bony, vibrating hands.

"Isaac! Look out!" screamed Jenna as she tackled him out of the way from another water tentacle.

They barely missed it as it came crashing down onto the bridge.

"Shüza!" swore Jenna under her breath as she slashed at some of them and blasted others with fire.

"Isaac, we have to—" she cried out.

"No!" he interrupted. "Not yet!"

After some time of dueling the ocean waves and Dark Majesty tentacles that both came rising up to assault them, Jenna had finally had enough.

"Isaac…" she shouted in a weak and feeble voice, "I can't go on…"

Seeing this as a perfect opportunity, the conductor furiously weaved his hands through the air in repeated pulling motions as Isaac stared up in awe at the massive black-and-blue waves that were coming up and over the bridge.

The conductor's hands were vibrating like crazy as he charged his Dark Majesty.

"Jenna!" screamed Isaac as he dashed toward her.

The careening wall of water came thundering down as the conductor slammed his hands forward.

"Arrgghh," grunted Isaac under the tsunami-like wave that was consuming his barrier.

"Isaac…" mumbled Jenna weakly as she looked up at him. "I'm so tired… Forgive me."

"No way, Jenn, get up!" he exclaimed as he reached out a hand to her.

She slowly pushed herself up as she stared at the glowing light that emanated from the etchings within his palm.

With her last strength, she gripped his hand and instantly received a surge of vitality and strength.

The barrier began to fizzle and dim as it weakened from him imparting some of his Majesty to Jenna.

"Stay with me, dear!" Jenna yelled as she gripped her rapier in her free hand.

"Are you ready?" she demanded. "Can you do this last thing with me?"

"Y-yes!" he said.

Suddenly, the spark that existed between them now felt like a glowing bonfire that was ready to be unleashed. For the way she looked at him, and the way he looked at her, might've forever changed the way they viewed each other.

Jenna stood next to him as she pointed the gleaming sword forward.

"Ready? One… two…"

"Three!" they shouted together as one of his hands latched onto the hilt of the sword with hers.

"Haaaaaaa!" they bellowed as Isaac lowered the barrier.

Whatever water was surrounding them was now instantly evaporated or banished as the raging, exploding, consuming storm of fire and light erupted from their palms and sword and descended upon the conductor like a flamethrower against a fly.

"Holy mother of…" muttered James as he descended the stairs to view the power of their combined Majesty.

"Isaac! Jenna!" he cried out from behind them.

After a few more moments, they ceased the attack.

Shink, shink! rang his daggers as he unsheathed them and bolted out, more than ready for combat.

But to all their surprise, the conductor was gone.

"Did we do it?" Isaac muttered as his vision was focused down the bridge.

"I'm not sure how anything could've survived that," Jenna slightly laughed.

"From the looks of it, I'd agree!" exclaimed James as he turned around and sheathed his daggers.

"Aaaaannnddd that's why I don't piss either of you off." He smiled.

But Isaac and Jenna could hardly say anything as they viewed his visible transformation.

"Why are you two looking at me like that?" he asked them, still unaware of his changes.

"James," Isaac quietly said, "what… happened up there?"

Jenna grabbed Isaac's hand and then walked up and grabbed James's icy hand.

"I'm sure we can all talk about it over some nice, hot—shüza, James, why are your hands cold as ice?"

"Language!" exclaimed Isaac, with a hint of sarcasm.

"Language my nothing!" retorted Jenna as she placed his hand upon James. "Feel that!"

"Again, what happened, James?" Isaac restated as he gripped James's icy hand.

Jenna took their hands again and hurried them along. "I can't wait to hear all about it too, Isaac, but right now, we need to get off this bridge."

"I agree," said James stoically. "Probably wouldn't be too good if Vergaus came back."

"Wöntylnas?" Isaac and Jenna said in sync.

"Yeah, I mean," he replied as he suddenly got irritated, "just, ugh. Never mind!"

And in all their cases, they couldn't have run faster as they headed back to the castle.

CHAPTER 16

The Town of Wyllmourn

Knock, knock, knock!

"Come in!" shouted James.

He was lazily resting upon his bed, directing streams of snowflakes and ice flurries around the room, when Isaac opened the door and entered.

Sniff, sniff. Was that— It was! James nearly fainted as he sat up and looked at Isaac.

Isaac was holding a plate of steaming hot boar, garlic mashed potatoes with fresh cubed butter on top, and a side of kinberry sauce in one hand, with an apple rollover in the other.

"How are you doing?" Isaac kindly asked, clenching down on his jaw to prevent it from chattering. The steaming plate of food was really noticeable against the arctic temperatures of James's room.

"How'd you know I'd be in here?" James asked as he sat up.

Isaac set the food on his lap and sat down next to him on the bed.

"Well, two reasons. One, I can always find you because I know your energy, and two, the frost that's collected beneath your door and out into the hallway was a pretty good giveaway," he finished with a wink.

"Oh, shüza!" James exclaimed. "My bad, my bad, mate!"

Isaac could only laugh. "Don't worry about it! My only concern is the unlucky servant who might pass by and—"

Boom, boom! Clink, clatter, slam!

With wide eyes and pursed lips, Isaac and James looked at each other and burst into laughter at the audible crashing of items on the other side of the door.

"Oi…" James muttered as he stood up and tiptoed over to the door. "My bad… You think they're okay?"

Isaac shrugged.

"Only one way to find out."

James opened the door. To his horror, he saw Jenna, sitting on the floor covered in garlic mashed potatoes, roasted boar, kinberry sauce, an apple rollover, and some mulled kinberry wine.

"And you wonder why I don't do anything for you," she said with a hollow voice and half-smile.

Isaac quickly rushed out and helped Jenna up, brushing some of the food off her.

"Excuse me!" he called out to a servant who had just come around the corner. "Could we please get some—"

"Don't bother," Jenna interrupted. "I've got it. All of it. It was my fault, and no one should have to clean up after my mistake."

James and Isaac helped her up as they assisted in the cleanup.

"No, no… it's my fault," James said sadly. "I'm really sorry."

"Well, if you're so sorry," Jenna poked at him playfully, "then cast some of your Water Majesty and clean me up!"

James leaned against the wall as he confessed, "I can't. I've tried. That's what I was doing in my room!"

"Still ice and snow, huh?" asked Isaac as he sat next to him.

"Yeah…"

"That's so crazy!" Jenna chimed in. "Forget the fact that it already takes an unbearable sacrifice to charge it, nooo, then it has to go ahead and alter Majesty too!"

Isaac's expression softened as he looked down.

"What's wrong, Isaac?" she asked with concern.

"Well… what if it changes your Majesty too? What will your sacrifice be?"

Jenna brushed some of the food and debris off herself as she sat down in front of them.

"Please, Isaac, you know me. And you know my life story. I really don't have anything to give, so I can hardly imagine it'd be that big of a sacrifice!"

"Be careful what you say now!" he warned.

"Haha!" James laughed as he helped brush off some of the food from her. "She does have a point though, and she's a pretty bitter person. I can't imagine it taking much to charge her sphere."

"See? Let's listen to the guy who's already done it!" she exclaimed. "Besides… I can't wait to see what kind of cool Majestic beast I get too!"

Isaac sighed as he helped both of his friends up.

"I just wish… that somehow, I could take the burden off both of you."

"Puh-lease!" they both reprimanded him, nearly in unison.

Jenna gave him a strange, fierce look.

"I'm pretty sure that the healing and barriers that've saved our lives multiple times count as 'taking burdens off.' Wouldn't you agree, James?"

"Oh, too right, you!" he agreed. "No one compares to you, Isaac Erbrecht. You are the most incredible man ever sent to grace Vaerün."

Isaac shook his head in embarrassment.

"Stop that, both of you!" he exclaimed.

To his relief, a few servants came rushing around the corner to help clean up.

Jenna caught their attention as she began walking away.

"Where are you going?" Isaac called after her.

"To change! That'll give James enough time to go and get his own food."

"But I've already got—"

He was silenced as Isaac suddenly cupped a hand around his mouth.

"All right, Jenn! Thank you!"

"Don't forget we're supposed to meet up with King Närveid!" she called back. "Meet us in the throne room when you're done!"

"Sounds good!" Isaac smiled as he finally let go of James's mouth when she was out of sight.

"Good goin', mate…" he whispered gratefully. "'Cuz that wouldn't've ended well."

King Närveid was nothing short of shocked and devastated on hearing of James's sacrifice.

Following the discussion, a lively debate ensued as to whether Jenna should activate the weapon housed in Fürnas. Ultimately, she won—as she always did.

As their audience with the king concluded, he humbly requested the Majesticians to stop at Wyllmourn, a small branch-off town of Wöntylnas inhabitants that desired their own independence.

"And you want us to give the founder this sword?" Isaac asked as he accepted the sheathed blade from the king.

"Please," he answered. "It'd mean so much to my cousin, dünréld, and so much to me. He's been requesting it for some time now."

"With all due respect, Your Majesty," said Jenna as she unsheathed and observed the blade, "why this particular sword? Surely he has access to many others?"

"I'm not proud to admit it," the king replied, "but I'm sure James here has told you that the people of Wöntylnas are rather… superstitious. And I'm afraid that Dünréld is no exception."

"He thinks it possesses some sort of 'protective' powers," James added.

Jenna raised an eyebrow. "Yeah, I get that, but protect him from what? The Kreaux?"

"No one's exempt from Kreaux attacks," responded Isaac. "Surely your cousin knows that?"

"I'm not sure that's it," the king answered. "In his letters, he describes a man who keeps coming to Wyllmourn. He says that more and more of his people change with every visit."

"Change?" Jenna leaned in. "What kind of change are we talking about here?"

"I don't know," said the king as he shook his head. "And to make matters worse, he stopped responding to my letters a couple of weeks ago."

"No wonder you need our help," muttered James as he observed the blade.

"There may be more to it than just handing a sword over, that's for sure," Isaac added as he equipped it around his waist.

"Was that some pessimism I just heard from you, Isaac?" Jenna laughed.

Isaac's eyes grew wide as he waved his hands.

"What? No! I'm just worried that... grr! Forget it. Let's just go!"

"Haha!" James laughed. "No worries 'bout us, King Närveid. We'll send word as soon as we figure out what's going on."

King Närveid stood and humbly bowed to the Majesticians as he expressed his gratitude upon their departure.

"Thank you so much, all of you. You leave with my blessing."

Isaac, Jenna, and James ignored the pointing Wöntylnas inhabitants as they rode through the marketplace, first district, and onto the massive bridge connecting the kingdom to the mainland.

Isaac beamed as he patted his white stallion.

"Rather generous for King Närveid to lend us some of his finest horses!"

Jenna used the opportunity to act like she was talking to force the people out of her way.

"Considering that James just fulfilled one of the greatest requests from the founding king of his kingdom, yeah, I'd say it's the least he can do."

James laughed as he kicked back on his horse and waved goodbye to the astonished individuals blurring by.

"Can't argue with either of you! It's about time we left this hellhole of a kingdom."

Isaac kicked his horse and rode up beside James, patting the sheathed sword attached to his belt.

"So, our first stop is Wyllmourn, right? How long till we get there?"

James's mouth twisted left and right as he thought about it for a moment.

"It's actually a straight shot down the southern trail. We'll know we're close when the trail begins to run parallel with the western oceanic cliffs."

"Ooh!" Jenna awed. "Sounds pretty!"

James nodded and then leaned forward, cracking the reins and galloping even faster.

"It is! But with the way we're moving, it'll take us a couple of days to get there. So let's kick it up and get there by nightfall! Any objections?"

"None!" they responded in sync.

Words couldn't describe how happy they were to be back out on the mainland of Vaerün.

The crystal clear, blue ocean waves gently crashed against the shore to their right, absorbing and reflecting the golden beams of the opposing eastern morning sun.

Although the morning was cold, the combination of the fresh new day and salty ocean air made it quite pleasant—revitalizing, even.

Isaac took in a deep breath as he fully lay upon the mane of his galloping horse.

"Have either of you had it where you've been sick," he said lazily, "and it felt like it'd never go away?"

Both of them responded affirmatively, in the same disgusted, grudging way.

Isaac bobbed up and down every once in a while as his horse hit slightly rough patches of terrain.

"That's... kinda how Wöntylnas felt. Y'know what I mean?"

James let out a sarcastic, "Hah!" as he answered, "Except in Wöntylnas's case, it was like a disease."

With her gorgeously long, dark-brown, reddish-burgundy hair flowing in tandem with her jacket-dress combo, Jenna agreed and posed another thought.

"It's such a shame because it's such a beautiful kingdom!" she exclaimed.

"That's what happens when you get spoiled on riches, prosperity, and secure protection from the Kreaux," James shrugged.

Isaac pushed himself up a little as he concernedly said, "I fear for Wöntylnas. It's always the people and places that declare to be 'invulnerable' that suffer the worst."

"You better say it!" Jenna clapped as she suddenly dashed ahead.

The late afternoon sun began casting its patchwork patterns of light upon the stony plains around them, the sky gently pushing patchy white and whitish-gray clouds in a northeast direction.

"I swear, that girl can sleep through anything," said James in a subdued voice as he and Isaac observed the sleeping Jenna, collapsed on her peacefully trotting horse.

"Well," said Isaac with a slight wince, "when you've gone through hell most of your life, like she has, you learn to rest whenever you can."

"That really is a shame," mumbled James. "I can't help but wonder how her 'sacrifice' is going to go."

Isaac said nothing for a moment and then responded, "I don't know. To be honest, I'm trying not to think about it... I don't want to imagine anything bad happening to her."

James gave a squinted smile to Isaac. "You... care for her, don't you?"

Isaac's face instantly grew hot as he responded, "Of course! More than anything!"

"No," said James, waving his hand. "I mean, you really care for her."

Isaac's eyes darted this way and that as he tried to think of a clever response. But always striving to be honest, he quietly admitted, "Yes. I really do."

James looked forward, giving a slightly melancholy smile.

"That's so awesome. I'd be lying if I said I wasn't jealous."

Isaac rode a little closer to him. "What? Jealous? You have nothing to be jealous of! Why, I can only imagine how many girls would love to be with you!"

With a sincerely nonchalant and hopeless expression, James shrugged.

"Nah, mate. But it's all right. I honestly don't care anymore. As long as you two are happy."

Wow. He really must have sacrificed his hope, thought Isaac as he looked down for a moment.

"Well, if it means anything, it's not like anything's going to happen between us anyway," he muttered.

James instantly gave him a mixed look of shock and glare.

"What?" he almost shouted. "And why not?"

Isaac looked dead ahead as he calmly answered, "Jenna doesn't care about me like that."

To get back at Isaac for his time pretending to be asleep near the Wéljelnin pass, Jenna, too, was pretending to be asleep. But she nearly blew her cover as she heard these words.

Come on, James, fight for me! she practically exploded in her head.

"This is a joke, right?" asked James coldly. "Please tell me this is a joke."

Yes! Get him, James! Get him! she continued to shout in her mind. I always knew you had my back!

"I'm afraid I don't understand you," admitted Isaac.

James looked forward as he chuckled and shook his head.

"Mate...," he muttered, "I don't know if you're blind or if you choose to ignore it, but that girl has more fire for you than the very Majesty she wields."

Isaac swallowed nervously and asked hoarsely, "You think so?"

"Hah!" James bellowed accidentally. "I'm not even going to entertain this."

In desperation and sincerity, Isaac pleaded, "No, please tell me, James! Please!"

"Mate," he responded flatly, "ugh! How do I put this?"

For James had kept a secret. And that secret was that he could read people's minds, just like King Wöntylnas of old.

"Just tell me!" demanded Isaac.

"Fine!" James retorted as he rode up close and began whispering to him.

Jenna's heart nearly beat through her chest as she was no longer able to hear their voices.

Damn it, James! she bellowed in her mind. *You better not be filling his head with junk!*

"I understand," Isaac nodded, a smile forming on his face as their horses separated a little. "Thank you for telling me."

"Anytime, mate!" James beamed.

"So…" Isaac muttered, "about your sphere. And this new companion of yours… Ruvíag, was it?"

"Aye, aye!" he confirmed. "That's him! Beautiful creature, you'll soon see."

"Or hopefully not!" Isaac laughed, and James agreed, knowing it would mean battle.

"That's so fascinating to me," Isaac pondered out loud.

"How so?"

"Well, according to your experience," answered Isaac, hand on his chin, "your sacrifice was your hope, but how does Ruvíag tie in with that?"

James mirrored Isaac's gesture, placing a hand on his chin.

That, James, is your hope, he recalled Lucy's words in his mind, though he still wasn't sure how to apply them.

"To be honest, mate," he answered out loud, "I have no idea. But I'll think on it!"

Isaac smiled and nodded. "Then I shall too!"

"What's wrong, Isaac?" James asked, observing Isaac's expression melt.

"Just a lot on my mind, is all," Isaac answered with a half-smile. "There's just so much we have to do."

"Like what?" James asked, head tilted—a habit he'd picked up from Isaac.

"After Wyllmourn, we head to Fürnas for Jenna," Isaac explained. "Then we have to go up to the Wölnas Kingdom."

"Right?" James motioned for him to continue.

"And even with that comes so many issues!"

"Like what?" James pressed.

"Well, the doors only open for the Majestician of that element. Wölnas is a kingdom of wind and storm."

"Oh, I getcha!" James interjected. "You're saying that since you're a light Majestician, you fear it might not work for you. Right?"

"Exactly! And what a wasted trip that'd be!" Isaac exclaimed. "Not to mention that the kingdom is haunted beyond measure. I simply don't want to put us in unnecessary danger."

James massaged his black (and now silver-streaked) goatee as he thought.

"Minus that, is there anything else?"

"Of course." Isaac nodded. "After learning what we have—and I agree with you—the conductors are obviously the Majestician Kings of Antiquity."

"Right," added James.

"As you know, we had to duel with Vergaus, the water conductor, while you climbed the tower."

James rolled his neck as he added, "Got it. You're worried that we'll have to duel Coltin, the fire conductor, as Jenna climbs her tower."

"Not just that," said Isaac. "What if we have to keep fighting them? And to top it off, we still need to find this Gage Grünas."

"Right, right!" said James, spinning his hand through the air. "The earth Majestician."

"And then even after we get all the weapons... then what?"

James laughed a little. "I'm surprised to hear you talk like this, Isaac!"

"What do you mean?"

"Well," said James, looking off a little, "you're always unfailingly optimistic. And right now, you just seem a little worried."

"It's not that I'm worried." Isaac smiled as he immediately demonstrated his strength. "You simply asked, and so I told you what was on my mind."

James blinked and gave a blank look.

"Well, damn. I guess you shut me up."

Both of them laughed before James finished by asking, "Is there anything else you'd like to talk about? You know I'm all ears!"

"Thank you very much, James! Actually..." muttered Isaac.

And so for the next four hours, Isaac learned all about James's childhood.

Jenna yawned and stretched as her horse came to a stop. She was a little surprised that she slept so long, but her eyes easily adjusted to the moon and starlight above.

"Hey, guys… everything okay?" she asked sleepily.

But Isaac and James said nothing, their focus locked on the huge, wooden, broken Wyllmourn gates some fifty feet away.

"Are you sure this is the right place?" Isaac asked. "You know there are lots of broken-down ghost towns and villages—remnants from Kreaux attacks."

"Only one way to find out," James said. "Isaac! Can you cast some Light Majesty over the archway of the entry gates?"

"Absolutely!" he answered.

He placed both hands together, palms up, and a burst of light exploded out of thin air. He then took it in his right hand and directed it forward and through the air.

'**Wyllmourn**,' read the broken, dangling sign atop the rotted wood of the archway as the light swooped past it.

As the light came flying back to Isaac, he momentarily suspended it in the air.

"*Hm…*" James thought. "What do you two think we should do?"

"I keep trying to tell everyone," Jenna chided, "but no one wants to listen! I vote we burn all these stupid, spooky ghost towns to the *ground!*"

"How can we be sure that no one is here, though?" James asked with a slight smile.

"This doesn't make sense," Isaac said in deep thought. "The king said that Dünréld only stopped responding two weeks ago. This town looks like it's been abandoned for years!"

"Not to mention that the air reeks of Kreaux," James spat.

"Again," Jenna said with a sassy smile, "what better way to put it out of its misery than to burn it to the ground?"

"I really think we should investigate," Isaac said boldly as he galloped forward.

He was headed off as James quickly rode in front of him.

"Whoa, whoa, mate!" he shouted. "Before we go charging into a potentially Kreaux-infested village, can we at least do so when the sun comes up?"

"I'm with James on this one," Jenna agreed. "Although, I still think…"

"That's fine." Isaac smiled. "We can camp out for the night and investigate first thing in the morning."

James and Jenna cheered as they immediately turned their backs to Wyllmourn.

"Where are you going?" Isaac asked as they rode past him.

They momentarily halted as Jenna said, turning to him, "Um, not everyone is as brave and fearless as the great Isaac Erbrecht!"

"Too right, you there!" added James. "I need at least five miles away from here before I can truly rest. And even then, that's pushin' it!"

Isaac couldn't help but laugh as he followed his friends to a safer distance from the eerie gates of Wyllmourn.

It felt like a *'Let's talk with James!'* kind of day as Jenna, now fully awake, sat by the campfire with him, while Isaac rested on his makeshift 'cloak pillow' a short distance away.

"You nervous?" James asked as he rested on his side, head propped on the palm of his hand, elbow on the ground.

"I would be lying if I said no," she softly said.

After a few seconds in silence, she asked, "Can I… ask you something?"

"Anything, Jenna!" he instantly answered.

"Was it…" she asked with a winced expression, "painful?"

James's eyes rolled as he gave a shocked expression.

"Oh, my word, it was a pain like I've never experienced. And trust me," he said, leaning forward, "I've experienced a lot of pain."

Visions of his childhood and all the bullying instantly flooded back into his mind.

Jenna gulped and said nothing, resting her chin upon her folded arms on her knees.

"But," James said, startling her a little, "next to Isaac, you are the strongest person that I've ever met. You're gonna smash it!"

She raised her head a little, giving a slight smile. "You really think so?"

"My word, what is it with you two today?" James asked with a large smile, rolling his eyes again.

"Haha, what do you mean?"

"First Isaac, and now you!" he exclaimed. "Both of you are thinking and acting like I've never seen before."

"Sorry…" she apologized, resting her head again.

After another moment passed, she looked at Isaac and then back to James.

"It's funny, you know?" she asked.

"What's that?"

"I so desperately want to protect him," she admitted.

James stared at Isaac. "Nothing wrong with that!"

"But the funny part," she continued, "is that that man needs no protection from anyone. I truly believe he is more powerful than even he knows."

"While I do not disagree," James said with a raised finger, "do not sell yourself short. You're an incredible Majestician."

"Thank you, James," she said humbly.

He couldn't help but smile as he observed her staring at him. Her face looked like someone deeply in love.

"You love him, don't you?" He couldn't believe he asked it.

Jenna felt as though someone had just opened a hole beneath her heart, one that led all the way down through Albÿuron and suddenly dropped it in.

"I'm sorry?" she hoarsely asked.

"Hahaha!" James sincerely laughed. "No, I'm sorry. I don't know where that came from."

Her face broke into a massive smile as she pressed her cheek into her arm.

"Do you want to know the truth?" she asked.

He stopped laughing and eagerly leaned forward.

"Well, yeah! Of course!"

"I have never loved anyone as much as him in my entire life," she confessed as her eyes began to grow glossy. "Not even my own parents. He is my everything, and I would do and give anything for him."

"Well, I'll be..." James muttered, leaning back and quietly asking, "Jenna?"

"Yes, James?" she whispered.

"That is absolutely beautiful," he whispered back. "Don't ever let that go."

"Never!" she nearly spat back.

"So... when are you going to tell him then?" he eagerly asked.

"My, my, aren't you nosy!" she giggled before continuing, "But to be honest, I don't know. It's just so hard!"

"That much I can imagine!" James admitted, grabbing another log and tossing it onto the fire.

"Not only that," she went on, "but I don't want to make things awkward."

He gave a strange face. "Awkward?"

"Well, duh!" she reprimanded. "Let's say he does like me back—then what? It'd be weird to have him and you around, and just... ugh!"

"Nonsense!" he sharply exclaimed. "Horse shüza! I couldn't possibly be happier. Especially since I know how much he loves you too."

Jenna's face practically exploded in a smile as the campfire suddenly erupted, forcing James to shield his eyes.

"He loves me too? Really?" she demanded, and he immediately hushed her with a repressed laugh.

"He does," James simply answered. "More than you can even begin to comprehend, miss."

With a small laugh and a look that said, "I can't believe it," she asked, "How do you know?"

"I cannot tell you right now," he said, "but please... you must trust me on this."

Jenna sighed as she lay back again.

"I do. Thank you for telling me."

James flipped his hand through the air. "Sooo? When are you going to tell him?"

Hmm, she thought for a moment, while looking up at the crescent moon, galaxy markings, and infinitely numbered stars.

"After I get my weapon," she finally said.

"That's odd timing, isn't it?" he asked with a raised eyebrow.

"You might laugh at me, but… I think that it'd be *perfect* timing."

"And how, may I ask," he laughed, "do you figure that?"

Jenna reached out a hand and waved it, forcing the flames to consume the new log.

"Like I just said," she whispered, "it may sound strange, but I want to be able to protect him. And with this new weapon, I feel like I'll be able to."

James gave her a look with a raised eyebrow that said, "Really? Just… really?"

She simply ignored him as she looked away.

"Or at least put me somewhere near his level? I don't know."

"Jenna," he said frankly, "you don't need power, nor do you need to be able to protect someone, to tell them that you love them."

"I'm not asking you to agree," she said. "I'm simply asking you to respect my wishes."

"Oh, of course!" he immediately responded. "It's none of my business anyway!"

With a slight smile and a suspicious look, she had to ask, "Why are you so interested in all this, anyway?"

James's face instantly turned serious.

"To be honest," he muttered, "we've all been through so much. You and Isaac, especially!"

"Thank you, but—"

"Vaerün's darkness grows with each passing day," he continued, "and its salvation rests upon us, demanding nearly unbearable burdens."

With a sincere expression, she continued to listen.

"Both of you are already so powerful… but to add one more power, a power that governs the unbreakable heavens above, I'd think you nigh unstoppable."

"I know, James!" she exclaimed. "That's why I'm itching to get to Fürnas so I can get my—"

"I'm not talking about that weapon, Jenna!" he argued.

Her heart began to race as she quietly whispered, "What power are you talking about then, James?"

He fully sat up and sighed as he rested for a moment before answering, "Love, Jenna."

"Just kidding about the sunlight then," Jenna said sarcastically.

"Right?" James demanded. "With this cloud cover, we might as well have entered last night!"

Isaac could only smile as they approached the large, broken gates of Wyllmourn. The sky was very dark and gloomy overhead, even amid the morning sunlight, adding to the eerie, still air of the quiet ghost town.

Indeed, the air was so still that you could actually hear the creaking sound of the "Wyllmourn" sign overhead as it hung from a rusted nail. The sound—*eargh, eargh, eargh*—echoed as it gently swayed back and forth. (But how was it doing that? There was no wind, not even a breeze!)

Caw, caw! shrieked the crows perched upon the borders surrounding the gates.

Isaac, Jenna, and James dismounted their horses, who immediately galloped back to the campsite, whinnying in fear.

"That's not a good sign either," Isaac mumbled as he looked back over his shoulder and watched the horses disappear.

"Who wants to go first?" Jenna asked, her hand outstretched to the gates.

"I'll go," Isaac nodded bravely, his boots stomping in the muddy puddles of water.

Ever determined and always curious, he stepped onto the fallen, angled door and jumped down into the town of Wyllmourn, followed by James and Jenna.

"Wow," James muttered as they looked around.

The air was very hard to breathe; it was as if someone had poisoned it. A strange, gray, wispy fog loomed everywhere.

As they ventured down the wet, muddy path, they looked left and right, observing the wooden houses with dead flowers stuck to their planters and boxes. Many of the homes had broken windows, and they nearly threw up as they walked past a rotting stand with moldy and decayed fruits and vegetables. But strangely, not a single fly was buzzing around!

Jenna choked and coughed, holding up her dress and breathing into it—though it did little good.

"Okay, so," she mumbled through her dress, "all in favor of me burning it to the ground?"

They all came to a stop.

"I!" muffled James through his cloak, raising his free hand.

"I know this is bad," Isaac said without covering his mouth, "really bad. And if you two don't want to stay, you have my blessing to return to camp."

He began walking forward again. "But I must find out what is going on here!"

Jenna's and James's eyes darted left and right as she held her rose-etched rapier, and he his daggers, ready for anything to jump out at any moment.

But Isaac continued forward, leading the way with a brave, determined look, hands swinging gently by his sides.

"You know," James whispered to Jenna, "sometimes I think he does it just to impress you."

"Naaah…" she replied. "He's always been a badass like that."

Reeeeeeee! shrieked the bloodcurdling sound of a Kreaux as it dashed across in front of them.

Perhaps for the first time ever, none of them fired any Majesty.

"Um," Jenna coughed. "Was that a Kreaux? It was so small!"

"It gave a very similar shriek to one!" answered James, holding up his gleaming daggers.

"I'm not so sure it was…" muttered Isaac as he suddenly walked off the path and approached a door to one of the houses, still intact with all its windows and door.

"Isaac!" cried Jenna. "What are you doing?"

Knock, knock, knock! thudded the wet, wooden door under Isaac's fist.

"Aww, look at that," James said. "Even in a hellhole like this, he still maintains his manners!"

"Hello? Anyone home?" cried Isaac, placing an ear to the door. Nothing—no response.

"What a shame, no one's home, so let's—" Jenna started.

Eaaarrrgggghhhh, creaked the door as Isaac pushed it open.

With a burst of light from his upheld palm, he walked in.

"Are you sure you want to be with this man?" James asked, looking at Jenna, who was already looking at him.

"It's for reasons just like this that I give a resounding yes."

And with that, she disappeared into the two-story home, followed by James.

The wooden floor creaked beneath their feet as they looked around.

Chills ran up Isaac's spine as he entered the kitchen to find a neatly decorated table with recently placed cups, folded napkins with silverware on top, dead flowers in a vase at the center, and multiple plates with rotten food upon them.

His hair stood on end as he heard the piercing squeals and shouts of Jenna and James.

Thump, thump, thump! thudded his boots as he ran up the stairs.

"Agh!" he yelled as his foot slammed through one of the rotted, wooden steps, forcing splinters into his ankle.

He bit his lower lip to stifle the scream as he foolishly pulled it up and out (instead of further breaking it down and then pulling it out).

"Jenna? James!" he called as he entered the first two rooms, finding nothing but moldy furniture and beds.

But when he entered the third room, his heart sank as he, too, had to repress a scream.

Visions of the Wölnas ghosts he'd seen when clasping Professor Vandergaus's hand to heal him flooded his mind as he stared at the two dead bodies propped up in their bed, resting against the headboard.

Their mouths hung open, revealing black holes—just like the empty sockets of their eyes. Their flesh was a sickly gray, yet showed little signs of decay. And although the smell was atrocious, it was, once again, strange to see not a single fly buzzing around.

But worst of all, it looked as though they were staring directly at him.

"J-Jenna. James," he hoarsely whispered. "Come with me."

Neither of them said anything as he grasped their hands and led them out of the room.

"Oh, and please watch out for the stairs—be very careful," he muttered as his mind tried to grasp not only the horrifying vision but also the pain of the wooden needles undoubtedly fixed in his bleeding leg.

No one spoke until they exited the house, Isaac gently closing the door behind them.

"What… was that?" Jenna suddenly demanded.

"That was no ordinary blight," added James. "You don't think it's the Kreaux, do you?"

"Not the Kreaux, precisely," said Isaac as he walked past them, wrapping his cloak around his leg to cover it, "but something very similar."

"Isaac, please!" called out Jenna after him, who was still continuing down the path. "Where are you going?"

"Come on, mate!" shouted James. "Let's leave this place! There's nothing here but death and decay!"

"Again," said Isaac as he turned around, "you two are more than welcome to leave. But I promised King Närveid I'd deliver this sword, and I'm not leaving until I find his cousin!"

And so once again, Jenna and James stared at each other and followed their beloved friend and leader.

Reeeeee! shrieked the same high-pitched squeal as before.

"Damn it," bellowed James, "then come on out, you little blighta!"

Isaac motioned his hands up, stopping his friends, as a young boy came running out of the mist. His hands flailed wildly, and his eyes were completely white. His gray skin was covered in countless boils, and his fingernails were sharp and claw-like, like the Kreaux (although his were white instead of black).

"Isaac, what are you doing?" hissed Jenna as he slowly walked forward and kneeled down.

James motioned a hand in front of her, dagger in hand, additionally silencing her as he watched Isaac.

"Battered and broken, we appear to be..." Isaac's Majestic, healing words came as he kneeled before the boy. "Tossed and turned by our enemies."

Glowing tears of yellow light rippled down his face as he reached out to the boy, his palms casting intense, furious Light Majesty.

"But upon thy glorious light we stand," he began to finish, when suddenly the boy pulled back his razor-sharp claws, preparing to stab Isaac through.

"Isaac, noo!" screamed Jenna as she tried to run forward.

"Knowing our deliverance is always at hand!" roared Isaac as he threw his arms around the boy, sending out a cascading wave of blinding light.

Jenna and James slowly lowered their hands from their faces as they saw Isaac embracing the young boy—and he back.

Jenna's mouth dropped as the young boy slowly pulled away from Isaac.

He was completely healed. And although it wasn't bright and shimmering like Isaac's, his hair was a beautiful blond. His charming blue eyes were young and innocent.

Isaac still had his arms around the boy as—who would've thought?—his mother came rushing out from the fog.

Her reaction was what any mother's would be, after not only finding her son but also learning that he'd been healed. She had been searching for him for some days now, despite having no rest or food.

Her sunken, weary expression showed just that, even beneath the thick scarf wrapped around her mouth and nose.

"I'm afraid I don't know what's happened," she honestly said as she held her boy and wrapped a thick cloth around his mouth and nose.

"A strange man in black armor suddenly started appearing over a month ago," she whispered.

"And that's when everything changed?" asked Isaac.

"Yes," she nodded. "Dünréld, our mayor and founder, has been trying to receive more food rations from Wöntylnas, with not much avail."

James pressed his cloak against his face. "You've been having difficulty with your crops?"

"At first, no!" she answered. "But a couple of months ago, they suddenly began to wither and die!"

"That is odd," said Jenna with a raised eyebrow, "especially since Feraahnin is a thriving time for crops."

"Exactly!" she agreed. "And for some reason, Wöntylnas didn't respond. That's when the strange man in black armor appeared. He said our food problem reached him and that he was sent by King Närveid!"

"Fascinating… please continue?" Isaac asked, squinting his eyes.

"Although we didn't see the arrival of any caravans carrying food or supplies, the next day, carts appeared—placed in scattered areas around Wyllmourn, overflowing with fruits, vegetables, and even bread!"

The three friends looked at one another as she finished, "At first, it was delicious. But after a couple of days, everyone began to grow ill—very ill… although the food kept coming, and we continued eating it."

"Right?" Isaac motioned.

"But somehow, it began to rapidly decay—faster than any food I've ever seen! And slowly, this poisonous fume began to consume the air. Many have already died."

"How did you manage to stay alive?" inquired Jenna.

"We're one of the only ones with a cellar—a perk, I suppose, of living in a home with Dünréld."

"Are you his sister then?" James asked.

"No!" she answered, almost offended. "I'm his wife!"

"His wife!" they all exclaimed in sync.

"Yes! And I would've left sooner were it not for me striving to find my son, who disappeared some days ago!"

"But what about your husband?" Isaac quickly asked. "Where is he?"

She pointed down the path. "He's been badly infected, in a very strange way. If he's still there, you'll find him in the town manor at the western end of Wyllmourn."

"Then we shall find him," Isaac returned. "But for now, please, m'lady, take your son and leave this place."

Her eyes widened in shock and gratitude. "Head east. You'll find our camp. Eat and drink as you please. Then take one of our horses and return to Wöntylnas!"

"Oh, thank you, thank you!" she could barely exclaim as her brown eyes filled with tears.

With a quick hug, the three Majesticians said goodbye to her and her boy.

"Wait!" she exclaimed, turning around. "What are your names?"

"I am Isaac Erbrecht!" he answered.

"I'm James Vandergaus!"

"Call me Jenna Coltier, m'lady!"

With a final bow, she said, "All of you… nothing short of godsends." And with that, she and her boy disappeared into the fog.

"As if one problem wasn't enough," muttered Jenna.

"Right?" shouted Isaac. "Who on Vaerün is this man in black armor, and how does one conjure a poison *this* powerful?"

"I was talking about the food. And one of our horses," Jenna mumbled again.

"That's okay, Jenna!" James said as he walked past her and clapped her on the shoulder. "You and Isaac can share a horse!"

Her face practically exploded in a smile as she rocketed into the air. One can imagine her gratitude as Isaac, deep in thought trying to solve the mystery, was unaware of her reactions.

"Dünréld is alive then," Isaac suddenly said as he looked forward. "We have to save him!"

"Shüza, Isaac, come back!" shouted James as he quickly followed, joined by the gracefully skipping Jenna.

One surprise led to another as they reached the town manor. Several infected individuals attacked out of nowhere, although they were no match for the trio's Majesty.

"I can't help but be intrigued," murmured Isaac as he looked at one of the bodies of those who'd just attacked. "How does a poison kill some and infect others?"

"Everyone's body responds in different ways," answered James as he stood next to Isaac, wiping the black blood off his silver daggers.

"Learned that in one of your research books?" mocked Jenna.

"Again, don't blast the power of research!" he retorted with a wagging finger.

Reeeeee! shrieked innumerable voices all around them as they stood in the large courtyard before the manor.

With their backs to one another, the three Majesticians raised their palms and weapons, ready for combat, as masses of infected citizens emerged from the fog, claws and fangs bared and ready to strike.

There was only a momentary pause before the fighting ensued.

"Haa!" Jenna shouted as she backflipped out of the way, dodging the razor-sharp claws that were about to come down on her, in turn launching a roaring blast of fire from her palm.

Shink, shink, shink, shink! rocketed a flurry of icicles from James's daggers as they repeatedly stabbed the air.

The grotesque sound of the infected, squealing zombies filled the air as they fled or were destroyed upon impact by Isaac's rippling Light Majesty—cast by his dancing fingers as he elegantly turned and spun around, tapping and touching the air in ceaseless movement.

Uuuggghhh! they vomited as Jenna slammed her rapier through three of them at once and kicked them off with her foot, followed by a cleansing wave of fire.

Boooom! exploded the repelling rays of Light Majesty as Isaac cast back the advancing hosts.

"Haha." James laughed maniacally as he forcefully gripped his left hand to his right wrist. With his right palm upheld, his dagger began to spin at blurring speed, a freezing storm launching forward from his direction and line of sight as he slowly turned.

"Hey, thanks for that!" shouted Jenna as she zipped and dashed around. It was like it was snowing, frost and ice flying through the air as her rapier met the iced zombies, instantly turning them into frozen powder.

"Keep it up. We're doing—"

"Jaaaaammmessss... Vaaandergaaauuussss!" hissed the voice upon the air, like a stinging, poisoned blade.

All three of them quickly turned to see a man slowly descend the steps of the manor.

"I'm going to guess," James said in a hushed tone, "that that is Dünréld."

"Makes sense to me," agreed Isaac.

Although not as foreboding as one of the conductors, he was definitely high on the freaky factor.

His eyes were glued shut. And his long, greasy black hair dangled before his boil-covered face. His black coat was covered in (what looked like) vomit and Kreaux matter, and his dark-gray pants were ripped and frayed, revealing the pale, gray skin beneath. Although his lips barely moved, his voice carried through the air like a hiss.

"Isaaaaac... Eeeerrrbreccht..." he hissed as he nearly tripped down the stairs, his hands lulling in front of him from outstretched arms.

Jenna raised her palm and hardly hesitated before launching a fireball at him.

"Yeah. How about, no?"

All three of them blinked as he instantly dodged the fireball, which flew past and exploded into the building behind.

Isaac pointed at him as he continued to descend the stairs.

"May I get a repeat of that, please?"

"Sure, but let me try," answered James, jabbing the air in a flurry, unleashing a stream of ice daggers.

In a dark blur, Dünréld zipped and dodged every single ice dagger.

In another sudden blur, he was instantly before Jenna, hacking and slashing at her with unbelievable speed.

"Okay, so what?" she mocked as she parried his claw attacks. "I'm not special enough for you to say my name? Rude!"

"*Eaaarrrrrggggghhhhh!*" shrieked the glass-shattering sound of his cry as he jumped back, outstretching his hands.

The trio looked around as they were suddenly overwhelmed with infected zombies.

It took some time before they began to whittle down the numbers. And like many fights before, it didn't come without suffering. Jenna had received a gash so large on her left arm that it was unusable, forcing her to fight with her nondominant right hand.

James had received a deep laceration in his back, staining his dark-blue vest and cloak black from blood. And, in addition to his splintered and bleeding ankle from earlier, Isaac's chest had just been slashed by claws. Although only three of the blades landed, they left a successful, bleeding blow, turning his white coat red.

"Isaac!" shouted Jenna and James in sync.

Time seemed to stand still as James watched his friends engage the horrendous monsters. His face scrunched up in anger, rage, and untamed fury as thoughts raced through his mind.

The Kreaux… his suffering… the suffering of others… his uncle. These poor, unsuspecting people… and his sacrifice. Oooh, the sacrifice! How it made his blood boil!

Before he knew it, his hand was reaching for the rippling blue sphere entangled in the Majestic net—attached to his belt.

With thoughts of righteous fury and untamed anger, he gripped the sphere in his right hand and held his left hand up.

"Ruvíag!" he belted, his voice echoing. "Come forth!"

In a dazzling burst of rippling white with blue snow and frost, the howl of a wolf pierced the air, sending a hope unlike any other through Isaac and Jenna's souls.

"*Haaaaa!*" he screamed as he dashed and blurred through the air, his silver daggers spinning and slicing at breakneck speed.

The sickening (but justly so) sound of rending flesh filled the air as Ruvíag shredded foe after foe, tossing them this way and that. The zombies flew like rag dolls from his razor-sharp maw.

For a moment, Isaac and Jenna were spellbound. How could they not be, watching the incredible spectacle before their eyes? This was a power and Majesty like they'd never seen.

In another blur, James jumped upon Ruvíag and bolted their way in a blast of snow.

Isaac shielded himself, for it looked as though they were charging straight for him!

After a few seconds, he slowly opened his eyes as he heard the repeated *crunch, crunch, crunch* of Ruvíag's maw.

Right behind him stood Ruvíag and James, with the body of Dünréld in his jaw.

What? Isaac thought for a moment before Jenna approached him.

"He tried to get you," she shakily said. "Dünréld... he was going to kill you. His claws came together and—"

"It's okay, Jenna," Isaac said as he held her. "I'm all right, thanks to James and Ruvíag."

"Wanna help?" James boldly asked. "Or would you like me to clean this up?"

They couldn't help but laugh as he motioned to the fleeing zombies, darting this way and that to escape.

"To be honest," said Isaac weakly, "I think... I just want to get out of here."

"Does Ruvíag have room for two more?" Jenna politely asked. "At least to get us out of Wyllmourn?"

Suddenly, the dead and mangled body of Dünréld flew through the air as the frost wolf humbly bowed and then kneeled.

"I suppose you have your answer!" beamed James as he extended a hand to both of them.

Ruvíag dashed down the muddy paths of Wyllmourn, his mouth constantly open as he unleashed roaring frost breath upon the infected, trying to stop them from leaving.

"Interesting experience, I have to admit!" exclaimed Isaac.

"Oh, I'm not complaining," muttered Jenna as she lovingly wrapped her arms around him.

James smiled and laughed.

"A lil' different from a horse, right?"

Their conversation came to a quick halt as the fog cleared, revealing the massive, broken-down gates and a host of infected.

"Hang on, mates!" shouted James as he gripped his loyal frost wolf.

Isaac threw his arms around James, and Jenna threw hers around him as Ruvíag buckled down and, with a mighty growl, leapt from rooftop to rooftop, over the large wooden barricaded walls.

"Whoa, whoa, whoa," Isaac repeated as the ground came fast at a straight nosedive.

Poor Ruvíag whimpered as he slammed to the ground, absorbing most of the blow, though Isaac, Jenna, and James still felt the impact.

"I know, mate. I'm sorry," James comforted as he rubbed the wolf's head. "But can you please get us at least partway to our camp?"

Isaac and Jenna looked over their shoulders as the zombies poured over the broken-down gates, rushing toward them with flailing claws.

"James?" muttered Isaac as he nudged him.

"Come on, bud. You can do it. I know you can!" James encouraged.

"James?" shouted Jenna as she rocked back and forth.

Reeeeee! squealed the zombies as they nearly reached them.

"Ruvíag… please, save us! You're our only hope!" exclaimed James as he gripped his beloved wolf.

And with those words, Ruvíag's back paws dug into the dirt as he launched forth, sending a billowing gust of snow behind him, barely missing the swiping claws.

Jenna placed a hand over her heart to calm down.

"Thank heaven above for you, James."

Ruvíag growled a little, then instantly stopped as Jenna patted his butt.

"And of course, you too, Ruvíag! You saved us!"

With a howl that accidentally summoned a snowstorm, the frost wolf expressed his happiness.

"Aggghh!" Isaac suddenly shouted as all the pain hit him at once.

"Hang on, mate, nearly there!" assured James as Ruvíag ran faster.

Isaac's eyes slowly closed as he muttered, "I'm just going to… rest for a moment."

"I don't appreciate how greedy he is," mumbled James in the darkness.

"Isaac? Greedy?" demanded Jenna's voice.

It didn't take long for Isaac to realize he must have fallen asleep on the way back to camp.

His eyes shot open as he demanded, "You think I'm greedy?"

Jenna slightly jumped back, nearly dropping the wet cloth she was holding.

"Well, yeah!" James laughed. "Somehow you always manage to take the most blows for us! Can't you share a little?"

"Haha." Isaac laughed a little as he rested back on the makeshift bed made of his and James's cloak. "No way. I'd take 'em all if I could."

"Then I suppose you won't argue to us tending to you for a moment, now will you?" Jenna questioned as she looked at him, then to James.

"Which one do you want to tend to?" he asked, pointing. "His chest or leg—"

"Chest!" she accidentally interrupted before calming down. "I mean… chest."

James immediately smiled as he pulled back Isaac's pant leg and observed the countless brown flecks and red marks from the splinters.

"Oi..." He winced, knowing how much it would hurt, "I'm sorry, mate. But this is going to hurt."

"What's going to—Agggghhhhh!" Isaac screamed as James created two tiny ice needles, acting as tweezers to pull out the splinters. Between the sharpness and freezing temperatures, Isaac nearly fainted as he slowly pulled them out.

"No, no, look at me!" Jenna comforted, placing a hand on his face and forcing him to look at her rather than the surgery James was performing.

She had to swallow a few times as she unbuttoned his coat and pulled up his shirt, revealing the three deep gashes across his strong chest.

With another wince, he had to look away as she dabbed the hot, wet cloth on his wound, sending that all-too-familiar stinging feeling through his body.

"Wait a sec," he murmured, noticing the dried, black blood and gash on her arm. "No!" he shouted. "Stop! Both of you need healing!"

Unfortunately, he was outnumbered as James further stuck in his frozen tweezers and pulled out an extra-long splinter.

"Like hell we do!" he shouted back. "For once, could you please let us tend to you?"

"Yes, but first let me—"

"No!" Jenna shouted in agreement with James. "He's right! As much as I love you, would you please just shut up and sit back?"

And although she didn't directly say it, Isaac's face grew exponentially hot as she placed him and "love" in the same sentence. Somehow, the pain seemed to melt away as she lovingly dabbed at his chest, washing away the dried blood.

"I swear... and I just stitched up our clothing," she muttered as her face, too, turned red, clearly aware of what she'd just said.

"Oi, don't worry about that!" James exclaimed. "I don't mind doing it this time around."

"You really don't?" she gratefully asked.

"Not at all! I actually enjoy it... helps calm my nerves."

But Isaac wasn't listening. He was too busy staring at Jenna's beautiful face. Every hair on his body stood on end as her long hair brushed his chest, twisting and gliding in the wind.

"Ugh… I'm so sorry!" she said embarrassedly. "As if you're not suffering enough, now you have to—"

"No, no! Please! I love it… please leave it," he interrupted, looking away.

With that enchanting smile of hers, she intently stared at him.

"Very well, then…"

Thus, the power of love—even amid surgery and the glaring noonday sun above—caused Isaac to comfortably fall asleep.

No! Isaac yelled in his mind as his eyes burst open.

The sun was setting, and Jenna was asleep on his abdomen, while James had somehow fallen asleep on a nearby rock.

No, no, no! he continued yelling. *I need the sun! Please hold on for a few moments longer!*

So very gently, he slowly reached back, pulled his cloak around, and gracefully placed Jenna's head on it.

She immediately took in a deep breath and smiled as she recognized Isaac's scent—even amid her sleep!

He couldn't help but get emotional as he stood back and observed his dear friends.

One can already imagine how uncomfortable it would be to sleep on a rock, but how much worse it must have been for James lying belly-down (obviously avoiding the massive gash on his back).

And his sweet and most precious Jenna… Isaac's eye twitched as he took a closer look. *Were those tendons?*

Isaac placed a hand over his mouth as he became overwhelmed with emotion. Instead of helping themselves or even allowing him to help, they chose to address his wounds—the fresh white cloths around his chest and leg a clear indication.

Arrggh, no! he yelled again in his head as he quickly tiptoed some ten feet away and then ran west about twenty feet.

The sun would set at any moment.

His hands flew into the air as he quickly said, exasperated, "Battered and broken, we appear to be… tossed and turned by our enemies."

With its last rays, the sun set. At first, he was shocked. His mouth dropped as a tear ran down his face. But refusing to give up, he blurted out, "But upon thy glorious light we stand… knowing our deliverance is always at hand!"

His breathing was heavy but slow. His large, graceful hands stretched high overhead.

Please… please. Please! he repeated as his lip quivered.

Dark thoughts entered his mind as a voice whispered, *See? You shouldn't have used your Majesty to heal that little boy! And now you don't have the strength to heal your friends! Hahaha!*

With a blank expression, he tried to ignore it. But it continued, *And what a shame. Heaven's light has abandoned you. You know they're not going to make it. You saw those wounds! Why didn't you just do it when the sun was right above you? It's because you're so selfish! You enjoyed them serving and waiting upon you.*

"*Arrrgggh!*" Isaac shouted out loud as he stretched his hands further.

His breathing stopped as his eyes widened, then squinted. For there, upon the red-and-orange horizon, erupted a sudden flash of light. And after a few seconds came twisting, golden beams of sunlight. Through the air they flew at incalculable speeds.

"Yes!" he excitedly shouted as he jumped up and down, hands still outstretched.

Zeeeeearrrggghhhh! they roared as they rocketed down and into his palms.

He momentarily levitated in the air as the force of the heavenly rays lifted him off the ground. His whole being glowed by the time he touched down again.

With palms before him, holding the searing, dancing rays of light, he gracefully walked back to their camp.

Jenna and James weakly sat up, slowly waking. It was as if the sun had reversed course, rising from the west instead of the east, as they watched Isaac approach, glowing brightly.

"Upon thy glorious light we stand…" echoed the pulsing words of His Majesty as the light furiously danced within his palms, "knowing our deliverance… is always at hand."

They shielded their eyes as the rays, like missiles, bolted through the air and careened into them.

The feeling was indescribable as the twisting, gleaming rays of heaven wrapped and enfolded their bodies and wounds, instantly healing them.

"But Isaac… why?" Jenna could barely utter as emotions consumed her.

After their work was done, the streaming rays zipped into the air and back into Isaac's palms.

"Before thy throne…" Isaac's voice echoed, "we shall always hail!"

Vooom! bounded the rays of light as they launched through the air and west, disappearing over the horizon.

The soft sound of grass underfoot was all that could be heard as Isaac approached his friends.

"Jenna, could you please—"

Boom! roared the firepit as she instantly brought it to life, giving light to the now-darkened surroundings.

"Thank you," he nodded, plopping down in front of it.

For a few minutes, it was silent. Isaac stared into the fire, while Jenna and James exchanged glances, queuing each other to speak.

"Th-thank you—" Jenna stammered first.

"No," Isaac interrupted, "thank you. Both of you. You didn't have to do that!"

"Don't be silly," said James as he jumped down from his rock and plopped next to Isaac. "How many times have you saved us?"

"Yeah, but—"

"He's right, Isaac. So please, let's leave it at, 'You're welcome' and 'Thank you!'"

Isaac slowly nodded in agreement, staring into the fire.

"So…" he asked, "where to next? Fürnas?"

"Actually, we're not too far from Fährlund! Can we stop there first?" James asked excitedly. "Seeing as how we've lost half our provisions and one horse, it'd be nice to restock there!"

"Sounds good to—"

"We can't," Jenna interrupted. "I guess you don't know, but… Fährlund was destroyed some twenty years ago, during the great Kreaux siege."

James's expression instantly melted.

"Is that the truth? Why didn't anyone tell me?"

"Did you ever ask?" Isaac prodded playfully.

Jenna dusted her hands off as she stood up.

"Trust me, I know because our surrogate mother, Tabatha Tromsdotter's brother, was once the mayor of Fährlund. She was devastated at his loss."

James looked away in shame and embarrassment.

"I'm so sorry. I didn't know."

Isaac looked up at Jenna, as if requesting her to say something consoling.

"But who knows?" she said, taking the hint. "Maybe they rebuilt it? Besides, we'll come across it regardless as we continue onward to Fürnas!"

James flopped down on his back, instantly thanking Isaac now that he could lie on it again.

"That's true, but… what if it's like Wyllmourn? We don't need to go through that again."

Isaac placed a hand on James's stomach and nudged him back and forth.

"Definitely. And we won't! How about this. Since it's along the way, we'll obviously be able to see if they've rebuilt or not."

"And if they have," Jenna continued for him, "we'll stop! But if not…"

"We continue onward to Fürnas," finished James.

Isaac flopped down next to James and looked up at the stars.

"When should we leave, then?"

James took a deep breath and let out a huge sigh.

"If we leave now, we'll reach Fährlund by morning."

Jenna started packing some of their supplies and attaching them to the horse saddles.

"Let's go then! Because if Fährlund is destroyed, that means we'll reach Fürnas by evening."

In surprise and slight hesitation, Isaac propped himself up.

"Are you two okay to travel? Don't you want to rest more?"

He coughed a little as James clapped him on the back and jumped up.

"I don't know if you'll ever be able to experience the healing power of your Majesty, mate, but trust me when I say that it makes you a brand-new person."

Isaac gave a suspicious look to him, then to Jenna, who agreed.

"It's true. You're amazing, Isaac! I've never felt better."

He couldn't help but wince a little as he pushed himself up, assisted by James.

"Haha." James laughed sympathetically. "I only wish we could do more for you."

"Nonsense!" Isaac quickly rebuked. "I'd never make it without you two!"

Jenna galloped in front of him, reaching out a hand.

"We feel the same. Now please, let us do some of the work for you, okay?"

"Thank you," he said gratefully as she and James helped him up and into the saddle.

"Rest for a bit, mate!" James smiled as he mounted his horse. "I'm sure Jenna will take great care of you."

"She already has," whispered Isaac as he wrapped his arms around her.

"Are you okay, Jenn?" he asked as he felt her heartbeat like mad.

"O-oh! Yes! Trust me, I couldn't be happier," she said with a wink to James, who returned it.

"Wonderful," whispered Isaac as he rested his head against her back and shoulder, instantly falling asleep.

CHAPTER 17

Return to Fürnas

"*Don't take it personal, dear. It's not her fault,*" spoke the gentle, kind voice of Lucy inside Isaac's dream.

Once again, he was in a black space, seeing absolutely nothing.

"*I could never blame her. But why can't it be something else? Anything else?*" he pleaded.

"*You know how they work, Isaac—the weapons,*" replied the voice.

"*Yes, but…it's not fair! Why do I have to pay the price for someone else's mistakes?*"

"*Because no one other than you is strong enough to pay the price.*"

"*But the worst part…is that she won't even know.*" He began to sob. "*And just like everything else, I'll be the one to suffer the most.*"

He could hear nothing other than her weeping, for she said nothing.

"*Please…can you tell me something?*" he asked.

"*What is it, dear?*"

"*Who…are you?*"

After a moment, she boldly said, "*I'm your—*"

Isaac bolted awake as the strong sound of horse whinnies filled the air. He quickly took in his surroundings. The morning was a little misty, and the air was wonderfully clean. The sun had risen but was hidden behind some of the small hills to the east. And as he looked past Jenna, there, down the southern trail, stood the ruins of Fährlund.

"Does that answer your question, James?" Jenna bitterly asked.

"I'm really sorry. I didn't know…" James trailed off.

"Don't be hard on him, Jenn…" consoled Isaac as he squeezed her hand. "It's all right."

"Well, on the bright side," James said optimistically, "at least we can head straight to Fürnas. I'm so excited to see it!"

"Me too!" Isaac piped up.

"Quick question," Jenna asked, "should we go around or through the ruins?"

They looked down the hill, truly observing Fährlund. The unkempt path continued down and straight through the ruins. The terrain surrounding the old town was incredibly steep as Fährlund was built upon a hill.

"We can go around," answered Isaac, "but it'll take more time."

"I don't have a problem going through," James shrugged.

She turned around and looked at Isaac and then at James with a serious look.

"Are you prepared to engage in combat should we encounter the Kreaux?"

Isaac and James stared at each other, then shrugged nonchalantly.

"I'm good," they replied in sync.

Jenna could only shake her head and laugh.

"Boys," she muttered.

"Ha!" she shouted as she cracked the reins, descending the hill.

Perhaps it would've been better if they had encountered the Kreaux, for Fährlund's desolation was nearly more than they could bear. As their horses slowly clopped upon the cobblestone streets that now had weeds growing in between, no one said a word. They were too busy looking all around at the ravages from the Kreaux siege, over twenty years ago.

Many of the houses, lined next to one another, had gashes and claw marks running through their wooden borders and walls. And nearly all of them had repulsive black stains and scars from fire damage.

Isaac pushed back some of the weeds that had grown up to their height (even upon their horse) as he stared at the war-devastated Fährlund.

"No matter how many times I see the same image, it always disturbs me just the same."

Jenna hacked down some of the weeds before them as she unsheathed her rapier.

"That's because it's wrong. It's like we're viewing something that never should have happened."

James's reflection stared back at him as he looked into a passing, grungy window in one of the houses.

"It's true. Even now, if I close my eyes…I can still imagine how this town used to operate."

He closed his eyes, momentarily losing himself in memories. The citizens greeting one another as they passed by on the streets. The laughter of children as they played and ran around…the mouth-watering smell of home cooking and baking. The beautiful sunrises, with breakfast, before toiling in the fields, in the homes, and shops. The high noonday sun with iced tea, peach pie, and lemon tart underneath the café umbrella. The setting of the twilight sun, with the company of loved ones at the comfort of a home-cooked meal at the dinner table.

"James?" Jenna asked, snapping him out of it.

He placed a hand to his head as he shook it. "S-sorry about that. You said Nann used to work here?"

Isaac tilted his head and leaned forward. "You told him about her? Awww. When'd I miss that?"

She shook her head and playfully whipped him with her hair. "That's what happens when you fall asleep, dear!"

He could only laugh as he squeezed her, alleviating some of the sorrowful tension from the surrounding atmosphere.

"And live here!" Jenna finally answered. "Isn't it amazing how much can change in such a short amount of time?"

James galloped next to them. "Oooh! Do you know where? I'd be curious to see where she stayed."

"From what she said, you can't miss it," said Jenna as she looked dead forward. "It's atop the highest hill, on the main street of Fährlund!" she said in a southern accent as she copied Nann's voice.

"Then we're bound to run into it," included Isaac, "since we're already, I'm assuming, on the main street."

Jenna sadly looked down. "That is, if there's any shop left."

As they climbed to the top of the hill street, there, on the right, stood Nann's old shop, perfectly intact. The sign "Nann's Bakery" barely moved from the slight breeze, although the letters were washed out and the wood was cracked.

All three of them dismounted as they jumped down and walked up to the shop.

"You okay?" Isaac whispered as he rubbed Jenna's back.

Unafraid to show her emotions, she began to cry. "I just…miss her, that's all."

"Me too, Jenn," he quietly said as he wrapped his arms around her. "But I have a feeling we'll see her again!"

"You really think so?"

"Yes! I really do!" he sincerely answered.

James walked up to the door and tried to open it, but it didn't budge.

"Ha ha," Jenna laughed as she wiped away her tears. "That's Nann for you."

Isaac and she looked at each other as they said in sync, in her voice, "The only time you lock the door is if you're not coming back!"

"Wow," said James shortly. "What a way to think. If that's the case, then do you mind if…?" he hinted as he slightly kicked the door.

Jenna laughed as she agreed, "Not at all, go right on ahead."

Boom! sounded the splintering door as James smashed it open with a powerful kick.

This time, the emotions hit Isaac as he could barely smell the faint scent of baked goods. Dusty and quiet sat the neatly placed tables, vases still upon them. Jenna swiped her hand across the counter as she walked up to it and observed the gleaming, polished wood freshly revealed underneath.

Eeeeeee! shrieked a sound very similar to the Kreaux.

Before he could say anything, Jenna and James already had their palms raised, fire and ice glowing in each one, ready for combat.

"My apologies," Isaac said frankly as they noticed him behind the counter. "Probably should've assumed it'd do that."

They sighed, ceasing their Majesty, realizing that the sound came from him opening one of the rusted oven doors.

"I think…I've seen enough," Jenna quietly said as she looked down at the dusty wooden floor.

James stood in the archway behind the counter and pointed behind him. "You mean you don't want to go upstairs?"

"No," she quietly said, "I don't. I want to leave this place right now."

Isaac placed a hand behind James as he kindly pushed him out. "Please forgive us. This is a little hard."

"No apologies necessary!" Éynath exclaimed as he began walking out. "It's my fault, and I'm sorry."

Jenna waved her hands in agitation as she said, "There's too much apologizing going on here. Everything's okay. I just don't want to be here."

Isaac was the last to leave the small, untouched, abandoned shop as he lingered in the doorway and gazed around one final time.

"How ironic…," he whispered to himself, "what I wouldn't do, Nann, to have just one more bite of your peach and kinberry pie."

But he hadn't a clue as to just how ironic it was—none of them did. For little did he know that he was standing in the exact same spot his father once was, speaking and (questionably) flirting with the woman who'd be his son and goddaughter's surrogate mother.

"Shall we continue then?" he asked as he attempted to close the mangled-up door.

It only took a second to see Jenna and James already mounted upon their horses.

"O-oh. I suppose I have my answer then."

And thus, they continued down the broken, ruined path of the main street of Fährlund. Indeed, it was the very same path that

Garon Erbrecht and his men had taken over twenty-one years ago—the same path to the Fürnas Kingdom.

How she held it together, no one knew. For nothing could have brought Jenna Coltier more familiarity, hope, despair, and reminiscence than the vibrant, fall-colored canopies overhead.

Thud, sounded Isaac's boots as he jumped off his horse, approached the wooden archway, and ran his hand along the cool, polished wood.

"Fürnas Kingdom," he boldly stated as he read the etched words above.

"Whoa, wait up!" he hollered as he caught up to Jenna and jumped back on his horse.

James couldn't hold his mouth any longer after over an hour of traveling in the enchanting, perpetually autumn forest kingdom.

"And you say that Wöntylnas is nice? Please! It doesn't hold a candle to this!"

"It is impossible to compare raw beauty against man-made," agreed Isaac.

Striving to maintain her composure, Jenna said nothing.

"Is she okay?" mouthed Isaac to James.

James observed Jenna closely as he brought his right fingers to his forehead. *I'm sorry to do this, Jenna,* he thought. *Just want to make sure you're okay.*

Voom...voom...voom...voom, rippled the thoughts and words as her ethereal voice echoed in his mind, *Please, let there be someone...anyone that's survived. Please...oh, please, Almighty Creator! I'd be happy with even just one!*

He swallowed. And then he looked at Isaac. A single tear ran down his face as he quickly wiped it away.

Isaac's eyes grew wide in fear and anticipation.

"She's fine," mouthed James as he nodded.

Phew... he thought as he sighed. *Thank heaven.*

After passing so many empty cottages and homes, she'd nearly given up hope. The first cottage they passed was empty. As was the third...and fourth, and so on.

But to her incredible and outbursting joy, she nearly fainted when she saw the glowing light of a candle flickering through one of the windows. At first, it was a little hard to notice, for the bright beams of orange-and-yellow light that descended through the colorful leaves overhead camouflaged very well with the candlelit window.

Thud! sounded all their boots as they landed upon the soft, moist, leafy ground.

"Hello?" Jenna fervently asked as she slightly scrunched down and approached the door. "Is anyone home?"

At first, there was no answer.

"Hello?" she tried again. "Please! Please! Let there be someone home!" she cried out as she knocked again and again and again.

She suddenly burst out crying so badly that she could barely breathe as she melted against the door and slumped onto the ground, tears ceaselessly flowing down her face.

Before Isaac and James could comfort her, the door cracked open.

"Wh-who's there?" sounded the quiet, nervous voice of a young man.

With an expression that looked as though she'd just been gifted Vaerün, Jenna immediately stood, brushing the tears from her face as she stammered, "Why, I'm Jenna! J-Jenna Coltier!"

"Liar!" screamed the voice as the door slammed shut. "Jenna Coltier died over twenty years ago!" shouted the muffled voice through the door.

"No, please! Please don't close the door!" Jenna desperately screamed as she began knocking at it again.

"Jenna," Isaac calmly but boldly said as he walked up, "calm down. I have an idea."

"Young man," he cried out as he pressed his face against the door, "she can prove that she is indeed Jenna Coltier!"

"How?" demanded the muffled voice.

"Well, let me first confirm that you are indeed of Fürnas, and not just some squatter!"

The door quaked for a moment as something was obviously hit or thrown against it in anger.

"How dare you accuse me of such treason! For I was born and raised here. It was here that I witnessed the death of my parents and countless citizens during the Kreaux siege over twenty years ago!"

James gave a nervous look to Isaac that said, "You're pushing it, mate."

"I have one last question for you," continued Isaac in his strong but calm voice. "What separated Jenna from everyone else?"

"That's your question? I don't have time for this! Leave me be!"

Isaac had to motion for Jenna to calm down as he tried one last time, "If that's truly how you feel, then we shall leave you be. But I promise…that you will never forgive yourself for missing the opportunity to meet Her Royal Highness."

With dreadful anticipation, he at last responded, "She was a fire Majestician. The first to be born in over a thousand years ago. And her eyes danced with a living light, like no other."

James gave a scrunched yet surprised look that said, "All right, all right. He's got it."

"Watch from your window," continued Isaac, "as she casts her flame Majesty! If you truly are of Fürnas…you'll know she's the last fire Majestician."

Everyone's heart raced as they looked at one another and waited for a response.

"Very well," finally sounded his voice.

With a motioned hand and smile, Isaac prompted Jenna.

Fsssshhhhrarrggghhh! roared the dancing fireball as she tossed it back and forth between her palms. With cartwheels, side strafes, and spin kicks, she continued to keep the fireball airborne. So as not to catch the surrounding area on fire, she ceased the flame in a light explosion and then held her breath in anticipation.

Click, sounded the lock as the young man slowly opened the door. He, like Jenna, was breathing heavily and had tears streaming down his sharp green eyes. His brown hair was rather messy, although he was not at all unkempt.

"It is you…," he stammered as he nearly tripped out of his home, "Jenna Coltier, my beloved princess!"

For a split second, and for the first time, Isaac felt the sting of jealousy as he watched the young man and Jenna embrace. To his credit, it did look as though a long-lost couple had finally been reunited. With the tears and embrace and…hold it now, was he kissing her cheeks?

"You're alive!" they both said in sync as they gave each other one final squeeze.

James silently walked up next to Isaac as his freezing breath whispered in his ear, "Do they know each other?"

Isaac shrugged as he guessed, "I don't think so."

The answer came seconds later as the young man looked at Isaac and James, then to Jenna as he said excitedly, "My name is Éynath! I am delighted to meet all of you! Please, please come in!"

Without hesitation, Jenna immediately entered, followed by James, and then Isaac, who ran a moment behind as he tied the horses up.

"Oh, that smell," Isaac said, enchanted, as he opened the door and took a deep breath.

The smell of a delicious, well-seasoned stew struck his nostrils in perfect harmony with the additional scent of freshly baked bread.

"You're Isaac Erbrecht?" shouted Éynath excitedly as he quickly sloshed the bowl of stew onto the table and eagerly rushed up to Isaac.

"I…I am!" stammered Isaac as the young man embraced him, and he him.

"I cannot tell you what it means to meet you!" muffled his voice in Isaac's coat.

Isaac gave an inquisitive look to Jenna as she returned a look that said, "Just wait for it."

"I met your father, Garon Erbrecht!" Éynath exclaimed as he pulled away.

Isaac's heart fell as his legs immediately grew weak.

"Y-you met my father?"

Éynath's fingers intertwined with Isaac's as he brought him over to the table and sat him down next to Jenna and himself, right in front of a fresh, steaming bowl of stew and steaming bread with butter melting into it.

Isaac felt a little ashamed as he missed out on Éynath's words for the next minute or so, as he stared at the mouthwatering food in front of him.

"And that's how I met him!" proudly finished the words of Éynath as he gripped Isaac's shoulder.

"O-oh!" Isaac quickly said. "That's incredible!"

"You look so much like him," Éynath said as he grabbed Isaac's chin and carefully observed him.

"I told you Fürnas inhabitants are the most hospitable people you'd ever meet!" Jenna exclaimed with a proud smile. "Isn't that right, Éynath?"

"Oh, yes, yes, Your Majesty!" he quickly said with a wide grin. "But I'm sure you're all starving. Please dig in!"

He didn't have to tell them twice! His sentence was barely finished as the sound of forks clattering against plates filled the room.

Jenna slammed her fist on the table as she caught Éynath staring into Isaac's eyes for the umpteenth time.

"Éynath...dear," she attempted in patience, "is there something wrong with Isaac's eyes?"

"No, no, Your Majesty!" he immediately defended. "Not at all! They're just so stunning! I've never seen eyes like his."

Isaac blushed a little as he scratched the back of his head. "Thank you, Éynath. But all our eyes move just the same!"

"Yeah, I get that you're all Majesticians," he said as he looked at all of them, "but the last time I saw yellow eyes like that was in one of the Vulföth many, many years ago."

Jenna's heart squee'd at the thought of one. "Awwww! I haven't seen a Vulföth since I was a little girl!"

"They were going extinct, you know!" he exclaimed in sorrow.

Her face immediately went stone-cold as she responded, "I know. Have you seen any recently?"

Éynath sighed as he looked down at the table. "No, Your Majesty. It's been a number of years now."

Isaac and James looked at each other as they raised their eyebrows, then shrugged.

"Thanks again for boarding us this evening, Éynath!" James said as he scooped up another bite of his cold stew that had now been sitting for some hours. The time passed quickly as they had talked about a lot of things.

"Are you kidding?" Éynath quickly responded. "It's the least I can do for the princess of Fürnas and fellow Majesticians! The honor is all mine."

James gave a sneaky smile as he pushed his bowl out of the way and rested his arms on the table. "So…if you don't mind me asking, would you tell me all about Fürnas?"

"Pssshhhh," blurted Éynath. "Please! You're asking me? Surely Princess Jenna has already told you all about it?"

But Jenna didn't answer. She was too busy staring at the falling leaves just outside the window.

"Éynath," she suddenly asked, turning to him, "forgive my boldness, but which room might I be staying in? I'd like to rest for a moment."

"O-oh!" he stammered as he tried to stand up. "I'll be more than happy to—"

"No, dear," she comforted with her waving hands. "You stay seated. I'm more than capable of following directions too!"

With a humble smile, Éynath answered, "Go up the stairs. Take a left. Your room will be the second door on your left."

"Thank you." She gracefully bowed her head. "Good night, everyone."

"Good night!" gleefully replied James and Éynath.

However, Isaac couldn't be fooled as he gave a concerned look. She simply gave him a tired smile and wink and walked up the stairs.

"Before I forget," added Éynath as he stood up and added more wood to his stove, "Isaac and James, your room is also upstairs. Make a left, first door on your right."

"Awesome!" James grinned as he rubbed his hands together. "First night in Fürnas. I'm stoked!"

"I can only apologize that you and Isaac have to share a room," he said as he poured some fresh water into a dented metal pot. "Would any of you like some mulled kinberry cider?"

Isaac's eye twitched as he robotically turned around. "Mulled. Kinberry…cider?" he whispered.

James busted out laughing as his palm clapped down on the table repeatedly, shaking the dishes.

"Oh, mate…if only you knew who you were talking to. For Isaac is the connoisseur of kinberries!"

"Is that so?" asked Éynath happily. "Well, then you're going to love this. Especially with the added orange zest and cinnamon. I just ground it this morning!"

Isaac couldn't get that mug fast enough as he instantly sat at the table.

"James, could you—"

"Ha ha! Don't worry, I got ya covered, Isaac," said James, already knowing what he was going to ask as he gripped the mug. His pale hand momentarily shimmered with blue frost as he let go. "Still nice and hot, but not unbearably so!"

Éynath kicked his feet up on Jenna's open chair as he threw his arms behind his neck. "So…you want to know about Fürnas, right? Ask away! I'll be happy to tell you all that I know."

"I bet you get this from everyone who visits, but…" James asked as he pondered, "does it really stay fall here, all year round?"

"Yessir," said Éynath as he sat his steaming mug down after just taking a drink, "Aahn, all the way through Wölntaahner."

"That's incredible!" he exclaimed in amazement. "Isn't it, Isaac?"

No wonder Jenna couldn't stop staring. It's so beautiful, he thought, obviously not paying attention to the conversation.

He had to blink a few times to snap out of the entrancing view of the falling leaves outside the window as James snapped his fingers.

"Huh? What? Oh! Sorry!"

"Bah to you, Isaac!" James said as he playfully pushed him. He then leaned in and covered a side of his mouth as he whispered to Éynath, "Don't ever try to have a conversation with this guy when Mother Nature's around. You'll end up talking to yourself!"

Isaac shook his head in dismay as he returned his focus to the falling leaves.

"I still don't understand how I'm the only one who finds our world to be so beautiful and miraculous."

"So uh…I hate to bring it up, but…" said James awkwardly, "you said your parents passed away during the Kreaux siege over twenty years ago?"

"That's right," Éynath quietly said as he swirled the mulled cider in his mug.

"Then…you've really lived here? In this same spot? For all these years? Why didn't you leave?"

"Didn't have anywhere else to go," he honestly answered. "Not only that, but nothing else compares to the comfort of Fürnas."

"Definitely," said Isaac as he turned around. "It's beautiful here. And although the temperature is quite cool, the spirit here is very warm."

James suddenly spat as he started laughing.

Éynath and Isaac gave him a dirty look.

"No, no!" he defended. "I'm sorry. It's just that I can only imagine what poor Éynath's reaction would be if he were to ever go to Wöntylnas."

"Never," he coldly responded as he stood to get more cider. "I have no desire to visit a place that poisons its citizens just to get gain!"

"Oi! Isaac! Where are you going?" James suddenly asked as he noticed him walking up the first few stairs.

"I'm just going to lay down for a bit…feeling a little tired. Don't worry! I'll be back."

"And we'll be here!" James grinned as he held up his mug. "Enjoy your rest."

Isaac nodded and humbly bowed to Éynath in gratitude as he quickly ascended the stairs.

And although he was feeling a little tired, he was much more concerned about Jenna.

"Jenna, darling, are you okay?" Isaac quietly asked as he lightly tapped on her door.

There was no response.

He waited for a few moments and then figured she'd fallen asleep. Consoling himself that he'd talk to her when she woke up, he trudged into his and James's room.

Two beds were neatly sitting side by side, with a hand-carved, wooden nightstand in between them. An ornate red-and-white bowl sat upon it, with all sorts of sticks, branches, and cinnamon sticks poking out.

He took in a deep breath as he approached the bed before him and slumped down upon it. His hand gently glided across the old, hand-stitched quilt. It smelled old but sweet and clean.

Jenna... Must stay awake...until I...make sure she's okay, he thought as he fought against his drooping eyelids that felt like massive anvils.

Although he put up a good fight for a grand total of seventeen seconds, he lost as he utterly clonked out.

"Please don't blame her, dear. It's not her fault!" Repeated the same words of Lucy inside his dream.

Once again, he was in a black space and could only communicate back and forth with this woman's voice, whom he knew not.

"I'm not blaming her or anyone! I just don't understand why we didn't have any other options!" he shouted.

"Sometimes life forces us to take options that we least desire. Trust me when I say that I've been there myself."

"But again, I'm going to be the one that suffers the most! I just want a break."

"Do you really believe that?" she asked. *"I'm surprised, Isaac. You always manage to put others before you. How do you know that she won't be affected more than yourself?"*

"I... You're right," he said, ashamed. "I'm sorry."

There was a pause, and then Lucy said, *"It's only natural for you to feel this way. Don't be sorry. But you're running out of time. Perhaps you should tell her?"*

"I promise I will. But only if you do me a favor?"

"What is it, dear?"

Isaac paused and then asked, "*Will you tell me who you are?*"

He eagerly awaited as she whispered, *"it's not wise to ask questions that you already know the answer to."*

His eyes slowly opened.

Tick-tock. Tick-tock. Tick-tock, clicked the peaceful pendulum of the clock on the wall.

The warm light of the lampposts outside his window cast a lovely glow into his room. At first deceived, he soon realized it was still dark as he got out of bed.

A strange excitement overtook him as he entered the hallway and noticed that Jenna's door was open—her room was empty!

Thud. Thud. Thud. Thud, thudded his boots as he as quietly as possible tiptoed down the stairs.

He snickered a little as he saw James and Éynath completely knocked out on the table. He further smiled as he saw the puddle of drool forming on the wooden surface, cascading out of James's mouth.

Argh, he grunted in his head as he opened the squealing front door. With a racing heart and strained vision, he stared at Éynath and James, then slowly walked outside. Thankfully, they didn't budge and were still lightly snoring.

Phew! He finally let out a breath of relief and closed the door.

His vision darted right and left as he observed the street.

No, not right, he thought. *I'm sure she'd choose to go left!*

And with his streaming white cloak flowing behind him, he darted left, down the street, and into the deeper heart of the kingdom.

No one could argue Fürnas's beauty. The pastel and cream-colored homes, with their wooden borders, tiled rooftops (covered in leaves!), bay windows, and winding stone paths leading from the cobblestone streets to their front doors, were perhaps the most enchanting homes in all of Vaerün.

"Incredible," he uttered as he reached out to the streaming light that ceaselessly flowed from the ornate white lampposts of the streets.

His hair suddenly stood on end as a gentle breeze blew past him, carrying the hypnotizing scent of cinnamon and rose. He turned around to see, standing there, some fifty feet away, Jenna Coltier.

As though she'd cast a summoning spell on him, he suddenly felt himself slowly walking toward her…and then jogging…and then running!

Her back was to him, for all he could see was the rippling, flowing mass of hair that extended well past her waist. The rose etchings of her red, black, and white dress waved and turned in the breeze, amid the flowing leaves all around her.

His heart pounded like crazy as he got closer…and closer…and—wait, stop!

One of the punishments of being new to Fürnas was that he was quite unaware as to just how slippery fallen leaves were upon cobblestone streets (and any hard surface, for that matter).

Please don't let her have seen that, he thought as his eyes were clenched shut.

For he had lost his footing and had not only slipped out but continued sliding…and finally came to a stop.

"Hee hee, hee!" He heard her giggle, although he refused to open his eyes.

"You could've just said you wanted to go leaf sliding."

Veeerrry slowly, he opened his eyes…to see her standing over him, with a hand outstretched.

His strong hand reached out and grabbed her delicate, smooth one.

"Up you go!" she giggled as she pulled him up.

"Th-thank you…," he stammered, beyond embarrassed.

"Were you worried about me?" she asked as she turned around and walked forward.

"Well, I, uh…I mean, it's, uh…we're just…and…," he bumbled as he followed her.

She suddenly came to a stop and then turned back around, facing him. She gripped his arms and, without letting go, brought him in front of her.

"Your red face matches quite well with the leaves," she observed.

He coughed as he bumbled back, "Your, uh…red, everything goes well with…the…kingdom."

She couldn't help but burst out laughing.

At first, he felt like a fool, but then he, too, joined in.

Once the laughter calmed down, he sincerely asked, "Are you okay? I know it must be so hard to come back here."

She sighed as she continued looking past him. He attempted to turn around to see what she was looking at but was stopped by her strong hands each time and a finger wag that said, "Ah, ah, ah!"

"To be honest?" she said. "I couldn't be happier to be back. If I had my way, I'd never leave."

"Then let's not!" he blurted out as he gripped her arms. "Let's stay here!"

"Stay? Here?" she flirted, "Why, Isaac Erbrecht…you haven't even seen my castle yet! What if you don't like it?"

He gave her a look that said, "Really? Just…really?"

She started laughing as she ran her fingers through his shimmering blond hair that was beautifully brought out by the glowing lampposts.

He had to gulp so that he could talk again.

"You know that that is the last thing I could care about."

"Is that so?" she asked with a suspicious smile.

"It is." He nodded as he momentarily looked past her.

She slightly turned around, still refusing to let go of his arms as she asked, "What is it? What's wrong?"

"Can I…ask you something?" he hesitated.

"Isaac, you can ask me anything."

"Well…," he hesitated once more, before finally asking, "I noticed a lot of homes that have either been untouched by the siege or have been rebuilt. And a lot of them had lights coming through the windows!"

She looked past him and then into his eyes. "It's true. What about it?"

"Well…" he mumbled, "aren't you happy that your people are alive? Why didn't you meet any more of them?"

She thought about it for a moment before answering, "For one, I don't know if they're my people at all. They may be squatters or immigrants. I don't know for sure whether or not they're my people."

"But how will you know, if you don't try?" he demanded.

"Isaac, dear..." She quietly laughed. "Squatters, immigrants... my people or not, it's not considered polite to bang on people's doors, demanding answers to questions at four in the morning."

His face instantly fell. *Yeah, Isaac. Congratulations! You're a full-fledged jackass,* he thought. *You've seen how many clocks, and you didn't think to look at one of them?*

Jenna giggled as she rubbed his arms. "Don't be embarrassed. It's okay! I'm sure you have a lot on your mind."

"Me?" he exclaimed as she smiled and hushed him. "I'm sure you are! Aren't you worried about charging this stupid...weapon thing tomorrow?"

"You mean today," she corrected with a wink.

"Choosing to ignore his sour look, she continued, "I would be lying if I told you I'm not."

"Then don't! Please don't do it!" he demanded with slight panic.

"I just..." She trailed off, then suddenly asked, "Can I be honest? I'm really scared."

His whole world felt like it came crashing down. The last thing he wanted was to hear or feel that she was scared!

"Do you want to know what comforts me?" he asked as he stared into her eyes. "I truly believe that once our work is done, we shall be given back whatever was taken or sacrificed."

"But, Isaac..." she stammered as she looked down and then up, revealing the tears in her eyes, "what if...what if it kills me?"

"Now that's just madness!" he bolted. "If it were to kill you, who would wield it and—"

"That's not what I mean!" she interrupted, shaking her head. "I mean, what if my sacrifice leaves me with a broken heart? How could I possibly go on? I don't want to fail you!"

"Jenna," Isaac said sternly as he placed a hand to her beautiful face, "please...don't talk like that. For all you know, it could require something you're least expecting!"

"Yeah, but James—"

"Never mind James!" he interrupted again. "You cannot base your experience on someone else's! Yours may be much different than his and possibly not even bad at all!"

"That's true," she whispered, and then looked him in the eyes with a solid expression. "But just in case everything goes wrong… there's something I've always wanted to do to you," she whispered as she leaned in.

Isaac gulped as his eyes transfixed upon hers and then down to her lips.

"Y-yes?" he barely choked out as he slowly leaned in.

She slowly raised her hands as if preparing to touch his face when suddenly, she shoved him back.

"What?" he demanded as he began to lose his balance.

So many thoughts stormed through his mind as he fell backward.

"How could she? Why? And why is she laughing?" These were some, to name a few.

"Agghhh!" he bellowed as he found himself zipping and zooming down the incredibly steep street.

The houses and lampposts grew blurrier and blurrier as his speed picked up. Leaves were flying everywhere!

"Woohoo!" audibly cried Jenna, not too far behind him.

"Whoa…whoa…whoa!" he hollered. "How long does this go dooooownnnn?"

Suddenly, he found himself laughing. And he was not just laughing but hollering with laughter! He hadn't had this much fun in, well, ever.

"Woohoo!" he cried as he joined in with Jenna.

Not only was it a rush; it was beautiful too. His eyes looked left and right as he stared at the enormous trees and their vibrant-colored canopies.

"Agghhh!" he cried out one final time as he noticed a massive pile of leaves that was all but too fast approaching.

Whooooosshhh! stormed the red, orange, yellow, and brown leaves as he and Jenna blasted through them.

It took a moment for him to catch his breath, not only from the rush but also from the laughter! And he wasn't alone, for Jenna was lying flat on her back, rolling left and right, doubled over in stitches.

One might've thought he was angry—no, pissed—as he marched over to her!

"Oops..." she said as she reached out and scooped a pile of leaves over her face.

They flew through the air as his hands reached down, grabbed her hands, and pulled her up.

"Is that how you feel?" he demanded as he shook her, her innocent-looking eyes and blank expression staring back.

"Is that...reaaallly how you feel?" He shook again. "Tell me!"

She said nothing.

"Not saying anything, huh?" he huffed. "Well, fine!"

He immediately let go of her and looked to the side, then back into her eyes.

"You want to know how I feel then?"

And before she could say a word, he kissed her. And with arms adoringly wrapped around his neck, she kissed him back.

Through the air, she spun as the swirling leaves trailed her weaving hair and dress.

For a moment, they may have slightly levitated off the ground as gleaming Majesty twisted and shone from their beings.

Such a gorgeous scene could hardly be described.

With her arms around him, and his hand behind her head, his white cloak and gleaming blond hair shimmered in contrast with her rich, brown hair and dress, adorned with the passionate autumn colors storming around them; all was paradise.

After what they may have wished to be eternity, he pulled back and adoringly stared into her dancing eyes.

"So..." she whispered as she caressed his handsome, etched face, "that's how you feel then."

"It is," he fervently said.

And then they kissed again...and again.

"You're right..." she said in between breaths. "Perhaps we should just stay here."

"Can we please...?" he sincerely and lovingly asked as he repeatedly kissed her. "I don't ever want to leave."

He pulled back for a moment and smiled as she lightly laughed.

"What is it, Jenn?"

"Like father, like son, I suppose!" she exclaimed.

Eyebrow raised, lips to the side, he asked, "What do you mean?"

A wave of goosebumps flooded over him as she gently ran her fingers through his hair.

"Garon…he loved it here. So much…that he did not want to leave."

Isaac looked up and into the enchanting canopy and then all around him.

"I can see why. I've never been to a more peaceful place."

His happiness quickly faltered as he saw her expression melt.

"Jenn? What's wrong?"

She held onto him tightly and then gripped him close.

"Just a bad thought, that's all."

"What do you mean? What bad thought?" he asked as he pulled her away and intensely stared into her eyes.

With some coercion, she finally admitted, "Well…you're kind of following in his footsteps."

He gave her a suspicious and concerned look that asked for more explaining.

"It's kind of funny, actually!" she said. "He came from Wölnas. Then stopped in Fährlund, like us…stayed here in Fürnas, like us… and then went back up to Wölnas, with Lucy…and didn't return."

"That's right," he said as he looked at the ground. "We have to go up to Wölnas after your…well, after we're done here!"

There was an awkward silence. Trying to think of anything to bring comfort, he said, "Hey! Pretty cool that Éynath got to meet him personally, right?"

"Oh my gosh!" she screamed, momentarily causing him to panic.

"Éynath! James! We have to go home! They're probably freaking out, wondering where we are!"

However, unbeknownst to them, the kitchen table was now covered in drool not only from James but Éynath too.

"You're right," agreed Isaac. "We should get back as soon as possible."

"Wh-what are you doing?" she shyly stammered as he picked her up and carried her upon his back.

"It's a long trek up." He motioned forward. "And you have some pretty heavy-duty stuff to do today. I'd like for you to get some rest."

"No way!" she rebuked. "Put me down so I can keep you company!"

"Right now," he calmly said, "nothing would make me happier…if you'd just do this for me."

It didn't take much persuasion until she finally said, "Fine. Gosh! You're as stubborn as I am!"

He laughed. "I don't think anyone is as stubborn as you, Jenn."

"Thank you so much for your hospitality, Éynath," Jenna graciously said as she embraced him in the doorway. "How can I ever repay you?"

They'd just finished eating breakfast and were now prepared to head to the castle.

Éynath paused for a moment and then shyly admitted, "It would mean Vaerün to me, Your Majesty…if, when you're done with your adventure…"

"Uh-huh?" She inquisitively nodded.

"And you return here, to Fürnas. Could I please be one of your servants, in the castle?"

She was shocked! What a request!

"Are you kidding me? Éynath, dear, of course! But not as a servant!"

"What then, Your Majesty?"

Isaac whispered into her ear, giving a suggestion.

"Yes. I agree." She nodded. "You'll be our chef, Éynath! For your cooking is out of this world. It has all the authenticities of Fürnas!"

He squealed for joy as he jumped up and down and gave all of them another hug goodbye.

"That was very kind of you," said James as he rode next to Isaac and Jenna.

"No, it was kind of him," she returned, "to not only house us but to feed us."

"And provide that cloak for you," interjected Isaac.

"Trust me," she said as she wrapped the dark-brown cloak around her and pulled the hood overhead. "You'll thank me for this.

Because if these really are my people, can you imagine how they'd react to see me?"

James growled as he blurted out, "I still can't figure out why you don't want them to know it's you!"

"Because, in case you've forgotten," she chided, "we're on a very important mission, and that would drastically slow us down."

"That, and they might not let her leave," added Isaac.

"I know, I know…" James mumbled sadly. "It just makes me sad, is all. It'd be such a reunion! Can you imagine it?"

"And it shall be!" She laughed. "So let's hurry up and get it over with!"

James grumbled under his breath as he said, "So she says, acting as if it's some small feat to banish the Kreaux from Vaerün."

Isaac laughed as she returned, "I heard that, James!"

It was painful for Jenna not to say a word to the kind greetings of passersby as they headed up to the castle. Perhaps most painful of all were the memories and feelings that came flooding back with each step.

"Have this many people truly survived?" she asked in her mind as she heard the numerous citizens hailing and greeting along the way.

Her emotions had only a moment to settle before all grew quiet once more. But they kicked right back up again as Isaac whispered to her, "We're here. It's safe."

As if she'd just jumped into freezing cold water, she took an enormously deep breath as she pulled off the cloak.

Her head barely moved as her eyes did most of the observing—for they scanned the white-and-red stoned steps leading up to her castle. The painfully familiar white marble towers with red-stoned rooftops and golden spires stared back at her with radiant luster.

Isaac and James could barely keep up with her as she ran with all her might up the countless teeming steps and suddenly stopped dead in front of the humongous white wooden doors of the castle.

Her hurried breathing echoed back into her ears as she held her face right in front of the door.

"My…home," she barely choked out as her white-gloved finger traced the red indentation of the Fürnas emblem upon the door.

Eaarrrrgggbhh…errrnn…errnn…errn, groaned the castle doors as they swung open.

Isaac had to catch Jenna as she nearly fainted upon walking in. For her, it was as if she'd just seen a ghost.

There, just as she remembered it, stood the same white marble pillars with a hint of red in them. Above them, but not currently alight, hung the grand, opulent gold-and-silver crystal chandelier overhead. All the tables and artwork upon the walls were covered with thick, white-linen cloths.

Clip, clop…clip, clop… echoed their boots as they fully entered, dulled every now and then as they stepped on a dead, stray leaf or two.

Isaac and James looked at each other, trying to figure out what to say as Jenna slowly approached some of the furniture, pulling the cloths off.

"It's just like I remember," she whispered as she ran her fingers along one of the arms of the luxurious couches.

"Oh!" she suddenly exclaimed as she ran to a corner side table and ripped the cloth off.

Please be here. Please be here. Please be here, she repeated as she thrust open a drawer and shoved her hand in so deep that her arm was disappearing into it.

"Wow," muttered James to Isaac, "that's some drawer."

"Ha ha!" she cried as she pulled her hand out, holding up a small, ornate lockbox.

"What's that for?" Isaac asked with a smile.

She closed her eyes as memories began to flood her mind.

"It was a gift…" she quietly said, "from Chef Türethen. Every night, when everyone was asleep, he'd come and place some hard candies in here for me."

"Think there's any left?" James asked as he pointed to it.

"I'm not sure you'd want twenty-year-old candy, James," she coldly said. "Besides, I don't have the key."

Isaac barely pulled his out when she said, "And no, Isaac, yours is way too big for this."

"Do you know what happened to the key?" James asked.

"Yes, and no…" she said with a sad look. "While Garon was here, I let him in on the secret. He, like Isaac, looooved sweets. And so I gave the key to him."

James nearly jumped back, appalled.

"You knew how to share at that age?"

At first, she gave him a sour face. But as if a most powerful memory had just hit her, she slammed the lockbox down and nearly tripped on the dead leaves as she bolted up the grand staircase.

"Wait, Jenna, I'm sorry!" he cried as he and Isaac pursued her.

Down the halls they flew, trying to ignore the obvious bloodstains and claw gashes upon what could only have been the beautiful floors and walls.

Over the suits of armor they jumped, through the cobwebs they flew, and under the broken pillars they dodged.

"I don't get it," James said to Isaac. "Why does the foyer and other parts of the castle show no signs of damage, yet other parts do?"

"Hmm…" hummed Isaac as he dodged a spear, stuck in one of the walls. "Well, for the foyer, perhaps they wanted to fix it out of respect? Although, I admit I'm not sure about the rest."

Flight after flight they climbed.

Ooooh, James grimaced in his head, *that must've been a bad one,* as they ran past a particularly badly bloodstained landing of stairs, gash marks, and fire scarring everywhere.

As they reached the fifth floor, they were grateful to see no signs of battle damage.

"Ah, this must be the floor we need," Isaac said to James as they ran across the pristine, unmolested marble floors.

The murals of the high-vaulted ceilings were magnificent and looked as though they were painted but a week ago. The eastern sunlight poured through the oversized, magnificent windows as it brought the whole hall to life. Indeed, all that was missing was the lighting in the fixtures and chandeliers overhead and the people.

Otherwise, it felt as though the castle was still fully operational. The feeling was both haunting and comforting at the same time.

Up another flight of stairs they ran, then another, and another!

"Any clue where we're going?" James asked Isaac as they both kept their attention dead-focused upon Jenna, some ten feet in front of them.

"Not a clue," he honestly replied.

Over the catwalk they ran, giving Isaac and James only a moment to take in the incredible view of trees and spires surrounding them.

After what felt like forever, they finally stood in front of a cherry wood door. Jenna thrust it open and ran in, humbly followed by Isaac and James.

"Thank heaven it's all intact!" she squealed with delight as she took in the scene that was her room.

How bizarre it must have felt to be the last person to touch your possessions and then to return many years later to see everything still there—unmarred, untouched, and exactly where you left it.

"Here's my comb," she quietly said as she approached her nightstand, "just where I left it."

She then dashed over to her dresser.

"And here's my dresses!"

She suddenly burst out laughing.

"What's up?" James asked, "What's so funny?"

"Isaac!" she blurted out as she pointed to him. "Oh my gosh! Isaac, do you not know the last time we were in this room was during that Kreaux siege, over twenty years ago?"

Isaac swallowed as a chill ran down his spine.

Jenna picked up dress after dress as she tossed them onto her huge, elegant, four-poster bed.

"I was trying to figure out what to wear that awful night when we fled! And you helped me choose!"

Isaac shuffled his shoulders uncomfortably.

"You're...welcome? I guess?"

Objects and possessions flew across the room as Jenna tore through drawer after drawer.

"I'm sure it's not my place to say, but..." Isaac asked as he approached her, "but...is everything okay?"

"Yes!" she huffed, still flinging things. "I'm just trying to find—got it! Yes!" she screamed in excitement as she held up a dark-gray-and-black plaque, jumping up and down.

"What, what, what?" demanded James. "What is it?"

"It's his plaque!" she shouted as she twisted and turned, hugging it.

James looked at Isaac, who simply shrugged his shoulders, obviously just as lost as he was.

"It's your dad's!" she shouted as she opened Isaac's hands and thrust it upon them. "See?"

Isaac read aloud the words engraved upon it:

To Garon Erbrecht,
Beloved and Honored Godfather to the
Princess Jenna Féralen Coltier
Officially declared by Their Majesties:
King Verolt Coltier
Queen Layna Coltier
Princess Jenna Coltier

Isaac felt a little strange after he'd finished reading.

"My father is your...*godfather?*"

"Oh, don't be like that!" She laughed with an added slug to his shoulder. "It's just a title. And it has nothing to do with you and me! Okay?"

"But—"

"That's so cool!" interrupted James.

Jenna stood proudly as she said, "Well, thank you! I had it made because—"

"Your middle name is Féralen? That's beautiful!" James exclaimed.

Isaac and Jenna looked at each other with blank expressions.

"Don't be offended, Jenn," Isaac smiled. "He has a short attention span."

"Your room is beautiful!" James shouted as he ran up and touched the walls. "I can't believe you lived here!"

Isaac gave her a look that said, "See what I mean?"

She gently took the plaque out of his hands, hugged it, then carefully wrapped it in one of her old dresses… Placing it in one of the drawers, then slowly closed it.

"Wait, where are you going?" James inquired as he turned around to see the empty room.

"Hurry up, or we'll leave you behind!" cried her voice from out in the hallway.

"Don't you want any of your stuff?" he curiously asked as he joined them and motioned back to her room.

"Sure!" she gleefully said. "Are you willing to carry all of it for the rest of our journey?"

"O-oh…" he mumbled. "Hadn't thought of that."

"Whoa!" the men shouted as they nearly bumped into Jenna in one of the hallways as she came to an abrupt halt.

"Sorry," she quickly said, obviously in deep thought.

"What now?" James carefully asked. "Need to find something else?"

"Isaac," she said, snapping out of it, "do we need any more money?"

"Err…I don't think so?"

"Are you sure?"

Obviously offended, James stepped in front of Isaac, hands fanned out.

"No, we don't need any more money! We haven't even used the gold that King Närveid and my uncle have given us!"

"And I'm not too sure we'll have need of it in the haunted, ravaged kingdom of Wölnas either," Isaac said sadly.

Jenna placed a hand on her hip as she stared at them intently. After a few moments, she threw her hands into the air.

"All right, all right! I get it! Just wanted to make sure. Can you blame a girl for trying?"

"Not at all, princess." James bowed, only to be met with a slap to the back of his head.

"I have to admit, I am a little surprised at you, James." Isaac smiled.

"And just what do you mean by that?"

"What he means," chided Jenna, "is that he's shocked that you don't want to see a vault brimming with gold and silver!"

James's expression melted as his knees gave out, forcing Isaac to catch him.

"That's. What. I. Thought," Jenna said as she leaned forward and tapped his nose.

"Isaac," she said seriously as she stared at him, "do you know how to get to the throne room?"

"If it's anything like Wöntylnas's Castle, then yes."

"Perfect! Go down two more flights of stairs. Head east down the hall, then turn right at the first corridor. That's the grand hall. Continue down and through the double doors, and you'll be in the throne room."

James gave a concerned and suspicious look as he asked, "Isaac's not coming with us?"

He received a strong clap on the back as Isaac answered, "Nah. Stuff's never really interested me. Enjoy!"

"Ah, but—" he tried, but Isaac was already gliding down the stairs, his white cloak flowing behind like an angel's garb.

It only took a moment for James to get over the concern as he looked at Jenna, who was excitedly rubbing her hands together.

The throne room doors creaked open as Isaac entered. Somehow, this room reminded him so much of his (now destroyed) concert hall back home in Aerlund.

Minus the white-and-red pillars, substitute the marbled floors for wooden, and switch the thrones, far down the hall, with his concert grand piano, and you've got it! Even the consecutively lined, huge eastern windows, with their morning sunlight pouring through, were the same!

Clip, clop…clip, clop…clip, clop… echoed the slow tapping of his boots as he headed down the hall.

Although it wasn't his kingdom, nor was it his home, so many feelings ran through his mind as he stared through the glowing dust before him, visible in the radiant beams of light casting through the windows.

Please don't let him take you! echoed a voice, so suddenly, in the hall.

At first, his heart nearly gave out. And then he began to question his sanity, for there was no one there! And although it was sudden, the voice was not at all threatening or unpleasant. In fact, it was very loving and tender.

"I'm sorry?" he asked aloud as he turned around, finding nothing except the vast, open hall.

He wants you, Isaac! Please don't let him take you! furthered the voice.

Okay. So, he wasn't going crazy. There really was a voice speaking to him!

"Who wants me?" he shouted as he spun around. "Is it a conductor? Are they going to attack us?"

His mind raced as he feared engaging a conductor while Jenna charged the weapon, immediately bringing him back to the tower bridge of Wöntylnas.

And please don't blame her. It's not her fault, dear! cried the voice once more.

"Blame who? Whose fault? Arrggghhh!"

"Isaac?" echoed Jenna's voice behind him.

She and James came rushing up. And James had a nice, new pouch attached to his belt—obviously, a few gold coins from Jenna.

"Who are you talking to, mate?" he kindly asked.

"This…woman! Can't you hear her?" Isaac demanded as he spun around with a slightly crazed look in his eyes.

Jenna and James looked at each other in concern.

"Dear…did you get enough sleep last night?" she asked as she tried to place a hand on his shoulder.

"No!" he rebuked, "I mean, agh! Let's just go."

Thunk. Thunk. Thunk. Thunk. Thunk, stormed his boots as he continued down the hall.

"Is he okay?" James whispered to her.

"He's been having dreams of this…woman who keeps warning him."

James swallowed as he asked, "A woman? Like who?"

"I don't know," she sadly answered. "But I'm afraid that if he doesn't find out soon, it's going to drive him crazy."

His eye twitched a little as he instantly recalled meeting his mother, Lucy, upon the Wöntylnas tower, who asked him not to tell Isaac that he'd met her.

"Yeah," he mumbled, "I can see why."

"Isaac! Dear, it's okay! Don't let it get to you!" Jenna shouted as she ran ahead.

He paused as he massaged his head, then joined his friends at the back of the throne room.

Jenna ran her fingers along the dusty, golden handles of the double doors.

"Heh…the last time I passed through these doors, I was running for my life with my—"

Isaac placed a hand on her shoulder as she looked to the ground, her hair sweeping over and covering her lamenting face.

It was amazing how quickly she coped with things! It only took her a minute before she straightened up and pulled the doors open.

To Isaac's and James's surprise, they were standing on another landing. They could either go left, down, and around the descending stairs, or to the right, which led up a long corridor with a very slight incline.

Despite their poking curiosity, they followed Jenna, who went up the long corridor to the right.

"Look familiar?" she asked as she pointed to the large stone door, with the Fürnas emblem engraved upon it, as they reached the end of the hallway.

"I only wish it didn't," said James as he looked away.

Chapter 18

Jenna's Sacrifice

Isaac's breathing quickened as he tried to stop her, but to no avail; she'd already placed her hand upon it.

Boom! The fanning red-and-orange aura of Fire Majesty exploded from her palm, cascading across the door. Without hesitation, the door immediately flew open, revealing an all-too-familiar scene.

Before them extended a large, white stone bridge with red railings. Like Wöntylnas's, it stretched out some distance, ending at the beautifully ornate white-and-red tower that ascended into the heavens.

"Please wait," Isaac said, running after Jenna and taking her hand into his. "What do we do if—"

"You'll be just fine." Interrupted Jenna, "If he does show up, I know you'll kick his—"

"That's not what I mean!" he interrupted.

She gave him a rather stoic look, trying to hide her emotions.

"Everything's going to be okay, Isaac! Aren't you the one who always says so?" she asked as she turned around and continued down the bridge.

Clap, clap! thudded his back as James landed upon it.

"Best start following your own words, mate!"

Despite their nervous and apprehensive feelings, no conductor showed up. And so, with weapons drawn and Majesty at the ready, they crossed the entire bridge in unnecessary suffering.

"Sacrificial tower or not, it's gorgeous," awed James as he stood before the entryway and looked up, followed by Isaac and Jenna.

The pinkish-peach sky overhead, with its orange-like clouds, gave the tower a sense of tranquility and dreaminess.

"All right," said Jenna, breaking the trance. "I'll be back. You two, be good!"

"No worries here, princess!" James bowed, smiling.

Isaac began to panic, though he suppressed it as he tried to follow her. "Wait, please don't—"

Boom! blasted the red, magical aura of the archway entry, knocking him back.

Jenna watched, with tears streaming down her face, as Isaac punched, kicked, and blasted the barrier with his Majesty.

"No. No. No. No! Jenna, please don't!" he screamed and cried as the rippling barrier refused to budge.

Confused, James tried to console him. "Isaac, don't worry. She'll be alright!"

"No!" Isaac shouted as Jenna blew him a kiss and dashed up the winding staircase.

She paused on the ninth step as she heard the sobbing Isaac belt out, "Jenna! I love you!"

She froze. Her heart pounded. Every fiber of her being told her to turn around, run back down those stairs, throw her arms around him, and confess, "I love you too, Isaac!"

But fearing that it would make her task that much harder, she did not. And so, she continued running up the stairs.

Ugh... How high up does this thing go? she wondered, much like James had with his tower.

The wind whistled and howled around her, up and down through the enormous space.

Come on, Jenna... You've been through much worse than this. You can do it! she thought, charging up the stairs, her hand gliding along the gold-and-red railing.

The sunlight grew brighter and brighter as she finally reached the top.

Clip, clop…clip, clop. She slowly walked out onto the huge landing at the top of the tower.

"Oh my!" she thought excitedly as she ran over to the northern side and looked over.

Far below, the multicolored trees of Fürnas looked like red, yellow, and orange specks—as if a painter had dotted the ground with a brush.

"Woooow!" she wheezed, as her gaze fell upon the tall, white-and-green tower of Grünas far to the northeast, then the massive, white tower of Laniakéa in the center of Vaerün.

Her heart sank as she barely made out the top of the purple-and-dark-gray tower of Wölnas to the north.

"But wait… Where is…?" she muttered as she dashed across to the northwestern side.

"Oh! There it is!" she exclaimed, smiling as her hair whipped and danced in the sweet-smelling breeze.

She now had a perfect view of the blue-and-white Wöntylnas tower, not too far to the northwest. Her spirits lifted as she gazed upon the shimmering ocean far below, which fully filled her southwest, west, and northwestern view.

As she admired the panorama, she suddenly felt a creepy, prickling sensation—as if something dark was watching her from behind. Slowly, she turned around and quickly noticed the red-and-white-marbled pedestal standing at half her height, some eight feet away.

Thanks to James's experience, she did not underestimate the small, empty glass sphere that rested within the top depression of the pedestal as she approached it.

Before she could even deliberate, a blinding flash of light forced her to cover her eyes.

Her shock and amazement could not be understated as she saw, standing before her, Lucy Erbrecht.

"Hello, Jenna," wisped her ethereal voice. "I am so happy to see you again! What a vision you are… absolutely beautiful."

Jenna took slow steps forward, squinting and hesitant.

"It cannot be. This is impossible," she quietly muttered. "Is it really you?"

"I'm afraid it is. I wish we could have met under more pleasant circumstances—just as James and I did."

Jenna nearly fell over.

"What? You've met James? How?"

"I was there to bring him comfort when he offered his sacrifice for Vaerün—just as I am here now for you."

Jenna was positively dumbfounded. She didn't even know where to start, and everything became more complicated as Lucy said, "I'm sorry, love. I don't have much time to be here with you. I can only imagine what's going through your mind—"

She was interrupted as Jenna threw her arms around her and broke down crying.

The care for time was swept away in the divinity of emotions as Lucy wrapped her angelic arms around her beloved Jenna.

"My darling Jenna… You've been so good. So strong."

"Why? How?" she pleaded. "What happened? Are you… dead? Where's Garon? And Isaac! Your son is—"

Lucy's undulating, streaming blond hair wrapped around Jenna, offering comfort.

"I know, dear. I wish so much that I could answer all your questions, but I am restricted and cannot."

"What? Why?" Jenna cried.

"It could potentially alter the future, and that is something we simply cannot risk."

"But… but… Isaac… have you met your son?"

Lucy's arms squeezed tighter around her. "No one can fathom… the earnestness in which I wait to meet him next, upon the Wölnas tower."

Jenna pulled away, looking into Lucy's dancing blue eyes.

"But then I—"

"Please don't tell him!" Lucy quickly urged. "It's not time for him to know yet."

Bitter—that was the first emotion that struck Jenna upon hearing these words. How could she not tell Isaac that his beautiful, gorgeous mother stood before her? How could she keep from him the very woman he had wept over and longed to meet? Nevertheless, she gave her word and promised not to tell him.

"This... weapon," Jenna said as she approached the pedestal. "James already told me everything about it, but do you know what it will require of me?"

Lucy's expression immediately fell.

"It will require the thing you hold most precious."

Jenna's white-gloved hand gently pressed over her mouth as her eyes closed, tears flowing down her face.

"I have just one question," she bravely stated.

"Yes, my dear?"

"Will it ever be... restored?"

Lucy closed her eyes, placing a hand on her shoulder.

"The greatest challenges in life require the greatest faith. That is all I can say."

Jenna slowly lowered her hand and opened her eyes. As if made for her, her knees fell perfectly upon the cool, smooth, kneeling stone.

"May our almighty Creator only know... just how much I love him."

She pulled off her white gloves, laying them beside the pedestal before placing her hands on the glass sphere.

At first, just like James, nothing happened.

She looked up at Lucy, who grimaced.

Figuring that she wasn't meant to do this, she tried to move her hands away. And then... as if that little sphere were alive and had greedily said, "And just where do you think you're going?" she found herself stuck to it, her hands unmoving.

"Lucy... Lucy?" Jenna began to panic as her breathing quickened, still trying to pull her hands away.

Lucy's grimace deepened as she walked over to the now-screaming Jenna and fell beside her, wrapping her arms around her.

"Whatever happens, Jenna," Lucy whispered, "Don't ever give up!"

"Agggghhhh!" Jenna screamed as red auras of her Fire Majesty repeatedly fanned out.

"No!" she screamed, thrashing her head as if talking to someone. "Those are mine! Don't you dare touch my memories, you—"

"Jenna? Are you okay?" asked a young, ten-year-old Isaac as he entered her bedroom in Aerlund.

Jenna was sitting on her bed and had obviously been crying.

"O-oh!" she stammered, sitting up quickly. "Yes, thank you! What are you up to?"

He gave her a blank look for a moment, his big yellow eyes staring at her as if observing her soul.

"Do you know what a piano is?" he sweetly asked as he sat next to her.

Jenna gasped, immediately thinking of Lucy, her parents' old adviser. "Yes! I most certainly do! Why do you ask?"

"Well," he said, slightly tilting his head, "Nann says that I should learn to play since my hands and fingers move the same way when I cast my Majesty."

"What a great idea! We can get you one right away!"

Isaac jumped up and stared at her. "No."

She couldn't help but laugh. "No? What do you mean, 'no'?"

He folded his arms and gave her a slight glare. "You have to promise me two things first!"

"All right, then… What is it?" she asked kindly, leaning forward.

"One," he said seriously, "you have to sing with me in duet. Your voice is beautiful!"

"Very well…" she agreed humbly. "And two?"

"And two," he suddenly beamed as he threw his arms around her, "no more crying… please? It breaks my heart when you cry because I feel your pain no matter where you are!"

Now she was curious. "What? How can you possibly do that?"

"I can feel people's emotions and sometimes see them too!" He smiled proudly. "But for some reason, yours stands out most of all."

Jenna's eyes burst open. The pain was unlike anything she'd ever experienced. Just like how a vast majority of us hate to vomit and are delighted when we think it's over—only to find there's more enduring to wade through—so did she as another memory flashed through her mind.

"What are you doing here?" Jenna spat as she stabbed an approaching Kreaux in the foot, then instantly spun around, decapitating another.

She had been fighting for the past two hours outside the borders of Aerlund. She was tired, pissed off, and just wanted to be done with the fighting. But for some reason, the Kreaux just wouldn't stop coming! And now, even worse, here came Isaac, running up to help her—always trying to help her! Didn't he know that she could take care of things?

"I'm sorry," he said as light waves coursed from his palms, obliterating the ruthless Kreaux. "I was just getting worried about you."

"Well, don't!" she yelled, dodging the massive club of a Praetor that was just about to come down on her head. "As you can see, I've been holding up just fine, thank you."

"Look out!" he shouted as she jumped back right into the arms of a Kreaux.

The gleaming tip of her rapier blasted through the Kreaux—visible through his back as she reverse-stabbed him.

Shuuuck. It sliced as she rapidly pulled it out, dodging the massive club again as it came down upon the Kreaux she'd just stabbed, instantly crushing him.

"Damn it, Isaac, I don't need your help!" she swore as she flipped and turned through the air, launching herself around with her fire casting.

"If you really don't want me here, then I'll leave," he humbly said, dodging the unceasing attacks of claws and fangs.

"I reaaally don't!" she snapped back, dodging the Praetor club again, this time coming down on the Praetor's extended arm with her honed blade, slicing it clean off. "So just go home! And don't come back again!"

"As you wish." He bowed as his attacking Kreaux fell to the ground from his light streams.

"I mean really." She couldn't help but continue. "I already have to live with you and see your ugly face every day! And now the only time I get, you have to come out and spoil it! Just… piss off!"

His heart fell as the warm gathering of tears filled his eyes. Without saying a word, he turned around to leave.

Even the Kreaux momentarily paused, as if to say, "Ouch. Really, girl?"

"Isaac... wait, I'm sorry," *she said with immediate regret.*

But she was interrupted as a Kreaux took advantage of the opportunity.

Shiiiink! *His long, razor claws pierced right through her chest.*

With a twitching head and a gargling mouth, Jenna slowly looked down as she fell to her knees, blood pooling everywhere.

The Kreaux unanimously cheered, except for the Praetor, who was stomping behind her.

You see, he wasn't finished and was still quite bitter about losing an arm.

High above her, the massive, white-boned club was raised, and with all his force, he brought it down.

I'm sure the Praetor wasn't expecting to lose his other arm... nor both legs, and part of his head, as he flew some fifty feet through the air.

Voom, voom, voom, voom, voom! *rippled and shone Isaac's light barrier as he stood next to Jenna, arms and hands outstretched.*

One could only feel sorry for the surrounding Kreaux as he exploded the barrier, inflicting instant destruction upon them.

And so for the first time, Jenna watched Isaac as he angelically spun and danced around, his ferocious, determined, yet calm face gracing the air. The rippling and whirring streams of his blinding Light Majesty twisted and rocketed through the air as if a thousand needles had come to life and were seeking their targets.

At least... she thought as she stared at the breathtaking scene, I get to see something so heavenly and beautiful before I die.

She no longer thought these words before Isaac was kneeling beside her, his hands and fingers outstretched to the high noonday sun overhead. She was fairly out of it, for she couldn't even understand his words as he recited his healing incantation.

What kind of man... she muttered, has access to the power of the sun?

For his hands were glowing and shimmering so brightly that they looked as though they'd momentarily become tiny suns themselves.

"Haaa!" *he roared as the glorious rays enveloped her dying body.*

Her eyes burst open as she immediately sat up and observed herself. She was completely healed! But how? Surely that injury was fatal! It wasn't like that time when she'd simply broken her leg.

All was quiet as she looked around. Mangled Kreaux and their body parts lay scattered all around. They'd won!

"Isaac," she hoarsely and emotionally whispered, "how? And... why?"

He looked around and politely answered, "Well, because you needed help! And if we lost, they would have taken over Aerlund, and—"

"That's not what I mean!" she yelled, a tear rolling down her face. "Why did you do it? I just said such terrible things! And yet... you not only rescued me, you saved my life! Why?" she demanded.

His beautifully long, blond eyelashes slowly fanned up and down while he took her hands

"Because I love you, Jenna!"

All went black in her mind for a moment as another scene began to appear.

She was walking down the street of Aerlund and had just finished speaking with Nann and Isaac in front of their home.

"I finally get to leave Aerlund... even if it is just for a few days!" she thought happily as she began walking down the trail.

And then her blood ran like lava. Her hair stood on end. Her heart pumped and raced as she heard him call out, "Even Isaac... I love you!"

Red lightning bolts exploded in every random direction as they launched from the charging sphere that was now glowing with a bright red flame.

Jenna was crying so hard that it was literally unbearable for Lucy to watch. Her eyes were squeezed shut, mouth open so wide that her stretched lips began to crack and bleed amid the drool running down. Her screaming so loud that even Lucy had to cover her angelic ears.

"**I CAN'T!**" she utterly bellowed. "Lucy! **LUCY**, please! Nooo! **NOT ISAAC!** Not *my* Isaac! God, please! **Save me!**"

Although I wouldn't want to be in Jenna's shoes (nor any of theirs, for that matter), I especially would not want to be in Lucy's.

For her tears, horror, and overwhelming emotions were not far behind Jenna's.

To witness someone willingly surrender their most precious, beloved, and treasured possession—so priceless that all the platinum and gold in Albyüron could never compare—freely given in faith alone, without any guarantee, to banish the darkness that haunts their cherished Vaerün… It would take an immense strength not only to watch such a sacrifice but also to offer aid and comfort in that moment.

The incredibly long hair of Lucy and Jenna, along with their dresses, furiously whipped and cut through the air as the effects of Jenna's sacrifice reached a tempest-like storm.

Even amid the gale winds, Lucy could clearly make out Jenna's nonstop cries and soul-wrenching screeches.

"No. No! **NO!**" cried Jenna as her head slammed left and right.

Lucy's arms flexed as she grabbed Jenna's head, trying to prevent her from breaking her neck from the intense thrashing.

"Oh, merciful, no! ***Please!***" she screamed at the top of her lungs. "Not that! It's… ***agggghhhh!***"

Her eyes and mouth suddenly slammed shut, as if a force had most cruelly said, *would you shut up?*

And as the unimaginably sharp, searing feeling poked around her mind, it ruthlessly grabbed hold of her most treasured memory as she viewed it for the last time.

"Is that how you feel?" Isaac demanded as he shook her.

What could she say? All she could do was give him her innocent-looking eyes and blank expression.

"Is that… reaaallly how you feel?" He shook her again. "Tell me!"

But she couldn't say anything.

"Not saying anything, huh?" he huffed. "Well, fine!"

He immediately let go of her and looked to the side, then back into her eyes.

"You want to know how I feel then?"

"You don't have a—" she thought.

And before she could say a word, he kissed her.

The floodgates of her emotions came crashing down as her powerful, loving feelings for him surged throughout her entire being.

How long I have waited... she thought as she wrapped her arms around his neck, to finally kiss these lips.

Through the air she spun as the swirling leaves trailed her weaving hair and dress.

For a moment, they may have slightly levitated off the ground as the gleaming rays of red-and-yellow Majesty twisted and shone from their beings.

With her arms around him and his hand behind her head—his white cloak and gleaming blond hair shimmering in contrast with her rich, brown hair and dress, adorned with the passionate autumn colors storming around them—all was paradise.

No... she additionally thought. *Please, don't end.*

He slowly pulled away, and both of their eyes melted as they looked at each other.

"So..." she whispered as she caressed his handsome, etched face, "that's how you feel then."

"It is," he fervently said.

Hoping that it would all come to an end, she was gravely disappointed as one last memory was stolen from her.

She had just begun running up the stairs of the tower. Isaac and James were out of sight.

"I wish so much that I could just turn around, and—"

"Jenna!" shouted the strong, masculine voice of Isaac.

"I love you!"

Rrrrrr... aggghh! Jenna hollered and screamed as she ripped her hands away from the sphere, her mind returning to reality. Her exhausted body fell backward as she gently landed in the lap of Lucy.

The light began to return as it had all but gone dark while Jenna charged the weapon.

"*Wh-what?*" Jenna thought.

Tap... tap... tap-tap, fell Lucy's tears upon her tired and drained face.

Lucy's hands were clasped over her mouth, and her eyes were squeezed shut. She couldn't stop crying.

"*How?*" she thought. "*How can I possibly help my precious son next? This is more than I can bear.*"

"L-Lucy?" Jenna shakily asked as she reached up a hand to her tear-stained face.

And that was the last thing she remembered saying as she fell unconscious.

The black, blurry background of her dream suddenly shifted as she saw a version of herself walking toward her.

"*Why did you do it?*" asked her doppelgänger. "*Was it worth it?*"

"*Was what worth it?*" she asked curiously.

"*You sacrificed your love for him. Are you even aware of what you've just done?*"

She thought about it for a moment, then answered, "*Yes. I have just charged a weapon of unprecedented power in order to save Vaerün!*"

"*That is true,*" *nodded her doppelgänger.* "*But at a price... that you haven't nor will you fully comprehend.*"

Jenna blinked her eyes open. The setting sun accented the already peach sky and orange clouds of Fürnas, all around her.

"Are you okay, dear one?" asked Lucy as she combed Jenna's long hair with her fingers.

Jenna let out a deep sigh as she stood up and looked around. Her attention was rapidly grabbed as she stared at the blazing red sphere, sitting in the pedestal.

"I'm... not so sure," she answered honestly.

"Dear... do you know what you've just given up, to charge that weapon?" Lucy asked.

Jenna thought for a moment and then replied, "Yes. It was Love."

Lucy placed a hand over her mouth as she shook her head.

"Faith... hope... love... what will be next?"

"I'm sorry?" Jenna asked.

Lucy weaved her fingers through the air, casting another golden netting, this time for Jenna's belt, to hold her sphere.

MAJESTY

Jenna gave a slight nod of gratitude as she attached it to her belt.

"Take your weapon, Jenna," said Lucy kindly but boldly as she pointed to it.

Jenna approached the pedestal and picked up the small, red glowing sphere.

"Hard to believe that something so small could possibly be a weapon."

Lucy gave a half-smile as she said, "It's not the sphere that's the weapon."

Jenna didn't even have time to ask what she meant as the sphere began to glow and vibrate within her palm. She seized upon it with her other hand as five fireballs launched out of it.

Through the air they danced until they collided together.

The sound of a horse whinnying echoed through the heavens around them as a black horse with a flaming mane, flaming eyes, and flaming tail galloped down next to her.

Jenna's lip quivered as she brushed the fiery beast. "I think… I finally understand, Lucy."

"What is it, Jenna, dear?" Lucy asked.

"The spheres. The weapons—they are our strongest feelings… our most precious possessions, literally brought to life."

Lucy couldn't possibly smile wider as she walked up next to Jenna and joined in petting her horse.

"You've got it. The spheres absorb your most powerful thoughts and feelings and bring them to life as an embodiment to fight alongside you."

Jenna smiled as she rested her head against her horse.

"Majesty is undoubtedly one of the most powerful forces upon Vaerün," continued Lucy, "but what's even more powerful… is your most sacred convictions."

"So then…" Jenna continued, "my most powerful weapon, even above my Majesty, is my love for Isaac."

Lucy smiled and nodded. "As is James's hope, and Gage's—"

Jenna stood up and gave a suspicious look. "Wait a second. Did you just say Gage's? Has Gage already given his sacrifice?"

Lucy shook her head and repeatedly waved her hands. "You will find out in due time! I promise! But for now, let me ask," she said as she looked up at the tall, grand beast. "What will you call your most powerful weapon?"

"Antéum," Jenna instantly replied, without even looking at her.

"Antéum? Doesn't that mean…"

"Yes," said Jenna as she kissed him, "it means, '*my love*,' in Fürnasian."

With a wave of her hand, Antéum leaped in the air and vanished in a burst of flames. She then took the flaming sphere and sheathed it in the golden netting attached to the left side of her belt.

"I'm so sorry, Jenna," stumbled Lucy as she began to watch Jenna descend the steps.

"Lucy," she responded courageously, "if you think that I'm going to give up my love that easily, then you've lost your mind."

A large smile erupted on Lucy's face as Jenna continued, "Forget about sending the Kreaux back to oblivion because when I'm done? There's going to be no, 'oblivion' to return to."

"That's my girl," said Lucy proudly.

"And it's strange," Jenna furthered, "I always thought my life was just one big hole of gaping emotions. But now? I literally know what it feels like to have that gaping hole."

Lucy said nothing but continued to listen.

"And weapon or not, I'm sure you learned at least one thing while staying in Fürnas."

In unison, Lucy and Jenna said, "We're the most giving people you'll ever meet. But take from us, and you shall have not only heaven to pay back but hell too."

The following laughter provided a little comic relief.

"Jenna!" called out Lucy as she watched her head disappear down the steps, "I… I love you!"

In great anticipation, Lucy waited as she stared at the back of Jenna's head (the only visible part). And then Jenna's hand rose up as she continued descending completely out of sight.

Chapter 19

Light Falls

"So that's what the weapons are!" exclaimed James as he held up his blue sphere and examined it.

At first, Isaac refused to believe that something so personal could be taken and sacrificed. But it didn't take long for the devastation to set in as Jenna repeatedly told him to leave her alone.

Even amid his pitiful breakdowns and unrelenting crying, she only grew more agitated. The message fully sank in when he tried to hug her, and she slapped him across the face—hard. He still bore the imprint, and they had just finished climbing down the castle steps and were now upon the main pathway.

"All right, so," Jenna said stoically as she grabbed the brown cloak off her horse and threw it around her. "Our next stop is Wölnas, right?"

James was kneeling, holding the sobbing Isaac as he looked up at Jenna, who had just mounted her horse.

"Oi! Y'think you can have a little bit of a heart? Isaac has—"

"What part of 'my love was sacrificed' do you two not understand?"

James was tempted to blast her off with his ice Majesty when she added, "I mean, I knew that men were stupid, but really, this is taking it a bit far."

Isaac ceased crying. James huffed as he stood, his palms glowing and cracking with his repressed, freezing Majesty.

"Don't have time for this," Jenna said flippantly as she turned the horse around. "Hurry it up, cry it out, then meet me at the northern archway, in the woods."

"Oi, wait!" shouted James as he pointed to Isaac. "You and Isaac have been riding together this whole time! So now you're just—"

"I'm sure you two will make a beautiful couple!" she said sarcastically as she flipped her hair.

Crack! went the reins as she dashed down the path, leaves scattering in her wake.

"Ugh!" shouted James as he launched five ballistic icicles from his palms. Through the air they flew, shattering in an explosion of snow against the trees.

"This is horse shüza! As if she wasn't hard enough to deal with before, now she's been upgraded to mega bitc—"

"It's okay, James," Isaac said as he pushed himself up. "Somehow, I knew this was going to happen."

James calmed down, observing him as he asked, "How on Vaerün could you possibly have anticipated this?"

Isaac sighed as he closed his eyes. "I had… warnings. In my dreams. A woman kept telling me to 'forgive her' and 'It's not her fault.'"

James gave him a blank stare, his eyes half-closed.

"Isaac Erbrecht," he said as he patted him on the back and mounted the horse, "you are one heavenly of a man to have to go through all this shüza because let me tell you—"

Isaac smiled gratefully as James extended a hand and pulled him up.

"There's no way, on the Almighty's lush green lands of Vaerün, that I'd ever go through what you do."

"Thank you, James. I really appreciate that."

"Arggghhh! Shüza!" swore James loudly, his thoughts briefly wandering to his mother, Lucy, and how he wasn't able to tell Isaac about her.

"Ha ha, what's wrong, James?" Isaac asked kindly. "Really, it's okay! I'll get over it."

"That's not it!" he retorted. "Not it at all! Why does one man have to go through so. Much. Shüza?"

Isaac thought for a moment, then sighed. "It's not... that bad. Others have it so much worse, I'm sure. I'm just thankful to be alive."

James growled as he caught some falling leaves. "Even now, look at you! You do know that you're next on the list for your weapon... right?"

"Oh!" Isaac shouted. "Speaking of weapons, we have to return to Wöntylnas. I need to give King Närveid his sword back!"

James burst out laughing.

"What are you laughing at?" Isaac asked nervously.

"Oi, sorry, sorry!" James exclaimed, wiping away a tear. "It's just, did you see the way Rúviag flung the mangled body of dünréld through the air, after he tried to get you? Priceless!"

Isaac was appalled at first but then couldn't help but laugh as he remembered.

"That's nothing! You should've seen the time Jenna and I—"

"No, no, none of that!" James said with a smirk. "But yeah, we should return that sword. It'd also be wise to stop in Wöntylnas to get another horse."

Isaac tossed his head back and forth. "Not to mention some more supplies."

"Now don't get me wrong," James joked, placing his gauntleted hand upon Isaac's that was wrapped around his torso. "I know how much you're loving this, but it just can't last, darling."

"Oh, but, sweetheart," joked Isaac back, "you know that you're my only rebound!"

Both of them burst into laughter.

"Okay, okay, so..." James smiled as he tried to calm his laughter, "we have another thirty minutes or so till we catch up with Jenna. Do tell about the funny times with you and the Kreaux?"

The thirty minutes flew by as Isaac told him of the many times they'd morbidly played with the fallen Kreaux, including, but not limited to, Isaac running around with one of the arms, trying to catch a head that Jenna tossed through the air.

Or... the time Jenna demonstrated her hairstylist techniques and makeup skills. (The pigtails one with the red blush was the best!)

Or... the time Jenna would launch them toward Isaac with a heat blast, and Isaac would have to time it just right to explode them through the air with a force field. (The farther they flew, the more points he got!)

Or...

James was wheezing in laughter by the time they reached the entryway to Fürnas.

"What're you laughing at?" Jenna asked curiously as she saw them approach.

Since James couldn't talk, Isaac had to answer, although he was laughing himself.

"I was telling him about the times that you and I used to make games out of the fallen Kreaux."

Jenna raised an eyebrow and shrugged. "Sorry, but I don't recollect."

"Oi, come on!" roared James in laughter. "How can you not remember putting pink-and-red blush on one, with pigtails? That is genius!"

She tapped her forehead repeatedly, trying to recall. "Hmm... that does sound—"

Whatever remaining doubts either of them may have had were banished as Jenna screamed in agony and gripped her head—a small, circular flash of red light appearing beneath her dress coat, revealing her sphere.

"Right, then," Isaac said dejectedly. "That's the last time I try to have her remember something from our past."

"I don't think it's that," James whispered to him. "I think it was locked away, on account of it being a fond memory between you two."

The glowing light dissipated. Isaac and Jenna both stared at the ground.

"Soo..." James broke the silence. "Isaac has a point. We need to return this sword to Wöntylnas."

"Pssshhh!" mocked Jenna, pointing to the sheathed blade. "You really think anyone in Wöntylnas needs it? Isaac should just keep it!"

"Whoa, whoa!" she exclaimed as James gave her a death glare. "Why the gaze of icy death? I'm sure when King Närveid finds out about his cousin, he'd want Isaac to keep it!"

"No, we should return it," added Isaac. "You know I don't like using swords anyway, Jenn!"

"What?" she shouted. "You don't like to use swords? How on Vaerün do you even fight?"

Isaac and James sighed.

James then rode up next to her and poked her. "Question, would you be upset if someone took something from Fürnas and didn't return it?"

"Well, duh!" she shouted. "I just told Lu—"

Isaac gave her a strange look, then to James, who was giving her a look that begged, "No, no! Don't say it!"

"Am I missing something here?" he asked suspiciously as he looked back and forth between the two.

"Of course not!" shouted James.

"Not like it matters." Jenna shrugged. "He'll find out soon enough anyway."

Both of them gave her a look that said, "What's your problem?"

"Well, whatever," she said as she looked down the northern trail. "Nightfall will be upon us soon. Let's get close to Fährlund, then set up camp."

"Close to Fährlund?" Isaac slowly asked. "Isn't that—"

"If you two can keep up with me," she rudely interrupted, "we'll get there sooner than you think! And after that, we'll head straight to Wöntylnas."

"Ignore her, mate," James whispered to him. "She doesn't mean it."

"Right!" he spoke up as she gave them both a funny look. "I was just telling Isaac that, after Wöntylnas, it's only two days to Wölnas!"

"Again," snickered Jenna, "that all depends on how fast you ride."

James's knuckles cracked as he rolled his fists and glared at Jenna, who was now riding away.

Thank heaven for Isaac, who placed a hand on his shoulder to calm him.

"Trouble doesn't last always, for this, too, shall pass," he said kindly.

"While I don't disagree with you, mate," James said as he rolled his head and cracked his neck, "sometimes I'd just love to… whup her. Y'know what I mean?"

Their horse whinnied as he cracked the reins, following at a distance behind Jenna.

"I mean really," he continued, "she sacrificed her love, not her couth."

Isaac couldn't help but laugh as he gratefully thanked his dear friend.

James stared at the broken-down ruins of Fährlund, some half a mile north of them. It was well past dark, and the moon was on a cycle where it was barely visible, giving hardly any light.

"I don't care if we had a full moon!" argued James. "I still don't think we should camp this close to Fährlund! It's just… bad energy!"

"No, you're just lazy and tired," snickered Jenna. "And don't want to fight the Kreaux, should any attack us!"

"You're damn straight there, miss!" he bellowed back. "You've already made us ride nearly most of the bloody night away! You intent on making us suffer more?"

"Look, I get it," she said sweetly as she tapped the part of her dress over her sphere. "I get that you're afraid to use your power. And I get that Isaac doesn't like fighting."

She suddenly looked at him and gave him a dirty, sarcastic look.

"No offense, Isaac. But who doesn't want to use a sword? And beyond that, who doesn't like to use a weapon, in general?"

"What's your point?" James growled as he raised his fist.

"My point…" She sighed sweetly. "Is that you boys aren't strong enough to do what needs to be done. And so I am graciously offering my protection."

She suddenly whispered to herself, "Why a princess has to protect two full-grown men in the first place is beyond me, but…"

"Even though you two should be offering to protect me, the princess of Fürnas!"

"We don't need your protection, princess," James howled as he sarcastically bowed. "And if you're so big and bad, then how about you just go on ahead and camp out in Fährlund?"

Jenna started giggling, only causing James to get angrier.

"You really think I need to prove myself to you?" She sighed again as she shook her head. "Oh, all right then… have it your way. Good night, boys, see you in the morning! Be sure to meet me at the northern entryway at dawn, or I'll leave you behind!"

The sound of cracking, subzero temperatures, roaring blizzards, and freezing ice pulsed through the air as James raised his hands, preparing to fight.

Jenna turned around just in time to witness Isaac wrap his arms around him, instantaneously calming him down as his Light Majesty twisted and flashed around him.

"Wow… really?" she asked as she looked Isaac up and down. "That's your Majesty? Hah! No wonder you don't fight!"

"Damn!" swore James as she rode up the path and at last disappeared into Fährlund. "Isaac, mate, I'm sorry, but if this continues, I cannot do this."

"It's all right, James," he said as he hugged him. "If there's one thing I know about Jenna, it's that she always hides her pain beneath bitterness."

"That much would be true if she could remember anything! But you saw it yourself," he said with a wave of his hand. "She doesn't remember anything!"

Crack! whipped the reins as James sent them forth, choosing to go the longer way around Fährlund rather than through it.

"Do you think she'll be okay?" Isaac asked concernedly.

"Hah!" he mocked, "Trust me, mate, with the way she's feeling right now, I'm pretty sure she could take out that whole town, need be."

Neither of them said much as they finished setting up their makeshift camp.

Since they didn't have Jenna's fire, Isaac unleashed a dancing orb of light that hovered above a circle of rocks they'd put together.

With their arms folded around their legs, they could only hear the nearby crickets, in addition to the pulsing, near-singing, gentle hum of his coursing Majesty.

"Can I ask you something?" Isaac asked quietly without looking up.

"Of course, mate. Ask away."

"Is it true that you don't have a single remaining memory after you charged your weapon?"

James thought about it and then nonchalantly tossed his head back and forth.

"While I truly cannot recall the memories, nor the feeling of hope that was taken from me," he admitted, "I can feel the wound it's left. It's hard to describe."

Isaac looked up for the first time, his yellow eyes perfectly reflecting the suspended light above them.

"Can you... *try?*"

James leaned back upon his palms as he looked into Isaac's eyes. "It's there but not there at the same time. Does that make any sense?"

Isaac shook his head. "No."

"Argh..." He grunted. "It's like... it's still *there*, but it's been, I dunno... locked away...? Or... covered with a blanket or something."

"I understand," muttered Isaac as he looked down again.

James gave a half, quirky smile as he offered some encouraging words. "But... want to know something cool?"

Isaac immediately perked up and nodded.

"Every time I summon Rúviag, it feels like I've just been gifted the feeling of hope, for the first time."

"That's amazing!" shouted Isaac as he nearly fell forward. "Do your memories come back too?"

"No," said James with a quizzical smile, "but it almost feels like Rúviag is saying, 'I'm just borrowing them for a little bit. Don't worry, I promise to give them back!'"

Isaac tried to repress a benevolent snicker as James, offended, asked, "What? Why are you snickering, mate?"

"I just think it's funny, that's all," he admitted. "For someone who's sacrificed all of his hope, I've never seen you more hopeful."

"Bah," said James as he flopped down upon his back. "I just do a good job hiding it, that's all!"

"Whether that's true or not," Isaac said, "I just wanted to thank you. Despite everything terrible that's happened, you truly have given me the most hope out of everyone. And for that, just… thank you."

"Oi, now, come on, mate!" James shyly said as he brought a hand over his face. "You're making me blush!"

His blue eyes reflected the twinkling light of the stars overhead as he carefully observed them.

"Y'know," he said, "I agree. I think she's putting on a front because she's so hurt. Don't you?"

He sat up and asked, "Isaac?"

But Isaac was fast asleep.

"That's right…" whispered James. "Rest, mate… you, too, have been dealt a heavy blow today."

The twilight sun cast its dazzling rays of reflecting light ever so brilliantly upon the massive white-and-blue bridge of Wöntylnas.

Isaac was massaging his head, and James had a look that said, "Please spare me."

The past day had been nothing but unpleasant as Jenna continued to jab, poke, and make fun of them

"Do you know what I think?" James asked sincerely as they were halfway down the bridge.

Jenna looked forward and gave an exhausted sigh. "There's no telling what is going on inside that frozen mind of yours."

James gritted his teeth as he said, "I really think that this is how you've felt about both of us this whole time, and now you're just using that stupid weapon as an excuse to treat us how you really feel!"

In shock, she turned to him and said, "My goodness, did you come up with all that on your own? Or did you have the aid of your saintly comforter behind you?" she asked, motioning to Isaac.

"Ooooh… he's cute!" she suddenly said as she stared at a muscular, scantily dressed man who winked at her in passing.

Isaac's guts twisted and turned as he felt ready to vomit.

"Aww… what's wrong, Isaac?" she playfully asked. "Not your type?"

She then looked at James, raising an eyebrow and giving him a disgusted once-over, before looking forward again.

"No, I forgot that James is the perfect match for you."

"Oi, oi!" James shouted as he pulled on the reins, bringing the whinnying horse to a halt, for Isaac had just jumped down and ran over to the side of the bridge.

Isaac received multiple stares and nonstop ridicule as he repeatedly vomited over the side, between his heart-wrenching tears and wailing.

Jenna looked over at James and asked, "And you mean to tell me that I fell for a man like that? Please! The only thing he has going for him is his—"

She was cut short as James leaped through the air, slashed the reins of her horse, slapped its butt, and forced it down the path.

"Why you—" she began as she painfully landed on her foot, slightly twisting her ankle.

The passersby gasped as he walked up to her, slapped her across the face, and shoved her back, nearly pushing her off the side of the bridge.

His blue eyes, with their dancing light, were moving like mad, revealing the untold fury barely being contained within his spirit.

"Let me make something very clear to you… right here and right now." He hissed, "You may pretend that you don't feel anything. You may pretend that you've forgotten it all. You may even pretend how much you hate."

He turned around and pointed to Isaac, many feet away, then faced Jenna with tears in his eyes.

"But don't you dare hurt that man any more than he already has been."

Shocked and appalled, she listened as he continued, "If you refuse to respect the fact that that angelic, divine, and most gracious man has already suffered more than you or I can possibly bear, then at least respect the fact that he's saved your sorry ass on countless occasions!"

And with that, he shoved her back, nearly pushing her over into the rolling waves far below.

"Why, I oughta—" she said as she went to unsheathe her rapier and grab her sphere.

He instantly turned around and threateningly raised a finger. "I dare you," he whispered in the most menacing way. "I don't care how badass you think you are 'cause, guess what, princess," he said as he held out his hands and motioned to the water that completely surrounded them, "right now, you're in my element. And with the way I'm feeling right now? You do not want to test my patience."

The light in her eyes was furiously dancing. Truly enough, if she could have, she would have strangled him... right then and there.

And yet... why did she look as though she'd break down crying at any moment?

"Oh, and another thing!" he said with a smile as he turned around again and held a finger in front of her. "If you continue to treat us like this, I can promise you that we will ditch you. And, hmm..." he hummed as he brought a hand to his chin, "last I just checked, a little over a day ago, you don't have anyone to return to in that big ol', empty castle of yours. Now do you?"

Her knuckles grew white as she was itching to run him through.

"And as we've heard so many times since your 'precious sacrifice,' you no longer love Isaac!" He gave a twisted smile as he motioned to him. "And so I'm sure you won't mind that I house him here, in the loving company of not only myself but also with King Närveid and my loving uncle, Professor Vandergaus!"

Before she could say a word, he wrapped it up. "And one last thing..." he said as he turned around for the final time, "keep acting like this, and not only will you lose your God-given Majesty, you'll lose the one thing that cares for you, more than you can even begin to comprehend: Isaac Erbrecht."

His face turned a little as his eyes squinted. "And let's say you do get your memories back. How devastated would you be, to have every memory... every thought and emotion restored, only to find that the man that you love and adore beyond measure now can't stand you? And hates your guts?"

James laughed as he looked at Isaac, who was still vomiting, and then to Jenna.

"Oh. What am I saying? He's too benevolent to hate anyone. Even a sorry, wretched, lame excuse of a person like you." He reached behind him and motioned to Isaac again. "No, he'd rather bend over a bridge and vomit in tears and devastation rather than hurt you. So yeah! Wouldn't that be fun?"

He snickered and shook his head as he finally walked away. "Nah. Not for me. Sounds like a hell far worse than what the Kreaux are even going through."

What could she say? What should she say, after such words? And so she could only watch as James rubbed his hand along Isaac's back and then embraced him for comfort.

Her sphere began to dance and vibrate as she, more than anything in Vaerün, wanted to cry. Just... cry! And let it all out!

But... the stabbing, searing pains of the sphere kept her from doing so. And so all she could do was watch as James helped Isaac up and into the saddle, and both of them continued down the bridge.

The following morning...

"Now you go ahead and order whatever you want!" roared Chef Volkan as he eagerly handed today's menu to the sniffling Isaac.

"I don't know what happened," he continued, "but you better believe that whatever you order will be finished off with a 'kinberry' something!"

Isaac gratefully bowed his head to Chef Volkan, who threw his massive arms around him and then trudged back into the double doors of the kitchen.

James was staring out the western window, observing the familiar, stunning ocean view.

"I'm... sorry," he said as Isaac sipped on his cinnamon hot cocoa.

"For what, James?"

"It's probably my fault that she hasn't shown up yet." He slightly laughed as he took a sip of his own cocoa.

Isaac accidentally blew bubbles in his as he went to take another sip.

"Well, to be fair, she may still be on her way. You did make her walk all that way, without a horse."

"Too right, too right." James's head bobbled nonchalantly.

"So! What are you going to get for breakfast?" Isaac eagerly asked as he followed with, "I think I'm going to try the stuffed crepes with sautéed kinberries, fresh roll with honey butter, boar links, eggs over medium, and… the roasted, garlic hash potatoes."

James could only give him a flabbergasted look as he congratulated with a slow clap. "Well done, mate… well done!"

"At least, I think that'll be enough to start me out."

They were only halfway through their breakfast when Professor Vandergaus walked up.

"Uncle!" James shouted.

"Jéid!" Isaac eagerly said.

Jéid motioned for them to sit back down as he pulled up a chair.

"It's nice to see you again. I hear you've already charged two out of the weapons?"

Isaac and James looked at each other, then back at him.

"How'd you know about that?" James asked.

"Your friend Jenna, of course! Of whom I've also heard that you made walk all the way to the castle."

"Now just hold on one sec," tried James before his uncle laughed and calmed him down.

"Whoa, whoa, James! No need to get riled! She knows what she's done, and she's going to apologize to the both of you."

James's fork clattered down as he angrily dropped it, crossed his arms, and stared out the window.

"I don't want her apology. So she can give both of them to Isaac."

"It's all right." Isaac smiled. "She's been through a lot. And like I told James, she's always had a way of taking it out on the wrong people."

Jéid unbuckled his cloak and draped it over the back of the chair. "Do you mind telling me what happened?"

"Not at all!" beamed Isaac as he additionally asked, "Have you eaten yet?"

"Nope!" he jubilantly replied, then looked at James. "Do you mind getting me a menu, nephew?"

"It'd be my pleasure, Uncle!" he exclaimed as he jumped up and gripped his uncle's shoulders, then headed off to grab a menu.

"You've been through a lot… haven't you, Isaac Erbrecht?" Jéid asked sadly.

Isaac simply smiled as he answered, "Everyone's been through a lot, Jéid. Like James, Jenna, and now myself and Gage, all of us have our own burdens we must bear and sacrifices we must give."

Jéid barely nodded his head as he looked down in deep contemplation. "Speaking of Gage, I take it you haven't met up with him yet?"

Isaac shook his head. "I'm afraid not. Although, I cannot wait to meet him!"

James just returned as he sat a fresh glass of ice water and some mulled wine in front of Jéid, in addition to the menu.

"Oh, thank you!" he happily said as he took a sip of the warm wine. "How'd you know I needed some of this?"

James brushed his cloak out as he took a seat. "Why, 'cuz it's cold outside, that's why! Now, what words could've been spoken while I was gone so as to bring you two down? Is it Jenna?"

"No," defended Isaac, "we were just talking about Gage."

"Gage? Gage Grünas? What about him?" Jéid asked.

Jéid took a sip of his water and then motioned to Isaac.

"I was just about to ask young Isaac here, if he was still intent on heading up to Wölnas."

"Darn straight he is!" James answered before Isaac even had a chance. "Isn't that right, mate?"

Again, before Isaac could answer, Jéid interjected. "Well, if I may add my two copper, I'd really think it wise that you meet up with Gage first."

"What? No way!" shouted James. "We don't need him! We've already gone this far without him. Are you saying that we're not strong enough to—"

"That's not at all what I'm saying," interrupted his uncle. "I just have some concerns! And they're rightly grounded!"

"I'd like to hear them." Isaac stated, "Please tell me?"

"Don't need no dumb earth Majestician… don't need no dumb Gage," grumbled James as he stuck his tongue out.

Jéid grasped his hands around the steaming glass of mulled wine, as he explained. "As you know, before you reach Wölnas, you have to travel through the northern Algár Mountain Pass."

"We know that, Uncle!" snickered James.

"But before you do…" Jéid continued, ignoring his nephew, "you'll find yourself upon the Algár Plains."

"All right?" gestured Isaac.

"It's not like what it used to be. The unrelenting storm over Wölnas occasionally throws itself beyond its bounds as it reaches over the mountains and drenches the plains."

"Okay, so we'll get a little wet. Is that your concern?" James snarkily asked.

"The footing is poor," he whispered, as if a ghost had entered the room, "very poor. You will not be able to take your horses across that terrain should a storm kick up."

Isaac looked at James as he said, "That is a concern."

"Meh…" James shrugged. "But what are the odds of that? Wölnas doesn't overthrow its storm often. I'm sure the footing will be fine."

"Were that all, I'd agree," continued Jéid. "But… over twenty years ago, when the Kreaux Siege took place, a portion of Wölnas must have attempted to flee."

Isaac's expression melted as he asked, "What makes you think that?"

Jéid shook his head, as if he'd just seen a ghost. "Splintered wooden carts, rusted metal, and shattered caravans riddle the plains like a graveyard."

Even James gulped as he heard this news. "What do you think happened?" he nervously asked.

Jéid took a long drink of his wine before he answered, "I believe some inhabitants attempted to flee Wölnas when the catastrophe struck. And…"

Isaac brought a hand over his mouth as he shook his head. "They never made it."

Jéid slowly nodded as his eyes glistened. "That's right, Isaac. They were probably hopeful as they'd just made it over and down the Algár Pass and onto the plains."

"But… the Kreaux must have caught up with them. And…" James faded out.

Jéid looked up as he took in a deep breath, then down to the two men. "I've experienced bad energy before. But let me warn you…," he whispered as he leaned forward and pointed a foreboding finger to Isaac and James, "that nothing compares to the darkness and despair that thrives upon those plains, through that pass, and especially in that forsaken kingdom."

Isaac and James gulped at the thought.

"So yes," said Jéid proudly as he brought a hand across his chest, "forgive your silly, overprotective uncle, James, for wanting you and your friends to be as protected as possible."

"It makes sense," agreed Isaac. "Not only would the extra Majesty be useful, but since Gage is an earth Majestician, he could secure the footing for us, just in case the storm overflows!"

Jéid smiled as he leaned back and threw his arms in such a way that said, "And I rest my case."

James let out a long, deep sigh as he thought about it. "I mean really though," he suddenly blurted out, "do you blame me for not wanting to travel clear across Vaerün, all the way to the eastern Grünas Kingdom, when we can just head directly north to Wölnas?"

"Hey, you can do as you wish," snickered Jéid. "And no, I don't blame you. I just wanted to make sure you fully understand the risks, that's all."

"And for that we thank you," answered James for Isaac. "We'll take it into consideration."

The timing couldn't have been better as Jéid's hot, steaming breakfast plates were served to him.

"Beautiful... just... beautiful," Isaac thought as he entered the castle ballroom. Tip, tap... tip, tap... tip, tap, sounded his boots as they tapped upon the white-and-blue, polished granite and marbled floors beneath his feet.

The monstrous chandeliers overhead emanated a comforting, soft blue-and-yellow light. And he was positively mesmerized at the view of the cascading waterfalls that shimmered and moved through the surrounding northern, eastern, and western windows.

Indeed, one may have thought that this was a room constructed by heaven—so elegant was the hall and its furnishings.

He couldn't help but jump in the air in excitement as he rushed up to the matte-black concert grand piano in the center of the hall. He quickly lifted the fallboard, lid, and pulled out the piano bench.

Ding! sang the single note he depressed as the acoustics brilliantly reflected around him.

I wish... for light, he prayed as he began playing on the perfectly tuned instrument.

"Agghh..." winced Jenna in pain as she stood outside the ballroom doors and listened to the alluring, bewitching music that was coming through from the other side. A sharp pain stabbed at her mind as she momentarily held her hand upon the platinum handles.

Isaac, Isaac... Isaac, Isaac, whispered the name again and again in her mind as the sphere vibrated a little upon her belt. Her legs nearly gave out on her as she pushed open the doors and walked in. A powerful sense of déjà vu struck her like a Praetor's club as she looked down the hall at Isaac.

Streaming rays of light were zipping and flashing through the air, some of them even enveloping around her, as if alive, before they joined once more in their freedom.

Why? she thought as she placed a hand to her throat. *Why do I have the strangest desire to sing? I don't even know what he's playing.*

What a beautiful feeling of hope, happiness, and joy that filled her soul as she slowly approached the performing Isaac.

Haven't you hurt him enough already? criticized a voice in her head as she once more wanted to sing. *Now you want to ruin his beautiful music with your toad voice? Just leave him alone!*

She stopped dead in her tracks. It was as if someone had just brought her entire world crashing down.

For a few more moments, she listened to the music. And then she turned around to leave the hall, which was a shame since she was only about eight feet from him.

Her heart plunged as the music stopped. And behind her back, she heard his voice call out, "Jenna?"

She closed her eyes and swallowed as she turned around to face him.

"H-hello, Isaac."

"I'm so happy to see you!" he beamed as he jumped up and went to hug her but then brought himself to a complete halt.

Why? Why do I want him to hug me so badly? she practically yelled in her mind as she noticed his sadness. *And yet at the same time, I don't want to be anywhere near him!*

Neither of them said a word as each was trying to figure out what to say.

"So…," they ended up saying at the same time.

"I'm sorry about earlier," she blurted out. "I really am. I didn't mean to act so harsh, and it's just been—"

Isaac simply held up his hand, stopping her. "Jenna. It's okay. Really, it is. I already knew what was going to happen."

Her face twisted up as a number of emotions hit her. "What? You did? How?"

"Like I told James…," he said, "I had multiple warnings in a dream, from a woman."

She took another step closer. "A… woman? Do you know who?"

He shook his head no. "Although, for some reason, her voice sounds so familiar!"

Her face accidentally erupted in a smile as he asked, "What? What are you smiling at? Do you have a clue who it is?"

Jenna bit her lower lip as she looked at him. "Let's just say… that you'll meet her much sooner than you think. And she cannot wait."

Isaac couldn't help but smile or help his curiosity. "How can you be so certain?"

"You're… just going to have to trust me on this," she painfully answered.

Jenna walked around a little as she stared at the hypnotizing view of the waterfalls crashing down on just the other side of the windows.

"They sure knew how to build it, didn't they? This whole place."

He stood up and followed behind her, at a distance, as he additionally observed. "It's unbelievable. Hard to believe it's been here for over a thousand years. And somehow, it still looks new!"

"I only wish I could've met the architect and builders," Jenna sighed as she placed her hand upon one of the windows. "The designs are exquisite. King Närveid is very lucky to live in such a place!"

"King Närveid!" shouted Isaac as he patted the side of his belt. "I was supposed to give his sword back and—"

Jenna started giggling as she repressed the slight pain that was creeping upon her from the sphere. "I hope you don't mind," she said, "but I returned the sword for you. I figured it was the least I could do since I treated you so badly."

His heart rate returned to normal as he said, "Thank you very much. Wait, you went in my room?"

Her eyes widened as her blood ran cold. "O-oh! I mean. Yes, but I didn't take or look at anything else! And—"

Isaac started laughing as he waved his hands, "No, no! It's all right. Don't worry! Thank you for returning it for me. Was he grateful?"

She turned around and looked out the window at the waterfall as she shrugged. "For which part? No, he wasn't grateful to hear that his cousin had become an infected zombie, only to be mangled up and thrown out by a wolf that can hardly be described."

Her smile was contagious as she turned around and looked at him. "But! He was grateful to have the sword returned and gives you his personal thanks."

Bashful, he nervously looked around. "It's nothing… really."

"However, I was right!" She laughed. "I told you that he wouldn't mind if you just kept it! That was the first thing he asked!"

James couldn't help but smile as he entered the large hall and watched as his friends were smiling and laughing.

"Oi!" he shouted as he walked toward them. "I just knew I'd find you down here!"

"James!" beamed Isaac as he approached. "Good to see you!"

"Likewise!" he returned as he gave his best friend a strong, "manly" hug.

James gave a slight glare and raised eyebrow at Jenna, who gave the same look in return. It quickly came to an end as they busted up laughing and embraced each other.

"I'm really sorry… about how I acted earlier," apologized Jenna as she embraced him.

"No worries, no worries, miss," accepted James as he held her.

She pulled away and flicked his ear as she exclaimed, "Oh, but how about not making me walk all the way to the castle from the bridge next time you reprimand me?"

Before James could answer, Isaac interrupted, "There won't be a next time."

"You got that right!" shouted James as he held up a letter. "Speaking of 'not having a next time,'" he continued, "guess who wrote you a letter, mate?"

Isaac tilted his head back and forth as he accepted the letter from James. "To me?" he asked as he read the front. "From Professor Minlöuian?"

Everyone eagerly awaited as he opened the envelope and read the letter within.

Dearest Isaac Erbrecht,

I hope this letter finds you soon, for I haven't been able to locate you in person. King Närveid just informed me that you and your friends have left on a very important mission.

How I wish that I didn't have to do this in a letter and how I so desired to apologize in person, but this is how it must be.

I am terribly, terribly sorry for treating you the way that I did, Isaac Erbrecht. You must know, as I now confess, that you are one of the most talented pianists that I have ever met. And begging most humbly for your forgiveness, as well as to confess, most embarrassingly, my crippling faults, of which I fell snare to jealousy. For never, not in all my fifty-plus years of teaching and instructing of the pianato, have I ever met a caliber of student such as yourself.

You intrigue me, Isaac Erbrecht. Your visage and countenance shine as the glorious heavens above. And begging most humbly, and boldly, I beseech you to return at once, upon your arrival back to Wöntylnas, to resume lessons.

However, these lessons shall not resume as we last left, oh no, for I desire to watch, observe, and learn of the way in which you play and compose—in that, you do so in such a way as I have never before seen. Yes, I admit, I desire to be the student! And should there be anything that you may still desire to learn of me, it is yours to be had.

Should my grievous behavior still be inflicting upon you, wounds of paramount significance, may I please, although unworthy, ask a request? Please come to my home, for I desire, above all else, to apologize to you in person. This letter will not and cannot do any justice to the above-stated.

Even understandably so, should you not desire to resume instruction, I humbly plead this final request: please meet me just one last time so that I may tell you just how sorry I am.

JUSTIN HENDRICKSON

Hoping that this letter finds you in brimming and radiant health, until next we meet.

Most sincerely,
Mrs. Minlöuian

"Well, now how abou' that?" bellowed James as he clapped Isaac on the back. "I told you, Isaac!"

"Exactly what did you tell him?" asked Jenna as she picked up the letter that Isaac just dropped from the blow.

"I told him," he continued, "that his spirit and optimism is so contagious that it cannot help but affect even the most bitter of people."

Isaac gratefully smiled as James placed a hand on his shoulder and added, "And trust me when I say that not many are as bitter and wretched as Professor Minlöuian."

Jenna rested upon the piano as she asked, "So what are you going to do, Isaac?"

"Nothing," he simply responded, much to the surprise of his friends.

"Nothing?" they both demanded.

"Piano can wait," he courageously said, "after we're done with our current task at hand."

"Which reminds me...," mumbled James, "Isaac! Care to recap to Jenna, here, about what my uncle told us at breakfast?"

"Oh!" he exclaimed. "That's right!"

Jenna listened to every detail as he recapped to her the potential dangers of the Algár Plains.

"I can see the wisdom in Professor Vandergaus's words," she agreed. "But I also see the wisdom in James, in that it'd be a waste of time to travel all the way across Vaerün."

"That's right!" hollered James indignantly. "And say we do travel all the way to the Grünas Kingdom. Then what? What guarantee do we have that Gage will even join us?"

"I agree," said Jenna. "But what do you think, Isaac?"

"To be honest," he said, "I don't know. Both sides are an equal gamble. But my heart leans toward the safer option, of course."

"Phooey to safety!" mocked James. "Since when have we ever been safe? Why, this whole journey of ours has been nothing but perilous, backbreaking, dangerous, treacherous—"

As James continued to go down the list of words, Jenna addressed Isaac.

"To be honest, I have to agree with James. We've never been safe, but that's why we've been given the power we have!" she exclaimed as she held up her hand, creating a fireball. "To create our own safety!"

James finally finished his list as he said, "See? Now for once, I agree with her!"

Isaac sighed as he took everything into consideration. "Very well. You two are my most beloved friends. If you think we'll be all right, then... I trust you."

James and Jenna gave each other a double high five as they cheered.

"Brilliant!" yelled James. "So when do we leave?" Then he added, "If we leave well before dawn, we should reach the Algár Plains by late afternoon!"

Isaac held his breath for a moment as a foreboding feeling crept upon him. "All right then," he said as he shook off the feeling, "let me go ahead and prepare—"

"No need!" exclaimed James as he jumped on Isaac's back, giving him a noogie. "I already got everything prepared! Water... food... supplies... and another horse."

"Awww...," said Jenna sadly, "but you two looked so cute on that horse together!"

Both of them gave her a flat expression that said, "Really? Just... really?"

"Whaaat?" She giggled.

"And on that note," Isaac said as he turned around, still carrying James, "I'm getting some lunch. You two wanna join?"

"Count me in!" bellowed James as he gave him another noogie.

"Me too!" clapped Jenna. "I heard that Chef Volkan's preparing some roast boar burgers with sweet potato fries and a relished sour sauce of some sort for dipping."

"Hey! Wait up!" she shouted as Isaac's speed tripled.

James yawned as he rested against the neck of his horse.

"Let me know when he gets here," he sleepily said as he closed his eyes.

Jenna had her arms crossed and was tapping them in irritation. "I don't understand him," she said. "What on Vaerün could you possibly have to take care of at four in the morning?"

The Wöntylnas bridge around them was elegantly lit amid the darkness as the white light of the lampposts gave their illustrious glow upon it.

"I'm going to let you in on a secret," he yawned.

"And what could that possibly be?" she irritatingly asked.

"Don't ever question what's taking a man so long, first thing in the morning. For all you know, he could be having a really bad case of the—"

"Aaannnd on that note," she blurted out, "here he is! Thank heaven."

Sure enough, Isaac came galloping up on his white stallion.

"Sorry about that, you two! I just had to take care of—"

James started giggling as Jenna interrupted him.

"No, no! That's okay! We don't need to hear about your issues."

"Excuse me?" he asked as he shortly followed, "You know what? I don't even want to know. Let's just go!"

Crack! snapped his reins as he flew past them.

"Oi!" hollered James, "Left, mate! Go left!"

"Don't be too harsh on him," said Jenna. "After all, the sun hasn't even risen yet."

To Isaac's surprise and relief, James and Jenna did most of the talking. Whenever they had time to talk, that was considering they were charging full speed ahead toward Wölnas most of the day.

Although they were heading his favorite direction, north (yes, having a favorite direction does exist!), he couldn't help but feel a certain sense of... dread and unease—as if something bad were about to happen.

He nearly jumped off his horse and flew into the forest trees overhead as he heard the same familiar words, from that same familiar voice.

No, Isaac! Don't let him take you!

His face was dripping with sweat, and he was huffing as though he'd just ran from a behemoth Praetor.

James and Jenna instantly stopped talking as they both rode up beside him.

"Are you okay, mate?" asked James.

Jenna raised a hand to touch him, but a magnetic-like force pulled her back, preventing her from doing so.

"You're so pale, Isaac. Are you sick?"

"It's not that," he said, after taking a deep breath. "It's this... voice. I keep hearing it in my head."

Jenna and James looked past him and at each other, then back to him.

"Don't worry. That'll go away really soon," said James.

"How do you know? What are you two not telling me?"

"You're just going to have to trust us!" exclaimed Jenna. "It's going to be wonderful. You'll see!"

Isaac placed his face in his palms as he spoke through them.

"It's torturing me. And I'm sick of hearing it. When will it go away?"

James pointed forward, north, down the forest path.

"We're almost through the Mülgfen Woods. It lets out directly onto the Algár Plains!"

"And from there," joined Jenna, "it's a straight shot across the plains, up and through the pass, then down into Wölnas!"

"Forgive my rudeness, you two," said Isaac as he was now massaging his face. "But I'm well aware of the geography. Why are you telling me this?"

"Because, mate," James said as he handed Isaac a canteen, "it is in Wölnas that you'll find the source of that voice."

"On the tower, to be exact." Jenna pointed.

They had to turn around as Isaac still hadn't moved, from when they continued forward.

"Am I really going crazy?" Isaac asked. "Can neither of you truly feel this awful, foreboding feeling?"

James and Jenna gave each other a sorrowful look as neither of them felt it.

"I'm sorry, Isaac, but… no. We don't," said Jenna.

"Maybe you just need to eat, mate?" asked James, trying to give comfort. "Bread can only hold you for so long, you know."

Isaac's vision vibrated a little as he nudged his stallion and joined them.

"Yeah…" he murmured, "maybe that's what it is."

"Don't worry!" exclaimed James after he took a drink from the canteen that Isaac handed back to him. "If you like, we can set up camp early when we get to the foothold of the Algár Mountains."

"And I'll cook up something delicious for you!" attempted Jenna, in the consoling.

"Thanks, you two," said Isaac quietly as they all continued.

The jokes that James and Jenna were telling each other came to an abrupt halt as they heard the sound of thunder overhead—beyond the green canopy of the forest trees.

"Did you hear that?" Jenna nervously asked.

"I did, but I can't believe it," answered James.

"It was thunder," Isaac spoke up as he nudged his horse again, continuing down the path.

It didn't take but another half a mile as a northern wind came whistling past them. Green leaves were whipping through the air as the trees unrelentingly lost them.

"Should we turn back?" shouted Isaac to his friends.

"Just a random storm, mate!" replied James. "Let's keep going. The plains might be fine!"

"I don't know, James, maybe—" started Jenna.

But then as suddenly as it had come, the storm had now completely stopped.

Even the surrounding forest trees that looked as though they were about to fall over and be ripped up from their roots at any second now sat quite still—with only a gentle sway remaining.

"See?" James smiled. "Just a random passing storm! Everything's fine!"

Jenna gave him a dirty look, and Isaac said nothing.

"Come on, don't look at me like that!" James said as he laughed. "Besides, look ahead! There's the opening! Wouldn't it be a shame to turn around, only to find out that we did so for nothing?"

Jenna gave a look to Isaac that said, "Are you sure about this?" But Isaac bravely looked forward and followed James.

Professor Vandergaus couldn't have been more right. For even if the sun overhead was able to fully bathe his light upon them, rather than trying to fight past the dark storm clouds, it wouldn't have made much of a difference.

The plains looked like a handcart graveyard. Random pikes of molded, splintering wood stuck out of the damp earth like a nail out of a misplaced board. The bright orange of the rusted metal parts laid bent and twisted, sticking out from the sunken caravans.

Eee...eee...eeeee, eee, squealed the barely turning wheel of a broken handcart.

"Whoa, whoa!" cried Isaac as he tried to calm his horse, who'd just sunk his entire back and left leg into a mushy patch of earth.

Jenna's hair stood on end as she looked behind her.

The view of the forest was barely there, offering a tiny glimpse of hope.

"James," Jenna called out, "I'm starting to think we should turn around—"

"It's okay, Jenna!" he rebuked. "Isaac's horse is fine. See? He's free!"

Jenna shook her head. "That's not it! Look at the footing. Your uncle was right! What if it gets worse? And not only that... this ground is perfect for the Kreaux to—"

"Please don't finish that sentence," Isaac pleaded. "That's been one of my biggest fears from the get-go."

James looked around at the grim scene and attempted to offer some encouraging words.

"Come on, you two. Look how far we've come! Here, follow me, I'll lead the way. And if it gets too bad, I promise we can turn around!"

Jenna had to do a double take as she saw what she thought to be a white, dead hand sticking out of the ground—the dark-brown flecks of dirt making it even more noticeable.

For reasons unbeknownst to her at the time, she looked to Isaac for comfort.

"Did you see th—"

"Yes," he instantly answered, cutting her off. Whether he was pissed off or just focused, it was hard to say. Nevertheless, his attention was dead focused on James, some eight feet in front of them.

"If you look closely, they're everywhere," he added.

Jenna's heart plummeted. Her blood ran cold. And her hair stood on end as she, surely enough, looked around to see the white, protruding hands and fingers that flecked the dark-brown plains all around her, amid the unending wreckage.

"Isaac, you don't think those are—"

But she was interrupted as her horse whinnied, his feet also sinking into the earth.

No, it was not just his feet but the whole front of his body!

Isaac watched in horror as he motioned for Jenna to get off.

"Jenn! Get off! Get off him before—"

His words fell, as though someone had just cut them from his tongue, as he watched her horse nosedive headfirst into the sludgy mud, his head and entire front half of his body sucked down into the gunk.

"James! **James!**" Jenna cried as she barely got off him in time and stared in horror as his back legs were flailing and kicking about.

James had just barely turned around, when the back legs of his horse fell into the mud and forced him to jump off.

Isaac's eyes darted left and right at the two beasts as he tried to figure out what to do.

Jenna was crying in exasperation and was about to launch a fireball at the mud before Isaac stopped her.

"No! Jenn! Wait!" he cried as he looked to James. "James! Come here! Freeze this portion of the ground! Hurry!"

James had to watch his own footing as he carefully (but quickly) made his way over.

"What? Mate, that's just dirt! I can't—"

"There's enough water in it to freeze! Just do it! Do it, or her horse is going to die!"

James's heart was pounding as his raised palms began to crackle and flicker from his ice Majesty.

"But…but what if I accidentally—"

"**Just do it!**" both of them screamed.

Fuuuussshhhh! blasted the icy waves from his palms, instantly freezing the mud that her horse had fallen into.

"Haaa!" hollered Isaac, his hands twisting through the air, rays of light streaming from his fingers and forming a glowing net that wrapped around the horse, pulling it free along with the frozen earth.

"Smash it, Jenna!" he cried, struggling to maintain the massive weight.

Boooom! roared her fire, doing as she was told. Frozen chunks of earth flying every which way.

It took about twenty minutes before she'd successfully calmed her horse down, in addition to them rescuing James's horse and calming *him* down as well.

"Please," Jenna shortly said, after they were all upon their horses again, "may we leave this forsaken place?"

James sharply laughed as he said, "Are you kidding me? We did not just go through all that, only to turn around!"

"Wait, please, James," Isaac tried,

"No! We've got this! Just… trust me!" he yelled as he continued forward. "And follow my lead!"

All they could do was look at each other as they shook their heads and continued to follow him.

To all their great relief, the ground seemed to solidify a little bit, although not much. But the debris and scattered wreckage was just as bad.

"See?" James confidently said. "I told you everything would be okay!"

A drop of sweat rolled down Jenna's face as her mind began to play tricks on her, for she couldn't stop staring at the dead hands and feet that were now sticking out from the damp earth.

"Jenna," Isaac said as he pulled her back to reality, "are you okay?"

How can you be so calm, Isaac? she thought as she stared at his strong, kind, and soothing glowing eyes.

"N-no, I'm not," she honestly answered.

Fearful to ask but always desiring to help, he asked, "Is there… anything I can do for you?"

She had to think about that for a moment. Suddenly, a memory ran through her mind, and she replied, "Actually… I think there is."

He couldn't help but smile.

"What is it?"

"That time I was being really cruel to you and James…" she trailed off, "just a few days ago. You calmed him with your Majesty. Do you think you could—"

But she didn't even have to finish the sentence. Isaac's hands were already twisting and elegantly moving as the living streams of light flowed and danced toward her.

Never, as she could recall, had she felt so much hope, so much comfort, so much tranquility, and peace of mind. So much ____ as the twisting rays of light enveloped and consumed her vision.

"Feel better?" he softly asked as he finished.

She wanted to cry as she answered, "You have no idea… Thank you, Isaac."

"See that?" James excitedly shouted as he pointed north. "Those are the Algár Mountains! We're nearly there!"

Isaac and Jenna joined in with him as they stared at the massive, black-and-purple-looking mountains some five miles north from them.

"And that," he added as he pointed to a small, winding, snake-like incision upon the mountain, "is the Algár Pass!"

Jenna pointed up as she said, "I just hope we can get there before it rains. These clouds aren't looking too favorable."

"Don't jinx it!" he demanded as he cracked the reins and continued on.

"No, please don't, please don't!" exclaimed Isaac as a loud crack of thunder sounded high above them.

"Just a few more miles!" shouted James as the wind began to pick up. "We can make it!"

Jenna nearly fainted as she felt something cold, wet, and rubbery grip her leg. Without moving her head, she looked down and let out a squealing scream.

There, attached to her leg, was one of the dead, white, clammy hands.

Shink! sliced her rapier as it instantly swept through the wrist.

Isaac and James weren't sure whether they wanted to help or laugh as they watched Jenna's horse turn and kick around as Jenna's hands were flailing in the air, sword in hand, with the white hand still gripped to her leg.

Their heads and necks moved in perfect sync as they watched her jump down and decimate it off with a roaring fireball.

Whatever thoughts they may have had about laughing were now completely gone as they watched a series of hands launch up, latch onto all four of her horse's legs, and instantly rip it under the dirt.

"Whoa!" howled Isaac.

"Holy shüza!" screamed James as both of them barely had time to scramble off their horses as they, too, were instantly sucked underground.

Horror, sorrow, and devastation may have set in, if they weren't immediately forced to combat with the Kreaux who were tearing out of the earth to fight them.

"Go!" screamed Isaac as he motioned to the north. "We have to get off the plains!"

"Or at least get some better footing," shouted James as his daggers cleanly sliced through a Kreaux head that just popped out and was trying to bite his ankles.

Whether Jenna was squealing in anger or fear, it was hard to say. For her rapier was making quick work of the Kreaux hands, claws, and heads that were revealing all around her.

"There!" hollered Isaac as he pointed forward to the "driest" portion of a random clearing.

"Get. Off!" Jenna screamed as the upper half of a Kreaux body that popped out and was trying to get her exploded in a wave of black blood and guts.

"You look lovely, princess!" James bowed as he swiped his daggers past the hands that were trying to get him.

She may have done something unladylike to him as she wiped away the black blood from her face.

"Haaa!" The three of them shouted as they blasted themselves forward onto the harder ground, free of protruding hands, heads, legs, and other random Kreaux body parts.

"All right," muttered James as he had his back to Jenna and Isaac. "Isaac, you take the north. Jenna, you take the southeast, and I'll take the southwest."

The Kreaux were surrounding them in countless numbers as they burst through the ground like cockroaches, out of their nesting grounds.

Ca-rack-rack-rack-rack-rack... snapped the thunder and lightning over them as a horrible storm began to brew.

Arms and limbs flew everywhere as Jenna jumped from Kreaux to Kreaux, dismembering them with her rose-etched rapier.

"Thanks for that!" shouted James to the air.

The sudden downpour of rain had just turned into his personal dart arsenal.

Sh-sh-sh-sh-sh-sh-sh-sh-sh-shink! whistled and flew the icy darts as his calmly moving, frost-enveloped, blue palms unleashed the incalculable, tiny missiles upon the advancing Kreaux.

"Isaac!" cried Jenna. "Look out! Haaa!"

The five forward front flips were an impressive sight but not nearly as impressive as the streams of fire that launched from her succession.

Boom! Boom. Boom, boom, boom! exploded the searing flames upon the unsuspecting Kreaux behind Isaac as he launched his concussive waves of light upon the Kreaux before them.

"Thanks, Jenn!" he called out.

"Any time!" she replied as her rapier met the legs of the Kreaux behind her.

Uggghwagghhh, sounded the grueling sound of the Kreaux as their faces exploded in a burst of Majestic light right in front of James.

"Oi! You rock, mate!" He laughed in excitement. "Here, allow me to return the favor! Ha!"

James thrust his dagger through the air as it suspended directly above Isaac's head.

His hands began to move in swaying, blue, rhythmic patterns as he conjured and charged a freezing ball of energy.

"Ha!" he cried as he unleashed it. Through the air it flew, higher, higher, higher, and then it stopped!

"Arrrgghh!" he hollered as he slammed his blue fist to the ground.

At the same time, the freezing ball of energy came thundering down as it crashed into the high, levitating dagger, unleashing a fury storm of ice daggers into every single Kreaux around Isaac, causing instant destruction.

"And that, mate," James cockily said as his dagger whistled like a boomerang through the air and back into his hand, "is how it's done."

"Oh, is that how we're going to do it?" Jenna laughed as she was gracefully jumping off Kreaux head after head, surgically injecting the tip of her rapier into their heads, giving them but a moment to realize what happened before they collapsed to the ground.

Zeargh. Zeargh. Zeargh. Zeargh! whistled and zoomed Isaac's rays as he unceasingly cast them.

"Please, both of you, just—"

Boom… boom… boom… boom… echoed and pulsed the air and ground around them.

All of them paused, even the Kreaux.

Boom… boom… boom… boom… It was that same, awful, gut-wrenching feeling that had washed over them when they engaged the—

Boom! exploded the earth around Jenna as Coltin, the fire conductor, appeared before her and, with him, countless Kreaux, including the hulking Praetors.

"Jenna!" roared Isaac and James as they tried to fight their way to her, only to be engaged by Coltin's summoned Praetors.

"You aren't worthy of the name Fürnas, princess!" hissed Coltin's voice, through the oozing, dripping Dark Majesty of his overdrawn hood.

"Heh…" snickered Jenna as she gripped her rapier in both hands.

Fffsshhrawrggh! it bellowed and roared as it burst to life with her Fire Majesty, her dress and hair dancing furiously from the emanating power.

"Far more worthy than you," she said as she tightened down on her sword, then yelled, "A wretched, filthy, unworthy sellout of a king!"

Boom! Shink, shink, shink, shink! sparked and roared his black sword against her flaming one as blow after blow they fought.

"Shüza!" swore James as he strafed—just in time to avoid the club that was hunkering down to crush him.

"Haarrrrrr…raagghh!" howled Isaac as his rippling light wave caught, deflected, and repelled the club of another Praetor that was coming down upon him.

"We need to help her!" shouted James as he slid beneath the Praetor's leg and turned around.

Fffheeewwwww, howled his palm as it pressed against one of his daggers, freezing it with his Majesty.

Who would've thought James could move so gracefully? It was as if he wasn't even touching the ground as he dashed back, then ran forward with such speed, his steps taking him up the back of the

Praetor as his freshly imbued dagger sliced all the way from the bottom of the tailbone up and through the Praetor's head.

Thud! slammed the Praetor as he crashed down, face-first, ran through by James.

Isaac's eyes darted to admire his incredibly powerful friend. "Look at you, Jame—. Look out!"

James barely ducked in time as the rippling, dark-blue-and-black water tentacle of Vergaus, the water Conductor, came bolting past him.

"Up we go!" yelled James as he threw his momentum up and forward, turning himself around to face Vergaus.

He was tossing his black water daggers back and forth and looked just like Coltin—minus the different weapons.

"Isaac, mate," shouted James as he repeatedly froze the water tentacles that were zooming their way, slashing them to the ground. "Take care of the Praetors. I've got this!"

Isaac boldly nodded as he engaged the six surrounding Praetors.

Jenna's and Coltin's flames collided in a violent explosion of light and dark fire, as both slammed backward.

Before she could get up, he'd already zoomed in front of her, sword pointed straight at her breast.

"Oh, come on," she chided. "You honestly think that's it?"

Her right hand instantly seized the sphere at her belt as she roared, "**Antéum!** Come forth!"

Coltin looked up, right on time, as her whinnying, flaming horse came charging at him; flames flooding all around the heavenly steed.

Through the air he careened as the impact from Antéum's head sent him slamming down into ground in a succession of over nine times.

Were he not imbued with the powers of fire and hell, he'd certainly have been a goner.

Jenna was hardly surprised as he quickly regained and levitated in the air like a string puppet. He was looking straight down, hands out to his sides.

She had to slightly squint her eyes as his red-and-black flames filled the air.

"Ha ha ha!" He laughed menacingly. She flipped and dodged as the streams of dark Fire Majesty honed in on her like heat-seeking missiles.

"*Wait, how'd he do that?*" she demanded in thought to know as she rocketed forth from an explosion of fire.

During his unleashed streams, he'd somehow dashed behind her and unleashed a fireball upon her back.

Certain that one of her legs had just broken as she continued to slam down into the ground and up into the air, she couldn't have been more surprised when she landed solidly upon Antéum's back, who'd just caught her.

"You know…" she wheezed in fury as she rolled her whole right arm in a clockwise fashion, "I really liked having my left leg. So do you mind if I take yours?"

Antéum's head rolled in clockwise unison with her arm as a flaming wheel began to appear before them.

"Oh, wait," she snickered, looking dead at him, "you don't have a choice."

Like a dragon unchained, the fiery wheel ignited and roared to life, spiraling through the air with searing intensity as Jenna's hand and Antéum's head propelled it forward in a blaze of unstoppable fury.

Straight toward Coltin it flew; wrapping around his legs and instantly exploding.

"**Aaggggggghhhrrrrr!**" echoed the bloodcurdling sound of his screaming. Leg literally obliterated in a heat-filled storm by Jenna.

James's frozen daggers crackled with energy, unleashing torrents of snow and ice with each strike, colliding in a storm of frost against Vergaus's shadowy blades; the air between them alive with the clash of elemental fury.

"Why…" whispered the chilling voice of Vergaus as he creepily floated in the air, "did the last water Majestician have to be so weak?"

"Weak?" bellowed James as he rolled a series of icy, streaming bolts through the air and toward Vergaus. "Just try me, you freak!"

Vergaus held his hands in the air as he charged his Dark Majesty. "Freak? Isn't that what they called you? Ha ha ha ha!"

James's eyes widened as a monstrous wave of water came crashing down toward him.

Vergaus watched as his entire wave began to freeze. In anger and agitation, he quickly charged, then unleashed a continuous series of monstrous waves. After the last one, it being the most powerful, he eagerly watched and waited.

Surely, there was no way anyone could've survived that, especially a weak Majestician like James, right?

A glimmering and most dazzling display of blue-and-white light coursed through the waves that Vergaus had just cast.

"Aarrooooo!" hollered Rúviag as he and James blasted through the frozen waves that they'd just blocked.

James had fused both ends of his daggers together and further imbued them with his ice Majesty as they formed a single double-blade. His slicked-back hair was let down and entirely ragged. And above all, he was pissed.

Vergaus had to retreat back to the ground as a blasting wave of frost launched straight for him from Rúviag 'smouth and James's blade.

Through his Kreaux he dashed and ran as Rúviag ripped and shredded through them, chewing them up and spitting them out as the worthless trash they were.

Shink, shink, shink. *Sh-sh-sh-shink!* hissed and sang James's ice blade as it made quick work of the Kreaux that they were bolting past. Arms, hands, legs, torsos, you name it, were flying every which way, cut off so cleanly that any surgeon would have to be impressed.

And in fair fear, Vergaus was momentarily fleeing for his life.

The circular rings of rainbow light unceasingly rippled through the air as Isaac unleashed his mighty Light Majesty upon the Praetors.

Every bit of his training was tested as he dodged club after club that swung over him, across him, and even attemptedly through him.

I only wish Mrs. Minlöuian could see this, he thought as he played upon the air, the living streams of light racing through the air and through the Praetors.

Three of them fell, but eight more had just launched out from underground.

Sweat dripped down his face as he lifted his hands high above.

Voom. Voom. Voom-voom-voo-voom! rippled his bastion of a barrier as it sustained the unfair blows of the massive clubs that were unrelentingly crashing upon it.

"Impressive, Isaac Erbrecht," hissed a voice through the air.

The hair on his neck stood on end as he shook his head in an attempt to dismiss the petrifying voice.

*Think, Isaac... **think!*** he demanded of himself, as an idea suddenly popped into his head.

"Haaa!" he shouted as he forced his hands out, exploding the barrier and casting the Praetors momentarily back.

"There is truth, there is light," he whispered as his hands and fingers moved so fast that they were but blurs of light.

With acrobatics that'd put a choreographer to shame, when he was done moving, a most intricate of patterns completely composed of light was etched and beaming off the ground.

Hands outstretched, light glowing and cascading from his being, he levitated some fifteen feet in the air. While looking high above, a gentle ray of light pierced the clouds and surrounded him as he cried, "Grace me with... thy ultimate might!"

The glyph on the ground exploded, releasing a storm of countless living streams of light as they wrapped around every single Praetor.

"Haaaa!" he bellowed as his hands came thundering down, rays of light instantaneously obliterating the trapped Praetors as they roared from his palms.

He took a deep breath as he slowly landed to the ground. Over a hundred feet away, on his western and southeastern sides, he could see James with the booming flashes of blue water and ice as he dueled Vergaus and the roaring flashes of red flames as Jenna and Coltin engaged.

Always the calm and courageous one, he had to constantly remind himself that everything was going to be okay as he strove to repress his huffed, panicked breathing.

Isaac's head darted this way and that as he tried to figure out who to help first—as both were equally matched in their furious battles.

I guess… I'll have to try and help them both, he thought as light began to emanate from him, his hands upturned, palms glowing, white cloak dancing furiously from his emanating power.

His hands began to vibrate as he was about ready to unleash his Light Majesty when…

Zeeearrrgggghhh!

Isaac vibrated and convulsed as the black, purple, and blue lightning struck him.

"Now, now, Isaac," hissed the unfamiliar voice, "let's play fair, okay? As it's clearly one against one!"

Thankfully, his courage and strength overpowered the blow as he quickly regained himself and jumped up to see another robed conductor.

Lightning was crackling and zapping all around him as his nocked black-and-purple bow was pointed dead at Isaac.

"Wh-who are—" Isaac stammered.

"Now that's just insulting!" the conductor laughed. "Didn't you ever do your history?"

Isaac fully stood up as his palms roared with light.

"You're… No. It can't be." He squinted, then whispered, "*Gerund Wölnas!* Is that even possible!?"

"Yay!" jumped Gerund. "Five points for Isaac! Whoops."

He went to clap but accidentally unleashed his nocked arrow as it came bolting toward Isaac.

Zeearrggggh. Boom! it sounded as it flew through the air, crashed into Isaac's rapidly cast barrier, and then off into a bystanding Kreaux.

"I don't care who you are," Isaac said indignantly as he unleashed wave after wave of light. "You will not stop me from saving my friends!!"

"My, *my*," chided Gerund as he repelled the light with his lightning. "I'm sure Garon would be most disappointed to learn that his son has become such a brat."

Albeit curious, Isaac didn't have time to ask any questions as he just had the time to create a barrier to protect himself from the lightning arrows that were raining down upon him from Gerund's blurring hand, nocking and releasing arrows at incalculable speeds.

Sweat began to form on his brow again as he sustained the siege. And then with his palms outstretched, he brought them in front of him as he angelically floated in the air.

James, Jenna, and their counterparts couldn't help but pause for a moment as they turned and watched the unimaginably glorious scene. To them, it looked as though a blinding orb of light had begun to levitate in the air.

"Oooh... pretty cool, huh?" continued chiding Gerund as lightning crackled and exploded around him, he, too, levitating and following in the air and still firing arrows upon Isaac's barrier. "Looks like we both can fly!"

"I already told you..." bellowed the angelic, near-singing voice of Isaac, "you will NOT stop me from saving my friends!"

Gerund sighed as his lightning bolts and arrows continued to deflect Isaac's streaming light.

But he wasn't fast enough.

"Aggghhh! Shüza! You *stupid*, shining, blight of heaven," he swore as three of the streams pierced straight through his left side, two of them piercing his right leg.

"Coltin! Vergaus!" he hissed. "I've had enough of this! Take the brat out!"

James and Jenna watched in horror as Vergaus and Coltin launched through the air at an impossible speed and unleashed their most powerful waves of Dark Majesty upon Isaac's barrier.

The light of his bastion-like barrier was barely visible as the three dark conductors unleashed their full-blown fury upon him.

Coltin and Vergaus were circling on the ground, below him, as they held up both of their palms, black fire and water exploding up and surrounding the barrier in such force as to cover it.

Isaac's barrier began to fizzle and vibrate as Gerund put away his bow, held up a pointed finger, and pointed the other—a direct conduit of lightning flowing through—and unleashing upon the barrier.

No, Isaac... don't give up! boomed the familiar, angelic voice inside his mind as blood began trickling down his face from sustaining the ferocious siege.

P-please, Isaac said in his mind as a tear rolled down his face, *whoever you are, help me. I can't take this. I'm not... I'm not going to make it...*

His whole being went erect as his eyes and outstretched hands unleashed blinding rays of light.

Jenna and James gasped as they watched the clouds part above. A glorious, heavenly angel descended through the light-filled portal and momentarily held in the sky.

"She's going for Isaac!" cried Jenna out loud as she sat upon Antéum.

James's mouth dropped further as he whispered, "Is that... It is! *Lucy!*"

Neither of them could say a word. As a matter of fact, it took a moment for them to realize that the blinking, moving light that was dancing through the air was her—kicking the living crap out of the three conductors with her sword of light and shield of truth.

Spellbound and unaware of what was going on, for the trance he was in, Isaac slowly lowered to the ground, hands still held overhead, eyes still consumed with light. His barrier ceased upon contact as his feet gently touched the ground.

What could Jenna or James say as they watched the three conductors crawl upon the ground?

Lucy slowly and elegantly walked up to her son, who was still entranced and unaware of what was happening.

"My precious, most beloved son," she whispered as she brought her hand to his face, tears streaming down her own. "Look how handsome you are. What an amazing, selfless, heavenly man you've become."

With a slight pause, she continued, "I'm so sorry. I wasn't supposed to meet you like this. And so for now, it's best that you know not about our encounter... but the time will soon come—"

"Really, Lucy?" thundered and roared a voice so evil and so penetrating the very ground slightly shook, as if repulsed to hear it.

"The déjà vu is uncanny. Don't you think?"

Lucy panicked as her eyes looked around.

"No! It can't be, Isaac—"

James and Jenna merely squeaked as they watched in the most inexplicable horror.

For there, behind Isaac, appeared a man in black armor so quickly that they didn't even know when he'd appeared.

And there, running straight through Isaac's and Lucy's chests, rippled and shimmered his long, black, dripping sword.

"Wouldn't you have learned the first time?" He laughed. "And this time, I didn't miss Isaac."

Jenna's sphere nearly exploded as she screamed at the top of her lungs, "ISAAC!!"

She couldn't even see where she was going. All she remembered was being surrounded by the unrelenting cataclysm of her Fire Majesty as she engaged the revived Coltin and nearly destroyed him for good.

The tears wouldn't stop rolling down James's face. He wanted to move, but he couldn't.

Isaac. Isaac... Isaac, he repeatedly thought. *It's all my fault. Oh, heaven... forgive me. My beloved best friend...*

Shiiiiiink! sounded the black blade as Garon pulled it out of them.

"N-no. No... no," Lucy repeatedly whispered as she shakily leaned in and kissed her son. "M-my beloved... don't give in to the darkness."

Garon trudged over and picked her up as she fell to the ground.

"That's enough for now," Garon called out to his conductors. "Let's go."

As if nothing had happened, Garon and his conductors blasted into the earth, disappearing.

Rúviag and *Antéum* bolted toward Isaac, who just slumped to the ground.

"No, no, no. No!" screamed Jenna as her sphere was literally dancing upon her belt. "Isaac! Isaac!"

His lifeless body held in her arms as she pulled back his gleaming blond hair.

"Is... is he..." barely croaked out James as he touched his hand to Isaac's.

Whatever feelings of coldness that he was used to sent even more chills down his spine as Isaac's hand was positively frozen to the touch.

James collapsed to the ground as all his strength gave out.

Jenna rocked back and forth, with her dead, beloved Isaac in her arms.

Wh-what's that? James weakly thought as he saw something flying through the air and toward them.

It began to grow bigger and bigger and bigger until finally...

Whoosh. Whoosh. Whoosh. Whoosh, flapped the wings of the massive griffin as it landed.

"Well, that's no good," sounded a strong voice as though coming from the griffin.

Neither Jenna nor James said a word as they stared in devastation.

"Thanks, *Tyrnat*. You can let me down now."

The griffin's head bowed down to reveal a man sitting upon him.

He was wearing a green, gold, and silver warrior's chest plate, chain-mail leggings, greaves, platinum silver shoulder pauldrons, and had a gold crown with emeralds fastened within the spires.

"Now that's a shame," he uttered as he jumped down and approached them. "Now what are we supposed to do?"

"Wh-who are you?" demanded Jenna shakily.

"Really?" He laughed in his strong, masculine voice. "Surely you of all people should know!"

He unsheathed a massive hammer from his back and slammed it into the ground, sending a cascading wave of stalagmites forth, in addition to an earthquake.

As it calmed, he said, "I'm *Gage Grünas!* But you can call me *Gage*. Nice to finally meet you, Jenna and James!"

ABOUT THE AUTHOR

Imbued with an insatiable curiosity and an unwavering optimism, Justin Hendrickson sees the world as a canvas of endless possibilities. Known for his boundless light, infectious hope, and genuine sincerity, Justin's journey began amid the vibrant landscapes of Southern California.

From the sun-kissed beaches to the rugged mountains, Justin finds inspiration in the kaleidoscope of nature's wonders that surround him. It was amid these diverse landscapes that he cultivates his creativity, drawing from the intricate tapestry of life to fuel his artistic endeavors.

In addition to his profound connection with nature, Justin's passion for music serves as a guiding force in his life. As a skilled pianist and composer, he weaves melodies that echo the rhythms of his soul, infusing his compositions with emotion and depth.

With an adventurous spirit and a heart full of dreams, Justin embraces each day as an opportunity for growth, creativity, and connection. Through his artistry and unwavering optimism, he seeks to illuminate the world with beauty, joy, and unending inspiration.

www.ingramcontent.com/pod-product-compliance
Lightning Source LLC
Chambersburg PA
CBHW021331240825
31589CB00031B/172